THE TURNBULLS

Taylor Caldwell

PYRAMID BOOKS  NEW YORK

To my dear children

THE TURNBULLS

Pyramid Books are published by Pyramid Publications (Harcourt Brace Jovanovich). Its trademarks, consisting of the word "Pyramid" and the portrayal of a pyramid, are registered in the United States Patent Office.

PYRAMID PUBLICATIONS
(Harcourt Brace Jovanovich)
757 Third Avenue, New York, N.Y. 10017

He was insanely drunk . . . wild with desire . .
his hunger a raging madness that would not
be restrained. The girl was half-crying now, her
bodice torn, her skirts rumpled, her hair
on her shoulders. When he buried his mouth
in her soft, white neck, she trembled.

"A lass for a true man," said Andrew with an
admiring smile. "How'd you like to be alone
with her, Johnnie?"

From the great Taylor Caldwell, a soaring novel
of a tainted dynasty and a young man's sin that
hounded him across two continents, set in the
sprawling, riotous America of the mid-nineteenth
century.

"The lofty peaks of best-sellerdom are traditionally difficult to scale. . . . But there are three American novelists who have climbed to the top not once or twice but over and over again. In so doing they have established themselves as an elite among U.S. fiction writers. . . . All three are women: Edna Ferber, Frances Parkinson Keyes and Taylor Caldwell."

Life Magazine

Novels by Taylor Caldwell in Pyramid editions

BOOK ONE

CHAPTER 1

ON A certain cold gray morning, wet and misty, (December 15, 1850, in fact) a young man of about eighteen years turned in at Russell Square, whistling abstractedly to himself. The whistling was low, impatient yet thoughtful, and his black eyes were almost obscured by his thick frowning black eyebrows. He was somewhat above middle height, with a well-made and compact body, enhanced by a youthful swagger, and conscious of a fine new wardrobe. Only his general air of robust masculinity saved him from a secret dandyism, for he was extremely fond of excellent dress and the latest fashion. Even his abstracted thoughts returned at intervals to his buff greatcoat, (bought that very morning) with its three tiers of capes. He fingered the good stuff with his gloved hand, and as he did so, his sullen expression became more lively. In truth, sullenness sat uneasily on that handsome countenance, somewhat broad and dark-skinned, with an alert shrewd look full of intelligence, and touched with more than a little gay and ruthless brutality. His features, too, were broad and short, hinting of the Celt rather than the Englishman in a wide and vigorous nose, the slight tilt of his lively and restless eyes with their strong mobile brows, the firm full chin with its dimple, and the breadth of the cheek-bones. Youth, health, high spirits, simple selfishness and humour combined to make that countenance very prepossessing especially when something amusing made him part his somewhat heavy lips to reveal two rows of large and dazzling white teeth, enhanced immeasurably by the general darkness of his skin. If his face lacked subtlety and great intellect, the casual observer did not care, so full of latent laughter and deviltry was the whole expression.

He walked carefully, for all his speed and swagger, for the darker buff broadcloth pantaloons, (rather full and very long over the instep, secured by straps under the polished black boots) were also shining with newness, and the streets were livid with the running water of a recent downpour. Under the greatcoat was a flowered silk waistcoat, and a well-cut jacket with long tails, to match the pantaloons. His stiff white frills

5

seemed made of polished and fluted ivory; they were secured by a full black silk stock, carefully folded and knotted, and completed by the bland shining of a smooth pink pearl pin. He had a big round head, profusely covered by short black curls, and rakishly disposed upon them was a tall and gleaming hat. He carried a black malacca cane with a gold head, which he swung with a devil-may-care nonchalance. (That morning he had been faced with a problem: should he keep the great-coat buttoned, thus showing its perfect fit, or should he leave it carelessly opened, to reveal the waistcoat and the gold watch-chain in all their splendour? He had finally compromised by buttoning three buttons and leaving the others unfastened, so that an unusually strong gust of wind might blow the skirts apart, allowing the passerby a coy glimpse of the glory beneath.)

He was conscious of the fine figure he made, pleased that his shoulders were so broad, his back so tapering and military, his coat so excellently cut, his kerchief so delicately scented. A smile would widen his lips, and his teeth would flash. Then he would scowl, remembering, and his face would become lowering and uneasy, and heavily brutal.

That morning his father, James Turnbull, had received a regretful note from Dr. Thomas Carruthers that he, Dr. Carruthers, was greatly saddened at the inevitable decision to which he had been forced: namely, that young Mr. John Turnbull had been expelled that morning from the very select academy for young gentlemen, for "general conduct unbecoming to one of his station, and for setting a bad example to the other young gentlemen—conduct which must fill the breasts of the parents with alarm and dismay." Dr. Carruthers sadly hinted that young Mr. Turnbull was in an excellent position to enlighten his respected father on the reasons for the expulsion. The revered doctor, it appeared, could not, in self respect, enlarge on them.

"The damned old maid!" thought young Mr. Turnbull, savagely rattling his cane along a row of iron palings. He had seen that letter that morning on his father's breakfast plate, and knew its contents only too well. Had not the "damned old maid" read them to him at four o'clock on the afternoon previous? So, he had come downstairs rapidly that morning, gulped his breakfast before the appearance of his father, and had fled the beautiful old mansion with tail-flying precipitousness. For, in his pocket, was his monthly allowance, a sizable cheque, which he had astutely decided must be cashed immediately at the bank, before Mr. Turnbull read that deplorable letter. The usual obsequiousness with which Mr. John was received by the manager of the bank soothed his annoyed spirits, and he emerged into the morning streets, jingling and comforted. He hastened at once to his tailor, where he paid something on account, receiving, in turn, the fine new wardrobe, and extracting a promise from the tailor that on no account must Mr. Turnbull be informed that the bill was considerably in arrears, even after a substantial payment that day.

By the time John had reached Russell Square, where his betrothed and cousin, Miss Eugenia MacNeill, resided with her widowed mother, he was in high bad temper which not even the new wardrobe could completely dispel. Moreover, he was sorry for himself. He had not wanted to go to that bloody Academy, from the very beginning. The army was more suited to his fancy. But what could one do, when one's father was in trade? The army was forever closed to the son of a merchant, even though that merchant was received in the most gracious houses of the lesser nobility, and was known as a scholar, famous for his taste, as well as a blasted importer of goods from the Orient, and India. The thought of his father, however, softened young Master John's countenance, and it became more childish and thoughtful. The old boy was second to none in England, in trade though he was, and it was a cursed shame that the "old maid" should annoy him, especially after he had had such a long siege with his cardiac asthma. As for his own part in that annoyance, John passed it over nonchalantly, feeling more and more abused. What had he done? A little dallying in Soho, with discreet and cunning companions, who had been more adept at avoiding discovery than John, himself. Andrew Bollister, the prize pupil, had introduced John to that tavern, which he and other gay young gentlemen from the Academy frequented regularly. Gad, a man was entitled to one uproar, wasn't he? What if he had drunk too much last Friday night, and had smashed a few chairs and a windowpane, had sworn prodigiously at the trembling proprietor, and had been forcibly ejected? Was that sufficient for expulsion, and the annoying of the old boy? Certainly not! (John completely ignored the fact that for over six months his examinations had been total failures, that he had caned a young under-master who snivelled to Dr. Carruthers about him, that he had lead a riot at assembly out of sheer high spirits, and was guilty of running up accounts at the pastry shop near by and neglecting to pay them.) The affair in Soho was the last crime.

"It was the Army for me," muttered John, aloud, with increasing self-pity. He cursed the British system aloud, and felt much better. In his mind's eye he saw himself in a handsomely cut red coat, a sword, polished boots and a cocked hat. Ah, there lay his heart! But he was destined to become a merchant, also, to follow his father in trade. There was no hope for him. For a ha'penny he would run away to the Colonies, or to America, where no one had heard of classes and a man could carve a life to suit his fancy.

He reached Number nine, Russell Square, and gloomily lifted his eyes to survey the gray stone pile of his cousin's home. The upper windows were still discreetly shrouded in gray silk. But the shutters had been removed from the lower ones. A servant girl was sweeping the wet stone steps; another was polishing the brass knocker and name plate. Upon observing the resplendent figure of young Mr. Turnbull, the wenches gaped, curtsied and bowed, settling their mob caps more coquettishly on their pretty and blowsy heads. They moved aside. He nodded to them graciously, feeling quite the young lord. (Gad, didn't he look more the lord than Tony Broughton, that pallid young heir of Sir George, who also attended Dr. Carruthers' Academy?) He ascended the steps with an air, his every gesture stately and condescending. He tilted the tall brown hat at a more dignified angle. One of the maids curtsied again, opened the door for him, curtsied and peeped at him through bronze curls. He was hardly inside the door when the rain descended again, in sheets and waves. He congratulated himself on his good fortune.

Old Briggs materialized from the gloom of the vast marble hall, and with only a faint look of surprise, took John's precious hat and cane. Miss Eugenia, he informed the debonair visitor, had only just returned from certain errands for Mrs. MacNeill. He would inform her at once that Master John had arrived.

"The Academy is not in session today, sir?" asked the old man, fondly.

"Too much in session, Briggs, too much in session!" said John, airily, and with a tender air he glanced at the greatcoat now reposing over the butler's aged arm. "Careful with that, Briggs. It is dampish. Hang it where the air will reach it. Yes, too much in session, that damned hole! I've done with it."

Briggs, with the familiarity of an old servant, gaped ruefully. "Indeed, Master John! And you were to graduate in June, too?"

John smiled. "Not at the rate I was going, Briggs. Three years from June, more likely. Well, I've done with it. I expect to go into the business with my father, immediately. The old boy isn't doing so well, you know. He needs me."

Briggs adored him with his faded spaniel eyes. John's charm overcame many who were much more subtle and discerning than the butler.

8

"Ah, yes," he sighed. "But it must be a great support to Mr. Turnbull in his indispositions to know that he has such a son as you, Master John, begging your pardon."

John had serious doubts that his father rejoiced overmuch in this blessing, but he only smiled a little less brilliantly than before. He was experiencing a qualm. The fact that his father would not reproach him, would only gaze at him quizzically upon reading that accursed Carruthers' letter, did not lighten that qualm. He could have endured the disgrace more easily if his father had been more brutal and domineering and given more to violent tempers. He could meet him, then, on equal grounds.

He sauntered into the great dim drawing-room, and looked about him with his usual distaste. That distaste was not lightened by the thought that the furnishings were identical, in their restraint and cool elegance, to those in his own home. There was a robust and passionate warmth in him which made him distrait and uneasy, and very resentful, in the presence of people or rooms that were still and lofty, calm and elegant. Pale dim walls like these, all remote plaster and high carved moldings, chilled him and filled him with a sense that he was alien. There were faded green draperies at the tall narrow windows with their rounded carved tops, and every fold was formal and cold, the golden cords and tassels as motionless as though formed of metal. The polished floor with its marquetry pattern enhanced the chill and withdrawal of the room, and reflected, as ice reflects, the simple but exquisitely carved chairs and love-seats, all covered with faded petit-point or ancient tapestry or dimmed velvet and damask. There was very little of this furniture, and it was disposed about the room in formal positions, which were, however, not stiff or rigid. Here and there a Persian rug was laid, the colours indistinguishable, so faded and soft were they. An enormous crystal chandelier hung from the molded ceiling; it caught the pale and livid light of the December day, like motionless icicles. In one distant corner was a pianoforte, of gleaming rosewood. The simple carved tables were not loaded with velvet covers, nor dripping with tassels, but stood in cold and polished dignity near the love-seats and chairs, and bore only one or two delicate objets d'art on their shining surfaces: snuff-boxes, Dresden figurines, gilt sweet-meat plates, a crystal Oriental figure, or a tiny music-box. On those detested pale dim walls hung dark family portraits; John loathed those calm narrow faces, so colourless and aristocratic, those dark aloof eyes, those slender dispassionate hands aimlessly disposed. He did not see the calm and unshakable

9

strength in those faces, those white unringed hands. They were merely flaccid and bloodless, to him.

He shivered, and approached the low crimson fire that burned on the black marble hearth in the black marble fireplace with its white marble pillars. It gave out no warmth to him. It was a painted fire, depressing and lifeless. Over the mantelpiece was hung a round mirror in a carved gilt frame. It reflected back the cold gray windows, and enhanced the formal gloom and silence of the room. John turned away from the comfortless fire, and moved to the windows. He looked out upon the drenched and ashen garden, where the grasses were brown and soaked. Dead brown leaves were scattered about, holding livid trembling water in their shrivelled cups. The large oak tree in the center was black and blasted with winter, its sinewy trunk and twisted boughs gleaming with bitter moisture. The flower-beds were desolate with fallen stems and withered leaves. Along the red brick wall at the end of the garden the climbing rosebushes shook and bent under the wind and rain. The sundial, the bird-baths and the white stone seats were streaked with wet soot, and dripping. A few sparrows picked disconsolately at the ashy grass, tugged at reluctant worms. The windowpanes rattled in a sudden cold gust, and the rain lashed at them in gray streams. Winter, which John hated strenuously, was at hand, the desolate gray winter of London, seldom enlivened by clean bright snow. He could hear, but not see, the carriages which rolled hollowly on the road. There was an echoing booming through the great silent house, like the echoes of furtive sounds made in long caverns. To him, the mansion was filled with cold thin ghosts. He hated it. He glanced at the gaseous and ashy sky, swimming with darker-gray cloud shapes and mist, and shuddered.

Now the thought which had wandered vaguely and mutinously in his mind became stronger and angrily resolute. This dull and colourless land was not for him! This echoing drenched land, so filled with forms and stiffnesses and lightlessness was horrible to one of his temperament. But where could he go? Even as he thought this, despairingly, his father's thin and quizzical face rose up before him, and he experienced the old pang of love and devotion. Could he leave his father? But not forever! he thought, resolutely. Only for a little while, an escape. He would return.

He walked back to the fire, walking on the tips of his pointed boots so as not to awaken the long and menacing echoes. He fumbled in his pocket and brought out a cheroot. He glanced about the room, uneasily. Dare he fill this empty and majestic barrenness with smoke? Then, pressing his lips together, he bent and lighted the cheroot from the smoldering and falling fire, and smoked defiantly. For some reason, the act reassured him, comforted him. He watched the coiling of the smoke with delight. His broad dark face, so handsome, brutal and intrinsically merry, lightened. He smiled. His white teeth flashed in the floating gloom. He inhaled with intense pleasure.

He heard a soft, gliding footstep. Instinctively, he tossed the cheroot into the fire, then cursed himself for doing so. A scowl appeared on his face, and it became lowering and sullen, as he turned towards the footsteps. Nevertheless, his heart began to beat swiftly, with an old and familiar anticipation and helpless wildness.

On the far threshold, between the portals of the great austere doorway, a young girl stood, about fifteen or sixteen years old. In that pale and uncertain light, she was hardly visible, for she blended with it, was part of it, and part of the bare and silent room. Her quietness was its quietness, its stillness hers, its dim colours in her face and garments, its austerity and dignity and restraint implicit in her own. She was not very tall, but her slenderness had in its such composure and pride that she appeared much taller than in reality. Her figure was still somewhat immature, but exquisitely formed, and full of calm grace. She wore a dove-gray dress, with a tight basque over her dainty breasts. Her skirt was not the immense circle of the fashionable gown, but, like everything else about her toilette, restrained and in perfect taste, and only narrowly hooped. At her throat was pinned an ivory cameo, quite large in its golden frame. A frill of pure lace rose above it. She gave off the elusive cool odor of eau-de-cologne, fresh and lemony, suggesting clean virginity.

Her pale and quiet face was oval, and the colour of ivory, delicately touched at the cheek-bones by a rosy shadow. This tenuous colour was repeated in her composed mouth, somewhat thin, but beautifully shaped. Her nose, sharp and almost transparent, was perfect in its formation. The chiselled nostrils were like marble, and one hardly believed that they were the portals of living breath. Between the black thick shadows of her eyelashes, polished and pointed, her large gray eyes looked out serenely and dispassionately. There was no vagrant blue in that grayness, no tint of green or hazel. They were pure gray, like smoke, and strangely bright and steadfast and without fear or guile. Her expression revealed the unshakable integrity of her temperament, her fine intelligence, her chilly pride and breeding. Her dark hair was perfectly straight, parted in the middle, and drawn back in a smooth roll near her small ears, and caught in a net. Upon it, she wore a wide-brimmed gray hat, untrimmed except for the gray satin ribbons tied under her pointed white chin. Over her shoulders was thrown a gray Cashmere shawl, heavily fringed, and her little narrow hands were still gloved in gray kid.

She stood for a moment on the threshold, then entered the room, calmly untying the ribbons of her hat, and slipping off her shawl. She smiled slightly, and began to remove her gloves. She exhaled the fragrance of cologne, and the freshness of wind and rain. When she smiled like this, the formality and restraint of her face lightened, and she was all regal beauty, untouched and composed.

"John," she said. Her voice was soft and sweet, and very low, unhurried, without vulgar curiosity, though this was an unusual hour for her cousin to be calling upon her. Now that her hat was removed, one saw that her smooth hair gleamed, not a lock disarranged or blown by the wind, and that above her eyes were finely marked and tilted black brows.

John looked at her, and was mute, as always in the presence of this adored and reserved girl. Once he tried to imagine her naked, but even his lusty and ruthless nature had recoiled at the thought, as at a sacrilege. He had almost come to believe that she had been born this way, fully clothed in pale and elusive colours, always composed and virgin. He had seen and played with her, when they had been children, but he could not remember that she had ever been flustered, that she had ever pouted or been dishevelled or hot or petulant. Always, she had been clean and orderly, sure of herself, graceful, faintly smiling, well-bred and tactful. She had always given way before him, lightly and coolly, with an obliging grace and delicacy. Yet, though he had known her so long, and worshipped her from the very first moment, he realized that he did not know her at all. Was she ever discomposed, uncertain, unsure, sad, angry or petty? If she was, he had never witnessed it. Her character was a locked box to him. She excited him enormously. She was unexplored and provocative. She never failed to confuse him, even to anger him with her remoteness. Yet her mystery, her cold and aristocratic charm, was to live for him always, to torture him and humble him in his lustiness and earthy lack of true breeding. The world of books, of music, of painting and literature, was her world, in which he was a loutish and hating stranger. But he reverenced it, with fury, knowing it forever unattainable to him, and convinced, to the end of his life, that it was the only worthy world.

She was no intruder, as he was, in this room so frightful

to him. The dark and withdrawn portraits on the wall became alive in her presence, seemed to smile down upon her, recognizing her as the embodiment of themselves. Now the chill and the bareness lightened about her, became exquisite serenity for all their austere majesty. She extended her white unringed hand to her cousin, and he raised it to his lips with a sudden and impetuous gesture, full of passion and love. Her thin black brows lifted for an instant, then fell. She smiled again. The faint colour in her cheeks and lips brightened. He did not hear her caught breath. He could not know that under that dove-gray bodice her calm heart had quickened its beat, and that in those fragile violet veins the blood ran swifter. He would never know that at his touch her breasts became warm and full, and that a hot languor disturbed that quiet flesh. He only knew that when he approached her the icy aura about her dissolved. He thought this only a reflection of his own desire and love.

Remembering his manners, he ceremoniously led her to a seat near the fire, and put a hassock under those tiny slippered feet. He did this with the priest's reverence and adoration. He did not see how her hand crept out to touch his black curly head, and then withdrew swiftly. When he glanced up into her face, his own dark with congested blood, it was soft for all its quietness. She was removing her gloves with slow and graceful movements, and smiling at him.

He poked the low fire into a quick and crackling life, his gestures impatient and disturbed. She watched him. Her gray eyes were quick and bright. He sat near her, and leaned forward, impetuously. His mouth felt dry, and his heart was thundering. She sat upright in her chair, as became a lady, and waited.

"I have been booted out of Carruthers'," he said, bluntly. He could never speak to her with composure, or with a casual intonation. He flung all his words at her with an awkward and despairing violence, brutal in their incoherent intensity. He always cursed himself for this. Why could he not speak and behave to her as did that pallid milksop, Tony Broughton, with his leg-making and his bows and neatness? How ridiculous he must appear to her!

She did not answer immediately. She paled; the firelight, reflected on her cheeks, was a reflection cast on polished ivory. She was a carved and silent image, with a severe and withheld look and secret thoughts. Now there was a certain bloodlessness about her, and, with rage, he strove against it, as always.

"Do not look so condemning, pray," he said, with deep

sarcasm. "No doubt you are thinking that this would never occur to our pretty friend, Broughton."

Her large gray eyes regarded him inscrutably, and even with a slight contempt.

"Certainly, it would not occur," she answered. "Why need it have occurred to you? What did you do?"

She was like a wall of ice, against which he impotently, and with despair, thrust himself, hating her, adoring her for her perfection which could not understand his own imperfection.

"There were a number of things, not fit for your maiden ears," he said, with harshness. "Among them, petty gambling, debts, rioting. Do I offend you?"

There was an imperceptible movement of her smooth gray shoulders, as if she shrugged. But her eyes fixed themselves upon him, sternly.

"You are trying, perhaps, to be the young gay gentleman?" she asked. "You think you are romantic?"

He stared at her, with furious wretchedness. How could he explain to her his feverish revolt against gentility, against good behaviour which was without blood and life, against his own sense that he did not measure up to incomprehensible and elegant standards of conduct? How could he explain to her that he did not really know against what he revolted? He was always inarticulate. When he spoke, in a desperate effort to make himself comprehensible, he could only use the form and sound of violence.

"I do not think I am romantic," he said, in a stifled tone, clenching his fists. "Perhaps I am guilty of folly. What young man is not?"

"There is folly which is in good taste, and folly which is not," said Eugenia.

"Hah!" he snorted, "you imply there is a difference between a coarse carouser and an elegant rake? You are quite right, ma'am. I am a coarse carouser. I do not bow properly, nor make a leg magnificently when I smash windows and run up accounts at the pastry shop."

She raised her left eyebrow. Her look was long and disdainful.

"I am seen in Soho, instead of Vauxhall," continued John, with withering emphasis.

"I prefer Vauxhall," said Eugenia, in a voice in marked contrast with his own.

She held her transparent hands to the fire. He saw the modelling of each delicate finger, the coolness, the bloodlessness of it. But he was not repelled. His passion for her was only increased at the sight of her inaccessible hands.

14

She spoke, without looking at him: "Uncle James went to great effort to secure your admission to Dr. Carruthers'. The sons of tradesmen and merchants are not customarily admitted. He, himself, would not have cared for this, for he is a gentleman of discernment, and has a sense of proportion. Nevertheless, your mother had an elegant tradition——"

"Though she was nothing but a merchant-draperer's daughter, herself," interrupted John, loudly, with a derisive but painful smirk.

Eugenia continued quietly, as if he had not spoken: "It was his promise, on your mother's deathbed, that he would make a gentleman of you, John." She turned to him now, and that bright inscrutable look, somewhat hard and shining, came back into her gray eyes. "Though why he should promise this, and demean himself by the promise, is, I confess, beyond me. Through his own worth, his own qualities of character and spirit, he is admitted to the most elegant and noble drawing-rooms in London. There is none who would dare to impugn that he is not a gentleman, of the noblest tradition. He is accepted where many another would not be allowed to enter. And, because of him, you are also admitted. You are the first merchant's son who has ever been admitted to Carruthers'."

As this was all only too true, John's fury increased. But she heeded this no more than she did the storm and wind outside. She spoke, but it was as if she spoke only to herself:

"Young gentlemen's high spirits are often offered in apology for unpardonable conduct. I believe your conduct is unpardonable, but not because of high spirits, John. I do not believe that you are capable of innocent high spirits. You behave unspeakably because you think the other gentlemen at the school look down upon you, in uncivil snobbery. I believe you are fully aware of Uncle James's remarkable character, and that it infuriates you that your companions do not defer to you because of this character, and even behave contemptuously towards you."

It is true! he thought, wildly. He was incapable of analysing his own impulses, even his own thoughts and desires. He was trembling with angry eagerness, and his dark cheek flushed.

"Yes," he said, hoarsely. "There is much to be considered in that. They are nothing but milksops and feckless fools, none of whom I would desire as a friend. Nevertheless, because of birth, they believe they are better than I."

She gazed at him with delicate ruthlessness.

"Are they?" she asked. "Does your conduct warrant the opinion that you are better?"

He looked at her wrathfully. "I did no worse than Bollister. He becomes entangled with drabs—" He stopped abruptly, terrified that she would be offended. But no modest or indignant blush appeared on that gleaming ivory cheek. There was no distaste in her expression.

"There are things in society, however deplorable and unjust, which must be accepted, John. Do not believe that I agree with these traditions. But they exist. Mr. Bollister's father, grandfather and great-grandfather are nobility. You may be a worthier man, but you are not gentry. We must bow to these laws of society."

"I do not bow!" he exclaimed, starting to his feet. "I loathe society! I repudiate it. I scorn it! I shall not knuckle under to it!"

She smiled, somewhat disdainfully, as at the ravings of a schoolboy.

"What can you do? Can you change traditions single-handed, yourself? It is easier to change the laws of the realm than it is to change the artificial laws of a self-conscious society. Your father understands this. He has tried to imply it to you——"

"You are both in league against me! You always were! You used to sit beside him, when you were in pinafores, with your hair plaited, and you would both smirk at me as if I were a fool!" He stood by the mantelpiece, and now he struck it with a clenched fist. His face was alive with rage; his black eyes snapped and glittered, and there was something of hatred in the look he flashed at her.

She was not intimidated. "You are tedious, John. You are childish. No one has ever smirked at you. If the consciousness of your own shortcomings and impetuousness made you uneasy, and uncivil, it was your own fault, not ours. Because you felt you were not a gentleman born, you became a boor. That is an insult to your father."

He was silent. But his disordered breathing was loud in the echoing room. The day had become darker and grayer. The far corners of the room were lost in uncertain mist, as if the rising fog outside had penetrated to them. In contrast, the fire was vivid and scarlet.

"Because of the esteem in which your father is universally held, it may be possible for you to return—" said the girl, contemplatively.

"I shall never return!" cried John, furiously. And then, in wonder, fear and amazement, he knew this was true. Instantly, he knew that he would not, could not return, no matter if this was granted to his father. He was done with all that. He had left a hateful place. The world was before him.

Eugenia, who was accustomed to dismissing John's extravagances, knowing that he hardly meant them for more than an instant, suddenly knew that he meant this, that nothing would change his new resolution. She was alarmed. She looked at him with uncertainty, as if he were a strong hard stranger, and not the impetuous, wild and foolish cousin whom she loved.

"What, then, is your intention?"

He did not speak. He sat down, heavily. He leaned forward, his elbows folded on his knees, and stared at the fire, as if he was alone. The firelight, as at a signal, suddenly flowered into brilliant red flames, and lit up that broad dark countenance, those wide planes of his cheeks, that ruthless heavy mouth. It lay like a red glare in the sockets of his eyes. He was a stranger, and her heart hurried, with a mysterious excitement.

"What shall I do?" he said, very softly, and with a kind of fierceness. "I do not know, yet. But this I do know: I shall not return to that accursed place; I shall not go into my father's trade. It is loathsome to me. England is loathsome to me. I gasp in this wet and gritty air. I hate all that is within these little borders."

His hands clenched. He began to beat his strong knees with them. A terrible excitement filled him. He looked at her with blazing eyes, as if dazzled by something she did not see. A deep flush rose to his face, increased.

"This is no land for me!" he exclaimed, and his voice was hoarse and quickened. "I shall go to the Colonies—to America — Anywhere where a man can breathe, away from this effluvia of oldness and stench."

She tried to smile. How extravagant! But she could not smile. Instead, she could only place her hand upon her breast, with great agitation. He had never seen her make that gesture before. She, then, was not invulnerable. He had the power to distract her! He reached out and took her other hand. It was very cold, and trembling. He turned over that hand and kissed the palm with vehement passion. Never had he dared such familiarity before. He had touched her pale cool cheek with his lips; he had kissed the back of her hand on a few occasions. But this pressing of his mouth deep into her flesh, that demanding hot mouth, was something new and shattering. He felt strong and inexorable, and when she would withdraw her hand, he clung to it, and kissed it over and over, until she was still.

He looked up at her, the dark blood in his face making

his features thick and congested. And she gazed at him with the strange and frightened face of a woman, aware of passion for the first time, revolted by it, drawn mysteriously by it.

"Genie! Come with me!" he whispered, urgently. "We can be married by special licence. We can go tomorrow, the next day——"

His words forced her swift recovery from momentary confusion. She dragged her hand from his, and rose to her feet, trembling.

"What are you saying, John?"

He stood up, also, and caught her by her thin shoulders. His fingers went deeply into her soft flesh. He was no longer afraid of her, overcome by her. He only knew that he loved her beyond reason, and that he could not let her go.

"We were to be married in July, Genie, my love. On your sixteenth birthday. What does it matter if it is a few months earlier? You are not a child. I am a man. Let us be married at once, and then go away together, to the Colonies, to America——"

"You are mad," she said, in a low voice. Never had he seen her so pale and stern.

"I shall indeed go mad if I remain here!" he exclaimed. He reached out his hands to take her again, but she stepped backward, and caught at the arm of the chair from which she had risen. She lifted her hand with a hard cold gesture, which restrained him.

"You would run away, like a coward?" she asked, incredulously. "Only because you have been expelled from a foolish school? You are afraid to face your father, who would only laugh, because he is wise?"

Her inability to understand made him frantic. He must reach through that chill and obdurate flesh to the steely heart that lay under it. He must warm it with understanding. But words, as always, failed him. He could only seize them, like heavy stones, and fling them wildly at her:

"Is it possible you cannot see, Genie? Do you not know how terrible this place has become for me? I am not running away. I have talked to my father before, and he has frankly confessed that he would not care if I did not follow him into the trade. He is wiser than you, Genie. He has understanding." He flung out his arms, awkwardly, despairingly. "Cannot you understand that I must leave England?"

"Why?" she asked, in her incisive and softly ruthless voice.

He dropped his arms hopelessly to his sides, and gazed at her despairingly.

"Because of the fools who have sneered at you, looked

down upon you? And you have cared for this, with such a father?"

He shook his head numbly. She thought that he looked like a child, a great schoolboy, inarticulate and confused.

Finally he spoke, stiffly and painfully, as though words were sharp stones in darkness, over which he must pick his way:

"I must go away. It is necessary for me to go away. There was an etching in a book— It was called the Iron Maiden. It was a torture instrument, an iron cast of a woman, filled with sharp spikes. They—put heretics in the iron shape, and pushed the parts together. The spikes went into the heretic's body—that is how I feel. In England. I must go away."

She contemplated the crude image which he had drawn with his halting words, then, as the full import dawned on her, she shivered with disgust. What ungenteel extravagance! But John was always wild and extravagant, saying the most exaggerated and incomprehensible things. One had learned to smile at them, knowing that he meant only a small part, or none at all. He spoke always for effect. What had Uncle James called him once? A buccaneer. An audacious pirate. But buccaneers and pirates were such theatrical impostors. But Uncle James had not smiled when he had called his son these things. He had looked a little sad and thoughtful, and had sighed. That sigh had been very mysterious, almost as if there had been envy in it, or nostalgia.

Now she was truly frightened. She looked at John's vivid and desperate face, crowned by its disordered thick profusion of black curls. He was no Englishman, this big young man with the broad shoulders and the military waist and thighs. He was foreign. He was an alien. There was no thin blue blood of England in those riotous veins. His grandfather, Angus Burnley, had been a Scotsman. One could never trust or understand Scotsmen. They were dour or violent, and so unEnglish. They produced women like those dreadful Catholic Marys, wantons and trollops and murderesses. They spawned Lady Macbeths, and their husbands. Wild colourful creatures, lawless and passionate, grim and terrible, creatures leaping over their blasted hills with dirks in their teeth, great black-bearded creatures and women with flashing indomitable eyes, shrieking! Eugenia had often heard the Scottish pipers. The frightful wailing of the pipes had appalled and terrified her, so barbarous had it sounded, so inhuman, so ominous. They made her see distressing visions of white mountains and black caves, of empty moors dark under Northern lights, of green and purple seas, icy cold, dashing over savage wet rocks and hurling themselves against impregnable cliffs. And now, as she gazed affrightedly at John, she saw all these things again and shivered.

John saw the shiver, and was gloomily contrite. "I am sorry, Genie. The Iron Maiden isn't pleasant to think about, I grant you that. But that is what I feel, in England."

Eugenia sat down, without speaking, and looked at the fire, while John stood humbly and desperately before her. Scotsmen were blood kin to Irishmen. They were one and the same. And what were Irishmen? Clever English novelists and playwrights put them into books and plays, and always they were buffoons and shallow rascals, amusing but contemptible. They were servants by nature. They were cheats and liars, lovable in a crude and cunning way, drunkards and dancers and gay traitors. Scotsmen had this Irish blood in them, in addition to the passionate and cruel wilderness. Eugenia shivered again, and her face became pale stone.

"Come with me," whispered John. He dropped on one knee near her, but did not dare to touch her. He could only gaze at her yearningly. But behind that expression she saw all the violence of his nature, his loud contemptuousness, his extravagance and heat, his hatred for orderly discipline and restraint, his hot vulgarity. She was terrified of him, but most frighteningly drawn to him. She pressed the palms of her cold hands together to restrain their trembling.

"You have no conception of your duty, John? You would desert your father? You would ask me to desert my invalid mother?"

Now the uncontrollable violence swept over him again.

"Duty!" he cried. "Must we choke in this vile place because of duty to those who are about to die? We must smother in this wet gritty air, and allow others to feed upon our flesh?"

"Don't!" The word was a disgusted cry forced from her involuntarily. She was very angry. John had never seen her angry before. He stared at her, incredulous. Her bright gray eye flashed with a reflection of his own fury. Then, it was possible for her to be stirred, to be moved, to be infuriated! A tremendous joy broke in him, a great delight. He tried to take her hand, but she snatched it away.

"How can you speak so?" she asked, in a quivering voice. "Your language is ungenteel and revolting. You are not a gentleman. You can never be a gentleman. I must seriously reconsider—" She paused, then continued ruthlessly: "If you have no conception of duty, I must confess that I have. I cannot leave my mother, to go with you to a strange and impossible country. Even if she—were not here, I could not go. There are duties to be considered, disciplines, restraints."

He forced himself to speak quietly, though his heart was a burning pain in his chest. "You do not care for living, then?"

"John, you are incomprehensible. I do not understand your wild words."

"You are not a woman," he said, bitterly.

She gazed at him in stern affront, but did not speak.

John moved to the mantelpiece. He leaned his elbows upon it, covered his face with his hands. Then he began to speak, in low words which came with a muffled sound from between his fingers.

"I cannot stay here. I must go."

Eugenia composed herself. She said, coldly: "Assume, for a moment, John, that you have gone to America. What would you do in that uncivilized country?"

He dropped his hands and turned to her, and now he was burning with hope and eagerness again. "I don't know! But it will be something strong and fresh, something to pit one's strength against, something new and living."

She smiled her still bleak smile. "There are Indians, I believe, and terrible forests, and wild beasts of all kinds. And wildernesses, unbelievable mountains, and deserts."

"There are cities, too, Genie."

"Vulgar, uncivilized outposts, filled with disgusting mixtures of all lawless people. I am afraid you must excuse me from such a life, John. I am an Englishwoman."

He did not speak, but he regarded her strangely. She was suddenly terrified. She reached out her hand, so unusual a gesture for the controlled Eugenia, and laid it on his arm. It did not respond to her touch.

"You would not leave me, John?"

He averted his head. And then, sighing, he said: "I do not know, Eugenia. But I have not given up hope that you will come."

She pressed her hands together again, convulsively. Her terror mounted.

"John, please listen to me. Suppose that we wait a number of years, until our dear ones need us no longer? Suppose, then, that we go to India? You will be a merchant, an importer. We can spend a few months a year, in India. I have always wished to visit that exotic place."

He was silent. His head was bent. Then he said in a voice she had never heard before: "No. No. I want no part of the Empire. I can see that, now. I must go to America."

She was deeply offended, and outraged. She stood up, smoothing down her dove-gray garments with firm hands.

"I must leave you now, John. My mother needs me. You have spoken very wildly. You are not yourself. I must decline

to discuss this absurd matter any longer. I trust, however
that you will soon come to your senses."

He turned to her. He did not speak. She inclined her head
with a stately gesture, and floated out of the room. He made
no movement to halt her.

A few moments later he flung himself out of that hateful
house, which he could not endure, could never endure.

CHAPTER 2

EUGENIA had a certain bloodless capacity to force her
thoughts, however turbulent, into disciplined paths, quell-
ing even the very agitated beating of her heart. It was
as if she were able, by will alone, to direct the very movement of her blood, chilling it when too fevered. By the time
she had climbed, in her calm and stately way, to the upper
floor and her mother's apartments, her ivory face was as
composed as ever, her breath serene, her manner controlled.
But the faint tint of depression remained in her thoughts and
mind, like dissolved mud in clear water. However, upon
entering Mrs. MacNeill's chamber, Eugenia's smile was
lightly affectionate and untroubled.

The widowed Mrs. MacNeill was much given to vapours,
to elegant invalidism. In truth, she was quite a healthy lady,
with a greedy appetite. Her servants understood this; they
discreetly left the pantry doors ajar at night, revealing a cold
bird, a bottle of stout, a good cheese and butter and tart
already set out invitingly. No one asked who consumed them
during the darker hours, by the light of a candle in the
great brick kitchen. If Eugenia, and the servants, knew, they
were silent. Eugenia, at times, appeared anxious, and the
winged black brows would draw together thoughtfully, for
she knew that her mother's physician had ordered that lady
to remain on a delicate diet, for reasons of heart. But the
girl had neither the indiscretion nor the cruelty to reproach
her mother ruthlessly for her gorging at midnight. The
pleasant fiction was allowed to exist that Mrs. MacNeill "ate
less than a bird, poor lady." Trays taken to her chaise-longue
and bed were always returned hardly touched, while Mrs.
MacNeill, on the pillows, assumed an interesting posture of
patient suffering languor and mournful sweetness, the while
her daughter or her maid bewailed the fact that the tea was

22

only sipped, the fowl merely nibbled at, the muffins in their original pristine condition. And Mrs. MacNeill would listen to these lamentations with a martyred smile, many sighs, many humble pleading gestures and beseeching looks that implored forgiveness for the anxiety she was causing her dear household. "I am sure I am a great burden," she would murmur, closing weary eyelids, or rolling her eyes heavenward.

This hypocrisy, which a more robust and more obtuse nature would have found furiously intolerable, only increased Eugenia's pity. She knew that her mother was a foolish woman, selfish, avaricious, greedy and self-indulgent, obsessed only with her own desires and vanities. She knew that Mrs. MacNeill had no qualities of mind or spirit which would attract the interest and attention of others by reason of them, but that, unfortunately, she possessed in unusual strength the natural human desire for this interest and attention. Not being able to draw the love and solicitation of acquaintances and family because of a lovely temperament, spirited conversation, real sympathy or tenderness or awareness of humanity, she had, perforce, to command them by simulating invalidism. As she was very rich in her own right, she was given that attention and interest which would have been denied a more impecunious lady. These riches, perversely, for that reason, had forced her to resort to invalidism; had she been poor, she would have been denied this luxury, and forced to shift for herself.

Mrs. MacNeill lay in her immense musty chamber, the curtains drawn against even the feeble gray light of the December day. The curtains hung heavily about her canopied bed, where she reclined upon her ruffled pillows. A tiny chuckling fire burned on the black marble hearth. The shapes of her bulky mahogany furniture lurked in the fetid gloom, like misformed animals. Not for her the austerity and elegance which had created the other rooms in the mansion. Mr. MacNeill had been a gentleman of taste, for all his later tendency towards the bottle. But Mrs. MacNeill loved solidity and ugliness and "cosiness." Her carpets were thick and dusty, and crimson. Her silk-hung walls were also of crimson, shot through with threads of gold. Her draperies were crimson, splashed with poisonous green. The portraits on the walls were heavy with gilt. Here and there a pier mirror caught what livid light penetrated the chamber and reflected it like spectral shadows. The air was smothering in its odours of medicine, tea, attar of roses, dust and stale pampered flesh.

Eugenia gently lit a lamp near the bedside. Mrs. MacNeill winced. "I was drowsing, child," she whimpered, sharply.

"I have not slept a wink all night. But now, in your perverseness, you must disturb me. You were always an inconsiderate little creature. Never mind. Let the lamp alone. What has delayed you so long?"

Eugenia quietly sat near the bed and folded her hands on her dove-gray lap. She smiled with forced gaiety at her mother. If her marble nostrils drew together to shut out too much of the overpowering smells in the room, the movement was not visible.

As she lay on her plump white pillows, it could be discerned, by the struggling lamplight, that Mrs. MacNeill was a gross and vulgar woman. She was of a big frame, her large bones overlaid with billows of pale and lustrous fat, flabby and scented. These billows gleamed as if oiled, even through the thin and delicate cambric of her ruffled nightgown. Her body made a mound under the silken quilts, bulging and huge. In contrast with the general grossness of that body, her hands were tiny, plump and dimpled, and very white, as were her feet. She was inordinately proud of these members. Her shoulders, however, were mountainous, but as they were also white as snow, and gleaming, she was proud of them, also. She thought of herself as a "fine figure of a woman," as indeed she had been in her youth, when she had been much admired for her tall and luxurious figure and flamboyant colouring. But now the "fine figure" was dissolved in fat, the colouring much faded. However, her face was small and round, still, the skin milk white and smooth, with a pouting petulance which gave her the appearance of a stupid and pampered child. Her mouth was full and pink, if sulky and sensual. In the midst of this rounded and heavy countenance, the nose was only a tiny sharp peak, tilted upwards, with amazingly thin and delicate nostrils, somewhat pinched and shrewish. Her eyes, which a former suitor had declared were "twin pools of azure light, reflecting stars," were no longer large and limpid as in her youth, but sunken in the hillocks of her facial flesh so that they appeared to be unusually small and shallow, little round blue disks of polished china, lighted, now, not by stars, but by the restless and unsleeping malice of her soul.

It is a tribute to unfailing human credulity that Mrs. MacNeill believed, against all the evidence of her many mirrors, that she was still the lissome and majestic young Martha of her youth, that her masses of faded blonde hair (still curly and heavy) retained the golden shadows that once distinguished them, that her eyes still blazed with light blue light, and that she was still possessed of enchanting charms. When she could be persuaded to rise from her bed to greet guests in the stately and pallid drawing-rooms which she detested, her toilettes were magnificent and florid, looped, braided, draped and beribboned, with coquettish water-falls cascading from bared shoulders, her hoops extravagant, her jewels overpowering.

Because she was sentimental as well as gluttonous, (two attributes inexorably found together) she believed she was much adored, that her opinions on every subject were gems of wit, that her toilettes set the fashions among the ladies of London, and that she was a power in the city, that every one commiserated with her because she possessed an only daughter completely devoid of charm and coquetry. This latter delusion of hers was always loudly on her lips, especially in Eugenia's presence. "How I could have given birth to such a pale and miserable little mouse is quite beyond my comprehension," she would say, sighing, and fanning herself with a martyred expression. "When I was her age, I was the toast of London, if I may be allowed to say so, myself. I had sonnets composed to me. Young gentlemen glowered at each other, and fought duels for the permission to take me to Vauxhall. I was told, on high and incontrovertible authority, that the Queen, herself, once inquired of a certain gentleman, "Who is that magnificent creature in the blue velvet and pearls?'"

Her father, Robert Turnbull, (father of James Turnbull) had adored her. Her mother, the former Mary Chisholm, had become a widow at the age of eighteen. Robert, a widower with one son, (James) had taken her as his second wife. Mary, had presented him with Martha. So it was that she and James were children of the same father but not the same mother. This, she repeatedly emphasized, especially to Eugenia. She assured the girl that the mother of James was reputed to be a meagre and silent little creature, much like Eugenia, added Martha, candidly, and of a very obscure and humble family. In her conversations she ignored her father's antecedents, and stressed the aristocracy of her own mother, Mary Chisholm.

It is strange that Eugenia should love this foolish and venomous woman. But that love was daughter of compassion. Eugenia had subtlety and understanding, for all her fifteen years. Her life had been miserable, secluded and hard. She had retreated to the land of contemplation, her father's and grandfather's library, and in these dim cloisters had fashioned a calm dry philosophy of her own, which sustained her in all emergencies. If she was cynical, no one knew this but herself. She had come to suspect, with acrid amusement, all sentimentality, all vulgarity, all extravagance and violence, all

25

volubility and affectation, having discovered how cheap and sordid they were in her mother.

Now, as Eugenia sat so quietly near her mother, smiling her pretty smile, she was filled with anxiety. How fat poor Mamma was becoming! Her breath, too, was so wheezy and laboured. If only some way could be found to restrain her bottomless appetite! Eugenia resolved that she would have a quiet talk with the housekeeper, and try to persuade that formidable but sympathetic individual to leave out a smaller bird, a smaller cheese, and no stout or pastries. Mrs. MacNeill would not dare to complain. Her health, however, would benefit.

"Do not stare at me so emptily, child," Mrs. MacNeill said, peevishly, shifting on her plump pillows. She blinked angrily. "And do turn out that lamp. You have no consideration for me, at all. How insensible you are, Eugenia. A girl of sensibility would have more sympathy for her mother."

Eugenia obediently dimmed the lamp. Its flickering rays struggled in the musky air. "I thought that you might like me to read to you, Mamma," she said, in her soft and chiselled voice. "You were so interested yesterday in Mr. Dicken's last novel. You said it was so affecting, and that it quite made you cry."

Now that the conversation was about herself, Mrs. MacNeill was soothed. She sighed, heavily, and touched her eyes with a laced cambric handkerchief.

"I do not think I could bear it today, Eugenia. So affecting. When I saw Mr. Dickens last winter, at Lady Christopher's elegant dinner, I reproached him, very gently, for his assaults upon our gentler sensibilities."

Eugenia had heard this story a hundred times before, but this did not prevent her from leaning forward attentively, with every expression of interest.

Mrs. MacNeill shook her head sadly. "Such a coarse man, in spite of his genius, Eugenia. He laughed in my face. I told Lady Christopher later, with much agitation, of the whole incident. Do you know what the abominable creature replied? Mr. Dickens, I mean, certainly. He said: 'Madam, gentle sensibilities are a crime, an unwarranted extravagance and hypocrisy in England, while one man is jailed for debt, or one child starves, or one desperate woman is driven to the streets.'"

Eugenia murmured something inaudible. Her interest was not feigned. Though she had never met Mr. Dickens she seemed to see his face while he spoke to her mother, vivid and angry, his voice like a bull's, his eye flashing with ire and contempt. It seemed to be John's face. A curious warmth rose in her, and her quiet heart beat faster.

"I was quite taken aback," continued Mrs. MacNeill, with all the original indignation she had felt. "Such language in a refined drawing-room! But that is what comes of admitting the lower classes into genteel society. Do not tell me that he is a genius, and that genius transcends the borders of class!" Her high voice rose irately. "That is nonsense. The man is nothing at all! Later, though I can hardly believe it, it was reported to me that he declared that England was done, finished, that she would go down, choking, in the warm ocean of fashionable tea brewed in English drawing-rooms! How Lady Christopher and other ladies can endure such a wretch is quite beyond me!"

Mrs. MacNeill, fully aroused, lifted herself upon her pillows and glared at poor Eugenia as though the child was directly guilty for Mr. Dickens, and his appalling notions. And Eugenia blushed faintly. She had been thinking that Mr. Dickens was a brave and noble man, and that he had been quite right. Even to herself, she was perturbed. Such heresy was unfamiliar to her.

"Fetch me my shawl," said Mrs. MacNeill, irritably. For a moment, the conversation had turned from herself, and she was annoyed. Eugenia started, and lifted the India shawl from the foot of the bed and placed it tenderly about her mother's massive shoulders. Her mother's expression was mean and vexed, and preoccupied. When Eugenia sat down again, she surveyed the girl with sidelong and vicious glances.

"How pale you are! And yet, you have just come from an airing. When I was your age, I bloomed. The rain made my cheeks like twin roses, dewy and fresh. That iron Dr. Bloomsbury prescribed for you is like just so much water. And you have no figure at all. When I was your age, I was called a goddess, a Venus, and I was much admired in the shops, and in my carriage, and in every drawing-room. I had a sonnet composed to me, in which I was called a queen——"

Eugenia was silent.

"No figure," repeated Mrs. MacNeill with malevolent emphasis. "One would believe you were miserably frail, if one did not know your appetite.

"I sometimes believe," continued Mrs. MacNeill, with a glance of active dislike at her silent daughter, "that you miserable little creatures suffer from over-eating, and derive no nourishment, in consequence, at the table. Pray, would you consider informing me of what your breakfast consisted?"

There was a slight tightness about Eugenia's smile as she replied: "I had only a cup of tea and a muffin, Mamma."

Mrs. MacNeill eyed her with sullen suspicion. "Mrs. Barkley informs me that a rasher of bacon and two chicken legs are missing." The sullen suspicion became very wary and piercing.

"I did not eat them," said Eugenia, with cold tranquility.

"Have you considered who did?"

Eugenia was silent. The strange excitement was like a growing fever in her. On another occasion she might have shook her head, protesting her ignorance, and might have ended with murmured commiserations over the pilfering of servants. But today this hypocrisy was beyond her. She gazed at her mother intently, and now her fine lips, somewhat pale, curled a little.

Mrs. MacNeill was dismayed, and, as a result, infuriated.

"What empty eyes you have, child! So expressionless. And how little consideration you have for me. You are well aware, are you not? that I am of a frail constitution and confined almost constantly to my bed, yet the matter of stealing from the scullery and the pantry leaves you undisturbed. I thought, at your age, that you might take an interest in the affairs of the household."

"Mrs. Barkley is quite capable, Mamma. Does she believe the servants are stealing?"

"I do not believe the servants are pilfering, Eugenia," she said, in a voice that was like a vicious leer.

"Who, then," asked Eugenia, in a very composed voice, "can possibly be guilty?"

There were strange and unfathomable things happening in Eugenia's neutral heart that morning. When she asked her mother that embarrassing and unpardonable question, she looked at her serenely.

Mrs. MacNeill was thrown into virulent alarm. She eyed her daughter with a truly intimidating look. But Eugenia remained undisturbed.

"'Who can possibly be guilty?'" she repeated, with excessive viciousness. Her round blue eyes sparkled malevolently. "Do you know who I believe is guilty, miss? I believe it is you! You pretend to a feeble appetite in order to receive sentimental sympathy. You wish to harrow the heart of your poor prostrated mother with pretenses of a frail constitution. Perhaps you wish her to believe you have consumption?"

"I am in excellent health, Mamma." The thin corners of Eugenia's lips twitched for a moment. "Moreover, I am certain you do not believe I pilfer during the night. I sleep very soundly. Unless, perhaps, I walk in my sleep."

"Oh, no doubt you are a somnambulist!" cried Mrs. Mac-Neill, with hysterical emphasis. "My daughter trails through the house at midnight, gorging herself, all in the deepest slumber! That is a pleasant thought for a mother! I might be overcome if I did not know this is complete nonsense, and a childish effort to deceive me. Have I denied you anything, you ungrateful child? Is it necessary to steal, and deny the stealing?"

"It would not be necessary to steal, Mamma," said Eugenia, quietly. "If I became hungry at night, I would not feel ashamed. I would not even think to mention it. I would merely help myself, and neither comment on it myself nor expect my servants to comment upon it."

All at once an unfamiliar and sinking sensation of complete exhaustion and disgust came over the girl. Impelled by it, she rose abruptly to her feet.

Mrs. MacNeill's disordered emotions kept her silent a moment. Then, after a sly peep out of the corner of her eyes at her daughter, she sank back upon her pillows and touched her eyes with her handkerchief. She spoke in a faint voice:

"You are quite right, Eugenia. If you wish a small midnight repast, it is certainly not the affair of a servant, even of Mrs. Barkley." She was suddenly relieved. "I shall tell Mrs. Barkley, very firmly, that I have discovered who has been dining in solitude at night, and that my daughter is quite at liberty to indulge herself if she wishes, without having to endure the impertinence of underlings."

Eugenia's lips parted, and her eye flashed. Then she closed her lips tightly and said nothing.

Mrs. MacNeill was delighted. Colour came brightly into her massive face. "I shall also inform Mrs. Barkley that she is to see to it that the larder is always well supplied with cold meats and tarts, and a bottle of good stout. Or would you prefer milk, my dear? On second thought, it shall be the stout. My physician informs me that stout is quite the blood-maker, and very sustaining."

She took Eugenia's hand. The girl's fingers were cold and stiff. Mrs. MacNeill rubbed them abstractedly in the warm thick cushions of her palms. She felt she quite loved this child.

Eugenia removed her hand gently from her mother's grip, and brought her the magazine, *The Lady of Fashion,* which she had purchased for her that morning, and also the new lavender smelling-salts. She laid these upon the round hillock which was her mother's knees.

"Hoops, I see, are to be even larger this year," she commented.

The bed groaned ominously when Mrs. MacNeil pulled herself upright on her pillows with every indication of avid interest. Her heavy fair rolls of hair fell over her ponderous cambric shoulders. Her full cheeks flushed. Her small mouth, pink and sulkily full, became as moist and eager as a child's. Now one saw that her claims to earlier and magnificent beauty were justified. Even now, weighted down by her gross flesh as she was, she had a certain lush splendour. The two women bent over the book, ruffled the pages, and Mrs. MacNeill commented with cries of admiration, scorn, disdain or ridicule, depending on whether the majestic creations pictured in the magazine excited her envy that she could not wear them, or her joy that she could.

"The pink velvet, my love! Is that not superb? The lace draperies, caught up with those exquisite blue bows! How very French! But those shoulders! They quite make me blush——"

"They would be excellent on you, Mamma. I do not think them extreme. Was it not Mrs. Berkeley-Niscome who said that you had the most magnificent shoulders in London?"

Mrs. MacNeill preened. She glanced sideways at the rounded marble mass of one shoulder. "Oh, Alicia is known for her extravagant flattery. Let us see. With that gown I could wear my white ermine, of course. And my pearls. But just look at those hoops! I declare they become more immense every year."

"You could modify them, Mamma."

"Indeed! And ruin the entire effect? You never did have an eye for fashion, Eugenia. You look quite the drab shopgirl; not an inch of style. If hoops continue to expand indefinitely, I shall expand with them."

Doubtless, thought Eugenia, cruelly.

"Look at these jackets. How tiny compared with the hoops. Black velvet, it appears, is very chic for the jackets. With brilliant buttons." She burst into gay ridiculing laughter. "And those ridiculous little bonnets, with the plumes and ribbons! What will Worth think of next? Really, they are monkey-bonnets. We shall have to have a street organ with them, I daresay."

Eugenia smiled.

"Tippets are smaller than ever," Mrs. MacNeill continued, frowning. "Hardly more than a rope around the neck. And look at those mantles. There is a military flavour about them. That is the Queen's influence, of course. She adores the military, though how she expects to wear them, with that figure——"

She was annoyed that fashions seemed designed for the

smaller figure this year. As she stood nearly five foot seven inches on her bare feet, she felt that she had been personally scorned. She eyed Eugenia with disfavour. What a shrivelled little creature it was, hardly larger than a respectable doll! Worth must have a tiny mistress this year, to be so intrigued by demureness and meagreness.

The magazine fell open to pages dedicated to brides. Mrs. MacNeill was consumed by envy. Never had bridal gowns been so exquisite. They were like vast white satin bells, designed for diminutive figures full of grace and daintiness. Above their gigantic flowering the little bosoms were all discretion and modesty, with the necks closely encircled by discreet rounded collars foaming with lace and simple pearls. The buttons were all very minute, and of self-material.

"How affected," muttered Mrs. MacNeill, who had no illusions that young ladies, for all their demureness, were too innocent. She gazed enviously at the clouds of lace which composed the veils. She was furiously annoyed at the coy and blushing expressions on the tinted little faces. In her day, brides were regal, with long sloping shoulders, proud queenly heads, and elongated figures, high-waisted and imperial. That is what comes of having a Queen hardly taller than a child, she thought.

Then she had another thought. If Eugenia were to be married to that immense horrid ape in the summer, it was none too soon to be planning her trousseau. She studied the bridal outfits with more interest. That plain gleaming satin would be excellent for Eugenia.

She studied Eugenia with an abstracted but acute eye. What a pity it was that the little wretch would be completely thrown in the shade by her mother! She smiled pleasantly. The pink velvet, with a lace scarf over the shoulders, would drown out the effect of pale bridal white and pale stern little face.

Would that oaf remember where to put his feet? She thought of John Turnbull, and her expression became quite mean. She favoured her daughter with a malicious bright glance, then frowned pettishly.

"Eugenia, I presume it has never occurred to you that I do not particularly favour this marriage?"

Eugenia lifted one of her fine black brows.

"No, Mamma?" she asked, serenely.

" 'No, Mamma!' " mimicked her mother, pushing aside the magazine with petty savagery. "However, I am only your mother, an invalid, whose opinion cannot possibly be of any value. Did you ever consult me, Eugenia?"

"I did not think it necessary." Now the girl's face was as

cold as snow, and as chilling. "I thought it was understood from the very beginning between you and Uncle James."

At the mention of her half-brother's name, Mrs. MacNeill' large face became uncertain. She feared James, and respected him. He managed her affairs. He was the only creature she really trusted in all the world. Then she recovered her mean irascibility.

"I have nothing against James, heaven knows! If his son were only more like him! James, from the very first, recognized the superiority of my mother, his stepmother. He patterned his home after hers, this house, in fact. He appreciated her impeccable taste. Though I always thought dear poor Mamma's taste somewhat depressing. I never altered the house, however; the memories were too precious. Indeed, I have nothing against James. Are you implying, Eugenia, that I have?"

Eugenia was silent. She stood at the bedside, looking down at her mother. Her mouth was pressed so tightly together that it was a thin sharp line. Whenever she was displeased, and this was more often than any one ever suspected, her mouth took on this hard severe expression, and presaged the day when its hardness would become cynicism and indifference to every one.

Mrs. MacNeill was now working herself up to a fine rage, which had its roots in dislike for her daughter, and envy.

"But James' son! What an oaf, what a great lumbering fellow it is, with no wit, no conversation, no charm, and certainly, no intellect! He does not suffer these deficiencies from his father's side; my own father was a gentleman whose conversation was much appreciated in the best drawing rooms. No, it all comes from his mother, who was truly a vulgar loud creature, with cheeks like red apples and a great hoarse voice. Whatever James saw in her is quite beyond me."

"I did not know you did not like John," said Eugenia, in her neutral voice.

"How obtuse you are, Eugenia. You are positively stupid. Simply because I did not refuse my consent to your betrothal does not mean that I was delighted. If you had any sensibility at all, you would have realized that I felt that John was better than having an old spinster on my hands. saw no other young gentlemen besieging you. Though in my day, my papa was thrown in a frenzy regularly at the manner in which young gentlemen called at all hours with flowers, clamouring at the doors—Why, at times the street was so crowded with carriages and chairs that it was a positive Bedlam!"

"I regret that I was not half so popular," murmured

32

Eugenia. Her tone was so low that the irony and disdain were not audible to her mother.

Mrs. MacNeill was mollified at these humble words. She sighed, touched her eyes with her handkerchief. Then with an expansively yearning gesture, she took the girl's hands, expressing sympathy and consolation in every line of her thickened features.

"Well, my love, do not be so heart-broken. One is not responsible for lack of gifts of the face and figure. But it is not my fault, either. Perhaps I am somewhat to blame. But here you were, fifteen years old, and not another beau on the horizon. I was so melancholy that when John spoke for you, I had to resign myself. I fondly, and foolishly, believed that young Broughton was taken by you. But that was all a mirage, an illusion——"

Eugenia did not think it necessary to mention that Tony Broughton had asked her to marry him. The fact might excite her mother, but it would also present other complications.

"I was married when I was months younger than you, Eugenia. You were born on my sixteenth birthday. Your father declared that I was a dream of beauty, when you lay in my arms, though even then you were a dark wan little bird with the sniffles."

Eugenia, who was not sentimental, was not at all touched by this affecting picture of herself in her buxom young mother's arms. Mrs. MacNeill saw this, and was exasperated.

"So, one must resign one's self even to a deplorable marriage. But, candidly, I cannot see what attracts you in John. He is a fool and a popinjay. He cares for nothing but riotous and vulgar living. I assure you, my love, I would not be inconsolable if this marriage did not take place." She nodded her head, meaningly.

Eugenia stared at her. Her gray eyes dilated. A faint pulse could be discerned at the base of her slender white throat. Not to marry John! All at once the thought was full of agony. It could not be endured. Her heart thumped under the tight gray bodice. She had never thought before of what it would be like, not to marry John. Tranquil and composed by nature, she had a certain belief in the inexorability and the immutability of coming events, which stemmed from the decisions of the present. Now the devastating thought was presented to her. She had accepted John, believing herself in love with him in a calm and amused fashion, without wonder or ecstasy. She had always known him. He had been her vehement friend and companion, awkward and passionate. She had patronized him smoothly and fondly, without excitement. Now his face rose up before her, dark, vital and turbulent, and her heart opened and shut on a spasm like a prehensile fist. She could not endure the thought of not marrying him. A wave of swift heat passed over her cool flesh. Her thoughts and emotions swirled together in a brilliant explosion like burning chaff.

"Do not talk so, Mamma!" she said, in a voice that shook.

Mrs. MacNeill laughed lightly. She patted her daughter's rigid hand, which hung at the girl's side, trembling.

"Ah, do not be afraid, my little love. I realize if John were dismissed there would never be any one else. How pale you are, child. Is your mother so impossible, however, that you could not endure remaining with her until she is called home?"

Suddenly, without warning, and quite terribly, Eugenia burst into tears. She stood beside her mother, and made no effort to cover her face with her hands. Nor did she make a single sound. The tears simply gushed from her eyes and poured over her white cheeks in an acid flood. Her face was stark with anguish.

Mrs. MacNeill was astounded. She had not seen Eugenia weep since the girl had been four years old. Confusion seized her, as she attempted to remember what words of hers had evoked this appalling manifestation of grief. Then, recalling her last words, she was overcome and ineffably touched. The easy tears rushed to her eyes. She leaned towards Eugenia and enfolded the girl in her arms, dragging her across the bed, and holding her tightly to her billows of bosom. She rocked her feverishly and violently.

"My darling, my little bird, my love, do not weep so! You are breaking your mother's tender heart. So, it was unbearably affected at the thought of its mother leaving it, of abandoning it in the cruel cold world! What a sensitive little creature it is! Please forgive your mother, my pet, my angel! I am ill, it is true, but, please God, it will be many a day before I am called to be with your dear Papa—! It shall not be an orphan so soon as it fears——"

Eugenia lay supine in her mother's arms. A frightful exhaustion had completely overcome her. Her face was pressed smotheringly in the folds of fat which were Mrs. MacNeill's neck. She thought to herself, with terrible and aching intensity: Wherever you go, John, I shall go with you. Tomorrow—today— It does not matter. There is nothing in all the world but you, John, my dear, my darling.

CHAPTER 3

A FTER flinging himself violently from the home of his cousin, Eugenia, John Turnbull rushed down Russell Square in a veritable blind frenzy of rage, misery and despair. He was in a condition of turbulent revolt; he was filled with a universal hatred. He fled headlong, so that oncoming pedestrians sprang aside to let him pass, staring affrontedly at his dark and furious countenance. He saw no one, blinded as he was by his undisciplined emotions. The handsome coat with its three tiers of small capes flapped against his calves; the flowered silk waistcoat was displayed to the most casual and unheeded gaze. Once when two ragged urchins got in his path, he raised his black cane and struck at them with an oath.

The rain had stopped. The bleak wind came howling around the corners of gloomy houses and over the walls of drenched gardens. Heated as he was, John did not feel its assault. The air, gray and wet and full of grit, choked him, and he cursed it. His polished boots splashed in the running gutters. A low dank mist was drifting on the brick roads. Carriages rolled by, and curious faces peered forth at him. He could smell the mingled odour of acrid smoke, damp, chill and dirt which was the peculiar odour of London.

Now the streets became more congested. He had to pause, fuming, on the kerbs, to allow the crowded carriages, hucksters' carts and heavy lorries to pass. Far in the distance the dark gray shadow of the Tower loomed against the boiling and gaseous skies, and the formless bulk of the Houses of Parliament crouched over the city like a great beast. He was in the area of shops, of draperers' establishments, of tailors, hatters and booters. Always, they had fascinated him. But now he did not see them.

At length he hailed a hansom, and flung himself onto the damp leather seat. He smelled its mustiness. The horse clopped in the gutters, spraying cataracts of dirty water into the air. John stared blindly before him, glanced through the windows. He was consumed with a wild heat and fever. Sometimes he felt that he could not restrain himself, that he must leap from the cab and hurl himself furiously through the streets again. At these moments his hands would clench, and he would beat

35

them impotently on his knees. Then he was overcome with a febrile exhaustion, and he would lean back and close his eyes. But always he was pervaded by the most savage and desperate excitement. Remorseless hands seemed to be clutching his throat, cutting off his breath, accelerating his tumultuous heart. Sometimes he was overcome with a voiceless and formless grief and passionate desire. At these moments he saw the face of Eugenia, whom he loved unrestrainedly with all the depths of his uncontrolled nature. But he could curse her now, with dry weeping. She had betrayed him, abandoned him. He saw her cool gray eyes, those curious bright and steadfast eyes, which seemed the portholes of a shining but mute spirit standing on tiptoe to peer out on a world she dared not invade. Never had he desired her or loved her as he did now, when he felt that she had left him forever.

"I cannot stay in this abominable place!" he cried out, aloud. The coachman, hearing him, thought him quite mad.

When he cried out like this, he was suddenly and abruptly silent. He stared out at the passing streets and throngs, holding his breath, his lower lip caught between his teeth. Now the tremendous excitement seized on him again. Sweat appeared on his brow and on his upper lip. He took off his hat, and his tight black curls rose upward like a vital crest over his broad dark brow. He rolled his neck in his stock, and panted. But now his eyes were glittering and feverish. He smiled a little, and the smile was grim and resolute. He began to beat a tattoo on his instep with his cane. He seemed to hear strange far voices and strange vehement sounds.

He must have given some destination to the coachman, for he saw that they were approaching the section where he lived. He opened the flap of the cab and ordered the coachman to drive him into Soho. He could not see his father, yet. There was some immense and clamorous purpose rising in him which he wished to explore further. He moved restlessly and feverishly on the seat, biting his lip again, grimacing and smiling, nodding. He was frightened, but terribly exhilarated also.

He had talked wildly to his cousin, only half believing his own impetuous words. But now they came back to him, inexorable and demanding. Always, in his life, he had lived by instinct and intuition, rather than by cold and arid reason. Nor were instinct and intuition wild and vagrant things in him, a momentary or blind passion, forgotten almost as soon as felt. Rather, they were like great purposes in him, solidifying moment by moment, so that they became unshakable resolution. He was assailed by storms. But he seemed to absorb the very essence of these storms. The fury passed, but the resolution remained.

The next steps were not quite clear in his mind. However, he knew where they led. He left the details for a future but near date. He tapped on the flap and ordered the coachman again to drive him to Soho.

Through the dark and lowering city came the long rumble and clamouring of bells. John withdrew his repeater and stared at the round white face. It was three o'clock. Dr. Carruthers' would have been dismissed; the young gentlemen were either homeward bound, or gathering in favourite grog-shops and taverns for a last convivial beer or ale together. He would be certain to encounter his old companions in one of them. Now he felt an enormous healthy hunger, and a desire for human communication. He was no solitary. He loved companionship. The turbulent excitement and impetuousness of his nature languished, became frantic, in solitude. He must always communicate; he must always feel the warmth of others about him. Without them, he was a tempest in a vacuum, whirling soundlessly and impotently.

Arriving in Soho, that boiling pot of a hundred noisy races, he paid the coachman and rushed rapidly through the narrow crowded streets. He loved the smell of this part of the city, its foreign salty smell, its hot close smell, its loud voices and loud noises. Here he was no alien, among these aliens. He felt foreign and ostracised only among his own people. He smiled brilliantly at Jew and Latin, at Portuguese and Spaniard, and they returned his smile with the warm comforting recognition of brother to brother. Now he began to walk less hurriedly. He breathed deeply of the dark wet air. He looked into the windows of narrow dirty shops. It had begun to rain again. But here the rain had the mysterious quality of rain in far places, not the soaking cold effluvia of London.

He turned into the door of his favourite tavern. It was warm and close in here. The panelled walls of dark wood, impregnated by smoke and age, were the walls of home. The oak tables and benches were ancient, and gleaming in candle-light. At the end of the long narrow room a fire burned heartily in a smoke-blackened fire-place, and tossed its ribbons and streamers of rosy light on low beamed ceiling as cured with smoke as a rich ripe ham. Above the stained black counter were rows upon rows of copper and pewter tankards. A sweet yet sourish smell of beer, ale and spirits pervaded the tavern. The tankards twinkled in the candle-and-firelight; the fire chuckled. It was very quiet and warm and consoling.

John entered with a gay smile. But the tavern was empty. It was still very early. Mine host was sitting before the fire in his stocking feet, toasting his toes and smoking. He was a tiny but very fat man with a bald head. He was in his shirt-sleeves, his cravat hanging about his throat, for until the young gentlemen came in any numbers he did not resume his coat. He was an Irishman, shrewd, good-natured and obscene. When he saw John, he stood up and bowed genially.

"It's early you are, sir," he said, in his hoarse thick voice.

John flung himself on his favourite bench and leaned back against the wooden wall. He threw his hat down beside him. He looked about him and smiled.

"A foul day, Tim," he replied. The dark excitement was still vivid on his face. His voice had a quick timbre in it.

"I have been over the whole world," said Tim, leaning his hands on the table and bending towards John, "and never have I seen such a climate. Fit only for geese and English-men."

John laughed his usual loud and boisterous laugh. He ordered a tankard of ale. His temperament was nervous and high-pitched, and now it was vibrating in an even higher key than usual. Tim brought him a large and foaming tankard, and John drank it as eagerly as a desert wanderer might drink. He put down the tankard and beamed at the host. Tim beamed in return. The heartiest good-fellowship prevailed between them.

"I am going to America," announced John.

Tim raised his eyebrows. "So, it's to America you'll be going," he said, thoughtfully. "A fine land. But strange. A land for men."

He knew John's extravagances. He had no doubt that the young gentleman would be a visitor to this tavern for many years to come, growing older and staider, the life slowly dying from him, until he would come no more. Tim had seen this happen so often. He sighed gustily. It seemed very sad to him, and very dolorous. It made him quite melancholy. He liked John better than he liked the other young gentlemen, the Englishmen. He never thought of John as being English. There was a strange blood kinship between them. Those violent dark eyes, that turbulent smile, those tempestuous and undisciplined gestures, did not come from calm, slow English blood. It seemed very sorrowful to him that such a young man must degenerate into slowness and heaviness, the fire and virility forever quenched, the eagerness drowned forever in London rains and London fogs.

The door at the back, leading to Tim's living quarters, where he led a comforting domestic life with his fat shrewd English wife, opened and a girl emerged. John stared. He had never seen her before. She entered with demure and provoca-

38

tive steps, her eyes downcast, her hair covered with a fluted cap, and took up her place decorously behind the counters. She began to wipe the dark and gleaming surface with a white cloth.

"My niece, Lilybelle," said Tim, casting a fond glance over his shoulder. "Or, I should say, my wife's niece. Lilybelle Botts. The old woman hurts in her joints, and the colleen has come to help us."

But John stared, more and more delighted and intrigued. Lilybelle was a very pretty girl, flamboyant, and of colours that would appear vulgar to more reserved eyes. She was tall and slender, not more than fourteen, with a neat waist and a little high bosom, pointed and perfect. Her hips, too, were youthfully full under the long gathered black skirt, which was protected by a white ruffled apron. Her black bodice possessed short sleeves with ruffles of lace, revealing white round arms with dimpled elbows, and pretty white hands. Her face was round and plump, with a naughty arch expression for all its demureness. Her cheeks, full and pink, were very dewy and dimpled. She had a round pink mouth, with little white teeth which showed when she smiled her empty but mischievous smile. Her nose, tilted and pointed at the tip, had an impudent air, saucy and provoking. When she shyly lifted her eyes and glanced swiftly at John, he saw that they were brightly blue and full of laughter between thick yellow lashes. The mob cap only partly concealed shining auburn curls, as wiry and vital as John's own hair. One curl peeped from behind her little white ear, with much impertinence. She had a long slender white neck, with two little auburn curls falling over it in a most entrancing manner.

It was not only this obvious and pleasing prettiness which attracted John so intensely. The girl had a lusty and healthy appearance, warm and strong. She swung her hips naughtily; her step was high and dancing. The round mouth, though with a looseness at the corners, appeared about to burst into laughter at the slightest excuse. While she polished the counters, her arms thrust and moved with graceful energy, the black bombazine of her bodice straining in a most luscious fashion about her bosom and shoulder. John suddenly had the keenest desire to touch that young breast; he had no doubt that it would be firm and full under his seeking fingers. He could not look away from the girl. She delighted and excited him more every instant. What a figure that would be, divested of that long black skirt, stays and petticoats! He could see it as clearly as though she stood before him, naked. There would be the long line of waist and hip, smooth and white and gleaming, the dimpled knees, the slender ankles, the little white feet. But even more than all this, he felt the flash of hot recognition between him and the girl, the kinship of lustiness and turbulence, the wild life and vitality and lack of restraint. What a girl for a man's bed! There would be no fearful demureness, no coyness nor modesty, no pretenses or foolish whimperings.

He forgot Eugenia as though she had never lived. He leaned his elbows on the table and stared at the girl with all his zest for life, for flesh and colour and warmth, violent and unashamed in his restless black eyes. And the girl maintained her pretense that she was only a demure and innocent maiden, embarrassed by the stare of the young gentleman across the tavern. But in her every motion, every sway of her hips, every exaggerated swing of her arms which drew the black bodice tautly across her breast, there was saucy and impudent invitation and teasing.

"Fetch Mr. Turnbull another tankard, Lily, my love," said Tim, quite aware of what was going on under his nose. The girl obeyed. She approached John with downcast eyes, the dimple at the corner of her mouth twinkling. She did not glance at him. But she smiled discreetly, then retreated.

"A forward wench, and stupid," said Tim, in a low indulgent tone. "But a good hand for the old woman, and neat and quick. Lancastershire lass, where the old woman was born. Pert and naughty with her tongue, too, but good-hearted. The old woman fetched her two days ago, after her mother died. No controlling her. The old woman thinks to teach her her sums, and to read, but there's no need of that in a wench with such a face, eh, Mr. John?"

But John neither heard nor answered. The girl had just flashed an improper smile at him, and he was responding. His big compact body was thrilling with waves of warmth and desire. He felt that he had known Lilybelle all his life. Apparently feeling that he had seen enough of her for a while, she flounced and swayed out of the room and disappeared in the rear. He became angry at this, with a sense that he had been deprived. When he looked about him, antagonistically, Tim had retired to the fire again, and his meditations.

There was a riotous sound outside, and many laughing male voices, and the doors burst open. Several young gentlemen, joking and sparring, entered the tavern. When they saw John, they swore, then laughed again, boisterously, and swarmed about him. He rose with a sheepish smile, and shook hands with every one, suffering their crude jests. They hurled questions at him. He answered that he was finished with Carruthers. They flung themselves on the benches at the tables, pounded their fists and called for their favourite beverages. The quiet and cosy air of the tavern disappeared in tempestuous noise, laughter, shouting and jests. It was alive with gay young faces, fashionable costumes, the sparkling of youthful and arrogant eyes.

Andrew Bollister, John's particular friend, sat beside him, and questioned him smilingly. There was no obvious snobbishness in young Bollister, or consciousness of caste. He liked John, or so John believed. He was a slender youth, with a narrow and clever face, narrow slits of pale eyes, a long bony nose, and a thin mobile mouth which even in repose seemed to possess a restrained sneer and cynicism. He had a narrow and delicate skull, on which the pale fine hair seemed painted by the smooth gleaming strokes of a careful brush. He appeared much older than his twenty years, for there was a cold and quiet arrogance about him, a firmness of his thin broad shoulders, a certainty in the tilt of his sharp chin and the disingenuous glance of his hard and secretive eye. Whereas the body of John was compact and strong with muscle, the body of Andrew Bollister was carved and sharp in all its angles, inherent with assurance and elegance. His movements, though quiet and controlled, were quick, almost feline in their swiftness. His hand was small and narrow, and the lines of the pale quiet fingers had a certain delicate cruelty in them; the fingernails were colourless, almost livid. Everything about him was pale; he affected pale colours. He wore a light buff coat, with darker buff pantaloons. His studs were moonstones. There was no doubt that he was a great gentleman, reserved and polished, bloodless and accomplished. Even the lobes of his ears were bloodless and transparent, small and bony and pressed close against his fragile skull.

Andrew Bollister was never known to be crude or guilty of bad taste. He displayed no pettinesses or malice in his temperament. A disdainful smile, a shrug, alone expressed any disgust or aversion or dislike that he might feel. He was reputed to be honourable and discriminating, a master of good taste, an authority on fashion, a scholar and an artist. No one had ever heard him lie, or had seen him display bad temper or angry emotion. Well-bred and aristocratic (he was the third son of Lord Brewster) he exuded that ineffable and indescribable English atmosphere of caste and birth and position. He was witty and subtle, and his epigrams, spoken in a low and withering voice, were jewels of acrid understatement and cleverness. He did all things easily. His prowess on the playing fields was famous. Moreover, he displayed no less genius in the class-rooms. He was the undisputed leader of Dr. Carruthers'.

No one, not even his adoring mother, knew the cold violence, the bloodless cruelty, the monstrous vanity, the gigantic malignance, which lived in him. For he revealed himself to no one. And no one, even his victims, could guess at the immeasurable mercilessness which was part of his nature. They only knew that something in him made them tremble and shrink before that narrow and hidden eye.

At the present time, he seemed to be fond of John Turnbull, though two less congenial characters could not have been found in juxtaposition anywhere else in England. It was known that Andrew Bollister drank heavily, and that at times he could become coldly riotous. But during these occasions his face would become narrow and wizened, frozen in its intense control. The contrast between his acts and his facial expression was mysteriously appalling. Perhaps the bitter and icy violence in him found something congenial in the hot and innocent violence in John Turnbull.

John had been amazed and excessively flattered when the favour of Andrew Bollister had fallen upon him. He could hardly believe it. It had at first inspired his suspicion, for, intuitively, John was no fool.

However, he had at last been won over. His correct estimations of Andrew's character were forgotten. He responded with warmth and complete surrender. He was overwhelmingly flattered, and gave Andrew all his confidences, opening his vehement and tumultuous heart to him in a manner which would have touched a less implacable man. John did not know that Andrew hated him with a virulent hatred, and despised him for a low-bred boor and ridiculous clown. He did not know as yet that he amused Andrew, and that the latter was merely awaiting the day to visit complete discomfiture and misfortune upon him.

Now, as they sat close together, in the little glass world which Andrew knew so well how to enclose about him, shutting out all else, John poured out to his sympathetically listening friend all the events of the morning, all his anger and restlessness and passionate emotion. Andrew inclined his pale and narrow head towards him. His light and colourless eyes were fixed on John's face with unblinking and cool intensity. His expression was inscrutable and absorbed. John was intensely flattered and soothed. Andrew listened in silence, sometimes merely lifting a smooth pale brow, or inclining his head as if he agreed. His bloodless fingers kept up a soft and thoughtful tattoo on the polished dark table. The candlelight gleamed on his slender shining skull. He never removed his basilisk gaze from John's vigorous and expressive dark face; he saw every flash of those stormy and mutinous black eyes.

John began to speak of his cousin, Eugenia MacNeil. Now his face lowered, became vulgarly poignant with distress and and misery. He saw nothing, and heard nothing, of his other companions all about him; they were drinking and laughing, and flinging themselves about with abandon. But they had long ago learned that when Andrew was engrossed in one of them, he was not to be disturbed. They ignored the two as if they were not present, not even hearing the excited hoarse timbre of John's voice.

At the mention of Eugenia's name, Andrew's face changed subtly. It was not that there was an actual change in his quiet and sympathetic expression. Rather, it was as though a flash passed over it, like the reflection of bitter sunlight on arctic ice. In that flash, the thin long features of Andrew's face seemed to become transparent, fleshless. He had met Eugenia some months ago, in his own mother's drawing-rooms. He had attempted to approach her, strangely attracted by her calm and reserve; seeing, as few others could see, the tranquil and restrained beauty of her little face, the strength and fortitude in those bright gray eyes. Strong and lethal as he was, he had been drawn to kindred strength. But she had looked at him steadfastly, and had known him. She had withdrawn from him, and he had been unable to approach her again. Nevertheless, he never forgot her. Deep within that implacable and deadly mind a cold passion had been born. He had heard of John's betrothal to her. On that very day he had begun to manifest evidences of friendship for John. He had long marked him as an eventual victim. Now he began to move swiftly.

With the merest flick of his hand, not for an instant turning away from John, he had indicated to the watchful host that strong spirits be served John. So Tim, though uneasy, obeyed and John was unaware, in his excitement, what he was drinking. He was accustomed to his after-dinner port with his father, and his occasional whiskey and water, also with his father, and so the acrid sting of spirits on his tongue did not warn him, even if he had been in a condition to be warned. His glass was always unobtrusively full; he gulped it, as he talked vehemently to Andrew Bollister, waving his strong dark hands in uncontrolled gesticulations.

"I thought she would understand," he repeated, over and over, and more hoarsely as the minutes passed, and the fixed and sympathetic gaze of those brilliant pale eyes did not leave his own.

"I have always felt," he cried to Andrew, "that if I should

43

draw a deep breath, from the bottom of my lungs, that I should crack England at every worm-eaten seam! I have felt that if I stretched out my arms to their full extent, I would knock over these mean crowded buildings. There is no place to breathe in this country! I've got to get out, I tell you, Bollister! That is what I tried to tell Genie." He paused, and added bitterly, after another gulp at his glass: "She advised me, in so many words, to go home and wipe my nose!"

"Ah," murmured Andrew, delicately fingering his glass, and frowning as if sympathetically moved by these passionate words.

"So, I am going to America," continued John. The tavern swam before him in long concentric circles, touched with sparks. There was a drumming in his ears; his flesh felt light and floating. He was filled with exhilaration, sudden and intoxicating.

"Without Eugenia?' said Andrew.

In that, he made an error. Suddenly, John put down his glass and stared at him, paling.

"Not without Genie," said John, with slow quiet emphasis. "When I go, she goes with me, if I have to carry her to the ship, myself. Do you think I would not?"

He stared at Andrew, and now his black eyes were pointed.

Andrew laughed lightly. He lifted his glass and scrutinized the golden fluid which shimmered in it.

"That oughtn't to be a hard job," he said in his peculiar voice, which was toneless and shallow, without resonance or echo.

He seemed to reflect, and his pale brows drew together in concerned meditation. Then suddenly, as John watched him, his face lightened, became boyish with assumed eagerness and pleasure. He put his fleshless hand over John's big clenched fist which lay on the table.

"I have it! I have a relative in New York, Richard Gorth, my mother's brother. He is in the export trade. Cotton and such, you know. For the Manchester mills. There is a trade for you! There was a rebel, like yourself, Johnnie. When you arrive there, go to him, with my compliments."

John's eyes began to glitter. He smiled. He seized Andrew's hand and shook it violently. Now everything seemed to expand before him in seas of light. He heard far and colossal voices, shouting across roaring seas. Bursts of music seemed to crash in his brain. His exultation choked him, made his heart beat in great long thumpings. Nothing was impossible!

"There is a world for you!" exclaimed Andrew, with enthusiasm. His gaunt face was bright with evil. "A world for a John Turnbull! If I had the guts I would go with you. But

44

I haven't. I'm too lazy. But go on, with my envy. There's a lad!" And he clapped John on the shoulder and leaned back to look at him with intense admiration. John was not proof against that look from Andrew Bollister. He swelled. His face became congested. He moved it slowly and powerfully from side to side, smiling darkly. Andrew saw that power, and his thin colourless mouth drew in. So, this was no ox, then, after all. It was a wild bull, charging, ruthless and more than a little terrible. This bull would stop at nothing, would trample and gore anything that stood before his charging hoofs. The hatred that had always been amused and derisive became deadly.

He cast around in his glittering ordered mind for the next step. In the meantime, he dexterously refilled John's glass. The other young gentlemen had begun to throw dice. They leaned over a table, shouting and snapping their fingers, and laughing and groaning, their young handsome heads, dark and blond, close together, their shoulders pushing against each other. No one heeded these two talking so intimately in the corner, hemmed in by panelled walls and candlelight.

A vast heat was engulfing John. His broad and vital face gleamed with drops of sweat. Colour swelled in his wide and heavy mouth and encrimsoned his cheek-bones. His black curls rose fiercely all over his big head.

The warmth in the tavern increased. The fire rose and crackled. The air was pervaded strongly by the odours of beer and spirits. The beamed ceiling danced in the mingled light of fire and candles. The young gentlemen shouted louder. Tim watched the dice game, a white towel over his arms, grinning. Banknotes, gold and silver exchanged hands, with cries of joy, or groaning.

Where is the fatal spot in him? thought Andrew, again filling John's glass.

CHAPTER 4

IN THE meantime, the dull winter day was drawing to a close. The wind had increased; cataracts of silvery water gushed down the little panes of the tavern's windows. In contrast, the warmth and firelight and gaiety within the tavern became closer, more intimate, as night closed in. The crowds on the streets were thinning. A lamplighter, singing, splashed through the gutters, lighting the wan lamps.

John was drunk. But never had he been so happy, so exultant, nor felt so powerful, so unchallenged. He seemed to fill the tavern; his consciousness extended beyond it, so that he appeared to be aware of every corner of London, of the seas beyond England, of the whole world. Now everything was plain to him; he felt his strength as if it were universal. He felt that if he walked on the earth, its brittle crust would crack and splinter under his strong feet. Things which even he suppressed, beautiful, majestic and terrible things, surged into his flaming consciousness. He heard marching music; there was a blaze of banners before his fiery eyes. He saw shapes and forms of loveliness. A strange emotion devoured him. Every one else about him became little and weak, even Andrew Bollister. Nothing mattered; everything changed, became insignificant, passing, trivial. Only he, John Turnbull, was immutable, indomitable, restless, a fixed and burning star in the midst of silly fireworks.

Andrew, watching him, seeing those dark and brutal passions passing over that wide and ruthless countenance, seeing the strange flames in those black eyes, threaded with red and congested veins, acknowledged to himself that this was not the awkward, bumbling and noisy lad he had known in Carruthers'. It would not be easy to destroy him.

But, where was the fatal spot? Andrew looked about him with that slow and implacable authority which was so implicit in his colourless glance. His gaunt face tightened, became a pallid wedge of malignance. John still drank. He had subsided into a turbulent silence, in which his drunken breath was loud and heavy.

It became imperative to Andrew to find the spot immediately. Not only would there be the artistic satisfaction of destroying one who represented all that he hated and despised, but there would be the reward of Eugenia MacNeil. Only one glimpse had he had of that silent and graceful little creature, with the shining and intelligent gray eyes; only a few indifferent words had he exchanged with her. But the one cold and lethal passion of Andrew's life had been born in him in that brief interlude.

In the midst of his intense and vicious musings, the sound of a loud and rollicking shout intruded. He loked up, frowning formidably, enraged that his courtiers dare so affront him with their bestial noise. But they did not glance at him. A pretty tall young girl was entering, her eyes downcast, her body swaying coquettishly. She carried a tray of clean glasses. Her dimples came and went demurely about her round pink mouth. She might have been a nun modestly and fearfully entering a den of carousal, conscious of chaste charms, but praying that none would observe them. The young gentlemen, jesting, crowded about her.

Andrew stared at her with cold indifference, and with annoyance. How dared this trollop interfere with his cogitations! The glassy bell he had pulled over himself and John was shattered, letting in noise and disorder. Nevertheless, he turned to John, to resume the conversation, and to refill the other's glass.

He was surprised. John had half risen on his bench, supporting himself with those strong hands, which were still clenched. He had turned his big violent head in the girl's direction. He was smiling, broadly, the nostrils in his short and powerful nose distended. Unashamed lust and admiration flamed in his congested eyes.

Andrew looked from him to the girl, and then back again. He smiled. This, then, was the fatal spot! A whole plan, a whole design, slipped smoothly into place in his mind.

"Lilybelle!" shouted John, standing upright, and swaying. He swung out his arm in a big drunken circle. "Come here, Lilybelle!"

Andrew pulled him back upon the bench. John sat down, mechanically. But his face was still turned urgently towards the girl, who was coquettishly, and with giggles, fending off the lustful hands of her new admirers. She had heard John's shout; she was peering over a gentleman's shoulder at him, shaking her auburn curls, which danced under her fluted cap. In those shallow blue eyes was an answering urgency.

"A fine lass, a good plump wench," said Andrew, with admiration, to John's swollen and sweating profile. "An excellent girl for a man's arms. Don't you think so, Johnnie?"

John grunted. He did not turn his head. He had lifted his hand to the girl, with brutal command.

In some dexterous manner, she managed to elude the imploring gentlemen, who were delighted at this new vision of youth and beauty, and she came skipping and swaying to the table, arching her head and tossing her curls and laughing coyly, her admirers thronging protestingly at her heels. John reached up, ruthlessly, and dragged her down upon his knees. She struggled with him, shrieking modestly. Other hands reached out to pull her away. Bedlam reigned. Tim, anxiously approaching, said something, but his voice was lost in the confusion.

Andrew watched, leaning on the table with his elbows. This, then, was the proper plump pink heifer for this dark and charging bull! He missed none of the congested black-

47

ness of John's face. In his drunken lust, he was pressing the girl's breast with his big hands, completely ignoring the laughing others. He seemed absorbed in what he was doing, as though he and the girl were alone in a nuptial thicket designed for amorous beasts. There was a deep cleft of lecherous concentration between his swollen eyes, a lewd absorption. He did not appear to feel nor notice her light coy slaps of protestations, her attempts to leave his knees, her little shrieks which were becoming sincerely frightened. But when he buried his mouth in her soft white neck, she trembled, arched away her head, and paled noticeably. Tim appeared again in the confusion of heads and crowding shoulders. Some one swept him aside with an indulgent jeer.

Still frowning in a business-like and absorbed way, indecent to see, obscene in its implications, John was now bent on further explorations. What a bestial lack of control, what a display of animal urgency and swift animal purpose! thought Andrew. He leaned forward curiously, the better to see.

"Ho!" shouted the others, beside themselves with laughter. John pulled up the girl's skirt. Her plump legs in their white stockings were displayed. She kicked impotently. Somewhere in the background of riotous noise there was a thin and angry voice, helplessly protesting and threatening. The candlelight shone and wavered on a ring of lecherous young faces, sweating, nostril and eye dilated, mouths open on laughter and caught breaths. But John still appeared unaware of them. When the girl continued her struggles, desperate now, he frowned with enraged impatience, struck away her hands savagely.

He was insanely drunk. He was mad with the sensations of his new power, with desire that would not be restrained, with primitive purpose. The others no longer existed for him, were not even present. They were only the sound of trees in a forest, their faces struck with light beating down through thick crowding leaves. He was alone with young woman-flesh, and his hunger was a devouring madness in him. And with it was a wild desperation for which he had no name, only an awareness.

"Here!" said Andrew, suddenly, in a quiet but penetrating voice. This was really becoming too much, even in a joke. He stood up and literally tore the girl from John. He would not have succeeded, but obeying their leader's gesture, the others assisted. The girl, dishevelled, half-crying, her bodice torn, her skirts rumpled, her hair on her shoulders, (one of which was entrancingly bare) was literally lifted from John's arms and set down upon her feet. She pulled at her bodice and sleeve. She cried, and stamped her slippered foot. Several

48

laughing young gentlemen were forcibly restraining John, who was cursing and flailing about him with strong arms.

"Gad," said Andrew, with contempt, even while he smiled. His loathing for John became a mortal disgust.

John's black eyes suddenly, in the midst of his violent struggles, encountered Andrew's glance. And at that encounter with that pale and polished eye, John abruptly subsided. It was as if a bludgeon had been brought down with terrific force upon his skull, shattering his consciousness, reducing him to sprawling incoherence. Fear in the physical sense had rarely assailed John Turnbull. He had the brutal courage of the sanguine temperament, the confidence that issues from strong muscles, excellent health and omnipotent youth. But now a most horrible and nameless fear beset him at Andrew's look, and a long shivering passed over his collapsed body.

Andrew seated himself composedly, and with a wave of his thin white hand dismissed his grinning subordinates, who retired to the bar where they offered their amorous consolations to the weeping and stamping Lilybelle. She was quite dramatic, vowing vengeance, pleading with her admirers to avenge the insults upon her virginal person, weeping most entrancingly as she did so, and tossing her auburn curls with quite a devastating air of tearful rage. In short, she was enjoying herself lavishly. Her uncle hovered near her, but when he attempted to disband the consolers, she flashed him an angry glance, and he retreated once more, shaking his head and mumbling to himself.

Andrew leaned his thin sharp elbows upon the table, and continued to survey John with his strange half-smile, secret and malignant. Fresh whiskey appeared, and Andrew, with those elegant gestures which were so much a part of him, poured a prodigious amount into John's tankard. He indicated the vessel, with an inclination of his head, and like one drugged, John lifted it and drank again, deeply, feverishly, like one running away mentally from an ominous foe.

And now Andrew spoke in his light low voice close to John's ear, and with indulgence: "That was a display very interesting to observe, my Johnnie. I can't blame you, however. It is a bewitching piece, eh? She is much taken with you, too. Look what glances she flashes you, the minx!"

John looked up, obediently, and indeed Lilybelle was gazing at him over an admirer's shoulder. Encountering his look, she tossed her head quite vigorously, so that the swinging lamp overhead danced on every shining curl. She smiled a little, through her tears.

"A lass for a true man," continued Andrew, bestowing an

admiring and amused smile upon John. "How'd you like to be alone with her, Johnnie?"

John, whose face had again become swollen and suffused, his pulses throbbing, stared at the other man. There was a rough sound in his throat, like the voice of a bull.

"Now, in my City quarters," insinuated Andrew, softly, "a man can be alone with a baggage."

He poured fresh whiskey into John's tankard, and again the young man drank feverishly.

Later, when he attempted to remember what happened, he could not, giving up in despair. He recalled that lights began to wheel in long brilliantly coloured circles before his swimming eyes. He recalled voices that roared in his ears, retreated, like the sound of surf on a shingle. There were thundering sounds, mingled with wild maniacal laughter, murmurs,. hoarse rumbles. He thought that shining walls, opalescent and radiantly gleaming, were about him, shot through with threads of gold and scarlet. He was dimly aware of movement, that he was walking, leaning heavily on the shoulders of others he could not see. Hands touched him from everywhere in that blazing space; faces appeared and disappeared before him, disembodied faces with white dazzling teeth, forever present, forever vanishing. Once there was a blast of cold damp air upon his burning cheeks, sounds of horses' hoofs starting like low drumbeats then swelling to universal crashing in his intoxicated ears. Some one was nestling against him, warm, soft, murmurous. An immense nausea seized him. Voices shrieked and roared with laughter. He was caught up in flames that stretched to an endless black zenith. He saw their long radiant streamers ascending, himself with them, floating, soaring. Yet another part of him, suddenly, was in a dank dark room, lit with flickering pale candles which glimmered on white intent faces. It was very strange: he was in that room, yet also streaming heavenward in thin banners of fire and light. All at once it seemed very necessary to him that he reconcile this phenomenon.

In the midst of his concentration, he fell into a pit of blackness.

CHAPTER 5

Mr. James Turnbull sat before the low fire in his sitting room which adjoined his bedchamber.

The gray rain was hurling itself in cataracts against the windows, against which his valet had drawn the dark brown curtains. Mr. Turnbull heard the roaring sound of it; his house might have been under a waterfall. Occasionally there was a long loud rumble of thunder. But no lightning penetrated that silent dim room with the flickering fire. The curtains stirred in gusts that reached through the panes; there was an uneasy movement in them, as though enemies lurked behind their heavy and voluminous folds. Far in the depths of the great house there were echoing and booming sounds, discreet and disembodied. They enhanced the atmosphere of gloomy quiet and stillness in the sitting-room.

Mr. Turnbull sat in his great chair before the fire, his slippered feet on a hassock. At his right elbow stood a small table covered with a crimson velvet cloth, fringed with little gold balls. His lamp was lit. His pipe lay on the table, his deck of smooth old cards, and his little notebook, covered with black leather, in which he made his private and serene notes. The fire flickered. In Mr. Turnbull's quiet veined hands lay a copy of famous words uttered by famous dead men. He read this book many times. He never tired of it. Always, he found something new in it, some freshness, some poignant pertinence which struck his heart as though it was a cymbal and the word a muffled hammer. For Mr. Turnbull was of that species of rare and contemplative creature who live solely in the mind, and find there all solace, all irony, all joy, and all peace and adventure.

As only a true cynic can enjoy life utterly, (and Mr. Turnbull was a true cynic) he had no regrets, no anticipations, no disappointments. His was tranquillity, devoid of futile expectations. He lived easily, for nothing disturbed him overmuch. The fiercest hate, the mightiest love, the coldest wind and the hottest sun, which disturb more ardent men, never assaulted him. He knew these to be passing, and had long known that nothing is worth desire, regret or sorrow. Nevertheless, like all true cynics, he was all gentleness and all tolerance.

51

Mr. Turnbull was thin and slight, bowed and fragile of body. The thick fringed shawls over his shoulders seemed the habiliments of a mummy, for he seemed hardly to breathe. On his bald head he wore a knitted cap with a tassel. His dressing gown covered two narrow ridges that were his legs, stretched out towards the hassock. The hands that held the book were worn and delicate, and trembled slightly. He seemed to be sunken in profound contemplative thoughts.

His face had in it a strange resemblance to the young face of Eugenia MacNeill, for it was pale and closed and still, and immeasurably withdrawn. His forehead, gleaming and polished, was the most prominent feature of his countenance, and appeared to overshadow the long narrow nose below it, and the pale folded lips. When he sat like this, his gaze on his book, his whole face had an aspect of aloof dignity and remoteness, like the majestic expression of the dead. But when he lifted his eyes, one saw that they were full and gray and mysteriously lighted, and full of profound serenity. And then his thin withered lips betrayed their inherent but unmalicious irony, their wise tolerance and gentleness, as he half smiled at some thought of his own, or some inner comment on the words on the page.

His sitting room was almost bare in its simplicity. The walls, panelled with brown wood, were lined with books. There was a thick brown rug upon the polished floor. Between the bookcases, and over the mantelpiece, were exquisite small paintings of quiet landscapes, umber brown, dim green and golden yellow. Sometimes, as the fire leapt uneasily, light flashed on the landscapes, or shone brightly on the polished fenders.

" 'Le matin je fais des projets, et la soir je fais des sottices!' " murmured Mr. Turnbull, aloud, reading from his books. He smiled slightly, and glanced at the fire. What an old story that was! But it was also a story for the old. Such sadness should not touch the young, lest they grow cold, numb and impotent. But always, at the end, they knew this. However, when that knowledge came, it could no longer hurt them. An endless resignation came to them with cooling blood. And, at the last, the words brought no sadness, but only relief.

Mr. Turnbull had no longing for his youth, as he had no longing for anything at all. What a turbulent time was youth, indeed! He was done with it. He was done with its absurdity and its splendour. The old, finally, eat at every man's table, but reside in no man's house. But youth invaded all houses, blustering and noisy, contemptuous and boisterous. What guests in a serene house! He was glad that his curtains were drawn and his low fire was warm yet not too warm.

He continued to read through the quotations:

"Bid faith and hope alike adieu,
    Could I but add Remembrance, too!"

But a wise man discarded remembrance at will, thought Mr. Turnbull. To remember was endless pain. The man of strength refused, at last to suffer. He recalled Voltaire's: "Details that lead to nothing are to history what baggage is to an army—impedimenta." Memory was a detail. On the onward movement of a man to his grave, heavy with his years, he could not afford the impedimenta of memory.

But memory, thought Mr. Turnbull, though its outlines were forgotten, was still like the Old Man of the Sea, unseen but felt. It was a sore burden. Youth was strong because it had no memories. He had the sudden whimsical thought that if a man could forget completely, he would always be young. It was memory that slowed the blood, wasted the muscles, made the step falter and the eye grow dim. It was the remembrance of dead happiness, of dead hopes, of futility, of dreams that came to nothing but wry sad laughter, that killed a man at the last.

It was the old Voltaire, not the young, who had said:

"This world, this theatre of pride and wrong,
    Swarms with sick fools who talk of happiness!"

But Voltaire had never ceased to long for happiness, with a desperate and bitter despair. He, James Turnbull, had long ceased to desire it. Voltaire, in his eighties, had gone to his grave, still protesting, still vital—still young. How very sad! He, James Turnbull, would go to it with humorous resignation. He would go to it an old man.

Turning another page, his eye fell on a poem by Lucretius:

"No single thing abides, but all things flow.
    Fragment to fragment clings; the things that grow,
    Until we know and name them. By degrees
    They melt, and are no more the things we know.

Thou, too, O Earth, thine empires lands and seas—
    Least, with thy stars, of all the galaxies,
    Globed from the drift, like these, like these thou too
    Shalt go. Thou art going hour by hour, like these.

Globed from the atoms, falling slow or swift,
I see the suns, I see the systems lift
Their forms, and even the systems and their suns
Shall go back slowly to the eternal drift.

Nothing abides. Thy seas in delicate haze
Go off; those mooned sands forsake their place.
And where they are shall other seas in turn
Mow with their scythes of whiteness other bays."

Another old and terrible story, thought Mr. Turnbull, with calm serenity. All that was true was old. He contemplated the majestic words of the poem, removed and undisturbed.

And then, all at once, he was beset by a most frightful weariness and sadness, as if his soul, aroused from peaceful slumber, awoke with a loud and bitter cry of protest. So powerful was the assault upon the calm fortress of his mind that the book slipped from his hands to the floor with a dull thud, and his heart began to labour distressingly. He tried to calm the sudden onslaught upon his senses. But he had nothing but words and irony to meet that onslaught, which swept over him like a desperate army.

He became aware that his ancient valet was standing beside him. He looked up through dim and tormented eyes. The man was extending a white square towards him, an expression of distress on his nutlike face.

"Mr. Turnbull, sir, a letter for Mr. John."

Mr. Turnbull stared at the letter as if he could not recall what it was. Then he lifted his hand feebly and pushed it aside.

"Well, then, take it to Mr. John, Thomas."

Thomas hesitated, sucking in his lips and wrinkling his gray brows. He mumbled anxiously: "It's just that Mr. John did not come home last night, sir."

Mr. Turnbull struggled to recover himself. He repeated: "Did not come home last night." He smiled a little, undisturbed, and quizzical. "Is it possible that the young ass—? There was a letter from Dr. Carruthers, Thomas. Most probably Mr. John imagined I would be annoyed— What a young fool it is. Rest assured, Thomas, he will be at home at any moment, with his tail between his legs, sheepishly expecting some sort of a thrashing." He paused. "That boy has known me for nineteen years. He must be very stupid, I regret to say, if he believes I will be overly annoyed. I should never have sent him to Dr. Carruthers. That is the doing of Mrs. MacNeill, Thomas. As for myself, I am glad it is ended. All nonsense. He will settle down properly, now."

Thomas was relieved. He loved his master. He had withheld the news until it could be withheld no longer, for fear of disturbing Mr. Turnbull. He retreated.

Mr. Turnbull lay back in his chair. The ghastly emotion which had assaulted him had subsided. But it had left in its place a dull and numbing throb. So deep were its effects that he fell suddenly into a heavy slumber.

It was some time before he could be aroused from that slumber. It seemed to him that for ages someone had been gently shaking his shoulder. He opened his weary eyes to discover that Thomas was beside him again, his features knotting and wrinkling themselves in a most surprising manner. The man spoke incoherently.

"Mr. Turnbull, sir! Mr. John has returned. He begs to speak with you. There—there is a young person with him——"

Now real annoyance appeared in Mr. Turnbull's full gray eyes. "I was sleeping, Thomas. Tell Mr. John I will see him at tea."

Thomas wrung his hands, and so great was his agitation that it finally impinged on the awareness of his master, who sat up in his chair.

"Mr. John particularly begged, sir— It is extremely important."

"Well, then, send him in. The impetuous young brute."

Thomas retreated again. But Mr. Turnbull, for some reason, did not subside into his chair. He leaned his elbow on its arm and stared intently at the door through which John would enter. It was some time before the young man appeared.

Mr. Turnbull was greatly surprised at the aspect of his son. The young man's dress, always dandified and flamboyant, was crushed, bedraggled and dirty. His beloved new greatcoat hung on his shoulders and big body as if it were too large for him. It sagged, it swayed, in wrinkled folds. He had not bothered to remove it. He must have forgotten it entirely; his hat was in his hand. He cringed, stopping some feet from his father. His thick black curls were disordered. Beneath, there was his full face, now pasty and livid. His mouth was open and slack. But it was his eyes that attracted Mr. Turnbull's suddenly concerned attention. They were stricken, sunken and hollow. His whole appearance was stricken, terrified and undone, and very desperate. When Mr. Turnbull's eye met his, his own fell, and he cringed again, uttering a faint hoarse sound.

"Johnnie!" exclaimed Mr. Turnbull. "What is wrong with you?"

He held out his hand to his son. John approached with a feeble, swaying step, as if terrified. But he paused some distance from his father. The look of despair was vivid on his face, now. It was a child's face, most dreadfully frightened.

John's whole short life had been turbulent. He had always been in some trouble or other. He had always returned to his father, penitent, defiant, tempestuous, full of good intentions for the future. But never had he looked undone, as he did now. Mr. Turnbull conjectured that this was something extremely serious.

"Johnnie!" said Mr. Turnbull, not too disturbed. Yes, this must be extremely serious. But there was a protective and gentle sound in Mr. Turnbull's voice, as if he spoke to a wounded and desperate child. That voice urged his son not to be too wretched, that his father was at hand. He was fond of John, that absurd and violent young ass. He was frequently tired by him, bored by him. But he was always very fond, though they had never been able to approach a common meeting ground. Now he saw that John was in some sort of truly immense trouble, and his first instinct was to console, to soothe.

"Nothing is so bad as you might imagine," he urged, gently. "Tell me about it."

John, to his father's rising concern, trembled visibly. He moistened his cracked and swollen lips. His voice came in a hoarse croak, even as his eyes pleaded with Mr. Turnbull like the agonized eyes of a child:

"It is very bad, sir. You will never forgive me."

Mr. Turnbull smiled. He extended his hand again. "Is it the police? Well, no matter. We can adjust it. Come here, Johnnie."

John took one step, then halted again. He shook his head slightly.

"I—I am not fit to be in this room with you, sir," he whimpered.

Mr. Turnbull raised his brows. He had never heard John whimper before. His tired heart began to beat faster. Nevertheless, he smiled again.

"Let me be the judge, Johnnie. Rest assured, though, that you can tell me without my exhibiting excessive annoyance. And, how do you know that you are not fit to be in this room with me, after all? I've lived a long time, Johnnie. Come here."

Now, with feeble steps, as though he was blind, John approached his father, not looking away from him, the wild pleading and despair increasing on his livid and congested face. Now he stood before his father. His trembling had increased.

"Is it a woman, Johnnie? No matter. We can deal with women. Just tell me."

John tried to speak. But only a strangled and drowning sound came from his throat. His cravat hung loose about his neck, untied. He extended his hands to his father. Then they dropped limply to his side.

"It began with Andrew Bollister, sir," he whispered at last.

Mr. Turnbull inclined his head, and pursed his lips. "A reprobate, Johnnie. A young silver snake. Ah, yes, I can see whatever happened began with Bollister." He hesitated. "Then, it must be quite serious."

John suddenly wrung his hands. "I was wrong, sir. It really began with Eugenia. She would not go away with me. To America. It began then, sir. After Dr. Carruthers."

Mr. Turnbull was silent a moment. Then he said contemplatively: "To America. You wished to go to America, Johnnie? Why?"

But John could not speak for some time. Mr. Turnbull indicated a chair near him. "Sit down, Johnnie. You look thoroughly washed out. This appears to be a long story. We can talk better when we are at ease."

Automatically, still not looking away from his father, John fumbled for the chair, collapsed in it. He put his elbows on his knees, buried his face in his hands. Through his big trembling fingers his father saw his crisp black curls, so disordered and uncombed. Now heavy sounds, dull dry sounds, issued from John's hidden lips. They were the sounds of grief and despair that men make, not children. Mr. Turnbull heard them, and for the first time in John's life, his father felt for him a sudden and terrible anxiety, and alarm.

The firelight glimmered on John's heaving shoulders. His whole attitude was broken. Mr. Turnbull waited for some time. Then he said, very softly:

"Yes, Johnnie? You were speaking of America?"

John slowly dropped his hands. It was the face of a ruined man, not the face of a youth, which confronted Mr. Turnbull. Now there was a grim calmness in it.

"America, father. I—I had decided I couldn't stand England any longer. I wanted to leave. All at once, it was necessary for me to go." His voice was cracked and feeble, but no longer incoherent.

"Yes, Johnnie? I can understand. You are quite alive, and strong. Yes, I can understand. You see, we have been dead in England for a long time."

He hoped, by his words, to produce a shade less of despair on his son's countenance. But instead of that, the blackness

57

increased. John sat upright, rigid, heavy and stonelike of attitude.

"I had to go, father. I went to Eugenia. I asked her to marry me at once, and go away with me. She refused."

So, that was it! What extravagance and childishness of emotion! Mr. Turnbull was vaguely disappointed. He had believed John to be in truly dangerous trouble, a man's trouble. And now it seemed that this young idiot had taken a silly girl's hasty refusal to heart, and had gotten drunk, and wallowed in a gutter! What bathos! Mr. Turnbull relaxed in his chair, and spoke with cold indulgence:

"What, then, if the child refused? She can always be made to change her mind. Trust her mother for that. As for America, we can speak of that later, when you silly children are married. I suggest you bathe, change your clothes, and bring Eugenia to me. When would you like to be married? On Saturday?"

But John merely gazed at him steadfastly, the grimness and darkness increasing on his face, and the despair.

"As for America," repeated Mr. Turnbull lightly, "we can speak of that later. Yes, perhaps America would be best for you. Were you worrying about the business? Hang the business, Johnnie! I carried it on because of the curious and beautiful objects which passed through my hands. I will be glad to be rid of it. There is more than enough money— Did you believe I might roar at you because you wished no part in it?"

But still John did not speak. Now he had clenched his fists and was beating his knees with them. Some cold doubt began to insinuate itself into Mr. Turnbull's heart like a thin icy finger.

"You can be married whenever you desire, Johnnie," he said, in a somewhat weaker tone. He was conscious of the shaking of his heart.

"It is too late, sir," whispered John. His cracked lips had opened here and there, and Mr. Turnbull saw the tiny ooze of blood.

"Too late!" he exclaimed, sitting upright, and staring at his son.

John rose. He had to catch at the mantelpiece to keep himself from swaying.

"Yes, father. Too late. I am already married." His voice was a dull hoarse whisper.

Mr. Turnbull shrank in his chair. His veined hands gripped the arms. From the dark depths his eyes gazed speechlessly at his son.

"It began with Andrew Bollister," said John. "It began yesterday afternoon."

Mr. Turnbull did not speak. He listened to that low hoarse voice for what seemed an eternity. Disordered, disconnected scenes passed before his fixed eyes. There was the scene with Eugenia. Then the tavern. The entrance of young Bollister, and his companions. The pretty young trollop. The confusion, the drinking. The unspeakable vulgarity of what followed. The drunkenness. John's voice did not falter. He spoke grimly, in a man's harsh voice, not sparing himself, lashing himself, full of hatred for himself. He had not known what had happened. He had discovered it only an hour ago, when he awoke in young Bollister's City quarters, with the young trollop beside him in the bed. From her alone, he had learned that they had taken him for a special licence. Bollister had maneuvered it all, with his customary arrogance and assurance. There was the magistrate's office, where John had been married to the girl. A Lilybell Botts, niece of an innkeeper.

Suddenly, Mr. Turnbull was aware that John was not speaking, that there had been silence in the room for a long time, and that he had been unconscious of everything but his son's appalling story.

He looked up and studied John in profound quietness. A vast sickness churned in him. His very fragile bones were trembling. But John was calm, if his expression was coldly murderous and desperate.

"I shall kill Bollister," said the young man, in a low and savage voice. "After I leave this house, I shall kill him. It has all come to me: he arranged this. He wanted to ruin me. But why, I do not know. That does not matter. I shall kill him."

Mr. Turnbull struggled to speak. His voice came in a whisper.

"Sit down, Johnnie. You must give me a moment."

John sat down. He no longer was aware of his father. His thoughts were fixed on some deadly resolve. His eyes were terrible.

Long moments passed. Mr. Turnbull laced and unlaced his shaking fingers together. He gazed at the fire. He was filled with a sinking disgust for his son. But his fondness and concern increased, also. This was just like Johnnie. He, James, ought to have realized that some day such a situation would inevitably have had to arise. He had neglected Johnnie, smiled at him, indulged him, dismissed him. They had never spoken in confidence together. Of what could they speak? They had not a single thought in common. He had provided for his son with extraordinary affection and indulgence, had granted him everything. Ah, there was his crime! He had given everything to Johnnie, hoping only to be left alone in peace with his books, his curios, his paintings, and his thoughts. To have attempted to talk with Johnnie, to have attempted to probe into that turbulent and violent young nature, would have disturbed him unduly. He had let Johnnie go his tempestuous and foolish way, congratulating himself, in his imbecility, that he was not the heavy father, the heavy-handed father, who dealt harshly and uncompromisingly with wild sons. Yes, he had congratulated himself on his tolerance! His tolerance! It had been his indifference. He saw that now. He had not interfered with Johnnie because he did not wish to interfere, not out of noble motives, but only out of selfishness. He had wished only to cloister himself with his thoughts, to live in his own unreal peace. And his son had disastrously gone his irresponsible and silly way, with this result. He had never, in truth, had a father.

James thought of John's childhood years, those noisy, boisterous, and belligerent years. How the boy had bored him, and tired him. He had never tried to restrain him. He had had wisdom— (A strange thin laugh, full of acid, issued from James' bitter lips.) Yes, he had had wisdom. But he had never tried to impart a little of that wisdom to poor Johnnie. He had persuaded himself that Johnnie would not understand it, anyway, that he would resent it. So he had "nobly" refrained from inflicting it upon the lad. Johnnie would learn, he had told himself. Yes, he would learn; had learned. But with what agony, what ruin, what despair!

The words of a wise and tender father fell on the heaving hot soil of a lad's mind, and were apparently lost in the chaos. But in moments of stress they gleam with a vivid light in the morass, in the crevices of earthquakes. So James thought, now. But he had never planted these little bright lights in Johnnie's mind. He had thought himself unusually wise in not doing so. Now, he realized that he had been only too indifferent, too indolent. He had not wished to be disturbed in his cloisters. He had simply not taken the time. He had not disciplined his son. He had not warned him of the passions which await like mad beasts in the thickets of life, to destroy youth and hope and joy forever. Johnnie had gone his way, ignorant of the beasts. By his father's guilt.

Once James had told himself that he had too much respect for the individual soul to interfere with its thoughts, or direct its actions, or sickly it over with his own cast of pale thought.

Now he saw that in thinking this he had been merely freeing himself of the necessity of disciplining his son. The human soul entered this world full of primordial instincts, passions and furies, teeming with jungle lusts, bare of fang, and savage. Barely emerged from the ageless ooze, it had no reason, no restraint, no self-discipline. It was a stranger in a world of souls that had learned to wear pantaloons, to read, to control lusts and savagery, and to present, at least, a calm face to civilization. But he, James, had conveniently forgotten this. The face that John turned to the nineteenth century was an unbridled and vehement face, blazing with primitive passions. It was the face of a barbarian, a wearer-of-skins, a druid prancing beneath a moon.

I ought to have taken time to thrash him, to punish him, to restrain him, to discipline, brow-beat and control him, thought James. Now he felt his old passionate and selfish repugnance for action, for invading the mind of another lest his own be invaded. Hermits had no right to sons. They had no right to life.

He thought again of Johnnie's youth. After the death of Johnnie's mother, he had practically confined the young lad to spacious quarters on the third floor of the house on Grosvenor Square. There Johnnie had his own nurses, and later, his tutors. None dared oppose him. James recalled that a long procession of tutors had come and gone, bruised and terrified. He had only laughed indulgently. The boy had "spirit." So long as that spirit could be kept away from his own quiet rooms, he did not care what it did. The boy would "find himself." But souls do not find themselves in jungles; they must be led into the cities.

He recalled, most painfully and vividly, a certain Sunday afternoon when Johnnie was only twelve. The latest tutor had departed with portmanteaus and black eyes. The great house was dark and quiet, with here and there only a red fire to light the gloom. James had been sitting in this very room, reading, as always, his feet on his hassock. The silence and cloistered dimness of the house, the rain-locked city outside, all contributed to the tranquillity of his mind, his enjoyment of his thoughts. He had been reading Plato. Then, he had heard a sound at the door, and had looked up, irritably, to discern young John standing diffidently in the doorway, eyeing him with mingled shyness, fear and hopefulness. He stood there, scraping one boot against his shins, his big legs already bursting the seams of his tight pantaloons, his jacket sleeves riding up the large awkward young arms. As usual, his face was dirty, his hair uncombed. It was a gawky standing there, a tiresome, hot-blooded, noisy young creature, bored with itself, restless, with no inner resources. A youth hardly emerged from childhood. A tight shudder had passed over James' flesh at the sight of this raw and beefy youth, who appeared to make the very air about him palpitate with animal lustfulness and urgent stupidity.

He had said to his son, without inviting him into the room, and in fact, by every psychic and mysterious compulsion, had prevented him from entering the room:

"Well, Johnnie, have you gotten your sums for tomorrow, when Mr. Burrows is to arrive?"

His voice had been indulgent and fond, but also withdrawn and repelling.

Johnnie had said nothing. He had only looked a long time at his father, with a strange and miserable look, full of bleakness, wretchedness and uncertainty. Then, after a moment or two, he had backed away, had closed the door and had gone. His father had forgotten him immediately.

Now, he wondered what would have happened if he had bid the boy enter, if he had sat him at his knee, and gently probed that festering young mind, so obviously in distress, and so bewildered. What confusions might he have obliterated; what light he might have bestowed on that savage and pristine soul! What loneliness he might have banished. It was a strange thought, this, that Johnnie must have been lonely and beset.

"Johnnie," he said aloud, to the desperate young man sitting in his own ruin near him, "you must have been lonely." And in his voice there was humility, an anguished pleading for forgiveness.

John regarded him with blind eyes. He mumbled, as if from the very broken depths of him: "I have always been lonely." But he hardly seemed aware of what he had said.

James' ascetic face grew stern. Every man was eternally lonely, he thought, walled in by his own flesh, by his own inaccessible thoughts. But others, through love, might at moments exchange a muffled greeting with the prisoner within, might feel warm flesh and eagerness even through the stones. He had never approached the prison-walls of another human being. He had made his own fortress even stronger, so that finally he heard no word, no cry, from without. He had feasted on the words of dead men, like a vulture feeding on decaying flesh. He was fillled with a terrible loathing for himself.

How could he help Johnnie now, brought so low, to such ruin? By kindness, by further indulgence which must henceforth be suspect? No, only by the wise cruelty of making him face his acts for the first time in his life, by making him carry the weight of his own enormities on his own shoulders. If those enormities were also his father's guilt, that could not be helped.

He said: "Johnnie, I presume you have—cohabited—with this wench?"

John aroused himself from his lethargy of despair with a visible effort, and looked at his father with dull and swollen eyes. Then a dusky crimson ran over his cheeks.

"Yes," he said, hoarsely.

James sighed. He felt ill and disintegrating. He clasped his hands and gazed at them intently.

"She—she is a drab?"

John moved violently upon his chair. "No!" he cried. "She —she is a poor little creature, very young! I—I do not blame her, father. It is I who am to blame."

It is I who am to blame! James felt a lightening of his grief. It was a man's cry, this, a man come to full estate. When one could cry out so, against one's own self, then the long and agonizing journey toward redemption had begun.

He, James, must be cruel, if Johnnie were to be saved. He saw this, now, so clearly. All his life he had been delicately cruel in his gentle selfishness. Now he must be ruthless. Or Johnnie would be forever lost.

He made his voice calm and judicious:

"You have been very foolish, Johnnie. But you have not murdered any one. Short of murder, a man can build his life again, if he is brave enough to accept the consequences of his own acts."

He paused. His calmness had affected John. He was leaning towards his father, his congested and exhausted face intent.

"You have married this—girl, Johnnie. From what you say, she is no strumpet. Not of your class, perhaps. That is, she was, no doubt, brought up in poverty and ignorance. That can be remedied—by your own hands, if you are strong enough, and wise enough. Too, the girl is probably healthy. That is an excellent thing in a wife. She must be somewhat of your own kind, or you would never have been drawn to her in the very beginning. There were times when I did not think that Eugenia——"

He paused, for John had uttered a truly agonized sound, and had gotten to his feet. He dropped his arms on the mantelpiece; he lowered his head upon them.

James stood up. He put his hand on his son's head, with speechless sympathy. John was unaware of him. He was swallowed up in his abysmal grief. So, thought James, he loved that pale cold little piece, who seemed more my own daughter than Johnnie seemed my son.

"Johnnie," he said at last, when the sobs were quieter, "let us be as calm as possible. Let us think, and talk."

John lifted his head from his arms. His face was bruised and contorted, streaked with scarlet. He fell in his chair as if his big shapely legs could not support him any longer.

They sat across from each other with the firelight on their faces.

"Johnnie," said James, "I have never tried to restrain you, to force you to face your own consequences. Now, you must restrain yourself, and take up your own responsibilities. I have never taught you this. It is late, but perhaps not too late, to force you to do this now. It will be very hard for you. I could have made it easier, so that at your age self-restraint would have become a habit. It is too late to regret the past. We must go on from today."

He paused. John listened.

Now it was becoming difficult. "You are a man, Johnnie. You are nineteen years old. Many young men of your age are already married, and have a child. With my stupid assistance, you have prolonged your childhood into manhood. In some wild and precipitous fashion, you have escaped my folly and have burst into full estate. You think you have done this disastrously. But perhaps this is not so. Perhaps the future will prove that you have been wise, even in your ignorance."

John muttered hoarsely: "I don't understand, father. Is there no way to get out of this abominable marriage?" A pale flash of hope appeared in his desperate eyes.

James was silent. Most certainly, there were many ways, for men of wealth and substance, and especially for the son of James Turnbull. For a moment James' aching heart betrayed him. It would be such an easy thing to accomplish, this. But to what end? What would Johnnie gain? It would only topple him from his new and precarious manhood, back into the tinkling foolishness and tempestuous folly of childhood. From this scrape he would learn that he need not restrain himself, that always there would be some one to rescue him from his own folly in the nick of time. The ruin of his life would throw this smaller ruin into significance. There would be no end to the ruin.

No, from this youthful wreckage he must salvage what he could to raise a firmer and stronger house in which to live. It would be hard; it would be heart-breaking. But if Johnnie were to be saved, he must face what he had done.

"No, Johnnie," said James, in a firm low voice, "there is no way. You have done this. From this place you must go on."

The wild hope that had flashed in John's eyes was quenched. Now they were just dull black circles, in the suffused flesh of his face.

"I can't go on," he stammered, brokenly.

James smiled. "We can always go on, just one more step, one more mile. Nonsense, Johnnie! You will remember this lesson: that what seems impossible is not impossible for the wise man. Only fools cringe and whine. You are not a fool, Johnnie, though you are considerable of an ass."

That calm and quiet voice had its effect on the young man. Unconsciously his bowed shoulders straightened. The slack hands on his knees tightened a trifle.

"I will see this girl—your wife—in a few moments, Johnnie. Doubtless she is strong and young, and very healthy. It may be best for you, after all. You must forget everything else.

"The day after tomorrow, there is a packet sailing from Liverpool, the *Ann of Argyle*. To America. You, and the girl, will be on that packet. I shall give you one hundred pounds, and one hundred pounds only. Go to America. You have wanted this. I can see now that it will be most excellent for you. You will make your mark there. Of that I am very sure.

"Yes, we have been dead a long time in England. Before very long the stench of our decay will fill the world. So far, we have befooled the world that we are still alive. But, we are not, our Queen to the contrary.—I believe that in America the world has had a rebirth of youth and strength and limitless power. It is a land for young men, for men like you, Johnnie. Go there, with my blessing.

"But what you do in America you will do for yourself, with no assistance from me. Thousands have gone there with much less than one hundred pounds. It is almost a fortune."

He paused. John's expression was dark and twisted, rebellious and frantic. James appeared not too affected by this. He looked steadfastly into his son's eyes, though his heart ached for his own ruthlessness.

"I have given you two thousand pounds a year for your own, here at home, Johnnie. That was intolerably stupid of me. You know nothing of money. But, in America, you will learn. You will stand or fall by your own strength or the lack of it. In some way I know that you will stand."

"You are booting me out, then?" asked John, brokenly.

"Certainly not. I am giving you an opportunity to be a man, Johnnie."

He continued: "You have always been irresponsible, lawless

and stupid, Johnnie. I blame myself for this, in part. You have played too long with your toys. It is time to put them away."

But John was not listening. He was gazing slowly and despairingly about the dark and quiet sitting-room, like one who has been condemned to hopeless exile. How he had hated this room, this house! But now it became a haven, warm, fragrant with home, secure and safe. From this house, this room, he was to be thrown into danger and uncertainty and struggle. He could never return. The future seemed like a bleak and bitter plain to him, with frightful stony mountains in the distance, with empty winds about him, and one with him whom he loathed and detested. He had contemplated this exile with longing, only yesterday. But it had been joyous and adventurous exile, with Eugenia.

As he thought of his cousin, his heart divided on a blazing pang of pain, and tears rushed into his eyes for the first time. He turned aside his head to hide them from his father, but James had seen.

He could not endure his son's suffering. He had inflicted this upon him. But there was nothing he could do, for Johnnie's own sake.

"And now, Johnnie," he said, very quietly, "you will bathe and dress, and then go to Eugenia, and tell her."

John started up, as if struck. "No!" he cried, wildly. "I can't do that, father! I will write her—I'll—!" His voice broke. He wrung his big hands together.

But James was inexorable. "Johnnie, you must do this, believe me. It will be painful. That cannot be helped. A letter is a coward's way. Only cowards write the things which they dare not say, or shrink from saying."

He lifted his hand. "Go, Johnnie," he said, very gently. "And send in the girl to me. You need not return until you have spoken to Eugenia."

CHAPTER 6

JAMES TURNBULL awaited the entry of his son's wife. He who had lived so long in calm detachment, experienced an enormous pain in his head and his heart, a long and throbbing aching like an abscess. Did emotions, smothered and repelled and choked, wait in ambush in a man's soul for the hour of resurgence? Then was a man unfortified against them, and completely undone by them.

Nevertheless, his manner was quiet and stern as he waited. He had turned his chair from the fire and was facing the door. There was no sign on his face or in his manner of the exhaustion and anguish he was suffering. Only his thin frail hands were clenched on the arms of the chair, and his bright gray eyes, full and brilliant, were unusually vivid in that narrow and ascetic countenance. The fire was burning strongly behind him, and so the girl who entered so timidly, and with so much hysterical and defiant fear, could not discern his body or his form in the chair, and saw only those eyes and those white tense hands in the vague lamplight. They appeared disembodied and affrighting to her, and there rose a low whimper in her throat.

James gazed at her, and he thought: It is only a terrified child.

Poor young creature, and very pretty, too, in a coarse and common way. He saw that she was tall, and of a luscious figure, for all her youth. Her round face was pale, but her full loose mouth was red, as though she had a fever. The round blue disks of eyes were strained and hunted, their natural protruding quality enhanced. He saw that her taste was not at all bad, and he, who considered an error in taste worse than an error in morals, was pleased. She wore a tiny jacket of black wool over her black bombazine skirt and bodice. At the collar there was a thin white line of linen, grotesquely nunlike under that bold if frightened child's face. A little black bonnet crowned a tumbling mass of auburn curls, which spilled down upon her shoulders, and the white ribbons were tied with pathetic coquetry under her dimpled chin. Her hands, which he suspected of vulgar size and coarseness, were thrust into a diminutive muff of some coarse black fur.

Terrified though she was, she tried to assume a bold and defiant air, and held her head high. Yes, she was quite handsome, poor child. Moreover, to James' sudden and mysterious relief, he detected vitality in her, strength and audacity. Her strength was an animal's strength, sanguine and hot, quite unlike that of Eugenia's which was steely, cool and intellectual. Stupid, yes, most deplorably stupid. The big pouting lips were somewhat gross, and too highly coloured. The tilted nose might almost be a snout, the nostrils large and distended. In better times, those smooth cheeks would be flooded with coarse colour, a milkmaid's colour. In ten years, she would be fat and florid. Not unlike Martha MacNeill, thought James. At this thought, he smiled slightly. And those big empty blue eyes were as shallow as water in a glass. If there was a soul behind all that health and strength, it was a little unformed soul, still in embryo. He doubted that she would ever be disturbed by even its smallest movement or pulsing.

He had seen a thousand such girls in the fields, in the little villages, clacking along in their clogs, their coarse cotton skirts draped high over thick ankles, their bright hair frowsy, their red hands swinging pails of milk as they came homeward in the sunset. He almost heard again their loud boisterous laughter.

Yet, he was not too unhappy. This vitality matched John's virility, this coarseness his own violence, this health his own health. He had long been uneasy over the bethrothal of John and Eugenia. Would that intellectual bloodlessness, that calm aristocracy, be enough for the strength and recklessness of John Turnbull? Would it not at the end chill and destroy him? It was unfortunate, of course, that at the end it was a milk-maid, a Lancastershire lass, with whom John had become entangled. But, at the end, again, might it not be better? James could not conceive of a Eugenia in America. America was for the John Turnbulls. And the Lilybelles.

Nevertheless, for all his philosophizing, he felt a great sickness and sinking. He assured himself that it was a snob's illness, the sneer of the bloodless at the sight of the noisy sanguine. His aristocratic mind shrank from the girl. And now he knew that it had shrunk from his own son.

The girl stood far from him. She was trembling. Those bright gray eyes, so formidable and bloodless, terrified her more and more. She curtsied, over and over. She caught her lower lip with her little white teeth. In a moment, James discerned, she would burst out into tearful howls.

"Come here, child," he said, very softly, and gently, and with a lift of his hand indicated the chair in which John had sat, very near to him.

His voice, coming out of that bodiless gloom, and accompanying his eyes, frightened the girl still more. She burst into tears. They ran over her quivering cheeks, lay in the corners of her slack red mouth. She crept nearer to him, not daring to look away from him; as if he was a horrifying spectre. Her curtsying became more frenzied as she approached him. All the events of the last hours, and the entry into his enormous grand house, overpowered her. She sank upon the chair, and then perched on its edge, weeping, wiping away her tears with the muff.

James waited. He was full of pity for her, and more than a little sad amusement. Delicate of perception as he was, he guessed her bewildered and frightened thoughts. A Lancaster-

68

shire farm lass suddenly precipitated into the house of gentry, unwanted and terrified! He knew that her sense of propriety was more outraged than his could ever be. It was strange that it was the lower classes who were the most insistent upon class. It was a fetish with them. Democracy came from the aristocrats. But it was the poor, the rootless, the oppressed and the harried, who upheld the false traditions of nobility. It was they who were the inherent enemies of democracy, who would oppose it, at the last, with all the oxlike obstinacy of their natures. Perhaps they had more common sense, therefore, than the aristocrat, who maintained that all men were equal. The masses had more wit. The leaders of revolutions were born to aristocracy, ease and power. They believed that the masses desired ease and power also, and burned with indignation that these were denied to them. Hence, revolutions led by nobles, by the privileged.

But in destroying the privileges of the naturally superior, the leaders destroyed the simple faith of the masses in government; they destroyed their belief that there were some born, by the Grace of God, to direct and rule them. This created in them a vast confusion and resentment. Hence, chaos. The masses demanded superiors to respect.

So, James knew that the girl's propriety had been outraged. She had been victimized, she believed. James subtly guessed that she had vaguely believed that John, because of his manner and loudness and recklessness, was no gentleman at all. Probably only a prosperous grocer's son, or the son of a successful fishmonger or hatter, of a little better station than herself, but of her own class. Her awakening had confused and disorganized her. And so her defiance, and her terror, and her bubbling indignation.

As she sat there, wiping away her tears unashamedly with her muff, and whimpering, her indignation gave her a pathetic dignity. James waited for a long time.

Then he said, still very gently: "It is Lilybelle, isn't it? John mentioned your name."

She flung up her head, and her tear-stained face flushed. "Lilybelle Botts, if it please you, sir." Her voice was coarse and common. James, in spite of himself, winced.

Suddenly, she loudly burst into incoherent speech. It was not her fault. Mr. Turnbull must understand that. She was a girl as knew her station in life. She had been brought up proper, to mind her betters. She had been taught to keep a civil tongue in her head, and keep her place. It was not her fault!

"Begin from the start, and tell me," said James, feeling a

69

sudden warm sympathy for this girl and her outraged propriety.

She whimpered, gulped and sobbed, her hands clenched in her muff. But her eyes regarded James with that terrified defiance, humility and simple dignity. Her mother was a respectable woman, with no nonsense about her, and she, Lilybelle, had been brought up proper, and had gone to church regular like, and could do plain sewing and cooking. (Poor young creature, thought James, with some urgent tenderness.) And then her aunt had brought her to London, to help her in the inn. She had respectable ways, had Lilybelle, and her aunt knew this. Everything had gone well, until yesterday.

The girl's sobs increased. Her face was darkly flushed. Her voice became heavy and hoarse, as she stammered out the rest of the story.

The young gentlemen were very noisy, it seems. Lilybelle thought they must be drunk. She did not know. Her father, who had died when she was a little girl, had been known to take his beer proper on occasion, but he had never been drunk. He had been a respectable tenant farmer, and knew his place. So, Lilybelle had never before had any experience with drunkenness. He, Mr. John Turnbull, had been more boisterous and noisy than any of the others. He had been quite bold, like. The girl coloured more violently than ever, and dropped her eyes. Then, her inherent propriety asserted itself, and she jumped to her feet. Her instinct told her she should not sit in the presence of this great gentleman.

James, respecting her propriety, did not ask her to seat herself again.

She continued, incoherently. All at once John had approached her, and had seized her arm across the counter. He was accompanied by another young gentleman, very handsome and pale and laughing. (That would be Bollister, thought James, grimly.) John, drunk and shouting, had insisted that she marry him, and at once. Uncle Tim had tried to interfere. John had swept him aside with one flicking movement of his big arm. He had lifted the girl from behind the counter. It had all been very confusing. He had quite overpowered her. Before she knew it, she had on her bonnet and tippet, and there was a carriage. She was literally thrown into the carriage, and John had crawled in after her, with the other young gentleman. Another carriage was called, and other young gentlemen followed. She had been terribly frightened, but excited. John seemed so handsome and masterful. She had no idea who he was—

A special licence had been procured, and they had been

70

married by a magistrate in a dark little office. Then, the whole procession had gone to a strange flat in London. By this time, James discerned, the girl had been stupefied with excitement and fright.

Now the girl was silent. But her face was heavily flushed, and she had dropped her eyes. James delicately refrained from questioning her further.

After some long moments, she resumed again, haltingly. She had slept a little, while John snored in his drunkenness beside her. She had awakened, to tears and despair. After awhile, he awoke, and seeing her there, and questioning her, had cursed her with wild fury and rage. He had wept, and struck her.

She turned her round face aside, and indicated a dark bruise along her chin. James' quiet brows drew together, and his lips narrowed to a thin line. But he said nothing, though there was a steadfast spark, now, in his gray eyes.

But Lilybelle apparently regarded the bruise as of no significance, and was not offended by James' silence. In truth, there was even a small pride in her display of the bruise.

John had risen, had dressed in black and sultry speechlessness, and then had abruptly informed the girl that she was to accompany him to his father, who would "see to it that this bloody nonsense was ended immediately." And now, here she was.

James studied that pretty and stupid young face with an almost passionate intensity. His lack of contact with humanity had sharpened, rather than dulled, his most subtle perceptions. He knew that this girl, though stupid and illiterate, had the cunning and shrewdness of her class in full measure, as well as its brutal common sense. He finally glanced down at his transparent clasped fingers and spoke gently:

"And so, Lilybelle, what do you think is the best thing to do?"

He had expected her to hesitate, but she spoke in her loud and forthright voice with a look of surprise: "Do, sir? But Mr. John said you would do it!"

James reflected wryly: So, the young scoundrel came home with his tail between his legs, believing I would extricate him from this abominable mess at once.

He said: "But, Lilybelle, you are a young person of some intelligence. I would prefer to know what you desire."

His manner had some kind deprecation in it, and so she became bold and even somewhat disdainful, as though he had lowered himself to her level, either in weakness or in his own confession of inferiority to her. She preened a little, and said in a mincing tone: "I am a respectable girl, Mr. Turnbull, as was never in any trouble before. I'm not one to go where I'm not wanted. So, I'll go my way and Mr. John can go his own way. Best that all this be forgotten."

James frowned meditatively. He said, with some sharpness: "But, my dear, you are now a married woman. You could not return to your home——"

She tossed her head so that the auburn curls bounced. "I've got my marriage lines, sir. You or no one else can take them from me." Feeling superior now to this senile old gentleman who showed her such consideration and respect, (probably recognizing that she was not one to be toyed with or fooled) she sat down again, arched her neck, bridled, and surveyed him with fierce and triumphant defiance.

James was kind-hearted, for few occasions had risen in his life for ruthlessness. He thought to himself: One cannot be too benevolent with this class. They take advantage. This thought distressed him, for it was no part of his nature to exert himself vigorously. He saw that he must do this now.

He leaned towards the girl and spoke with cold authority: "Ah, so you have your 'marriage lines.' That is enough for you, perhaps? You would go home to your mother, with your 'marriage lines' and forget all this?"

She was taken aback, more by his tone, than his words. But her slow wits gathered themselves together finally. She tried to summon her earlier defiance, and spoke sulkily:

"I thought as you would make it worth my while—." And then she cringed.

"Worth your while how?"

She was silent.

"You mean, you thought I could buy you off? How old are you, Lilybelle?"

She whimpered: "Fifteen, next March, sir."

Fifteen, then. James lay back in his chair and looked at her as coldly as he would survey an animal. She was no child, this, either by reason of age or by class. They knew how to take advantage, this class. They were predatory and cunning, for all their servility and respectfulness. At the end, the superior encountered the obstinacy of the inferior, and were confounded. He felt an outraged anger. He saw much, now. Johnnie had been a fool. But he had been helped in his folly by this girl. He, James, doubted very much that she had been forced into this marriage, as she had implied. Yes, he had her cunning to deal with, and deal with it he would.

"You shall not have a penny from me, Lilybelle," he said, calmly, and even with a smile.

She stared at him. She retreated a step, as if in sudden fear.

"No," he continued, "you shall not return to your home

with a fist full of money, Lilybelle. I can extricate my son, if I wish. I can prove that he was not responsible for this marriage, that he was tricked into it. Do you know what penalty the law exacts from a woman who humbugs a man into marriage with her? You are a clever girl. Think of this for a moment."

He spoke with such authority and ease that she did not even question his insinuations, or doubt them. She stared at him with pale terror, her big loose mouth fallen open in an expression of complete confusion and dismay.

"Even if I did not wish to prosecute you, Lilybelle, you would return home without your famous 'marriage lines.' You would be neither maid nor wife. Have you considered there might be a child, Lilybelle? What then? You could not go to your home under those circumstances." He leaned towards her and said, softly: "It would be the streets, then, for you, my lass."

She cried out, frantically: "A hundred pounds, sir!"

James shook his head. "Not a penny, Lilybelle."

Completely demoralized, now, she wrung her big calloused hands in her muff, and began to sniffle. "I've been hardly done by, Mr. Turnbull, me as was a respectable girl, even if I don't know my letters and my sums! You've got to remember that!"

"You've done 'hardly' by my son, too, my dear girl," said James, though now his treacherous heart was touched by her distress. Yes, this business of being ruthless was too much for a hermit. He decided that he did not like it. "You humbugged a drunken lad into marrying you. You want to deny this? Remember, Lilybelle, who you are! Remember that my son's friends will rally to him, and not to you. Have you ever been before the Assizes, Lilybelle?"

She was wild with terror. She retreated precipitately. But James forced himself to his feet, and halted her flight with an outstretched hand.

"That's no good, Lilybelle, your running away. Come back. We have other things to discuss."

She came back, her eyes fixed on him, hypnotized with fear. She trembled violently. He sank back in his chair and surveyed her blandly.

"Let us talk of all this, Lilybelle, quietly, like sensible people. You have married my son, drunken though he was, and not knowing what he did. That is done. You are his wife. I propose that you remain his wife."

She could not believe her ears. She gazed at him, stupefied.

"I will be frank about John, Lilybelle. He is a young fool, and a wastrel. I have given him money, because I did not

73

wish to trouble myself with disciplining him, and watching his expenditures." Now he spoke with an air of great candor, while the girl, still trembling, listened, only half understanding. He added, abruptly: "My dear, why did you marry him? I want the truth, now, and nothing but the truth."

She opened her mouth to whimper lies, but meeting that steadfast and bright gray gaze, she bowed her head and whispered: "It's no use, sir. He—he was a fine gentleman. He—he quite swept me off my feet."

"But you were drawn to him, eh? From the very beginning."

She nodded her bowed head.

"You liked him, and he appeared to be a fine gentleman, perhaps some one of your own class, but more prosperous, eh?"

Again, she nodded.

"And you thought such a marriage would be advantageous?"

She wept loudly in answer.

"Well, then," said James, "we are getting somewhere. So, you liked him, and he appeared to like you. You had much in common. Excellent! This forms a basis for a very sound marriage, indeed. So, you will remain John's wife."

"He don't want me, sir," she stammered, through her sobs, and now she lifted her head and looked at him with real grief. "And I'm not a one to force myself——"

"And, not wanting to 'force' yourself, Lilybelle, you decided the next best thing was money?"

He was touched, and a little pleased. He reached towards her and took her strong young hand, turned it over, and looked at its callouses. She looked down at him as he did so, weeping as openly and loudly as a child, and with a child's simplicity. Then he glanced up at her, still retaining her hand, and smiling.

"Lilybelle, how would you like to go to America, with Johnnie?"

"America," she repeated. But the word evidently only stupefied her.

"Yes, to America. They tell me it is a remarkable place. You would do well there, you and Johnnie. Yes, you are much alike. You would be excellent for him. You would be able to keep him under control. I am sure of this. You will make him a good wife, Lilybelle."

He stood up, then, and with only a little repugnance, and much sadness, he drew the girl to his frail chest. She dropped her head on his shoulder, all her defiance gone, and sobbed

74

loudly and without restraint. And he smoothed those coarse but vital red curls with a thin hand suddenly tender, sorry for her. What will become of them? he asked himself. Am I wise in this? Or is this just my old inertia asserting itself? How much that we do is the result of wisdom, and how much only laziness and negative denial of more vigorous conduct?

He called for tea, and led the girl back to her chair. With his own hands he removed her bonnet and her jacket. And as he did so, she smiled up at him pathetically.

Yes, it was a strong young thing, this, a proper mate for Johnnie.

CHAPTER 7

EUGENIA sat in her quiet and gloomy chamber with her needlework. Though she had thrust aside the heavy draperies on either side of the great tall window, very little gray light penetrated into the misty dimness of the room. The canopied bed, prim and white and smooth as a bank of snow, was only a shadow in the far corner. The high ceiling was fretted with the faint rosy bars of the fire which burned almost silently on the black hearth. As she worked, the girl was hardly conscious of what she was doing. At moments she lifted her smooth brown head as if listening. But she did not hear the roaring lash of the rain that assailed her windows, nor the wind which rattled them furiously.

Her "indestructible calm," as James fondly called it, was not disturbed this morning. But a shrewd observer would have detected a faint quick glow in those pale cheeks, coming and going like a reflection of the fire. Her small and delicate body retained its stillness, as always, its tremendous control and poise. The little feet on the footstool did not move restlessly. She sat, as always, very straight and elegant, her brown velvet gown falling in heavy rich folds from the curve of her dainty thighs and marvellously slight waist.

The room was chilly. Over her shoulders was laid a brown Cashmere shawl. She bent her head over her work. The needle flashed precisely in her little pale fingers, so transparent and bloodless. Once or twice she smiled. It was then that she would lift that proud small head and stare at the fire, the smile and the glow in her cheeks quickening. Authority, inflexibility and pride, always so evident in her, were softened this morning into something, which, if gentler, was still strong and determined.

She heard the hollow booming of the house about her, coming from a distance. Her mother still slept. It would be an hour before Martha would awaken with her petulant demands. In the meantime, Eugenia waited. She waited for her cousin John, to whom she had written the evening before. The embroidery increased and brightened under her fingers, blooming softly in its delicate design. She did not see it. In her mind she saw only the strangest and most exciting things, novel and delightful. She saw her cousin's strong dark face and restless black eyes. Visualizing him, then, there was just the faintest sound of a caught breath in the dank dimness of the chamber.

Fog rolled up to the windows in weird shapes like spectres, curiously peering within. It deadened even the few street sounds of Russell Square. When a dray passed, the echo only reached Eugenia's little white ears, and it was like an echo rising up from a bottomless pit. Nevertheless, it seemed to her that the chamber was full of rich warm things, moving in excitement and mysterious gaiety. The mirror over the fireplace reflected the gray wet windows and the fog shapes. But for Eugenia, as she glanced at it absently, it was full of colourful visions.

There was a tapping at the door, and she sprang up with more eagerness than she had displayed in many years. She ran to the door, and flung it open. A housemaid in cap and white apron stood there, tenuous in the gloom. The wench stared at her young mistress, gaping, for Eugenia's aspect, so eager, warm and flushed, was a strange and unusual one to her. She stammered that Master Turnbull awaited Miss MacNeill in the drawing-room.

"Yes!" breathed Eugenia, and now the round white throat fluttered. She flashed by the staring housemaid, and glided like a brown swift vision down the stairway, her hooped skirts billowing about her, the brown shawl streaming. But once at the threshold of the drawing-room, she was forced to pause, putting her little trembling hand to her heart, her breath catching. Then, summoning all her decorum, she advanced, with a smile, into the room, arching her smooth and shimmering head, her manner serene.

John, who was standing with bent head near the fire, turned slowly as he heard her light and gliding footstep. He had bathed, replaced his dishevelled linen with fresh, and had combed his hair. But his inner despair and wretchedness and sick hopelessness could not so easily be disguised. Pale, distraught and sunken-eyed, he stared speechlessly at his cousin, advancing with so much smiling tranquillity in his direction.

He had dreaded this moment. Beforehand, during his walk to Russell Square, he had told himself that he could not endure seeing her again, that it would be unbearable to look into those bright gray eyes, so like his father's, so suggestive, like his, of things hated and loved and never to be understood, but only to be resented and humbly adored.

He looked at his cousin, and his heart was pierced with the most appalling anguish. He had loved her, and had resented her, feeling boorish and inferior in her presence, leaving her either with exaltation or burning irritation and humiliation. But now, as he stood before her, gazing at, but not taking her extended hand, he felt that he was dying, that he must control himself or he would burst into dreadful tears.

Eugenia was puzzled for a few moments, as she looked at that ghastly and sunken face above hers. Then she smiled, secretly. Poor darling Johnnie! He had come to tell her, then, that he was going away, that he must leave her, remembering her decision not to go with him! Ah, but she had such a delightful surprise for him! In the meantime, she would remain aloof, delicately but lovingly teasing him, until her sudden capitulation and surrender would transport him into the most delirious joy.

She seated herself with her dainty air of authority and composure, and, tilting her smooth brown head, gazed upward at him with those large gray eyes filled and dancing with firelight. He stood on the hearth, and looked down at her. The black misery of his face grew more intense. It was apparent that he was most terribly ill. Ah, but it was not to last long, she smiled to herself. And now she breathed a little faster. A hot and delicious tremor ran along her nerves. Her heart was trembling.

"John," she said, very softly. "You received my letter, then?"

He started. Her voice called him out of his black pit of agony. Her face swam below him, its pallor warm and tremulous, the lips, usually so pale and composed, full and rosy and faintly smiling. She had always seemed to be standing at a little distance from him, even in their more familiar moments, untouchable and mysterious. But now he felt that she was closer to him than his heart and his breath, and so ineffably dear that he became frantic with his grief.

He half turned from her and put his hand over his eyes. He could not look at her. With his face still hidden by his hand, he spoke hoarsely and slowly, as if his throat had been torn, and was bleeding.

"I am going away, Eugenia."

She was silent. He heard the dropping of coals on the hearth. Through his sheltering fingers he saw their red hearts, luminous in the gray ashes, bursting open in little showers of sparks. He heard the howling of the wind, the battering of the rain. He shivered, for a sudden icy chill beset him, crept over his body in freezing waves. He thought incoherently: I shall tell her I am going to America. But, I shall not tell her the other. When I am gone, she can learn this from my father——

Yes, that would be best. She had made her decision yesterday. She would abide by it. In all the years he had known her, she had never turned aside from a previous decision. He had found her cold obstinacy infuriating, had often flung himself out of her presence in a flaming rage. Now, that obstinacy was his only strength. His habitual easy cowardice drew a long and quivering breath. It whispered to him that he would be allowed a last kiss from her, if he did not tell her. He would be permitted to touch that little white hand just once again, affronted and angered though she would be at his decision to leave her and go to America. For that kiss, for that touch, he would have to pay only the small price of silence.

"I am going away," he repeated, and now his voice was stronger, if even more despairing. He dropped his hand, and looked again at her, expecting to see her face smooth and withdrawn and haughtily indifferent, as it had been only yesterday.

He was not prepared for her smile, tremulous and tender, for the quick light colour on her cheek, for the strange shy brilliance of her eyes. He was not prepared for her to rise like this, in her small and delicate beauty. Bemused, stricken, he could only stare at her, and at her extended hands, at the gentle humility of her attitude.

"John," she said, softly, almost pleadingly, "take me with you." And now she caught her breath on something like a joyful sob, and the brilliance of her eyes increased.

For several moments he did not understand. His mouth dropped open, with an imbecile expression. His cheeks fell inward, and his whole face became wizened. There was a sudden wild roaring in his ears.

Then, all at once, he understood. Now the agony and the horror and the grief which he had been able partly to control fell on him with unendurable torture. In a swimming darkness, he cried out, loudly and chokingly: "No! No!"

He heard her cry out, confused and frightened: "John! What is it? Are you ill? John, didn't you hear me? Johnnie, dear, I said I would go with you!"

In his terrible suffering he did not feel her hand on his arm. But he saw her face terrified and white, close to his. There were tears in her eyes. She had begun to shake him a little. Words came from her lips but he saw only their movements in the midst of chaos.

As for Eugenia, some premonition of disaster struck at her, so that her hand finally fell limply to her side. The expression on John's face horrified her. She stepped back a pace or two, regarding him fixedly, "What is it, John?" she asked, in a faint whisper. And then, louder, in a kind of fearful frenzy: "John! What is it?"

He tried to speak. He put his hand to his throat, moved his head. He turned away from her, and rested his head on the mantelpiece, and she saw his profile, stark and drawn, his lips fallen open.

"Genie," he said, and in that one beloved sound was all his sick anguish.

She approached him again, involuntarily drawn to him with the frightened impulse of her love. She pressed her cheek against his shoulder. "Yes, John? Yes?"

She was bewildered when he started, and drew away from her, his forehead still on the mantelpiece.

"It's too late, Genie," he whispered. "You can't go away with me."

A quick furrow appeared on the smooth delicacy of her brow. She lifted her head proudly, though her lips dried suddenly.

"Why not?"

His big young body appeared to shrink in the fashionable coat. He lifted his hands and pressed them against his cheeks, so that she no longer saw his face.

"I'm married, Genie," he said, and his voice was dull and faint.

Slow and ponderous moments passed one by one. It was not for some time that he realized, in all his endless misery, that there had been a long silence in the great quiet drawing-room. He had been too engrossed with his own suffering. But becoming aware, after that prolonged silence, that she had not spoken a single word, he painfully dropped his hands and turned to her.

She had seated herself again near the fire. She sat very straight and stiff, looking at the incandescent coals. Her hands were clasped lightly on her knees. An intense coldness and composure emanated from her, and her features were rigid and very calm. There was a carved quality, too, about the folds of her brown velvet dress as it fell to her little instep.

She felt rather than saw his movement towards her. Still gazing at the fire, she asked, quietly: "When did you marry, John?"

"O Genie!" he cried, in his hoarse and stricken voice. "How can I tell you? It was last night, Genie, after I left you—after you told me you would not go with me——!"

She turned her head slowly towards him, with an expression of frozen incredulity. Her hands tightened convulsively on her knees.

"Last night!" she exclaimed. "Impossible!"

In spite of her control, she gasped, and her clasped hands lifted rigidly in the air, then slowly dropped.

He could not speak again. He could only look at her, at that aghast little face with the bitter lips and the outraged eyes, in which the dazzling light was like the reflection of lightning on ice. Never had he seen such an expression on that beloved face before, and it was this, even more than his own torment, which made him cry out, move towards her, sink on his knees, and lay his head on her unresponsive lap. He put his arm about her waist. He cried out again: "O Genie! Don't look at me like that! As if you hated me. I can't endure it, Genie!"

For a moment there was a convulsive movement throughout all her slight small body, as if she would repulse him with disgust and loathing. Then, he felt a relaxation in her, as if she had collapsed. But she said nothing, only sat there, not feeling the weight of his head, nor the frantic grasp of his arm.

"Forgive me, Genie," he said, brokenly. He moved on his knees, as if he writhed. He kissed the soft silken velvet which covered her thigh; he rubbed his cheek against it. He put his other arm about her, pulled her desperately towards him. She resisted for an instant, then relaxed again, as if all her powers of repulsion had disappeared.

But he felt her hardness, her outrage, her unremitting cold anger. So small a thing in his hold, but unbending as steel, and as inflexible. Too, she had an unsuspected physical strength, for, despite his frantic grasp of her, she put her hands on his head and forcibly lifted it. She looked down at him with a cold and forbidding look, stern and implacable. But when she saw his face, blotched, raddled with tears and suffering, the eyes suffused and sunken, she faltered, and the hard hands on his head became gentler. But she forced him to look at her.

"Tell me about it, John," she said, very quietly.

He would have turned away from her, in his shame and unendurable agony, but he could not. He tried to find words, but they were like hot fragments on his tongue. Now the enormity of the story he must tell her appeared to him to be too frightful for speech, too shameful.

Never, in his turbulent life, had he known, or acknowledged, that certain acts of his had sprung from a weakness of character, from some rotten spot of softness. Weakness in others had been abhorrent to him, had elicited loud condemnation and expressions of disgust. Weak men were not "English," and men who were not English were in some way contemptible; the worst could be expected of them, dismissed with a shrug of the shoulder. "Character" was "English." Never had he suspected that perhaps he did not have complete "character."

Now, it came to him with ghastly force that what he had done had sprung from some treacherous weakness in himself, unacknowledged or unknown. For a moment or two, in the midst of his struggle for words to tell his story, and immediately after his blinding insight into that unconscious weakness, he was stunned, appalled, stricken with terror.

"I am a weakling!" he exclaimed, in the strangest voice. "Yes, that is it: I am a weakling! I never knew it before. That is how it happened." His humiliation, his horror, increased. He became frantic. He got to his feet, and looked down at the girl. But he did not see her. He saw himself.

Though he was not aware of it, he had taken another agonized step towards maturity. He was still too juvenile of nature to understand that awareness of inherent weaknesses and strengths grows in proportion to a man's spiritual stature.

"A weakling?" repeated Eugenia. Her pale lip shook, became rigid. She did not understand weakness. She detested it. It became more shameful than ever when it was self-confessed. She believed men decently hid weaknesses as they hid their nakedness. There was no hope for a man when he acknowledged that he had this rottenness in himself, when he displayed it as a leper displays his sores: for pity. Eugenia did not know that a confession of weakness was the first step towards strength, that only the complete coward is capable of self-deception.

She stood up, and it was incredible how much contempt, how much inexorableness, her small and delicate body could convey.

"How were you weak, John?" she asked, mercilessly. Deep within her she was suffering desperately, overcome with desolation. But he could not know this, from her aspect, from the ruthless piercing of the gray eyes fixed upon his.

He pressed the palms of his sweating hands together. He stared at her, his horror, his loathing of himself, increasing. He began to speak, incoherently, stammering, his words rushing out as poison gushes from an abscess:

"When I left you, Eugenia, I—I thought the end of the world had come. I went to a tavern—it was a place in which we usually met. The men from Carruthers, Eugenia. There was a girl there, a barmaid——"

He paused. Eugenia flinched. She lifted her hand and put it on the mantelpiece. Her fingers clenched on the cold stone. But she said nothing. Her eyes became more ruthless, brighter than ever with her condemnation and disgust.

John's feverish gaze, wandering, fell at last on that little hand on the mantelpiece. For some unfathomable reason, he could not look away. He saw the strained and transparent knuckles, the faint pink delicacy of the nails. The whole appearance of the hand had a curious and fragile cruelty.

His words continued to rush out, disjointedly, with great speed:

"It was Bollister, Andrew Bollister, who came in with the other chaps. We—drank." He paused, flung out his hands despairingly, his eyes pleading with her abysmally. "Genie, I swear I don't know how it happened! But—when I woke up—the girl was there! I don't know!" He rubbed his trembling hands over his face. "It seems I married her, the night before. It was Bollister who arranged it——."

Now his expression became black and savage. He clenched his fists and beat them with slow and terrible force on the mantelpiece near her own hand.

"I am going to kill Bollister," he muttered.

Eugenia sat down, very slowly. She gazed at the fire again. She was very white. Even her lips had turned white. She spoke very quietly, after a long interval.

"John, have you told your father?"

"Yes," he answered. His voice was muffled; the savagery was still vivid in his black eyes, and his tone was absent. "I took—her—to him. We had a talk, first. I thought—he might get me out of this. But he told me I had to live up to my bargain."

He drew a deep breath, as if he smothered. A dullness and heaviness had come out on his face.

"He said I—we—must go to America. It was best."

Eugenia lifted her head alertly. Now her gray eyes glittered.

"Uncle James said this, to you? You are certain? He wished you to remain married to this—creature?" Her light voice was hard and swift. "Why?"

He shook his head. Again he covered his face with his

hands, "I don't properly know. It was something about it being time for me to be a man. I'm a fool, Genie. I've always been a fool. Father made me see it. He was right. I know he was right."

"You mean to imply," cried Eugenia, "that it is your intention to continue in this impossible situation?"

He did not hear the catch in her throat; he did not see how she suddenly pressed her hands to her breast as if to quell an intolerable pain.

"What can I do?" he muttered, dully. "Father will not help me. He was quite determined. Genie, you don't know what a fool I've been all my life!"

"Uncle James will not help you?" repeated Eugenia, insistently.

He shook his head. He turned away from her, abruptly, so that she might not see the burning tears which stung his eyelids.

Eugenia was silent. That stern young face became bitter, and vengeful. Her throat throbbed. She swallowed to quiet it. The firelight lay in the sockets of her eyes, and flickered over her pressed and stony mouth.

"Perhaps you don't quite understand," said John, almost inaudibly, his back almost completely turned to her. "I—something took place between us, Genie. She—she is my wife."

Still, Eugenia did not speak. But a fiery blush darkened her white cheeks. She lifted her head as if stung, and again an ineffable look of supreme loathing and disgust flared over her features.

Then she spoke in a practical voice, without emotion: "You were dragooned into this impossible situation, John. Your—weakness—played a large part, one must admit. But, one must also remember other things. I can't understand Uncle James. Has he forgotten me? He always seemed very fond of me——"

Now her voice broke. She recovered herself sternly, however.

He turned to her swiftly, dropped to his knees again, and took her cold little hands in his. Now, though she struggled for composure, her mouth trembled if her eyes were still steadfast.

"O Genie, forgive me, my darling!" he cried, hoarsely. He kissed her hands with vehemence. "Do you think I'll ever forget you, wherever I am? Don't you know how all this is killing me, my darling? There isn't anything else left for me, in the whole world, Genie."

She looked down at him. She tried to retain her inexorable sternness, her cold condemnation. But she could not. Her mouth trembled more and more, though her eyes remained dry and excessively bright. Then, with a faint and shaken sob, she dropped her head on his, and her cold hands quivered.

"O John," she whispered. "O John!"

They clung together, these two poor young creatures, in their desolation and their anguish.

A long time passed, while they neither moved nor spoke, their arms holding fast. Now Eugenia wept. John could not bear it. Her tears came reluctantly, for she rarely cried, and the fount of weeping within her filled painfully.

But, in the meantime, the girl's contained heart grew more icy, more swollen with misery and grief, more vengeful and determined. She felt for John only overwhelming love, however she despised his weakness and folly, which had led to this hour of suffering. But for her uncle, James, she felt hatred and bitterness.

Defeat was not familiar to Eugenia. There was the quality of implacability in her, and an almost virulent obstinacy. She did not relapse into frantic resignation. She did not sorrow or mourn. Her quick sharp mind, so disingenuous despite her youth, was already planning. Strength returned to her.

She gently released herself from John's arms.

"I think you had best go now, my dear. You see, I must think."

He stood up. The face that looked down at her mutely was no longer young, with softnesses about the mouth and eyes. It was grim and desperate.

"Genie, it is goodbye, you know."

She smiled faintly, and her eyes narrowed.

She repeated: "You had best go now, John."

She rose, and before he could stop her, she had glided silently from the room, her smooth gleaming head high on her throat, her step unhurried but determined.

CHAPTER 8

JAMES frequently remarked to himself that it was the passionate, the emotional, those given to profound frenzies and furies, who reached numbness first and most completely. The men of reason, he said, unfortunately rarely knew this anesthesia. As their emotions were rigidly pale and controlled, so could they keep their thoughts and passions within the cold borders of complete consciousness. Therefore, their suffering was unremitting. It was a chronic ache, very seldom lessening, always endurable. And invariably devastating, however long the final disintegration was delayed. Their pallid torment was a slow ulcer which eventually poisoned their souls, the venom cumulative, the end completely destructive.

But the wild and passionate spewed out their poison at healthy periods, exorcising the devils which beset them. A numbness followed this salutary catharsis, during which the vital forces could gather strength again, and fortitude. Rarely, a scar remained. Or, if it remained, it only throbbed at far intervals, never enough to destroy the organism. Sometimes the wild and passionate, feeling that vague throb, were hard put to it to remember the original wound, feeling only a passing dim anger, an uneasy despondency, or, at the worst, a desperate and turbulent resistance.

So it was that John, having left his cousin, was suddenly seized by a profound numbness, in which external objects took on a shifting grayness and unreality. He moved through a gray dream. He felt in himself a vast and ragged wound, diffused and empty; he was conscious of its swift bleeding, but the first anguish was gone. He looked about him at the streets; they were the streets of a dull nightmare. He hardly felt the stones under his feet, and the dank and gritty windiness and rain did not exist for him. Nor did he think acutely of past events, and the miserable black future ahead, nor of his grief and his exile. He only knew that London was strange to him, like an alien city in which he had no interest, which was devoid of memory for him, and which was only part of his vague if circumambient illness. His mind could not think; it had passed the point of endurance.

Then, as he stumbled along in a streaming crowd of wet and scurrying people, jostled by them, pricked by the points of their black umbrellas, a hot and vivid pang of pain and rage struck deep at his anesthetized heart, and he halted abruptly, staring wildly before him. He stood in the midst of the buffeting throngs, the rain streaming in his face, utterly immobile, with his eyes, blazing and fixed, seemingly fastened on some terrible thought, some savage decision. His big hands slowly clenched; his body tightened. The pale and livid light of the day flashed on the teeth which his lifted lips revealed.

Andrew Bollister remained, with a few others, in the classroom after Dr. Carruthers' had been dismissed. There were two passages of Cicero which engrossed his attention. It was not that he was particularly interested in the sonorous phrases which he was translating, nor did their majestic meaning inspire in him any exaltation or joy in their stateliness. But it was part of his nature that he allowed nothing to conquer him, nothing to appear difficult to him. Even the smallest and most insignificant event was a challenge to that frightful and frozen egotism of his. He would set himself to conquer and subdue it. Nothing was too small for his attention, and his relentless pursuit of it.

Only that morning he had discovered that one of his boots had slightly less sheen upon it than the other. No one but Andrew Bollister would have observed that small deviation. In truth, he had to examine the offending boot in both daylight and candlelight before he was certain. When he was finally convinced that his suspicions were correct, he had called "Boots" from his cave near the kitchen and had thrashed him soundly with his cane.

It was not his fastidiousness which had been offended. It was something more profound, something which did not spring from cruelty, or at the last, from pure egotism. It was as if he dared not for a moment relinquish his control of things. Let his control slip for but an instant, even if it was only the delay in the bringing of his breakfast, and there would be a breech which might widen to let in the floods of destruction. Had any one of intuition told him that he was beset by a constant and mortal fear, he would have stared with incredulity, and with a smile.

He would have smiled even more if he had been told that his pursuit of Cicero had its roots in his fear. But there was a grimness in his expression as he pored over the book in the flickering lamplight of the room, which was empty except for himself and two or three other young men. He bent his pale and polished head over the pages; his eyes, almost as pale, were fixed unrelentingly on the words. His hand, that long and almost fleshless hand, wrote the slow translation on a sheet of paper. His intensity of purpose was inexorable. He exuded an air of frozen steeliness, as if this was a matter of life and death that he was pursuing. As indeed it was. A failure in translation might be the first breech in the iron wall.

His long and elegant profile, all thin sharp lines like a bitter cameo, had no expression upon it but motionless implacability. He thought of nothing else but the conquest of the passage. The events of the night before were waiting, like a neat pile of books, for his later study. But at this hour only Cicero mattered.

He felt, rather than heard or saw, the sudden disorderly

tumult at the door, the caught breaths of his companions. His pale and slender brows knotted in renewed concentration. His hand moved steadily. He would not look up until he had completed this last sentence, no matter what the provocation.

Then, in the very midst of his absorption, he felt a hand seize his shoulder. It was a powerful and violent hand. He was whirled to his feet. The pen fell from his fingers, spluttered upon the exquisite neatness of the paper. It was the disruption of his preoccupation that made him blink and stagger in the grip of his assailant, and not fear.

He found himself looking into the wild and savage face of John Turnbull. He found himself being shaken as if he was a rag in John's grip. He heard strange distant sounds coming from John's contorted lips. But his mind, that strange and terrible mind, still, like a mad shining engine, pursued the last words of Cicero down the vanishing track of his absorption, even in the very midst of his sudden awareness of John's presence and the tightening of his own body.

John had him by the throat. He towered over him, his face black and inhumanly changed by his fury and hatred. The lamps flickered as if a gale had surged into the classroom. In the doorway crowded a few of the curious and eagerly anticipatory. The other young men in the room had gotten to their feet, and were staring avidly.

Andrew had seen his bellicose father in a rage. Rage had often broken about that polished head, but he, himself, cool and invulnerable, had never been disturbed by it. So many had hated him, even when he had been a child. But never had he seen a face like this, and a nameless prickling went along his nerves like a trembling warning.

Nevertheless, fear in the physical sense had never assailed him. It did not assail him now. He felt, for a fleeting instant, only a malevolent amusement, followed by instant outrage and disgust. Had John threatened the malignant core of him, he would have been frightened. But John threatened only his body, and his final reaction was loathing that his enemy dared to touch his flesh.

"Let me go, you fool," he said, in his quiet and toneless voice. But he did not struggle. To struggle would have been the fatal mortification which could have attacked his psychic vulnerability. He fixed his pale and gleaming eyes upon John's countenance with an expression of supreme contempt and indifference.

It was this look which increased John's fury and hatred to insane heights. Had Andrew trembled, had he exhibited terror, part of his vengeance would have been satisfied. To see that bloodless face, narrow and handsome, change and be-

87

come fearful, to see those eyes shaken with personal fright, to feel that thin flesh quiver, to see that haughty mouth open on a cry, would have been more satisfying to John Turnbull than any crushing or bleeding of Andrew's physical body. Then would have been alleviated his ancient sense of inferiority to Andrew Bollister; the fear expressed in the face of his enemy would have freed him from an old disease. Then would he have been delivered from past uneasy torment and misery. In his conquest of Andrew would have been deliverance for himself.

But even in his madness he knew that he could not conquer this immortal enemy. He might beat that frailer flesh into a pulp. But there was an invulnerability there, contemptuous and sardonic, which he could not conquer. It was an invulnerability which would remain disdainful of him, which, at the last, would reduce him to the old position of inferiority and impotence.

It was this, then, that made him burst into a wild and vicious oath, which made him, almost with despair, raise his knotted fist and plunge it into that faintly smiling face. He felt Andrew's skin and flesh soften under his knuckles. He felt the sudden bending of Andrew's knees. But he had the strangest and most maddening feeling that he really had not touched Andrew at all. He uttered a loud cry, almost like a sob. Even when Andrew's blood poured from his nose, John glared at it furiously as though he had been tricked.

He heard angry voices about him. "Unfair! This isn't a fair fight, Turnbull. You can't strike a man without giving him a chance to defend himself!"

He heard the outrage and disgust in those voices. He knew that they thought him a man without sportsmanship. In other words, he was no longer "English." Even as he clutched the half-fainting Andrew, he knew, with a dim and childish wonder and bewilderment, that he was not "English," that he had never been "English."

He cried out: " 'Unfair!' Was this snake 'fair' to me?"

Then he lifted his fist once more, and struck again, and again.

Andrew made no attempt to defend himself against those blows. To have done so, to have been inevitably defeated in a physical contest with this superior enemy, would have struck at that unfathomable vulnerability in himself. If he did not resist against superior force, that vulnerability would remain intact. He never resisted when inevitable defeat faced him. He never attacked if he knew he could not win. If John Turnbull was not "English," Andrew was the very epitome of "Englishness."

He felt his senses slipping away. To the last he thought: If I do not resist, I remain unconquered. It was this final thought that made him smile faintly before he collapsed.

John's hand opened convulsively. Andrew crumpled at his feet. But even if his body lay there, silent and bleeding, he was undefeated. John had not touched him in the slightest. He began to sob aloud, drily.

CHAPTER 9

JAMES TURNBULL read the cold and peremptory note sent him by his niece, Eugenia:

"If it please you, Uncle James, I should like to have a moment or two *alone* with you this evening, during which we can discuss certain matters of importance."

He smiled sadly, and turned over the stiff little sheet of paper in his thin fingers. The note brought Eugenia's small and indomitable face before him, and he saw those brilliant large gray eyes, so like his own. He understood her; hence his fondness for her. John had never been a true Turnbull. But all of the characteristics of the true Turnbull were in this frail female creature. She was lucid and reasonable. Subtle appeals to emotion would only bring a pale and scornful smile to her lips. James' sadness increased. He knew how truly vulnerable the reasonable were, immune to the warmth and passion of emotion, and with only the bleak bitterness of logic to sustain them. Theirs, no psychic intuitions to console; theirs, no sudden swellings of the heart in nameless rapture. They were never seduced or bewildered. But neither did they hope. The emotional could be reconciled, led to beautiful renunciations. But the men of reason never truly acknowledged defeat, however loud and clear their philosophical protestations of acceptance of it. For their very reasonableness prevented them from sublimating defeat into spiritual glory. No wonder, then, that the reasonable never became leaders of men, never conceived crusades, never overturned worlds or invented gods!

James felt more compassion for Eugenia than he had felt for his son. John would never be hopelessly befuddled by reason. He would proceed by his emotion. He would never be able to see both sides of a question. On this knowledge, then, James based his hope for his son. But for Eugenia there was no hope. Her reason would compel her to see the ugliness of facts and living, uncoloured by passion and faith. The emotional sometimes became cynics. But skepticism was reserved for the unfortunate who were afflicted with true reason. It was theirs at birth.

Understanding this, and how he must make Eugenia, whom he loved so dearly, unhappy and embittered, James sighed, and sent a note with a messenger to her.

"I will be alone tonight, my dear," he had written, gravely.

But not more alone than I have ever been, he reflected. And not more alone than any one else. Those who wrote, or said: "I shall not be alone tonight," did not know they were guilty of unconscious irony.

At eight o'clock, precisely, Eugenia was admitted to the vast dark library where her uncle awaited her. Here the ponderous gloom was only accentuated by the scattered oil lamps, by the dark fire at the farthest wall. Hundreds of forgotten books looked down in their dust and leather upon the heavy oaken furniture and the crimson rug. James sat before the fire in his leather chair, smoking with an appearance of thoughtful tranquillity.

He rose slowly when Eugenia entered, holding his pipe in his hand, his tasselled cap giving his long ascetic face a look of frivolity. Eugenia advanced into the room, clad in black silk with a black fur jacket, a wide plumed hat on her haughty and gallant young head. There was nothing disordered or hasty about her appearance. The cold serenity and sternness of her pale face, the aristocratic lift of her head, and her "indestructible calm," inspired, as always, James' admiration and respect, and his love. Also, strangely, his pity. Always, he pitied his niece: the unbending were capable of such enormous and hopeless suffering. Their tears were heavy with iron, and as slow and reluctant.

She gave him her gloved hand, rose on tiptoe to touch his bent cheek with her cool lips. Then, seating herself, after he had removed her jacket, she regarded him steadfastly. He sat near her, smiling painfully. Their bright gray eyes were reticent.

"I believed it was time that we had a talk," said Eugenia, in her firm light voice.

"Yes, my dear?" murmured her uncle, affectionately. He leaned forward to poke the fire into a warmer blaze. Eugenia watched him indifferently. Her composure was amazing.

James continued his murmur: "It has all been so very sad,

so unfortunate. I am glad, my love, to see you endure this unpleasantness so calmly."

She did not reply. He glanced at her with some timidity. Was that a grim faint smile on her young mouth?

Then she looked at the fire. The shadow of that suspected smile gave her an expression of implacability and sardonic strength.

"I have been wondering, dear Uncle James, just how much I must endure. And by whose guilt."

"Guilt, my dear?"

She turned to him fully, with quiet bitterness.

"Yes, Uncle James. Your guilt. John has told me how you have refused to help him. I have come tonight to persuade you to reconsider."

James stood up. She had not said: "I have come tonight to try to persuade to reconsider." In the small omission of two words was the whole key to her character. He had always known she was hard. He had sometimes thought her hardness came from pride, which might at times be vulnerable. But now he saw that her hardness was no product of another characteristic, but a strong characteristic in itself.

He felt his tired heart sink. This was going to be very bad indeed. Poor child. His own harshness emanated from wisdom. But hers came from a bottomless egotism. He remembered his grandmother. Eugenia was much like that terrible woman, who had ruined a number of lives. But James was not concerned with that. His whole fear was that Eugenia might ruin her own life. There was a terribleness in her, too.

He knocked his pipe carefully into the fire, bending forward so that his lean and emaciated figure was lighted by the incandescent coals. He was trying to find words to say, gentle words, reasonable words. Then he knew he must be cleanly brutal.

"I am afraid," he said, gently, seating himself again, and looking at her with forthright sadness, "that everything is too late. Matters are out of my hands. John, and his wife, are already on the way to America. They left this morning."

He watched her with tender closeness. Would she weep? Would she cry out? Would she rise, full of exclamations and wild denunciations? She did none of these. She only grew very white, and her features froze into a look of desolate hatred and despair. Her gray eyes blazed. Her lips turned to stone. But she did not clench her hands, nor move even slightly on her chair. Her straight and narrow back did not, even for an instant, bend or tremble. In truth, she seemed to gain in stature, and become more rigid.

There was a long silence between them, while they regarded each other. There was no sound but the dropping of coals in the room.

Then, not looking away from him, and with the blaze sharpening like lightning in her eyes, she said, very quietly: "So. You refused to help him. You ruined him, after all. Why? Did you hate your own son so much?"

There was a malignancy in her voice. But that did not deceive James. He knew that she was suffering the agonies of the reserved, so much more poignant than the loud emotional. How could he have ever thought that her affection for John was coolly indulgent and indifferent?

Overcome with his pity, he stretched out his hand to her, and said: "My poor little love. Believe me, it was for the best. I would have spared you this; I would have done anything in the world to spare you. Except to destroy John's only opportunity to become a man."

She did not glance at his hand. But her face darkened and grew more still.

"I don't understand you, Uncle James." There was a cold scorn and an increasing hatred in her tone. "You imply that if John had married me he would have been destroyed. Is that what you mean?"

James was silent. He rested his hands, palm down, on his knees. He regarded her with sorrowful intensity. Now a certain tenuous implacability, matching her own, appeared sternly about his mouth.

"I did not imply that, Eugenia. But now that you have said it, I see that it might have been true."

Her expression did not change, except, perhaps, to grow more stony and inflexible. If she had been abominably hurt, she betrayed no sign of it. She waited.

He continued, in a lower and even more saddened voice: "I had often wondered, Eugenia, why you held Johnnie in some affection. Was it childhood propinquity? Was it an inertia on your part, which forbade you to search for a more congenial companion? I do not deceive myself that it was the result of any urging on your Mama's part." He added, with a hint of a grim smile at the corner of his melancholy lips: "You are not a young lady to heed tears or urgings when your own mind has made its decision. Then, what turned you to Johnnie?"

James' pity grew. However, he waited obdurately for her reply. She moved very slightly, and spoke in a dry pent tone which was infinitely pathetic to his ears with its evidence of a control beyond her years:

"It did not occur to you, Uncle James, that I may simply love John, without reason or explanation?"

Poor child, poor child, he sighed over and over in himself. Yes, she loved that rascal, Johnnie. And she was not one who forgot love, who gave love easily or loved lightly. Love became part of the very fibre of that tough heart, interwove itself with its muscles and its veins. To tear it away would be to tear away tendons, leaving a mortal wound behind.

For her own sake, then, he must be ruthless, even cruel. Would the wound heal? Or would it leave twisted scars behind? He believed it would be the latter. He believed that Eugenia would be maimed forever. Now a real bitterness rose in him against his son, that foolish, turbulent wild young fool! How often the Johnnies of the world became the recipients of the strange and hard and reluctant hearts of the Eugenias!

He interlaced the fingers of his hands together very tightly, as they lay between his knees, and regarded her with quiet but passionate earnestness:

"You are hating me, my love. I am wounding you. But I have always been able to talk to you, not as an uncle to a young niece, but as one human being to another. We need not lie to each other.

"Let us look at Johnnie: Here is an irresponsible, selfish, uncontrollable young barbarian, who has refused to become a man in spite of his nineteen years. He is the sort who is precipitated into manhood by some momentous event, not by natural growth, or wisdom. His cocoon must be rent by force, external force, otherwise he must remain a silly and overgrown child until his beard is gray.

"There are so many of such men in the world, who are a burden first to their parents and teachers, then to their wives, and finally to their children. They inspire contempt and laughter and scorn in others, even if they also inspire protection and love. Eternal children, Eugenia. Who desires them? Only the fools."

He paused Eugenia did not speak or move. The ice in her eyes hardened, brightened.

"Sometimes these men are lucky. Sometimes a kind fate deprives them of protective and maternal wives, such as you might have been, Genie. Sometimes that kind but harsh fate precipitates them into events which set their irresponsible heels on a hard sure road. Such an event has happened to Johnnie. I might have saved him, continued to keep him in swaddling clothes, inured against the consequences of his own acts. But I have not done this. He committed a grave folly. I have forced him to face it, to accept it, to profit by it, to learn by it."

He dropped his head on his breast. "I might have saved

93

him, if I had earlier taken an interest in him. But I only wanted him to leave me alone, as I have always wanted to be alone. No matter. I did him a wrong. Then, after he had done this appalling thing, I saw that the final opportunity had arrived for me to save him. It was my guilt that he has to learn the lesson in one supreme and terrible hour, instead of over a period of nineteen years. Do you think it was easy for me, my child? But it had to be done. I have suffered, as he has suffered, as you are suffering. That does not lessen my guilt. In my heart, I have asked Johnnie's forgiveness. I ask yours, now."

"And," said Eugenia, with low bitterness and hatred, "you believe it is 'saving' John to force him to accept a—trollop—as his wife, to go away into exile, almost penniless, to abandon his friends, and the girl to whom he had given a solemn promise?"

James was silent a moment, then he said steadfastly: "Eugenia, my love, I believe that."

She spoke with an icy passion: "You did not consider me?"

He said, looking at her fixedly: "Yes, I considered you. But you were not as important to me as Johnnie."

He knew that she was strong, that she could hear truths calmly, even if with anger and hatred.

"Genie, let us be frank. It would not matter to you if Johnnie remained an eternal child. You would have married him, knowing what he was. In fact, you would have preferred it if he had continued to be irresponsible and weak. Why? Because you are an arrogant, dominant woman, who loves power. Johnnie's weakness, his compliance, his yielding, to you, would have tickled your egotism, and would have finally made you a most horrible woman, a really terrible woman, a tyrant dominating and terrorizing your husband and your children. Deep in you, you love Johnnie less than you love power. That is what I meant when I said you might have destroyed Johnnie."

She looked at him, with all her cold naked fury in her eyes, all her indomitable resistance to him. But he knew that he had struck her to the heart, also.

"I overlook your insults, Uncle James. I am not concerned with myself just at present. I am thinking only of John. Did you ever give a moment's thought to his happiness? He will never be happy again!"

As if she had said something heinous, something intolerably affronting to him, something most contemptible and indecent, he regarded her with a stern expression, even an outraged one:

94

"Happiness! Are you a fool, Eugenia? I have been talking gravely and solemnly to you, and you insult me with idiotic prattlings about 'happiness'! What a childish remark! What an absurdity! Only idiots talk of happiness, only dreamers and half-wits. Consider for a moment: Have you ever known a single man or woman who was happy? No! Only a child has flashes of happiness, because it lives in unreality, in dreams and folly. Perhaps a drunkard has those flashes too, or an opium eater. But that has nothing to do with the world of living. I am speaking of life, not the dreams of fools, drunkards, opium eaters and children!"

He stood up, as if shaken to his very depths, and regarded her with dark and moved affront. "I thought you were a woman, Eugenia. Knowing the circumstances of your life, I thought the word 'happiness' would bring a bitter and disdainful smile to your lips. I would never have believed that such as you would mouth it, ridiculously. You are either a child, or a fool!"

She did not answer him. But over her face passed a gleam like the flash of a sword, and he saw her enmity for him, her hate, her eternal vengefulness. He had caught her in a folly; she would never forgive him for showing her her own nakedness, her own ridiculousness.

After a moment of the most intense silence, he continued sternly, even brutally: "I have forced Johnnie to sink or swim. What happens to him now is his own responsibility. I can do nothing else."

He looked at her with sudden warning sharpness: "There is nothing you can do, Eugenia. Nothing you dare do."

She rose, took up her jacket and put it on. She pulled on her gloves. All her movements were measured and calm. Only at the last, when she was ready to go did she look at him. And now he was overcome with pity again. This poor, poor child, so unbending, so implacable, but so vulnerable too, so pathetic. He knew only too well how she was bleeding in her heart, and what anguish she was enduring. If she would only weep, so that he might comfort her! But such as Eugenia never wept, repudiated consolation as the last and supreme insult.

"Genie," he began, then was silent.

He saw her smile, dark and repellent. Then, without a word, she glided away from him. He watched her. Her narrow back was so straight, like steel enclosed in silk and fur. Her tread was unhurried. Her head was high and stiff. But if her attitude was indomitable, it was also unbearably desolate.

When she had gone, he sank back in his chair, and a mortal

disintegration seemed to pervade him. He covered his face with his hands. There was no sound in the room but the dropping of the coals, and long, painful, continued sighs.

CHAPTER 10

M R. BOB WILKINS had not attained to his very satisfactory status in life without his shrewd and sly, and yet intrinsically good-tempered understanding of his fellowmen. If that understanding was leavened with malice, it also owed much of its validity to a boundless curiosity, and even to a kind of left-handed sympathy and foxy tolerance. Mr. Wilkins was a born scoundrel. He had a high respect for the nastinesses of law and the lack of openmindedness of the police. He was too intelligent to do anything which might bring him anything more onerous and disagreeable than a long and thoughtful stare from the gendarmery. At the crucial moment when that stare might be suddenly and violently transformed into action, Mr. Wilkins was simply not present, or, if forced to be present, his life and his activities took upon themselves the blameless innocence and blandness of a lamb cavorting on spring hills.

Mr. Wilkins was a plotter, but without drama. His plotting had the outward appearance of a gay Punch-and-Judy show, so that every one was convinced that he was animated only by high spirits, with perhaps a touch of whiskey-jauntiness. Nor was that plotting nefarious, designed to bring confusion and ruin to others. It was simply planned to bring the largest possible profits to Mr. Wilkins. He was an excellent servant to those who bought his services. So long as he was in their employ, (at a most respectable sum) the employers could be certain that he would not betray them. But they were never certain just when their employment of Mr. Wilkins terminated. They never knew the exact and crucial moment until something occurred to throw them into devastating and appalled rages. When they attempted to seize upon Mr. Wilkins, they discovered, to their confoundment, that Mr. Wilkins had already severed relationships with them and was now happily employed by others. "I'm a man as is loyal," he would say virtuously. "I'm not a man as would take a chap's money and turn and bite him. When I does something agin him, I'm no longer his man."

Mr. Wilkins, then, despite his great talents, and despite his funds of humour and saltiness and great entertainment value, was not at all liked by those who had previously employed him.

"Lawsuits?" he would say, tapping himself on his round and sturdy chest, and grinning. "I've got more lawsuits hangin' around my neck than any other man in the world! Like a bloody necklace!"

He was proud of his lawsuits. He regarded the baffled pursuits by bailiffs with as much pride as a great actor regards the pursuits of his adoring audiences. It was all only a compliment to his genius. The bailiffs did not worry him. He would always rely on the laughing employer of the moment, (appreciative of Mr. Wilkins' temporarily bought talents) to extricate him from a situation which showed disagreeable symptoms of becoming embarrassing.

Mr. Wilkins, in short, skimmed on the thin ice of the law with grace and finesse and skill. Being extraordinarily intelligent, he had little fear of breaking through that ice. "The law is an ass," he would quote, blandly. Too, he knew that the bailiffs were only the hunting hounds of disgruntled and howling ex-employers. "I've got me books that is open to the world!" he would exclaim, with injured innocence. But the books he kept in his mind were safe from the law.

In conclusion, Mr. Wilkins had long ago arrived at the great truth that a man's best friend was himself. If he took good care of Mr. Wilkins, he was only demonstrating the fact that he was no fool. Integrity paid poor dividends in this world of knaves. Integrity was the virtue of eternal servants. It was the last consolation of those who had failed. Mr. Wilkins did not care to die fruitlessly. He preferred to live richly.

Mr. Wilkins often declared, with an admirable lack of modesty, that he had "a nose." In the physical sense, this was very obvious. In the figurative sense, also, it was only too true. He could "smell out" an unusual personality, however innocuous or drab or desolate it might appear. He had rarely erred. His passion for Mr. Wilkins made that nose his most valuable instrument. He never wasted the sensitivity of his nose on those who could never advance the black figures in Mr. Wilkins' innumerable bank-books. When his nose began to "twitch," (a quite subconscious phenomenon) Mr. Wilkins alertly began to search all those nearby for the only one which had tickled his olfactory organ. The latter detected an object far in advance of Mr. Wilkins' vision. For instance, Mr. Wilkins might go about for days, even for months, without his nose once twitching, though during that time he might

97

have encountered thousands of fellow beings. Then, all at once that unfailing tickling began, and Mr. Wilkins would begin to sniff greedily, his eyes piercing through all those nearby. Was this he, or this one, or again, this one? Eventually, like the nose of a retriever, Mr. Wilkins' nose would suddenly point. And the unconscious man at whom that nose pointed would mysteriously find himself the puzzled recipient of Mr. Wilkins' genial and open attentions, always begun with the utmost friendliness and innocence.

Nor was Mr. Wilkins ever rebuffed permanently. Some there were who would stare haughtily, or would shrug and walk away. It was quite useless. Mr. Wilkins would strangely be at hand in the most unlikely spots, and just when the pursued had decided that the bounder had finally been thrown off the scent, there was Mr. Wilkins again, jaunty, affable, grinning and gently persistent!

The objects of Mr. Wilkins' nose were not confined to one walk in life, nor one trade, or class or occupation. Thus it was, in the service of Mr. Wilkins, that the nose had led him into the strangest bypaths. Mr. Wilkins had an extraordinary knowledge of importing and exporting, of the cotton trade, of the slave trade, of the gold trade, drug traffic, and the financial markets of the world. It was even said, by those who had come to not liking Mr. Wilkins, that he had been engaged in the bawdy trade, but this Mr. Wilkins would deny with authentic indignation. Not that he would have refused such a connection had it been offered him. It was simply that no such a connection had as yet been suggested. Therefore, he was still entitled to his virtue in this respect, and could boast of it.

All things were for sale in this most entertaining world. Mr. Wilkins, therefore, felt himself a legitimate bargainer in the universal bazaar.

Mr. Wilkins had not been aboard the *Anne of Argyle* two days out of Liverpool, when his nose began to twitch. He looked about at the some two hundred and fifty passengers, a motley crowd if he had ever seen one! But the nose did not yet point, though its twitching became more excited every hour. Among that passenger list was some one who was going to be very important and valuable to Mr. Wilkins In the meantime, he prowled about the ship, beaming, joking, making himself very entertaining and popular with every one, waiting for the moment when his nose would unmistakably point.

There was nothing about Mr. Wilkins to inspire the slightest suspicion even among those who are born with an unremitting distrust of all other men. He was very short, not more than five foot three, and very bulky, though not fat. He gave the impression of enormous physical strength, and this he had. He was built on the lines of an oaken cask, with all its suggestion of sturdiness and thick durability. Too, like that cask, he appeared full of potential joviality and high spirits and wholesome satisfaction. One thought, as one thought of the cask: "Nothing there thin and acid, sir!" There was a hint of Yuletide festivity about Mr. Wilkins, too.

Mr. Wilkins' penchant for loud and gaudy clothes endeared him even to the elegant and fastidious. It was all part of his "amusing" personality, and assured the spectator that there must be some frank and simple innocence in Mr. Wilkins which inspired such flowered weskits and big gold watch-chains, such light-coloured and buoyant pantaloons, such pointed and polished boots, such flowing, long-tailed broadcloth coats and extravagant cravats and florid ruffles at his wrists, such amazingly high and gleaming hats. Mr. Wilkins took such evident and candid enjoyment in his lavish wardrobe that even the sourest were forced to smile affectionately, as at a big and engaging child. He talked of his wardrobe with sparkling eyes and great pride to all who would listen, and would often drag reluctant gentlemen down to his stateroom in order to display it. But, in truth, Mr. Wilkins' wardrobe and his conversation about it were only part of his trade, and a very shrewd part. Mr. Wilkins knew how necessary it was to give the impression of simple and even vulgar innocence and harmlessness.

Mr. Wilkins carried with him a great cane with a lavish gold head, intricately chased and molded. It was almost as tall as he. He would rest his hand upon it with an air. This further amused those who imagined they could easily exploit Mr. Wilkins, for Mr. Wilkins had such a manner of being innocently open to exploitation by more cunning and intelligent gentlemen.

For the rest, Mr. Wilkins' large round head was completely bald, and rosily glittering. Beneath a vast and shining forehead, which wrinkled sweatily when he was excessively earnest, was a round and bulbous face, "larger than lifesize," to quote a malicious wit. It was also a cherubic face, healthily pink, with three double chins which seemed to rest on his barrel chest, so short was his thick neck. In that infantile face was a pair of bright hazel eyes, surmounted by two tufts of sandy eyebrows, so thick, so bushy, that they stood out between his hairless head and the rest of his face like shelves. This gave his pudgy and artless profile an extraordinary look, for the tufted brows were the most aggressive feature he possessed, and were noticed far sooner than was his round bulb of a red nose, and his little round fat mouth, always smiling. He had tiny white teeth, glistening with sound health, and two engaging dimples sunken deeply in his rosy and quivering cheeks. From the side of that high domed head protruded two big pink ears, which had the habit of blushing furiously.

Mr. Wilkins' eyes were very unusual, for all their ordinary colour and shape. It is true that they were very small, and sunken in rings of sanguine flesh, and the lashes were short and colourless and quite bristling, as if forced outwards by the press of heavy skin. They were exceedingly bright and restless, alive and alert. But even that would not have aroused attention. It was in their expression that they were extraordinary. For, despite their openness (a look carefully cultivated by Mr. Wilkins) he had not been able to conceal a certain glassiness and opaqueness, like polished glass, a certain lack of that quality which is called "humanness." They were not fish-like, nor wild and savage. In short, they lacked "livingness," in spite of their constant movement and brilliance and animation. It was as if he kept them on "the jump" to hide that betraying and basilisk stare.

Mr. Wilkins' character was very bewildering, and inconsistent to the superficial. For he was a bad man, an evil man, a conscienceless man. Had he been merely selfish, that could have been forgiven. But he was beyond selfishness, as a stone was beyond it. He was also very kind, given to strange and impulsive acts of generosity. He was understanding and subtle, and just. If he had an affectionate and ingratiating manner, this was not always pure pretense. He exuded jollity.

All this was very deceiving to the superficial and those who had certain rigid notions with which to measure whether a man was good or evil. Mr. Wilkins was evil. If he also possessed attributes fondly considered "Christian and good" that did not detract from his wickedness in the slightest.

When he discovered, (very rarely) a man or woman who was truly gentle and noble, truly sweet and good; in short, truly harmless, then that man or woman had a loyal and passionate friend for life, much to his or her bewilderment.

But, to return to a certain activity of Mr. Wilkins' olfactory organ:

It took Mr. Wilkins two days to become acclimated to the sea, which he disliked ardently. It made his nose run, and men whose noses have a tendency to run are not at their best, either mentally or physically. But after two days his head was quite clear and active. His nose had begun to twitch.

Genial, loud, ingratiating and benign, always helpful with a rug or a chair, always interested and sympathetic and considerate, Mr. Wilkins roamed the packet, looking for that one human being which had excited his nose. Was this he, or he, or she or she? Another day passed, and another, and still his nose had not "pointed." But Mr. Wilkins knew that the man, or woman, who had activated his subconscious smell was on this heaving packet.

He was not too disturbed at the delay. The journey to America would take considerable time, perhaps three weeks. For it was an old vessel, only lately equipped with the new steam engines, which were uncertain at the best. It also possessed sails, for those emergencies when the steam power was likely to fail. It had failed two days out. The billowing dark sails were already tilting and bellying against a wild dark sky. Many of the passengers had retired miserably to their staterooms or their bunks (depending on their class). Mr. Wilkins was not annoyed by seasickness, but he realized that he must have patience. His quarry might be retching in the subterranean regions.

It had been all of five years since Mr. Wilkins' nose had informed him that some one who would be of immense value was in his vicinity. He had sometimes been apprehensive that he had lost his extraordinary capacity. Now he was delighted. The capacity had lain dormant for lack of proper excitation.

He became quite ebullient and proud. His eyes were everywhere; he sniffed. He prowled in the lower passageways of the staterooms. He even ventured to the darker and more oderiferous regions where the poor sweltered and shivered and vomited in complete misery. But one inhalation down there assured him that his prey was not in the steerage. It was somewhere among the staterooms.

In the meantime, he made himself much loved and liked among the passengers. He, better than the ship's harassed doctor, knew the best remedies for seasickness. He carried the most efficacious in a bottle in his capacious coat-tails. One swig and the victim began to take an interest in life again, and thereafter followed Mr. Wilkins about like a devoted dog. After a few days his entourage resembled the train of a royal personage. One could hear his laughter, his jokes, his gay and hoarse and booming voice everywhere. What did it matter if his speech and grammar were vulgar, reeking of a Cockney strain? What did it matter that he was no gentleman? Some of the more aristocratic of the passengers declared that he was "nature's gentleman," without benefit of the artifices of breeding. He was an "excellent soul," to quote those who under happier circumstances might have snubbed or ignored him.

Mr. Wilkins was enjoying himself immensely. He was a gregarious soul, despite his affable hatred for his fellowmen. Nor, unlike his mentor, Lucifer, did he affect friendship for his own ends. He had his ends. In the meantime, let the wine and the laughter flow, without hypocrisy. It was not inconsistent with Mr. Wilkins' character that he truly enjoyed alleviating the sea-miseries of his fellow travellers. He truly hated the sight of suffering, unless he afflicted it himself. Then, it was only revenge.

Then, on one of the worst nights, when the black wind and the black night seemed to howl together in demonic fury, and practically every one but the crew was below battened decks, Mr. Wilkins' nose implacably "pointed."

The barometer had been falling steadily all day, to the Captain's anxiety. The weather had been unremittingly gloomy since the ship had left Liverpool, and the ocean had behaved itself as the Atlantic usually behaved itself at this time of the year. So, it was not until the barometer had displayed ominous signs that the Captain had become apprehensive. All hatches had been battened down, and the decks forbidden to the passengers, even those who gasped and declared they would die downstairs.

At twilight, the storm had swooped down from the cosmic places where such evils lurk, waiting. There was no rain, only a steadfast and rising gale which lifted the racing waves to mountainous heights. To the Captain's gratitude, the steam engines had finally spluttered into activity, and he was able to order the reefing of the enormous sails. The Captain had never overcome his fear and distrust of the sea. And he knew that few seamen really loved it.

After tea, the passengers had repaired to the crimson-plush-and-gilt salon, where a few simpering ladies with "voices" had been prevailed upon to regale their friends with simple and sentimental songs. Mr. Wilkins had led them with booming gusto. Then followed charades. The passengers sat about on little gilt chairs. Some of the gentlemen smiled painfully, yearning for a forbidden smoke. The lamps, fastened in their sconces on the walls, flickered and flared with the lurching of the ship. Many of the faces which the lamps revealed were clammy and pale. These turned instinctively to Mr. Wilkins, whose beaming rosy smile was very reassuring. Even when the whole salon tilted, and suppressed shrieks rose to the ladies' lips, Mr. Wilkins only increased his loud melody and laughed even harder.

But the heat and the smell of the oil lamps eventually unnerved Mr. Wilkins. He did not like heat; he did not like the too close press of the others. He decided to go out "for a breath of fresh air."

He found his way barred by two robust young sailors. But Mr. Wilkins, who was such a favourite with every one, finally prevailed on them to allow him to go on deck.

For a moment, reeling in the impact of wind, he wondered if he had not been too sanguine. He caught at posts and protuberances as he cautiously made his way to the rail. There was a blowing light at bow and stern, and the portholes made round rosy glows along the side of the ship. This light revealed the stark and oily swells of the billows rushing past. They were like the glistening backs of enormous whales, and Mr. Wilkins watched them, fascinated. He gripped the rail, and allowed himself to lurch easily with the pitching of the vessel. The icy gale, laden with salt, roared by his ears. He could hear the uneasy groaning of every timber. The sky was black, not a star visible.

Mr. Wilkins was happy. He did not need to smile. His short sturdy body braced itself against the wind. He wore no hat, and he felt trickles of cold currents laving his bald head. He hummed hoarsely to himself, pursing out his lips, tapping an accompaniment on the iron rail. Sometimes he lifted his big face to feel the battering of the gale. A strange wild excitation filled him. There was nothing in his physical body which resembled Lucifer, his guardian saint, but there was such a resemblance in his soul. Suddenly he wanted to howl with the wind, to throw up his arms in savage imprecation and evil joy, to utter strange deep gibberish as if in black ecstasy.

Then, suddenly, he was still, tense, his hands gripping the rail. He sensed he was not alone. Moreover, he sensed that the some one for whom he had been searching was near by.

He turned slowly. That mysterious prescience of his sent a prickling along his nerves. Had he had hair, it would have stood on end.

He could see nothing in the darkness. Inch by inch, he moved along the rail, blinking rapidly as the salt spray stung his eyelids. Who, besides himself, had been allowed to go upon deck?

All at once his sliding hand encountered the rough stuff of a sleeve. Some one was standing beside him. He controlled an impulse to continue his explorations of that sleeve. The roar and shrieking of the gale was more deafening than ever.

Mr. Wilkins, literally trembling, cupped his hand to his mouth and shouted: "Good evening! Wild night, ain't it?"

The sleeve moved impatiently, withdrew from Mr. Wilkins' touch. He felt, rather than heard, a movement as if some one was retreating from him. He was filled with panic. What if this creature removed itself, disappeared again, was lost to him? He might never find it again, for if it had remained hidden before it could easily do it again. Was the creature a criminal who secreted itself during the day, from the sight of others? Did it come up only when it knew it would not be seen? Mr. Wilkins guessed this vaguely. He dared not lose him now. His nose was twitching frantically.

It was no time for amenities. Mr. Wilkins' hand reached out desperately in the darkness. It closed upon the sleeve, which jerked angrily. He moved closer to the man who owned it. Yes, it was a man. Mr. Wilkins was happy. He had had a few dealings with extraordinary women, and though they had been profitable they had also presented difficulties not encountered in men. Sometimes Mr. Wilkins had had to be a lover to advance his ends. Hating every one as he did, he did not overmuch enjoy amorous episodes. Too, he especially hated women.

"Blasted storm!" he roared, retaining his grip on the sleeve.

There was no answer. But Mr. Wilkins felt a face turned towards him. It belonged to a tall man, he knew, for the impulse of the eyes was high above him.

Mr. Wilkins shouted with laughter. He put all his geniality, all his bluff fascination into that laugh.

"How'd ye get above? Bribed the lads, eh?"

The man must have felt his personality. The jerking of the sleeve stopped. Mr. Wilkins felt his shrug.

"Yes," came a voice to him on the wind, curt and surly. There was a relaxation in the unseen body near him. Ah, then it was no criminal. Mr. Wilkins was happy again. He did not object to criminals, but their necessity for unobtrusiveness often delayed important things while certain precautions took place.

"I like storms," said Mr. Wilkins. His confiding tone was no mean accomplishment in the face of the gale. "Makes a man feel he can fight 'em. Resist 'em, like. Eh?"

There was a silence.

"Now," said Mr. Wilkins, "there's some as don't like storms. Genteel critters as loves a fire, and a bed and curtains. But there's hardy souls as loves to show anythin', even a storm, that he's a better man. That's it, eh?"

There was another silence. But Mr. Wilkins knew he had an intent audience.

He breathed ostentatiously, as if enjoying the buffeting of the wind and the sting of the spray.

"Give me a man as can take his storms! There's a man as is a man, I say. Nothin' can do him in. Let the whole bloody world kick him abaht, and he'll come up sparrin', just. I'd not give tuppence for a chap as must whimper downstairs and pull down the blinds. He's soft, he is. That's not the sort that does things in this world! Eh?"

The other was still silent. But Mr. Wilkins sensed his painful listening.

"There's Ameriky," continued Mr. Wilkins. "Wot sort of chaps made Ameriky? The soft ones, with gloves and gaiters? Nah! It was the chaps as had iron in their souls. There's a place for iron—Ameriky!"

He had moved closer to the other. He was leaning affectionately against the stiff arm. It was a big arm, muscular and strong. The arm of a man.

"I know!" shouted Mr. Wilkins. "Ain't I one as helped 'em? Give me a chap with iron, and me brains is at his service. There ain't nothing we can't do—together."

There was a gruff sound in the darkness, a contemptuous sound.

"I'm one as who doesn't force hisself," said Mr. Wilkins. "It's the background for me. Let the other chaps have the bugles. Power behind the throne that's Bob Wilkins, sir!"

"You're mistaken—Mr. Wilkins," said a young hard voice. "I'm no 'man of iron.' I'm a fool, Mr. Wilkins."

A fool. The astute Mr. Wilkins knew that once a man confessed he was a fool there was no end to his capacities. Provided, of course, that he didn't carry the thing too far. And from the derisive and embittered tone in that young voice Mr. Wilkins discerned that if the speaker carried other things too far this was not one of them.

He chuckled. He twined his arm affectionately in the arm of the other man.

"Where's the man as ain't been a fool once or twice in his life? A woman, now. There's critters who makes fools out of Samsons. Why, they've even made a fool out of Mr. Wilkins, sir!"

There was a convulsive movement in the arm he held. Ah, so it was a blasted woman, eh?

He enlarged: "A man as ain't had a woman make a bloody fool out of him once or twice ain't human. I've got no time for him. And I'm a proper man with time, sir. Essence of somethin', ain't it? Well, now. I does business with men as is men. And a man ain't a man as hasn't had his breeches pulled by a lass or two. Beggin' yer pardon, sir!"

He heard a sudden shout of laughter near by. He felt the other turn fully to him. He could not see the face, but he guessed it was a strong and turbulent face, with some ferocity in it. Mr. Wilkins joined in the laughter.

The ship reeled and shuddered under their feet. They clung together to hold themselves up. They laughed and laughed.

Finally, Mr. Wilkins said jovially: "May I enquire whom I have the honour to address, sir?"

The laughter ceased abruptly. There was a withdrawing movement. Then a relaxation, and a shrug. "What the hell does it matter what my name is! But it's John Turnbull. Not that it means anything to you, Mr. Wilkins."

Turnbull? Turnbull? Mr. Wilkins' sandy tufts of brows drew together in the blackness. Where had he heard that name before? Never mind, it would come to him.

He said, jovially: "Your servant, Mr. Turnbull. Now, as the bloody storm's getting worse, how about a nip in my cabin?"

CHAPTER 11

"Now 'ERE," said Mr. Wilkins, proudly producing a bottle and holding it high so that it caught limpid golden lights from the lamp, "is somethin' a bit out of the common. It's Irish, sir, not that I'm one as holds much with the Irish. Queer chaps."

He had not taken a very thorough look at his new friend since entering the cabin, but now, as he did so, he felt a momentary consternation after his remarks about the Irish. For this was a Celt face glowering at him in renewed and sullen silence. Now, Mr. Wilkins had had dealings with Irishmen before, but preferred any other race. They inevitably saw through the heartiest suavity, being past-masters in the art of false ingratiation, themselves. They could out-lie Mr. Wilkins, and do it with a grace and finesse which he admired and envied. They could out-cheat him, too, and when he laughed too loudly they laughed even louder, so that it was a matter of conjecture as to who was laughing at whom. They were no gentlemen, and were very frank about admitting it. Mr. Wilkins preferred to deal with gentlemen, for, in the final summing-up before relationships were broken between Mr. Wilkins and the latter, there were some things to which gentlemen would not "stoop." But there was nothing, Mr. Wilkins would reflect with some apprehension, to which Irishmen would not "stoop." Gentlemen would threaten to break Mr. Wilkins through law. But the Irishmen had had the unpleasant habit of simply threatening to break Mr. Wilkins, and not in the financial or legal sense at all.

Mingled with his consternation was an immense disappointment. He had vowed, after his last melancholy experience, to have no more dealings with the Irish. He saw no reason, nose or no nose, to alter this decision.

Nevertheless, he allowed himself to hope a little. "Not Irish, sir, I hopes?"

The scowling face lightened somewhat as its owner threw himself heavily on the carved plush sofa near the wall. "Not Irish, Mr. Wilkins. English. Like you."

Mr. Wilkins felt a rush of warm delight. With a flourish, he poured two glasses half-full of the whiskey. "Cockney, sir, a proper Cockney! That's Bob Wilkins. And proud to say it!"

He had allowed himself only a brief glimpse at the face of his visitor. Now, beaming, he sat himself carefully on the edge of a little plush chair, and held up his glass to the full extent of his short fat arm. Lounging at ease was not possible for one of Mr. Wilkin's general architecture, and so he always sat in an attitude of alert and jovial smartness, his short plump thighs apart so that the excellently tailored broadcloth acquired a high sheen across them. Too, his latest weskit, gleaming with colours "rich but not gaudy" added a pleasant touch to his wardrobe.

Now, in the light of the swaying and flickering lamps, he studied his guest, while the latter glanced with uneasy appreciation about the cabin. It was large, and spacious, with a good sound walnut bed, a commode, a fine rug, a mahogany wardrobe, a sofa, and two or three smaller chairs of plush and gilt. It was heated by a small round iron stove, very grateful after the cold black wind outside. Here, the storm was less evident, the swaying almost pleasant. Curtains of red plush were drawn across the portholes, behind which the gale mourned and howled. Mr. Wilkins' luggage, very elegant and of the best leathers, was disposed neatly beside his bed, and locked with sturdy brass locks.

So, thought Mr. Wilkins, his face quite pink with the exertions of his friendliness and the warmth of the cabin, this was one who knew "good things," and was at the present time not in possession of them. The young man's clothes showed distinction and taste, and were of even better material than Mr. Wilkins' own. His watch-chain was not quite so heavy and opulent, but it was delicately chased and finely wrought. The ruffles at his wrists, and his cravat, though not ostentatious, must have cost a pretty penny.

Turnbull. Turnbull. Even while he smiled and smacked his lips over the whiskey, Mr. Wilkins ruminated. He would have it in a moment.

In the meantime, without at all giving the appearance of it, Mr. Wilkins studied every feature of the lowering young face opposite, which had sunken into a dark apathy and abstraction. The young man held his glass, but had not begun to drink of it yet. He appeared to have fallen into a sombre revery. A big handsome face. Mr. Wilkins was slightly disappointed at the youth of it for a moment. But he read that countenance astutely. Power there, and turbulence, and lack of discipline. A wild and disorderly mouth and look, vehement black eyes that could become passionate and fierce, a short and bellicose nose, a good hard chin and a deep dimple in it. The black curls on the large round head told of virility and strength of body. A willful devil, a bad one to cross. Murder wouldn't be beyond the blighter. Nothing would, in fact. If the angles were still faintly soft with youth, that would alter in good time. There were clefts beside that large full mouth, which would certainly become ridges in later years. Yes, a bad un. But an excellent one for Mr. Wilkins' money!

Mr. Wilkins loved big men, muscular men. The little chaps were their own masters. Bloody little devils as knew their own minds and stuck to 'em. A man couldn't do much with 'em, for they were diseased with conceit. The big men were rarely conceited. Not that they were soft, though, thought Mr. Wilkins, shaking his head slightly to himself. But they had presence; they had wit. Despite the evidences of tumultuous passions on the young man's face, Mr. Wilkins did not doubt that he could see things that were to his own advantage.

Mr. Wilkins loved the fashion in which John Turnbull's coat fitted his shoulders and his narrow compact waist, the elegance with which the light pantaloons draped themselves over his good long legs. He admired the slenderness and arch of the restless feet in their boots of finest polished kid.

"Your health, sir!" exclaimed Mr. Wilkins, though he had already drunk half the whiskey.

The young man started, raised his eyes as if confused and bewildered at finding himself here. He looked at the glass as if seeing it for the first time. Then he put it to his lips, hesitated, then, as if seized with desperation, he swallowed half of it quickly. He did not splutter, turn red, or choke, though it had been a formidable swig. Ah, so then he could drink too, might even be guilty of drunkenness on occasion. Good. Mr. Wilkins despised and feared men who did not drink. They were bloodless; they were cold and calculating. Moreover, it had been Mr. Wilkins' experience that men who did not drink were liars and passionless and extremely dangerous. Worse, they did not possess that wild ruthlessness so necessary for success, and the enrichment of Mr. Wilkins. They kept their slimy wits about them, and men who kept their wits about them rarely rose above the status of clerks, if they were poor, or rarely became masters of fate, if they were in better circumstances. Give Mr. Wilkins wildness and savagery and a good drinking capacity: men like that never recognized boundaries or limits. The long patience of the teetotaler led to nothing but a quiet deathbed.

Mr. Wilkins knew that the way to receive confidences was first to be frank and open himself. He engaged John's eyes, inclined his head with an even wider and more affable smile, drained the last of his glass. He filled the stateroom with the warmth of an amiable and affectionate disposition. His bald rosy head twinkled in the lamplight. It was very cosy here, with the stove and the drawn curtains.

He saw that his guest was wretched and furtive, filled with some heavy and rebellious misery. He must discover what that misery was, and then alleviate it.

"Your first trip across, sir?" he asked, with an open and loving look in his protruding hazel eyes.

"Yes," said John, curtly, looking into the depths of his glass and shaking the golden contents.

"My tenth, sir!" beamed Mr. Wilkins. "I enjoys it. Though," he added with a wink, and putting his finger along the side of his nose with the most engaging of sly expressions, "though it's business with me afore pleasure."

John was not interested. He raised the glass and drank the rest of the whiskey with a gesture of wretched defiance.

"I'm a man as likes company," confided Mr. Wilkins. "Friends. Wot's life without friends? And then, you asks, why aren't you married, Mr. Wilkins? Why do you travel alone? Ah!" said Mr. Wilkins, with a sigh, "that's a story in itself!"

The young man studied the bottom of his glass.

"A bachelor, I takes it, sir?" asked Mr. Wilkins, sympathetically.

The young man continued to scrutinize the glass for some moments. Then he looked up. He laid down the glass on the table with a sort of suppressed violence.

"No!" he said.

Mr. Wilkins exhibited extravagant evidences of delight and surprise. "Why, confound you, sir, you're a happy man!" he ejaculated, as if John had imparted to him an astounding revelation. "A happy man, I repeat, sir! Would this be your honeymoon, beggin' your pardon?"

He leaned towards John, his cherubic face red with pleasure, though inwardly he was cursing the unknown girl who might prove a temporary obstacle.

"Honeymoon," repeated John, slowly, as though savouring the word in all its repulsion. His expression darkened still more. He grinned, very unpleasantly. "You can call it that, Mr. Wilkins. I've been married less than a week."

So! thought Mr. Wilkins, he hates the lass. A hasty marriage, like, or a forced one. All the better! The girl was disposed of.

He jumped to his feet, positively radiating his delight. "We'll drink to the leddy, sir, that we will! A honeymoon! Ah, I envies you, Mr. Turnbull!" He poured fresh whiskey into the glasses. His broad pink forehead was pricked with little drops of hearty sweat. Though he did not look directly at John, he saw that the unpleasant grin had become a vicious grimace.

He sat down again, slapping his thigh with one hand while he raised the glass with the other. They drank again. "Ah," breathed Mr. Wilkins, deliciously.

Then he assumed an expression of acute concern. "The little leddy wouldn't be seasick, would she, Mr. Turnbull?"

"Yes, very seasick," replied John, and he smiled again, as if the thought gave him a grim and malicious pleasure.

"Then," said Mr. Wilkins, with increasing concern, "I've got just the thing for her! One swig, and they're up dancin' like a bloody fairy."

He produced the bottle from his coat-tails, and regarded it with reverence. It was an oily brown liquid, leaving residues of little brown flecks on the glass. John shuddered at it.

"If a man wasn't sick before, I'll wager he'd be sick after a swig of that glue," he said, disdainfully.

Mr. Wilkins betrayed no offense. He looked at John earnestly.

"You're wrong, sir! Very wrong indeed. I've seen 'em dying like flies, and green as grass, and I've put the bottle to their lips and 'ad 'em up singin' in no time. No time at all! It was given to me by a Dutchman, a trader. Right out of the jungle, sir. Medicine men. Proper chaps with the herbs, those lads."

He swirled the contents about in the bottle, took a neat swig, himself, pursed up his lips and shook his head seriously. "Wholesome as milk, Mr. Turnbull."

But John was interested. "Dutchman? I—I am interested in trade. My father is an importer, a merchant."

At the mention of his father, his dark face saddened, became gloomy.

Mr. Wilkins stared. Turnbull. Ah, he had it. James Turnbull. Importer. His face reflected a genuine if puzzled delight.

"Mr. James Turnbull! Thought as I'd heard the name before. Ah, a fine gentleman, Mr. Turnbull!" His face became even more genial, if slyly arch. "You wouldn't be goin' to Ameriky to arrange a little trade for your Pa, would ye, Mr. Turnbull?"

John's expression darkened into complete sombreness. "No," he answered, shortly. "I'm on my own. I've got to make my own way."

Thrown out, with a clout, Mr. Wilkins reflected. A marriage against the Old Boy's wishes, like. Cut off with a shilling.

John pursued hurriedly, as if he wished to change the subject: "You spoke of Dutchmen. I thought, perhaps, of not stopping in America, but of going to the Indies. I knew something of trade. I—I had intended to go into the business with my father. Do you know anything about that?"

Mr. Wilkins was silent a moment. He wet his fat pink lips and scrutinized John with unusual intensity. Was there a conscience there? Or had it been obliterated by bitterness and resentment? He judged that John had little money. Men like this, violent and turbulent, never reconciled themselves to poverty, could forgive anything which alleviated that unendurable condition. Still, there might be a conscience. He proceeded to answer John very cautiously, watching him closely:

"Trade? Well, now, I'm not one as actually engages in trade, not direct, like. I'm what they call in Ameriky a go-between. I arranges things. I make plans, and brings the proper chaps together, so they can do business. When everything's done to satisfaction, I collects a fee. Very discreet. From both. They trusts me. They knows as I'm a chap who's got his finger in every pie. Nothing's too strange or pecooliar for Bob Wilkins. I'll take a go at anythin'. For a fee. 'Wot's your proposition?' I asks. Then they tells me. I says, even if I'm still in the bloody dark, 'I'm the one for you, sir, just.' Then I scurries abaht and learns what I can. I've got a nose, sir." And he grinned at John cunningly, with high good humour. But John was regarding him impatiently.

Mr. Wilkins leaned towards him and spoke in a soft and confidential voice, leaning his fat little hands on his fat broad thighs:

"Now, I'll tell you sir, just between us two, wot I did a few years ago. In a way, it don't sit well in me belly. But a chap's got to live, and if there's others as makes a livin' in a way I don't approve of, well, that's not my business. You understands, sir?"

John said nothing. But his black eyes narrowed and glinted as they fixed themselves intently on Mr. Wilkins.

Mr. Wilkins saw that look, and was content. He proceeded with more confidence, his head on one side, his glassy hazel eyes noting every expression on the other's face, as a physician watches every faint shadow of pain which might give him a clue:

"Well, now, sir, as I said, there's chaps in rum businesses. You knows your history, sir? Well, seems like a hundred years ago a yeller chap in China, the Emperor Yung Chen, got 'is wind up abaht his people taking opium. A sour-faced chap, I'll wager. There's some allus sniffin' abaht doin' good and interferin' with the innercent pleasures of the miserable. Not that I'm one as thinks opium's innercent," and he chuckled amiably, still watching John with that hidden shrewdness. "But if the yeller chaps wants their opium, says Bob Wilkins, let 'em have their opium. But the Emperor thinks it's 'is bloody business. So he ups and slaps on a law as says his lads can't have the bloomin' stuff."

John did not speak. But the rigid folds about his big heavy lips grew thicker. Mr. Wilkins, perceiving this, was more and more pleased.

He continued, sitting on the edge of his chair and leaning towards John, and reducing his affable voice to a confidential whisper:

"I don't know why I'm tellin' you this, sir, except you looks as if you can keep your lip still. I'm not one as goes abaht spillin' his guts to every Tom, Dick, and Harry. But there's somethin' abaht you, sir——

"Well, now. There's English and Dutch gentlemen who looks at China, and says to themselves: 'Here, here, there's a chance for business down there in the bally place!" I'm speakin' of the East India Company, sir. So, what does they do? Easy, sir! They starts to ship chests of opium into China. Twenty thousand chests a year! Who gives 'em the idea, sir? Why, Bob Wilkins! I says to 'em in plain words: 'If the bloody yeller fellers wants their opium, against the sour laws of their Emperors, why not let 'em 'ave it?' It was Bob Wilkins as brought the proper English and Dutch chaps together. Of course, there was a little bribery at the China ports to get the bloody stuff in—" And now Mr. Wilkins chuckled hugely, slapping his thighs, and throwing back his head, but not so vigorously as to leave one instant during which he was not watching John.

John's face became inscrutable, but the desperate defiance increased in his eyes. Mr. Wilkins read that look with subtle completeness. A year, a month, even a week ago, he thought to himself, that young dark face would have expressed loathing and disgust of Mr. Wilkins. Perhaps, even yet, those sentiments struggled in that furious young heart. But, if they did, the bitter defiance, so desperate, so bewildered, had already begun to shout them down with contempt. Ah, good. There was nothing that became so completely relentless in the end, so completely implacable, as an originally good man turned, by some circumstance, into enraged resentment against the world.

Mr. Wilkins took out a silk kerchief, and wiped his forehead and his eyes, as if his mirth had exhausted him. He shook his head over and over. Then he regarded John with gentle affection, and winked.

"It was Bob Wilkins, sir, as arranged the bribery. Nothin' piddlin' about the East India Company! Pounds flowed through me hands like water. And into me banks. I turned a neat profit, sir."

John's eyes quickened. "And then came the Opium War," he said, disdainfully. "What did you do then?"

Mr. Wilkins burst into rolling mirth. He slapped his thighs over and over. He let his tongue hang over his lips, and even his three chins became encardined. He coughed, and choked.

"Wot did Bob Wilkins do then, you asks, sir?" His voice came, muffled and stifled with his mirth. He winked over and over so rapidly that his right eye shed tears. "Ah, didn't I tell you as Bob Wilkins was a foxy chap? I seen the writin' on the wall, sir. I seed the War comin'. Was the Emperor goin' to stand by and see the East India Company a-pushin' its chests of opium in and not open his mouth? No sir! Bob Wilkins sees this. He's got a nose and an eye, if I says so myself. So, Mr. Wilkins goes to the Emperor, and says: 'Now, see here, my yeller friend, wot're ye goin' to do? It's war, sir. Are ye goin' to fight the English and the Dutch with bows and arrers? No, ye've got to 'ave guns!' And the Emperor sees me point."

He paused, wiped his face and forehead again, with vigorous flourishes. He beamed with delighted modesty.

"So, I rushes back to Ameriky with a secret letter from the Emperor. To a certain lot of chaps, English and Frenchmen, who've got a new armaments business in a place called Pennsylvania. Barbour and Bouchard. A new little business, full of ginger, run by a young un with an eye. Ernest Barbour. And I says to Mr. Ernest Barbour: 'Now, then, me hearty, there's goin' to be a war between the Old Country and China. The yeller chaps ain't got the guns and the powder. I'll put you into a fine little business, for a fee. But ye've got to button up your breeches and move fast.' I've said Mr. Ernest had an eye? A bad un! He see me point at once. A bad devil to do business with, and a cool un. But Mr. Wilkins is a match for him, sir! So, Mr. Ernest says: 'But wot abaht the bloody ships? Who'll ship the guns and powder to China?' So, I goes to a chap as runs a cargo business in Californy, and arranges for the shipment. For a fee. Bob's a good lad for a fee! So, off goes the guns and powder to China. And, in the meantime, Bob's been busy. 'E's gone to the East India Company, and confidential like tells 'em abaht the guns and powder goin' off to China. Was they upset! So I soothes 'em, and tells 'em 'ow I knows a little concern in Pennsylvania as can give 'em the best in arms, for a moderate price, and Mr. Ernest does more business through Bob Wilkins. First shipment's gone off to China, and damn me if it ain't followed by another to the East India Company! Then off I goes to England, and see Robsons and Strong, the big armaments concern, and I tells 'em about the East India Company and China, and I says: 'Are ye goin' to let the bloody Chinks murder Englishmen?' So, smellin' the wind, off they goes to some lords in the Government, and the military chaps, and the Robsons and Strong shops begin to hum like hell!

"So," concluded Mr. Wilkins with intense satisfaction, and holding up the fingers of his left hand as he checked them off with the index finger of the other, "Bob Wilkins collects 'is little fee from China, from the East India Company, from Barbour and Bouchard, and from the shippin' company, and from Robsons and Strong. Grateful they all is to Bob Wilkins. 'A proper chap, Wilkins,' they says to themselves. 'A good chap to keep us in the wind. One as 'as a nose. A proper one to remember.' And they remember. Nice little bits of business comes my way regular like from all of 'em."

John had listened with absorbed attention, his expression becoming more and more inscrutable. But a dark and bitter smile played about his mouth. He regarded Mr. Wilkins with a strange glitter in his eyes.

"Conscience, of course, Mr. Wilkins, doesn't enter into your little—negotiations?"

Mr. Wilkins stared at him in tender affront. "Conscience, sir? Wot's conscience got to do with it? 'Ere's China wantin' to keep out the bloody opium, and the East India wantin' to get it in, and hell waitin' to pop, and chaps like Barbour and Robsons and Strong waitin' to make a bit of money! So Mr. Wilkins sees a way to satisfy everybody and keep everybody happy. 'Give 'em wot they want, Bob,' says I to myself. For a fee. If I don't do it, some other clever chap will. Wot's wrong with a bit of business, gotten honest like?"

John did not answer. But the dark unpleasant glitter brightened in his eyes.

"If I'd tell you, sir, the bits of business Bob Wilkins turns over regular like, you wouldn't believe 'im! And all up and above board. Give 'em wot they want, is me motto."

John turned away and stared at the floor. The cynical smile remained on his lips.

"I keeps me accounts in me head," said Mr. Wilkins, tapping that organ significantly. "No bits of paper lyin' around just beggin' to incriminate me clients. I forgets nothin'. Relies on me nose. Just like tonight."

John looked up quickly, scowling.

Mr. Wilkins nodded fondly. "Just like tonight, I repeats, Mr. Turnbull. When I spoke to you up there on deck, I says to myself: 'Bob Wilkins, there's a chap for your money! 'E's got wot you're lookin' for.'"

John's face expressed his complete incredulity and disdain. He raised himself from his elbow and fixed his eyes on Mr. Wilkins, who nodded over and over, beaming, tapping his nose.

"I've got a nose, sir, as knows. I smelled ye out. Right up there on deck. As a matter of fact, I've been lookin' for ye for days. Not that I knowed who'd you be. But I knowed as there was a chap on board for my money!"

John burst into wild laughter, shaking his head, still astounded.

"You're wrong, Mr. Wilkins! I haven't a penny in the world beyond one hundred pounds, and my passage, for me and my—wife. Look again, somewhere else, Mr. Wilkins. If you think you can turn a 'bit of money' in any connection with me, through my father, you've made a serious mistake. You see, Mr. Wilkins, my father kicked me out. For my own good, it appears. I'm little better than a pauper, Mr. Wilkins, going to America without the slightest idea of where I'll land or what I'll do."

Still laughing wildly, John stood up.

"So, Mr. Wilkins, it's good night, and thank you for a drink and an interesting story."

He held out his hand. Mr. Wilkins, remaining on his chair, looked at that hand, then slowly took it. He did not release it. His warm moist fingers closed strongly about the other fingers. He felt their texture, harsh and strong and unshaken. A good hand.

He smiled up into John's face. He put into that smile all

his true affability and affection and understanding. That big cherubic countenance, so rosy, so engaging and candid, glowed like a full moon. The little round eyes twinkled, taking on the appearance of sparkling agates, pale gray shot with streaks of brown and yellow, and his thick tufts and sandy eyebrows raised themselves with quizzical fondness. In spite of himself, the hard iron core which was John's desperate heart began to dissolve.

"Did I ask you for money, Mr. Turnbull? Did Bob Wilkins speak of money? Far be it. Mr. Turnbull, sir, I've spoken only, in a way, of making your fortun. Yes, Mr. Turnbull, it's your fortun as wot I was speakin' of. Throw your lot in with Bob Wilkins, and your fortun's as good as made."

John stared, and then his brows knotted darkly.

"Why should you want to make my fortune for me, Mr. Wilkins? What am I to you?"

Mr. Wilkins tightened his grip on the restless hand he held. He spoke with solemn earnestness: "Mr. Turnbull, didn't I tell you I've got a nose? And me nose never deceives me. Am I a bloody philanthropist, out doin' good for every bounder in sight? Not Mr. Wilkins! I'm a one as is frank, Mr. Turnbull. I want to help you make your fortun. For a fee. I thought as that was understood."

"I'm no opium smuggler," said John, with a faint smile. But his fingers ceased their restless movements to release themselves.

Mr. Wilkins shook his head sadly. "Did I say anythin' abaht opium smugglin'? You does me a wrong, Mr. Turnbull. I knowed you at once as a chap that'd put up with no humbug. 'There's an honest man, Bob Wilkins,' I said to meself. 'It'll be honest business for you when you work together, and no humbug.'"

John was silent. His young eyes, so unused to duplicity, and, in fact, so unused to human nature, tried, in bewilderment, to read Mr. Wilkins' open countenance. But he could read nothing there but the utmost sincerity and affection.

"Now, it's not like I'm satisfied," said Mr. Wilkins, with moving candour. "I've done a bit of a job in England just now for a chap. Cotton patents—y'know, mills. My client is one who's lookin' for himself, and he thinks as 'e's payin' too bloody much for the weavin'. So, he sends Bob Wilkins to do a little research abaht gettin' around the patents. The job's done. That'll be two thousand pounds in Bob Wilkins' pocket. But I don't stomach this client. A bad un, in a foxy fashion. Stab 'is own brother in the back. So, it's out for Bob Wilkins. I'm lookin' abaht. I'm a free man, Mr. Turnbull. I'm done with Dick Gorth."

"Gorth!" exclaimed John, visibly starting.

"Ah, you know the name?" asked Mr. Wilkins, quickly.

A deep and violent flush passed over John's face, and he bit his lip. He slowly sat down again. "Tell me," he said.

CHAPTER 12

HAD ANY ONE spoken to Mr. Wilkins of the strange dark grandeur inherent in a human soul, he would have stared and thought the speaker mad. For Mr. Wilkins had never met that grandeur, had not even suspected its existence. The world was a jungle to Mr. Wilkins, filled with distorted animal shapes, predatory and ferocious, where a chap needed his wits about him if he was not to be devoured. Mr. Wilkins indulged in no philosophical meditations upon this ancient fact. He accepted it and lived accordingly, never once condemning or complaining or indulging in epigrams. He even found the world a pleasant and amiable place, where a clever chap could come to a temporary armistice with the animal shapes and even drink happily with them, keeping a wary eye out in the meantime. He had not made the world. But he was convinced also, that no god had made it, so, no one was to blame. Blame was the last thing Mr. Wilkins would have entertained.

But for those who by reason of youth or innocence or vulnerability of heart were made to endure torment, he had the strangest and tenderest of compassions. Not only would he attempt to console or alleviate, but would set himself out to avenge them. He never questioned this strangeness in himself. It was there, like all other facts. In avenging the helpless, Mr. Wilkins felt a high frenzy in his heart, and nothing could have exceeded the virulence and the relentlessness of his attack. He rejoiced in the most cruel of plots. Perhaps he was a sadist. Perhaps, in the depths of his hidden soul, he was a kind of reformer. He had never conjectured that at the end the two were the same.

He had no sooner entered the dark and narrow cabin of John Turnbull, and given one glance at its cold disorder and wretchedness and the face on the tumbled pillow in one of the bunks, than he smelled the deep and uncomplaining misery of the helpless once more. The lone lantern was swinging on the streaked and wooden wall, filling the cabin with a wan dim light. There was no curtain over the bleak porthole, washed with spray. The bare floor was littered with garments, boots and other pieces of baggage and apparel. There was an ashen chill in the air, reeking with suffering.

Mr. Wilkins thought it was a child's face on that pillow. It was so young and so bewildered, so channelled with tears. It was such a pretty little face, too, and Mr. Wilkins had a soft spot for prettiness, especially in children. The rich auburn curls spilled on the dirty pillow, framing wet cheeks, a trembling pale mouth and stricken round blue eyes. Its very stupidity enhanced that look of helpless sadness, that childish look of undeserved pain and bewilderment. He had seen that look in the eyes of beaten horses and dogs, in foul English orphan asylums, and in the eyes of beggars' children shivering in rain and snow. It was a look that did not implore or demand or cry out against life. It was its dumb and hopeless acceptance that set hot things stirring in Mr. Wilkins' heart.

He gazed in silence at the child in her bunk, and felt behind him the sullen and tempestuous presence of his new friend. The child did not speak. Her big coarse hands lap emptily on the dirty coverlet, palm up. She gazed back at Mr. Wilkins, her eyes expressed no surprise, no question, nothing but pain, blank and dark.

Mr. Wilkins felt, rather than saw, so many things. And John Turnbull, waiting in gloomy silence behind him, did not know that at that instant he had been presented with a most terrible enemy. He had afflicted the helpless. For that, he had admitted Lucifer.

"Well, now," boomed Mr. Wilkins in sudden cheeriness, producing his bottle, and beaming at the child on the pillow. "I've just been told there was a little leddy down here in need of Dr. Wilkins! Right you are, Miss! I've come to get you up in no time."

The girl still gazed at him with that look of suffering which caused Mr. Wilkins such strange wrenchings in the region of his heart. Then, in the very depths of those round blue eyes, so empty and motionless, a spark of desperate pleading rose.

"This is Mr. Wilkins, Lilybelle," said John, in a cold and emotionless voice. "My wife, Mr. Wilkins. Lilybelle, Mr. Wilkins believes he has a cure for your sea-sickness."

He withdrew from the two of them, and stood near his own bunk, his dark face closed and heavy.

The girl's lips quivered. But she did not stir even a finger. Ah, thought Mr. Wilkins, it is not the sea-sickness, then. For, for one moment, he had seen the shrinking and wrinkling of the girl's eyelids as her glance had touched John, the sudden faint drawing together of her flesh as if she expected a blow.

Mr. Wilkins saw that she was no child, after all, but a well developed young woman of about fifteen. But always, he thought, this would be a child at heart, helpless and vulnerable and bewildered, despite the good strong body and the strong hands used to work and long patience.

He approached the bunk, beaming like the sun, his head on one side, his hand shaking the bottle archly. The girl watched him come. Her eyes widened; the look of frightened pain increased in them. Mr. Wilkins looked about for a cup or a spoon. There was a dirty cup on the table near the bunk, filled with tea-leaves and a little dark fluid. He tossed this into a pail near by, and poured out a generous dose of his medicine. Then, with the utmost tenderness and gentleness, he presented it to the girl.

She stared at it, then at Mr. Wilkins' vast rosy countenance. Their eyes met. Then slowly, though the girl did not look away from Mr. Wilkins, but seemed to cling to his face in a kind of suffering mournfulness and despair, tears rose in a flood to her eyes, rolled over her cheeks. Her breast heaved and trembled. Her lips parted and uncontrollable sobs burst from her pale and swollen lips.

John uttered a low and impatient exclamation, filled with disgust. But Mr. Wilkins did not move, did not lessen his smile. His hand continued to extend itself with the cup towards Lilybelle. However, had there been any one there of sublety to see, he would have perceived that something passed between Mr. Wilkins and Lilybelle. It was as if, recognizing in a world of bewildering enemies and oppressors, a potential friend with a voice promising succour, and expressing sympathy and kindness and tenderness, the girl had cried out for help in an agonized voice.

John did not understand any of this, but he vaguely experienced a resentment and dim anger. He felt himself thrust aside, an alien, in the midst of two who had mutually recognized each other. If he did not know that he had gained a terrible enemy, he knew, confusedly, that Lilybelle had gained a friend.

"Nah, nah," said Mr. Wilkins, in the most soothing and soft of voices, "if the little leddy will just sip of this nice medicine——"

Still weeping and shuddering with her sobs, catching her breath as a hurt child catches it, the girl obediently let Mr. Wilkins put the cup to her lips. She drank, choked, swallowed, her tears mingling with the potion. And, as she drank, her pleading eyes, swimming with tears, did not leave Mr.

Wilkins' face. She seemed to believe that so long as she gazed at him she was not entirely bereft.

Mr. Wilkins had learned several things from John's uneasy and taciturn mutters just before they had left his stateroom. He had learned that this had been a "hasty marriage," and vaguely gathered that Mr. Turnbull had not "approved," that he had given his son one hundred pounds and passage and had packed him off. But there had been something in John's reserve which made Mr. Wilkins believe that all of the story had not been told. Like a faint scrawl underlying blacked-out words in a letter, Mr. Wilkins had felt some subtle emphasis on things which had remained unsaid. When John had spoken of his wife, it had not been with obvious distaste and in his actual voice. What he had omitted, however, had been very poignant and eloquent to Mr. Wilkins' trained ear. He had "smelled" hatred.

Whatever the girl had done, Mr. Wilkins did not particularly care. He observed that she was of a much lower station than was her young husband. That did not matter, either. What did matter to Mr. Wilkins was that she was defenseless, that she was being made to suffer, that she was the victim of chronic hurts and cruelties. Perhaps she was a trollop; perhaps she had inveigled and tricked this young jackanapes into marrying her. No matter. He had made her suffer, and she had no defense. That was the unpardonable crime to Mr. Wilkins. To afflict the helpless was the one thing Mr. Wilkins could not forgive.

He laid the cup down on the littered table, still glowing like a beneficent sun. He sat down on the edge of a stool, and put his hands on his spread thighs. He regarded Lilybelle benevolently, still with that warm kindliness in his glassy hazel eyes. But now those eyes were like agate marbles with a light behind.

The girl lay back on her pillows, gulping down her sobs. She directed one fearful and cringing glance at her husband. Her pale cheeks paled even more. She returned her drowning gaze to Mr. Wilkins.

John stirred. He came forward slowly and stood at the foot of the girl's bunk. "Better, Lily?" he asked, coldly.

Still gazing at Mr. Wilkins, the girl's head moved affirmatively on her pillows.

"I've never known it to fail!" exclaimed Mr. Wilkins. "The little leddy will be as right as rain in no time. Mark my words."

He turned now to John, smiling broadly. He winked. "Your husband and me 'as 'ad a very interesting conversation, Mrs. Turnbull. A proper talk. I'm to make his fortun in Ameriky."

John coloured. He dropped his eyes to his boots, and his big mouth set itself sullenly. "Santa Claus," he muttered.

Lilybelle's swollen eyes lightened with pathetic eagerness. Her head moved more strongly on her pillows. She spoke now, in a voice hoarse with tears: "Oh, Mr. Wilkins, that's very good of you, just!"

Lancastershire lass, thought Mr. Wilkins. He smiled widely.

Lilybelle now looked desperately at her husband, all her desire to placate him out on her poor face like a blaze. "Mr. Turnbull, that's very good of Mr. Wilkins, ain't it?"

"Very good," said John, with sardonic heaviness. "The only thing, Lilybelle, is that I think Mr. Wilkins is just a little too sanguine."

The blaze vanished from Lilybelle's face, and the look of bewilderment returned. It was obvious that she did not understand. She looked at Mr. Wilkins humbly, waiting for translation.

"He means, Mrs. Turnbull, ma'am, that he don't believe I'm capable," he said, with good humour. "He thinks I'm a proper liar. Well, we'll see."

He took Lilybelle's hand and patted it paternally. That hand was very cold and tremulous. But it began to warm. She smiled at him vaguely. She was feeling much better. The retching quiver in her stomach was subsiding. The chill in her feet was less. Slowly, a languor began to steal over her, comforting and gentle.

Mr. Wilkins looked at John. "You've called me Santa Claus, Mr. Turnbull. Now, that's not fair to you, or me. Bob Wilkins don't do anything for nothing. Fee only. If I help you make your fortun, it's understood I make a fortun, too."

Now he gazed into space, and his smile took on a curious and peculiar quality, as if he looked at a seething world of men. "I allus gives people what they wants," he said, in a strange and echoless voice, musing and withdrawn. "Allus what they wants."

Mr. Wilkins soon took his departure. At the very last, he winked gently at Lilybelle, and she smiled drowsily in return. He had hardly closed the door when she fell into a deep and motionless sleep.

By the light of the swaying lantern, John undressed. It was bitterly cold in the little narrow cabin. Shivering, he reached for the lantern to blow it out. He held it in his hand and looked down at his sleeping young wife. Her face was still blotched and stained with tears. The auburn lashes quivered on her pale cheeks. Her white lips trembled slightly.

He looked at her with hatred and loathing and despair. He

121

had taken her body several times during this voyage, but always with that hatred, always with that despair and loathing. His violence was part of his revenge on her, and, in spite of her stupidity and ignorance, she knew it. She loved him, and he terrified her with his black rages, his curses, his roughness. Once, when she slept, he had cried out in anguish: "Eugenia! Eugenia!" She had known, then, that he was calling for some one whose place she had usurped.

During these rocking days of misery and illness, she had wildly contemplated throwing herself into the sea. But her wholesome love of life, her simple peasant affirmation of living, had made her shrink instantly from the idea.

She believed, in her ignorant simplicity, that some day he might at least tolerate her, that he might allow her to understand him, or permit her to serve him. That was all she desired. If once she touched him and he did not recoil from her, that would be enough. If once she spoke, and he listened, not with averted head, but with polite decency, she would be satisfied. She asked for so very little.

"I've wronged him," she would whisper to herself. "I've done a wicked thing to him. Please God, let me help him."

Only that morning, while he had been dressing in his black silence, she had timidly stammered that she was a good cook, and "a proper manager." For some time she thought he had not heard her, then suddenly he had given her the most glittering and malevolent of glances, and had flung himself out of the cabin, leaving her to weep alone for hours.

Now, as he looked down at her, a very swirl of aching visions passed before his mind's eye. He saw the austere and elegant parlours of the Turnbull and MacNeill mansions. He saw the face of Eugenia, and his heart twisted with real agony. He saw all that he had lost, and he gazed at it with the desperate eye of the exile. Because of this drab who lay there before him, he had lost his home and his love, his prospects and his father, and all that had been his life.

He lifted his arm with a fierce and involuntary gesture, the lantern swinging in his hand. He had only one desire, to smash that lamp down upon the sleeping face of the miserable girl. He lusted to obliterate her features with one bloody and lacerating blow. There was a redness before his eyes, fiery streaks before his vision. In the very act of bringing the lantern down, he caught himself. Then, bathed in sweat, trembling violently, he stood there, panting, filled with horror.

Finally, he blew out the lamp, and in the darkness crept to his soiled bunk. He drew the cold sheets over him, shivering.

The ship rocked in complete blackness. The wind screamed outside. John turned his face into his mussy pillow, and it became wet with the most terrible tears he would ever shed.

CHAPTER 13

WEATHER meant nothing to Mr. Wilkins, not even this weather in New York. The sky might be gray as an old woman's hair, and streaked with boiling black whips lashing through layers of spinning clouds. The raw wind, blowing in from the ocean, might be as cold and penetrating as death itself, reaching for bone and warm flesh with inexorable tendrils. Heaps of dirty melting snow might be piled high along the crowded streets, and the air might have in it the wet astringent smell of ashes and soot. But it still meant nothing to Mr. Wilkins, wrapped in his greatcoat with its beaver collar, his tall brown hat set firmly on his bald pink head, thick gloves of good leather and fur on his hands, and his cane flourishing gaily as he strutted along.

He glowed at the world, his smile broad and jovial. Drays and wagons of all kinds splashed through the black slush and running waters of the streets. Carriages rolled arrogantly by, phaetons, buggies, victorias, carryalls, fringe swaying, harness gleaming, whips curling, horses prancing disdainfully, the occupants within the vehicles peering through polished windows at pedestrians struggling against wind and a new harsh rain which had begun to fall. Women held their skirts high, battled with umbrellas. Men turned up their collars and clutched their tall hats. Ragged urchins shrieked the afternoon papers, and between times made balls of the dirty snow to hurl at a particularly high and resplendent hat. Though it was hardly past two, lamps were already lit, sending their flickering yellow light over wet and irritable throngs. Shop windows, steamed and streaked, gushed rays of golden light out upon the wet pavements. Crowded buildings, their browns and grays running with water, huddled together, doors opening and shutting swiftly.

Mr. Wilkins loved New York as he had never loved his native London. He loved its quick and riotous roar, though the long sustained mutter of London had never thrilled him. The roar of New York was the voice of young men, hot and tempestuous, alive with greed, gaiety, richness and rapacity.

But the mutter of London was the mutter of old men, still potent, still dangerous, still looming over the City like bent and evil spirits. If there was evil in New York, it was a vital and laughing evil. The wickedness of London was the wickedness of ancient things, corrupt, filthy and broody. The very dirtiness of New York was exciting. There was virility in the ashen air, and a limitless power, boisterous, clangorous and violent. Moreover, there was hope. There was always hope when a city was in flux, coming into being. But London had long ago done with flux. It had petrified in its darkness and immensity. There was only dusky rigidity there, and hopelessness. "What we will shall come!" cried New York. "What has been is to be," muttered London.

"Mark my words," Mr. Wilkins would say with unusual seriousness to those who laughed at his predictions, "New York will soon be the center of the whole bloody universe. Mark my words!"

The stinging rain on Mr. Wilkins' face did not annoy him in the least. He buried his chins in his beaver collar and chuckled. He lifted his polished boots as high as possible, and daintily stepped around puddles. Fog was coming with the rain. It swirled in yellow wisps about the lamps. The streets were becoming more narrow, more dirty, more crowded. The squat dark buildings bent towards each other. Now Mr. Wilkins could smell the strong fishy odour of the dark ocean heaving sullenly behind the warehouses which were beginning to replace the shops and business buildings.

"Ah!" sniffed Mr. Wilkins, as if that primordial stench was the very perfume of Araby. There was salt in the vicious wind. It brought a ruddier tint to Mr. Wilkins' rosy countenance. He bought a paper from a shivering urchin, handing the lad a round silver dollar, then walking away hastily with a wave of his hand. The boy stared after him, stupefied, looking first at the shining circle in his dirty fingers, then at the back of Mr. Wilkins' sturdy and resplendent figure.

Mr. Wilkins was happy. He had returned to New York. He was among his own again. His mind, which had threatened to become fat, was churning pleasurably. By the time he had reached a certain gloomy warehouse, blank and reeking in the lamplight, his strut had in it the lilt of a dancing step. He stood for a moment to watch the passing of a clamorous horse-car, the gray horses bent and steaming, the bells deafening. Lanterns swayed inside, so that it was a rolling cabin of yellow light and huddled bodies in the midst of dark rain and wind and fog. The windows had become steamed; there were little rubbed circles on them, through which anxious eyes peered. Mr. Wilkins smiled after the car, his sandy tufts of eyebrows quivering.

There was little traffic in this dark and misty South Street, narrow and lined with the great bleak warehouses. The rain rushed in stormy torrents over the broken wooden pavements. Here and there a lamp tossed its yellow light in the wind. The roar of the sea behind the warehouses penetrated far up the river. Mr. Wilkins could hear its tumultuous harsh sucking around the quay. Dolorous moanings penetrated the foggy afternoon, for the river was busy with cargo ships and tugs. Night was settling down over the city. On a level with the pavements lamplight flickered through little dirty windows. Beyond the sound of the storm and the whistles of the ships, there was silence in South Street.

Mr. Wilkins approached the door of a certain warehouse, on whose blank front was painted the words: "Richard Gorth, Cotton Exporter." He pushed open the door, and found himself in a gritty office, lined with the high desks of bookkeepers. About eight old men bent over ledgers, their green eyeshades casting sharp shadows on their gray faces, their shirt sleeves protected with black paper, their knees drawn up on their stools. Over their heads swung dirty oil-lamps, which hardly lightened the cold and ashen gloom.

"Good afternoon!" roared Mr. Wilkins, flourishing his cane, his face seeming to send out rays of its own. Immediately a warmth penetrated the vaultlike chill. Every hopeless old face turned towards him with one accord. Every pale and sunken lip burst into a broad and delighted smile. Every man slipped down from his stool, and immediately Mr. Wilkins was surrounded by incoherent old men, each reaching eagerly to shake his warm plump hands. The diamond on his right ring finger glittered bravely and agilely, as his hand was pumped by one man after another. And he looked into each pair of faded eyes with a real and tender compassion and affection. He listened to their anxious exclamations as they brushed off the drops of rain on his greatcoat. He watched another old gentleman sedulously polishing the gold head of his cane. Another knelt stiffly to wipe off the mud from his shining boots with a thin white handkerchief. Every eye glowed with passionate devotion and joy in his presence. The room resounded with tremulous and broken voices, with Mr. Wilkins' booming Cockney voice laden with its rich jokes and deep rumbling laughter.

A chair was dragged from a distant corner for him, brushed off with half a dozen handkerchiefs. He was induced to sit in it, surrounded by these wretched and ancient starvelings, with their pathetic veined hands so wasted by hunger and endless toil and the stains of imbedded ink. He saw their painful neatness, their darned linen and polished and patched old boots. He saw the wrinkles about their tired eyes, the weariness in their delighted smiles. That familiar lurching began again in the depths of his strange and evil heart. These, too, were the dumb and helpless ones, bewildered and unasking.

He knew the history of each and every one. He inquired about each man's health, the health of his wife and family. And he listened with intentness and sober interest to the faltering replies, spoken in cracked and patient voices. They were children to him, though even the youngest was old enough to be his father. As he listened, his keen and searching glance saw the sunken and feverish gleam of the eyes under the shades.

He began to cough, as if embarrassed. He brought forth his fine linen kerchief, and coughed in it. His apparent embarrassment grew.

"Well, now," he began, "blast me if I had time before my passage back to buy you chaps anythin'. Wot with the bloody weather over there, and rushin's abaht, and me cold, I was fair put to it to do me own job."

He fumbled in his pocket as every old man heartily disclaimed any expectancy of a gift. It was enough for them, wasn't it, Joe, Harry, Will and Jack, that Mr. Wilkins had returned safely, the weather being what it was this time of year? Every gray head nodded vehemently; every eye burned upon Mr. Wilkins with deep love.

He coughed again. "Well, now, it's nice of you chaps to say that! But, I didn't forget you. I said to meself only this morning: 'Bob Wilkins, are you one as forgets old friends, partiklarly old friends as works for Gorth? No, Bob Wilkins,' I says to meself, 'never be it said of you that you forgets.' "

He withdrew a thickly stuffed leather case and opened it, revealing sheafs of banknotes. Under their stupefied eyes he withdrew eight of them, each of the value of fifty dollars. "It's Christmas soon, lads!" he cried, jovially, and thrust into each numb and trembling hand one of the banknotes. Then he stood up, shaking himself like a fat dog. No one spoke. Every eye gazed in complete stupefaction at the banknotes. Not one man there earned so much in a month as this.

And then a thing happened which seemed quite terrible to Mr. Wilkins, and caused him an acute and genuine embarrassment. For, all at once, the old men began to weep, soundlessly, standing there under the swaying oil-lamps, their heads bent, their eyes fixed on the banknotes in their hands.

There was complete silence in the dusky room. Each man was alone with his emotions, with his thoughts, and his own tears. Mr. Wilkins scowled, poked at the floor with his cane. The lurching in his heart was an actual physical pain. He knew that none of these old men saw the money; they saw only what it would buy in terms of warm mufflers, in new boots, in medicine for sick old wives, in fuel, in food, in relief from constant terror. And all this seemed very dreadful to Mr. Wilkins. He could never endure the tears of children and the old.

Despite his short bulk, Mr. Wilkins could move like a swift shadow when he desired. Before any of the old men was aware of it, Mr. Wilkins had gone. A door had shut softly behind him. In the dark corridor beyond, he stood for a few moments, wiping his steaming face. There was a fierce look in his eyes.

Then he smiled again, tilted his hat, opened another door. He found himself in a large and warm familiar office, where a fire burned between two high and luxuriously curtained windows. There was a thick soft rug under his feet, dark crimson and velvety. The walls were panelled in gleaming wood, along which were a few heavy chairs covered with crimson velvet. In the center of the room stood a great mahogany desk, polished and rich, littered with papers and with silver objects. At this desk sat Mr. Richard Gorth, busily signing letters under the bright light of a hanging crystal chandelier.

"Ha!" shouted Mr. Wilkins, removing his hat and bowing elaborately.

Richard Gorth started, and looked up with that sharp and piggish alertness which distinguished him. He was as short and casklike as Mr. Wilkins himself, but where Mr. Wilkins gave the impression of jovial rotundity, Mr. Gorth's figure was all hard compactness for all it resembled a broad squat keg. Moreover, his thighs were not plump, as were his agent's. His large belly sloped down to lean shanks, so that he resembled a fat egg standing on end on two wooden sticks. His arms, too, were lean, ending in narrow voracious hands, bony and veined. Like Mr. Wilkins, he had practically no neck, but he had no triple chins. His face was broad and angular, rather than plump like Mr. Wilkins', and of a dull and pasty colour with a streak of rough red on his hard cheekbones. Like Mr Wilkins, he had a broad and flattish nose, but whereas Mr Wilkins' was a red and shining blob, his gave a snoutlike impression. If Mr. Wilkins had a round and rosy little mouth, fat and smiling, his was a mere broad slash in his face, implying, in its colourlessness and its viselike quality, all cruelty, meanness and avarice. His eyes, too, were not round and protruding like Mr. Wilkins', but were of a shallow grayness, bleak and dead, like the eye of a cold dead fish. There was even the glaucous veiled quality of that fish's eye over them, like phlegm. He was not bald, like Mr. Wilkins; he had rough gray hair growing at strange angles over his bullet-shaped head.

Whereas Mr. Wilkins' expression was warm, rosy and sympathetic, Mr. Gorth's was all harshness, cunning and brutality. He affected a severity in dress, quite unlike Mr. Wilkins' resplendent attire. Almost always, he wore black broadcloth, well cut and rich, with plain white linen and a black stock. He was secretly proud of his little effeminate hands, and kept them exquisitely manicured. But he could not conceal their malevolence and their cruelty and their greed.

Upon discovering Mr. Wilkins, he smiled grimly, and a baleful light invaded his pale slits of eyes. He stood up, and, leaning across his desk, he extended his cold dry hand to his agent. All his movements were swift, if abrupt, giving evidence of his enormous vitality.

"Well, well!" he exclaimed, in his hoarse and toneless voice. "So, you have returned. A week early, too. Sit down, man. From the look of you, you were successful."

His eye bored into Mr. Wilkins' glassy hazel eyes, which revealed nothing. Mr. Wilkins sat down, carefully lifting the tails of his coat, and laying his tall hat on the shining desk. Still beaming, he daintily removed his kid gloves, smoothed them, laid them beside his hat. He carefully balanced his cane against the desk, and crossed his fat legs.

"Aye, if I may say it, sir, I was successful," said Mr. Wilkins, in his suetty voice.

Mr. Gorth sat down slowly, never taking his hard stare from Mr. Wilkins. His slash of a mouth smiled faintly.

"Then, we shall celebrate, shall we?" he said.

He produced keys and unlocked a drawer in his desk, bringing forth a bottle of brandy and two little silver cups. He filled them precisely, not a drop too much or a drop too little. Then he replaced the bottle, and pushed a cup towards Mr. Wilkins, who raised it high. Mr. Gorth touched that cup with his own, and they drank slowly.

"Ah," murmured Mr. Wilkins, smacking his lips. Mr. Gorth's livid tongue licked the corners of his mouth in order not to lose a drop. Mr. Wilkins glanced approvingly at the fire, and about the office.

"Good, this, after that blasted ship," he said.

Mr. Gorth's eye had never moved from his agent's face. His pale brows drew together, impatiently. But he knew Mr.

Wilkins. One could never hurry him, foul vulgar Cockney though he was. Mr. Gorth was a gentleman, and an Englishman. It was necessary to hire such as Mr. Wilkins, but Mr. Gorth never forgot the difference in their stations. It infuriated him that such as he had to defer on the pleasure of this abominable upstart and thief, who, by rights, ought to be sojourning in Old Bailey.

"Shall we get down to business, eh?" said Mr. Gorth, trying to smile pleasantly, but only succeeding in bringing a most disagreeable expression to his countenance.

But Mr. Wilkins seemed fallen into deep thought, which gave him pleasure, for he kept smiling and nodding in a mysterious fashion as if communing with some unseen friend. Mr. Gorth's little hands clenched and tightened on the desk. After a moment, he ostentatiously drew out his big gold watch and frowned at it. Mr. Wilkins remained oblivious.

"Well, now," said Mr. Gorth, in a sarcastic tone, "if it is not too much trouble, Mr. Wilkins, I'd like your report. After all, I am a busy man."

"Ah, yes," said Mr. Wilkins, softly, putting down his cup, "you are a busy man, sir."

He fumbled in the tails of his coat and brought out a thick envelope. Mr. Gorth eyed it voraciously. Mr. Wilkins laid his pink hand on the envelope. He smiled with tender embarrassment, and actually blushed. He cleared his throat.

"There's the little matter, sir, of a cheque," he murmured.

Mr. Gorth scowled. "Why should I pay you before I know the value of what you have brought?"

Mr. Wilkins sighed. "You must trust me, Mr. Gorth, beggin' your pardon. Am I one as 'as got a reputation like I have without gentlemen trustin' me?"

Mr. Gorth threw himself back in his velvet chair, and gazed at Mr. Wilkins with a look that never failed to intimidate. But Mr. Wilkins was not in the least intimidated. He stared back at Mr. Gorth, his glassy eyes shining but opaque.

Mr. Gorth coughed roughly. "You have me at a disadvantage, Mr. Wilkins," he said, ironically. "But it seems I must trust you, eh?"

"You really must, sir," said Mr. Wilkins, with gentle regret.

Mr. Gorth thrust his hands deeply within his pantaloon pockets. His pale smile was grim and dark. Then, shrugging, he drew his chequebook towards him, dipped a pen in the inkwell, and wrote upon the cheque. He tore it out of the book with a thin and savage sound and tossed it at his agent. Mr. Wilkins lifted it, gazed at it, tilted his sandy tufts of brows with a satisfied air, and carefully tucked the little paper in his weskit pocket. Now he assumed a look of business-like efficiency. He tossed the envelope neatly across the desk, and Mr. Gorth seized on it with a pounce, tore it open and began to scan the contents with swift darts of his eyes. Mr. Wilkins, in the meantime, leaned back in his chair, one foot swaying, smiling at the ceiling.

There was no sound in the room but the dropping of coals, the hiss of smoke, and the dry quick rustling of the papers which Mr. Gorth was perusing with malignant smiles. Occasionally he muttered: "Ah!", in a tone of intense satisfaction.

Finally he exclaimed loudly, with exultation, slapping the papers:

"Ah, old Appleton in Massachusetts will pay well for this!" Then he looked piercingly at Mr. Wilkins, and smiled his malignant smile again. "You know, of course, Mr. Wilkins, that Old England could have you extradited as a thief, for stealing these patents from the cotton mills there?"

But Mr. Wilkins was not startled. He raised his eyebrows with injured innocence. "Well, now, Mr. Gorth, is American cotton mills goin' to be hamstrung forever by those English rascals? 'Ere we got 3,500,000 spindles in Ameriky, but England's got 21,000,000. Ruinous, sir! Right is right, whether it's law or no law. 'Ere they're floodin' the bloody country with cheap cotton goods, and what's to become of our own mills? I ask you, Mr. Gorth, what's to become of 'em?"

He seemed very wrought up, and leaned towards Mr. Gorth, his face expressing patriotic indignation and concern. But Mr. Gorth merely leaned back in his chair, smiling unpleasantly, and waited.

Mr. Wilkins waved his hands. "We've got the best of conditions, right 'ere in New England, Mr. Gorth, sir. Water, cheap labour, coal, and the world's best business ability! That's wot we've got, sir! And wot does England do? Hides her bloody patents from us, smirkin' all the while, and floodin' Ameriky with cheap cotton goods, all to the disadvantage of our on workmen. 'Tisn't right, sir, damned if it is!"

He thumped his fist resoundingly on the desk, and glared righteously at Mr. Gorth, who laughed shortly.

"It seems we have a patriot here," he said, in a meditative voice. "You aren't an American citizen yet, Mr. Wilkins?"

"Not yet, sir, but soon! Another six months, and it's done."

He smiled genially. "And if you think, Mr. Gorth, after me 'avin' 'elped you, with your own blasted cash, that you can do me in with the law, for—'elpin' myself to English patents, well, then, you don't understand American patriotism. There's some in Washington, all worked up abhat the cotton industry, as will thank Bob Wilkins."

Mr. Gorth laughed loudly. "I thought you had a sense of humour, Mr. Wilkins! Don't you understand that I'm grateful to you? Why, you don't know what this means to me, Mr. Wilkins. I'm a patriot, too. Why, I'm an American citizen! Damn me, if we won't be manufacturing cotton goods here very soon, with these patents, so that we can produce them in New England cheaper and better than in the old country. I'm grateful to you, Mr. Wilkins! You've saved me thousands, I might say even millions, in cargo costs alone! New England gets my cotton, now."

He smiled delightedly at the papers in his hands. "Why, with this patent, we'll double the mule for 300 spindles to 600 in no time. And this power loom, too! Gad, Mr. Wilkins, this means the beginning of a cotton industry in America beyond that ever dreamed of in England, thanks to you!"

"There's some as would be grateful to you, Mr. Gorth, for sendin' me for these patents," said Mr. Wilkins, slyly, watching his patron very closely meanwhile. "Down in Washington, like."

Before he could stop himself, Mr. Gorth said brutally: "You've got no proof, Mr. Wilkins." Then, he bit his lip and his eyes narrowed upon Mr. Wilkins so that they were only gleaming slits in his broad face.

Mr. Wilkins shook his head, smiling widely. "Now, 'aven't I, Mr. Gorth?" he asked, very softly. " 'Aven't I, just?"

There was a deep silence in the room, while glassy hazel eye and baleful gray eye engaged each other.

Then Mr. Gorth laughed loudly, reaching forward to pat Mr. Wilkins on the hand. He winked. "We have our secrets together, Mr. Wilkins. I still insist you have no sense of humour."

"There's sense of humour, Mr. Gorth, sir, and sense of humour. It hurts me, sir, to 'ear you talk, even in a joke."

Mr. Gorth waved this sad comment aside with a light lift of his hand. "A sense of humour, Mr. Wilkins, a discriminating sense of humour, is what makes the difference between vulgar barbarians and Englishmen. And, at the last, we remember that we are Englishmen, don't we?"

To celebrate this happy remembrance, Mr. Gorth brought forth the brandy again, and the two little silver cups. This time, with an abandoned air of extreme and reckless generosity, he filled Mr. Wilkins' cup to overflowing. Mr. Wilkins, willing to forgive, was his happy self again. He tossed down the brandy, and then helped himself to another cup. Mr. Gorth winced, though his smile remained fixed.

"That is rare Napoleon, Mr. Wilkins," he said, delicately.

"And blasted good, too," Mr. Wilkins replied approvingly. "You are a gentleman as 'as taste, sir."

Mr. Gorth became curious. "I don't imagine you used such as this Napoleon during your—little transactions—did you, Mr. Wilkins?"

With another cup near his lips, Mr. Wilkins winked. "Perhaps I did, sir, and then again, perhaps I did not. The least my employers know about me methods, Mr. Gorth, the better for all concerned." He tapped his brow with one knowing finger. "The more I keeps in me own mind, the less others get to know. And that's capital, sir."

"You are a clever man," said Mr. Gorth. "A very clever man. We'll have other business to do together very soon."

He watched Mr. Wilkins toss off another cup of brandy. His brutal features hardened, for all the smile of his long and colourless mouth.

Mr. Wilkins put down the cup, wiped his lips appreciatively with his handkerchief. His complexion had become quite crimson, and there were little beads of sweat not only on his brow but all over his pink dome of a head. He settled back in his chair and regarded Mr. Gorth seriously.

"There's another thing, Mr. Gorth, sir, as 'as been givin' me thought. They say in England as there is to be trouble between the North and the South in Ameriky very soon. Blasted abolitionists, and such up 'ere."

"Nonsense, Mr. Wilkins! Civil war! Pah! Sheer nonsense." Mr. Gorth, however, leaned towards Mr. Wilkins with quickened interest. "But just for the sake of discussion: in the event such an impossible thing should occur, what would be the sentiments of England?"

"For the South, Mr. Gorth. I know that for a fact. There's sympathy there, for the South. Why? There's a lot of talk abhat the right of secession of States. Freedom, like."

Mr. Gorth scowled. He uttered an indecent expletive to express his contempt for the noble sentiments of his former countrymen. "Hell, Mr. Wilkins. That's just an old pose. What they're after is to help destroy our Northern industry. We're going to be formidable competitors, Mr. Wilkins, of all of Europe. That's what England can't stomach. Let us get into a Civil War, and we're ruined for years. That's what England hopes for. I know all the tricks! Every time England comes out nobly for the rights of man, watch your purse, Mr. Wilkins, watch your purse!"

Mr. Wilkins grinned. "I do that, Mr. Gorth."

Mr. Gorth had relapsed into deep and somber thought. This however, did not prevent him from removing the brandy bottle, replacing it in the drawer, and locking it up.

"I know what the South's after," he said. "Taking the cotton trade away from New England. Cheap slave labour. Abominable! How can we compete with slave labour? Why, damn it, industry will steadily move South. Either the whole damn country should be slave, or free. No half measures."

"You'd prefer it slave, Mr. Gorth?" asked Mr. Wilkins, with a cunning smile.

Gorth's slit of a mouth twitched humourously. "We'd make a lot of money then, Mr. Wilkins!" he said, heartily. "But that's too much to hope for."

"It's practikly slave labour in India," mused Mr. Wilkins, with a quickened eye. "Mark my words, India's the next logical place for our cotton mills! But England'll get there first, mind you. She allus does. We've got to look for a better place, all our own. I've been thinkin' of Japan."

"Japan?" Mr. Gorth stared. "You're daft, Mr. Wilkins."

"Not I, sir," said Mr. Wilkins, shaking his head vigorously. "There's Japan, with all the women and the children. I'll wager you could get 'em to work for practikly nothin'. Nothin' at all. A few cents a day." He grinned. "Bringin' 'em the blessin's of civilization into the bargain, sir, and no questions asked."

But Mr. Gorth gazed at him with opaque thoughtfulness.

"Mark my words," said Mr. Wilkins, "there's many a spot on this old earth that could do with a bit of civilization, and a job in the factory or the mill. Wot did the old chaps fight for? Land, sir, land. Wot'll they fight for in the future? Cheap labour, sir, cheap labour! Mind you, I understand these things. I've got a nose. Cheap labour, and markets. That's the ticket, Mr. Gorth. I've got a nose!"

Mr. Gorth mechanically stared at the organ under discussion, but said nothing. But the malefic glitter in his eyes increased.

"Who pays bloody labour the most, sir?" continued Mr. Wilkins. "We does. 'Ow long can we compete with a world of cheap labour, I ask you? Not long! So, it's us for un-Christian countries lyin' abhat just abeggin' for us to move in and civilize 'em."

Mr. Gorth remained sunk in thought.

"Our own mills and factories in heathen lands, Mr. Gorth," said Mr. Wilkins. "We'll be doin' 'em a favour. Give 'em an interest in life, besides dancin' around in their heathen temples and sleepin' under the bloody palm trees. Make 'em share the white man's burden, like," and he laughed richly.

Mr. Gorth's inner eye saw vast and overwhelming visions. He sucked in his breath.

"And wot with steam," said Mr. Wilkins, "the stinkin' world's 'arf the size it used to be."

He added: "But we've got to move quick, like, or England'll be there before us, with parsons and prayer books and beads and factory plans." He chuckled: "Bringin' in Jesus along with the looms and the machines. That's the ticket! Nothin' like Christianity to 'elp an honest man get cheap labour."

Mr. Gorth's thoughtful eyes pointed themselves directly at Mr. Wilkins. He smiled malevolently.

"There are times when I think you are a cynic, Mr. Wilkins."

"Not I!" exclaimed Mr. Wilkins. "I'm all for bringin' in religion with the jobs! Two best blessin's of civilization, sir. Keep 'em quiet with religion, and you'll have no trouble. Keep 'em lookin' at the starry heavens, and they won't think whether you fill their bellies or not."

"I still think you are a cynic," said Mr. Gorth.

Mr. Wilkins said nothing. Mr. Gorth was not a very imaginative man, or he would have detected something sinister and virulent in Mr. Wilkins' smile. However, he felt something like a dark shadow steal through the warmth of the room, as if an evil emanation had diffused itself there. He turned in his chair and poked vigorously at the fire.

Then he directed his attention to Mr. Wilkins.

"You saw my nephew in England, while you were there, as I requested you to?"

"That I did!" Mr. Wilkins spoke ardently. "A fine young chap, that he is. Just the ticket for you, Mr. Gorth. I approached the subject delicate, like. The lad's been waiting around, 'oping that his two older brothers'l die off and leave him a clear path to the title. But he's lost 'ope, in a way. Brothers remain 'ealthy. When I hinted to him wot was in your mind, he seemed uncertain. Seems there's a lass he's after just at present."

Mr. Gorth frowned. "Who's the girl?"

"Good family, sir, and you can set your mind at rest abhat that. Daughter of a widow with ten thousand pounds a year. Niece of Mr. James Turnbull, the importer. You've heard of him, sir?"

Mr. Gorth's frown disappeared. "So the girl's acceptable, eh? Turnbull? No children there?"

Mr. Wilkins hesitated a moment. Then he said evasively: "There's a son. So, the lass won't inherit there. But there's enough money without that. Your nevvy won't stir until the lass gives her word, yes or no. I think it will be yes." Mr. Wilkins pursued up his round fat mouth inscrutably.

"Ten thousand pounds, and Andy's own five, is quite respectable," mused Mr. Gorth. "But you think he will come? I've always fancied Andy. A hard young scoundrel. Gad, it's hard luck I have no children of my own." And he thought of his barren wife with gloomy hatred.

Mr. Wilkins clucked sympathetically. Then he uttered a slight exclamation. "Ah, I'd almost forgot. In comin' over, I met a young chap on the ship. The son of that very Mr. Turnbull, uncle of the lass your nevvy's after. Turned out with a shillin', for marryin' beneath his station. He told me this one night, after some drink. Hard to get anythin' out of him at first, but trust Bob Wilkins. Told me the whole bloody story, and it's a rum one, too. He'd be valuable to you, Mr. Gorth. Well eddicated and such; public schools. Good strong mind. I as much as told 'im I'd speak up for him to you."

"Why, damn you, Mr. Wilkins," said Mr. Gorth slowly. "Am I to find employment for every worthless young rascal in England? You've taken a lot upon yourself, I must say."

Mr. Wilkins winked. "I think not, Mr. Gorth, I think not. The lad's got intelligence, and he's ready for anythin'. Remember, in a way, like, he'll be a connection of your nevvy's, if the lass says yes. Nothin' like keepin' things in the family."

Mr. Gorth stared fixedly at his agent. "You've got something up your sleeve, Mr. Wilkins."

"Nothin' but Christian charity," protested Mr. Wilkins, virtuously. "Can't I do a chap a good turn without gettin' the wink?" He laid his finger along the side of his nose. "I tell you again, Mr. Gorth, I can smell some one as will be of value. I smelled out this young chap afore I even saw him."

Mr. Gorth smiled unpleasantly. "Well, then, send him in. Mind you, I'm promising nothing, Mr. Wilkins. What can he do, if anything?"

"He can keep your books, and learn the business, like. Trustworthy. When I saw him, I said to myself: 'Bob Wilkins, there's a young chap as one can trust.' You haven't a bloody man around here you can trust, Mr. Gorth."

"That I haven't," replied Mr. Gorth.

Mr. Wilkins rose, picked up his hat and gloves and cane. "Then, if it's convenient, sir, I'll bring him in tomorrow."

Mr. Gorth, with unusual urbanity, shook hands with his agent. "There'll be other bits of business for you soon, Mr. Wilkins. I can rely upon you?"

Mr. Wilkins, out in the dark little corridor outside the office, hesitated. He glanced at the door leading to the bookkeepers' room. Then he shook his head. He let himself out at another entrance.

CHAPTER 14

Mrs. MacNeill was extremely ill. Whatever of pretense she had used in the past, her present illness was not assumed, though self-induced by spite, rage, hatred, obstinacy and brutal determination to have her way.

So far, this determination had been ably and coolly frustrated by her daughter, Eugenia.

The girl would sit almost all night beside her mother's fretful and feverish bed, unspeaking, as calm and dignified and contained as always, would leave, at dawn, for physical refreshment and a change of garments, for a light breakfast and a cup of hot tea, then would return to her mother's side to perform the arduous work of bathing her and combing her heavy plaits, of making her bed and bringing her the morning tray. There were those who asked why a nurse was not engaged for these onerous and burdensome tasks, too heavy for the slight strength of the girl. But Eugenia did not complain. She knew that her mother was punishing her most cruelly, and that if she died she would occasion Martha no grief but a vicious satisfaction, an intense relief. It was a battle to the death between these two women now, open and savage, and one would eventually expire of exhaustion or the other of pure spite. Up to this early evening, it appeared that Eugenia would be the final victor, for, despite sunken eyes surrounded by purple patches, an emaciation so marked that the delicate bones of her face and neck and hands were sharply outlined under pallid and transparent skin, an exhaustion so acute and enervating that she floated like a ghost and hardly appeared to have a physical being, there was about her that accustomed strength of hers, prideful, haughty, reserved and full of authority. These were more evident than ever. As her flesh wasted, her mental and spiritual attributes seemed to gain in stature, so that one felt the steely quality, the inflexible coldness, the rigid implacability, with uncomfortable awareness.

"It is a thing which never would have been dreamt of with regard to myself!" Mrs. MacNeill would cry in a voice of wailing vitriol from her heaped pillows. "Mamma and Papa would have died of shame, and as for myself, I should have sunken ten feet deep in the earth for very mortification! Oh, it is intolerable, it is unendurable, that Martha Turnbull should have come to this, that she be afflicted with a daughter that not only is jilted in the very face of London, but refuses to accept a far better offer, an offer which will enable her to hold up her head again and sweep off in a grander carriage than the one offered her before!"

More and more beside herself, Mrs. MacNeill must be lifted high upon her pillows, gasping. Eugenia watched this with the face and stillness of a statue. No one could guess that her throat was as dry as dust, that salt filled her mouth, that her heart rolled on sick waves of blackness.

"If this had happened to a thousand other girls, it would have spelled a melancholy end for them," sobbed Mrs. Mac-Neill, wringing her hands. "They would have been the laughter of London. A young female who is jilted has no refuge but the chimney corner, and her needlework. What gentleman is attracted to a young lady who has been scorned by another gentleman?"

How could she know of the bottomless sadness and disgust which pervaded her daughter, the bitter unreconciled grief, the harsh resolution? How could she know of the shame which choked and sickened her, the same of a proud and coldly passionate spirit pilloried in the stocks of vulgarity and outrage? But Martha MacNeill, petty, shallow and stupid though she was, understood quite a little of this. She found the false consolations soothing, though quite disingenuous about their sincerity. But she found the contempt heaped upon Eugenia some recompense for her daughter's flouting of her, and some revenge for herself. Ah, she would soon see that proud and haughty neck bent in snivellings and weakness!

But though none guessed it, Eugenia had reached the end of her endurance. On this dark and somber February afternoon, as she sat near her mother's bed and was forced to suffer the agonized humiliation that was a daily occurrence, she resolved, in her stony and embittered young heart, that she would endure no more. She reflected on the letter she had sent that morning to Andrew Bollister, and the grimmest of smiles touched her cold pale lips.

"I have never seen so unfeeling a child!" her mother sobbed. "Have I desired anything for myself? Have I not gladly borne every sacrifice for you? Have I lived for any one but my child? What have I asked of you? Only that you make an incredibly brilliant marriage, suitable to your station, one which will redeem you in the eyes of all of London! A girl of sensibility and intelligence would rejoice at being delivered from an unsuitable marriage, and would thank heaven on her knees that such as Mr. Bollister had deigned to look at her! But my sufferings, and your advantages mean nothing to you, you wretched little creature!"

Eugenia did not speak. It was as if she were deaf, or entirely alone. She moved deftly about the chamber, drawing the curtains, urging the fire to renewed activity, gathering up shawls neatly, arranging the tea-table for her mother. All this finally done, to the tune of Mrs. MacNeill's lamentations, the girl then glided from the rom and went to her own chamber.

She lit a lamp near her commode, then gazed steadfastly at her reflection in the glimmering mirror. Behind her, the austere room was dim, floating in shadows. The lamp carved her young face starkly out of the shifting gloom, so that it was molded of sharp black and white lines, the expression of bitter pride and unbending authority and endurance heightened to a great intensity. Her head was lifted stiffly and tilted. The lamplight made her large gray eyes more brilliant, more brightly hard and fixed. Her character, rather than any softness of beauty had made her face arresting and strange in its outlines, and these outlines were now intensified so that the angles of her cheek-bones, the sweep of her white forehead, and the sharpness of her firm chin gave an aspect of indomitable and icy emaciation to her countenance. It was a terrible thing that so young a face had this aspect, and a very sad one, also. Its rigidity, its inflexibility and inexorable self-control were pathetic in their implications. The nostrils of her fine clear nose were dilated, white and carved as marble, and her pale mouth was compressed in a harsh line.

She held her unyielding pose for several mintes, gazing at her reflection. But she hardly saw it. She stared indifferently at the purple shadows about her eyes, and her ghastly pallor which spoke of exhaustion of body as well as of spirit.

Then, most moving, a tear started to her eye, dropping sluggishly as though half frozen, and fell over her haggard cheek. She watched it abstractedly, then calmly wiped it away with her handkerchief. She turned resolutely from the mirror and went to her wardrobe, withdrawing a gown of black silk with a round lace collar. She moved more quickly now, divesting herself of her plain brown garments, standing for a moment or two in the lamplight in her billowing cambric petticoats, her young arms, so thin and so white that they were almost transparent, shining like stone in the dusk, her childish shoulders so slender that the bones were visible

138

in their swift movements. The black gown rounded itself over enormous hoops, swayed and tilted about her, revealing the ruffled drawers at every swift step. She fastened a huge gold brooch at her throat, eyeing it gravely in the mirror. It was inlaid with black enamel and small pale pearls. Then she brushed the sleek parting of her shining brown hair, tucked in a stray wisp that threatened to curl against her ear. Her severe aspect satisfied her at last. She touched her wrists with eau de cologne, and swept from the room, descending the staircase like a rapid ghost in swirling and rustling hoops.

The drawing-room fire was burning sulkily. One lamp had been lit on a distant table. All was heavy silence there, dank and chill. Eugenia seated herself before the fire, and stared somberly at the restless coals. There was no change in her expression, but at intervals her throat moved and trembled, and she swallowed convulsively. There was something terrible in her control.

At last she heard the faint and melodious tinkling of a bell in the thick silence, and the footstep of the butler. For one instant her rounded young breast rose on a quick breath, and then was still and calm again. She rose, rested one hand on the mantelpiece, and turned her face, so like a white mask, towards the doorway.

Andrew Bollister, austere and elegant in black broadcloth, entered the drawing-room, moving with his accustomed grace and stillness. His pale hair, shining as though painted on his narrow skull with a brush dipped in silver gilt, caught rays from the lamp. His eyes gleamed and flickered in his long keen face with its ridged and slender nose. His subtle mouth, so cruel, so delicate, curved slightly in its ghost of a smile.

The eyes of the girl and the eyes of the young man met for a long and inexorable moment. Then she extended her hand to him. He took it into his own, which was no less chill and impassive. Gallantly, he raised it to his lips, then held it firmly. His smile brightened, yet did not warm. However, those malignant eyes of his, the colour of winter ice, glowed strangely.

With a firm movement, she withdrew her hand and seated herself. But she did not remove her unconquerable gaze from his face.

"Please, sit down," she murmured. "I must have a talk with you, Mr. Bollister. That is why I asked you to come."

He sat down near her, carefully lifting his coat-tails, and then stiffly leaning towards her with an attentive look. For a few instants, she could not turn away from him. Then she stared at the fire. Her lips hardly moved as she spoke:

"Mr. Bollister, I must ask you to cease your persecutions of me. I must ask you not to write me or attempt to see me again."

She waited. He did not answer. Impatiently, then, she turned her face to him. His smile was broader now. Something strange and violent stirred in her heart, and she cried out in a shaking voice:

"I must appeal to whatever honour you possess, Mr. Bollister! I am a young and defenseless female, and have a right to demand some consideration, some mercy, from you! Your ceaseless persecutions of me, your appeals to my mother, have made my position unendurable in this house, have caused me shame and great wretchedness. There is nothing left for me, therefore, but to appeal to your honour——"

She paused. There was a hard choking in her throat. She put her handkerchief to her lips.

He looked at her for a long time before he answered, and an expression of serious meditation replaced his malicious smile. Then he said: "Miss Eugenia, I have only asked you to marry me. It is extraordinary that you should find this offensive. An honourable offer is not usually regarded with such aversion, even if it must be refused."

She started to her feet, overcome with the strangest emotions. Her heart beat wildly. She had to repress sobs which rose from some agitation which she could not explain. He rose more slowly, and stood looking down at her with the utmost gravity.

"I have refused you, Mr. Bollister, many times!" she exclaimed, hoarsely. "An honourable gentleman would have found the first time sufficient. But, apparently you have no honour, Mr. Bollister, no self-respect. You have written to my mother, and have appealed to her in my absence, so that you have inflicted suffering upon a girl who has done you no harm. I must ask you, then, for the last time, to remove yourself from this house, and accept your dismissal."

Her control was unbearably shaken. Tears rolled down her cheeks. The hammering of her heart increased so that she had a momentary terror that she would suffocate. He regarded her in silence. But his face changed, became harder, yet oddly moved, and he half lifted his hands as if to take her, and then let them drop to his sides. He spoke quietly:

"Miss Eugenia, I will ask you only once more to listen to me, and not with repugnance, but with serious consideration. Then, if you ask me to go and never annoy you again, I will accept my dismissal, and our paths will not cross unless by accident."

He paused. She touched her cheeks proudly to remove the

tears. His low and toneless voice, so without resonance, seemed to fill her ears long after he had done. Her agitation was like a storm in her heart; she felt impelled to weep with a nameless passion.

"Well," she said, hardly able to speak. "I am listening, Mr. Bollister."

He took her hand again. It trembled in his, but she did not remove it. He led her back to her chair. She sat down, shivering uncontrollably. The pain in her breast, so urgent, yet so inexplicable, increased, so that she was flooded with desolation. He drew his chair closer to her, leaned forward so that his face was very near hers. She saw its hardness, its subtle malignance, its rigorous calm. Her heart swelled again with that nameless and wild emotion, and her eyelids fluttered.

"Why have I pursued you, Miss Eugenia?" he asked, softly. "Because we were made for each other, deny it vehemently though you will. We are alike; we understand each other. You will repudiate what I tell you now, cry out your denial, but the truth remains that you love me as I love you. Had I not been assured of this knowledge from the beginning, I should have removed myself from your presence long ago."

She stared at him, incredulous. Then she uttered a short and caustic laugh.

"You are amusing, Mr. Bollister!" she exclaimed. "I assure you that I have no regard for you whatsoever, not even liking!"

She clenched her fingers together, and shivered again. Her breast lifted, and trembled, and her lips shook.

He smiled faintly. "Miss Eugenia, I have said you would deny it. You are still bewitched by some infatuation which is ludicrous. But the time will come when you will realize the truth, that you love me, that we belong to each other, that for either of us to have married any one else would be little short of bigamy." And he laughed lightly.

She regarded him, white with anger and affront, as though he had vilely insulted her. But the wild passionate clamouring in her breast grew even stronger.

"I do not give up my own so easily," he whispered, and now he took her hand, and pressed his lips into the quivering dry palm.

She flung back her head, rigidly, closing her eyes. A violent current passed through her whole body.

"No one has ever known you in the slightest, but I," he pursued, still very softly. "You thought you had been loved, and believed that you loved. But that was not true. You have never loved any one, before. You love me, Eugenia, and I have never loved any one but you. Look at me, please, my darling."

Irresistibly, she was compelled to look at him. But she forced her expression to remain cold and remote, and inexpressibly contemptuous and amazed.

"Ah," he murmured, looking into her eyes. "What a proud little thing it is, to be sure! You see, only I understand such pride."

He gently dropped her hand and stood up, looking down at her with new sternness. She felt a sudden bereavement, and a new desolation.

"I am proud, too, Eugenia," he said, and his voice was cold and harsh. "That is why, even before I received your note, I determined that I would see you only once again, and then, if you were obdurate, I would remove myself forever from you."

He smiled slightly.

"It seems that every one is going to America. That is where I am going very soon, also. My uncle, Mr. Richard Gorth, has some thought of making me his heir to his cotton importing business. His agent had talked to me a few weeks ago, and I have determined to go. I have waited, however, for your final word."

Her wet face changed strangely. She rose very slowly, and gazed at him with her large gray eyes. She was shaking visibly.

"America!" she repeated.

His smile was secret, and grimly amused. "Yes, America. I presume you have heard of it, Miss Eugenia?"

She was unaware of his malicious undertone. She pressed her clenched hands to her breast, and continued to gaze at him. And he waited, his smile more secret and amused and knowing than ever.

She caught her breath, slowly sank into her chair, as though her strength was gone. The rosy firelight played over her rigid features. She seemed to have forgotten Andrew Bollister. Her fingers convulsively knitted themselves again, the knuckles starting out from the frail flesh.

Then she spoke, in so low and breathless a tone that he had to lean down towards her to catch her words:

"Mr. Bollister. I have reconsidered. I will marry you."

For a long time he merely stood there near her. Then he knelt beside her, and gently took her into his arms. She resisted a moment. Their faces were close together. Her features became contorted, then softened and dissolved in a storm of mysterious grief and weakness. Tears ran down her cheeks. He kissed them away, with the greatest gentleness, holding her tenderly. She suffered his caresses. Her sobs were loud and unrestrained. Finally, as if with despair, she dropped her head on his shoulder. Her arms lifted without volition, wound themselves about his neck, and clung to him with an odd fierceness. Her soft breast pressed itself against his chest, and he could feel the thundering and pulsing of her heart.

An hour later, Eugenia crept into her mother's room. Her face was flushed, her movements uncertain as if she walked in her sleep. Mrs. MacNeill laid aside the rich novel she had been avariciously perusing, and looked up at her daughter with her usual hatred. She burst out into reproaches.

"So, my daughter, my unfeeling child leaves her mother alone to suffer and repine, neglected, while she amuses herself in her naughty satisfaction!" she cried. "But, why do I reprove you, you little wretch? Why do I waste a moment's grief upon you?"

Eugenia's breath was disordered. She attempted to speak. Then, with a gesture clumsy with despair and haste, she extended her little fleshless hand. A large gem flashed upon one finger. Mrs. MacNeil stared at it, stupefied.

"I have accepted Mr. Bollister," said Eugenia. Her voice was changed and muted.

Mrs. MacNeill uttered a great triumphant cry. She reached up for her daughter, caught her in her big fat arms, and dragged the flaccid girl down upon the bed, clasping her against her vast and heaving breast. Eugenia did not resist. She lay there like a slender dead thing, her lips smothered in a welter of perfumed laces and warm heavy flesh.

"O my darling!" screamed Mrs. MacNeill, beside herself, convulsively showering kisses upon that cold young face with the closed eyes. "O, how happy you have made me, my pet, my love, my dearest one! O, I shall die for very joy, my sweetest, my child, my little angel!"

But Eugenia said nothing. Slow tears poured from under her lashes, wet the laces upon her mother's bosom with their saltness and their endless and painful bitterness.

CHAPTER 15

I F Mr. Bob Wilkins was insensible to bad weather, he was appreciative of good weather, and especially of the spring in New York. Ah, what cool wine was in the air, what refreshment, what stimulation, what sparkling effervescence! None of that dang murkiness of London, that livid pale light lying like glimmering reflection on the dour fronts of sooty buildings! None of that fetid odour of centuries to choke the streets and fill the alleys with a miasma like a palpable mist! None of that powerful and crushing gloom of a city standing in fog to its knees and glowering at a world! What London had done was accomplished. What New York was to do was like a bright delirium in the air, feverish, joyous, youthful and thunderous.

He breathed deeply. Unashamed, he would strike his cask-like chest with his gloved hands, turning his head from side to side with that beaming, sunny look which distinguished him. He would swagger and strut, flourishing his cane, tilting his hat at a precarious angle, his gilt buttons shining, his gaiters immaculate, his boots glistening, his coattails fluttering, his linen polished by hot irons until it glittered. He attracted smiles as a mirror in the sun attracts light. His feet came down on the pavements lovingly. Nothing was too small, too insignificant to catch his delighted attention. He fed pigeons as they fluttered down from shining roofs, the sun on their wings. He patted horses, watched them drink sympathetically. He touched the heads of children playing in the Sabbath sunlight. He watched the gay passage of carriages with fondness of a well-fed uncle, and tipped his hat gallantly to young ladies who fluttered along the walks, stepping aside with elaborate courtesy to permit the passage of their huge billowing hoops. He loved the spring glow on the fresh faces under the tiny bonnets, and glanced happily at violets tucked in neatly at gentle bosoms. At these times, he was not Lucifer, but Puck.

He had walked miles, for the sheer joy of walking. Now he turned down West Fourteenth street, and glanced complacently at the old houses, which, mingled with heavy old trees, lined the length of the street. The trees were full of green and fragile mist, the black boughs struck with pale bright light. The patina of spring polished every long shrouded window glimpsed through awakening branches. Occasionally, he passed a house in whose stable-yard he could discern a stolid cow contentedly munching at the new grass. The air was still cool, strong with the winds from the sea, but the sun lay warmly gentle on the slate roofs and the brown stone steps of the houses, and the rough cobbles of the street. The sky above was pale but brilliantly blue, with swift white clouds like small sails briskly fleeing across it.

The houses were old, but solid, with tiny front gardens in which crocuses and other early blossoms were already in colourful bloom. Mr. Wilkins saw the brilliance of tulips, red, yellow, purple and pink, standing in their bristling thickets of stiff green leaves. The gardens were protected by low iron railings, or white picket fences, and from these gardens rose the steep brown steps to the firm doors of the houses, on which brass knockers blinked ruddily in the sunlight.

Mr. Wilkins looked at the houses with increased complacency. A fine old street, this, not yet decayed, and still faintly haunted by the shades of Dutch burghers despite the infrequent horse-car which rocked its noisy way through the Sabbath calm. He reached an old brown house, four stories high, a tall and severe house with long narrow slits of windows fully eight feet in length. The windows were polished vigorously; shutters were thrown back to reveal crimson draperies. The house itself stood on a wide lot, carefully landscaped, if meagrely sprinkled with little trees. At the end of the lot was a stable; a cow and a calf grazed obliviously, and from the stable came the stomping of an impatient old horse.

Mr. Wilkins mounted the steps with a stately but benevolent air, and lifted the glittering knocker. The street, whose quiet had just lately been rocked by the clatter of a horse-car, had subsided into breathless, sunlit silence, disturbed only by the echo of the knocker. The door, after an interval, was opened by a kitchen girl in cap and white apron, her stout Irish face flushed from the stove, her black hair in little tendrils falling about her neck. When she saw Mr. Wilkins, she curtsied briefly, and returned his beaming smile with one as broad, as she held the door wide for his entrance. The "missus," she informed him, was out for her constitutional. Mr. Wilkins nodded gravely. He had not come to see Miss Beardsley, the elderly spinster in decayed circumstances who owned this house. He had business with the lodgers he had cajoled her into taking under her severe and immured roof. These lodgers lived on the third floor, beneath the servants' quarters. "And very comfortable, too," thought Mr. Wilkins, as he climbed the dark and narrow staircase, carpeted in frayed Brussels fabric. The house smelled of wax and soap and polish; its air was quite chill, but fresh as only extreme cleanliness can be fresh. There were no fires today, for Miss Beardsley was very frugal, and believed in fires only when snow lay on the ground. Mr. Wilkins had his suspicions that Miss Beardsley was not quite as "decayed" as her sparsely furnished house and sombre garments would lead one to believe. In fact, Mr. Wilkins suspected that she was miserly. However, he had no objection to miserly people. It was his experience that miserly people had great self-respect and were exceptionally clean, neat, and competent. It was the generous people who lacked pride, and were apt to be slovenly, careless and incompetent. Give him, within reason of course, a penny-pincher to a penny-thrower. The penny-pincher, more often than not, was a solid citizen, full of honour, uprightness, integrity and intelligence, while the penny-thrower could rarely be relied upon to keep his word and usually had no character.

The paradox to Mr. Wilkins, however, was that miserly people had their price, and it was not always an honourable one, despite their usual integrity and righteousness. But the generous, though giving the impression of carelessness and haphazardliness, frequently could not be induced by money into dark by-paths. By love, yes. But not by money. Whereas the miserly could be bought by cash; they remained obdurate to the pleadings of love.

Mr. Wilkins, at the end, preferred to deal with miserly people. Once their cupidity was aroused, there was nothing they would not do.

As he knocked softly at a tall white door, he reflected whether his new protégé was miserly or generous. He inclined to the latter belief. However, he was comforted by his observation that a generous man turned furious and resentful could give many a lesson to the greedy. What be lacked in calculation, he made up in ruthlessness, when his angry passions were aroused. It was not money he was after, but revenge. Mr. Wilkins, instinctively distrusting the generous man, was not yet certain that revenge was as firm a foundation to build upon as avarice. Revenge, in a burst of contrition, frequently tumbled down the largest edifices, whereas empires themselves, built on avarice, could resist the onslaughts of centuries. Mr. Wilkins' dealings, in the past, had been almost exclusively with avaricious men. Now he had the new excitement of dealing with a generous one, potential with earthquakes and cataclysms. Yes, he had quite a new interest in life.

The white door opened, and revealed Lilybelle on the threshold, dressed in glimmering mauve satin with gigantic hoops, the bodice a froth of white lace. Her rich auburn hair was caught in a net, and bedecked with little mauve bows. Under that hair, her round face, so pretty and so stupid and vulgar, was flushed on one cheek, as though she had just risen from a couch. Mr. Wilkins, who saw everything, discerned that the mauve satin was quite crumpled, and stained here and there from careless eating. But she was a beguiling picture, even so, with her full luscious figure and bold bosom and plump white neck, even if her expression was chronically baffled and sulky.

She was delighted to see Mr. Wilkins, and stretched out her big warm hands with joyous pleasure, seizing him and pulling him into the room. She knew he was genuinely fond of her, and she was gratefully fond of him. Moreover, the day had been unbearably dull, and he was a happy diversion. She greeted him loudly, her voice already promising that hoarse booming quality which was to distinguish it in later years.

"Mr. Wilkins, sir!" she cried, boisterously, blinking her round blue eyes at him, and hoping that he would not observe their reddened and swollen rims. "Mr. Turnbull, Mr. Wilkins is 'ere!" Vitality, coarse but strong, gushed from her. She dragged Mr. Wilkins irresistibly across the floor, as a heedless exuberant child drags a puppy. Mr. Wilkins, laughing and chuckling, clutched his hat, gloves and cane, and tried to keep his balance, trying, also, to protect himself from the whirling and bouncing of the enormous hoops which buffeted him. During all this, he was not unaware of the fluttering lace drawers revealed to the knee by the hoops, and the tidy sturdiness of the good ankles in white stockings.

The room into which he had been dragged was large, awash with the glittering and colourless sun. The tall thin windows blazed with light, the draperies impatiently thrust back, the shutters flung out, so that one saw the spring sky, the ruddy brick of the opposite houses, and the soft green fog in the trees. Miss Beardsley's lodgers occupied this room and a small adjoining bedroom, both of which were furnished in her severe sparse custom. The floors, of wide oaken boards, were dark and unbelievably polished, so that they were like brown mirrors. Over them were carefully scattered a few little rugs, at strategic spots. The tiniest of fires burned in a black marble fireplace, and the white walls increased the sense of shining chill and astringent cleanliness of the apartments. The furniture, too, was very austere and stiff; a mahogany rocker or two, with upright uncomfortable backs, a cane sofa, a few tables covered by stiff linen or crimson velvet, an ancient rosewood spinet, a wardrobe of some mouldering black wood, intricately carved, a massive bookcase boasting formidable tomes untouched for generations, and a really beautiful little mahogany desk, made up the furnishings of the sitting room. Beyond, Mr. Wilkins could see the bedroom, with its enormous canopied bed and its fringed white coverlet reflected in the darkly shining floor, its one gloomy commode and its single rocker. Miss Beardsley had wasted no carpet here, and there was no fireplace. The ceilings were so tall that all furniture was dwarfed to insignificance.

Nevertheless, despite the formal stiffness and lack of comfort of the apartments, it was all so clean, so polished, so fresh, that it had a kind of hard dignity and much gentility. Mr. Wilkins, who loved space and glittering austerity in the homes of others, admired these apartmests. (As for himself, give him roaring fires, thick carpets, close warm furniture, and velvet and plush!)

John Turnbull sat in a rocker between the two windows, a big ledger on his knees, a pencil in his hand. He rose slowly upon Mr. Wilkins' entrance, and bowed slightly, with surly reticence, and without a smile. His dark face was sullen.

"Ah!" exclaimed Mr. Wilkins, placing his hat, cane and gloves in Lilybelle's eager hand, and favouring her with a fleeting smile of genuine fondness, "a lovely day, sir, if I may say so, a lovely day! I've been walking for hours, sir, and what a pleasure it is! I said to myself: 'Bob Wilkins, why not drop in on your young friends though I doubt you'll find them in on such a day.' It's quite a surprise to find you here, Mr. Turnbull."

Lilybelle, who had been standing and gazing at Mr. Wilkins with affectionate joy and pride, as though he were a creation of her own, now drooped her full red lips in a childish expression of artless sadness. She glanced timidly at her husband, and faltered:

"Don't blame me, Mr. Wilkins. I thought a walk would do us good, but Mr. T. had some work from the office to do. Very important work," she added hastily, cringing a little from John's expected displeasure.

John reseated himself slowly, and indicated a chair for Mr. Wilkins with an inclination of his head. Mr. Wilkins sat down, placed his palms on his fat spreading thighs, and beamed heartily at his young friend. He raised his sandy tufts of eyebrows archly.

"Diligent, I see, Mr. Turnbull, diligent! Ah, that's the ticket! I've good reports of you from Mr. Gorth. Make yourself indispensable, I says; then they can't do without you. First step to success; indispensability. That's in the copybooks, eh?"

John shrugged. He closed the ledger and placed it on a table.

"Ah," murmured Mr. Wilkins, to cover the awkward silence. He looked at Lilybelle. The girl had seated herself, after a fearful glance at John, on the sofa, where it was evident that she had been reclining before the interruption. She tucked her feet under the hem of her mauve gown. All at once, she appeared smaller, and shrunken, and very cold.

"I've been off on a bit of business of me own," said Mr. Wilkins, his voice hearty and rich in the chill silence. "That's why I 'aven't looked in on you, sir. But, now I'm back, and we can go into certain matters, eh?"

At the sound of his reassuring voice, Lilybelle sprang up again, eagerly. Her blue disks of eyes were suffused with the ready tears always so near the surface. "Tea!" she cried. "I'll go down to the kitchen and bring up a pot!"

John glanced at her with cold contempt and reproof. "You know very well, Lily, that Miss Beardsley doesn't approve of your dirtying her kitchen. I thought she had made that plain to you before, when you've sneaked down there and attempted to brew yourself some of your precious tea."

"Don't think of it!" cried Mr. Wilkins, vigorously. "I've 'ad me tea, only an hour ago! We're not tea-drinkers in this country ma'am."

He paused. Lilybelle had subsided again, in a huddled heap on the sofa. Mr. Wilkins murmured softly to himself, and chuckled, as if he had rich and fruity thoughts. John bit his lip impatiently, and scowled. As if he had spoken, the girl trembled, gazed at him with sudden alertness. Her lips quivered; her eyes filled with tears. Her expression was terrified, but worshipful.

Then John, unable to contain himself, burst out savagely: "I've wanted to talk to you, Mr. Wilkins! I've done what you told me, but there seems no rhyme nor reason to all this. Especially under the circumstances. It is only a matter of time until Mr. Gorth learns, from his nephew, of our last meeting. It will be all up then, Mr. Wilkins. He won't continue to retain in his employ a man who smashed up his precious Andy as a farewell token. It is only a matter of time—"

Mr. Wilkins continued to chuckle, to nod his bald and rosy head, to arch his brows, as if he had not heard. Then, after John had uttered a helpless and disgusted exclamation, Mr. Wilkins spoke, very softly and affectionately:

"Don't upset yourself, Mr. Turnbull. In fact, I've dropped in to have a little chat with you on the subjec'. It will be a surprise to you, sir— But, before goin' any further, I beg your leave, sir, to permit me to remember your lady's birthday."

"Birthday!" ejaculated John, with another scowl. He looked at Lilybelle. Electrified, and as naively joyful and expectant as a child, Lilybelle bounced off the sofa. "Birthday!" she cried, clasping her hands to her breast.

Mr. Wilkins nodded with great pleasure. "I remembered, ma'am, that you mentioned your birthday, when I saw you last, and though it's a great impertinence of me, I remembered it. I said to myself: 'Bob Wilkins, Mrs. Turnbull is a daughter to you, like, and in a strange country, away from kinsfolk and 'ome, and it's only right, considerin' her husband is a friend, and son, like, to remember her birthday. If it's not impudence," he added, with a humble inclination of his head towards John, who had begun to smile disagreeably.

John waved his hand with some mockery. "It is very kind of you, Mr. Wilkins, I'm sure." He turned to his wife, whose full young face was flushed with joy and anticipation. "It is kind of Mr. Wilkins, isn't it, Lily? By the way, how old are you now, my dear?"

"Fifteen," she quavered, mechanically, not removing her dilated and shining gaze from Mr. Wilkins.

"Quite ancient," muttered John. Nevertheless, his sombre look changed to one of uneasy compassion and reluctant softness. He rubbed his mouth with a finger, and sighed to himself.

Mr. Wilkins, quite crimson with his pleasure in Lilybelle's childish anticipation, and quite grinning from ear to ear. fished in the tails of his coat and produced a flat white box. Lilybelle involuntarily uttered a shrill cry, and reached out to snatch the box, as a child would snatch. "Lilybelle!" said John, with stern disgust, and his voice was like a whip. And, as if a whip had lashed her, she cowered, drawing back her hand, biting her lip, blinking away her fresh tears.

But Mr. Wilkins pushed the box towards her as if he was entirely unaware of everything. Lilybelle, recovering herself with easy delight, took the box and opened it with shaking fingers. Then she uttered a cry of extreme joy. She lifted out a heavy bracelet of carved and pierced silver, crusted with turquoises, a Chinese bracelet all twisted dragons and curved tails. She held it in her hand, stupefied, entranced, her cheeks flushing deeply, her mouth opened on a soundless cry of amazement and ecstasy.

"Only a little thing," murmured Mr. Wilkins, deprecatingly. "From China. Only a little token, Mr. Turnbull."

"Oh," sobbed Lilybelle, fumbling with the clasp, and frankly weeping with her rapture. She opened the trinket, and put it over her wrist. But her wrist was big, and try as she would, she could not make the clasp meet. She struggled furiously, while Mr. Wilkins watched in helpless dismay. She pressed so hard that edge of the silver cut her flesh. Some of her auburn curls came loose, and fell over her brow, in her desperate concentration on making the ends join. She caught her lip between her pretty little white teeth; sweat sprang out on her forehead, and about her mouth. John leaned forward the better to watch, and not to miss anything.

But, in spite of her struggles, in spite of the wounding of her flesh, Lilybelle could not bring the clasp into position. It remained a full three quarters of an inch agape. The girl sobbed heavily, pushing and pulling at the bracelet in her frantic efforts. Evidently John found something ludicrous in the frenzied struggle, obdurate and blind, of his wife, for he suddenly burst out into a harsh and uncontrollable laugh.

As if that laugh had turned her to stone, Lilybelle paused in the very act of her distracted struggle, her right hand clutching the bracelet, her head bent. She stood motionless, becoming very pale and still. She no longer sobbed, but tears coursed down her cheeks, paused at the corners of her lips, rolled down her chin. Mr. Wilkins, with a faint and smothered sound, stood up, stretched out his hand to the girl.

But John, scarlet with his mirth, said: "Lilybelle, can't you see that bracelet was made for a LADY with a fine and slender wrist, and not for you? I should think even a fool would have discovered that immediately?"

Some evil and desperate bitterness seemed to break in him, then, sweeping away his last precarious restraint, and in a hurried and muffled voice he continued: "They don't make jewelry and trinkets for barmaids, Lily! They don't anticipate that barmaids and country wenches will be so fortunate as to step out of their stations and be able to afford bracelets, or possess friends who will present them with such baubles. Give it back to Mr. Wilkins, Lily, at once."

Mr. Wilkins, with the strangest and mutest of expressions, gently lifted the bracelet from Lilybelle's bruised wrist. He weighed it in his hand, but looked only at the girl. She dropped her head on her breast. Her soundless and motionless anguish was most moving to see, at least to Mr. Wilkins.

"It was made for a little maid's wrist," said Mr. Wilkins, in a soothing and regretful tone. "I should have seen it. It's me that's stupid, ma'am. It's for a child, Mrs. T. And if you'll permit me, beggin' your pardon, I'll take it to a proper chap who'll do it up right for you, in no time. A trifle more silver at the end, and it'll be capital."

Lilybelle lifted her head slowly, and turned on Mr. Wilkins such a white and stricken face, such pale lips twisted in such agony, that he felt a stronger lurching in the region of his chest. She tried to speak, to smile, then, with an abrupt and mournful sound as if her young heart were breaking, she turned in a wild tilting of hoops and ran from the parlour into the bedroom, closing the door behind her. She did not bang the door, but closed it with painful care and softness, and this seemed most terrible and revealing to Mr. Wilkins.

Very thoughtfully, he replaced the bracelet in its box, and gazed at it with hatred. He put it back in the tail of his coat, with quiet motions. John was smiling disagreeably, but with some shamed discomfort.

"I ought not to have said that, I presume," he remarked, angrily. "But, she ought to realize some things."

"Not at all," said Mr. Wilkins, abstractedly. "It is a child's trinket. I'm very sorry, that I am, sir."

John said nothing. He merely stared at Mr. Wilkins, gloomily. And Mr. Wilkins returned that stare with a curious point of light deep within the glaucous depths of his protruding hazel eyes.

Then, after a long moment, Mr. Wilkins' expression changed again, became as affable and bland as ever. He said, briskly: "Well, now, we'll get down to our little talk, Mr. Turnbull, sir. May I ask how matters are proceedin' for you?"

John moved restlessly. "Mr. Gorth—seems pleased, I must say. He has a nasty temper, but he's been generous and patient, to a certain extent. I have nothing to complain of, I admit. I'm learning the business rapidly, as you suggested."

Mr. Wilkins nodded. "Excellent, sir, excellent."

John gave an impatient and irritable gesture. "But where is all this leading to? Not that I'm ungrateful; I'd be a puppy if I were. Mr. Gorth has been more than generous with regard to salary. I am receiving seventy-five dollars a month, fifteen pounds," and his lip curled with acrid contempt as he remembered that fifteen pounds had been a mere item to him before his marriage, "and after I pay Miss Beardsley forty-five dollars for our lodgings and our meals, I have a considerable sum left. I repeat, I have nothing to complain of. As you know, I am Mr. Gorth's confidential secretary——"

"Excellent," repeated Mr. Wilkins, with a twinkle of delight, and moving his round fat mouth in an expression which John found somewhat obscene.

"But, where is all this leading to?" said John, with increasing impatience and annoyance.

Mr. Wilkins put a plump finger archly against his nose. "When I undertook to make your fortun, Mr. Turnbull, it was with the agreement that no questions be asked. You've got to trust Bob Wilkins, as is one who knows wot he's doin'."

John's right fingers began to beat a hurried tattoo on the arm of his chair. He studied Mr. Wilkins darkly.

"It's fantastic, Mr. Wilkins."

"Patience, Mr. Turnbull," purred Mr. Wilkins. "It's comin' abaht the way I intended. I had a very edifyin' conversation with Mr. Gorth yesterday. Pleased with you, he was."

"Wait until he hears from his nephew. He won't be so pleased," said John, with an unpleasant smile. "What then, Mr. Wilkins? I'll be given the sack."

Mr. Wilkins commenced his rich chuckling, turning quite purple with his inner mirth. He regarded John merrily. "It may surprise you, sir, to know that he's 'eard. I told him wot you'd told me, on the ship."

"What!" exclaimed John, sitting up.

Mr. Wilkins nodded, chuckled again. "Surprised isn't the word, Mr. Turnbull. And flabbergasted, he was. And then, he laughed. Laughed, sir, like he'd never stop."

John slowly sat back, stupefied, his black brows wrinkling.

"Mr. Gorth likes a man," continued Mr. Wilkins, with pleasure. "I've got to give the devil his due. You went up in his estimation like nothin', sir."

John was without speech. He stared at Mr. Wilkins, unblinkingly, and with suspicion. He never forgot, and crudely never allowed Mr. Wilkins to forget, the difference in their stations. And now, as he stared at the strange Lucifer who had taken over his fortunes for some mysterious dark reason of his own, his big handsome features tightened.

"What is all this to you, Mr. Wilkins?" he asked bluntly, as he had asked a hundred times before.

Mr. Wilkins shook his head fondly. "No questions asked, Mr. Turnbull," he said, lifting an arch and admonishing finger. "That was agreed. I make your fortun—you make mine. Fair enough, isn't it?"

"You are a philanthropist, Mr. Wilkins," John remarked, scornfully. "I can't make your fortune. And I can't see how you can make mine."

"But you want your fortun made, eh?" said Mr. Wilkins, cunningly. "Anythin' short of murder to make it?"

John compressed his lips. But there was a sudden swift violence in his eyes, as though he looked at a vision Mr. Wilkins could not see.

"Ah," murmured Mr. Wilkins, with ineffable satisfaction.

He coughed. "And now for a bit of news, Mr. Turnbull. Mr. Bollister's comin' to Ameriky. He's expected in less than a week."

John sprang to his feet. He glared down at Mr. Wilkins. He turned quite livid. But his voice was very quiet and dull.

"Well, Mr. Wilkins, that's the end. He'll have me put out."

He sat down again, quickly, as if he had become ill.

"It's the end, Mr. Wilkins. Well, that appears to sever our connection, doesn't it?"

But Mr. Wilkins laughed gently, twinkling more than ever. "Not at all, Mr. Turnbull. I've 'ad quite a talk with Mr. Gorth. In fact, he's to invite you to a little dinner he's to give for his nevvy. Command performance, like. All this told me in confidence."

John's face turned black and vicious, and aghast with outrage.

"That is intolerable!" he ejaculated violently, striking the arm of his chair with his fist. "So, I'm to be made game of, am I, for the pleasure of that reptile? Intolerable! You'll reckon without me in this, Mr. Wilkins. Whether you want to end it or not, I'm ending it now!"

Unable to contain himself, he rose, began to pace up and down the room, all the old wounds open again, burning with pain.

"You don't understand, Mr. Wilkins. There is more here than what appears on the surface. I have no words for it, but you must take my word."

"I can see you're makin' much ado about nothin'," said Mr. Wilkins, soothingly. "Mr. Groth's got a 'igh opinion of you, Mr. Turnbull."

John wheeled on him savagely. "Why is Bollister coming here?"

Mr. Wilkins hesitated, and then began to bite his finger thoughtfully.

"It seems he's to be Mr. Gorth's heir, like," he said, with caution.

John burst into furious laughter, bitter and hopeless.

"So, that's it. Well, Mr. Wilkins, you are a fool if you can't see the way the wind's blowing."

But Mr. Wilkins was not disturbed. He looked at John

with great candour. "I can assure you, Mr. Turnbull, that nothin' of the kind's to 'appen. You've got to trust me, sir. Besides, it won't be long. I've told you that, 'aven't I? A few weeks more, and we're done. Not that Mr. Gorth's to know, as we said."

John fumed. His pain was much greater than even Mr. Wilkins shrewdly suspected. He said, flatly: "I don't know where all this is leading. But you've got to understand, Mr. Wilkins, that I'm to be faced with a mortifying experience, if I do as you wish me to do."

Mr. Wilkins spread out his hands. "Mortifyin' experience or no, sir, we've got work to do, you and me. It's only a fool as throws up the sponge when things is comin' his way."

John was baffled. "You're beyond me, Mr. Wilkins."

Mr. Wilkins studied this statement for a moment or two, and seemed innocently gratified. "I am that, sir, and beyond other chaps, too. Ive 'eard that before. Allus be beyond other chaps, Mr. Turnbull, and you've got the world by its tail."

John compressed his lips irritably. But his thoughts were elsewhere, depressed and turbulent. He sank into depths of dejection and misery, his hands thrust in his pantaloon pockets, his head bent forward a little, his eyes fixed starkly off into space.

Mr. Wilkins studied him fixedly, forgotten by the other. Quite apart from everything, he liked to look at John, for he admired handsome men, and especially tall and well-formed men. He admired them as a stable-owner admires race-horses, for the potentialities such creatures contain for their master.

"I can't do it," muttered John.

But Mr. Wilkins ignored this. He went on, with careful delicacy:

"It seems as Mr. Bollister's bringin' his bride with him."

John's head jerked around, swiftly. "He's married, then? To whom, Mr. Wilkins? Oh, that's impossible that you should know," he added, with a gesture of impatience at himself. He continued: "I can't seem to make you understand, Mr. Wilkins. My position was much different in England. My father is a wealthy man. Bollister and I attended the same Academy. We were of equal station, for all his father has some mouldy title." He hesitated, looking at Mr. Wilkins sharply. But Mr. Wilkins apparently found no slight false-hood in this, but gazed at John with sympathetic attention. John resumed: "And now, he'll come here and discover me to be little better than an office clerk to his uncle! Are you too obtuse to see all this, Mr. Wilkins?"

"Mortifyin' in a way, I admit, sir," said Mr. Wilkins, gently.

'But things is different 'ere, in Ameriky. You're the better man, Mr. Turnbull. That's evident, ain't it? Besides, I've told you it won't last much longer. I've got plans for you."

John glanced with meaning bitterness at the locked mahogany desk. "Or perhaps you've just got plans for yourself, Mr. Wilkins. You've asked me to trust you, but how am I to know I'm not just a cat's-paw for you, after all?"

Mr. Wilkins smiled blandly. "There's no way for you to know, Mr. Turnbull, I admits that. You've got to take me on trust."

He took out his big gold repeater and looked at it. He rose. "Well, now, sir, I must be leaving." He paused. "You've got the copies, like, eh?"

John smiled sombrely. Then he took a key from his pocket, went to the desk and unlocked it. He brought out a thick sheaf of foolscap paper, closely covered with his black and angular writing. He held the sheaf in his hand, turned to Mr. Wilkins, and smiled with great unpleasantness. "It's all here, Mr. Wilkins. All the contents of Mr. Gorth's confidential business files. All his most closely guarded business dealings and connivings and skullduggery, all his market reports. Everything that could ruin him."

A vast stillness had come over Mr. Wilkins. He did not stir even a finger. But he gazed at the thick sheaf in John's hand like a man enthralled.

"Why should I give it to you?" continued John. "Why should I trust you?"

Mr. Wilkins slowly lifted his eyes and looked at John. He whispered: "You've got to trust me, Mr. Turnbull, sir. You've got only my word for it. Wot could you do with that information? Nothin', nothin' at all. It means nothin' to you."

"Perhaps," said John, with a disagreeable grin, "you've picked me up and used me just for this very thing. To get you this information, to be your thief and dupe."

Mr. Wilkins' ruddy colour had faded to such an extent that there were only mottled spots left on his round and suetty cheeks. But his eyes, so strange, so exultant, so terrible, now, did not leave John's face.

"I've said," he whispered, "that you've got to trust me. I say it again."

There was a sudden hard silence in the room. The pale sunlight brightened to a vivid glow at the windows. The chill seemed to grow more intense.

Then John shrugged, enraged at his helplessness and impotence. He thrust the sheaf stiffly at Mr. Wilkins, and said harshly: "Take them. Perhaps I'm a fool. I probably am. I can't help it, it seems."

Mr. Wilkins took the sheaf. He ruffled the pages quickly, his eye flicking over line after line, darting like an avid beetle. He seemed to forget John. His beaming smile became evil, gloating, deeply satisfied. "Ah," he murmured at intervals. John watched him with a dour and heavily suspicious look.

Mr. Wilkins glanced up. His plump face glowed like the sun itself. He clapped John on the shoulder. "Capital, sir, capital," he said, and his voice was curiously breathless. Then, his exultation overcoming him, he cried: "It's more than I expected! Mr. Turnbull, your fortun is made. And mine."

"That is very agreeable," said John sourly. Nevertheless, his heart had begun to beat with unusual rapidity. He went back to the desk and brought out a stout manila envelope. He reached for the sheaf, but Mr. Wilkins, archly and naughtily shaking his head, took the envelope himself and carefully and lovingly put the sheaf in it. He tucked it under his arm, held out his hand.

"Mr. Turnbull," he said solemnly, "allow me to congratulate you. Your servant, sir."

"Or yours," said John, with a glower. But he took Mr. Wilkins' hand.

When his strange and inexplicable visitor had left, John experienced a nameless depression of spirit. He paced back and forth, up and down, the room, chewing his lip, striking the fist of one hand in the palm of another. His thoughts were turbulent, confused, sick with pain, shaken with uneasiness. The thing he had done was reprehensible, dishonourable, and even, he thought, despicable. He shook his head savagely, as he thought these things, and allowed his galling bitterness to wash away any qualms he felt. His head began to ache furiously, with a heavy pain. He flung himself into a chair, covered his face with his hands. An utter sickness and lassitude overcame him.

The sun fled from the window. A dank dimness and chill pervaded the apartments. Somewhere a clock faintly chimed the hour. A carriage rolled over the stones of the street below, followed by the rocking and clamour of a horse-car. Coals dropped on the hearth. A long slow shivering passed over John's body.

He had written his father once since coming to America. But he had received no reply. He lifted his head as he thought this, and his eyes became suffused, his lip shaken.

If, he thought, I had received only a word from him, a single word, I would never have done this!

His heart felt wounded and sore. He swallowed convulsively, as if to keep back a sob, for he was still young, still vulnerable, unused as yet to villainy and duplicity.

A single word, he repeated to himself. And then, "Eugenia," he whispered.

At last, feeling bruised and aching in every muscle, he pushed himself to his feet. He lit a lamp, looked about him at the chill stark gloom of the big parlour. He shivered again. He poked up the fire, all his movements sluggish. A single rosy streamer of light struck the white ceiling.

He heard the faintest of dolorous sounds, and glanced quickly at the closed door of the bedroom. His face wrinkled with sad and involuntary disgust. Then, sighing, he opened the door and went into the chamber which he shared with Lilybelle.

The girl was lying across the bed, clutching the white coverlet, her face buried in the pillows. Her crushed mauve satin, the heaving lines of her young figure, her tumbled auburn head, all spoke eloquently of the hopeless desolation which pervaded her, and her helplessness.

"Lilybelle!" he said, harshly.

She pushed herself upright, not looking at him, wiping her tears away with the backs of her hands, childishly. He stared at her quivering back, and something seemed to break in his heart. He went to her quickly, sat down on the bed and pulled her roughly into his arms. Her head fell on his shoulder. She sobbed aloud, clutching him with desperate and clinging arms, and hands.

"Oh, Lilybelle, you are such a fool!" he said angrily. "You cry over nothing, like an infant." Nevertheless, he kissed her with violence, and great pain.

CHAPTER 16

Mr. Wilkins descended the stairs slowly. Once in the square and dusty hall below, so cold, clean and bleak, he lurked about a few moments, chewing his finger-nail in deep thoughtfulness. Then he tapped gently on the forbidding front of a oaken door off the hall, and assumed his usual expression of radiant affability.

Kitty, the Irish maid, opened the door and glowed upon him. The "missus," she informed him, would see him immediately. Mr. Wilkins, hat and gloves elegantly in hand, his cane tucked under his arm, bowed and beamed his way into the tall dim parlour, where a dark floor glimmered like a shadowed mirror, and where panelled walls, grim and lofty, reflected that dim light. Here was the same gleaming bitter cleanness and dignity of the upstairs apartment, enhanced by austere polished furniture, and very little of that. Miss Beardsley, who did not believe in "pampering" others, nevertheless did not carry this to extremes for herself, for a low red fire crackled on the tiled hearth of a mahogany fireplace. Nor did Miss Beardsley care for too much sunlight in her house. It "faded" the furnishings. So heavy crimson draperies were drawn over the high windows, a narrow crack between them allowing the entry of pale and furtive light. Near the fire, in a high ladder-back straight chair, Miss Beardsley sat in formidable stiffness and majesty, her knotted livid hands folded on her bony knees, her white-capped head as rigid as if upheld by a board. Indeed, there was something wooden about all of Miss Beardsley, from her lathe-like back and front, her broadlike shoulders and sharp angles.

Dressed in black wool which revealed no softness of outline, and with a black fringed shawl about her broad thin shoulders, she was the picture of a spinster, grim, relentless, suspicious and gaunt. Under her white cap, her hair was black, threaded with silver, and drawn severly in a net to a high position on her head. She had a long cavernous face, with a wide thin mouth, tiny acidulous blue eyes, a wide low forehead, and a bony Phoenician nose. Nevertheless, she exuded that nameless air of breeding which always inspired Mr. Wilkins' sincere respect. This was a gentlewoman, full of integrity, righteousness, "character" and haughtiness. Nothing, Mr. Wilkins reaffirmed to himself, would shake that stony woman, except money.

Miss Beardsley's attitude, though stately, expressed a frozen quality rather than repose. As she saw Mr. Wilkins, she inclined her head with majesty, and indicated a chair near her with a slight motion of her mottled hand. Mr. Wilkins repressed a shiver at the barren coldness of the room, but sat down with every manifestation of affectionate geniality and pleasure at finding himself in this virginal presence.

"A beautiful day, Miss Beardsley, a beautiful day!" he said, with rich enthusiasm. "I trust you enjoyed your constitutional?"

"I walk for my health, not for frivolity," said Miss Beardsley, in a frigid voice. "I remember it is the Sabbath, and while I walked, I meditated upon the weakness of human nature. It is a very interesting subject, Mr. Wilkins. One sees much food for thought while pursuing one's way through the city."

"Oh, I agree with you perfectly, Miss Beardsley," said Mr.

Wilkins, with a knowing look, a momentary quenching of his brightness, and a deep sigh. "One can't 'elp but think of the frailty of human natur in the raw. Revealing, I allus says."

Miss Beardsley inclined her head with severe approval of these worthy sentiments. If it could be called that, her attitude relaxed just the slightest. She echoed Mr. Wilkins' sigh, touched her dry eyes with the corner of a stiff linen kerchief, and assumed a look of noble and unflinching suffering.

"On the Lord's Day, one would expect sober faces upon the streets, and meek and meditative attitudes. But one sees nothing but the most sinful gaiety and heedlessness. One might even say, thoughtlessness. There is no dearth of gentlemen and ladies walking in the parks, idling away precious time, though the churches are more than half empty. One can only fear what the end will be, in this new Babylon."

Mr. Wilkins was not certain what Babylon was, but he nodded heavily, sighed again, tilted his head and stared despondently at the floor.

Miss Beardsley cleared her throat ominously, and stared rigidly before her. "It is the Catholic influence, certainly, Mr. Wilkins. We ought not to have allowed those professing that heathen faith to enter America. It has destroyed our reverence for the Sabbath, for the Holy Book and our Protestant austerity and lofty simplicity. I fear that this is just the beginning, that eventually we shall see the influx of impossible persons of strange ideals and stranger ways of life. America, as we know it, will be destroyed. I can only prophesy, Mr. Wilkins, and you need not look incredulous or doubting, that we are to be devoured in the wrath of God, as Sodom and Gomorrah were devoured, or Nineveh."

As Mr. Wilkins had very little acquaintance with the Bible, he said nothing, but only sighed over and over, shaking his head.

"I love my country," continued Miss Beardsley, in a tone of low and noble anguish, "and it is a great trial to me to discover her in the throes of dissolution."

"Ah, perhaps not," breathed Mr. Wilkins. "I have such faith in Ameriky."

Miss Beardsley gloomily considered this for a moment, then, after a sad glance of acknowledgment at Mr. Wilkins for this sentiment, she shook her head, bowed her spade-like chin on her flat bosom, and sighed.

"I hope we shall not disappoint you, Mr. Wilkins," she said, in a fatal tone. "I cannot reassure you with real sincerity. The city is rife with sin and darkness. One dares not think how close and terrible the end is to be."

She sank into melancholy. Mr. Wilkins did not see what her expression intended to convey to him: meek and long-suffering holiness and regret. He saw the real expression, mean and hating envy of all that was alive and warm and full of colour. He saw that Miss Beardsley was a quite malignant and virulent woman. In other words, an excellent woman "for his money."

"You are a busy lady, Miss Beardsley," he murmured, leaning towards her with deep reverence. "And I'm not one as imposes on others. I'd like to 'ave a word with you about certain young persons now under your roof."

Miss Beardsley lifted her head. In the dusky cold of the room, her little blue eyes glittered with eager malevolence. She pressed her lips together, smoothed her brow with one finger, as if a pain had suddenly invaded it.

"Ah, yes, certainly, they are protégés of yours, are they not, Mr. Wilkins?" She hesitated elaborately, then, with an air of determined courage she said: "I also wished to talk with you, Mr. Wilkins, about them. I fear I cannot accommodate them any longer."

"No!" exclaimed Mr. Wilkins, in a tone of strong consternation. "'Ave they offended you in some way, Miss Beardsley?"

She compressed her lips until her mouth was a mere livid slit in her horsey face. She regarded Mr. Wilkins with grim sternness.

"Not exactly, Mr. Wilkins. That is, young Mrs. Turnbull has not offended me. It is evident that she is a young person who has married out of her station. However, I admire her for her admission of this, and her desire for improvement. I find her respectful, and eager for proper training, and very complaisant and obliging. One of the servant class, I presume, but not forward and above herself. At your own request, and hers, very respectfully advanced, I have endeavoured to supply her with the rudimentary conduct becoming a born lady. I must admit that she is an excellent pupil."

She paused. Mr. Wilkins leaned forward with every evidence of absorbed attention.

"I have acquired a fondness for Mrs. Turnbull," resumed Miss Beardsley in a severe and uncompromising tone. "I think I could do much with her, as you requested, Mr. Wilkins. It is Mr. Turnbull that I find objectionable."

"I regrets to 'ear that," said Mr. Wilkins, in a concerned voice. "I know 'e's a blasted opinionated beggar, beggin' your pardon, ma'am, and given to violence and such. But 'e's a gentleman, and I'm one as knows that."

"A gentleman is as a gentleman does," Miss Beardsley remarked, with a swift toss of her head and a sniff. "I find him boorish and impossible, and quite rude. He appears to be of the opinion that I am a professional lodging-house keeper, and treats me in a very cavalier and demanding fashion, and, though you will scarcely believe this, with disdain."

"And I was partiklar to inform him that you was a lady of breeding and famly," mourned Mr. Wilkins, "and that you accommodate him and his wife out of friendship for me."

Miss Beardsley sniffed again, with dolorous offense, but did not answer.

"What 'as he done?" urged Mr. Wilkins, sorrowfully.

"It is more Mr. Turnbull's attitude than what he has actually done," said Miss Beardsley with reproving severity. "He has no consideration for my sensibilities. He smokes cheroots in my dining-room, though I have specifically informed him that it is offensive to my nostrils, and has a tendency to darken the walls. Worse than that, Mr. Wilkins," and she gazed at him formidably, "I have smelt liquor upon his breath, and even while passing his door. You can hardly believe that Mr. Wilkins? I assure you that I am not one to indulge in vagrant imaginings. I had rather a sharp talk with Mr. Turnbull on the subject, and he replied very offensively, and asked me if I was receiving my rent on time, and, if so, that he would thank me to mind my own business."

"I can 'ardly credit that!" cried Mr. Wilkins, with horror.

Miss Beardsley smiled darkly. "I assure you it is quite true. You can see, therefore, that despite my liking and patronage of young Mrs. Turnbull, I cannot continue to shelter them."

Mr. Wilkins shook his head over and over to himself, as if he was too aghast to speak immediately.

"Sad, sad," he murmured, at last. "And 'ere I was about to inform you, ma'am, that within a few weeks these young persons would be renting your second floor apartments at a rent, say, of seventy-five dollars a month, with appropriate adjustments for dining privileges."

Miss Beardsley turned her head to him alertly, and frowned.

"And Mrs. Turnbull was athinkin', too, of engagin' a personal maid for herself, and another for the apartments, and settin' up a genteel establishment," continued Mr. Wilkins, studying the floor mournfully.

Miss Beardsley cleared her throat. "How can that be, Mr. Wilkins? You informed me that Mr. Turnbull was receiving but seventy-five dollars a month at the firm of Richard

Gorth, and that he can pay me but fifty dollars for the apartments he now occupies."

Mr. Wilkins winked ponderously. "Ah, but there will soon be another song to sing. I can't tell you much more, ma'am. 'E's got go, that one, and there is some gentleman who is much interested in Mr. Turnbull's talents."

Miss Beardsley reflected on this in silence. She pursed her lips, scowled, rubbed her brow, touched her eyes with her kerchief. Mr. Wilkins staring at the floor again, apparently saw nothing of this.

It's be cruel to put Mrs. Turnbull on the street now, just when she's profitin' so proper like from your instructions, ma'am," continued Mr. Wilkins in a tone that suggested inner weeping.

Miss Beardsley said thoughtfully: "We have been doing some exercises with the backboard, and I have been preparing a lotion of honey and milk of almonds for the child's hands. I have had excellent hopes for her. Her taste is somewhat extreme, but we were to shop for a more restrained wardrobe, one of elegance. She really is very civil, poor young creature, and anxious to learn. I have offered to teach her her letters; she is quite illiterate. And to instruct her on the piano. Her gratitude is truly touching."

She lifted her head again with noble resolution. "Mr. Wilkins," she said, in a ringing voice, full of dedicated exaltation, "I would be failing in my duty to a fellow creature if I did not continue my instruction of Mrs. Turnbull. I must be at hand to console her, on the inevitable occasion when she learns the true character of her husband."

Mr. Wilkins, who had been smiling under his nose, now glanced at Miss Beardsley with genuine concern. "True character,' ma'am?"

Miss Beardsley nodded grimly. "I blush to mention this, Mr. Wilkins but one Sunday I was walking in Jeannette Park, and discovered Mr. Turnbull in the riotous company of a young person who was evidently no better than she should be." She looked at Mr. Wilkins portentously.

Now Mr. Wilkins was truly concerned, without dissimulation. He scowled so deeply that his jovial and rosy face was wrinkled in heavy folds. He chewed the corner of his lip. Those hazel eyes gleamed, for an instant, with the baleful look so few ever were permitted to see, and then only at the destructive end.

He rose. He bowed to Miss Beardsley. "I can see, ma'am, that Mrs. T. will need a—a sister to console her. Out of your Christian charity, ma'am, I have observed that you are eager to offer her this consolation, in her time of wretchedness. I can rely upon you?"

He extended his hot plump hand to the spinster, who took it with her air of grim and stately resolution. They shook hands solemnly.

"You can trust me, Mr. Wilkins," replied Miss Beardsley, in strong tones, dedicated and steadfast.

She rose, her narrow hoops swaying stiffly about her. "You will partake of a small collation with me, Mr. Wilkins?"

Mr. Wilkins, who was acquainted with the "small" and secret collations of Miss Beardsley, accepted with grateful alacrity. He accompanied his majestic hostess into the dining-room. She was very tall, and his head hardly rose above her shoulder. The dining-room was hardly less chill and gloomy than the parlour, and as sparsely if elegantly furnished. But the table was spread with a white lace cloth, exquisite and fragile, and the heaviest and most lustrous silver. Kitty was admonished to set another place, and Mr. Wilkins, after bowing and drawing Miss Beardsley's chair for her, seated himself with a fat grace opposite her. There was a cold bird, some excellent hot breads, a salad, rich seed cake and lemon tarts, and a bowl of red apples and nuts upon the table. Miss Beardsley requested Kitty to bring in the blackberry cordial, "as a stomachic, of course, Mr. Wilkins. It increases the circulation on a chilly day. I find it invaluable when one is threatened with a cold."

Mr. Wilkins had already enjoyed the potency of the blackberry cordial on other occasions, and inclined his head with graciousness. Miss Beardsley, with many elaborately graceful gestures, and with due solemnity, filled her glass and Mr. Wilkins' with unusual lavishness today. Her tight black sleeve revealed the hard boniness of her large wrists. Now that she had relaxed, she even indulged in a grim coquettishness, and replied to Mr. Wilkins' toast: "To a beautiful and noble lady," with a coy inclination of her head and a gaunt simper.

At the end of the meal, they were in a mood to complete affinity and secret geniality. Mr. Wilkins had had four glasses of the cordial, and Miss Beardsley three. He leaned towards her, and with much winking and noddings, whispered:

"A word to the wise, ma'am, and from one as knows the way the wind's blowin'. Sell your Gorth shares, and buy Livingston Cotton."

Miss Beardsley was all attention. "But, Mr. Wilkins, Gorth pays 12% on the preferred stock. And Livingston is a very small firm, very small indeed, Mr. Wilkins! And quite strug-gling——'

Mr. Wilkins was all significant solemnity. He raised his glass and eyed it with approval before looking at his hostess again, who was regarding him with avid speculation and passionate interest.

"Miss Beardsley, ma'am, 'ave I ever advised you wrong? You've made some proper profits on my advice. So again I advise you: sell Gorth, buy Livingston. In six months you'll thank me on your bended knees."

BOOK TWO

CHAPTER 17

No, NO, my dear," said Miss Amanda Beardsley in a pained voice, lifting her hand in an attitude of august patience, "a lady never cranes her neck to study the sway of her hoops or the folds of her gowns. A lady is oblivious of her garments. She glides, floats, in a radiant dream, always assured, always gracious. It is impossible to glide, to move with discretion and modesty and grace, if one is wondering as to the effect of her toilette."

Lilybelle Turnbull meekly paraded the long narrow parlour, trying to restrain her free milkmaid's stride into a gently tripping motion, small steps, toes pointing delicately. The big buxom girl literally sweated with her concentrated efforts, in order to acquire the necessary mincing walk. Her new black slippers, laced about her strong neat ankles with black satin ribbons, pinched her sturdy toes. Her full luscious figure was displayed very bewitchingly in a purple velvet gown with enormous tilting hoops. The very low neck revealed her milk-white full throat and shoulders; the latter were entrancingly dimpled. But when Lilybelle glanced down at the bodice a most becoming blush rose to her full smooth cheeks, for the division of her plump and pretty breasts was plainly visible. Her skin had a pearly translucence and glow delightful to see. Once or twice she furtively tugged at the edge in an effort to raise it to a more modest line. It was bordered in a wide band of imitation seed pearls, which glistened in the lamplight. Cascades of heliotrope lace drifted over the hoops, caught here and there with tiny cherry velvet bows. Her rich auburn curls were drawn back from her low white brow, fell in clusters down the nape of her neck almost to her shoulders.

A pretty creature, thought Miss Beardsley without envy, for she was fond of the girl, but over-coloured, over-flamboyant, and a trifle vulgar. Those cheeks were too full, too bright with colour, too lavishly decorated with dimples. Her round blue eyes could never remember to lower themselves with becoming demureness and decorousness, but must stare blankly if shiningly at any speaker. Her mouth, too, was not the fashionable dainty rosebud, sweetly pouting, but was big, generous, and very red. The nose, too, was unfortunate, with its resemblance to a pretty snout. Worst of all, the expression was forthright, childishly naive and stupid. Her large coarse hands, in the purple lace mitts, displayed awkward gestures, and she had a habit of trying to hide their imperfections in a fold of her gown.

However, thought Miss Beardsley, it is a veritable Venus, if somewhat overblown. She was pleased at the docility of the girl, at her passionate admiration of her mentor, at her eagerness to learn, her meekness under reproof. Miss Beardsley knew that here was no mouse of a girl, vapid and weak of temperament, but a sturdy peasant girl with a hot temper, a wild generosity of temperament, and a coarseness and vitality of emotion and speech. It was something to have obtained the adoration and admiration of such a one, and Miss Beardsley's tiny avaricious eyes softened a little. There was a fresh strong odour about the girl, an emanation of her flesh, which suggested warm sweet hay and foaming milk. Miss Beardsley had sprayed her subtly with eau de violets, and hoped that this would be discerned rather than the sweetness of her white flesh.

"Again, my dear," she urged. Lilybelle obediently paraded up and down. Now one saw that a backboard was strapped against her back. This was unnecessary, however, for Lilybelle had a straightness and buoyancy of carriage. The backboard was only to prevent her from turning her neck. She was very excited at the prospect of the party to which she was going within the hour, but very close to tears, also. Would she disgrace John? Would he be ashamed of her, among his fine friends? At the thought, the tears gushed over her eyelids, and splashed over her cheeks.

"Now, that will never do," admonished Miss Beardsley in a severe and bracing tone. "No, no, my child, how many times must I tell you not to wipe your eyes or nose on the back of your hands? Where is your handkerchief?"

Lilybelle fumbled blindly at her sleeves and her bodice. Sighing audibly, Miss Beardsley picked the kerchief from the floor, and gave it to the girl, who sniffled in it, then blew her nose vigorously. Miss Beardsley winced at the earthy sound. "That isn't done, Mrs. Turnbull. A lady wipes her nose invisibly, turning aside her head daintily. And she never, never, makes a noise doing it. That is very vulgar."

Lilybelle gulped, then suddenly giggled hoarsely. "Lady or not, my nose runs, and it won't stop with a bloody little wipe!" she exclaimed.

Miss Beardsley clapped her lean hands to her ears with a

pious ejaculation of horror. "My dear child!" she groaned, "how can you use such language! Have I not told you that ladies at all times must use the most decorous and restrained of language? Whatever would Mr. Turnbull say if he heard you?"

At the mention of her husband's name, Lilybelle's face became sullenly distressed. She twisted her handkerchief in her hands, and her bronze eyelashes flickered. Immediately, all her vitality and buoyancy disappeared, leaving her a mere big hulk of a young woman, awkward and uneasy in her purple velvet and cherry bows.

"I can't help swearing!" she burst out, abruptly. "Things is sometimes too much!"

Miss Beardsley shrewdly understood. She said mildly: "You wish your husband to be proud of you, don't you, Lilybelle? You wish him to approve of you? How can he do these things if you swear and are obstinate? You have only yourself to blame."

Lilybelle drew a deep shaking breath, and her hands clenched on the handkerchief. Her blue eyes flashed, and she said impetuously: "Miss Beardsley, ma'am, there's no pleasin' Mr. T.! He hates me. He never wanted—" She paused, and gazed at Miss Beardsley affrightedly, covering her treacherous mouth with her fingers.

But Miss Beardsley, understanding many things, continued in a practical voice: "Perhaps you haven't done much to please him, Lilybelle. Tonight he is taking you to a grand house, where you will meet fine ladies and gentlemen. If you give him occasion to be proud of you—and you are really improving—I am sure he will be very pleased with you. Now then, shall we walk a little more, sliding the feet instead of lifting them, so that the hoops do not swing so violently from side to side? The essence of the secret is that the hoops may sway so gently as hardly to be noticeable. They must give the impression that they are propelled by wheels rather than by the motion of one's feet."

Miss Beardsley mentioned "feet" with a pained look, as though they were members of the body whose existence must be ignored as much as possible.

Lilybelle shook her head so that the auburn curls flew and caught sparks of reddish light from the lamp, wiped her eyes roughly, and paraded up and down while Miss Beardsley critically watched every movement with growing satisfaction. Yes, there was a large grandeur about the girl, in spite of the vulgar high colour and the superabundant curves. Her waist, however, Miss Beardsley noted with regret, was not getting smaller, but really larger, and the bosom's swell was increasing. This could not be from overindulgence at the table, for the girl's hearty appetite had shown symptoms of failing. A possibility occurred to the virginal mind of Miss Beardsley, and she blushed. She remembered that at times Lilybelle had precipitously left the table in the midst of a meal, and had fled from the room, not to return.

A baby in my house would be impossible! thought Miss Beardsley, with annoyed asperity. Consider the probability of diapers floating in her fine austere garden, and the wails of an infant in the night! It was not to be thought of. She must find a way to express her objections with the utmost delicacy to Mr. Wilkins. Then, as she thought of it, staring broodingly at Lilybelle, she felt a dim pang. Poor young creature, with such an unbearable husband! Too, she, Miss Beardsley, would be quite desolate in her lonely house if Lilybelle should go. The girl's admiration and worship of her would leave a blank behind. No one had ever admired Miss Beardsley before, and she found the experience very pleasant and warming. I shall think of this later, she thought to herself, and uneasily suspected that she was losing her "character."

Following this train of thought, she said aloud: "Lilybelle, you must remember that a true lady is distinguished by 'character.' It is a very mysterious essence, and can only be acquired, when one is not born with it, by unremitting discipline and determination. It is composed of restraint, control, integrity, self-respect, honour and an acute awareness of what is proper and dutiful. It is polished, too, by graciousness, decorum and good manners. A woman who possesses it need have nothing else. A woman who does not possess it can have everything else and she will have nothing. Do you understand?"

Lilybelle paused in her pacing and gazed at Miss Beardsley blankly. Then she said in her loud and hesitating voice: "Yes, ma'am, in a way, I think I do. I was brought up proper like, and taught not to lie or steal or gossip, or be greedy. My Ma says a lass must mind her tongue, and be kind to her neighbours, and speak well of others. That's character, she says. Fine manners is for the gentry, she says. But poor people must have character."

For some reason Miss Beardsley felt a queer embarrassment. She said lightly: "I would say that fine manners are the outcome of character, Lilybelle." She paused, and looked strangely at the girl. "What did your mother mean when she said poor people must have character?"

Lilybelle fumbled for words, knitting her light brows as she concentrated. "Well, ma'am, I suppose it's this way: if you've got money, you only need manners. You don't need character. Everybody'll like you just for your money, if you don't up and offend 'em too much. But a poor man's just got himself, and he must needs make the best of himself. He ain't got any money to apologize for him."

Miss Beardsley was startled. She eyed the girl searchingly. Was the child unconsciously subtle? Was she deeper than suspected? But Lilybelle gazed back at her with simple candour.

"Lilybelle," said Miss Beardsley, with an unusual softness in her hard tones, "you are a very good girl. I am sure that no one could help but love you."

Lilybelle's full round face changed; her mouth trembled, and tears of gratitude and pain filled her eyes. She caught Miss Beardsley's mottled and bony hand and kissed it impulsively. "O ma'am!" she cried, "if that was only so!"

Miss Beardsley, unbearably and mysteriously touched, sighed. She touched the bent curls with a gentle hand, then pressed strongly upon them. "Dear child," she murmured.

She had never been so stirred in all her barren and fruitless life. And because of this, she was acutely embarrassed. She patted Lilybelle's head again, then rose briskly.

"I see you have such a lovely turquoise bracelet, my dear. And I believe that somewhere I have a silver and turquoise necklace to match, which belonged to my mother. Allow me to beg you to wear it with your costume."

Lilybelle was so young that her moods could change quickly. She wiped her eyes vigorously, tossed back her curls, and smiled down at her bracelet. "It was Mr. Wilkins as give it to me for my birthday." Then remembering the painful episode of the presenting, her mouth shook. Then she continued bravely: "It was too small. Mr. Wilkins took it to a proper man who made it bigger."

Miss Beardsley left the room to get the necklace, and Lilybell stood and stared at her reflection in the long pier mirror. After casting a furtive glance at the door through which Miss Beardsley had disappeared, she preened to her heart's content, struck attitudes, curtsied, dimpled, and arched her neck. She took a simple delight in her handsomeness. She minced about, her arms extended, her curls swaying. Then, as she heard Miss Beardsley's slithering step on the polished floor without, she stood rigidly like a soldier at attention.

The necklace, all spun silver and round mottled turquoises, dangled from Miss Beardsley's hand. She clasped it about Lilybelle's neck. Ah, a lovely effect, if somewhat theatrical. Yes, Lilybelle looked like some young stage person, of whom Miss Beardsley did not approve. But all at once a vision of the pale and decorous and dun-coloured ladies which Lilybelle would meet in Mr. Gorth's fine house swam before Miss Beardsley's eyes. She smiled slightly and grimly. Among that drab assemblage Lilybelle would blaze like a bird of paradise. What a sensation she would make among the gentlemen! As if her vitality was not enough, her vigour and her flamboyancy, she would dazzle and confuse with her colour, height, figure and strong beauty. Miss Beardsley was satisfied.

Impulsively, she laid her long lean hands on the girl's shoulder and kissed her cheek. Surprised at this, but immensely delighted, the girl flung her arms about her mentor and squeezed her with such joyous strength that the breath was quite crushed from the older woman's lungs. But under her discomfort her heart was beating with a strange warmness, and her mean little eyes were blinded in mist. The strangest thought came to her: This might be my daughter, if I had married!

They heard the front door open, then shut with a loud bang, and then John's hard impatient footsteps ascending the stairs. Lilybelle rushed to the door of the parlour and shouted: "Mr. T.! Do come here and look at me! I'm grand!"

John, halfway up the stairs, paused, scowling, his hand on the banister. Reluctantly, his face dark and repressed, he descended the stairway, and came slowly into the parlour. He shot a swift glance at Miss Beardsley, and his mouth tightened. The old bitch! he thought, for the liveliest hatred existed between him and his landlady. Then, looking at Lilybelle for the first time with a seeing eye, he was taken aback. He was stunned by her beauty and her spectacular costume. He stared, his mouth dropping open.

All day he had fiercely contemplated not going to the dinner at the Gorths'. The humiliation, the misery of old memories at the sight of the loathed Andrew Bollister, were more than he could think of without despair and hatred and fury. If he did not appear, it was probable that the offended Mr. Gorth would sack him. That would not annoy him too much. It was unendurable to continue to be employed by the uncle of Andrew Bollister. But that very afternoon Mr. Wilkins had appeared like an apparition, without warning, at his side as he laboured over his desk, and had whispered swiftly:

"Trust me, Mr. Turnbull, sir! I'm one as knows wot 'e's doin'. Three months, like, and it'll be done! But go tonight. You'll understand, soon, wot I've been gettin' at."

John, who had not had an hour of ease since his betrayal of his employer, and who had spent sleepless nights wondering what his strange rotund patron was to do with the important information which he, John, had stolen, had regarded Mr. Wilkins with unfeigned detestation. And Mr. Wilkins saw this, and knew it. If he was to have John completely, John must go to that dinner. Until he did, he would always be wavering, always unsure, always tormented by a conscience which even now could lacerate him. For Mr. Wilkins well knew who the bride of Andrew Bollister was, and he knew that she was the cousin of John Turnbull, and once his betrothed. Until John saw her as the wife of his enemy, he, Mr. Wilkins, could never be entirely sure of him.

"I don't think I will go," muttered John, doggedly, with fire in his dark eyes as he looked with disgust at Mr. Wilkins.

"You must," said Mr. Wilkins, urgently, and he was very earnest about this. "Give me three months, sir, and it'll be done. In the meantime, rein in your hosses."

He had persuaded John, who had gloomily and irascibly agreed to go. But all the way home the young man had been tortured by memories, griefs and hatreds. He finally came to the conclusion that he must go alone. He would present his apologies to Mr. Gorth and his lady, saying that Mrs. Turnbull had been "unwell," and had been unable to avail herself of the gracious invitation. John could not endure the thought of entering that elegant drawing-room in the company of his coarse and vulgar barmaid wife, and watching the venomous derision and satisfaction in the eyes of his old enemy, who had brought him to this pass. At that thought, John felt maddened, felt the old lust for murder, and had stood immobile for some moments on the street, clenching his fists. It was too much! Lilybelle should not go.

Now, here was Lilybelle, decked out in splendour, glowing, radiantly if too strikingly beautiful, and too colourful. After her first impulsive movement toward him, she had shrank back, and now stood perfectly still, her arms a little lifted at her sides, her head thrown back, her body upright and a trifle rigid. Yet, despite her immobility, which resembled a statue's, she palpitated. Everything about her was sparkling and welling. John, for really the first time, saw the pearly translucence of her neck and bosom and shoulders, the brilliance of her curls, the redness of her lips, the stateliness and full-blown beauty of her figure.

She was gazing at him eagerly, with shyness and hope, for all her new restraint. He saw that she was much improved, and vaguely remembered that lately her voice was softer and quieter, her manners better. (He had not known of the secret sessions with Miss Beardsley.)

And now he thought: Gad, she will make a sensation! No doubt Andrew, who had arrived a week ago at his uncle's house, (though not yet having appeared at the warehouse) had already regaled his relatives with the story of John's downfall, much to their amusement. They had doubtless invited John and his wife for the pleasure of watching his discomfiture and mortification in the presence of his barmaid wife, who they had been told was a coarse and illiterate creature. Ah! but they would laugh on the other side of their faces tonight!

He smiled, and his smile was dark and excited. Now, if he could just persuade Lilybelle to hold her tongue and keep her silence, all would go well! He extended his hand and indulgently turned her about, in order to look her over. He missed nothing. The girl glowed and trembled under his touch on her bare arm and shoulder.

"Is she not beautiful?" said Miss Beardsley. John started at the unexpected sound of her voice.

He knew she was a lady of breeding, and had mistakenly suspected that she despised him for his mésalliance with a barmaid. He had thought that she detested Lilybelle, and had only suffered her presence in her house for the sake of Mr. Wilkins, and himself. What could a lady like Miss Beardsley have to do with a Lilybelle? He had suffered excruciating torments when he imagined what Miss Beardsley must think of his wife, and her secret derision.

Yet, here was Miss Beardsley surveying Lilybelle with pride, as though she had created her, and with deep affection. There was no patronage in her august manner, but only real if cold delight. Her head was on one side, her hands clasped before her. She resembled a gaunt but benevolent old vulture. There was real tenderness in her eyes.

More and more confused and startled, John gazed again at Lilybelle. Now if Miss Beardsley really found Lilybelle presentable, and worthy of her patrician admiration, he could be certain that others would find her so, too. John was incredulous, but oddly intoxicated.

"I will do, Mr. T.?" asked Lilybelle, timidly. She gazed at him with frightened adoration, for even her simplicity divined that strong and turbulent thoughts were assaulting him.

"Of course you will do!" replied Miss Beardsley vigorously, divining John's emotion with extraordinary acuteness. "You will be quite the belle of the ball, Mrs. Turnbull. You will create a sensation. New York ladies are so dull and spiritless. You will quite dazzle every one. You look quite— French," she added, with only the slightest distaste at the word.

Miss Beardsley's words (as she suspected) were the final undoing of John, and all he needed to convince and fortify him.

"Where did you get that necklace, Lily?" he asked, and in spite of his attempt at sternness, his strong voice was gentle and indulgent.

Lilybelle's fingers flew to the jewelry, but Miss Beardsley said calmly:

"It was my mother's, Mr. Turnbull. No one has ever worn it since her death, for I have never before seen any lady worthy of wearing it, or one who could confer such distinction upon it. It completes Mrs. Turnbull's costume, does it not?" And she looked at John fully and blandly, without her usual coldness and dislike.

John was stupefied. He bowed stiffly. He said: "You have done my wife an honour, ma'am."

"It is she who honours it," replied Miss Beardsley, with dignity. She turned to Lilybelle: "My dear child, I have not lent the necklace to you. I beg you to accept it. My mother would have been delighted."

"Oh, I couldn't," murmured Lilybelle, overcome with delight, but gazing fearfully at her husband.

"Don't be so uncouth, and so ungrateful," said John with severity. He turned to Miss Beardsley again, and bowed more deeply. "My wife accepts, ma'am, with tremendous gratitude." In spite of himself, his voice faltered, and he said on a rush: "You can't know how happy you've made me, Miss Beardsley!"

Lilybelle listened with bewilderment, staring first at one and then the other, but Miss Beardsley smiled grimly and imperceptibly under her long Phoenician nose, and inclined her head.

"I am afraid the other ladies will be sadly neglected tonight, Mr. Turnbull. But don't let her head be turned, for she is so young. She must not forget," and she turned with a stately sternness to Lilybelle, "that her first duty is to attend upon her husband, in spite of the compliments she will receive."

"Oh, I will, I will!" murmured Lilybelle, quite overcome, and close to tears. She did not know what all this was about; it was sufficient for her to realize that John was pleased, not angered. She did so fear his rages.

"I hope," said John, with Miss Beardsley's own severity, (which seemed to league him as an adult with her in the face of Lilybelle's youth and inexperience) "that she will be an honour to you, ma'am." He felt the most mysterious affinity with his hated landlady, and exchanged a subtle smile with her.

"Come, my love," he said, taking Lilybelle by the hand, "I must dress. Have you thanked Miss Beardsley properly?"

CHAPTER 18

M̲R. RICHARD GORTH, among guests and friends, was known as a jolly soul, ready with rich ruddy laughter and a jest. One careful to observe, however, would have detected the fact that he laughed the loudest and with the most sincerity and spontaneity when some one's good name, foibles, eccentricities or character was under discussion, or preferably, under doubt. Let a woman's reputation be winked at, a man's honour or integrity questioned, a joke told against a friend, and then came Mr. Gorth's shaking harsh mirth accompanied by a cruel harsh glitter in his eye. It was also observed, however, that Mr. Gorth, though encouraging the speaker, and laughing most enormously at his tale, rarely added anything to it, or made an original observation of his own about the person under discussion. This gave him the name of not being a gossip, of never "saying a bad word about any one." If he repeated what he had heard, (and he always managed to do that) he gave due credit to the informant, and quoted exactly, with perhaps a chuckling and deprecating word of his own. "I fancy it is all fabrication," he would say. Thus it was that he also had the repute of defending others. It was convenient. Mr. Gorth had ruined more men and plunged more women into despair than any other man of his acquaintance.

He deceived every one except his wife and Mr. Wilkins, and a very few others.

Tonight, the occasion for his mirth was his trusted secretary, John Turnbull. "Oh, come now," he said, several times to his nephew, Andrew Bollister, "you aren't implying that Johnnie isn't to be trusted?"

To which Andrew would reply in his toneless and neutral voice: "Johnnie can be trusted. He hasn't the brains to be anything else but trustworthy." A remark which made Mr. Gorth appreciatively hilarious.

The dinners were excellent in the Gorth mansion on lower Fifth Avenue, for despite the fact that Mr. Gorth was an Englishman, he was a gourmet. He had brought a French chef, whom he had discovered in a Parisian café, to America, at a fabulous salary. Again, despite his English blood, Mr. Gorth was a cosmopolitan. His home, of chaste white brick, with a white door decorated with brass knocker and fittings, was in remarkably good taste. He had, in the course of his business, travelled in the Southern States, and had been most agreeably impressed by the lovely architecture of the planters' houses. But he was clever enough not to try to reproduce it exactly in the bleaker and more sterile atmosphere of New York. He contented himself with the general façade of a planter's home, eliminating the pillars and upper gallery, thus presenting to the quiet stretches of Fifth Avenue a distinctive and dignified home, smooth and white of face, tall yet wide, gracious and symmetrical. But the great tall windows were there, low of sill, protected halfway by wrought iron grills, gracefully curved. The front doors were enormous, also grilled, and the narrow lawns in front of the house were an incredible emerald green despite the heat and dust of the summers.

Like many men with dirty souls, he had a passion for order and cleanliness. If there was soot in the neighbourhood, it appeared to avoid staining even one white brick of the Gorth mansion, or dulling the glittering expanse of the mighty windows. Even the trees near the kerb were perfectly matched, never revealing a perforated leaf or a blasted twig. Each day two servants washed outer window sills, polished knockers and plates, dusted grills, scrubbed doors, rubbed up windows, picked up stray leaves or chaff, swept walks and washed doorsteps. In the midst of tall narrow brownstone palaces, severe and ugly, the Gorth mansion was a jewel of white and orderly beauty. Yet, it was not incongruous, not at all suggestive of the South. It fitted its surroundings.

Mr. Gorth's taste extended to the furnishings of his home. His wife, (the former Arabella Worthington of Philadelphia, and a descendant of the original Quakers) could not be trusted, in his estimation, to furnish even a kennel. (Though she had furnished the original fortune which had enabled Mr. Gorth to steal the business of his former employer, Nathan Appleton.) Mrs. Gorth ran rather to the lush opulence of New York than to the taste of her forebears, and would have filled her house with massive mahogany and tortured ebony, thick dark carpets and heavy drapes with huge gold tassels, and bathrooms all carved oak. But Mr. Gorth personally selected every article in the house himself. There were no ornate vases, no fringes, no fretted wood, no plush or velvet here. He had combed Europe thoroughly for the finest pieces of furniture, simple and waxed to a shimmering patina, but irreproachable and pure of line and exquisitely executed. He had avoided anything Latin, for Italian and Spanish furniture gave him a gruesome feeling, and was vaguely suggestive of plague, Popery and vermin. It did not matter to him whether the piece were antique or new, so long as it carried with it an impression of dignity, simplicity and unaffected beauty. He had a love for Oriental rugs, but not the Turkistan, which he declared made him think of American Indians, with its dark patterns, geometrical lines and raw colours. Only the Persian pleased him, for their delicate colouring, flowery grace and subtle blending of tints appealed to him enormously. These rugs were spread on floors so polished that they glittered in the faintest light, and gave an atmosphere of freshness and airiness to every room. Hating clutter, he had few pieces of furniture even in his drawing-rooms, and the upholstery was of damask, dim silks and faded tapestry. He ran to the Chippendale, but not the Chinese motif. His fireplaces were of pure dull white marble, and the ornaments also suggested the Chippendale, and the Dresden. (He loathed Chinese bric-a-brac, and could see nothing lovely in Japanese prints, either. Perhaps the latter's lack of a third dimension irritated him for some obscure but interesting reason.) Mrs. Gorth would have loved to have cluttered the chaste austerity of the mantelpieces with vases and clocks and other decorations, but Mr. Gorth left them severely alone, enhanced only by an oval mirror over them or an excellent portrait.

Andrew Bollister, who had the conviction that America was a country of rude barbarians, was quite astonished to discover such taste, such beauty, such light and airiness in his uncle's home. He could find nothing which offended his own meticulous taste. The dining room, with its creamy walls, its polished floors, its light and beautifully carved mahogany furniture, entranced him. The cloth was of the finest lace, the silver thin and fragile, the china pure white and delicately embossed. Moreover, the dinners served to him were distinguished by the most subtle flavours, the service impeccable.

Mr. Gorth had been readily accepted into New York's budding but tight society. This was partly due to his wife's unassailable position, and partly because it was well-known that Mr. Gorth himself came of an excellent upper class English family, if one somewhat impoverished. Now that the Irish, and other "lesser breeds" were invading New York, it was more necessary than ever to narrow the confines of true society in order not to admit one who had the slightest taint in his ancestry. The rich Mr. Gorth, therefore, with his Quaker wife, his lovely home, his excellent cook, his reputation as a host, his irrefutable taste, found every desirable door open to him. The great leaders in trade and finance came here freely, pressed invitations upon him, and plotted their skullduggeries and impressive thefts with him in his gracious library panelled with white wood. He had a faintly patronizing air towards them, for, after all, they were of Dutch ancestry, and not to be considered in the same class with an Englishman. Moreover, their origins in America were not of the most savoury, and in spite of their mansions and their wealth, one could not forget fur caps, leather coats and the pungent odour of Northern trade. So, Mr. Gorth was not above playing pranks upon them, to lower their dignity, and so he would often invite an obscure little trader to dine with more august company, or include such as Mr. Wilkins for their discomfiture. He knew that new aristocracy was very sensitive, that a lady whose grandmother had dwelt in a log-cabin or had scrubbed the floors of her betters was easily bruised in her sensibilities, and that a gentleman whose father had cleaned his own trapped skins with a dull knife, and had used raucous and illiterate speech, could not bear the presence of any one who was not of the most refined and irreproach-able family. Mr. Gorth, whose own family was truly ancient and cultured, if of the smaller gentry and nobility, found all this diverting and amusing. The portraits in his drawing-rooms were authentic, which could not be said of the por-traits in the other mansions in New York, and he could point to a painting of a fine lady of the sixteenth or seventeenth century and say: "This was my great-grandmother, or my great-great-grandmother, Lady Elizabeth Cowles-Broughton." He had no particular pride in ancestry, and found it some-what foolish and ridiculous, but it delighted him to see awe and furtive discomfiture on the faces of his New York visi-tors who had secretly purchased old portraits in Holland, England or France, and now palmed them off as representing illustrious forebears. "You see, I have the Astor nose," a lady would languidly say, indicating the cracked dim countenance of some female who doubtless would have expressed horror at this infamy and sudden relationship had she been aware of it. So, Mr. Gorth found his dinners very diverting and extremely amusing, as he found all pretense and falseness and shallow mean lies.

"These Americans," he would say to his wife, observing her wincing and dull flush, "are all the descendants of gaol rats, petty criminals, drabs and harlots, incompetents and little adventurers. It does me good to discomfit them."

In a way, however, Mr. Gorth was a true democrat. He did not truly estimate a man on the basis of his ancestry, but on the firmer ground of his ability, his superior genius in the field of larceny, his rascality which might approach the point of genius, and his machinations. Let a man reveal these admirable traits, and he had all Mr. Gorth's admiration, and was assured of a frequent chair in his dining-room. Especially, if he could increase Mr. Gorth's fortune by a hint here and there. Therefore, Mr. Gorth was indeed a real democrat, the forerunner of those who would build America to the highest eminence in world affairs.

They were awaiting the arrival of their dinner guests, seated in the airy drawing-room. Mr. Gorth allowed his satisfied eye to dwell upon his nephew, of whom he was more fond than he would admit. Andrew was at home here in this mansion, seemed more fitted to it than his uncle, himself. That suave urbanity, that cold malicious amusement, that slender elegance, completed the effect of distinguished and flawless perfection. Even his neutral voice, considered and cold, enhanced the air of civilized completeness.

He had listened to his uncle's cautious if enthusiastic approach with utter smiling impassivity. He was properly grateful, attentive and respectful. He showed no resistiveness, no superiority. Mr. Gorth again was satisfied. As the days had passed since Andrew's arrival, he became more and more certain that the lad would become a permanent fixture in Richard Gorth, Cotton Exporter. He had not yet entered the offices or the warehouses, but he had shown secretive interest, had asked intelligent questions, had made strangely astute suggestions. Tomorrow, he was to visit the warehouse.

Moreover, he and his uncle had understood each other from the start. They had seen each other only once, a year ago, in England, and immediately a great and edifying rapport had sprung up betwen them. This was the son I should have had!

Mr. Gorth had contemplated some difficulty in the person of the young lady who had married his nephew. She had a mother, it was reported to him, a sufferer from some sort of some obscure ailment. She might not desire to live in America, away from friends and family, and so might persuade Andrew to return. Young English ladies were notoriously disdainful of America, and coolly amused at its roughness and uproar. But to Mr. Gorth's amazed and delighted gratitude, young Mrs. Bollister had expressed her considered opinion that she would like to remain in this new land, and her quiet approval, calm and toneless, conferred a compliment upon America which Mr. Gorth sardonically told himself ought to be received with humble and adoring gratitude by that country. Though he was proud of his English ancestry and birth, he secretly loathed and despised and ridiculed the English for a race of people who had a delusion of superiority, a delusion shared with their cousins, the Germans. He admired his countrymen for their ruthlessness, but derided them for covering this ruthlessness with a polite and moral polish, as if Biblical texts and noble sentiments uttered in measured tones would deceive others as to the underlying exigency and greed. "Be a scoundrel, but don't be a damned hypocrite about it," he would say. "Stand on your sins, and be proud of them, and damned to the rest of the world." It was the Englishman's refined aversion to admitting his rascality which so annoyed Mr. Gorth, who had no such reticence himself.

He had quickly taken the measure of young Mrs. Bollister. Ah, a ruthless piece, cold, authoritative, determined, inflexible and relentless! And a lass with a mind, and with hard sharp thoughts of her own, too. An excellent wife for Andrew, one of his own kidney. Mr. Gorth was gratified at the strange resemblance between the young man and his bride. A fine pair. He had soon discerned that Andrew, despite his reserve, was overwhelmingly in love with his young wife, and for some mysterious reason, seemed to be constantly amused by her.

Mr. Gorth, even while he conversed with his nephew tonight, kept glancing furtively at his newly acquired niece. Not pretty or buxom, perhaps, not of any obvious or startling loveliness. But he was a connoisseur, and the blatant never appealed to him. He admired her hauteur, the cool disdainful curve of her mouth, the tilt of her small gleaming head, the large chill brilliance of her gray eyes. This was a lady, and Mr. Gorth excessively admired ladies. Their control and repression hinted of delightful things when the icy barrier was broken down. There was no opulence about them, no obviousness, and Mr. Gorth loved the subtle.

Though so small, she had an admirable and perfect figure, he thought. Her taste was perfect. Clad tonight in rich wine-dark silk, the bodice a waterfall of deep creamy lace, her neck and little white shoulders revealed in their dainty perfection, her smooth brown hair parted and rolled with simplicity and decorated by one or two dark red rosebuds, he could find no fault in her. About her neck she wore a slender chain of garnets, and there was a bracelet of the same stones upon her wrist. When she breathed, so quietly and slowly, little jets of crimson flame danced over her white skin. She sat with grace and silence in her armless chair, the voluminous hoops belling about her, and her whole attitude expressed compact control, authority and pride.

Her manners, too, were exquisite, perfectly suited to every occasion. No wonder she made poor Mrs. Gorth look like an elderly spinster servant despite the new French gown of vivid blue velvet which the lady had donned this evening.

For Mrs. Gorth had no taste at all. The blue velvet, with the immense hoops, the lace and bows and intricacy of her toilette, were grotesque on that large masculine frame, enhanced the yellowish cast of her coarse skin which no emollients could soften, and increased the sallowness of her big lean arms and leathery neck. Mrs. Gorth had never been a beauty. Her fortune had been her chief attraction, but until the scheming Mr. Gorth had chanced by, no suitor, however indigent, had been able to overlook that furtive cavernous countenance, those little muddy brown eyes, that hawklike nose, that mean tight expression full of piety, envy and spite, that little puckered mouth pursed so primly into a look of chronic meanness. Her dull brown hair was coquettishly dressed this evening in a coiffure of lank curls, utterly unsuitable.

Even her hatreds were not strong, though constant and poisonous. When she saw her husband's affection for his nephew, she hated Andrew with a vitriolic detestation quite unusual for one of her monotonous temperament. She hated Eugenia for her youth and delicate breeding and exquisite manners. She regarded both as interlopers, but was helpless to destroy them. Since their coming, she prayed nightly that they might remove themselves, or die.

She sat on a love-seat of buttercup satin with Eugenia, her jaundiced long face set in an expression of prim politeness, apparently listening to the girl's quiet and even voice. But her sluggish little brown eyes were fixed upon her husband, as usual. She tried to listen to everything that was said everywhere, for she was suspicious by nature, and either hoped to hear a derogatory remark about herself or a vicious remark about an absent acquaintance. She fingered the greasy curls at her ears and at the yellow nape of her furrowed and oily neck, and occasionally, as Eugenia paused, she pursed her dry and puckered lips in a mechanical smile. Mrs. Gorth exhaled an odour of musk, for she was lavish with scent as if to hide the stench of her own spirit. Eugenia found the odour unbearable whenever Mrs. Gorth would lift her fan of blue ostrich feathers to create a restless breeze about herself. Then would Eugenia lift her own fan, of white lace, and create a gentle counter-wind.

Andrew had expressed himself with frank surprise that evening that America was far more agreeable than he had expected. With smiling candour he informed his uncle that he had not expected such genteel and civil gentlemen and ladies in New York, but rather bluff coarse traders and buxom peasant wives. Richard Gorth smiled. "You were not really mistaken, Andy," he said. "Your first impression was quite right. But they are slowly acquiring a gloss."

Mrs. Gorth broke feverishly into speech, in the middle of some remark of Eugenia's, which indicated that she had not been listening to the girl at all:

"Oh, these Americans are so unrefined, Andrew! You have no idea! It is a great trial to entertain them!"

Her voice, uneven and cracked, made Andrew wince. He raised his blond brows courteously. "But you are an American, are you not, Aunt Arabella?"

A rough flush rose under her yellowed skin and she tossed her head uneasily. "I never was, at heart, Andrew. Not at heart, even though I was born here. And now I am an English subject, through your uncle."

Andrew's brows remained elevated, though he said nothing. But Richard Gorth scowled, and his pale eyes, so like Andrew's, shot a baleful gleam at his wife.

Because he found looking at his wife so oppressive, he glanced at Eugenia for refreshment. Andy was a lucky dog to be able to sleep with this formidable young creature and conquer her. Mrs. Gorth, seeing his glance, gave Eugenia one of her own, furtively malefic. She whined, after a titter: "O Mr. G., you know you really find Americans odious! You've said so, yourself."

Mr. Gorth looked at her with bland brutality. "Only to you, my dear," he said, smoothly. "And only when I mean it."

This passed completely by Mrs. Gorth, who looked blankly baffled as usual whenever her husband made one of his ambiguous remarks. But Andrew touched his delicate lips with the tips of his fingers to hide his smile, and looked swiftly at his young wife. She had lifted her fan swiftly to cover the lower half of her face, and her eyes met Andrew's. Before she could control herself she had exchanged a look of complete accord and discreet and mirthful understanding with him. Then as if she remembered that she disliked him, that she truly loathed him, she cast down her lashes, dropped her fan, and allowed him to see that her face was stern and withdrawn. For some reason this amused Andrew.

As if she felt his thought, she looked at him straightly with intense coldness, and lifted her head with bitter hauteur. This further amused Andrew. He bit his lip. Only last night she had clung to him with wild grief, weeping in his arms, and then as his tenderness deepened to passion, she had thrust his arms from her and had fled from him. But he remembered how soft and misty her gray eyes had appeared for an instant or two, how bewildered, how shamed and lost. He felt

182

that she was one of those who, once convinced of a thing, once set upon a thing, must, to maintain their own confidence and self-pride, cling to it grimly, and would pursue it until exhausted.

Since she had known that John was to come that evening, she had displayed a hard repressed restlessness that day. She seemed to lose flesh even in a few hours. There were mauve shadows in her cheeks, and her eyes were over-brilliant. Her emotions communicated themselves to Andrew, in spite of his self-control.

It was then that Richard Gorth, who had spoken often to his nephew about John Turnbull, made his remark that he trusted his new secretary. Andrew had replied in his languid and sardonic tones, but he watched Eugenia as he spoke. Her lips had parted, pale and dried.

Andrew had not yet told his uncle of his last meeting with John, but now he did so, with so much wit and vivid detail that Mr. Gorth listened with delight. But Eugenia's small pointed face became transfixed as though she tasted immense sickness in her mouth. As for Mrs. Gorth, she smiled with sly pleasure, and licked her lips furtively.

"He appeared to think," said Andrew, with a lift of his bloodless hand, "that I had something to do with his marrying that impossible barmaid. A plot, sir, nothing less than a plot. Of course, I did not struggle with him. That would have been quite beneath me. The strange thing is that I had no real animosity towards him at any time, though I always considered him a boor—" He inclined his head towards his wife apologetically. "Please forgive me, my dear, I often forget he is your cousin." He resumed: "Because he was so loud and boisterous, he had few friends at Carruthers'. He always seemed excessively uphappy, too, and I was quite sorry for him. I had the impression that he was lonely and bewildered, so tried to be a friend to him."

At this, a strange dark gleam passed over Eugenia's face. It was a brief and evil light, and seeing it, Andrew was sincerely disturbed. He frowned momentarily.

He continued, with less assurance, and more incisively: "I repeat, uncle, that I have no animosity towards him, and am pleased that he has obtained a post in your firm. I only hope that he has become less violent and unreasonable, and that he will realize that I do not intend to come into conflict with him. I hope, too, that he has not forgotten that it was I who recommended that he approach you for a post before we had our—disagreement. I even suggested that I correspond with you on the matter. Apparently, though, by some fortuitous

183

circumstances connected with your Mr. Bob Wilkins, this was not necessary."

"Wilkins," said Mr. Gorth meditatively, "says he has a 'nose,' and that that worthy organ detected Johnnie long before he actually saw him."

"A mystic," commented Andrew with a smile, but with an uneasy eye on his wife, who seemed to have sunken into some deep apathetic meditation of her own.

Mr. Gorth laughed. "A fat rosy mystic, then, if he is. But you'd go far before you'd find a more subtle and useful man. By the way, he is dining with us tonight, also."

At this, Mrs. Gorth broke out into a flutter. "Dear me, Mr. G., I did not know this! You never condescend to inform me about my own guests, and I find this very distracting. Is it not bad enough to entertain a—a creature who served liquor to coarse gentlemen without being afflicted by Mr. Wilkins, who is no gentleman, and has no gentility?"

"I take exception to your remarks, ma'am," replied her husband. "Mr. Wilkins has my highest respect. He has a great heart. He has assured me of that, himself," he added, with a wink at his nephew.

Ignoring his wife, then, and her whining flutters, he continued to discuss Mr. Wilkins with his nephew. "A rascal, Andy, if there ever was one. A mountebank, malefactor, and blackguard and thief. But a very useful man. And quite delightful to converse with, his remarks always distinguished by shrewd wit and pungent observations."

"I found him very interesting, when he visited me in England," said Andrew, abstractedly. He was filled with a cold and wandering apprehension as he gazed at Eugenia out of the corner of his eye. Now he acknowledged to himself frankly that he had believed that upon meeting her cousin and his wife, upon hearing this conversation about him and observing Mr. Gorth's faintly contemptuous if indulgent attitude towards his new secretary, she would be embarrassed, her pride aroused, her native inexorability awakened and strengthened. But nothing that had been said about John had caused a flush to appear upon her cheek, an embarrassment to make her lips uncertain. She seemed to be congealing into a statue of ice. For the first time he guessed the full depths of her strength and implacability and pride. And, he thought, her vengefulness. For now, she suddenly lifted her eyes to his, and he saw her naked hatred, her wild and frozen antagonism for him, and her despair.

CHAPTER 19

THE FIRST guests were arriving, a bevy of ladies elaborately dressed and begemmed, fluttering their fans and conversing in the bright twitters suitable to the occasion, and elegant gentlemen in gleaming hats and cloaks. Behind them, like a fat and jovial rooster, Mr. Wilkins beamed sunnily. Mrs. Gorth rose with magnificence, and discharged her duties as a hostess. Behind her stood Eugenia, in her deep and, to Andrew, her suddenly terrible silence. She was deathly pale. But she smiled frigidly at her aunt's guests, and her curtsey was controlled and graceful. She acknowledged every introduction with dignity, her head tilted. Her breeding antagonized the ladies, charmed the gentlemen, but intimidated them. Though so small, so slight, so silent, she threw the ladies, for all their finery, quite into the shade, made their dull haughty faces appear plebeian and coarse, their studied manners affected. There were thick diamond necklaces galore, and heavy diamond bracelets, but Eugenia's delicate garnets made the former take on a vulgar look, and dimmed them to a glassy lustre. Her contained and perfect gestures seemed to make their own gauche and awkward, her cool tranquil voice, when she spoke, contrasting so acutely with the voices of the ladies that they sounded too shrill, too hard and too loud.

No one but the watching Andrew saw the rigid intensity under her quietness, but later Mr. Wilkins was to discern this also. Now that ebulient and cherubic gentleman came forward, bowing at each step, blushingly affable, radiating cheer, respect and passionate admiration. His bald pink head almost touched his knees when he was presented to Eugenia, and this combined with his lavish and courteous speech spoken in purest Cockney, brought the first involuntary smile to the girl's face, even though the barely perceptible gleam of moisture on her brow testified to the inner stress and anguish which were almost destroying her. She surveyed his gray broadcloth, cut cunningly over his plump belly, his polished boots, his astounding weskit, his fluted linen and amazing cravat, and her lips drew in involuntarily.

As for Mr. Wilkins, though he appeared not to be doing anything of the kind, he was keenly studying and analysing the young lady. In a few seconds, he had such an understanding of her as to be almost incredible. Her faults and her virtues were arranged in orderly columns in his mind, and her probable responses to all circumstances and provocations.

When she glided away to assist her aunt with the ladies, he looked after her with a malignant smiling point in his eyes. Then, with this same expression, his eye passed over all the others. So Lucifer might gaze. He knew them all; he had assisted them all, "for a fee." These were the courtiers of his vast kingdom, the nobles of a foul world of greed, rapacity, cruelty and murder. In a way, they were his servants, his panderers, for all he appeared to serve and pander to them. He looked at the smirking and attitudinizing ladies, the bowing and grinning gentlemen, and his round fat mouth twisted. He could destroy them all, if he wished. The thought of this power did not exhilarate him. He only hated them the more. He accepted their lofty condescension, their agreeable smiles, with the proper servility and eagerness, but he knew how they searched him, wondering how they could use him again. Within five minutes at least six gentlemen had furtively whispered in his ear, asking his opinion about certain stocks, suggesting that he call upon them in their offices.

He was relieved that John and Lilybelle had not yet arrived. He wished to be on hand when John encountered his cousin. It was very important for this to be so. Then he could judge.

The voices in the drawing-room rose to an amiable confusion. Fans fluttered, hoops tilted and swept, tittering laughter mingled with the booming of men's mirth. The radiant lamplight gleamed down upon jewels, bare necks and. arms, and dainty slippers gliding over the soft luminous rugs. The fire on the white marble hearth roared and snapped. Mr. Wilkins was not unsusceptible to beauty; he looked at everything approvingly, nodding his head sagely, meanwhile, as two gentlemen simultaneously tried to get his large roseate ear.

Then, Mr. and Mrs. John Turnbull were announced. The name evidently meant nothing to those assembled, for they turned and stared curiously at the still empty archway. Mr. Gorth hurriedly explained that the gentleman was his new secretary, also cousin to his new niece. Faces became satisfyingly respectful and anticipatory.

John and Lilybelle appeared in the archway, and a deep silence fell in the room. The young man and his wife were suddenly transfixed by two dozen pairs of staring eyes and blank secretive faces. They stood there, dazzled and confused, more than a little awkward and distrait, and unsure of themselves, John's handsome face darkly flushed, his eyes glittering belligerently, his big round head with its black curls held in a defiant attitude. As for Lilybelle, lurking timidly at his side, her gaudy beauty appeared overwhelmingly theatrical. She was obviously frightened, for her cheeks flushed and paled, and her large hands fumbled with the cherry bows on her purple velvet gown. She knew that John was suddenly and wildly ashamed of her, that some vast wretchedness and despair had taken possession of him, and that because of all this, he was frantically enraged.

Because of his own tumultuous emotions, John could not at first distinguish or recognize any particular face. Mr. Wilkins took this opportunity to pluck fervidly at his host's sleeve. Mr. Gorth had taken a step or two towards his new guests, and glanced down impatiently at his agent.

"Mr. Gorth, sir, beggin' your pardon—a word," whispered Mr. Wilkins, urgently. "It's somethin' I've just come across, today. That bloke, there, I didn't know. But your nevvy's wife was the lass he was goin' to marry, and which he was done out of, by Mr. Bollister."

Mr. Gorth halted abruptly, and glared at the other. His strong rectangular face suddenly became suffused with hard colour. "The devil," he muttered. "The devil, Mr. Wilkins." He paused, and then said viciously: "You knew this, Mr. Wilkins!"

"Not till today, sir, not a bloody thing," repeated Mr. Wilkins, with such a sincere and artless air that Mr. Gorth was almost persuaded to believe him. "I'd 'ave told you, sir. I tried, tonight, but there wasn't no opportunity."

Then Mr. Gorth knew that this creature lied. His fists doubled. His pale eyes stretched until they were a whitish glare. If he had known, even an hour ago, he would have sent a hasty message to John announcing that the dinner had been postponed. Even half an hour ago, he thought, furiously. It was too late, now. What had this mountebank in mind, this affable thief and liar?

He and Mr. Wilkins looked at each other steadfastly. Mr. Wilkins' round pink countenance expressed nothing but sympathetic concern. Mr. Gorth ground his teeth together, turned away and proceeded towards John, followed by the twittering and awkward Mrs. Gorth, whose simper was very patronizing and arch. Mr. Wilkins, after a faint smile, followed them unobtrusively through the passage made for them by the guests.

Mr. Gorth was maddened. The purplish flush had receded from his face, and it was now as gray as winter ice. He was in a devil of a predicament. Even his short acquaintanceship with John had assured him that here was a character full of violent impulses and tumultuous reactions. There was no predicting what he would do in a few short moments. Mr. Gorth's rage mounted. But, as he looked at John, now not more than two feet distant from him, he was seized with a harsh and reluctant pity and a real concern. He had come to be fond of his secretary; he relied upon him, admired the dogged and angered persistence with which he attacked a problem. He trusted him. Now he must appear to the young man to be an enemy, one plotting with condescending contempt behind his back for his discomfiture and humiliation and pain.

He seized John's cold and clammy hand, and forcibly turned him slightly from the others. He took no notice of Lilybelle, though before he had heard the devastating revelation from Mr. Wilkins he had been struck by her beauty and her lavishness of young figure. Mrs. Gorth, nonplussed at the sudden action of her husband, stood uncertainly behind him.

Mr. Gorth, by his sheer will, forced John to look at him directly and to forget his embarrassment for a moment while he listened.

"Johnnie! You must understand. I didn't know until a moment ago, when that stinking Wilkins told me. If I had known, whilst you were still at home, I'd have sent you a message. I'm damned sorry, lad."

His rage and indignation temporarily choked him. His iron fingers tightened on John's hand. The young man, who had been smiling mechanically, now frowned. But he answered quietly enough: "It's quite all right, sir. I knew Andy Bollister was your nephew, that he would be here tonight. There's no love between us. But I hope I am gentleman enough not to cause you any awkwardness."

Mr. Gorth's purplish slash of mouth divided, and John saw the glisten of his yellow teeth in something which had no resemblance to a smile. He heard a quick harsh sound as his employer drew in his breath. But he lifted his head angrily when he detected pity and impotent fury in Mr. Gorth's glacous eyes. Their fishlike quality had disappeared.

But despite these evidences of fulminating wrath, Mr. Gorth's rough voice was still quiet: "It's worse than that, my lad. Brace yourself. You are a man, and you must face this." He paused, then said in an even lower voice, hurried and pent: "Andy's wife's your cousin, Johnnie. Did Wilkins know? Didn't he tell you?"

John listened. All expression vanished from his face. He

stood and looked at Mr. Gorth. His flesh took on the hue and texture of stone. Mr. Gorth felt the hand he held grow cold and stiff as ice. He felt a strong rigour pass over John's body, an arching rigour like the last convulsion of a dying man. Then he looked away from Mr. Gorth and stared blindly, like a statue, at the opposite wall.

Mrs. Gorth coughed delicately behind her husband. "Really, my dear," she simpered. "Your guests. You must introduce me." She ignored poor Lilybelle, standing a little apart, her face puckered in an expression of childish perturbation.

Only three of the guests, Andrew, Eugenia and Mr. Wilkins, saw anything strange in this quick interchange between Mr. Gorth and his new guest. To the others, this seemed polite exchange of greetings, with perhaps a private aside, and they elaborately took up their conversation again until such fit time as they were introduced to the new arrivals. But Eugenia stood in silence, no less pale than John. She had understood that John knew of her marriage to Andrew, but all at once she was overwhelmed with terror and faintness. For, as she saw his look, she knew that he had not been informed, that Andrew had kept his silence for just this hour of sadistic pleasure, that his uncle had been ignorant of everything. As for Mr. Wilkins, lurking modestly near his hostess, he said nothing, and wore only a fixed and sympathetic smile. Once he glanced at Lilybelle, and thought: Ho, my lass, we've got our revenge, eh?

"Believe me," said Mr. Gorth urgently, ignoring his wife, "I didn't know, Johnnie. Think I'd humiliate you like this?" He wet his dry lips. "Don't give 'em the satisfaction, Johnnie. Buck up. Brace yourself. You are a man."

John's face changed again. It had a look of death upon it. What a hellish trick to play upon this young and vulnerable man, and under what circumstances! He had thought his own ruthlessness immune to compassion for others. Had he been only a spectator, and had had no personal fondness for John, he would have enjoyed this. There was no enjoyment in him now.

He urged again, putting his hand on John's sleeve, careless of whatever his guests might be thinking: "Buck up, Johnnie. They're looking at you. You'll not give them the satisfaction, eh? You're a man, Johnnie."

John did not move or answer. He seemed so stunned, so frozen, that he might have been blind or deaf. Mr. Gorth eyed him apprehensively. How soon would the reaction come? What would it bring with it? With a strange helplessness, he turned to his wife, and said: "My dear, let me present Mr. Turnbull and his lady."

Mrs. Gorth, who had noticed nothing except that her husband had been remarking something inaudible to the young man, arched her neck, smirked condescendingly, and croaked: "It is a pleasure, I am sure, Mr. Turnbull."

John heard her voice. He turned his dull glazed eyes upon her. His lips moved slightly. But that was all. Then, stiffly, as if his arm was made of wood, he indicated his wife.

As if John had spoken to introduce his wife, Mr. Gorth, in relief, turned quickly to Lilybelle, nudging his wife sharply to draw her attention to the girl, for she had begun to stare in puzzlement at John. "So, this is Mrs. Turnbull," said Mr. Gorth, in loud delight, taking her slack hand and bowing over it. The girl surrendered to him, limply, for she saw nothing but John and his anguish. She did not know the cause. It was enough for her that he looked like death, itself. Wild panic suffused her. Her mouth fell open on what sounded dangerously like a sob. When Mrs. Gorth curtseyed only very slightly, the girl turned to the woman with an abrupt start, and gazed at her with glazed eyes. Then, after a moment or two, her shaking knee bent stiffly.

The moment had arrived to draw John and his wife into the circle of the guests. Sweat bedewed Mr. Gorth's fixedly smiling face. He took John's arm with exaggerated familiarity and pulled him along at his side. He uttered a few bright words. John walked beside him, blindly, moving as stiffly as a marionette. His head was bent a little; his feet stumbled. Mrs. Gorth followed with the silent and trembling Lilybelle.

Mr. Gorth hoped savagely that that accursed Andrew and his wife would be the last to be introduced. He observed that they had withdrawn to the fringe of the group of guests. For one moment he saw Eugenia, and he understood a great deal. But Andrew was smiling wickedly to himself.

As for John, after the first crushing immensity of the horror which had fallen upon him, he felt nothing at all. Colour, light, movement, walls, floor and men and women had merged together in a great blinding swirl before him. He felt himself swaying and tottering, and all at once it became most enormously important to him that he keep his feet. There was a frightful rocking nausea in his middle; he felt cold wet fingers running up and down his back. His physical sensations were too intense to admit any thought to their crowded arena.

Mr. Wilkins followed behind the ladies. He walked gently, on the balls of his feet. Had any one noticed him at the moment, he would have seen him nod very softly to himself.

Now Mr. Gorth had a sudden inspiration which so relieved him that he felt quite weak, and there was a rush of salt water into his mouth. He began the introductions. The ladies curtseyed, the gentlemen bowed stiffly. Mr. Gorth, still holding John's arm, felt his automatic dazed response, and knew that he saw nothing. He raised his voice loudly and genially:

"Mr. Turnbull has just informed me that he must leave almost immediately, on some important matter. I am sure that we are quite regretful."

This surprising remark, and John's own face, which in contour and tint resembled wet clay, would have immediately engrossed the curious attention of the guests had not Lilybelle compelled every eye with her height, figure, toilette, bright hair and pretty wholesome freshness. The ladies only half heard Mr. Gorth's soothing regretful words, for they were enviously and maliciously studying every curve of Lilybelle's arms and neck and bosom, calculating the origin of the purple gown, estimating the value of her turquoise jewels, concluding that the tint of her curls was artificial, and that she was quite astoundingly vulgar, and not at all genteel. Literally yellow with envy, they lifted their fans to their lips and tittered meanly behind them, and archly whispered to their neighbours. If Eugenia's elegance had made them appear gross and cheap, Lilybelle overpowered them so that they resembled dun peafowl. As for the gentlemen, they were overcome with admiration. Such glowing health, such pearly translucence of exposed bosom and neck, such glorious shimmering hair, such vitality of line and movement, intoxicated them. There were furtive lickings of masculine lips in the wretched Lilybelle's wake, and glances too bold, eager and lustful. "Gad, a beauty!" they whispered to each other. "A lusty piece," said others. "What a warm baggage, what an armful!" said still others. It was no wonder, then, John's obvious illness, his somnambulant walk, his blind staring eyes, escaped all but the most passing and indifferent attention. If any one did remark it, he concluded that all this was but the natural reaction of a young ill-bred man in the midst of superiors.

Mr. Gorth had faced many difficult and dangerous experiences in his exigent and relentless life, but none of them affected him as did this experience. He was vaguely astounded at his own inner shaking and disorganization. The pangs of pity were so unfamiliar to him that he hardly recognized them. These unpleasant sensations increased as he approached the worst moment of the ordeal.

Eugenia stood beside her husband, but slightly behind him,

her head bent, her face half concealed by her fan. But under lashes, fixed and rigid, she watched the approach of John and his wife. Her white fan emphasized the gray pallor of her small face. One flicker of her eye had passed over Lilybelle, and her eyelids had contracted, and she had winced a little, not with affected fastidiousness, but with real revulsion. The knuckles of the frail hand that held the fan turned white and blue.

Andrew waited easily, slightly smiling, his slender head with the painted silver-gilt hair gleaming under the light of the great crystal chandelier. He himself, felt no apprehension, but only a wary amusement and quiet disdain. He loved the discomfiture and misery and pain of others, and enjoyed them objectively, especially if he despised them. He watched John's blind approach, saw that he walked as if drunk or wounded. His eye flickered over Lilybelle, and he felt a momentary surprise and curiosity. Though his taste rejected the flamboyant and the too gaudy and obvious, it was, nevertheless, aroused to a more sturdy interest. Too, he was faintly annoyed. The girl was very suitable for stupid old Johnnie, if the fool would only see it. Much more suitable than Eugenia, standing in such a vacuum of silence and coldness beside her husband, and affecting him whether he would admit it or not with her bitter stillness. There was a kind of physical harmony between John and Lilybelle, as there was between Andrew and Eugenia. If only old Johnnie, and that silly little Eugenia could see that! reflected Andrew, with fresh surprise.

Now the meeting was inevitable, was at hand. Richard Gorth, smiling fixedly, his harsh face furrowed with his efforts to maintain an appearance of ease and heartiness, lifted his eyes and met those narrow glinting ones of his nephew. The smile remained, but Andrew, to his languid inner mirth, saw the sudden savage fury that boiled in his uncle, a fury which would have intimidated any one else but Andrew. He felt a rustling movement near him; Eugenia had uncontrollably started, and he laid his hand lightly upon her arm. But that arm jerked away from him as though convulsed.

The moment had come. "You know Andy, Johnnie! And, we've a surprise for you!" exclaimed Mr. Gorth, feeling as if his casklike chest was contracting painfully about his heart. "Your cousin, Johnnie, Mrs. Andrew Bollister! Thought we'd keep it a surprise for you, finding her here in New York! Mrs. Turnbull, ma'am, my nephew, and his lady, Mrs. Turnbull."

Andrew, smiling, bowed. Eugenia moved slightly, in a

curtsey. But John neither bowed nor inclined his head. He stood and looked at Andrew and Eugenia, slowly, steadfastly. The blindness was gone from his eyes. There was a terrible quiet awareness in them. And, as John stood there, so rigid and impassive, without a word or a movement, the suave smile faded from Andrew's face. He regarded John without flinching, but his lips tightened slowly, and he appeared to recoil without actually making the slightest motion.

John gazed at Eugenia, and she returned his gaze proudly and silently. But her eyes pleaded desperately with him, hopelessly. He made no gesture of recognition. Very slowly, Eugenia's pale face flushed deeply and thickly, and her throat contracted.

Andrew had not expected this. He had not dreamt of such control on the part of his enemy. He had wondered if John would break out into wild threats and imprecations, and create a disturbing scene, which would furnish him, Andrew, with amusement, and great entertainment for the guests. Then Uncle Richard would be impelled, later, to sack the blackguard without Andrew lifting a single finger to bring about that pleasant culmination. He had half believed that John might attempt to assault him, which would be very ludicrous, and bring forcibly to Eugenia's mind the impossible and odious character of her cousin.

But John betrayed no indication that he was about to explode into unseemly violence. He stood there before his enemy and his cousin for long moments, only his eyes aware of them, and they were appalling in their expression, so full of loathing they were, so full of frozen abhorrence and detestation. It was as if he found them too abominable for petty violence, too despicable for a word from him.

Andrew found all this very extraordinary and baffling. John was not proceeding according to type, and in accordance with former indications of his character. Before silence, before immobility that suggested a deep horror of him and his wife, Andrew was impotent. Richard Gorth, seeing all this, felt a sudden slackening of relief in himself, and sudden malignant gratification. Andy was not to have his circus, after all. As for Lilybelle, she stood forgotten.

Then John turned quietly to his wife, and spoke softly: "Come, my dear." He took the girl's trembling arm, and piloted her back through the now completely silent and curious guests towards the door. He moved without haste, and with a strange new dignity, his head high, his eyes ahead. If there was a taste of death, of mortal illness, in his mouth, he did not betray it. It is true that deep blue lines had appeared about his white lips and about his eyes, but there were no further signs of the bottomless agony within him.

A carriage was waiting in the quiet street outside. John helped his wife to enter. In a controlled voice he gave his destination, and the carriage started up. It was Richard Gorth's vehicle; that quick-witted gentleman had ordered it for his departing guests.

Lilybelle was terrified. John sat beside her as if made of stone. Something awful had occurred, but the girl could not understand it. A streetlamp shone on John's stiff features, which had a kind of contortion upon them as if he had been seized with physical anguish, with overpowering torture. Breath was suspended on his lifted and twisted lips.

She forgot her own terror in her overwhelming compassion for him, and touched his arm, murmuring to him. He started violently. He turned and stared at her, awareness of her presence slowly and horribly dawning upon him. He struck off her hand; he thrust her from him so ferociously that her head crashed against the window of the carriage. He cried out, his hoarse voice broken by the most appalling dry sobs:

"O damn you, damn you, damn you! You drab, you trollop, you slut—you foul thing!"

Later that night, when the guests had departed, and Andrew and Eugenia were about to go to their apartments, Richard Gorth suddenly and brutally turned upon them.

"You," he said to his nephew, "you damnable blackguard! Why didn't you tell me that you had married the woman you had done him out of? You told me nothing but that she was his cousin, you scoundrel and liar!" He choked, coughed, turned purple. "I can see it all now! I remember how you came mincing to me, saying how capital it would be to surprise your old 'friendly enemy,' introducing him unexpectedly to his cousin! Never at any time did you inform me that he didn't know she was married to you, but you were quick enough to urge me not to betray your accursed simpering secret! Oh, it would be capital, it would!"

Andrew tried to smile and shrug. "It was impossible for me to know, uncle, that he would misunderstand this way. He was always an unreliable and unpredictable scamp. After all, he was married, himself. Why should it have mattered to him who Eugenia married, after he had jilted her? Did he expect her to sit in the chimney-corner the rest of her life and mourn after him?"

Richard Gorth stared at him, baffled. Andrew's words were reasonable enough. But he shouted, turning an even brighter purple: "Oh, use your smooth words to me, you liar! There's more to this than what meets the eye, I can tell you!"

He swung upon Eugenia. "And you, ma'am, it was a cruel jest to play upon your cousin! How could you look at his face, tonight, without shame?"

Eugenia did not answer him. But she lifted her head proudly and looked at him. The gray brilliance of her eyes was suffused with tears. She rose with haughty dignity and left the room. Richard Gorth watched her go, confounded. Yes, there was more to this than what met the eye.

Mrs. Gorth, in the background, tittered happily to herself.

CHAPTER 20

THE SPRING night was warm and exhilarating. Mr. Wilkins had enjoyed the walk from the Gorth mansion to the residence of Miss Amanda Beardsley on West Fourteenth Street. Standing before the latter house, he looked up to the third floor, where a light still burned. He nodded his head with satisfaction, opened the front door with the key recently and amiably furnished him by Miss Beardsley in order that he might visit his young friends without the inconvenience of waiting for admission, and disturbing her own household at odd hours.

He climbed the stairs softly, like a fat cat, for his step was very light. He reached the door of the Turnbull apartments, saw a gush of light exuding out from under it into the dark corridor. He tapped gently, then opened the door.

His first impression was of complete confusion, though not an article of furniture had been disturbed and the polished floors gleamed in the light of a lamp on a distant table. The disorder apparently came from John Turnbull, who had been pacing wildly for hours up and down his severe gaunt living-room. He had torn off his coat and cravat, and was in his shirt-sleeves, which were rolled back revealing his strong brown arms. His neck, so like a corded column of brown marble, was also fully displayed. He had run his distracted hands so often through his hair that every thick black curl stood upright all over his big round skull in damp and vital springs.

Mr. Wilkins' entry had evidently interrupted hours of

frantic pacing, for John stopped abruptly in the very motion of walking. Seeing Mr. Wilkins, a look of the most frightful hatred and fury shot across his haggard and distraught face, and he uttered a hoarse and incoherent imprecation. Lilybelle was nowhere to be seen. Mr. Wilkins thought that he heard prolonged moaning from the other room.

If Mr. Wilkins was momentarily taken aback by the expression in John's eyes and upon his face, he did not betray this. He, himself, had assumed an aspect of mournful solicitude, tempered by grave indignation.

He held out his hands, and said in a rich trembling voice: "My poor young friend! Wot I've suffered for you! And wot a dastardly plot to 'oomiliate you!"

Never was compassion more rosily expressed, never were bright tears so obvious in the opaque hazel eyes, never did a fat round mouth reveal so much righteous anger and grief, never did hands tremble so convincingly! Even John in his wretchedness and madness could see all this. The fury and hatred sank into sick dullness on his face, whose grayish cast deepened. Then once again it was alive with wild despair and loathing, and he raised his clenched fists.

"Why did you not tell me before I went to that place?" he cried, in a choked and suffocating voice. "I could kill you, you piggish swine, you pink mountebank and liar! Why didn't you warn me? It was little enough to do!"

Mr. Wilkins' countenance revealed nothing but sorrow and vicarious suffering. He shook his head a little, dropped it, sighed.

"You knew who she was! I'd told you!" panted John. "Yet, you hadn't even the common decency to warn me!"

Mr. Wilkins lifted his head and gazed steadfastly at John, with such affection, such simple grief, such shock, that the young man's voice dwindled into a breathless squeak.

"Mr. Turnbull, sir," began Mr. Wilkins, sadly, "did you think it of me? You thought I knew, eh? That's a bad and ungenerous thought, Mr. Turnbull. True it is that you told me the young female's name, from the beginning, but never did I know it was one and the same as was married to Andrew Bollister. Not till tonight, sir, I swear it. 'Ow could I think a young female as 'ad given her word to you, before a certain night, sir, would up and marry your worst enemy? It ain't in hooman nature, sir, it isn't that. It's a plot, sir, an unChristian plot."

These words were so extraordinary, and Mr. Wilkins' attitude so humble, so grief-stricken, so sincerely sympathetic and indignant, that John fell into desperate silence, clenching and unclenching his hands, his distraught face wrinkling and twisting. But his loud and torn breathing filled the room.

Mr. Wilkins cautiously laid his hat, gloves and cane on a chair, shaking his head dolefully meanwhile. Then he straightened bravely and regarded John with noble affection. and determined courage.

"You'll not condemn a bloke afore he's heard, sir? It breaks my heart, indeed it does, that one as I've regarded as a son and a friend, and 'ose welfare's so close to me thoughts, should jump to unworthy conclusions. If I'd known, if I'd 'ad an inklin', sir, you'd never have gone to that 'ouse, or known nothin' abaht that young female. I'd have protected you, just.

"It wasn't five minutes afore you came, sir, that Mr. Gorth draws me aside, laughin' a little, and says: 'We've got a capital joke on Johnnie Turnbull, Bob! It's his cousin as is the wife of my nevvy, the female as he was goin' to marry before a better man whisked off with her. This will be amusing, Bob Wilkins!' "

John uttered a loud cry, and looked about him with a frenzied aspect, as though searching for a murderous weapon.

"And wot does I say, Mr. Turnbull?" continued Mr. Wilkins, advancing a step towards the delirious young man, but not removing himself too far from the door. "I says: 'For God's sake, Mr. Gorth, let's warn the lad! Send out a messenger, a footman, to warn him orf before he sets foot in this door! It's a 'orrible thing, Mr. Gorth, and I'll not be accountable. I love that young feller like a son! I'll not 'ave it, Mr. Gorth,' I says. 'It's not to be thought of,' I says. And wot does Mr. Gorth say, eh? He says: 'O come now, Bob, let's 'ave our joke! Andy insists on it. It won't 'urt Johnnie, and will put his back up.'

"And then," added Mr. Wilkins sombrely, "you comes in, sir, with your lady, looking like a princess and puttin' all the other ladies in the shade so that they quite turned yellow. It was a beautiful sight, Mr. Turnbull, and it fair broke me heart. It was too late to warn you. I could only 'ope you would conduct yourself with genteel breeding, as you did. It was proud I was of you, Mr. Turnbull, under such circumstances. I understood, then, 'ow it was I'd cottoned to you from the very start. It fair made me proud."

His voice shook; he cleared his throat courageously; he choked again, and wiped his eyes unaffectedly. He faltered, as if struggling with gushes of tears:

"And to think 'ow I've served Mr. Gorth! You'll pardon me, Mr. Turnbull, if I says me heart is breaking; me sensibilities allus rush to the surface when there's been injustice done. 'E knew, Mr. Gorth, as you was like a son to me, and that I brooded over you like a blasted hen over a chick. And so, it's a capital return 'e's made to me, treating you as he did. And me rememberin' 'ow loyal you've been to him, 'esitatin' over givin' me wot I needed! But in me heart I allus knew. That's why I arsked, Mr. Turnbull; that's why I insisted. Ye see, now?"

But John hardly listened. His features contorted sharply in a savage grin. "So, it was a capital joke, was it? It was a plot, was it?"

"That it was, sir! I can see it all now. It was done to both of us, to you and me. From the beginnin', it was plotted." He paused, then said resolutely, "So, wot's to be done, Mr. Turnbull? I'm your man. You can allus rely on me to stand by your side and defend you. Only an hour ago I says to meself: 'Bob Wilkins, you've done with Gorth. Him and you's got nothin' more in common. You've done with him, for good and all. It's you and Mr. Turnbull, now, against the whole blasted world.'"

As if his passions, his rages and despairs had overcome him at last, John suddenly fumbled blindly for a chair, fell into it, leaned his elbows on his knees and bowed his head in his hands. Mr. Wilkins looked at him; the most gloating and malevolent light flashed across his cherubic countenance. It was gone. His former expression of studied and eloquent grief replaced it.

"You and me against the whole blasted world," he repeated in a grave and sonorous voice. "Wot d'ye say, sir?"

But John did not answer. He sighed, over and and over. His hands clenched; he rubbed his fist grindingly against his forehead. At last he muttered in a stifled voice: "I can't endure it! I can't endure it, I tell you!"

"You won't 'ave to endure it, sir!" said Mr. Wilkins, sturdily, now laying his hand with strong affection on the young man's shoulder. "If you remember, I'd told you to stand it for three months longer. That was before I knew. Now, it's done. You'll not go back to that ruddy place. It's me and you against the world. Let Mr. Gorth whistle for us; he'll whistle his blasted throat dry. I've got somethin' in mind for you, sir, and a good thing it is."

He paused, then lowered his voice slyly, so that it had an insinuating and oily quality about it. He bent over John and whispered:

"There's revenge, sir, as goes out with fists and stones and brickbats. Vulgar revenge, as isn't liked by the police, and does no good, just makin' a laughin' stock out of a chap, or landin' him in gaol on his ass. No good at all, sir. And there's revenge as satisfies the cockles of his 'eart, and makes the other bloke gnaw his nails down to the quick, and ruins 'im. That's wot I've got in mind."

John lifted his head very slowly. He looked at Mr. Wilkins with haggard and sunken eyes, in which a black and virulent fire had begun to burn. Mr. Wilkins nodded with grim satisfaction and elation.

"That's wot I'm after, Mr. Turnbull: a proper revenge, for both of us. We'll ruin Gorth, that's wot we'll do. 'Ave I your 'and on it, sir? You and Bob Wilkins together?"

John gazed at the little fat hand extended to him in noble brotherhood, and he grimaced. "What can you do?" he asked, with profound and hating contempt, not taking the hand. But there was a note of hope in his tone.

Mr. Wilkins continued to extend his hand. He nodded again, with increasing exultation. "Leave it to Bib Wilkins, sir! I'm one as 'as ruined many a man who played a dirty game! There's many a one, in Lunnun and New York, as is grinding his teeth over Mr. Wilkins, and wishin' to God 'e'd never set eye on him or done him wrong. There's many as is bitin' the dust, now, this very hour, and regrettin' he was ever born. These is not idle words, Mr. Turnbull. I knows as wot I'm talking abaht. Are you with me, to the end, sir?"

Despite his despair and agony, despite his contempt and incredulity, John was struck by these words. His head ached with a splitting pain; there was a wide and throbbing wound in his chest. But now, as ever, numbness was coming to his rescue, easing the sharper agony of his torment. His fixed expression relaxed a little into one of grim and dawning hope and hatred.

"You can really do all this?" he asked. He cleared his choked throat, and rubbed his pulsating forehead.

"You can be sure of that, sir!" exclaimed Mr. Wilkins, strongly, lifting his rejected hand in a gesture like one taking a solemn oath. "I've made men; I can break 'em. You'll see! There'll come a day when you'll say to yourself: 'That Bob Wilkins is no fool. He's one as knows wot he's talkin' abaht, and no mistake.' That'll be the day when you'll be gloating down at Mr. Gorth, bitin' his fingers in the dust. And his precious silky nevvy with him, too!"

John sprang to his feet. He looked at Mr. Wilkins with ferocity, almost insane in its intentness.

"I believe you!" he said, in a pent low voice. "Damn you, I've got to believe you!"

He seized Mr. Wilkins' hand, and shook it frenziedly. Mr. Wilkins winced but continued to smile bravely and with high exaltation.

"You'll go to your bed, now, sir, and ye'll sleep, remem-berin' we've got work to do. You'll leave it to Bob Wilkins, 'ose never said an idle word. We've got our revenge to think abaht, our revenge on the Gorths and the Bollisters, and on females who've got no proper regard for the sensibilities of others. Eh?"

He reached up and laid his other hand on John's tall shoulder. The young man was trembling violently. He was gazing over Mr. Wilkins' head with a truly malign look, which destroyed, in one instant, all his youth and sanguine if uncontrolled generosity of heart.

"And now," said Mr. Wilkins, softly, "we'll 'ave that proper paper in your desk, eh, that you've not trusted Bob Wilkins with? That last patent, eh, as was goin' to Appleton? The one you've 'esitated to intrust to Bob Wilkins, and argued abaht?"

CHAPTER 21

Not far from the warehouse of Richard Gorth, Cotton Exporter, was the much smaller and much more dilapi-dated and failing firm of Everett Livingston & Company. At one time this firm had been exceedingly flourishing, and in command of the cotton export trade of New York. But the founder, and his son, the present Everett Livingston, had been distinguished by a rigid honour in all their dealings, and so were no match for the new species of trader which had sprung up in the past twenty-five years. The present Everett had discovered that fair dealing, scrupulous honesty and integrity could not survive in this new world of robber barons and expedient opportunists. But he was an old man now, and could not employ the tactics of his competitors. The habits of honour and honesty were too much for him; he had fallen into their set pattern, however much, at odd and silent moments, he wished he might be able to extricate himself. He was old, and he was unmarried. But Mr. Wilkins knew that in him was that inexhaustible greed which lived in all other men, and which was much more vulnerable, at a good opportunity, to vicious and rascally suggestion than it was in men more familiar with these things. "Give me a man as 'as been honest and aboveboard all his damn life," Mr. Wilkins would reflect, "and let him be down on his luck and starin' the work'ouse in the face, and there's nothin' 'e'll stop at, either for revenge or to 'elp 'imself."

Though he'd had only slight dealings with Mr. Livingston before, and then only obliquely in the interests of Gorth, Mr. Wilkins knew all about the old gentleman. He knew him for a proud and bloodless old bachelor, suspicious, rigid, of excellent and courtly breeding, impeccable old family, and high and relentless integrity. Mr. Livingston was close to seventy now, with a long and aristocratic face, sunken and lean, the skin pale and crumpled, the nose long and sharp and patrician, the blue eyes cold and repellent and full of suspicion. His white hair was sparse, but well-brushed and gleaming. The lobes of his ears were transparent and delicate, as were his hands. He spoke in a quiet but firm voice, and nothing disturbed his punctilious courtesy and elegant composure. When he looked at one, it was with such piercing and forthright attention that a pettier rascality than Mr. Wilkins' was immediately undone. His wardrobe was also distinguished by a refined elegance which all envied, and his walk and carriage were regal if somewhat stiff now.

Mr. Livingston was indeed a gentleman "of the old school," polished, dignified and upright, without passions or uncertainties, but very embittered during these past few decades. He was much travelled and cosmopolitan, and of exceptional discernment and taste. He spoke several languages, having attended the best universities in Europe, and his library, in his small and impoverished but still elegant home on West Tenth Street, was perfection and discrimination themselves. He had two elderly servants, man and wife, who had been in his service for over forty years and knew his tastes. His little house was so polished, so charming, so perfectly appointed, that all who entered were forever entranced.

Each Sunday, the ancient carriage was brought out to his door, surmounted by the elderly manservant in a patched and much worn livery, and Mr. Livingston, sitting upright in the vehicle, was driven to the small Episcopal Church on Broadway. Many New Yorkers in the vicinity were familiar with the carriage and its occupants, but Mr. Livingston was never known to nod or recognize any one. He sat in his carriage, upright as if carved, his gloved hands resting on his ebony cane, his tall hat shining in the morning sun, his many-caped coat brushed to the threads, his boots gleaming, his manner all authority and unshaking and royal pride. He despised the newcomers to his city, in which he had been born, and his father and grandfather and great-grandfather before him. He was of such family that his forebears had condescended with disdain to General Washington, and had considered him an insufferable and radical upstart. They had been irreconcilable Tories, and Mr. Livingston still draped the portrait of George III with the British emblem on his library wall. He spoke of the Queen with royalist reverence, and despised the raucous democracy of the new Republic. Because of his attitude, he had few friends, which did not disturb him. He would never have admitted the Astors and the Vanderbilts into his home anyway, under any circumstances. They were not gentlefolk. The Livingstons had nothing in common with them, would never have. They were of the hoi polloi, and their new affectations of "family" and tradition and aristocracy always brought a pale and virulent gleam of disgust and amusement to Everett Livingston's marble countenance. Otherwise, he ignored their existence.

Years ago, on the strength of Mrs. Gorth's forebears, Mr. Livingston had extended an invitation to dine to Mr. Gorth and his lady. He had also been impelled to this upon thorough if quiet investigation of Mr. Gorth's antecedents. Now Mr. Livingston would not tolerate a man of poor antecedents and obscure background in his home, no matter how upright, brilliant or noble such a man was, no matter how successful or accomplished. He preferred the company of his peers even if those peers were of poor and vapid quality themselves, and distinguished by no graces of character or soul. However, despite the fact that Mr. Gorth and his lady were Mr. Livingston's peers, or even "beyond" him, he could not endure them. This occasioned him much regret, and he turned with temporary relief to lesser gentlemen of his acquaintance who possessed finer and more lofty characters. But later he was very uneasy. Was it possible that he was becoming a democrat? This so horrified him that for six months or more he entertained nobody. He told himself sternly that he could not trust himself. That a Livingston could descend to entertain "nobodies" in preference to "somebodies" however contemptible, shook the whole foundation of his philosophy.

He despised trade, but as he was also possessed of a love for money, he told himself that he found something "earthy" in his firm. "Keeps a man's feet on the ground to occupy him. Brings him closer to the heart of things," he would say, with pallid sturdiness. He would have preferred, certainly, to have a private income far removed from the taint of "trade," but this not being possible, he brought "trade" in to the pure environs of his code and so purged it of grossness. This feat of egotism was very admirable, and astonishing.

At the present time the business of Livingston had so deteriorated that it brought in less than six hundred pounds a year. (Mr. Livingston preferred to calculate his income in British pounds rather than in vulgar dollars, a fact which embarrassed or coarsely amused those with whom he had dealings. "He thinks it gives an air of gentility to the damned transaction," one was guilty of saying.) Mr. Livingston had not been able to keep up with newer developments, with the new interlockings of the cotton trade with American manufacturers in New England, partly because of the rigidity of his mind which detested innovations, and partly because of his integrity.

There were those who fatuously declared that Mr. Livingston was possessed of a "genteel and patrician mind," unaware of and indifferent to the steady decay of his firm, that trade was "beneath" him. Like all fatuous and sentimental people, they were entirely wrong in their fond diagnosis. Mr. Livingston was only too poignantly aware of the decline of Everett Livingston & Company, and as he had the cold voracity of temperament which is one attribute of the aristocratic soul, and its secret and glacial rapacity, he was now at the point where he would do anything (provided he could retain to himself the delusion of integrity) to recoup his declining fortunes.

Mr. Bob Wilkins, who knew everything, it seemed, also knew this. Mr. Livingston, heretofore invulnerable to suggestion, was now a "man for his money." Mr. Wilkins' nose had lately begun its premonitory twitchings in Mr. Livingston's presence.

So it was, on this happy golden Spring morning that Mr. Wilkins alighted from his own carriage and entered Mr. Livingston's presence. He had been careful to observe the formal amenities, and had ceremoniously asked for the pleasure of this interview. Mr. Livingston knew Mr. Wilkins very well, if only from repute, aside from their very rare meetings. He had despised and ignored him as a vulgarian, a "feller," a panderer and servant to the less scrupulous and patrician. He had a vague idea as to the manner in which Mr. Wilkins served his patrons, for Mr. Livingston was no airy fool. Six months ago he would have ignored Mr. Wilkins' request, astutely understanding that where Mr. Wilkins entered he brought with him corruption, a stench, dishonesty, skullduggery and unashamed larceny. Moreover, he would have been appalled at the presumption of the "feller" daring to assume that such as Mr. Livingston would permit him to enter the aseptic offices of the company. What insolence to presume that Mr. Livingston would give ear to any foul suggestions of his!

Now Mr. Livingston also knew that Mr. Wilkins did not

bother with failures and potential failures, and that where he appeared there was the bright shimmer of possible gold, and the dazzling promise of unbelievable profits. Only two weeks ago Mr. Livingston had been inexorably faced with the probability of immediate bankruptcy. He had spent sleepless nights, contemplating the ignominy of such a thing occurring to Everett Livingston & Company. Why, this firm was rooted in the very history of New York, of America! It was not to be endured. It can be seen, then, that Mr. Livingston was in great if silent despair and shame previous to Mr. Wilkins' respectful letter asking for an interview at the noble man's pleasure.

He had sat immobile for hours, Mr. Wilkins' letter before him. He had no definite idea as to what Mr. Wilkins would suggest, but he knew it would be nefarious, involving all sorts of criminal and snide activities, all unscrupulousness. His first automatic reaction was to toss the letter aside in contemptuous silence. But immediately after this thought he was seized with such hope that he became quite weak, and trembled violently. Help was at hand, even if it was shameful and loathsome help. He paid Mr. Wilkins the compliment of conceding that Mr. Wilkins would waste no time on those who could not be salvaged brilliantly. He, Mr. Everett Livingston, obviously could be saved then, and not in a small fashion, but in a spectacular one. Mr. Wilkins did not play for pennies.

Mr. Livingston, meditating on these things, had covered his royal face with his long white hands, so delicately veined with blue threads. He began to sigh, over and over, with restrained sounds. But a lifetime of integrity was not strong enough to withstand the hope of rescue, the hope of profits. Mr. Wilkins never made a mistake. He knew that every man had his price, and that not two men in a single generation were ever immune to rascality, theft, and even murder. The rosy Lucifer with the infantile countenance knew his humanity too well. A lesser man, i.e., a nobler man, might have become a bitter cynic about men. Mr. Wilkins merely used them.

Mr. Livingston, after a whole day's desperate and agonized struggle with himself, had coldly if politely granted Mr. Wilkins this interview. Now, in his bare chill office, he awaited the arrival of the beaming saviour. He had never been of a warm and sanguine appearance. Today, he resembled a withered if imperial cadaver. He presented to Mr. Wilkins, as he entered bowing and sunnily dispensing his radiant smiles, the aspect of a severe and implacable judge. But Mr. Wilkins was not discomfited. He was even reassured. He knew the battle was already won. He had only to be discreet, with deference to Mr. Livingston's sensibilities. ("Let a bloke tell his little lies to himself as 'e's bein' honest and aboveboard all the damn time, and you've got 'im in the palm of your hand," he would say.)

One covert glance assured Mr. Wilkins that he had Mr. Livingston in the palm of his hand. There would be minor and dignified skirmishings of course, but such a clever chap as Mr. Wilkins would never present an opportunity for a serious argument, never give that latent integrity of Mr. Livingston's chance to assert itself. Everything would be quite frank and righteous between them. Mr. Wilkins, aside from his main object, was delighted. He loved such byplay. It refreshed his Satanic enjoyment at the spectacle of mankind's inherent virulence and hypocrisy.

Mr. Livingston inclined his head with haughty reserve in response to Mr. Wilkins' affable greetings, his expression of pleasure that he had been admitted to Mr. Livingston's august presence. This softened Mr. Livingston, brought him a mild relief. He gave a bleak and condescending smile, and indicated a chair.

Mr. Wilkins disposed himself in the chair indicated, with all decorum and stateliness, as befitting the occasion. If there was a preoccupied and serious air about him, that was well calculated, as was the wardrobe of smooth black broadcloth, severe white linen and black cravat. After the first sunny smile of greeting, he assumed an air of intense if funereal gravity, and looked at Mr. Livingston with respectful earnestness. All this was quite confusing to Mr. Livingston, who, on the few occasions when he had caught fleet glimpses of Mr. Wilkins, had designated him as a vulgar "feller," and one who was not likely to cross his patrician path except obliquely. Yet, here sat the "feller" now, looking quite the gentleman for all his rotund build, wearing an expression of severe dignity and grave alertness. Mr. Livingston was more and more baffled. Had his first impressions been wrong?

"You are a busy gentleman, sir," began Mr. Wilkins in a slow and unctuous voice, "and it is not my intention to consume too much of your time." Mr. Livingston, in response, inclined his head in an august manner. Had he been a man of humour, he would have smiled wryly, for no sounds of busyness were evident about them, but rather a foglike and empty gloom, as if all had moved away but the owner. The desolation of prostrate failure was all about them, in the cold bare office, in the lack of activity in the almost empty warehouse, in the dull far booming of harbour whistles, even in the gray set austerity of Mr. Livingston's countenance. Mr. Wilkins saw all this; he saw that only one sheet of foolscap lay on Mr. Livingston's small polished desk, and that there were no crumpled papers in the wastebasket.

Mr. Wilkins cleared his throat. He appeared to be thinking sad and embarrassed thoughts, for he stared at the floor and sighed. Then he lifted his pink bald head bravely and looked at Mr. Livingston fully with an air of desperate candour.

"I can be frank, Mr. Livingston, sir? I can say my say, and no offense? I can be assured that what I speak shall not leave this room?" His voice was strong and resonant, with just a manly tremor perceptible.

A crease appeared between Mr. Livingston's brows. He replied coldly: "I am not in the habit of betraying confidences, Mr. Wilkins. You can speak with all freedom."

"It is hard for me to speak," confessed Mr. Wilkins, looking aside as if sorely distressed and disheartened. "It is hard for me to tell one who is almost a stranger of the most dastardly plot and ingratitude it has ever been my ill luck to come up against. To no one else, sir, could I tell this story. But from the first I knew you as one who can be relied upon, and trusted, and can express himself with full indignation when somethin' comes up as would turn a heart of stone to fire."

The crease deepened between Mr. Livingston's brows at this extraordinary confession. A less naive and egotistic man would have smiled irrepressibly and have said: "Come now, man, let's halt this silly acting and get down to brass tacks." But Mr. Livingston, like all aristocratic egotists and lovers of self, was fair game for such as Mr. Wilkins, for he had the narrow innocence of his kind, and their complete and abysmal ingenuousness.

He said, with dignity: "This is very extraordinary, Mr. Wilkins. Please be more explicit." He added loftily: "If I can be of any assistance in righting a wrong, I am sure you need have no hesitation in confiding in me."

At these measured words, Mr. Wilkins suddenly became all ardour, all roseate passion. Tears actually swam in his eyes. He grasped the head of his cane with both hands, vehemently. He seemed to be having difficulty with his breath, and it was evident that he was overcome, for a moment, too deeply for speech. Mr. Livingston concealed his curiosity, but he felt a sharp sense of excitement.

"Did I not tell this to myself?" cried Mr. Wilkins, in a broken voice. "Didn't I say to myself just this morning: 'Go to Mr. Livingston! Tell him your story, Bob! There's a gentleman as will listen with sympathy and righteous indignation, out of his Christian charity and justice! Tell him 'ow you was betrayed, and your young friend with you, and 'ow there was some one plottin' to lay you both low and steal the very whites of your eyes! Tell him, Bob Wilkins, and you'll not regret it!'"

Mr. Livingston's curiosity betrayed itself in the sudden icy gleam in his eyes, in the sudden rigidity of the line of his emaciated jaw. Nevertheless, he became suspicious, and wary.

"I trust any revelation of yours will not bring unpleasant results with it, Mr. Wilkins?" he asked, with cautious hauteur. "Nor is it betraying the confidence of some one else? I cannot be party to a situation which would have disagreeable consequences."

Mr. Wilkins stared at him with such dignified wretchedness that Mr. Livingston became embarrassed. There was reproach in Mr. Wilkins' swimming eyes.

"Mr. Livingston, sir," said Mr. Wilkins, sadly, and in deep tones, "it is I as is the betrayed. O sir, wot 'as brought me to you? I do not know. But there's somethin', sir," and now Mr. Wilkins tapped his oaken breast solemnly and with measured strokes, "as 'as brought me to you." He implied that a mystic divinity or intuition had directed his steps to this office. He cast up his eyes for an instant with a look of profound piety. "If I'd stopped to figure it out, sir, in the light of cold reason, perhaps I'd not be here. But I'm one as goes by impulse, not questionin'. And I've never been wrong. 'Allus go by your mysterious impulses, Bob Wilkins,' I say to myself. And never 'as it led me astray, sir."

Mr. Livingston compressed his lips. He was impatient. But he found nothing ludicrous in all this. His curiosity increased enormously.

"Well, then, Mr. Wilkins, suppose you tell me? As you have remarked yourself, I am a busy man."

Mr. Wilkins inclined his head reverently in acknowledgment. "Don't I know it, sir! Don't I know that those as is noted for their honour and their integrity is always busy! Men you can trust! Rare in the world, Mr. Livingston, very rare. But there's a just Heaven!" resumed Mr. Wilkins after a moment, with a kind of elated and pious exaltation and enthusiasm. "There's a just Heaven! And when a chap does right, Heaven don't forget! Blessings, Mr. Livingston, come upon him, good rich blessings! Fortun allus attends the just and the upright."

Mr. Livingston's experience had never followed exactly this line, but he had never disbelieved in the bounty of Heaven upon those who deserved it. Sometimes Heaven was negligent, but never consistently forgetful. He leaned towards Mr. Wilkins with involuntary interest.

"It's yours to reject, sir," continued Mr. Wilkins, in that same high and hurried voice of exaltation. "Yours to reject, and nothin' else said outside this room. Yours to right a wrong and make a handsome thing of it, sir."

Mr. Livingston controlled himself. He forced himself to lean back with dignity in his hard chair. He began to tap his desk with his white and slender fingers, and regarded Mr. Wilkins intently. A febrile flush crept under his crumpled and imperial cheeks.

Mr. Wilkins, apparently still carried away by his enthusiastic and simple passion, leaned across the desk towards the old gentleman. "Mr. Livingston," he said, with shaking solemnity, "it's yours to right a wrong. And sir, wot d'ye say to makin' Everett Livingston and Company the world's leadin' cotton-print company?"

Mr. Livingston uttered a faint exclamation. Common sense returned to him. Angry and blasting confession sprang to his lips, repudiation of such impudent extravagance. For a blinding instant he saw Everett Livingston & Company for what it was, an obscure and dying little failure, surely beyond resurrection. Yet here was this insolent and ridiculous scoundrel suggesting the most impossible things.

"You aren't, by chance, Mr. Wilkins, making game of me?" he asked, in his quiet and disdainful voice. He made a slight motion as if to rise. "Let us be frank, Mr. Wilkins. Perhaps my company hasn't kept up with latest developments. We have preferred to pursue the old ways of integrity and close economy, detesting and suspecting the reckless extravagance and dangerous speculation of other companies. Because of our principles, our business has steadily declined. You are an astute man, Mr. Wilkins. You know all this very well. Yet, you speak quite wildly. Perhaps you have some dishonest scheme in mind. I can assure you now, sir, that I shall not countenance such a scheme." He added, with gloomy frankness: "Too, I doubt if any scheme of yours could possibly resuscitate us."

He was suddenly exhausted, and crushed. He sank back in his chair, dwindled and weak. He had never been so honest with himself before. Always, he had retained the delusion that though his company's trade had declined ominously and steadily during the last decade or so, it still retained its place in the world of affairs and was widely famous and respected for its integrity and fair dealings. He had deluded himself even in the face of evidence. Now, he looked starkly at the truth and was undone.

There was nothing Mr. Wilkins feared more than honesty and disillusion. Let a man look too long at the truth, and he was no longer a man "for Mr. Wilkins' money." Now there was no hypocrisy in the real earnestness of his voice:

"Mr. Livingston, sir, we all fall on evil days. Especially in a world of rascals and thieves. But, shall we lie down and let 'em trample upon us? Shall we doubt the ultimate triumph of an indignant justice? Surely, sir, you do not deny that justice, in retaliation, often offers us an opportunity to recoup our fortunes and lay low our enemies?"

Mr. Livingston was silent. He was still crushed by his wretched look upon truth. But a faint bright hope began to dawn in him. Mr. Wilkins, who had begun to sweat, sighed in himself with relief.

He clasped his fat little hands on the desk, and leaned urgently towards Mr. Livingston. "You 'ave asked me to be frank, Mr. Livingston. Wot you've said is no news to me. I know the Market. I've got good friends down on Wall Street. Jay Regan? You knows of 'im, sir?"

Mr. Livingston still did not speak. But his thin white nostrils dilated, and his glacial blue eyes widened.

"It was only yesterday," said Mr. Wilkins, his voice falling to a low whisper, "as I 'ad a talk with my good friend, Jay Regan, the great financier, a man as 'as an up-and-comin' eye out on the world. 'Wot of Livingston, Jay?' I arsks him. 'Wot's Livingston doin'?' And he says honestly, sir: 'Livingston, eh? A fine firm. Too bad it 'asn't done so well lately. Too bad no one's come along with new patents, Bob. Stock used to sell at five dollars. Now it's fifty cents. Too bad, Bob, with all its potentialities.' You see, sir, I'm one as can be frank, too, and you'll pardon this discussion of your affairs?"

But Mr. Livingston's old heart was trembling. He clenched his fine hands on the desk. A purple flush invaded his forehead.

"I've got Livingston stock," resumed Mr. Wilkins. "Would I 'ave bought it if I didn't 'ave faith in it, sir? And wot it can be? Bob Wilkins isn't one as buys at random, reckless like."

"Go on," said Mr. Livingston in a stifled tone, as Mr. Wilkins paused.

"I 'ad me talk with Regan," continued Mr. Wilkins. "And I said certain things to 'im. I said: 'Look here, Jay, if Livingston, now, with its reputation for doin' straight and aboveboard business should come into possession of the finest and most revolutionary patents for printing cotton cloth, so we wouldn't 'ave to send our cottons to England, and do business for ourselves, wot'd you say?' And he said: 'Why, damn you, Bob, you know damned well wot I'd say! I'd say, a hundred thousand dollars at once, damn you! About time, Bob Wilkins, that we stopped bein' robbed by England in the business. England uses our cotton staples, prints the cloth with her damned fine patents, and then resells it to Ameriky, and other countries. Show me somethin' as will enable us to compete with England, saving expenses, exporting, shipping, handling of raw material and finished products, and there's no limit to wot you can arsk! Let me see, now, Bob,' he continues, 'Livingston's got a little printin' concern in New England. But no good patents. No wonder it lies idle, when it could be the biggest concern in Ameriky, perhaps in the world. It should be, damn you, Bob! I'm a patriot, Bob, and we've got to get the trade in Ameriky!'"

Mr. Livingston stared, impassive. Then all at once he began to tremble. He turned as white as death, and a bluish tinge came over his face. He put his hand to his forehead, and it shook visibly.

He whispered: "But, we haven't the patents. The process. England has them, and we have no chance to get them for ourselves, or to improve upon them," he added, quickly.

Mr. Wilkins said, as if the other had not spoken: "There is a young gentleman I know, sir, who 'as patents, the best of 'em. Invented by himself. An Englishman, but sick of England and her ways. So, he brings the patents to Ameriky. Wot do I advise 'im? 'There's Gorth, Johnnie,' I says, doubtfully. 'I've done some business with Gorth. But I'm not certain of Gorth's honesty. I'll investigate.' So, I does. Gorth's all honey and promises and eagerness. Now, sir, I'm a chap as is trusting. I believes a man when he looks you in the eye and gives you his word. Trustin', ain't I, sir?" Mr. Wilkins permitted himself a twisted sad smile at his own expense, at his own naïveté, and shook his head drearily.

Then he looked at Mr. Livingston with an affectation of triumphant sharpness. "I believes Gorth, with reservations, sir. A cute customer. I investigates. Then I sees he's no man of honour. He interviews my man, and even hires him as his secretary. But all the while there's a plot goin' on to steal my man's brains, and give 'im nothin', and leave us both out in the cold. To steal his patents, sir, as he come by with his wits and his industry! 'Ow do I find out this plot? Well, sir, I 'ave me methods, and it's too complicated to say. I'm not one as jumps to conclusions, and I have to be certain. Now I'm certain. I've took my man away from Gorth. 'E's ready now, to do business with an honest and above-board concern, to dedicate himself to that concern. To make that concern the biggest in Ameriky, in the world, to emancipate Ameriky from English cotton mills, and bring prosperity to American mills, as is fittin'. Why, sir, with these patents there's nothin' can stop us!"

Mr. Livingston, dazed, took some long minutes to digest all this. He could not rid himself of the feeling that he was in the midst of some fantasy, some golden dream. He stared at Mr. Wilkins blankly, his thin face slowly becoming suffused.

He faltered, in a faint and grudging tone: "Has Mr. Gorth yet availed himself of these patents? If so——"

"Would I be comin' to you, sir, if 'e 'ad?" cried Mr. Wilkins indignantly. "Would I be arskin' you to cross even such as Gorth, if 'e'd yet invested 'is money in it, and gone ahead with plans? No, not even if Gorth is a thief and a blackguard, usin' my man's brains dishonest! First come, first served, even if a man's fit only for Old Bailey. That's Bob Wilkins, sir! I can tell you that 'e 'asn't gone ahead. I've thought he was dealin' with England, sly like, for a good sum. Promisin' not to compete, even if it means the ruin of American cotton industry by withholdin' the processes. For a good sum. Several hundred thousand pounds, sir. I 'ave me methods of findin' out such things." He elaborately hesitated, sighed, bowed his head as if in shame, and murmured: "I trust you, sir. I confess now that Gorth sent me to England just to make such a deal." He appeared suddenly frightened, and put his plump hand to his lips. "I ought not to 'ave confessed that to you, sir! You'll not think better of me for it. You'll say to yourself: 'Bob Wilkins's no better than Gorth, lendin' his talents to such chicanery and unpatriotic double-dealin'.'"

Mr. Livingston drew a deep and audible breath. He fixed his eyes sternly upon Mr. Wilkins. "A very unpatriotic and cruel thing to do, Mr. Wilkins," he said, severely. "Especially when your young man had confided these processes to you. Offensive you may think it, Mr. Wilkins, but I cannot refrain from expressing my indignation at such dishonesty. Surely you could not betray America, and your young friend, like this?"

Mr. Wilkins bowed his head humbly, and nodded slowly and despairingly. "There, sir, you've said it. I accepts my punishment. But, at the last moment I recoiled, sir. 'No, Bob Wilkins,' I said, 'you've not to do this. You owes a debt to Ameriky, and them as trusts you. Never mind the money, Bob Wilkins,' I says. So I comes back to Ameriky, hurried like, and takes my man away from Gorth."

There was a silence in the room, as Mr. Wilkins' head fell

lower and lower upon his breast in his complete and broken penitence. Mr. Livingston, now towering over the other in complete austerity and honourable indignation, gazed at him coldly. Mr. Wilkins' confession, his visible remorse, his attitude of penitence, removed from Mr. Livingston's not unastute mind the suspicion that there was something here that should be investigated. Men, he believed in his naiveté, do not openly confess themselves rascals and thieves and traitors if they have something nefarious in mind.

Then he forgot all this in the sudden and almost fatal surge of joy and liberation and hope. His breath came sharp and painful. His heart roared, and his pale and bloodless face dampened. He struggled before he could speak in a restrained if halting voice:

"Mr. Wilkins, you have suffered much for your treachery, I can see that. But you have tried to make amends. I hope you will let me help you. Bring your young man to me. I will interview him, at least. He knows something of the trade, besides the mere printing processes?"

Mr. Wilkins lifted his head. His countenance shone with delight, with gratitude. He half rose from his chair.

"Mr. Livingston, your words is balm to me! You forgive me! You understand the frailties in a man's heart! You 'aven't turned me out, as I deserve. Bless you, sir, bless you! You've given me 'ope, and you'll not regret it, sir. I swears it! 'Ere's me 'and on it!"

He thrust an extravagantly shaking hand in Mr. Livingston's direction, and after a moment's lofty and severe delay, Mr. Livingston took it. Mr. Wilkins affected to be overcome. He clung to that hand. He fell back in his chair, still stretching it across the desk, and he bowed his head again, heaving deep and broken sighs. Mr. Livingston felt himself in command of the situation, and deeply exalted and dazed.

When Mr. Wilkins could collect himself, he said: "This young chap, sir. He knows the export trade from A to Z. 'Wot about South Ameriky?' he arsks me, shrewd like. 'Wot are you doin' about South Ameriky, Mr. Wilkins? Are you lettin' England 'ave that trade, too, along with yours?' I was ashamed to confess we are, sir. And now, I'll bring 'im to you tomorrow, Mr. Livingston, and then we'll 'ave business to do with Jay Regan."

They stood up, shaking hands again, with restrained enthusiasm.

Mr. Livingston, swimming in his golden and imposing dream, was inclined to be magnanimous now. "You won't regret your honesty, Mr. Wilkins, I can assure you. There will probably be much in this for you. That is the reward of humility and honour."

Mr. Wilkins smiled a strange and hidden smile, which he concealed by bowing his head.

When the amiable "feller" had left, after effusive expressions of gratitude for Mr. Livingston's noble understanding, Mr. Livingston slowly lowered himself into his chair and sat motionless for a long time, staring before him with his frozen blue eyes. At moments a long tremor would pass over him, as if he were seized with a kind of solemn but repressed excitement. Then, at other moments, an uneasy shade would pass over his face, pinching it as though he felt a strange and unfathomable chill from deep within himself. Finally, a long time later, when he stood up, age and grim desolation had left him. There was a stiff grace in his long thin body, a quicker elegance in his manners. He smiled.

He was a scholar and a man of intuition, intellect and fine judgment, travelled and cultivated. It is only passing strange, however, that his seduction by Mr. Wilkins had been so easy, and so puerile, and that his own conduct had been as naive and shallow as an ignorant man's, that a whole long life's experience with men and affairs should have been nothing before Mr. Wilkins' raw brash flattery and acting.

Mr. Wilkins could have explained it quite airily, and truthfully.

"I allus gives 'em wot they really wants," he would have said, as he had said before, a thousand times. "Allus play on a bloke's instincts, and you'll never go wrong. Come to him with arguments for 'is mind and 'is reason and 'is conscience, and 'e'll slip away from you like a bloody eel. But get at him through 'is blasted instincts—that're allus right there under the surface of the finest snob—and you've got 'im! 'E's yours for life."

For Mr. Wilkins had come upon the most profound truth in the world, hidden from the most loquacious and pretentious philosophers and students of men: that mankind has always been, and always will be, the slave of its primordial instincts.

CHAPTER 22

Mr. Wilkins, rosily incandescent with his thoughts, made his tranquil and jovial way to Wall Street, where he had an appointment with the financial baron, Jay Regan. As he was well known there, and adored by the host of secretaries and attendants who swarmed in the outer offices like secret police or Praetorians, he had no difficulty in being admitted to his old friend. In fact, he was escorted to the very door by a platoon of the Praetorians, who seemed to sound a flourish of trumpets to announce the arrival, and then appeared to present arms and lift banners. Once, Mr. Ernest Barbour, of Barbour-Bouchard, has asked Mr. Regan if he were afraid of assassination, and Mr. Regan had replied with a grin: "Of course I'm afraid of assassination." And he had pointed to a black hole in the mahogany panelling behind his chair.

To the casual eye, it would seem absurd that any one should desire to assassinate Mr. Regan, for he had a big genial countenance, apparently frank and zestful, with deceptively kind eyes like sparkling pinpoints under bushy brows. He was quite a giant of a man, over six foot tall and heavily paunched, and he was as bald as Mr. Wilkins, with a head even larger, and very round. Broad of beam, weighty but swift of movement, ever smiling under a white mustache streaked with sandy tints, ever-agreeable and secretly mirthful, he inspired confidence, respect and liking. Surely no one with such a booming laugh, and weighing well over two hundred fifty pounds, with such a warm handclasp and candid affectionate glance, could be the desperate and lethal villain he was reputed to be. So he impressed the casual observer, who did not see the savage expression of the mouth under the mustache, when it was not smiling, and did not notice the cruel small hands, like a woman's, with the pale smooth nails.

His office was vast and luxurious, and he had amazing if opulent taste. Old Masters hung on the panelled walls, Rembrandts and Rubens. He loved warmth, even on this fine spring day, and a great fireplace leapt with ruby light along one side of the room. The mighty windows were draped with rich gold velvet, tasselled and fringed, and upon a round gleaming table near by stood an ever-ready selection of liquors to please the most fastidious taste. In a carved silver box on the immense carved desk were orderly rows of the best Havana cigars, and all the chairs were soft and inviting and carved also.

Mr. Regan greeted Mr. Wilkins with the most extraordinary amiability and evident pleasure. His tiny pinpoints of eyes began to sparkle with amusement. With his own hands he poured Mr. Wilkins a generous swig of whiskey, and presented the crystal glass to him with every indication of cordiality. They had done much business together in the past, snide but profitable business, and Mr. Regan had a profound respect for Mr. Wilkins' judgment. There was no insincerity in his expressions of delight at this call. Mr. Wilkins never wasted his time on piddling affairs. His visit heralded prospects of profits, and Mr. Regan had the highest admiration for profits.

"You haven't been in to see me since you returned from England, Bob," he said, throwing himself back in his gigantic chair and leisurely sipping his own potion. "What've you been up to, eh? I'll wager it won't bear the light of day, you scoundrel!" And with the utmost admiration and significance he winked broadly at his old friend. "Who've you been putting things up to, Lucifer?"

Mr. Wilkins laughed gently, swirling the golden contents of his glass and watching the sparkling ripples with approval. He shook his head, modestly. "You does me an undeserved wrong, Mr. Regan, that you do. I'm a chap as must make his way alone in the world—for a fee. Why, right here in New York there's those that swear by Bob Wilkins as they count their cash. I'm a benefactor, sir. A benefactor. I gives 'em wot they wants. Wot more can a bloke do? I can't abide to see them as could do well by themselves—and Bob Wilkins —going to seed, bitin' their nails, when a little suggestion here and there, a little cash, can smooth things out for them, like, and do good for themselves. Bob Wilkins don't like to see talent goin' to waste. It's sinful."

"Yes, you're a good substitute for prayer. I know that," said Mr. Regan, with a faint grimace of enjoyment. "Well, what were you up to in England, if I may be crude enough to ask?"

Mr. Wilkins smiled lovingly, as he contemplated his English activities. He looked at Mr. Regan archly. "Now then, does I ask you, Mr. Regan, wot you've been up to New York? Can't a chap 'ave his secrets? I can tell you this, though: I'm none the poorer for that dash across the pond."

"Oh, I'm willing to concede that, Bob," remarked Mr.

Regan, grinning broadly now. He leaned towards a neat pile of papers on his desk. "And, in the meantime, you've not done so badly here, either. Let me see. Yes, that railroad stock you bought is doing quite nicely. Up ten points since you bought it. That means another seven thousand for you. And to think you had to persuade me to invest in a miserable little affair which I doubted could amount to something! And now, thanks to the astute penetration you had with regard to the parties, we've both done well. But who but you would know that they would hornswoggle the former owners so neatly, and get the railroad away from them? But, of course, you had your hand in that, too! I ought to remember your genius."

"Could I see a railroad going to rack and ruin because the owners were fools?" asked Mr. Wilkins, virtuously. "Ameriky needs railroads, and needs enterprisin' blood to expand 'em. I saw that. I'm a benefactor, as I said, sir. Ameriky owes a lot to Bob Wilkins."

"That she does!" said Mr. Regan, heartily, with another wink. "What would America be without the Bob Wilkinses? And now, here's another thing. You've made ten thousand clear profit in that steel mill down in Nazareth. Not bad. And six thousand on those coal mines, since you persuaded old Carnegie to step down hard on those miners. Excellent, Mr. Wilkins! And all on your own, too."

"All on me own," repeated Mr. Wilkins. "Who the devil's goin' to care for a chap except himself? If I don't look after Bob Wilkins, who will? I never fancied bread and cheese in a garret."

Mr. Regan leaned back again in his chair to contemplate his old friend. There was amusement in his great expansive face, and cunning.

"Well, Bob, what're you up to now? This isn't just a friendly visit. I know you better than that. Are you still helping Gorth to corner the cotton export trade, and expand his printing mills in New England? Did you steal those patents from England, as I suspect you did?"

Mr. Wilkins piously lifted his eyes to the carved plaster ceiling of the room, as if calling upon heaven to protect him against this cynical accusation.

"Mr. Regan, I thought you was a friend of mine. You know I allus operates above-board. Honest Bob Wilkins, my friends calls me. And just, too. I got the patents, yes. It'd be wrong of me to deny it. But I bought 'em, sir, with me own good money. Advanced by Mr. Gorth, I admits. The English ain't above turnin' an honest penny, either. Can't blame 'em. But the patents is in me own name, sealed and registered, though Mr. Gorth don't known that yet. Right down in Washington they are."

Mr. Regan laughed with loud and vast enjoyment, slapping thighs like pillars.

"Bob, I'll do a little guessing. You brought the patents to Gorth, and then secretly patented them in your own name, shortly after your return. Am I right, eh? Come on, Bob, what're you up to? I'm an old friend. You can confide in me. Moreover, I have an idea your confidence will be profitable for me, and so I'll bear you no malice. What do you want?"

"Two hundred and fifty thousand dollars, Mr. Regan," said Mr. Wilkins, placidly, with a sweet smile. "Immediately. And two hundred thousand more, say, in about six months."

Mr. Regan emitted a long slow whistle of extreme admiration and surprise. He settled himself comfortably in a chair, as a man settles himself at a theatre. Then he said abruptly: "Let's hear it, Bob."

Mr. Wilkins immediately assumed a grave and business-like expression, which did not deceive Mr. Regan.

"I won't take too much of your time, sir. I'm not one as is frivolous and without regard for a gentleman's appointments. Don't think it. To make a long story short, I'm done with Gorth."

Mr. Regan twinkled. "A better opportunity, eh?"

Mr. Wilkins' expression became even graver. He seemed to sink into melancholy contemplation. "When a bloke's above-board, Mr. Regan, I'm the man for him. When he tries to do an honest chap out of his just deserts, then he's got no worse enemy than Bob Wilkins."

"You don't mean to say that Gorth cheated *you?*" cried Mr. Regan, diverted, and grinning. "Impossible!"

Mr. Wilkins allowed himself a momentary grim smile. "There's them that's tried it, Mr. Regan, but they got up very early in the morning. And much good it did 'em. No, Mr. Gorth didn't attempt to cheat *me*. It was my young friend, my protégé, like. A young gentleman of the best family and position, with brains, but too trusting. With patents for printing cloth right in this country, instead of sending our cotton to England, and buying the printed stuff back from 'em."

"Aha," said Mr. Regan. "Where did he get the patents? Stole them from England?"

"I takes exception to that remark, sir," said Mr. Wilkins, with dignity. "The young gentleman, himself, is from England. Only been here since Christmas. Got interested in the industry in the old country, and invented improvements.

New processes. In the course of my business in England, I come across him, and was interested. I persuaded him to come to Ameriky, and being of a trusting natur myself, I takes him to Mr. Gorth. Of course," he added, modestly, "the processes were patented in Ameriky. No use trusting too much. But Mr. Gorth doesn't know it, as I said. He's prepared, now, to manufacture the printed cloth in his own mills in New England, and has thought he 'as contrived to do it with our processes, and never pay us a penny for it. Then, in the meantime, he contemplates offering the English, for a nice sum, not to print the cloth in Ameriky. Blackmail, sir.

"Now, if the English ain't amenable, and the sum Mr. Gorth arsks is unbelievable, then Mr. Gorth is to use the processes in his own mills. In the meantime, as you know, Gorth's stock's fallen from $10 the share to $7. Mr. Gorth's goin' to depress the Market more, in order to buy it up later at about $3 or less the share. It's a plot, sir, a scheme."

"Ah," said Mr. Regan, suddenly alert, and scowling. "I noticed that. Wondered what was up. He passed the last dividend, due in January. I was wondering. So that's it, eh?"

Mr. Wilkins sighed. "That's it, sir." Then he smiled radiantly, lifted his right hand, and shook his finger, coyly. "But if Mr. Gorth lifts a 'and, I've got 'im. I've got the patents!"

But Mr. Regan was pursuing a thought of his own. "How do you know Gorth's scheme? I'm not fool enough to believe he's confided in you. How do you know he's going to run the stock into the ground, in order to buy it up cheaply, and watch it skyrocket after the processes are being used? Eh? How did you get onto his private papers?"

Mr. Wilkins coughed. "I have me methods, sir."

Mr. Regan studied him long and thoughtfully. Then he said suddenly: "This young friend of yours: where is he now? What has he been doing since he came to America?"

Mr. Wilkins regarded him with simple bland honesty. "He's been with Mr. Gorth as his secretary."

All at once Mr. Regan smiled broadly. "I see, I see," he remarked, nodding gently. He began to laugh with great softness.

Mr. Wilkins was not embarrassed. He joined Mr. Regan in his gentle laughter.

"Bob," said Mr. Regan, "you are a damned, stinking rascal. An utterly conscienceless thief and liar. I've seen some scoundrels during the past twenty-five years, but you, Bob, are stupendous. Why, damn you, you are postively artistic. I've admired ruthlessness and chicanery on a bold large scale. But now I see they're very crude, compared with your methods. Bob, it's too bad you weren't born in America. You could be President. I only wonder why you haven't gone in for politics."

Mr. Wilkins blushed at all this praise, and cast down his eyes. "I've done my bit in politics, Mr. Regan, though I'm one as likes to keep in the background. There's many a senator as owes much to me. I could write a book."

"I should imagine you could," said Mr. Regan, with passing grimness. He smoothed his mustache with his hand and stared at the other man with the pinpoints glittering under his brows. "For instance, I've heard of slave-running. You wouldn't have had your hand in that, would you, Bob? A nasty business."

Mr. Wilkins hesitated. Then, seeing something unusual in Mr. Regan's eyes, he shook his head sadly and virtuously. "Not I, sir. I don't help them as buys and sells human flesh, even if it's black. Freedom for everybody, I allus 'as said, and I says it again. Not that the Southern planters ain't got a side to their arguments. 'Ow they going to survive, and plant cotton and sell it, without slave labour? Can't afford to hire men for that. Besides, it's a plot against fine gentlemen, sir, and I'm against plots. These Northern chaps, these industrialists, can't compete with slave-labour, and they knows it. Let all the cotton mills get down there, and the Northern chaps is done for. It's a struggle, sir, for industry. If a war comes out of it, it won't be to free the blackamoor. It will be to see who gets the swag. But that's allus behind wars. Swag."

"Um," said Mr. Regan.

"Wot'll happen to the Market if slave-labour keeps growin'?" asked Mr. Wilkins. "We've got to think of that, sir. Wot'll happen to our mills, and our commerce? It's frightful to think of. I've had it in mind. That's why I didn't go in for slave-runnin', not that it wasn't offered to me."

But Mr. Regan was not impressed. "I've heard of that packet, the *Black Maria*. You had something invested in it, didn't you, Bob?"

Mr. Wilkins was momentarily nonplussed. Then he said sadly: "I did, sir. I admits it. But not now! Sold out months ago."

"Just after the *Black Maria* was sunk, wasn't it, Bob? You got the news before any one else? In the devil's own fashion."

Mr. Wilkins perceived that things were not going too well in this change of conversation. He coughed delicately. "I took care, though, sir, to inform you immediately that the packet was sunk off the coast of Africa. You remember that. You and I was the first to know. Not that you had anything invested in it, of course. It was just a bit of news I thought might interest you in a way."

Mr. Regan said nothing. His face was impassive. Then he moved in his chair. "Well, let's get down to business. You mentioned considerable money. You have a scheme. Out with it, then."

Then Mr. Wilkins outlined the plan he had earlier proposed to Mr. Livingston. Mr. Regan, beyond one or two noncommittal exclamations, listened intently.

"The first investment," concluded Mr. Wilkins, happy that his old friend appeared impressed despite a cynical and resistive expression, "would be just enough for installation of new machinery for the ney processes. We will need ready cash to get into operation, pay our workers, overhead, and raw material."

Mr. Regan was silent for a long time. Then he asked curiously: "I don't see how you got around old Livingston, who's the soul of honour. How did you do it, Bob?"

Mr. Wilkins replied with great nobility: "Mr. Livingston's a gentleman of character, sir. He was proper indignant when I told him as 'ow Mr. Gorth contemplates robbin' my young friend. I confessed to him, too, that at first I 'ad a 'and in it, too, and that I wanted to make amends and do the right thing by everybody."

"So, that's how you did it!" marvelled Mr. Regan, laughing visibly but silently. "Rescuing old Livingston from bankruptcy and complete ruin, and giving him at the same time an opportunity to make a new fortune! Excellent! What if he finds out the truth?"

Mr. Wilkins smiled gently. "Gentlemen as makes fortunes by doing good and honourable things never finds out the truth, sir. They don't let themselves."

There was another silence in the room, while Mr. Regan chewed a corner of his mustache and stared unseeingly at Mr. Wilkins. Behind those rapidly twinkling pinpoints of eyes his formidable brain was working with incredible swiftness.

Then he said: "Livingston will issue additional stock, at $1 a share, and I'll handle the transaction through my own offices. There'll be mortgage details, of course, which must be worked out adequately. That will take a little time."

Mr. Wilkins beamed like the sun at midday. He listened intently as Mr. Regan rapidly wrote figures on a sheet of foolscap, and explained them in an abstracted voice. An hour passed in this ineffable occupation and discussion.

At the conclusion, the gentlemen relaxed. Mr. Regan, quite in high humour, poured another drink for Mr. Wilkins.

"Where do you come in on this transaction, Bob? For, of course, you aren't solely interested in Christian justice."

"A man must live," replied Mr. Wilkins. "I will arrange it with Mr. Livingston. A fee of $5,000 for arranging this loan with you, sir, and 5,000 shares of the 100,000 which will be issued at $1 a share. And," he coughed, delicately, "a little fee of $5,000 from you, sir, for giving you this remarkable opportunity."

Mr. Regan laughed uproariously. "The devil, Bob! Well, I can't help but admire you! Excellent! When the time comes, of course, you'll have my check."

He felt quite a strong affection for Mr. Wilkins. They drank again, while railroad tycoons and mine owners chaffed impatiently in the ante-rooms outside. They would bring greater profits than this to Mr. Regan, but that gentleman, who admired skillful skullduggery, at times, more than he admired large profits, regaled himself in illuminating conversation with his old friend. Moreover, he well knew that some of those tycoons and owners now stamping up and down outside owed much to Mr. Wilkins. Mr. Regan learned much about human nature, listening to the bland remarks of Mr. Wilkins, and his acute and gentle observations. For Mr. Regan had his own personal reasons for detesting humanity, and he enjoyed the conversation of an artist in subtle revenge and seduction. Like many men of his kind, he always had a sharp ear for gossip and the revelations of shameful secrets.

Just before they bade each other an amiable au revoir, Mr. Regan, relaxed and amused, asked: "Bob, I've often wondered why you haven't married. A man of your talents and personality ought to have persuaded some fine lady to cast in her lot with you, and you have, no doubt, had many excellent opportunities."

Mr. Wilkins smiled musingly. "Well, Mr. Regan, I've been a busy man, goin' about the world fast, like. Not much time for lally-dally with the ladies. Not that I haven't 'ad my fancies, at times. But they was passing."

"You didn't learn much about females, then, eh?"

Mr. Wilkins was silent a moment. The gentle musing on his round pink countenance increased. But that strange and baleful glimmer appeared in his round hazel eyes. "I learned a great deal, Mr. Regan," he replied, in a very soft and meditative tone, oddly at variance with his malefic look, "a very great deal. Human natures, sir, is very bad. It's especially bad in females. Comes out clear, like, though the dears don't know it. I've 'ad me fancies, like I said. But later, I says to meself: 'Bob, why get entangled with a female, for all her pretty flesh and ways and her bright curls and coy glances?

221

Look under 'em, Bob, under all the smiles and the fans and the killing looks. Wot do you see, Bob? You sees vultures, Bob, damn man-eating vultures. You sees vampires. Wot've you got to do with bitches?' For, Mr. Regan, all females is bitches. A man'll 'ave some honour left in him, even at the last, even though 'e's been a blackguard and a murderer in his life. But females is born without honour. They lives to eat. Pitiless and ragin' creatures, under all the softness. I've 'ad me dealings with 'em, and I've never yet met a man as could hold a candle to a female when it comes to dirtiness and cruelty and real brutishness. They've got evil minds under their curls, Mr. Regan, and black hearts under their modest bodices. And treacherous as serpints. That's females, sir. I got this from me observations. Filthy they are, and relentless. No pity in their whole bodies, not a farthing's worth. Vicious to their daughters, slobbery with their sons. Drive their lasses to destruction, and rob their husbands to put loose money in their sons' pockets. There's material for speculation there, sir, for some honest philosopher and thinker. It would make rum reading, very rum."

A shadow of repugnance passed over Mr. Regan's large ambushed face. He coughed.

Mr. Wilkins continued to smile dreamily, but the evil glare in his eyes mounted to a blaze.

"Show me a female, sir, as 'as a heart with a little pity and goodness, and I'm 'er slave. There's nothin' she can arsk from Bob Wilkins that wouldn't be laid at her feet. Show me a female with honour and kindness and justice in her soul, and I'll fall down and worship 'er. Show me a female as ain't a born liar and monster, and Bob Wilkins will rise up and sing her praises." He tapped his oaken chest, and added, in a strange voice: "It'd do Bob Wilkins good, sir. It'd do a lot for Bob Wilkins."

Mr. Regan gazed at him steadfastly. He did not smile.

CHAPTER 23

L IKE many evil and malignant people, Mr. Wilkins loved animals, just as many of those who have dedicated their lives to their fellow men in all charity and heroism abominate the lesser beasts. Being what he was, he knew all this very well. In truth, he had often struck upon a very profitable partnership with a stranger on watching his tenderness with cats and dogs and birds. One instance was very close to his mind. He remembered that while strolling in a quiet little park he had come upon a tall emaciated gentleman who was absorbed in feeding pigeons. The creatures were floating about the gentleman like a veritable cloud of wings, alighting on his hat, shoulders, arms, feet and hands, and he was laughing softly and deeply in his throat as he stroked satin breast and small head. Mr. Wilkins was so struck by that look of passionate sweetness and love on the long gaunt face that he had stopped in his tracks. He had struck up a most genial acquaintanceship with the gentleman on the basis of their mutual love for animals, and a few hours later Mr. Wilkins had invested quite heavily in the *Black Maria* of infamous memory. For this was the owner and the captain, one of the foulest and most vicious of men, famous for his cruelty and lethal fury, a torturer and a murderer and a malefactor of the most hideous kind.

Mr. Wilkins, who knew his mankind too well, was not given to the sentimentalism of believing that "in every man there is some goodness," because of evil men's penchant for the lower animals. He found some mysterious but irrefutable connection between the fondness of men for those animals and their own fatal hatred for their own kind. He had come to the tenuous conclusion that evil men were drawn to beasts because the latter exhibited, unashamedly, the primordial and murderous impulses which animated themselves.

So Mr. Wilkins had a large assortment of cats and dogs and birds in his small but comfortable house on East Fifth Street. It was a pretty house of white stone with green shutters and squat red chimneys, an old house of various levels within, good fireplaces and thick pleasant rugs, presided over by an ancient crone whose malevolent society greatly amused and delighted Mr. Wilkins. There was a garden, too, all hollyhocks and lilacs, roses and tangled primroses, marigolds and pansies, and a delicate willow or two like fountains of fragile green cooling off the hot days. Like the house, it was old, also, and filled with sweet light and shadow. In this paradise of quiet and peace, Mr. Wilkins kept his beasts, romped with them for hours, and received and returned their abject adoration. For there was no doubt that the creatures loved him, doted on him, waited patiently for him. Seeing this from their back windows, his neighbours had come to the maudlin conclusion that he was a most excellent sweet gentleman, and, as they were wealthy enough, and scheming and greedy enough to be of past, present or future use to Mr. Wilkins, he was not displeased at their opinion. The few who did not exhibit affection for animals were sedulously avoided by Mr. Wilkins. They were not likely to advance his fortunes, nor, by pitiless exploitation and viciousness, their own.

This Sabbath morning, he was feeling some doubt and uneasiness, for his visitor was John Turnbull, and John was sitting on a marble bench under the willows with an expression of undisguised aversion for Mr. Wilkins' beasts. He was watching Mr. Wilkins romp with assorted dogs and cats, and his dark and violently sullen face was both disgusted and indifferent. Just as he had not taken to the creatures, the creatures had not taken to him, and dogs paused in their play to glance at him and growl deeply in their throats. The cats, subtly recognizing one who had none of their black and feline nature, avoided him with that ineffable delicacy and comprehension for which they are justly famed. All this rendered Mr. Wilkins uneasy. He suspected, then, that John was not entirely in his power, that perhaps at some dangerous moment he would revolt at some villainy and leave Mr. Wilkins, and himself, in a very precarious position. John had obeyed all his suggestions implicitly during the past few months, but it had been with dark and twisted smiles and sombreness.

Mr. Wilkins knew that every man had a touchstone. In most men, the lust for money and power led to one instinctive goal: women. The love for money and power, then, was a biological urge, as profound and fathomless as nature itself. That is why, he had concluded, when a man became old and impotent, his lust for these things diminished, and he turned to good works and philanthropies in lieu of the beds of females. The urge towards fornication and adultery and other ecstatic orgasms coincided with a man's teeming desire for bank accounts and gilt-edge securities, and were in direct ratio with each other.

But there were a few men whose urge in the direction of money and power was stimulated not by the desire for women, but for other if less substantial reasons. They were animated with a desire for revenge. Now, Mr. Wilkins had no particular quarrel with this desire, but he found it unreliable. Men who did not overly lust for women, and so for money and power, were always suspect. Their revenge would often dissolve into resignation, understanding or compassion. And where was Mr. Wilkins, then? Once the revenge was consummated, or abandoned out of pity or sadness, the man would frequently retire from the roaring arena, leaving his patrons or their friends in a state of complete ruin or bafflement.

Knowing this, and observing John's aversion for his beloved beasts, Mr. Wilkins had secret qualms and apprehensions. It was certainly too bad. John had done so excellently and incredibly well under his tutelage. There was nothing they could not do together, so long as John retained his grim and desperate desire for revenge. But that desire must be constantly stimulated, and Mr. Wilkins needed to exercise his imagination at all times. With some men, he had had to act as a panderer, forever producing some delectable and elusive female, especially if the man was growing old, in order to keep the lust for money and power active. But in a few others, like John, he must keep the lust for revenge alive. That was much harder to do. It was easier to keep a man's lower lusts in full bloom than it was to keep at high pitch a mental and spiritual passion, which might, at any moment, be destroyed by gentleness or compassion, or sheer ennui.

Too, he suspected very acutely that John was not by nature a vengeful man, or a cruel one, but darkly exuberant and passionate and generous, uncontrolled and vehement. Moreover, his life had not had hard and deprived beginnings, almost a necessity in those who aspired to power. Having experienced luxury and wealth and ease, he did not find life insupportable without them. Give Mr. Wilkins a man who had known arduous and tortuous poverty!

John obeyed, with commendable viciousness and determination, in his pursuit of revenge, and Mr. Wilkins had no fault to find with him there. But he could not predict when this driving motive would die away as suddenly as it had arisen.

So it was, that at last he wiped his red and steaming countenance, lovingly drove off his canine and feline worshippers, and came to the bench on which John sat in sultry silence. He knew that John despised him as the visible symbol of his moral degradation, and that gave Mr. Wilkins some bad moments. John's bank accounts and investments had reached a really formidable and delightful height, but the young man apparently had no care for them beyond their implicit promise that some day he would be able to undo his enemies. When that had been accomplished, or he no longer desired revenge, Mr. Wilkins would be impotent to influence him.

He sat down, chuckling, rubbing his handkerchief between his ruddy neck and his linen, while John stared bleakly before him at the sun-dappled grass.

"D'ye know who was here before you, Johnnie? None other than our old friend, Mr. Gorth!"

The reaction fully satisfied Mr. Wilkins. John turned to

him violently, and a savage gleam passed over his face. Mr. Wilkins nodded, smiling reminiscently.

"Came full of nasty accusations, he did. It seems that he'd been to Washington to patent those processes of ours, Johnnie." Mr. Wilkins chuckled so strenuously that he momentarily choked, and turned quite scarlet. "And wot did he find? He found 'em in Bob Wilkins' name! That was a bad blow to our friend. Came back ragin'. Found out, too, we'd turned 'em over to Mr. Livingston, and that the printing shops in New England was producin' the new processes. I thought he'd 'ave a fit, standin' there under that tree yonder. Called me a thief, me as 'ad brought them to Ameriky with me own 'ands. He was goin' to the police, he said, to get justice done." Mr. Wilkins' chuckle was deep and delighted. "And you know wot I says to 'im? 'Mr. Gorth,' I says with dignity, ''ow can you go to the police, or sue me, as you threatens? You'll have to show your own 'and, and 'ow you sent me to England to steal the patents. You'll 'ave to show you 'ad an intention of your own to use 'em. People won't like that, Mr. Gorth. I've kept your letters, and won't 'ave no hesitancy showin' them in Court, though it'll break me heart, you and me once bein' such friends.'"

"What did he say then?" asked John savagely.

"He went orf, breathing fire and flame. But he knew I'd done 'im in. There was no use him shouting or raising a stink. He knew it." He contemplated Mr. Gorth's discomfiture with a pleasant smile. "'E'd intended to depress the market price on 'is stock for 'is own reasons, but now the stock's gone down on its own. Down to two dollars. The chap's frantic."

"Good," growled John, clenching his big fists and beating them on his knees.

"I regretted to do it, as you know, Johnnie. But Bob Wilkins ain't one as will stand by and see another man 'oomiliated and treated bad as you was done, for no reason but wickedness."

A faint dark smile touched John's lips for a moment, but he made no comment. Then from an inner pocket he brought out a crumpled letter and tossed it to Mr. Wilkins. "I received this a few months ago from Gorth, after—that night. You may read it if you wish."

Mr. Wilkins opened it eagerly, after a long and furtive study of John's sombre features. Then he read, his round fat lips moving silently over each word:

"I cannot express to you, John, my real regret and anger over this occurrence. I assure you that if I had known, you

226

would never have been asked to come to my house and be confronted by Andy Bollister. You will grant me this decency, I know. I swear to you that I had no idea matters stood as they did. Though I regret that you have terminated our association, I understand that you cannot be a part of the organization which will eventually pass into Andy's hands. Please accept, however, this cheque for one thousand dollars as my expression of true regard for you. I hope you will do well in any other endeavour in which you may become engaged, and do not hesitate to ask me for assistance if you need it."

Mr. Wilkins was greatly surprised. He had not thought the felonious and corrupt Richard Gorth to be capable of an unselfish and charitable thought. He also saw that there was danger implicit in this letter, for though not visible at this moment, there was no doubt that John must have been inevitably impressed by it. Someday, perhaps, he would realize there was no hypocrisy in this communication from Richard Gorth.

So Mr. Wilkins laughed richly, and tossed the letter back to John. He regarded John with his glassy and protuberant hazel eyes humid with mirth.

"A foxy one, that Gorth!" he exclaimed. "A foxy one! May I arsk wot you did with that cheque, Johnnie?"

"I sent it back at once," replied John, angrily. "What did you think?"

Mr. Wilkins again experienced uneasiness. He would have been more reassured if John had kept the money.

"It was little enough, after your 'oomiliation," he said, thoughtfully. "But, mind, I'm not criticisin' you. You're a chap of honour, sir, as I allus said." He continued, with great and amused animation: "The man's a hypocrite, Johnnie. You was the one he blasted most. Accused you of ingratitude and such, and said things about you I wouldn't soil my mouth with in repeatin'. Betrayed himself, he did. Showed me the whole plot. D'ye know what he hinted? That your Pa intended to make your lady cousin his heiress, as he allus 'ad a soft spot for her. That's why you don't 'ear from your Pa."

John's violent reaction to this was even more pleasing to Mr. Wilkins than he had hoped. John sprang to his feet. His dark face turned ghastly. He could not speak. He looked down at Mr. Wilkins with a truly terrible expression. Mr. Wilkins nodded dolorously.

"I shouldn't 'ave told you of it, Johnnie. Mr. Gorth flung it into my teeth, vicious like. ' 'Is father's done with 'im!' he shouted. 'My nevvy's wife's goin' to get all the swag. Fifty thousand pounds! And all to go into Richard Gorth at the proper time.'"

John slowly reseated himself. His face gleamed with livid sweat. He clenched his lower lip in his teeth. Mr. Wilkins saw this, but he did not see the tears in the young man's eyes. Nor could he know of the consuming pain that almost broke his heart.

John thought to himself: I don't care a damn what he does with his money. It's his. I did a stupid and cruel thing to him. If only he had written to me! That is all I wanted. I wanted only to know that he'd forgiven me, and that he wishes me well, and that he hasn't forgotten me.

He put his hands over his face. For once in his astute life, Mr. Wilkins did not know the thoughts in the mind of another man. But some instinct made him say:

"I can only come to this conclusion, sir: that these schemers 'ave turned your Pa's heart away from you, and lied about you, to get the money rightfully belongin' to you. Done him in, as they tried to do you in."

John dropped his hands, and looked at Mr. Wilkins. His look of hatred, fury, despair, and malignancy quite satisfied Mr. Wilkins.

"If a man's determined to leave his money away from his nearest, one can't do anythin'," he said, sadly. "That's his privilege, unjust though it is. But there's a way open to the wronged chap. 'E can get his revenge on those as 'as cheated 'im and broke his father's heart with lies, and made a fool out of 'im.

"'Twas only last week I saw Mr. Bollister and his lady wife at the home of Mr. Astor. Right merry, they was, lookin' at each other fond like. Satisfied in their bad souls at wot they'd done for themselves, and against you."

John could not speak. Mr. Wilkins laid his hand sympathetically on his arm.

"It was lucky for you, sir, to meet Bob Wilkins on that packet. We've gone far together, and we'll go farther. I swear that, solemnly. Look wot we've done in ten months! Got practically control of Livingston. Money rollin' in. Mr. Jay Regan financing us. Stock up seven points in the market. Gorth chewin' his nails and watchin' his stock goin' down. You Mr. Livingston's manager, and trusted with everything! You livin' in style at Miss Beardsley's. But," he added, in a loud and triumphant voice, "we've just begun! It won't be long until we ruins Gorth complete, and his nevvy with him! We'll get control of Gorth, too, one of these days!"

John, whose youth and inexperience, and natural simplicity

of character, had precluded him heretofore from questioning the motives of others, suddenly had a sharp thought in
the very midst of his dream of hatred, revenge and despair.
He looked at Mr. Wilkins with straight hard eyes and asked
bluntly: "What has Gorth ever done to you, to make you
hate him like that, and plot against him?"

But he did not catch Mr. Wilkins unprepared, for that
clever gentleman, knowing his man, had already formulated
the answer to just this question some months ago. So, he
gazed at John with a countenance which he allowed to assume slowly an expression of reserved sadness, and he shook
his head, turning away at last, and sighing.

"I'm not one as airs 'is troubles, Johnnie. I'm not one who
goes abaht clamourin' for sympathy. That's not my way. The
least said the better. The way you were treated, a guest in
his 'ouse, was the last straw. Bob Wilkins is forbearin'. He
endures a lot before he revolts. He makes allowances. But
he can't abide them as betrays his friends. The last straw,
Johnnie."

"Very noble of you, I daresay," said John, with a cynical
half-smile. Then he relapsed again into his distraught black
brooding, and stared emptily at the sun-streaked wall of the
pretty little house. Mr. Wilkins, watching him, thoughtfully
chewed a nail.

"Don't take it to 'eart, Johnnie," he said, in a soothing voice.
"Mr. Gorth's only the first step. There's nothing we can't
do together. Mr. Regan was much impressed by you. You
can be a millionaire, Johnnie, with me helpin' you. You can
laugh in their faces, Johnnie."

John, who was suffering the hideous agonies into which
the tumultuous and sanguine and violent of temperament are
frequently plunged, said nothing. He felt as if his chest
was being crushed in inexorable iron hands, and as if an
intolerable weight was pressing upon his head. Everything
about him increased his anguish: the hollow light under the
trees, the streaks of sunlight on the dusty summer grass, the
lines of the chimneys smoking idly against the warm blue
sky, the very angles of walk and trunk and the very colours
of the languishing hot flowers in the tangled beds. There
was a burning dry sensation in his middle, an ache in his
brow, a sickness in his heart.

He who had been so careless, so exuberant and so zestful,
so young and lavish of nature, felt that never again would he
feel a single throb of happiness or peace or joy. He had been
flung into a horrible dark world of shades and gloom, where
nothing lived but vengeance and frantic sorrow. All the
forces of his soul revolted and cried against such a horror, so

foreign to him. He took no satisfaction or malignant contentment in revenge. It was a twisting pain that tortured him
far beyond what he could do to his enemies. He would have
done with it if he had known what to do. He would have
hidden himself far away, and would have forgotten everything, if "they" had allowed him to do so. But all the circumstances which surrounded him forced him to remember. And
more than circumstances, there was Mr. Wilkins constantly
goading him to remember, and inflicting upon him, in remembrance, all his frenetic grief, homesickness, outrage and
sadness. Sometimes, with a stab of real terror, he asked himself: "Why didn't some one warn me, my father, or any one,
that such people lived in the world? Why wasn't I prepared
to cope with them?"

He was tired to death even of hatred and revenge. Sometimes, he would say to himself, simply: "I want to go home."

But there was no going home now. "They" would not
permit that desperate flight. Sometimes, with that wild horror which was increasing in him, he would cry out in the
depths of his heart: "I can't endure living in such a world,
among such people! I can't endure going on hating and
plotting and lying and stealing! Life isn't worth living in
a nightmare!"

Sometimes he was so exhausted that he could feel nothing
at all. If only his enemies would allow him to forget them, he
would cease from plotting against them, and so have a little
peace once more. And then, in the midst of his sorrowful
weariness he would remember Eugenia again, with the mournful anguish with which one remembers the dead. It seemed
incredible to him that she had betrayed him, that she, according to Mr. Wilkins, laughed at him and hated him. And then
he would think: But it was I who struck her down, in the
beginning. She has reason to hate me.

Then he would be back on the treadmill of his red and
burning thoughts, his hatreds, his sorrows and his tiredness.
He must go on, doing evil things because those to whom he
did them would not let him forget them and leave them in
peace. It seemed appalling to him that those who had injured him constantly goaded him to revenge upon them.
How could they sustain such malignancy? he would ask himself, marvelling. How could they go about, laughing, eating,
drinking, sleeping, dancing, working, while their minds were
occupied with evil things? How could they bear living at
all?

For the first time in his life John was doing some real thinking, and the exercise, giving him a glimpse into the lives and
thoughts of others, sickened him, as if he was an alien from

some far planet dropped upon a hideous world. Deep within him was a bottomless pit of fear. He feared his fellowmen. They forced him to hate them.

Tormented and feverish with his thoughts, he rose abruptly, and looked about, dazed. "I must go," he muttered. He was unaware that Mr. Wilkins had been watching him with the most curious of expressions. A huge dog rushed up, lolling and drooling, and flung himself upon Mr. Wilkins with maudlin adoration. Mr. Wilkins embraced him. Evading wet lickings, he laughed up at John. But John had retreated a step or two with a look of dislike. The dog felt his emotion, grew rigid in Mr. Wilkins' arms, and growled savagely at the young man.

Seeing this, Mr. Wilkins drove off the snarling dog, and rose to stand beside his young friend. He put his hand affectionately on his shoulder. "A cup of tea, perhaps?" he urged. "A little swig?"

"No," said John, shortly. His breath was laboured. "I think I'll take a walk. I'm out of sorts, in a way."

"No wonder," remarked Mr. Wilkins, soothingly. "After last week. The missus is doing well, eh?"

At this mention of his wife, John's face became dark and closed. He turned aside. "Very well," he replied, in a dull voice. "She's a healthy girl. She expects to be up on Wednesday."

"You're a lucky man!" cried Mr. Wilkins, with enthusiasm. "A fine baby daughter, the very image of you! How I envies you, Johnnie!"

John's face stubbornly remained sullen for a moment or two, then involuntarily it lightened in spite of himself, into a touching look of young and embarrassed pride and affection. He laughed reluctantly.

"Oh, the baby's well enough, I suppose. Ugly little devil." He paused, and waited for Mr. Wilkins' protestations, which came with gratifying promptness.

"'Ow can you say that, Johnnie! A pretty little lady if there ever was one. Such black curls and big black eyes. Full of old Nick," and he poked John cunningly in the elbows. "There's one as will cause you some bad moments, when she's a young lady, Johnnie. Mark my words. Every lad in New York'll be after her, and no wonder."

John laughed that same reluctant laugh, as if natural merriment had rusted sadly in him. But the glow of pride lightened his tired eyes.

The two walked together to the gate, dogs and cats following in their wake. Then, with an exclamation, Mr. Wilkins had a joyful thought. Excusing himself, he rushed into his house, and returned almost immediately with a little square jewel box of old worn white satin. He opened it with elaborate movements of delight. There, on a cushion of blue silk was an ancient round locket of gold, encrusted with tiny seed pearls and inlaid with intricate designs in blue, black and scarlet enamel. The chain was of fine gold, strung with small but perfect rosy pearls. The workmanship was exquisite, and even John could not control an exclamation of admiring astonishment. Mr. Wilkins triumphantly thrust the box into the young man's hands.

"For the little lass!" he cried. "A present from old Bob! I looked long and 'ard for this, Johnnie."

"Thank you," said John, really touched.

"You'll give the little lass a kiss from me," urged Mr. Wilkins, beaming. "And my compliments to her lady mother."

John nodded. Mr. Wilkins locked the gate after him. Then Mr. Wilkins sighed, and let the sunny light fade from his countenance.

"From wot I sees, Mrs. Bollister will be presenting her husband with an heir, soon," he said.

The great and devastating black pain descended upon John again. The little light and pleasure which had come momentarily to him was gone. But he said nothing. He walked away, his big head bent. Mr. Wilkins watched him go, smiling slyly and evilly to himself.

CHAPTER 24

I SHOULD prefer, of course, a less pretentious name for a child," said Miss Beardsley, with some severity. "Such as Mary, or Jane, or Rose. But that is entirely your own affair, my dear Lilybelle. Lavinia, however, in my opinion, is a formidable name."

She opened a sheaf of yellowed white tissue and produced a most exquisite little dress of ivory satin, very long, and covered with webs of miraculously fine lace, so delicate that it seemed as if a breath would break the faery threads. The stitches were so lovingly done, so tiny, that they melted into the luscious fabric, and the little sleeves, puffed and lacy, caught the summer light that streamed in through the bedroom windows.

Lilybelle, lying upon her heaped and ruffled pillows, uttered an exclamation of reverential delight. She allowed the dress to be laid upon the bedclothes, but she held her breath and leaned back from it, terrified that her coarse, strong, young touch would destroy it.

"My christening dress," said Miss Beardsley, augustly pleased at Lilybelle's manner. "It was made in France, under my mama's supervision. It will give me great pleasure if little Lavinia wears it at her own christening."

"Oh, how can I thank you?" stammered Lilybelle, the tears thick in her big foolish blue eyes. She gazed at Miss Beardsley with swimming adoration.

Smiling austerely, Miss Beardsley smoothed the beautiful lace and satin with a gentle bony hand. For a moment the long gaunt face was quite gentle and sweet under the white cap. Then, all at once she sighed, as if some sad and nostalgic thought, impregnated with old dreams, had come to her.

She cleared her throat delicately after a moment. "Of course, I would advise—extra padding just behind. Or an extra thick folded napkin, to be inserted between the dress, and the—er—petticoat. Just for necessary protection."

"Oh, yes," breathed Lilybelle, enchanted. "You have to do that, I know. Babies get so wet, unexpected like. It—it wouldn't be nice if you were embarrassed, Miss Beardsley, you being the godmother and all."

Miss Beardsley smiled even more. She lovingly replaced the dress in its paper, which was redolent of camphor. "Lavinia Amanda Turnbull," she said. "Quite a formidable name for so small a girl."

She rose with a rustle of her black bombazine hoops, and with stately tread approached the belaced, beribboned and beflounced bassinet which stood behind a screen near the window. She bent over it majestically. There, on satin pillows, and under the whitest of woollen shawls lay the baby. It was a pretty child, for all it was less than two weeks old, rosy, plump, sweet-smelling. Its face was round, with a clear olive skin touched with bright rose, and long black lashes swept its smooth cheeks. An extraordinary thick mass of lustrous black curls covered the round head and cast a shadow on the white satin of the pillows, as if it threw out a dark light of its own. The little mouth was very red, and pursed imperiously, and there was a frown, curiously mature, between the dark brows. It was a discontented and haughty little face, even peevish, but very beautiful.

Miss Beardsley touched the warm cheek with one lean finger, and held her breath. A curious look of sadness and longing passed over her severe gray countenance. She whispered something inaudible, even incoherent, as if strange words rose from her hard and spinsterish heart.

The nursemaid, all starch and militancy, appeared as out of nowhere, a high white cap perched on her gray hair. But Miss Beardsley daunted even this grenadier, and she waited until that lady had withdrawn into the room again before picking up the child and taking it to the young mother. Lilybelle received her daughter with fatuous delight, simply and naturally bared her full and pearly breast, and placed the child at it. Miss Beardsley, who thought the procedure unesthetic, nevertheless found deep beauty in the sight, and only slightly averted her eyes as she seated herself again, assuming a stronger severity as if she implied that while all this was natural she deplored the ways of nature as being vulgar. But her dried and fallen breasts ached strangely, and she thought to herself: I must really see Dr. Burrows soon. There may be something wrong with my heart, though the Beardsleys were not given to such weaknesses.

It was she who had assisted the doctor and the nurse during the birth of the child, and she was still horrified, if oddly moved, at the memory. Nature was really quite vulgar, indeed, and quite shameless. She remembered Lilybelle's bare threshing limbs, and how she had repeatedly tried to cover them decorously from the doctor's callous eyes. She had winced and turned quite crimson at other revelations, also, about which Lilybelle, in her extremity, had shown no delicacy at all, but had kept her mouth open and fixed and screaming, her eyes distended with her agony. But Miss Beardsley had missed nothing. Some nameless urge had kept her riveted by the bed, covering up Lilybelle's panting breast when it was too exposed in its struggling abandon, drawing the sheet over the threshing round white thighs, to the doctor's impatience. "My dear madam," he said at last, bluntly, "I've got to see what I'm doing here, if you please. Children don't emerge coyly from under sheets while we avert our eyes. They come out quite boldly and shamelessly the way they went in."

This remark so revolted and horrified Miss Beardsley that she did not attempt to cover Lilybelle's legs again for some three minutes. She thought the doctor quite intolerable and disgusting. If he had no more delicacy or sensitive feelings than to aid and abet an abandoned nature in its raw exposures without apology, then he was no gentleman. He ought to be the one to be blushing, instead of herself, he belonging to that sex which in its vulgarity and shamelessness brought this upon demure young women, and forced them to submit to such a mortifying experience. If I were a man, she thought in outrage, I'd feel humiliated and degraded the rest of my life. She was confirmed in her opinion that men were an odious and disgusting sex, and not to be tolerated by gentlewomen, who were their helpless victims.

Lilybelle, being a lusty young woman, and no lady, screamed with heartiness and abandon. But this was more excitement than pain or fear. She screamed for her husband, who had been firmly told by the doctor to remain outside. She cursed, too, to Miss Beardsley's grim horror and the doctor's delighted appreciation. But she gave up the child in less than three hours, upon which the doctor commended her as if she had done this by some fine virtue of her own, and some personal will. Immediately after the child was born in a gush of blood and water quite overpowering to Miss Beardsley, Lilybelle had subsided like a rosy and smiling goddess upon her bed, had demanded to see the struggling and slimy little creature, and had asked for tea.

Miss Beardsley was very shaken, and overwhelmed. But she had gone out calmly enough to inform the anxious young father of the birth of his daughter. He had looked dully disappointed at the sex of the child, and so did not notice Miss Beardsley's bitterly condemning eyes and expression of loathing for him. He seemed entirely unaware that he ought to be grovelling and hiding his face in very shame for being a partner to this humiliation. He had burst past Miss Beardsley, without a blush or a murmur, though she stood near him in a grim and censorious attitude.

John had flung himself into the room and had rushed to Lilybelle's bed. He had forgotten that he hated and despised her. He had fallen on his knees beside her, had snatched up her hands and gazed fearfully upon her smiling and proud face. "You are quite well, Lily?" he had demanded, in a broken voice. "Quite well?"

And, from the new elevation of her womanhood and wisdom, she had smiled upon him gently, and had lifted her bitten lips for his kiss. He did not hesitate in giving that kiss; it was bestowed with simple affection and gratitude, and then he had kissed her hands, so warm and strong, and so suddenly gentle. He had not been very interested in the baby, and felt some repugnance for its noisy and crumpled red state, and some fear that it would remain hideous. Later, he had sat beside the sleeping Lilybelle, and the strangest sensation of numbness and calm and peace had come over him. It was the first time in nearly a year that he had felt the abatement of his misery.

It took him all of a week to remember that she had ruined his life, that he detested her, that he wished he had never laid eyes upon her. It took some remembering on his part to recall that when she had first timidly told him of her condition he had reviled and cursed her. And when he did remember, and revealed it to her roughly, she did not weep as she had done, nor look overly sad. She simply ignored it, with first a small sigh, and then a serene smile.

Each night he came in to see the baby, to ask curtly if his wife was well, to drop a cold dry kiss on her forehead, to answer her childish questions. And then he would leave her, not to see her until the next night. But in spite of himself, the child's suddenly blooming beauty entranced and fascinated him, and try as he would, he could not help feeling a surge of gratitude towards his wife for giving him this mysterious and lovely young creature, so like himself.

Miss Beardsley's affection for Lilybelle was compounded of egotism, vanity and gratification at Lilybelle's worshipful and reverential attitude toward her. In short, her affection was no different in any way from the affections of the rest of mankind. Moreover, the Turnbulls were financially secure, for the present at least, and this entitled them to a certain respect from Miss Beardsley. It is doubtful, however much her affection for Lilybelle and the child, that she would have tolerated any of the family had financial disaster overtaken them. "Friendship," she would frequently say, with firmness, "ends where money begins." She found nothing odious in her sentiments, which, again, she shared with many other people. Money was sacrosanct, a thing apart, not to be confused with any human relationship, but to be protected from that relationship at all costs. She would often assert that "money was nothing, nothing at all," but like all such protestors she did not believe it in the least. Had she been told that such sentiments were onerous, even dangerous, and contained no virtue, she would have been righteously angry. She and all her friends understood firmly that money had nothing to do with the virtues at all, should never be confused by them, and kept aloof from them.

Had, indeed, the Turnbulls become paupers, she would have turned them out without a qualm, and with only the loftiest feelings. They had violated the sacredness of money. Had they, under such circumstances, appealed to her charity, she would have been outraged, truly and sincerely indignant. They would have dared to step within the circle of forbidden ground, and the odium would have been theirs, not hers, upon her refusal to assist them.

But in the last few months her affection for Lilybelle had increased, for John had proved himself "worthy" of some consideration even from Miss Beardsley. The young couple had rented the whole large second floor from the amiable spinster, and there were four servants now to care for their wants. There was a nursemaid for the baby, a housekeeper, a cook and a housemaid, rooms for all of which had also been rented by the Turnbulls on the fourth floor among Miss Beardsley's two housemaids. There was, on this same floor, also, practically a self-prisoner in a miserable unheated room, a cousin of Miss Beardsley's, a middle-aged widow who had been robbed by a profligate husband before his death. It did not matter to Miss Beardsley that Mrs. Bowden was practically a pauper by no fault of her own. Her sole concern was that Mrs. Bowden was indeed a pauper, and thus less than a human being, and entitled to shrift from neither God nor man. Miss Beardsley severely collected five dollars a month from her cousin for that room, allowed her to devour the few lean leavings left over from her own meals, for another two dollars a month, and made it very clear to the hapless woman that, as she had violated the most sacred command of society by being a pauper, she must keep out of sight as much as possible. Had any one told Miss Beardsley that she was a monster, cruel, virulent and without gentleness of heart, she would have been dumfounded, and later, overcome with virtuous anger. She would have retired to her room in high insult and fury, and that night would have said her prayers in a quavering voice of rage, imploring the God of the solvent to forgive her denouncer for his crime and his ignorance.

But Lilybelle, not being possessed overmuch of Christian virtue, nor of Christian understanding of the heinousness of being a pauper, had discovered poor Mrs. Bowden in her eyrie and had set herself out to alleviate her wretched lot in furtive ways which Miss Beardsley would have found most stupid and outrageous. (How dare any one interfere with the just punishment of the insolvent? she would have asked. How dare any one insult the dignity of God by "encouraging" the existence of pauperism? Did not the Bible itself say: "These four count as dead: the poor, the blind, the childless and the lepers"?) However, Lilybelle, not being a true Christian, had her housemaid carry up well-loaded trays to the eyrie, and warm woollen garments, and a bottle or two of good wine. She had also, with a reprehensible slyness, had a little iron stove smuggled up to the roof, and bags of coal, and a vast quantity of candles. To demonstrate further her unregenerate and unChristian sinfulness, she often inserted envelopes with banknotes under Mrs. Bowden's door.

As the Turnbulls were now so prosperous, it is doubtful if Miss Beardsley would have turned them out of doors because of Lilybelle's heinous and indecent actions. But she would have been much outraged. However, her opinion of the lower classes' mentality and unChristian sinfulness would have been even the more confirmed. Lilybelle, for all her stupidity, understood this very well. But she was a generous and warm-hearted young fool, tolerant as only the expansive of spirit can be. Miss Beardsley had "her ways," and, according to Lilybelle, she was entitled to them for the sole reason that she was a human being. But Miss Beardsley, however much she was possessed of Lilybelle's admiration and sincere adulation, would have been astonished had she known that her protégé often had cunning and cynical thoughts about her.

Miss Beardsley had unbent so far (on the coming of the housekeeper, housemaid, cook and nurse) as to be tolerant of John Turnbull, even though he had afflicted a shamefulness upon a fellow woman. Because he, like Lilybelle, had had no extensive experience with humanity, he had come to the conclusion that Miss Beardsley was not at all bad, though peculiar, and so, at times, he could be gracious towards her.

Miss Beardsley, being softened by John's increasing prosperity, was given to short and reluctant remarks about him to his young wife, remarks touched with tolerance and austere approval. Too, she had frequently demonstrated her growing kindliness towards him and his wife. To the solvent, all things came, she believed. In giving Lilybelle little gifts, and the child, also, she demonstrated her basic philosophy, that to those that have more should be given. The mighty were very generous to each other, and that is as it should be.

Today, as she reflected on the baby, she remembered that Mr. Wilkins had told her that John was heir presumptive to a large fortune upon his father's death, and this increased her tenderness for little Lavinia Amanda, her godchild. There was no possibility, then, that this child would ever be a pauper, and so insult Miss Beardsley by her existence.

Therefore, though slightly disgusted by the method by which babies are fed, she found beauty in the sight of Lilybelle nursing her child. Lilybelle wore a nightgown of the finest cambric, floating with delicate lace at the neck and wrists, and over her plump young shoulders spilled the masses of her bright auburn hair. Her round face, so pretty and so stupid, had a kind of light over it as she brooded over the baby. Her big coarse hands were infinitely gentle, tenderly touching the sweating little forehead, or holding the red crumpled hand. She forgot Miss Beardsley. Her whole being was absorbed in the wonder and glory of this new life. The sunlight, pouring in the window, made a ruddy halo of her hair, increased the pearly tints of her shoulder and bosom. There was the strong and earthy holiness about her which sheds radiance on all young mothers. When she lifted her head, her bemused eyes were full of blue light, and her smile was soft and beautiful.

Miss Beardsley cleared her throat, and asked severely about Mr. Turnbull's health. Lilybelle's radiant expression changed. The light was more subdued, but her smile became broader.

"He is well, thank you," she replied, in the new measured tones which Miss Beardsley had painstakingly taught her, and which she conscientiously tried to employ on all occasions. The feeding having been concluded, the nursemaid inexorably removed the baby from Lilybelle's reluctant arms, and bore her back to her bassinet, where sundry things were done with napkins and cornstarch. Lilybelle's eyes followed the nursemaid somewhat resentfully. She was determined that as soon as she could leave her bed she would take care of her baby herself.

She leaned back upon her pillows, and smiled deeply and dreamily to herself. She glanced about her fine bedroom, so exquisitely furnished if sparse of those gimcracks and crowded plush beloved of the "lower classes."

"I trust," said Miss Beardsley, with austere delicacy, "that matters have adjusted themselves since the birth of the child?"

Lilybelle, not being a lady, found nothing offensive in the inquisitiveness which the better classes feel is their right with regard to less exalted personages. She answered with simplicity: "Oh, yes. In a way. He—ain't—I mean, isn't, quite so—flighty. But I always knew he'd come to that, and settle down."

She paused, gazed bemusedly before her, and settled herself comfortably on her pillows.

"It was very hard for Mr. T. I can see that now. What was I? Nothing but a Lancastershire lass, as couldn't read her letters nor do a real sum proper like, and helped her Ma on the farm and worked in her uncle's inn. And here was Mr. T., a gentleman—gentry. It was a far fall for him. It was no wonder he couldn't abide me at first."

"He shouldn't have married you then," said Miss Beardsley, censoriously, still being ignorant of the facts surrounding this marriage. "But once having married you, he should have made the best of it."

The light entirely left Lilybelle's face, but it retained its new calm and serenity. She continued, as if Miss Beardsley had not spoken: "But he seems more resigned, like, to things now. I knew it would be so.

"Wot—what—does a gentleman expect of marriage, any gentleman? A wife as knows her place and has respect for him, and minds her ways and her tongue. A wife as makes him comfortable. That's all. Gentlemen don't care so much for fine ladies as knows books and music. They thinks—think—they do, but they don't, really. Give 'em a wife as knows how to darn socks, cook a good meal, make a comfortable bed, and be there to hear their troubles and put up with their rages, all serene like, and that's all they ask. I knew it was only a matter of time before Mr. T. would come around. He'd find out, I says to myself, that even though I'm not gentry and don't know my letters, that I'm the same as any other woman after all. And more loving than most."

Miss Beardsley, though inflexibly opposed to the male sex, and outraged by Lilybelle's serene disposition of more refined and educated women, yet had to admit there was profound wisdom in her observations. But this only confirmed her opinion that men were a low sex, easily placated by creature comforts.

She said, admonishingly: "No doubt you are quite right, Lilybelle, though it seems a little deplorable. I am glad for your sake, however, that matters are adjusting themselves."

Lilybelle did not answer. Her smile was bemused and confident.

The door opened violently to admit John. His dark face was distraught and wretched, and his black eye, as it flashed on Miss Beardsley, had a dullness of smoldering misery. A moment later it turned upon Lilybelle, who smiled calmly and said: "Mr. T. you've missed the baby's feeding. Is it a fine day outside?"

But John said nothing. He walked across the sun-streaked floor to the baby's crib, and stood there for a long moment looking down at his first-born.

Miss Beardsley, who had perception, understood that she was not wanted here. She rose and with dignity said that she must really go and attend to some household matters. She left the room with stately quietness, and closed the door after her.

Lilybelle lay on her pillows and waited with that strong serenity which was like the earth itself. John, except at more violent intervals, had almost lost his power to frighten or sadden her. As he looked down at the baby, she looked at him. Her face became very soft and gentle and full of love.

He turned to her with abrupt and jerky movements, and she saw his suffering. It did not matter to her what had caused it. He was suffering as a child suffers, and the first thing a child desires is comfort and tenderness.

She lifted her round white arms to him speechlessly, and smiled a little. She had never done this before, but in her simplicity she did not reflect on her audacity, and that this gesture might be rudely repudiated, and with scorn and hatred.

He stared at her, his eyes flickering with fire. He stiffened. If there had been the slightest taint of cajolement or theatrical falseness in Lilybelle's attitude, he would have broken into harsh and furious laughter. But he saw nothing but the pretty young girl in her white bed, her lovely curling bright hair on her shoulders, and her expression of tenderness, sympathy and understanding.

Instinct, rather than desire, sent him stumbling towards her, made him fall on his knees beside the bed and drop his aching head upon her breast. He felt her arms enfold him with warmth and infinite love. He heard her speechless murmurs of compassion and love. The hot anguish in his heart mysteriously began to abate. The love of all simple women implicit in Lilybelle seemed to him like cool water washing over burning wounds, an undemanding love that asked nothing else but to comfort.

"O Lilybelle," he groaned, and pressed his cheek more urgently against her breast. "O my God, Lilybelle!"

"Yes, yes," she whispered. "Yes, my love."

CHAPTER 25

MR. LIVINGSTON surveyed his superintendent, John Turnbull, with his pale blue and watery eyes. He sat in stiff dignity behind his desk, his white hand lying impotently upon it.

He had absolutely no aversions or likings for his young superintendent, for he was a man of no strong emotions at all. John, to him, was only a piece of machinery, or a young human being who had been installed in Everett Livingston & Company for expedient reasons. Beyond that, he did not exist. He was useful. He was competent, restless and keen, and his dour expressions and occasional vehemences had not disturbed Mr. Livingston at any time. He had allowed John to have his way, knowing vaguely that behind John's decisions stood the form of the genial Mr. Wilkins.

But today he saw John as more than just a man who represented usefulness to his company. He had suddenly enlarged to Mr. Livingston, had annoyingly come close, had exuded a disagreeable warmth which had begun to thaw the edges of Mr. Livingston's remote personality. In short, he had forcibly impinged himself on Mr. Livingston's notice, and this was enough to arouse in that gentleman an active if frigid dislike.

He really saw John for the first time, and decided that the "feller" was objectionable. Did he not know that his function was to advance the prosperity of the company and not to intrude his humanness upon his employer?

"You were saying, sir?" asked John with impatient courtesy.

Mr. Livingston moved his head in his high starched collar, then regarded John with affronted dignity.

"I was saying that I seriously object to this importation of most—ah—objectionable persons into my New England mills. Really inexcusable creatures, Mr. Turnbull. I cannot understand what you are thinking of."

John compressed his big angry lips as he strove for a reasonable voice. "Mr. Livingston," he said at last, "you must really understand the situation. There are not enough men and women, or children, in the community about the mills to expand production. We have all the farm folk and the town folk we can procure. Now, with new mills we need more labour. It is very simple. Too, the natives demand too high a rate of wages. These French-Canadians will work for much less. We can hire their children for not more than two dollars a week. Surely you can see the possibilities?"

Mr. Livingston contemplated the possibilities, and his ascetic white face momentarily became uncertain and confused. He toyed with a paper knife.

John continued: "We can hire the men for seven dollars a week, the women for five. These people breed like rabbits. Most of them have five to eight children. For twenty-two dollars a week we can hire a whole family, whereas a similar family of old New Englanders would demand at least fifty. I cannot see how you can object to this, then."

Mr. Livingston rubbed his lower lip against the faint frosty line of his mustache. Then he said: "How young are the children you contemplate engaging?"

John shrugged. "The New Englanders will not allow their children under twelve to work, even for four hours a day, and all day Saturday, after school. They insist upon schooling. But the French-Canadians care nothing for schooling, and, in fact, their priests deplore it except in rare and unusual instances. We can hire children as young as seven years old for several hours a day."

Mr. Livingston rose with a graceful movement that even his age could not destroy. With bent head he slowly paced up and down the room. John watched him, then smiled darkly.

"Mr. Wilkins said to me yesterday: 'Do the little beggars good. Nothin' like hard work to keep down high feelin's from eatin' too much meat.' "

Mr. Livingston continued to pace the bare cold office as if he had not heard.

"Mr. Wilkins," continued John, the darkness of his smile increasing, "points out the mills in England, where children as young as five and six work ten hours a day. To their distinct betterment, he urges."

Mr. Livingston said in a low voice: "I've been to Manchester. I've seen the women and the children in the cotton mills." He shivered. "I've heard them coughing their lungs out, from the chaff and the fluff. I've seen the women and the girls in the coal mines—" He paused. His elegant and aristocratic face tightened. He continued, in a lower but firmer voice: "I'll not have such things in my mills."

For an instant an inscrutable look passed over John's features. But he said nothing just then.

Mr. Livingston continued, as if recounting a scene of indescribable horror to himself: "They crawled on their hands and knees, almost naked, blackened like blackamoors, streaming with sweat. They snarled and sobbed like dying animals. And the men who used them for this infamous thing sat in their country estates drinking their wine and fattening up their fine ladies and their strumpets."

John, who had risen when his employer had risen, played absently with the pens on Mr. Livingston's desk. He had looked up alertly once, then had become silent again.

Mr. Livingston drew a deep breath, for unaccustomed emotion choked him. "I'll not have this thing in America, at least not in my own mills, Mr. Turnbull. Not so long as I have one heart-beat left."

"I did not know you were such a democrat, Mr. Livingston," murmured John, sardonically.

But Mr. Livingston heard his words, and a dull flush crept under the crumpled parchment of his skin. He drew up, haughtily. "I am no democrat, Mr. Turnbull, at least not the sort you imply so unpleasantly. But, there are things men cannot do, in decency and honour. I shall not have babes in arms strangling in my mills."

John turned to him impatiently, but he said with enough respect: "Let us discuss this sensibly, Mr. Livingston. These French-Canadians are inured to hardship. Their priests have seen to that. They are ignorant, illiterate, stupid, greedy and dull as dogs. Work is nothing to them. The children work from the moment they walk——"

The flush increased on Mr. Livingston's face, and his blue eye flashed with unusual ire. "You don't see the implications of all this, Mr. Turnbull? Of course, you are an Englishman, who does not accord humanity to those who are poor and unprotected. But I am an American. I deplore many things most strenuously, and hope that the day will come when a worker will be regarded as more than a beast of burden. I love my country, Mr. Turnbull, strange as it may seem to you. And because I love her, I fear for her safety, virtue, integrity and health. There is a threat implicit in the entrance to America of such as these—these French-Canadians. Not that, of course, I do not feel the utmost compassion for them, and admit they are human, also. They are not responsible for their sad condition. But I cannot see that by allowing them to enter with their illiteracy, their stupidity, their adherence to a foreign, repugnant, and alien hierarchy, they advance the welfare of America. Nor are they of those honoured and persecuted men who have come to America to escape that very hierarchy, and to enjoy the blessings of liberty. They come solely for money, for even the pittance you would dole out to them."

He paused. John was looking at him steadfastly. But Mr. Livingston knew very little of men, could not read his expression.

Mr. Livingston continued, in a more hurried and stronger tone:

"Though this will no doubt bore you, Mr. Turnbull, I will recall to your memory the fact that America was founded by noble men who could not endure slavery, ignorance, persecution and superstition in their native lands. They came here to breathe the air of freedom, of—of liberation. Later, other men like them followed them, from France, from Germany, from England, and other nations. We give them all honour," and Mr. Livingston inclined his white and narrow head. "But these others, such as the wretches my competitors and other business men and industrialists are bringing here now on cattle boats—they are a menace and a threat to America. They come in their filth, like a pack of hungry and ravening wolves, escaping famine. America, and her ideals, mean nothing to these creatures. She is a land to be plundered. She is a land to be perverted by their own alien allegiances, their obnoxious religions, their desperate tyrannies. She is a land to be seduced and enslaved by the Papist hierarchy, to be brought under the thumb of Rome. Mr. Turnbull, sir, I shall not be guilty of such betrayal of my country, my people! The Anglo-Saxon Protestant ideology of America shall not be betrayed by conscienceless scoundrels, not for all the money in the world!"

He paused by his desk, and with his frail patrician hand he struck on it loudly and dully. He was trembling slightly. One parchment cheek was twitching, and the blue fire of his eye was strong and resolute.

"Mr. Turnbull, I ask you to reflect on the future of America, should these alien hordes inundate her, and breed as they do. What of the future, Mr. Turnbull? Or, perhaps, you do not care. But I do! America will become rich and powerful. She will excite the lust and greed of less fortunate and vigorous nations. What then? They will assail her. They will seek to overcome her. Who will defend her then? These dark aliens, these ravagers, who owe allegiance not to America but to their greed and their appalling pagan religions? I assure you, Mr. Turnbull, they will not! They will not love her, no more than any plunderer or devourer loves that which he has plundered or devoured. Nor, having by biological accident so little intelligence, will they be stirred by any battle-cries of 'liberty, freedom, equality!' They will be but sounding words to them. A man needs integrity and tolerance and intelligence to understand these precious things."

"You are looking too far into the future, sir," said John. His head was bent. He lifted the cover of a thick ledger on Mr. Livingston's desk and glanced at the contents absently.

Mr. Livingston drew a strangled breath. He stood by his desk, so straight, so thin and so rigid that he seemed to gain in height.

"I am thinking of the future of America," he said. "The future of a race of people that stemmed strongly from England! A future of men of integrity, strength, cleanness and intelligence. How dare I betray them, and their children and grandchildren? Is America to become the vassal of some benighted, foul and illiterate European nation? Is her best in blood and manhood to be destroyed by the same monsters that have destroyed Spain, France, Italy and Russia? Never, sir! Never, never!"

He was overcome with his own rare passion. He sat down, holding stiffly to the arms of his chair while he slowly lowered his trembling and emaciated body to its seat. "Never, never," he whispered, above the choking of his lungs.

John sat down also. He seemed very thoughtful. Then he quietly opened the ledger.

"Let us look at things more realistically, sir. Of course, the final decision is with you.

"Here is Appleton's Mills, and the reports of their progress. And Gorth's mills, and Brownings', all situated in the same localities as Livingston's. You have maintained a higher standard than theirs, with regard to labour. Your rates have been much higher. But, nevertheless, your workers have not produced more. In fact, they have produced less. Mr. Wilkins would have some pungent observations to make about that!"

He smiled humorously at Mr. Livingston, but that gentleman's white face remained frozen and rigid.

"Now, thanks to our new processes and patents, we have taken a huge spurt in the cotton industry," continued John, biting his lip and trying to control his own thoughts. "We have gone very far, in a year. Your competitors have shown much anxiety. In order to maintain their profits, they have been importing these French-Canadians, and even some shiploads of people from Europe. They are now abreast of us. They will go on, and pass us. That is inevitable. You cannot get sufficient labour in New England, even if your competitors let their American workers go to you. Which I doubt they will, considering everything."

He closed the ledger, and looked fixedly at his employer, who was even whiter if possible.

"Mr. Livingston, I can tell you now that if we refuse to employ alien labour we shall lose what we have already gained. You can't compete with your competitors in the market. Unless, of course, you sacrifice all your profits—to America."

He paused, and smiled his dark and ironical smile, which had something twisted in it. Then, as Mr. Livingston said nothing, he shrugged.

"I doubt, however, that your stockholders will be so patriotic, and so delicate about the welfare of America. They have invested because they saw the chances of good return. You owe a duty to them, also. In short, we hire foreign labour, or we go under. That will be the end of Everett Livingston & Company."

He added, very softly: "The end. Bankruptcy. Ruin. The disappearance of Livingston from the cotton trade."

Mr. Livingston suddenly came to life with wild and feverish passion. He cried: "We have the best processes! The buying public will not be deceived! We can do business honourably and survive!"

John smiled again, and fatalistically shrugged. "Then it becomes my unpleasant duty, Mr. Livingston, to inform you that Mr. Wilkins has instructed me to tell you that in the event you are obdurate he will not allow you to use our patents."

Mr. Livingston stared at him. He wet lips as dry and cold as death.

"He would do that?" he whispered.

John averted his head. Unseen by Mr. Livingston, his hands clenched in his pockets. He felt a great sickness all through him.

"You and he are Englishmen," said Mr. Livingston, struggling for speech. "You are brothers to Americans. You would betray all that your race—our race—has stood for in all these agonized generations?"

John rose. He could endure no more. "I have pointed out to you, Mr. Livingston, the inevitable results of your policy. My own feelings have nothing to do with it. You must make your own decisions."

He waited. Mr. Livingston's eyes, staring so feverishly at him, slowly dulled, until they looked like the glazed eyes of a dead man. His face appeared to dwindle, to become ancient and wrinkled. Some enormous and dreadful battle was raging within him, at some far and terrible distance.

"Ruin, with misguided honour, sir, or a realistic point of view with great profits," said John. He leaned a little towards his employer, and his broad strong nostrils dilated. Mr. Livingston, who did not see him, was not aware that a man's whole future life, his very soul, was dependent on his words yet unspoken.

He stirred in his seat. Very slowly, he lifted his hand and covered his face. There was something most terribly defenseless in the lines of that hand. In his sunken attitude, in his hidden face, was a whole world of men faced with loss with honour, or gain with dishonour.

He felt something slip under his other hand.

"The writ of permission to import," said John, very softly.

Mr. Livingston dropped his hand. His livid face was twitching. He stared down at the paper and it seemed to him that the printed words were written in syllables of ominous and fateful fire.

"Even if you do not, others will," said John. "You cannot hold back the tide. King Canute could not, either."

But, thought Mr. Livingston, in his desperate and fatal turmoil, it is not significant that Canute could not hold back the engulfing waves. It was enough for his soul that he had tried. At the end, only the individual man's soul mattered, even if he was defeated.

He looked at the paper. There lay ruin, or deliverance.

Honour or profits. His heart felt as if burning bands had encased it, and were crushing it.

Then he looked up at John, and even though he was young, John read the agony and despair in those old eyes. There was even pleading in them.

"You can do nothing against Wilkins," said John.

There was a long silence in the office, while the old grandfather's clock stuck five in the gathering winter dusk.

Then, as John watched with fixed and distended eyes, Mr. Livingston lifted the pen and signed the writ of permission. And it seemed to John that the whole air rustled and scratched with the pens of men signing away the future of America.

CHAPTER 26

JOHN reread, frowning, the formidable legal letter received by him that morning from Gillespie, Gillespie & Gillespie:

"As we have a matter of extreme importance to communicate to you, we should regard it as a favour if you should call upon us this evening at six o'clock."

John knew these solicitors by repute, a sombrely rich and austere firm engaging in nothing more reprehensibly illegal than estates, the wills of wealthy men and funds in trust for widows and children. After some puzzling, he came to the conclusion that this message concerned the estate of some prominent stock-holder in Everett Livingston & Company.

At six o'clock of this fine early April evening, he left his offices and called for his carriage. He stood on the steps of the warehouse, looking unseeingly at the blue sky glimpsed above the buildings. He could smell the salt odour of the sea. There was a wash of ruddy gold on the faces of the blank warehouses across the narrow street, and the upper dusty windows burned with a hot crimson. Even in these noisome and muddy streets the scent of spring was strong and fresh, and John became aware of it as one becomes aware of an old wound, half-forgotten.

This was his second spring in America, but the first one of which he had been conscious, and this only today. He had lived in a dull formless dream of pain, hatred, revenge and

248

despair. The emotions, he thought, can blind a man to everything external, and create, in the midst of pleasantness and joy, a core of black and sightless agony. Now he looked about him as if he had just come to America, and was seeing it for the first time. Everything had a bright shine of unfamiliarity and strangeness. He had seen this street hundreds of times, the warehouses opposite, the sky and the passing faces. He had smelled the sea and felt its harsh strong breath on his cheek. Yet, in truth, he had seen and smelled nothing of all this before.

His sense of strangeness increased. For the first time he had partially emerged from himself. For one instant, as he looked at the patch of burning blue above him, his heart lurched and lifted with the old passion of spring. And then he was plunged again into a deeper and more poignant misery. Not for him again the freshness and joy of the new season. He had hated too much.

He hated, with a monstrous hatred, those who had spoiled life for him by making him hate them. No man who has hated, he thought, can ever be truly happy again. A slow seeping poison invades all his days, even when the original ulcer has been forgotten. There is an eternal disease in his blood, which does not confer immunity to fresh assaults, but increases his vulnerability to every foulness. It is not the hated, then, who are the victims. The hater is the victim of those he has hated.

Now that his awareness was like freed blood flowing through twisted and tortured veins, he felt that his skin had been flayed from him, that every nerve was exposed and throbbing. The narrow shadow of the cobbled street, the face of the illuminated warehouses opposite, the washed blue of the sky, the very gurgle of liberated water in the gutters, were all like pulsations of his own emotions. He wished, desperately, that he had never become aware again. He was filled with fear of fresh assaults. Better to have remained in a formless sick dream, than to have awakened to a strong and vital reality implicit with potential pain.

At last he became conscious that a private carriage had been standing at the corner, waiting. But it was not his own. As he stared at it, the coachman slapped the reins on the backs of the two fine black horses, and the carriage moved towards him. The carriage, too, was black, blindingly polished, the fittings of bright silver, the wheels twinkling as they caught the late rays of the last sun, the gleaming windows reflecting the light.

As he idly watched, wondering what had delayed his own carriage, this strange vehicle drew to stop in front of him. He saw the bonnet of a woman inside, and her lifted gloved hand and her pale intent face. He stared uncomprehendingly, then all at once a wild pang divided him and the ground seemed to move under his feet. He could not stir from the spot on which he stood, though he desperately desired it, and there was a loud roaring in his ears.

The window dropped, and the woman leaned her head through the aperture. "John," she said, quietly. "Please. I must speak to you."

He did not move. He looked at the face of his cousin, stern and composed as he remembered it, but older and stiller. She was dressed in dark gray, with sables about the throat. Her gray bonnet cast a pallid shadow over a face even more colourless. But her gray eyes were more brilliant than ever, larger, more strained, and her mouth glowed vividly in this sterile background.

As he stood there, not able to move, aware only of new anguish and new hatred, the coachman, in plum livery, leapt down from his seat and opened the carriage door. John found himself, without his own volition, approaching the carriage and entering it, while his cousin held her gray hoops aside for his passage. Then he was sitting beside her. The carriage moved on in a dream of cloud and shifting shadow.

The first pangs and upheavals subsiding, John became numb and unthinking. His dark face was set and rigid under the narrow brim of his tall hat. The carriage clop-clopped through the deserted cobbled street, turned towards the sea, entered a small empty alley composed of the backs of great warehouses. Then, as if at a signal, it stopped. There was nothing now but the sound of the ocean. The alley was plunged in dun shadow.

During this short journey, Eugenia had sat beside her cousin, as silent and removed as himself. She, too, had looked straight ahead, her gloved hands in her lap, her head high, her face closed and quiet.

Now she turned to him, and in that still neutral voice he so poignantly remembered, she said: "I waited for you. I had to see you. There is so much to say."

The rigidity that had encased John was broken. He turned to Eugenia, and his dark eyes glittered and jerked with his pain and hatred and misery.

"We have nothing to say to each other!" he said, in a pent and stifled voice. He put his hand on the handle of the door, and drew himself to the edge of the velvet seat. "Nothing at all. I don't know why I came with you."

Her gloved hand moved to his arm restrainingly. Now her

face flushed and tightened. She spoke in the old tone of authority, but there was a pleading note in it also.

"John, you must listen. Do you think this is less painful for me? We are not children, John. There is much to say."

He felt, all through him, the old sickness and desire and passion, the old love. This was Eugenia, her flesh, her presence, her faint fresh scent, her beloved gray eyes and calm haughty face. All at once he wanted to groan, to cry out. He wanted, with one supreme and desperate effort of will, to obliterate all that had gone before. He had a sick and feverish feeling that if his will were only strong enough, he would find himself back in London, in Eugenia's carriage, and nothing of agony and horror and loathing between them, but only the old sweet quarrelsomeness, the old eager plans, the old vehemence battering at her steely will.

He looked down at her as she sat beside him, and he thought: I can't endure this. Everything else was gone, and there was only Eugenia. There had never been anything else! How could he have forgotten?

The gray eyes, fixed so urgently upon him, saw all his thoughts. They softened. They filled with tears. She turned aside her head, and he saw her profile, delicate and chill, but inexpressibly moved and shaken.

"John," she whispered. The frail muscles of her white throat stood out above the brown fur, and trembled.

"Genie," he said. Involuntarily, his hand reached out and seized hers crushingly.

She struggled to regain that steely composure of hers. The tears were so thick in her eyes that she had to distend her lids to hold them, sternly. She swallowed. After a moment she spoke again, tonelessly:

"I am a mother now, John. I have a little boy. Anthony."

She did not look at him. Her eyes were fixed on the opposite wall of the carriage. But she felt the grip on her hand loosen, slacken, fall away. The carriage was pervaded by a deathly coldness.

Then John spoke, and his voice seemed to come from a great distance:

"And I have a little girl. Lavinia."

Then he laughed aloud, shortly, with a sound under the laughter that seemed quite terrible to Eugenia. She covered the hand John had held with her other hand. The fingers still ached and throbbed. She felt the shaking of John's laughter, harsh and desolate and infinitely derisive and bitter, and a tremor ran over her body.

Then he took the handle of the door again, and slid to the edge of the seat. "Goodbye, Genie," he said.

Terrified that he would leave her, she caught his arm desperately in both her hands. "No, John. I've got to talk to you. I came three thousand miles to you, John!"

Then, realizing the appalling indiscretion of her words, her hands fell from his arm. She lifted them to her face, and sat motionless.

There was a long silence in the carriage, while she knew he stared at her, slowly thinking of what she had said. At last she heard his voice, hushed and infuriated:

"How can you say that? How can you lie so?"

She dropped her hands. The pressure of her fingers had left red streaks on her white face. Her eyes burned with gray and feverish light. But she said coldly and contemptuously enough:

"You can speak of lying? You can pretend to be the injured one, John? After what you did to me? Have you forgotten what you did? Have you forgotten the shame you put upon me, the desertion, the misery? Why do you pretend to be so heroic, so wronged? It was you who left me, ran away from me, after disgracing and wounding me. I did not leave you. Whatever I have done is your doing."

He stared at her grimly. But he knew that much of what she had said was true. She sat upright and shaking near him, and her eyes shot lances of contempt and anger upon him. He clenched his teeth together, and turned away. Finally, he said:

"I made you marry Bollister, certainly. You knew what an enemy he was to me. You knew he was—responsible—for what happened. Yet, you could marry him."

She cried out, in a voice full of trembling indignation:

"How can you be so weak as to say this! If you had not been weak no one could have hurt you, John. But it is so like you to blame others for your own fault. If Andrew was your enemy, he could not have hurt you if you had not allowed him to. It was your weakness that opened the way to him. It was your own weakness that made you behave so abominably, without self-control or self-discipline. Yet, it is so easy for you to exonerate yourself, to make yourself appear the wronged one, the virtuous one who was betrayed by others!"

Two years ago, John's stung fury, unreasoning and impelled only by the instinct of self-defense, would have lashed out at her, disregarding truth and logic. But he was a man now. He had thought much and endured even more. He could feel no sustained rage, after its first tearing assault. Suffering had opened the way to reason.

He looked at his cousin's wet and haughtily contemptuous

252

face. It was so small, so pale, imbued with such a delicate and unshaken strength. The lines of her mouth were hard; the exquisite distended nostrils seemed carved from marble.

He said, bitterly: "You are right, Genie. I was weak. I was stupid. I did a rotten thing to you. You are right to condemn me. But, I cannot understand you. Knowing what Bollister had done to me, through my own weakness, and what an enemy he was to me, I can't comprehend why you married him."

She was silent a moment. Her eyes did not leave his, though their sternness increased. She said unemotionally: "I have told you. He said he was coming to America. I married him, so I could be near you."

There was no shame, no hesitation in her voice. She looked at him steadfastly, without a blush or a shrinking. He felt her hard and uncompromising courage, matter-of-fact, and without bravado. He regarded her incredulously. He had forgotten how relentless, how ruthless, Eugenia could be.

As if he could not trust himself to look at her, he averted his head.

"And now?" he said, almost inaudibly. "And now that you are here, Genie?"

She was silent. He thought, as he waited, still not looking at her, that she was suddenly frightened, suddenly filled with fear. But when he turned to her again, she was as quiet and steadfast as ever, gazing at him with a world of proud and inflexible meaning in her calm eyes.

She was stronger than he, and that is why he did not take her just then in his arms, and satisfy the anguished hunger in himself. It was he who trembled, and not Eugenia. It was he, in a kind of strange shame and reticence, that was embarrassed.

He stammered, out of the welter of his emotions: "Tell me, Eugenia: do you—do you care anything for him?"

In a tone as measured and controlled as always, she answered: "No. I do not dislike, or hate him. He has been a good husband to me, according to his lights. I have nothing to complain of. I have a little son, too."

She spoke of her child with no emotion at all, as if neither her husband nor son mattered to her in the least, as if they were extraneous creatures with whom she had the most casual and indifferent of relationships.

The strangest emotions, rather than thoughts, swept over John. He could not analyse them. He could only gaze at this young hard creature, with her pale and beautiful face, her wide and faintly rosy mouth with its inflexible and remorseless lines, her unshaken and unreadable gray eyes, so brilliant and so unmoved. The reticence and delicacy inherent in almost every man, however gross, caused John to wince, to feel a slight coldness over all his flesh. Eugenia seemed incredible to him, unbelievable, and oddly unfamiliar. He thought confusedly: I never really knew her, never at all. The fear that all men of hot and generous impulses experience in the presence of calm and inexorable exigency and inhuman fixity of purpose invaded him now.

She said, still with firmness and calmness: "And you, John? Do you care for that—for your wife? And your child?"

Still confused and shaken by his emotions, John was silent for some long moments. Then, striving for her own detachment, and succeeding only in making his voice uneven and breathless, he said: "Lilybelle is only a circumstance to me. I hated her once. Detested her. She was repugnant to me. And now? I tolerate her. She—is nothing. She makes me comfortable. I have nothing in common with her." He paused, and now his voice was softer: "I have a very dear little lass, Eugenia."

Then, he felt a power in her, impassive, immovable. That power made him appear foolish and weak, too filled with human softness and irresolution. He turned to her. She was smiling a little, subtly, with a cold cruelty that paled and molded the lines of her mouth.

"All this has nothing to do with us, John," she said. She laid her cool hand on his. He felt its delicacy and deceptive frailness.

"No," he said, his heart plunging, "it has nothing to do with us."

They looked for a long time in each other's eyes. Then Eugenia's smile became incredibly soft and tremulous. A faint rosy light spread over her face, and it was young and tender again. Her lips parted. Her breath came through them, hurried and urgent. The marble of her throat dissolved into warm and pulsing white flesh, and, as she leaned towards him, the beautiful lines of her young breast seemed to swell, to seek to burst the tight gray bodice that enclosed it. She lifted her hands imploringly. They trembled, the fingers becoming soft and eager.

He tried to speak, and then was silent. Then he caught her in his arms and pressed his mouth hard upon hers. She melted against him. The bonnet fell down upon her back, and her shining brown hair, so smooth and orderly, loosened and rolled down over her neck and shoulders. He felt the wild and tumultuous beating of her heart against his. A wild rapture swept over him. His hands pressed her body, hot and seeking, and her firm flesh softened and yielded under them.

They were aware of nothing but their turbulent coming together, the satisfying of their desperate hunger. The shadows of evening closed about the carriage, entered it and filled it with darkness. The coachman on his high seat yawned, turned and tried to see in the vehicle. But he could see nothing. He heard nothing at all.

CHAPTER 27

JOHN lay tensely beside his wife all that night, unable to sleep for the feverish thronging of his thoughts. Lilybelle breathed softly and regularly, the night air scented with the sweetness of her warm flesh. But John was no more aware of her than if she had never been born.

There had been much said and promised between him and Eugenia. So much spoken until the carriage had been engulfed in complete darkness, and yet, they felt, at parting, that they had not said all that there had been to say.

Eugenia had informed him sadly that he had not heard from his father for the reason that James had suffered a stroke two weeks after the departure of John, that he had enforced a promise from Eugenia that John not be told. "There will be enough of adjustments and confusion for him," he had said. But, Eugenia hurried to reassure the anxious young man, Uncle James had shown much improvement later, and had been able to attend her wedding to Andrew Bollister. He had seemed quite well at that time.

However, the puzzled Eugenia commented, when he was informed that she and Andrew were to leave for America almost immediately after the wedding ceremony, he had acted quite strangely. Moreover, he had been actually incoherent, and had made remarks which she found it difficult to understand and interpret. He had urged her to make no effort to see her cousin in America. He had said he, John, was not to be made unhappy. That is why, said James, he had not allowed John to be informed of his illness, and why, now recovered, he had not yet written. John was to be allowed to secure a firm foothold in America before being reminded of his old home and his kinsfolk. (He had said other things to Eugenia, bitter, denunciatory and angry things, but these the young woman prudently refrained from divulging to John.)

"So," said John, in his aching love for his father, and his misery, "so that is why he didn't answer my letters." He had a sense of great desolation. If he had only known the truth, how different life might have been for him, and for others! But of this he dared not think just now.

He lay now and thought of his father. Then, as the thought brought nothing but pain, he thought of Eugenia, and his heart and his flesh burned with impassioned joy and a mysterious sorrow. How brave and resolute she had been to do the things she had done, for him! He was humbled and incredulous at the very thought, and unbearably elated. It had been enough for him, that evening, to hold her in his arms and kiss her lips, but he felt in her a surging power and restlessness, as if these embraces had not been enough, that it was necessary for much more to satisfy her. Nor was it solely passion, John recalled, with vague confusion. There was a greater urgency in the delicate and exquisite Eugenia, something sexless and indomitable and relentless, something which aroused a cold and nameless caution in him, and inexplicable resentment. For awhile, he had felt that he had been the weaker of the two, and that he had been exposed to a strange ruthlessness.

Let us forget what has gone, Eugenia had said to him, looking into his eyes. And, as she said this, he could believe, for high and blazing moments, that it would be possible. It could be possible to forget their marriages, their children, this alien land, and all the desolation, hunger, grief and wretchedness that lay between. They would make a world for themselves here, in which America and families could not enter. "A bit of England," Eugenia had said. And in that "bit" they would be free again, and young and untouched again, like children, wandering hand in hand in a universe created by themselves, eternally young and careless.

When he had suggested, in a restive surge of his old hatred, that Andrew would still be existing, and waiting outside the charmed circle of that golden universe, Eugenia's face had shown a faint dark shadow, and she had put her fingers gently on his lips. "What does it matter?" she had asked. However, she had changed the subject quite abruptly.

She had listened with tender sympathy to his account of how he had fared in America, and had uttered little cries of exultation. Tactfully, of course, she did not tell him of Mr. Gorth's angry denunciations of Andrew, and the furious arguments which took place regularly in the fine home on Fifth Avenue since Mr. Wilkins had displayed his astute duplicity concerning the new patents. It was not Eugenia's intention to soften John's rage against her husband and his uncle.

Like one remembering every detail of an occasion of great joy, John went over the events of that evening. He remembered, vividly, his heavy sadness because he had been unable to feel the Spring, and could only see it, and then, later, how the world had taken on vividness and a poignancy too sharp to be endured. He had left Eugenia, and had walked home, and all the air, the stars, the very stones under his feet, had seemed to sing, with a wild high agony of joy.

He had stood there, on the warehouse steps, waiting for his carriage, too leaden of heart to feel anything, and then Eugenia had come!

Then, all at once, he thought: Where had I been going? There had been an unimportant letter from the lawyers Gillespie, about some trivial matter no doubt concerning a stockholder. John smiled disdainfully in the darkness.

Suddenly, without any discernible reason, his heart began to beat with savage swiftness, and he sat up in bed, his ears ringing, his eyes smarting, his whole body pervaded with a sensation of disaster and terror. He got out of bed, trembling heavily. The windows were gray with dawn. He sat beside them, his throat dry and choking, telling himself incoherently that it was all nonsense, this fear, that it was the night, and his exhaustion, and the events of the past evening, which had brought this reaction upon him. But still, the fear mounted blacker, more nameless, and when Lilybelle awoke, with a murmurous sigh, and a smile, she found him sitting there, rigid and cold, in the light of the morning.

Mr. Aaron Gillespie, a little wiry man with a dry face like a sharp ferret, was surprised to find Mr. John Turnbull waiting for him at eight o'clock that morning.

"We expected you last night, Mr. Turnbull," he said, briskly seating himself beside his desk in the office that smelled of leather and legality and the mustiness of virtuous law. He eyed John curiously, and with a little hesitation. This young man with the pale dark face and sleepless eyes looked ill to him. Was it possible he had already heard?

"I was delayed, unavoidably," replied John. He moistened his parched lips. Then he could not longer control himself: "It isn't about my father, is it, sir? I don't know why," he added, smiling painfully, but fixing his eyes with pathetic urgency upon the little man, "but I've had that foolish idea all night——"

Mr. Gillespie was silent. He lit a cheroot so long that it looked ridiculous in his small gray face. He spent quite a time on its correct lighting, swearing genteelly under his breath at the spluttering "lucifer," and frowning severely at the lighted end as though it were culpable. And all the time John waited, sitting on the edge of his chair, his clenched hands pressed on the top of his tall hat.

Mr. Gillespie cleared his throat, and spoke quietly: "Yes, Mr. Turnbull, it is about your father." He paused and studied John apprehensively. An emotional beggar, from the look of him, and violent. Strange that such a big young man could be so volatile. Big men were usually calm and lethargic. He wondered if he should call in one of his partners to help him bear the brunt of what was likely to happen.

"You haven't heard from your father recently? About his illness?"

John was so relieved that he felt quite weak, and a light sweat broke out upon his face. He smiled slightly. "Yes, I have heard. From my cousin. Last night. But I understand he is better now."

Mr. Gillespie allowed a grave expression to come over his face. He nodded sombrely. "Yes, Mr. Turnbull. Very much better. Very much better, indeed. He will never suffer again."

There was a sudden silence in the room. Then, stiffly, as if pushed to his feet, John rose. He put his hands on the desk to support himself, leaning forward.

"You mean," he said, very quietly, "that he is dead."

Mr. Gillespie was quite relieved. He was not wrong, then, about the lethargy and lack of emotion in big men. For John had seated himself, and was sitting motionless in his chair, staring blindly before him. But beyond this, he showed no other emotion.

"Yes," said Mr. Gillespie, in a sepulchral voice, "he has passed on. Very calmly, in his sleep, I am informed by his solicitor. About six months ago."

After a long pause, John asked tonelessly: "I wasn't informed."

"No, it was by his request that you were not. Six months were to elapse. I may say, however, that I, myself, was not informed by my English associate until day before yesterday. I understand," continued Mr. Gillespie, clearing his throat, "that your father appeared to wish that you be better established before you were told. He seemed to be very solicitous about you."

John said nothing. He felt nothing in himself but desolation, too profound, too deep, for speech or thought. Later, there would come anguish and wild sorrow, but not yet.

Mr. Gillespie opened a drawer and proceeded briskly about the business. He laid a sealed envelope before John. "A letter to you from your father," he said. He rustled other papers. "And now, let us go into the matter of your inheritance:

"You are to receive fifty thousand dollars immediately, Mr. Turnbull. At the age of twenty-five, fifty thousand more, provided that you have earned, by your own endeavours, not less than fifteen thousand dollars. From what I have heard," and he smiled fondly at John, "you have already been able to accumulate much more than that already. So, there will be no trouble about that part of the will. Then, at the age of thirty, you are to receive the balance of your father's estate, provided," and now Mr. Gillespie betrayed some embarrassment, "that you are still living in connubial relationship with your present wife, the former Miss Lilybelle Botts. Unless, (and we hope this will not come to pass) she has already passed on."

But John had heard only the rumbling echo of his words. He had taken up the envelope and was opening it with stiff and icy fingers. His father's words, written in a painful and angular hand, lay before him:

"My dear son, this is a letter of regret and sorrow, and a plea for forgiveness. There were so many years when I might have been a father to you, but I had not allowed this, in my selfishness and stupidity. I might have saved you much regret and bitterness of heart, much disaster and pain. I did not do this. Not out of design, but out of ignorance and love of self and comfort. Perhaps this is the more reprehensible, the more unpardonable. I believe it is. That is why I implore you to forgive me, even though I will be in my grave when this is put into your hands.

"We often say 'but that is all gone and done with, and forgotten.' But nothing is forgotten. We cannot stay the widening rings in the water when we cast in our stone. The rings go on into infinity. Only compassion and forgiveness can make their effects endurable. But the stone remains, sunken at the bottom of our consciousness, and our lives. I cannot recall that stone. I only ask that by your own efforts, and your fortitude, you do not let it destroy your life. Otherwise, even in the grave, there can be no peace for me.

"I cannot say to you: 'be happy.' Those are the words of fools. I hope I have not been a fool, though I have been a criminal in my dealings with you. I can only say: 'be strong. Do not let others destroy your life. Your life is your own, sacred to you, and to God.' You have never heard me speak of God, except with a faint smile and a shrug. But now that I stand here alone, I know there is nothing but a man and his God, at the last. Remember God; think of the day when you will stand as I stand at this hour, and know there is nothing else. Be strong. A man needs all his strength to survive. He needs it even more when he loves. Men, perhaps, have not died for love, but they have been destroyed by it. You will know my meaning.

"Be true, not to other men, but to yourself. That is the first commandment. Never lie to yourself. Men lie more to themselves than they do to others.

"I wish I might look at your face again, my dearest son, and touch your hand. But that is not to be. That is my punishment. Forgive me."

John folded the letter slowly. He stood up. And then, without another word, he left the office.

BOOK THREE

CHAPTER 28

IT WAS very odd, but the flowers Lilybelle grew in her garden were as blowsy and opulent and warm as herself.

Others might grow the most genteel of little pink tearoses, properly behaved and correct of petal and leaf, but Lilybelle's roses were lush and riotous, huge, overpowering of scent, boisterous of leaf and thorn. But she loved them, and would bury her rosy plump face deep into their hearts, sniffing loudly, and with quite unrefined delight.

She had gathered a big basket of them this June morning, and was busily engaged in thrusting masses of them into every available Chinese and alabaster vase she could find in the pleasant brick house on West Eleventh Street, much to the aristocratic alarm of her housekeeper, Mrs. Bowden, who, however, loved her passionately. (Later, Mrs. Bowden would remove the masses, and allow only a few exquisite buds and blossoms to remain in each jar and vase. She would strip off most of the enormous leaves, and would pick off the happy insects.)

Lilybelle, in her morning gown of sprigged muslin, her hoops swaying vigorously, was a pleasant sight, for all she had taken on much white flesh. But her height prevented her from obesity, so that her appearance was warmly commanding rather than gross. Too, her face was full rather than fat, and if there was a suspicion of a double chin already making its appearance, it only served to enhance her air of lush generosity, health and vitality. Her white skin had pearly-rose undertones to it, and her big, if somewhat stupid and sensual mouth, was flushed with living scarlet, the lips always parting in smiles to reveal flashes of marvellously sound and snowy teeth. If her round blue eyes were often vacant and vague, they could brighten with an almost constant affection and good humour, and one forgot that the short wide nose had distinctly the appearance of a pretty snout. The vivid auburn curls no longer hung down her neck upon her shoulders, but were piled in lustrous and beautifully radiant masses upon her handsome head, and little coppery tendrils curled lovingly at the nape of her long white neck. Mrs.

Bowden thought her the loveliest (if the most buxom) lady she knew. Never were there such large white arms, with such dimples at the elbows. It made one quite forget that the hands were large and coarse, the nails square and too pink.

Mrs. Elsie Bowden, a brown spare little sparrow of a woman, followed her mistress about on the rose-disposing business, listening to the endless loud chatter of the young woman about household duties and the children, the flowers and the weather, and forthcoming meals. Mrs. Bowden listened with an attentive smile, and a fond look in her beady brown eyes. Dressed in brown cotton, over which was a black satin apron, white-capped and with white linen at the wrists, and with a huge bunch of jingling keys at her compact little waist, Mrs. Bowden was a wholesome and comforting small woman. She had a brown wrinkled face, wise and quiet, the arched and delicate nose of the Beardsleys, and a still puckered mouth. She was exceedingly intelligent and shrewd, uncompromising but gentle. She never forgot that Lilybelle, against all the stern and outraged arguments of her cousin, Miss Amanda, had rescued her from the misery of a cold back room and had taken her away to all this pleasantness, noise and gaiety and happy "dis"order of the house on West Eleventh Street. She had her own comfortable apartments on the third floor, a cosy bedroom and a fine sitting-room with a fireplace and plenty of coal, and fifty dollars a month to boot. She managed all the affairs of the household, including the nursemaid for the three little girls, four housemaids and the cook, and the two gardeners. She was friend and counsellor and guardian, and Lilybelle could not have done without her, in her vague frivolity, irresponsibility and quite complete helplessness to manage her family.

Lilybelle chattered about her children. The last governess had left, and Lilybelle discussed the new present incumbent with her housekeeper.

"Do you think Miss Hamlin really understands the children?" she asked, with a vague passing anxiety, as she stood off to admire the last enormous bunch of roses to be forced into the large Chinese vase on the polished grand piano. The drawing-room was quite enormous. Lilybelle had had no part in the selection of this furniture, at least. John, not knowing that he was doing so, had reproduced the austerity and elegance of his father's home in his own house. The gleaming floors, scattered with Persian and Turkish carpets, the few chairs in their quiet tapestries and damasks, the white walls and molded ceilings, the crimson draperies and white marble fireplace, all revealed an astonishing taste in John. But the room did not appeal to the exuberant Lilybelle, who privately thought it very dreary and cold and bare. She had been allowed to indulge her own taste, however, in the other rooms of the big colourful house. The drawing-room rioted in scarlets and blues and gilt and intricately carved black walnut furniture. The bedrooms were noisy with colour, and crowded to the very doors. If it was all very vulgar and riotous, it was also very gay and comfortable. "Homelike," Lilybelle would say, with satisfaction, avoiding the drawing-room except when stuffing flowers into every available receptacle, or when entertaining guests. (She was certain that the guests found the room as overpowering as she did, and was only happy when she led the way into her great and violent dining-room.)

She would have liked to have been allowed to do something with John's apartments, out of her love for him. But here he would not allow her to enter. His rooms were all leather, heavy mahogany, dull rich carpets and hangings, and quiet order. His father would have been quite astonished.

The two gardeners were always in despair over her, but adored her. Not for Lilybelle well-ordered and prim paths and well-behaved flowers. There must be a riot and thunder of hues, rose-covered arbours, intricate flagged paths, bird-baths, little bright pools covered with water-lilies, and shady retreats under thick trees, all with a fine disregard for symmetry and classical taste. It was in vain that the gardeners pointed out that the land was entirely too small for such exuberance, and it would need at least three acres, instead of half an acre, to contain all this without an effect of disorder and confusion. Lilybelle had her way, but so prettily, so affectionately, that she was always obeyed, and the gardeners toiled to bring order out of chaos. Too, she was always so contrite, so anxious to placate, when she had her way, that the gardeners usually assured her hurriedly that she had better taste than they had, themselves.

Unlike the usual run of gardeners, the elder gardener was always vastly relieved when Lilybelle swooped down upon the gardens and carried off enormous masses. It "tidied" up the place, in his opinion, to have such overwhelming armfuls taken away.

As Mrs. Bowden followed Lilybelle about, trying to extract orders for the day out of the loud and running remarks constantly bursting from her smiling mouth, the housekeeper assured her mistress that she considered the new governess quite satisfactory, and a good influence upon the children.

"She is quite civil, and refined," said Mrs. Bowden, in her gentle but resolute voice. She carefully adjusted the white cap with its fluted borders upon her little gray head. "And that is just what the children need. They have been allowed too much liberty, in my opinion. Miss Higgins was entirely too lax with them. That was because she was lazy, and preferred to munch with the maids in the kitchen to teaching the children good manners. You know yourself, Mrs. Turnbull, that their language was becoming quite outrageous. I have even heard Lavinia swear, and Louisa was becoming entirely too pert. Though," she added, with a soft change upon her stern little brown countenance, "nothing could spoil Adelaide, nothing in the world."

Lilybelle paused in her distribution of the flowers, and turned quickly to her housekeeper. Her big and highly flushed countenance became radiant, and foolish with love. "Oh, Adelaide, the little monkey," she said, with a deeper tone in her loud and careless voice. "You did always spoil her, you know you did, Bowden. And such an ugly little thing, too, not to be compared with Lavinia and Louisa, who are so beautiful, the darlings."

"I don't regard Adelaide as being ugly," said Mrs. Bowden, with spirit, and quite flushing in her indignation. "She has character, and refinement, and elegance. The child could not lie, no matter what happened. She is as straight as a die. You will forgive me, Mrs. Turnbull, but Adelaide is a lady, a thing I cannot say in all truth of Lavinia and Louisa, for all their handsomeness."

Lilybelle was not offended. She laughed comfortably. "Who cares if they are ladies or not," she said, giving Mrs. Bowden a brief hug, and having to bend considerably to do so. "You are an old bear, Bowden."

Her voice, under years of tutelage by Miss Beardsley, had almost completely lost its old country accent. But it could never lose its strong and vital coarseness, its evidence of vivid life and exuberance. She almost never committed an error in grammar, thanks to Miss Beardsley, though she could still only read the simplest of words. Miss Beardsley had finally given up in despair at making Lilybelle literate.

She paused, after the hug bestowed on Mrs. Bowden, to think about her youngest child. In spite of her words, the look on her face betrayed that Adelaide was her pet, her love, her darling, her Benjamin. She said, wishing to urge on the housekeeper to fresh praises of the child: "It's true she's clever, Bowden. Too clever, her Papa says. But such a little pale face, and such big brown eyes, and the lashes too long and black for real beauty. So solemn, too, like a little monkey. You hardly ever hear her laugh."

"Perhaps," said Mrs. Bowden, quietly, "she hasn't much to laugh about."

She hardly thought Lilybelle would understand this, for usually the young woman was so stupid and obvious. But to Mrs. Bowden's surprise, Lilybelle's large and pretty fat face suddenly clouded, and she seemed oddly distrait. She turned away and fumbled unnecessarily with the roses, and a thorn entered her thumb. She uttered a loud and really vulgar word, and thrust the thumb in her mouth, where she sucked on it vigorously. But her big blue eyes had a dark distress in them.

"Oh, Bowden, that ain't—isn't—so, and you know it," she said, her articulation somewhat obscured by the thumb. She removed the digit, and examined it with too much absorption. She continued: "The little lass doesn't make friends, not even with her own sisters. Keeps to herself, like a naughty little foreigner. No wonder they tease her."

"They're quite brutal to her, Mrs. Turnbull," said Mrs. Bowden, with fresh indignation. "I know it is not my place to remark on this, but I've desired to speak to you of it for some time. I trust you will pardon me. Adelaide is too proud to complain, too reticent. Too, she isn't very strong, and can't hold her own against those big and careless girls. They pounce upon her like young animals, and maul her unpardonably. Then she will creep off to her room, and never let any one see her tears. Perhaps she is foreign to them," added Mrs. Bowden, gravely. "Perhaps she is superior to them, for even though she is only eight years old, she quite surpasses them in her lessons. Even Miss Higgins remarked on that. And her music is really exceptional. The other girls are quite stupid at music." Mrs. Bowden hesitated. She would have liked to have protested at Mr. Turnbull's open and savage dislike of his youngest daughter, but refrained from doing so. However, her wise mouth tightened, trembled at the corners.

Lilybelle, despite her obtuseness, evidently caught a little of her thought, for she said, in a somewhat dull voice: "I wish Mr. T. could hear you, Bowden. Addy's plainness offended him. With all that long straight brown hair, so fine, and not curling proper in spite of rags and hot irons. The other lasses have such pretty curls, Linny's so black and rich, and Louisa's so yellow and bright. And they've got such nice colour, too."

"There are some," said Mrs. Bowden, severely, "who prefer delicacy of colouring and fineness of feature and decorum to obvious prettiness. I find Adelaide a true beauty. She will never be as tall as her sisters, but she will have grace and refinement, and true breeding. There are some," she continued courageously, "who prefer ale and whiskey, and those who prefer fine wine. Adelaide is brewed from the best, and her bouquet will be adequately appreciated some day."

The unstable Lilybelle glowed like the sun upon the little woman. Impulsively, she bent again and kissed her with generous abandon. "O Bowden!" she exclaimed, "I know it's so! Nobody could be sweeter or finer than my little darling! I always tell Mr. T., but he thinks I'm a fool. I know I'm a fool, but about her children, a mother knows!"

Swinging rapidly from delight to sadness, she said mournfully: "Mr. T. doesn't understand lasses. Because the older lasses make such a to-do over him, he thinks they love him quite to death. But they're so selfish, and grasping, even if I'm so fond of them, and say it myself. He doesn't know that Addy is the one who loves him, truly, and more than she does me, even if I'm her own mother."

"The child's affection for her Papa is excessively touching," agreed Mrs. Bowden, with sombre regret. "But, she can't express it. She can just look at him with her great brown eyes, full of tears. Gentlemen are so oblivious. I believe Mr. Turnbull thinks Adelaide is sulky and dull."

"Yes," agreed Lilybelle. "And it does no good for me to tell him."

Mrs. Bowden regarded her with secret compassion. She knew that Lilybelle's two older daughters despised her, mocked and ridiculed her behind her back, and reflected their father's attitude toward their mother with malicious and childish fidelity. They never obeyed her if they could help it. They played cruel little tricks upon her, laughing loudly at her confusion and bewilderment and hurt. Nor could Lavinia, for instance, be excused on the ground of too much youth. She was almost thirteen, and physically older than her actual age, practically a young lady now. And there was Louisa, so deceptively sweet and charming and dainty, as cruel and even more merciless than her older sister, a cunning shrewd woman at eleven. No, there was no excuse for them. For all their assurance and greed and realism, they were not worthy of such a mother, ignorant and stupid though Lilybelle was. Mrs. Bowden, having suffered at the hands of the clever and the exigent and ruthless, had the highest regard and appreciation for those who were kind and pure of heart, and generous. Kindness, to her, was more than beauty, gentleness more than elegance, and charity nobler than breeding.

There were other things which Mrs. Bowden might have told Lilybelle, but hot irons could not have dragged them from her. She could have told her, for instance, of a matter that was common and sniggering talk in the servants' dining-hall, and that was of a certain discreet little house on West Fifth Street, a blind and elegant little house of white wood with green shutters, where Mr. Turnbull and a certain highly bred lady met on regular afternoons, or evenings. Where the servants had obtained this information no one knew, and Mrs. Bowden had not only disdained to listen to the stories, but had ordered them to cease, in her presence, at least.

Pursuing her thoughts, Lilybelle said: "I've so wanted Linny to go to Miss Hartford's School for Young Ladies at Tarrytown, but Mr. T. won't hear of it. And Louisa ought to go, too. Such great girls to have a governess and a nursemaid! Makes them dependent, like. But Mr. T. will have his lasses at home. There will be a tutor, soon, he says. But you know how it is, Bowden," she added, helplessly. "The lasses are so forward and sharp, and there's no doing anything with them. I can't manage them, really, and we can't keep governesses. It's beyond me."

They went into the pretty if crowded morning room, where Lilybelle left the last of the flowers. Soft flowered curtains blew in the gentle summer wind, and the french windows opened on a slope of green that led to the brilliant gardens. Here canaries sang in white cages, and long streaks of sunlight sparkled on white ceiling and gay red walls and ruddy tiled floor. Lilybelle sat down and fanned her hot face with her kerchief. On her damp forehead the coppery hair curled in ringlets, and her white hands and neck glowed with a vibrant warmness. If she could only curb her appetite, thought Mrs. Bowden, with loving regret, she would regain her lissome figure and be most excessively handsome. But her expression, if stupid, was so kind and generous, and even sweet, that one could forgive her anything, even her enormous zest at the table.

They completed the long list of household matters, and Mrs. Bowden competently jingling her keys, was about to depart on her duties, when a housemaid entered to inform Mrs. Turnbull that she had visitors, Mr. Wilkins and Miss Beardsley. Lilybelle sprang to her feet, her sprigged hoops swirling, and uttered an exclamation of pleasure. But Miss Bowden's withered brownish lips pursed.

Lilybelle ran through the cool freshness of the pleasant house to greet her guests, while Mrs. Bowden, remembering that Miss Beardsley was her cousin, followed more slowly.

"Such a lovely day, ma'am, and not so hot as yesterday, and the lady and I thought we'd drop in for a minute," said Mr. Wilkins, as his hostess burst delightedly into the drawing-room. "She'd had her carriage ready for an airing, and I joined her. I trust we don't intrude?"

"Oh, no, I'm so glad you've come!" cried Lilybelle, shaking hands warmly with her old friend, and then turning to kiss Miss Beardsley heartily on that august cheek. She looked at them both, her eyes shining in the polished gloom. There was something childlike in her unaffected pleasure and affection.

The years had hardly changed Mr. Wilkins at all. He was one of those men who mellow rather than age. A little more rotund, a little pinker of bald head and face, a little slower of walk, and that was all the change discernible in him. His wardrobes were slightly more magnificent, his air more gallant, his manner more genial and affable, if anything at all. As for Miss Beardsley, she withered rather than aged, becoming leaner and sparer and more commanding. Under her black bonnet her hair was very gray and flat, but her face was still uncompromising and grim, her little sunken eyes sharper. Her black bombazine gown over narrow hoops was still stiff and proper, and she moved in as stately a manner as ever.

"You look very well, child," she remarked. "I've thought of you very often, even though I haven't seen you since Easter."

Miss Beardsley then became aware of her cousin hovering on the threshold and a tighter look appeared on her face. "Good afternoon, Elsie," she said coldly.

But Mrs. Bowden no longer lived in abject terror of her. All the memory of years of humiliation and suffering stood in her calm brown eyes. She inclined her head. "How are you, Amanda?" she asked, in a voice as cold as Miss Beardsley's.

Miss Beardsley gave her a long look of dislike. She had never quite forgiven Lilybelle for removing her victim from under her thumb, and now she quite hated her cousin. But Mr. Wilkins greeted her effusively, and asked about her health, to which Mrs. Bowden replied in a noncommittal and unbending voice. Then, inclining her head again, she glided away into the shadowy hall.

The guests seated themselves, Mr. Wilkins striking an attitude in a winged chair, Miss Beardsley sitting stiffly on the edge of a damask love-seat. Mr. Wilkins beamed fondly at Lilybelle, while even Miss Beardsley found herself helplessly unbending as usual in the presence of this young woman whom she loved as much as she could love any one. A radiant aura of health and vitality vibrated about Lilybelle, so that the air around her appeared actually luminous in the half dusk. She burst into a stream of bright and amiable chatter about a mass of inconsequentials, talking of her children and her garden, and laughing loudly with sheer happiness in the presence of her friends.

They would have tea with her, of course, in the garden, she said. She jumped up to ring for a maid, and gave the order. Then they all rose and went through the french windows out upon the brilliantly green grass, and then down the slope to a pleasant spot under the willows. A table was set there, and a lace cloth and silver placed upon it. Mr. Wilkins looked about him complacently, enjoying the fresh shade under the trees, and conversing amiably with his hostess. Miss Beardsley, who was never affected by weather, and inclined to be censorious even in the presence of flowers, eyed the flower-beds and the distant gardeners with a stern eye. She thought the effect of the gardens very blowsy. But so like Lilybelle, certainly. She, herself, disliked flowers very much. They were untidy, and encouraged insects. As for Lilybelle, she looked about her with beaming pride.

She is such a fool, thought Miss Beardsley, with regretful contempt. Is it possible she doesn't know about her precious husband and his lady-love? But there was no cloud in Lilybelle's blue eyes. She prattled on, endlessly. Mr. Wilkins appeared to enjoy her conversation, and his expression was smiling and gentle as he gazed at her attentively.

Lilybelle sent for her daughters, and as she waited for them she bridled a little with pride, and simpered. "They are really impossible," she said, articulating properly, with care, in order that Miss Beardsley might not be too ashamed of her former pupil's speech.

"And how is my godchild?" asked Miss Beardsley.

"As naughty as ever," said Lilybelle. Miss Beardsley looked annoyed.

"Nonsense. She is a girl of spirit," she said, reprovingly, and settled her mitted hands in her lap with a gesture that expressed her irritation. "Louisa is quite the ringleader, I'm sure, and little Adelaide makes her impatient, and no wonder."

At the mention of Adelaide, an alert point of light flickered in Mr. Wilkins' protruding hazel eyes, and he turned towards the door expectantly. But Lilybelle's radiant exuberance was momentarily shadowed with sadness and protest.

There were young fresh voices across the grass, and three little girls appeared in a flutter of white, pink and blue muslin and spanking curls, their neat young legs encased in ruffled drawers, their girlish hoops tilting and weaving, their light feet in black slippers tied with black ribbons. Lilybelle noted with fond regret that the moist heat of the summer day had already wilted Adelaide's painfully-wrought curls, and they had become long sleek lengths of light brown hair with a coppery overtone. It was her youngest child at whom she glanced first, and then with an indescribable melting of her whole expression. Adelaide was small and slight of build, seeming even younger than her eight years, and she moved quietly and softly and with a still pride. She had none of that spectacular beauty which seizes the casual eye in entrancement, for her little pointed face was pale and serious, the wide thin lips almost colourless, the little thin nose quite transparent and very delicate, and the large brown eyes too introspective, too quiet and reserved for the ordinary taste, for all that they had a liquid quality full of hidden light. That straight fine hair, long and gleaming, which caused Lily-belle so much regret because of its inability to retain tortuous curls, hung down her straight young back, and was confined about her head with a blue ribbon, which matched her blue muslin. To the connoisseur, however, Adelaide possessed real and transcendent beauty, reserved and cultured. To those who knew Eugenia Bollister, the resemblance between that lady and the little Adelaide was quite startling.

The vulgar eye, which would have touched Adelaide with indifference, would have brightened avidly, however, at the sight of her two older sisters. For Lavinia, the eldest, was a tall luscious beauty, black and brilliant and restless of eye, with a thick mass of black and lustrous curls falling heavily down her firm and pretty back. She had a round face like her mother's, but her colouring was clear and dark like her father's, and her pouting mouth, full and small, had a vivid and burning tint. She had John's firm short nose, belligerent and well-shaped, and his firm dimpled chin. Restless and in constant movement, she revealed an immense vitality and impatience. Her young figure was somewhat full for her years, but beautifully formed, and gave promise of splendid womanhood. Her expression, however, petulant and willful, unresting and quick, did not predispose the more discerning in her favour, however fascinating he might have found her true loveliness.

To those who admired blondes, Louisa was irresistible. Dainty, almost as small as Adelaide, exquisitely formed and as fragile as Dresden, Louisa delighted all who looked upon her. Her masses of soft golden curls lay on her pretty shoulders and about her neck, and curled over her brow and cheeks most bewitchingly. She had large soft blue eyes, demure and sweet, with golden lashes and brows. Her face was oval, and most entrancingly tinted in the softest shades, the tender mouth just faintly flushed with rose, the smooth cheeks pulsating with a lighter hue. Her neck was as white as her mother's, her little hands seemingly formed of porcelain with tiny rosy nails. She walked so gracefully that she seemed to float, and was a model of decorum. Her expression was so beguiling, so innocent, so charming and fair, that few guessed how selfish and cunning she was, how avaricious and full of treachery. Where her sister, Lavinia, while ruthless and bold, might at times display a rare kindness and generosity, Louisa was all greed, all cruelty and slyness. She rarely spoke a word that was not gentle or sweet, tactful or lovable.

"My darlings!" cried Lilybelle, holding out her large warm arms to them. They came to her, Lavinia with impatient speed, Louisa with a ladylike and mincing step, very proper and demure, and Adelaide more slowly, but with a bright urgency in her steadfast brown eyes. Lilybelle kissed them all heartily, but it was Adelaide's little thin hand that she took and pressed, and it was Adelaide who received her long and loving look.

The girls curtseyed properly to their mother's guests, and then Lavinia went to Miss Beardsley, whose favourite she was, Louisa seated herself daintily, as was becoming, at her mother's side, and Adelaide approached Mr. Wilkins, who had extended his hand to her. She shook hands with him gravely, looking at him with thoughtful eyes from under her long dark lashes.

And Mr. Wilkins returned her look, and he felt within himself that strange lurching in the region of his heart.

"And how is the little lass today?" he asked, his chuckling voice lowered to a fond intimacy for the child's own ear.

The brown eyes lighted with a smile, though her face remained serious. Those eyes were wise and pensive, full of restraint and shyness, and contained.

"Well, thank you, Uncle Bob," she answered.

"'And you, Uncle Bob?'" prompted Lilybelle, dotingly, with an eye to Miss Beardsley, who was listening with her pouncing expression of severity.

But Adelaide only smiled again with her eyes. Mr. Wilkins put his arm about her and drew her to his knee.

"The child," remarked Miss Beardsley, "has bad manners, Lilybelle. I hope the new governess will improve them."

She lifted her bony hand and touched Lavinia's curls with awkward affection. Try as she could, she could not conceal her deep attachment to the beautiful dark young girl. Lavinia's insolent face, so petulant and selfish in repose, smiled, and when it did so it was as charming as Louisa's. With the license of a favourite, she sat down on the grass beside Miss Beardsley and rubbed her cheek against that lady's arm, looking up at her with her great black eyes. No one, not even Lilybelle, had ever dared show Miss Beards-

271

ley that familiarity, but Miss Beardsley, far from being offended, smiled down upon the girl.

"I hope, my dear," she said, "that our French has much improved?"

"Not much," admitted Lavinia, saucily, with another smile, and a toss of her mass of black curls. "But then, these governesses are so stupid. I wish I could go away to school."

Because she was so volatile, her smile disappeared, and she frowned sulkily, glancing at her mother with a look of dislike and accusation.

"Why isn't the child allowed to go to school, Lilybelle?" asked Miss Beardsley, in an ominous voice.

Lilybelle flushed. She glanced at Lavinia pleadingly. "Linny knows," she stammered. "Her Papa wants her home. I am quite willing."

Miss Beardsley pursed her lips and tossed her head stiffly, giving Lilybelle the impression that her old friend was not convinced, and that she, Lilybelle, had been caught in a stupid lie. "It is absurd that great girls like these are under a governess," she remarked. "It is not my affair, of course, but Lavinia is my godchild, and I feel some responsibility towards her." She turned to Louisa, sitting beside her mother so correctly and decorously. "And you, Louisa, wouldn't you prefer to go away to school?"

Louisa hesitated. Then with the sweetest of smiles, she replied: "I prefer anything my parents wish, Aunt Amanda. What I wish is of no consequence."

Miss Beardsley tried to remain severe, but in spite of herself she softened. "A very proper sentiment, my dear Louisa," she said. "Young people these days are deplorably lacking in respect for their parents, and it pleases me to hear one girl, at least, who has this respect. Nevertheless, I think you and Lavinia should go away to school, where there are adequate teachers."

"Mr. T. is bringing a tutor here in September," pleaded Lilybelle, humbly, feeling herself in the wrong.

Miss Beardsley lifted her mitted hands in horror, opened her mouth to a dry O, and looked about her aghast. "Surely, my dear Lilybelle, you are not serious?" she exclaimed. "Mr. Wilkins, sir, have you heard this? Can I believe my ears? A tutor, a male creature, for these girls? How reprehensible, how indiscreet, how entirely improper!"

Lilybelle turned crimson in her misery. But Mr. Wilkins smiled most affably. "Well, now, I can't see that it'd be improper, ma'am," he said, soothingly. "I call it to mind that in the old country the lasses of the gentry had their tutors. And very well behaved they were, too."

Lilybelle gave him a grateful look. She was almost in tears. As for Adelaide, she pressed closer against her friend, and over her shoulder looked at her mother with strong and reassuring love.

"I'd like a tutor, Mama," she said. "I wouldn't like to go away to school." Her voice was light and fluting, but full of deep undertones.

"Mind your manners, miss," said Miss Beardsley, sternly. "I think you, more than your sisters, would do well away at school, where there is discipline, and children are taught not to interfere in the conversation of their elders."

Adelaide did not reply to this. She was not intimidated. She looked steadfastly at Miss Beardsley with her grave brown eyes, and that lady felt a surge of such active dislike for the girl that she could hardly restrain an impulse to reach out and slap that pale and pointed little face. Lavinia giggled maliciously.

"Oh, Addy's a prig, and a sly piece," she said. "They'd whip her soundly at school. I wish she'd go! She is so tiresome, anyway."

"Lavinia!" said Louisa, in a soft shocked tone. "How naughty of you to say that about dear little Adelaide. Your own little sister."

Lilybelle murmured in distress, but no one bothered to listen to her. "Oh, don't be a hypocrite, Louisa!" cried Lavinia, pettishly. "You know Addy's an odious little toad, and you'd be glad to be rid of her. But you never say what you think."

Miss Beardsley wound one of Lavinia's opulent black curls about her fingers, and said with a weak attempt at severity: "There are some people, miss, who'd do well to conceal their thoughts occasionally. You are very rude, Lavinia, and I am ashamed of you."

Lavinia flung back her head and laughed boisterously. Then she sprang to her feet, flung her arms about Miss Beardsley, and hugged that protesting lady with such vigour that she was almost strangled. "Oh, you are such a darling, Aunt Amanda!" cried the girl, "and such a prim old thing! I love you!"

Lilybelle, seeing that Miss Beardsley was quite placated, and that a deep flush had softened her gaunt countenance, and that she struggled with Lavinia fondly in an effort to straighten her bonnet, became quite cheerful, and said, in a loud voice: "Isn't this war terrible, Mr. Wilkins? I don't know what's to become of all of us, really I don't."

Mr. Wilkins assumed an expression properly serious and shook his head. "Ma'am," he said, in sepulchral tones, "the good Lord alone knows wot's to be the end. The Southerners, ma'am, are set on keepin' their miserable slaves, and we're set on 'em not keepin' 'em. Right will out, though. Justice allus triumphs."

"Not always," said Miss Beardsley, fatally. "I beg to disagree with you, Mr. Wilkins. I've seen wickedness triumph more often than good. It's the way of the world."

This remark so distressed poor Lilybelle, that she sank into confused gloom, and was speechless. Miss Beardsley shook her head over and over, grimly, and looked about her as if to defy any one to dispute her sentiments.

Louisa, in her soft ingratiating voice, spoke and glanced about for forgiveness in advance: "I know it seems impudent of me to say it, but I'm sure that we shall win. All those poor black people. Their condition is so horrible. We can't live half slave and half free."

"Pooh," broke in Lavinia, contemptuously. "Your noble remarks make me sick, Louisa. You're always quoting somebody. You never have an original thought. Just now you quote Mr. Lincoln all the time. Why don't you use your canary brain once in a while, yourself?"

"It would be better for you, miss, if you had a few noble sentiments of your own," reproved Miss Beardsley. "If your dear little sister has Christian charity, you might emulate her."

"Louisa hasn't any more Christianity in her than a pig," sneered Lavinia. "She's hard as nails, and all those yellow curls and blue eyes just hide what she really is. Isn't that so, Louisa?"

Louisa did not appear offended. She smiled gently, and looked upon her sister with smiling eyes.

Now Miss Beardsley, who was no fool, understood quite well that the two older girls were as good friends as it was possible for them to be, that though they might reprove each other in public, and indulge in recriminations and sneers, they understood each other, and, in moments of crisis, would present a crusty front to the world. Therefore, she was actively jealous. She wanted Lavinia to care for no one but herself, and would constantly endeavour to stir up dissension between the two girls.

Mr. Wilkins, that astute analyser of character, knew that Lavinia had a small sharp brain, abnormally active and clever, that Louisa had a far subtler mind, and was therefore more dangerous than her elder sister, and that Adelaide, of the three, had the only real intellect. He knew what enemies Lavinia and Louisa were to Adelaide, and he had long ago set himself up as her defender. He loved the child, as he

274

had never loved another living creature. For she was one of those rare souls which he instinctively revered: noble, truthful, simple and honest, and of the highest integrity. He had dedicated himself to her service.

Now he lifted her little brown hand, examined it minutely, then smiling at her fondly, he kissed the back of that hand. She regarded him seriously. He had not the slightest doubt that she understood all about him, that she was not deceived by any of his tricks. Yet, in spite of all that, she loved him in return.

He liked to sit here under the willows, drinking tea and eating thin bread and butter and jam, and tiny frosted cakes. He liked to look about the opulent gardens. He thought the sight of the three young girls on the grass, so blooming and fresh, the prettiest scene in the world. He thought their full-blown buxom mother the handsomest lady he had ever known, and because she had much of Adelaide's character, he forgave her her stupidity and obtuseness. Moreover, she was one of those helpless ones whom he was always defending.

As he looked at her without seeming to do so, he wondered if she knew about John and his cousin, Mrs. Eugenia Bollister. He believed she did. Females had an uncanny knack of knowing when their husbands were unfaithful. Yes, he was sure that she knew. Now that every one was engaged in conversation with each other, and she thought herself unobserved, the big pink mouth drooped forlornly, the round blue eyes were sad, and her whole expression was mournful and patiently enduring. But, if she was sorrowful, Mr. Wilkins was sure that she never reproached her husband, that she suffered his infidelities, indifferences and slights as her lot, believing that her own inferiority provoked these things.

The long yellow shadows of the sun crept over the hot green grass. The willows extended their drooping shade so that the party relaxed in deep violet shadow. Between the fronds of the trees the sky burned ardently blue, and the flowers took on a more violent confusion and oriental lushness. Somewhere there was the long whirr of a mower. The red brick wall surrounding the gardens blazed with climbing and flowering vines. Mr. Wilkins looked at the house, tall and pleasant, the windows blazing with sunlight, the curtains blowing in the warm breeze. Yes, John Turnbull had done himself well, reflected Mr. Wilkins, aided, of course, by the inheritance from his father. But most of all was due to Mr. Wilkins, so that gentleman felt much personal satisfaction. However, as he contemplated the peace and beauty of the house and the garden, his opaque eyes narrowed evilly.

Adelaide was seated on his knee, munching bread-and-butter-and-jam sandwiches. She rarely spoke. But her slow serious smile appeared whenever Mr. Wilkins glanced at her.

Miss Beardsley had launched into a vigorous diatribe upon the subject of women's rights, about which she was very militant. Mr. Wilkins had long observed that females who were ardent upon the subject (their faces quite swelling with their bile and indignation) were generally women upon whom no man had looked with favour. This, then, was their revenge upon the indifference of males.

"If we women could vote, we should most assuredly bring the millennium!" she exclaimed to the bewildered Lilybelle, who, not understanding much about the subject, was quite abject. In fact, as Miss Beardsley's ireful eye, accusing and fiery, touched her, she would shrink as if personally responsible for the dreadful condition of womanhood in 1863. "Gentlemen are venal!" continued Miss Beardsley. "They are prone to temptation and all manner of odious chicanery. Politics are a stench in the nostrils of the righteous and the God-fearing. Drink, theft, dishonesty and treachery are rife, because men have all their own way, without the stern and gentle restraint which females could exercise upon them. One has only to observe the saloons, the unspeakable districts where females of questionable character congregate, the corruption in politics, to see how utterly incompetent gentlemen are to conduct the affairs of the nation. Moreover, once women obtain their rights and their vote, war will forever pass away, and disputes will be settled amicably about international tables of Law. Too, we shall see more churches, more cleanliness, more decorum and integrity in public affairs when women vote."

Lilybelle, terrified at this barrage, nodded her head in dumb agreement, though she had not the slightest inkling about Miss Beardsley's vigorous remarks. The girls listened with deep attention. When Miss Beardsley had concluded, out of sheer breathlessness and fury, Lavinia said: "Why shouldn't we vote? You are quite right, Aunt Amanda. I'd like to show these gentlemen a thing or two!"

Louisa smiled gently, and inclined her head with modesty. "I prefer to leave such matters of politics in gentlemen's hands. I don't think it is genteel for females to interfere."

"You are a little fool!" exclaimed Miss Beardsley, irately. "What does a child of your years understand about such things?"

Mr. Wilkins became aware that Adelaide was quite tense. She was only a little lass, not quite nine years old, but her brown eyes were alight and eager. He smoothed a length of her long brown hair.

"And wot does the little gel think of this, eh?" he asked, fondly.

She turned to him and gazed at him earnestly. "I don't think ladies are any different from gentlemen," she said, in her light but penetrating voice. "I don't think ladies could make things better, just because they are ladies. I—I don't think if just a lot more people vote than they do now, that things could be made better. It's not the amount of people who vote, but the kind of people they are. And, I don't think ladies are nicer than gentlemen, or kinder, or gooder."

Miss Beardsley was outraged. She turned to Lilybelle with a momentous and baleful air. "Lilybelle, I am horrified. Why do you permit your children to interfere so insolently in adult conversations, especially when they are not very intelligent? Adelaide not only uses most abominable English, but she is a very stupid child indeed. You will oblige me if you will send her back to the nursery at once where she belongs."

Adelaide was not in the least crushed. She gazed at Miss Beardsley fixedly, and her wide pale mouth tightened. The other girls giggled and looked at their sister with smiling malice.

Lilybelle was quite broken. She looked from her old friend to her beloved youngest daughter. She faltered: "Addy, I am afraid you are very naughty. Please apologize to Miss Beardsley."

"What for?" asked Adelaide, clearly. "I'll be glad to apologize, Mama, if I know how I've offended Miss Beardsley."

" 'Aunt Amanda,' dear," murmured the agonized Lilybelle.

Miss Beardsley tossed her head. "Do not bother, Lilybelle. I do not care if your daughter calls me 'Aunt Amanda,' or not. In truth, I prefer that she does not. I cannot be aunt, even by proxy, to such an odious little creature."

"Nah, nah," said Mr. Wilkins, soothingly, tightening his arm about his favourite. "I asked the little lass. It's my fault. The lass is entitled to her own opinion, that she is. That's Ameriky: full of own opinions, and thank God for it."

Miss Beardsley was about to attack Mr. Wilkins, himself, when the distant white gate opened, and John appeared, walking slowly and abstractedly as always.

CHAPTER 29

JOHN TURNBULL was barely thirty-four now, but thin white streaks were already making their appearance in his thick black curls. Under their angry turbulence his dark face was chronically haggard and ravaged, with a feverish look, turned upon a speaker, was apt to be suspicious and had lost much of his youthful weight during the past ten years, and though not thin as yet, there was a gaunt look about his big body which was enhanced by his unremitting restlessness. His active black eyes were contemptuously unquiet now, rather than bold as once they had been, and his look, turned upon a speaker, was apt to be suspicious and heavily belligerent.

Mr. Wilkins, upon every encounter with his protégé, was struck anew by the thought that here was a man corroded and corrupted by hatred, a hatred thrust upon him rather than embraced with desire. Now, Mr. Wilkins had respect for a man who hated his fellows because of knowledge of them. It took intelligence, reflected Mr. Wilkins, to understand other men, and with understanding invariably came detestation. But he had no respect for a man who hated and destroyed himself in the hating, because hatred was intrinsically alien to his temperament. John had no comprehension of his fellow creatures. He struck blindly in the dark out of his own pain and weariness, his blows were the blows of self-defense, fierce and ruthless though they were.

John was still only half aware of the group under the green light of the willows. He walked slowly, his head bent, his face partially hidden under the brim of his tall hat. But he had a more imposing presence than ever, and his long buff coat and pale pantaloons were all elegance. Too, he had acquired an indifferent grace. He struck absentmindedly at the flowers with his cane, and even at that distance Mr. Wilkins could discern the brooding duskiness of his expression. Here was a man who had acquired much, and would acquire more. He had everything that one could desire, even the woman he loved. Yet, in his every motion, in his every glance, the misery of hatred was implicit and overwhelming.

Upon seeing her husband, Lilybelle's plump and pretty face

was illumined by a sudden radiant light, shy, fearful yet full of joy. She jumped to her feet, her sprigged muslin hoops swirling. But she said nothing. She did not advance to meet John. She clasped her hands tightly together, with humility and tremulousness, and her whole body was vibrant so that she seemed to shed a luminousness about her in the green translucence of the shadows. Miss Beardsley, seeing this, said: "Humph!" in a very uncompromising and disdainful voice, and settled her lean shoulders stiffly under her black lace shawl. But Lavinia and Louisa, with light screams of delight, sprang up from the grass and fled across it to their father, their hair flying in the sunlight, their pretty feet hardly seeming to touch the ground. They flung themselves upon him, and he opened his arms and received them, hugging them to him. Now the sombreness of his expression lifted, and he smiled and laughed a little with deep fondness, tumbling Lavinia's black curls and the masses of Louisa's golden hair. They wound their arms about him, each chattering vivaciously, Lavinia's somewhat loud and domineering voice rising above her sister's. Then, with a girl on each side of him, John came towards the others under the willows. The girls' faces were eager and mirthful and confident, their dainty little hoops swaying at every dancing step. Lavinia pranced rather than walked, impatiently, while Louisa moved with the utmost decorum and grace.

Adelaide, on Mr. Wilkins' knee, had grown very still. Her little brown hands lay quietly in her blue lap. She hardly seemed to breathe. She made no motion to go to her father. But her small pale face, turned towards him, was fixed, and there was no sign of emotion upon it except for a strange quivering at the corners of her lips. Yet Mr. Wilkins, that astute and penetrating gentleman, felt a little stricken and sick, for he had seen the look in Adelaide's great brown eyes, a starved and passionate look full of grief and love.

If only the little lass could speak her thoughts and say what's in her heart, thought the pink and affable Lucifer, with mysterious compassion. But he knew that profound emotions are silent, and the soul that is deeply stirred remains transfixed from the very profundity of its thoughts. And he also knew that of John's three daughters, Adelaide alone loved him, that the pretty pouting affection of the others was a mixture of vanity, cajolement, rapacity and self-indulgence.

Mr. Wilkins was not a scholarly man, but something stirred vaguely in his memory. Blast it, he had read somewhere of a situation like this, but for the life of him he could not recall it. Something poetical, or something. The thought nagged him, and his sandy tufts of eyebrows drew together. He was certain that if he could recall the thing, it would have some bearing on John and his daughters. But that came of practically having no learning: a man could derive no satisfaction from comparisons, or from recognizing some ancient truth. It had something to do with the theatre, Mr. Wilkins remembered, something about a man and his daughters, and a great terror and agony.

He tightened his arm about "the little lass," but she did not feel that comforting pressure. Her whole soul was turned like the light of a struggling candle upon her father. Mr. Wilkins could not endure seeing what there was to be seen on the face of this child. It wasn't right, he reflected, that a child should experience the emotions of a mature woman.

It was a good sight to see the handsome young father and his blooming young daughters coming with accelerated step across the grass. Some of the sombreness and abstraction had gone from John's eyes. He bent his head first to his right and then to his left as each girl demanded his attention. It was not possible to say which girl was his favourite, for he looked at each with similar affection.

Lilybelle spoke in her warm and husky voice, ingratiating and eager: "We are just 'avin' tea! You'll 'ave some with us?" In moments of stress, she lost the careful enunciations taught her by Miss Beardsley.

John glanced at her indifferently. His smile disappeared. Then, without answering, he bowed slightly to Miss Beardsley, and inclined his head in Mr. Wilkins' direction. "Well, Bob," he said. Lilybelle awkwardly pushed her own comfortable wicker chair in her husband's direction, and he sat down in it without another look at her. The two older girls collapsed prettily on each side of him, and Lilybelle busied herself with the tea and cakes, her big hands shaking a little.

"A fine day, a fine day!" boomed Mr. Wilkins, pressing Adelaide's hand with dumb reassurance.

John looked about the garden listlessly. "It is," he admitted. Then his eyes returned to Mr. Wilkins. "I've wanted to talk to you, Bob. Can you come in to see me tomorrow? Old Livingston came in today, and he's in a bad state."

"Ah," said Mr. Wilkins, soothingly. "I'll drop in tomorrow."

"I thought Mr. Livingston had practically retired these last years?" said Miss Beardsley, in the prim aloof tone she always used to John, whom she really detested. "After all, he is quite an old gentleman now."

John did not answer her, but Mr. Wilkins turned to her

affably. "Old gentlemen sometimes go daft," he said. "They get queer notions. Mr. Livingston still 'as the idea he manages things."

John did not speak, but he shot Mr. Wilkins a dour and unfathomable glance from under his angry black brows. He accepted the cup of tea which Lilybelle timidly proffered him, but still he did not look at her. Even while he helped himself from the silver plate of cakes he appeared unaware of her existence.

A surly brute! thought Miss Beardsley, tossing her head slightly and pressing her lips together. Not worthy of poor Lilybelle, even if she is ill-bred and illiterate. And he spoils those girls abominably.

Lilybelle, nervous as always in the presence of her husband, turned vivaciously towards Adelaide, with the simple and loving desire to call the father's attention to the child he had ignored.

"Addy, love, go at once and get your Papa a footstool," she urged.

Adelaide slipped down from Mr. Wilkins' knee, and now John looked at her for the first time. He scowled somewhat. "Why is that girl always so untidy?" he asked, with a sharp upward glance at his wife. "Her hair is always unbrushed and flying, and her frock is soiled and crushed."

Adelaide, standing near Mr. Wilkins, did not move. Her small thin body became rigid, drawn too tightly, like a string on a violin. Mr. Wilkins turned his eye upon John, and that sharp and ominous point of light began to glitter deep within its glassy depths. But his smile was immovably fixed.

Lilybelle, distressed and flustered, smoothed Adelaide's long brown hair with a tender hand. "It won't curl," she faltered humbly, as if this was some fault of her own. "It can't be helped. But Addy's a good little lass, ain't you, pet?" She bent and kissed the child's cheek. Adelaide bent her head towards her mother, then moved away towards the house. There was an odd and lonely desolation about her slight figure. John watched her go, uneasily scowling. (Ah, thought Mr. Wilkins, with satisfied viciousness, she reminds you of some one, don't she? and you hates her for remindin' you. Aye, there's some'ut about her that's like that fine lady of yours, but there's a spirit in the little lass that's worth two of her.)

Lavinia began to giggle loudly. "Every one says it's so strange that Addy could be our sister! She's so ugly. You must have had an ugly female ancestor, Papa," she added, with an audacious upward glance at her father, her bright black eyes dancing.

"Adelaide isn't ugly," Louisa reproved her, placidly. "She is very uncommon looking. She will never have style, of course, and will never be distinguished. She is a real little old maid. But there's something about Adelaide, in spite of everything."

"Breeding," said Mr. Wilkins, very gently. John glanced at him with sudden savagery, but Mr. Wilkins returned that look most amiably. "It's breeding," repeated Mr. Wilkins. "It's not every one as 'as it. It's born in the bone. It's better than handsomeness, for them that's got the taste for it."

Lavinia laughed boisterously, but Louisa gave Mr. Wilkins a secret and amused smile, not at all pleasant for all her natural loveliness. As for Miss Beardsley, she snorted in a ladylike manner and tossed her grim head. "Indeed, Mr. Wilkins! I always thought you a gentleman of discernment. Surely you can see that there is no comparison between Adelaide and her sisters!"

"I can see that, ma'am," agreed Mr. Wilkins, mildly. But Miss Beardsley had the disagreeable sensation that Mr. Wilkins was being ambiguous, and she tossed her head again.

Lilybelle was pathetically grateful. She shone upon Mr. Wilkins, and her smile was bright.

Lavinia became gaily flirtatious with her father, knowing how it pleased and amused him. She patted his hand lightly. "You are so handsome, Papa. Quite the handsomest man I've ever seen. And Mama is pretty. You didn't find Addy on the doorstep, did you?"

"How can you be so vulgar?" asked Louisa, sweetly.

Lavinia, with one of her tempestuous and ugly changes of mood, turned furiously upon her sister. Her face became quite dark and vicious, her under lip thrust out coarsely, her eyes snapping.

"I'm honest, miss, and you're not!" she cried, looking as if she would spring to her feet and assault Louisa at once. "You are a little grinning sneak, and you hate Addy like poison! I know. I like her a little, and sometimes I'm fond of her, but you'd kill her if you could! You're cruel as a snake, for all your fine smiles and your innocent looks!"

"Lavinia!" exclaimed Miss Beardsley, shocked. "What language! My dear child, this is unpardonable."

But Louisa was not disconcerted. Her smile was angelic, and she gazed at her sister gently. "Oh, that's just Linny's way, Aunt Amanda. She doesn't mean anything by it. I'm not in the least offended."

"Oh!" cried Lavinia, with impotent rage, clenching her fists and beating them upon her knees.

John laughed spontaneously, and ruffled Lavinia's curls so vigorously that they fell all over her enflamed face. She struggled with him, trying to beat off his hands, and he bent over the arm of his chair and easily tussled with her. Finally he pushed her backwards upon the grass where she lay a moment glaring at the sky through her tangle of curls. Then she burst out in her sudden loud laugh and sat up again, only the flush on her pretty cheek testifying to her late fury. But Mr. Wilkins alone saw the long red scratch on John's hand.

Adelaide now appeared, carrying a footstool. She placed it silently before her father, and without a glance at her, he lifted his feet and settled them on the support. He was much easier now, and his smile was without strain. When Lilybelle refilled his cup, he looked at her quite amiably, as if seeing her for the first time.

"Well, my love," he said, pleasantly indifferent, "did you find the day very hot?"

Overcome as always with joy, whenever John deigned to recognize her existence, Lilybelle stammered: "O no, Mr. T.! It's such a nice day." She thrust the plate of cakes at him again, and he took one, smiling a little.

He turned to Mr. Wilkins. "I've a pretty wife, haven't I, Bob?" he asked. "Don't you envy me, you old codger?"

"That I do!" agreed Mr. Wilkins, heartily. Adelaide was still standing near her father, gazing at him with that sad and hungry light in her eyes.

Lilybelle bridled and flushed. She was close to tears of delight. She sat down, overwhelmed, on the edge of a chair. She stared at John with adoration. He saw all this, and was not displeased. Now a younger look, a relaxed look, appeared on his face. He was no longer taut, no longer tense. He let his eye wander contentedly about the gardens.

Why! thought Mr. Wilkins, with great surprise. It's a fool, that's what it is! He don't realize, yet, but someday, when it's too late, probably, he will!

He and Miss Beardsley soon took their departure. Miss Beardsley kissed Lilybelle with that reproving air she always affected towards the young woman, and then kissed Lavinia with true fondness. She also bestowed a caress upon Louisa, who appeared sweetly grateful for it. She did not even see Adelaide, or ignored her deliberately. She shook hands in a stately manner with John, then preceded Mr. Wilkins down the garden path to the gate.

CHAPTER 30

THE HOT July silence shone about the house and the blazing gardens. There was no sound at all, except the sonorous and majestic sounds that rippled and swelled from the music room. They did not disturb the silence; rather, they enhanced it, giving it a profound meaning. The simple Lilybelle, resting from the heat of the day in her bedroom, was mysteriously stirred. Slowly, tears ran over her placid pink cheeks and stained her pillow. Her heart throbbed. She stared sightlessly at the ceiling, humbly reverent. The servants in the great tiled kitchen listened, speechlessly. The gardeners lifted their heads from the beds of flowers, and stood immobile in the cataracts of sunlight. Only the two girls, Lavinia and Louisa, were deaf to that stately thunder downstairs. They were quarrelling about their wardrobes in the large bedroom they shared together.

Miss Hamlin came briskly through the blue dusk of the hallway, her heels clicking under her gray bombazine hoops. She had a thin gray face, and a quantity of iron ringlets falling from her prim head. Her expression was tight and resolute, acquired from a long guardianship over young girls, whom she detested. She entered the music room.

There, in the dim barred light that streamed through the Venetian blinds at the immense windows, sat Adelaide at the piano. Miss Hamlin disliked Adelaide. She considered the child "quite gnomelike, furtive and incomprehensible." The piano was vast, polished and motionless on the glimmering floor, and there was something eerie and unearthly in the spectacle of the little brown girl perched on the stool and evoking from the instrument that divine and terrifying thunder of music. In spite of her dislike, Miss Hamlin listened with reluctant approval. The girl really had talent, though she was bearing down outrageously on the loud pedal. Adelaide did not see Miss Hamlin. Her head was thrown back, and from it flowed the pale brown lengths of her straight hair, touching the bench itself. In that shining dimness her pallid little face was rapt, the eyes half closed, the mouth stern and strong. For some reason that irritated Miss Hamlin intensely. She coughed raucously, and approached the piano.

"Really, Adelaide, you are making a furious noise," she said.

The girl started so violently at the sound of the governess' voice that she almost fell off the stool. Then she swung about and fastened upon Miss Hamlin so wild and fierce a look that the woman fell back a step, appalled. She could not believe, for a moment, that such a brown and silent child, so reticent and reserved, could be capable of such ferocity, and with only the slight provocation of being disturbed at her music. Even while Miss Hamlin was confusedly thinking this, the wild fire in those nut-brown eyes flashed away, and was replaced once more by the silent and waiting patience with which the woman was more familiar.

"Yes, Miss Hamlin?" murmured Adelaide. Her tanned thin hands lay quietly on the white keys. The diffused sunlight made a narrow and coppery halo about her small head.

"Really, Adelaide," said Miss Hamlin, catching her breath, "that was a very nasty look indeed which you gave me." She put her hand to her flat bosom and breathed loudly. "I didn't think you capable of it."

Adelaide said nothing. Because the sun was behind her, Miss Hamlin could not see her face. But what she had seen for just a single moment still dumfounded her. It was an evil little tigress, then, thought Miss Hamlin, viciously. Her first instinct upon seeing the child some months ago was justified. No wonder her sisters despised her, and her Papa actually disliked her. There was a meaning to everything, thought Miss Hamlin, with grim sententiousness. And you could always rely on these meek quiet people to hide terrible fires and violences; one could not trust them.

Adelaide slipped down from the stool obediently, anticipating her governess' next command. "You wanted me?" she asked, in her light low voice.

"Yes. But of course you knew that, Adelaide! You knew very well that you ought to be preparing for Mrs. Brotherton's little girl's birthday party instead of idling away your time at the piano. Not that I'm not pleased at your diligence," she added, remembering that part of her duty was to see that the girls practiced regularly, "but there is a time and place for everything. It is very late. The carriage will be here in fifteen minutes, and you haven't even bathed yet, nor decided what frock to wear."

Adelaide did not speak, but glided like a thin little gnome past the woman and went upstairs. Miss Hamlin followed, still very shaken.

Mrs. Bowden was in the two older girls' large sunny bedroom trying to quell the bitter argument which was taking place between Lavinia and Louisa. The great white bed with its canopy was heaped with colourful frocks, over which the heated debate was taking place. Lavinia's red firm cheeks were fiercely scarlet, and her brow was wet with sweat. She was gesticulating passionately, and her big black eyes were flashing flames. Louisa stood by, dainty and sweet as always, with not a golden lock out of place, and a provokingly angelic smile upon her face. Both girls stood in their ruffled pantalettes and voluminous ruffled and laced petticoats, their young arms bare, their smooth skin shining in the brightness that flooded the room.

Adelaide halted on the threshold. She must always wait like this, while her sisters made their decisions as to their frocks, so that later she might not overwhelm their effect by an indiscreet choice of her own. Miss Hamlin brushed briskly by her, and took charge, for Mrs. Bowden was fast losing her temper. "What is this, girls?" she asked. "Come, come! Haven't you yet decided what to wear?"

Lavinia turned upon her with vehemence. "Look here, Miss Hamlin, you've got to settle this! I want to wear my green tussah, and Louisa insists upon wearing her blue foulard. And you know very well what that will do to my green! She plots these things deliberately."

Miss Hamlin, trying to frown, turned to her favourite, Louisa, and attempted to speak sternly. "Louisa, you know Lavinia is the elder, and has the right of choice. Why can't you be amiable and civil? You could wear your white, and be very charming in it."

Louisa sighed, and let her golden lashes touch her cheek for a moment.

"Dear Miss Hamlin," she said, in her sweet and beguiling voice, "my white is badly soiled. My own green is apple, and will look quite washed-out beside Lavinia's brighter colour. It is too warm for my red, and brown makes me look so dull, and the sprigged muslins are not the proper thing for a party. My light rose is crushed, and there is no time now for a pressing. I cannot wear yellow, for we've decided that Adelaide is to wear her own yellow. What, then, am I to do?"

Presented with this momentous impasse, Miss Hamlin frowningly examined the frocks in question, while Lavinia breathed furiously at her shoulder, meanwhile flashing the calm Louisa very murderous looks indeed. Mrs. Bowden, exasperated, shrugged and removed herself to a position near Adelaide, who was observing all this confusion with remote detachment and indifference. She was accustomed to it.

"My pet," said Mrs. Bowden, "why don't you go and bathe, and then we'll tell you what to wear?" She touched

Adelaide's head with a gentle hand, and Adelaide gave her one of her rare quiet smiles. And when she smiled like this, her pale still face took on such a strange beauty that Mrs. Bowden felt her heart tremble. The girl turned away then, and disappeared into her own bedroom.

"Don't breathe so hotly on my neck, dear Lavinia," said Miss Hamlin, lifting one frock after another and studying it minutely. She dropped the last, and sighed, annoyed. But her frowning glance was for Lavinia. "Lavinia, Louisa is quite right. She cannot wear anything but her blue. You will have to decide upon something else. You could wear your pink, or your white, and there would be no clashing of colours at all."

"I shall wear my green!" shouted Lavinia, beating her clenched fists on the bed, and tossing her mass of black curls in a spasm of rage. "She's not to get her way all the time, Miss Hamlin! I've got the first choice. She'll have to wear something else."

Louisa, with a look of celestial patience, lifted her blue foulard and slipped it over her head. "There is nothing more to say, Lavinia," she said, softly. "You are being stubborn. You need not stand near me at the party. We can avoid each other, and so there will be no odious comparison."

Outraged, Lavinia stared at her, her mouth open, her eyes dancing with black fire. "What do you mean by 'comparison,' miss?" she screamed. "Are you insinuating that your miserable washed-out colouring can compare with *mine?*"

Smiling sweetly, Louisa did not reply. She turned her back to Mrs. Bowden to be buttoned. She smoothed the shimmering blue foulard with her pretty white hands, so plump and dimpled. Lavinia advanced on her, her fingers curling. "Answer me!" she bellowed.

"Girls, girls!" pleaded Miss Hamlin, angrily. "Let there be no more of this. Your Mama is suffering a bad headache today, and is trying to rest. Be more considerate. Really, girls, you are behaving yourselves in a very unladylike way, and I've never encountered girls with less sensibility." She took Lavinia by the arm. The girl struggled to free herself, her blazing eyes fixed on her sister.

"She's not to wear her blue!" she insisted, through clenched teeth.

Louisa gave her a look of weary sweetness. "Linny, let's be sensible. It's getting late. I can't wear anything but the blue. I'm very sorry. If I could wear anything else I'd do so, but it is impossible. You must forgive me. After this, you may have your choice and I'll abide by it."

"There!" exclaimed Miss Hamlin, with an affectionate look at Louisa.

"Oh, you infernal hypocrite!" shouted Lavinia, with ferocious scorn. "You and your meek tongue and smiles! The last time you insisted on wearing your green when I wore my red, and I looked like a barn on fire! You do these things on purpose."

"Have you no consideration for your mother, young ladies?" asked Mrs. Bowden, sternly. "She is ill today."

Lavinia turned upon her savagely. "Hell!" she cried. "Mama's always puling about, and there's no sense in encouraging her vapours. Go along with you, Bowden, and don't interfere."

"Lavinia!" said Miss Hamlin, clapping her hands to her ears. "Never have I heard such language, and such disrespect for parents. This is terrible!"

Lavinia, with one of her lightning changes of mood, laughed loudly and contemptuously. "Don't be an ass, Miss Hamlin. You know Mama's a fool. Every one knows it. So don't let us be so nice, and pretend. Mama can sleep when we've gone."

"Linny's quite right," said Louisa, looking in the mirror and carefully arranging a golden curl on her forehead. "We can't go about tiptoeing all the time, and holding our breath. Mama has all afternoon to sleep."

Adelaide appeared during the sudden hiatus that followed Louisa's words, carrying her soft yellow silk on her arm. She had brushed the straight streaming lengths of her hair so that they gleamed, and had tied a yellow ribbon about her head.

Lavinia, finding a fresh victim for her wrath, swung upon the little girl, and screamed with shrill disgust. "Oh, how bilious that odious little wretch will look, with all that yellow! Yellow dress, yellow ribbon, yellow eyes, yellow skin! How does she get all that brownness, and why doesn't she stay out of the sun! I can't bear it. I simply shall not go in her company. This is the final insult."

Louisa turned from the mirror and examined her small sister with a critical blue eye. She smiled amusedly. "As usual, Adelaide, you try to embarrass us. Poor child. It is not your fault, of course, that you are so plain."

Lavinia, scowling, stared at Adelaide. She thrust out her full red under lip. She rubbed her round dimpled chin with her hand, uneasily. Then she glowered at Louisa.

"Hold your tongue," she said, rudely. "Yellow is Addy's colour, and she isn't plain. Anyway, it's not her fault." She smiled now, at Adelaide, with a return to her volatile good humour. "You'll do very nicely, Addy. The yellow will be becoming, after all."

"Thank you, Linny," replied Adelaide quietly, allowing Mrs. Bowden to slip the yellow silk over her thin little shoulders. She looked at her sister with her inscrutable eyes, which were full of that liquid light peculiar to them. Lavinia smiled in return, but she was still uneasy. She and Louisa, in spite of their constant squabbles and recriminations, understood each other perfectly, and were very close. Nevertheless, Lavinia was fond of Adelaide, in a cavalier fashion, and knew that Louisa, in spite of her sweetness, hated the little girl. There was in Lavinia a faint detestation of those who hated without cause, for she was not virulent in spite of her natural brutality. Moreover, she had an uneasy compassion for the weak, even while she despised them.

Touched by the little girl's composure and defenselessness, Lavinia put on her bright green tussah, scowling meanwhile. She tied a wide green Leghorn hat over her black curls, while Louisa donned a similar hat of blue. With tender hands, Mrs. Bowden tied the yellow ribbons of a brown Leghorn over Adelaide's shining hair. How sweet the child looked! thought the woman. How noble and composed. The little pale face had an expression of tragic grandeur under the shadow of the hat.

Lavinia thrust a quantity of silver bangles over her wrists, stared at herself discontentedly in the mirror. But it was a handsome and vivid face that gazed back at her, and her eyes lightened. Louisa turned carefully before a pier mirror with sweet satisfaction.

"Rufe Hastings is home," she fluted. "I hear he is to be at Alice's party."

"Oh, you and your beau!" scoffed Lavinia. "I hope there'll be some interesting boys there. I heard, too, that that awful Irish person, Pat Brogan, is invited. Just because his Papa made such money in the paving business is no reason to invite Irish creatures. Papa says things like that are unthinkable in England. Pat's a Catholic, too," and she shrugged elaborately. "A Catholic! Imagine that."

"Patrick is very amiable, and lively," remarked Louisa. "And quite handsome."

"Lavinia is right," said Miss Hamlin, severely. "The most impossible people are thrusting their way into exclusive society. There is no excuse for the Irish. Coarse, ill-bred people. One does not know what the world is coming to."

Lavinia giggled. "Some one told me that a whole shipload of them waited for days outside of New York before they were allowed to enter, with all their verminous baggage and their hundreds of brats. I wonder who finally let them in?"

"Some one without a regard for America, you may be sure of that," said Miss Hamlin, portentously. "Such impudent and pushing people, too. And so very ignorant and presumptuous. I confess that it quite depresses me. No Irishman can ever be a gentleman. Rogues and rapscallions, and so naturally dishonest."

"I still think Patrick very amusing," said Louisa, gently. "And he has nice manners. And his Papa is very rich."

"No excuse for them," repeated Miss Hamlin, inflexibly. She turned to Adelaide, and thrust her sharply towards the door. "The carriage is here, young ladies. It is not necessary to see your Mama. She begs to be quiet."

"As if we'd bother," muttered Lavinia.

But Adelaide, escaping for a few moments, slipped into her mother's room to give her a soft kiss and a smile.

CHAPTER 31

D R. ALEXANDER BROTHERTON was the Chief of Staff of the Medical College of the New York University, and a rich man in his own right. His home on Fifth Avenue, of brown stone, was imposing and pretentious. His wife, the fluttering former Miss Cousins, was considered one of the leaders of New York society, and only those whom she considered rich enough, or impeccable enough, were invited to her mansion. The Brothertons had one child, a sickly little creature, upon whom they doted, and whom they considered the most beautiful little girl in New York. But, in truth, Alice was under-sized, scrawny, peevish and spoiled, with an overweening idea of her own importance. This was her birthday, and a most elaborate party had been prepared for her by her parents. Arrayed in white silk, sprinkled with satin rosebuds, her light yellow hair tied by a white ribbon, her pale and petulant little face composed in an expression of the utmost hauteur and refinement, Alice waited with her Mama to receive her guests.

The spacious rooms were filled with flowers in honour of the child, and in the great dining-room was spread a miraculous repast for the delectation of the young people. When the Turnbull girls arrived in their spanking brougham, they found the house already genteelly noisy with guests. Lavinia and Louisa were very popular, but the silent and shrinking Adelaide was ignored when she was not openly despised. There was a firm belief extant among her contemporaries that she was excessively ugly and unattractive, an opinion fostered originally, and with vigour, by her amiable sisters. Not one careless young eye took the trouble to question this dictum, and so Adelaide usually retired to a shadowy corner to hide her "ugliness" as best she could. She did not care whether she was ugly or not; it was a matter of indifference to her. But her sensitiveness could not endure the scorn of others. Not yet, at least.

She found a place in a bow-window, half hidden by heavy blue velvet curtains. From that vantage point she could observe the guests, without herself being observed. Her expression was remote and aloof. She was not unhappy. It would have surprised the others had they known that they existed only as noisy mannequins to this quiet little Turnbull miss in the shadows. In truth, she was glad that she was left alone. Lavinia and Louisa, as usual, had been absorbed among their many admirers, and were having an excellent time for themselves.

Adelaide amused herself by gazing out over long green lawns, brilliant in the July sunlight. Scattered oak and elm trees stood in pools of violet shadow. She could hear the whirring of lawn-cutters, and the distant barking of two gay collies, who romped occasionally into her view.

She did not hear any one approach her, and so started when a boy's voice said: "Hello, there. What is your name? And why are you hiding here?"

Annoyed, and flushing, she turned back to the room. A young fellow had moved aside the blue draperies which had partially hidden her, and he was smiling down at her. She gazed at him with cold resentment, which appeared to amuse him. He sat down on the window seat and regarded her with reserved sparkling eyes the colour of dark slate.

"What is your name, mouse?" he asked.

Affronted, Adelaide was silent a moment. Then she said haughtily: "Adelaide Turnbull." She did not ask him his own name. She only wished urgently that he would go away and leave her in peace. In a moment he would discover that she was very dull and plain, and would depart for the brighter companionship of prettier girls. She hoped he would soon discover all this, and retreat.

She did not feel any regret, though he appeared to be a very nice boy of some thirteen years, and a stranger. She did not recall having seen him before. He was very tall, and thin, with quite an elegant grace, and with a narrow fair face and sharply cut features, very firm and intelligent. His hair was a sandy-red, thick and straight, and his fine ears hugged his head in a very satisfactory fashion.

When she spoke her name, his face brightened with pleasant surprise. "Is that so?" he exclaimed. "Well, now. We are cousins, it seems."

"Cousins?" she repeated, incredulously. "I have no cousins."

He laughed a little. He had an air of ease and assurance, and his slate-gray eyes were kind and full of laughter. "Oh yes, you have! My Mama's told me about you, though we've never met. Your Papa and my Mama are cousins. So that makes me your second-cousin." He paused, and twinkled upon her. "Hello, cousin Adelaide."

"Hello," she murmured, still doubtful and confused.

"You've never heard of me? Anthony Bollister?" he asked.

"No," she said, firmly. "If you were my cousin, I'd have been told."

He laughed again, lightly. "Well, now, it seems our Papas don't like each other very much. Mama told me. But I know all about you. You have two sisters, Lavinia and Louisa. You see?"

Adelaide did not reply. But she was certain that if her Papa did not like Anthony's Papa, there must be a good and sufficient reason which she, as her Papa's daughter, must respect. No doubt Anthony's Papa was a disagreeable person. So her face became colder and more remote than ever.

But Anthony was not in the least disconcerted by her attitude. He gazed at her with considerable fond amusement. "I like you, mouse," he said. "You look something like my Mama, except that your eyes are brown and hers are gray, a little lighter than mine. Yes," he added, studying her critically, "my Mama must have looked just like you when she was your age. I think a lot of my Mama, and so I suppose that is why I like you."

"Thank you," said Adelaide, ironically, rising as if to leave him.

But he caught her hand and pushed her gently back upon the seat. Then the import of his words entered her full consciousness, and she blushed. No stranger had ever said he liked her before, and this was a handsome boy. Handsome boys always avoided her. She could not believe it!

"My friends call me Tony," he offered, in a confidential and affectionate tone. She liked his voice. It was firm and strong, and kind. She could not help smiling a little.

"Tony," she said, shyly, and blushed again.

"That's better!" he exclaimed, heartily, settling himself more comfortably on the blue cushions. Then remembering his manners, he said: "But you've no ice-cream or cake. I'll get you some at once."

Adelaide watched him go without his having paid the slightest attention to her anxious demurring. He walked easily among the other boys crowded about the tables, and she saw that they parted eagerly to make way for him, and tried to engage him in flattering conversation. But though friendly, he did not allow them to delay him. He filled a plate with ice-cream and cake, and secured a silver spoon. One boy must have asked him who was the favoured young lady, for he glanced merrily over his shoulder at the shrinking Adelaide. Other boys, following his glance, stared incredulously. Adelaide distinctly heard one say: "That kid? Why, she's only a baby, about eight years old! And ugly as sin."

Anthony ignored these remarks, and pushing aside his protesting and ridiculing admirers with his elbows he returned to Adelaide, whose little face was bright red with shame and anger. He apparently did not see this, but sat beside her again, and laid the plate in her lap. She stared at it miserably, her eyes full of tears. Her throat was choking.

"Go on, eat," he said, kindly. "You don't want me to feed you, do you?"

She tried to eat. The ice-cream stuck in her throat in an icy ball. She swallowed and choked. He gave her a large white handkerchief without comment. Her humiliation was complete.

"Go away!" she cried, strangling.

"What for?" he asked, bluntly. "I like you. I don't like the other girls much. I won't go away. I told you: I like you."

She struggled against her tears, while he watched her, no longer smiling, but very intent and serious. He waited until she was composed again, and saw that she was trembling and shivering.

Then he said: "The moment I saw you, I knew I'd like you. You are so different from the other girls. Foolish, silly creatures, always giggling and trying to flirt like their elders." He paused. "You are so pretty," he added, in a low and gentle voice. "So unusual. Your eyes are the prettiest eyes I've ever seen."

Her heart flooded with pure ecstasy and incredulous joy. She gazed at him with mute pleading through her wet eyelashes. He took her hand and pressed it warmly and firmly. "Nice little girl," he whispered. Then he filled a spoon with

293

ice cream and put it to her lips, and she took it with silent gratitude.

In the meantime, while Adelaide pathetically allowed her cousin to feed her, the sound of gay music had come from the parlours, and the young guests had joyously streamed away to dance. Dozens of happy and laughing voices mingled with the strains of piano and violin and cello and harp. Anthony and Adelaide were left alone in silence at the window of the disordered dining-room.

They looked at each other long and seriously, faintly smiling. The last of the ice-cream was gone, and Anthony helped Adelaide finish the cake. They enjoyed it immensely.

Then Anthony said: "Would you like to dance, Adelaide?"

She shrank back against the window again, her happiness fading away. "Oh, no!" she murmured. "I don't dance well." Then quite pale once more, she said: "But you haven't met my sisters. They are so very pretty. Every one says so."

"I've met them," replied Anthony, with the most miraculous indifference. "I think Lavinia is very bold, and I believe that Louisa is sly. I don't like them in the least."

Family loyalty made Adelaide protest indignantly: "Perhaps they didn't like you!"

He laughed. "Indeed they did! That's why I came here to hide in the window. And there you were, not at all like your sisters. Why are you so different?"

But Adelaide was speechless. After looking at her with his long and intelligent kindness, Anthony took her hand again, and stroked it gently. Adelaide resisted a moment, then submitted. His hand imparted to hers a most soothing and peaceful sensation, secure and warm and good. She smiled at him tremulously.

Two young couples came back into the dining-room on a wave of high excited laughter and gaiety. Adelaide, seeing them, tried to disappear into the shadows. For the girls were Lavinia and Louisa, accompanied by two vigorous boys, with whom they were flirting in the most indecorous manner.

Her sisters were hardly in the room when they saw the two lurking in the window, and Lavinia shrieked: "Oh, there's Tony, and that little toad! Whatever is he doing there with her?"

Anthony rose slowly. His sharp and finely-cut features became hard and cold, and his gray eyes resembled dark slate on a bitter winter twilight. But he bowed courteously to Lavinia, who was lumberingly coquettish, and at the serene and dainty Louisa, who swept her golden lashes on her cheek in a most devastating fashion. Adelaide, in spite of her shrinking, was more frightened by Anthony's stony change of countenance than she was of her sisters' teasing, and the stare of the two strange youths.

Lavinia bridled her head at her newly found cousin, and simpered. Her black eyes sparkled; her firm cheeks were very round and red. "Why did you hide yourself with that little wretch?" she demanded, in a cajoling voice. "We've looked all over for you."

"I found Adelaide very good company," said Anthony, coldly. He glanced tentatively at the other youths, waiting for an introduction.

"Good company!" shrieked Lavinia, with a burst of boisterous laughter. "She's only a child! And the nastiest little sneak." But there was no venom in her voice, and the restless glance she gave Adelaide was mirthful. "There, I'm sorry, Addy. But Cinderella always gets the prince, doesn't she?"

Adelaide was overcome with misery. Then, all at once, to Lavinia's startled confusion, that wild and fiery light which had so appalled Miss Hamlin flashed into the child's eyes as she looked at her sister. It was gone in an instant, and Adelaide was as still and silent as she had been before. But Lavinia gazed at her, her mouth momentarily agape.

Louisa prettily performed the introductions, sweeping her lashes up and down and speaking in her soft and mellifluous voice. "Anthony, Patrick Brogan, and Rufus Hastings, old friends of ours. Patrick, Rufus, Anthony Bollister is our cousin, our second cousin, to be entirely correct."

The youths bowed ceremoniously, but furtively eyed each other like young gamecocks. Anthony, after one swift and appraising glance, decided that he liked neither of the other two, though both were prepossessing in appearance. Patrick Brogan was about sixteen, a handsome twinkling young Irishman, tall and florid of colour, with little deepset eyes of intense dark blue, sparkling and smiling. His hair was very black and thick, with a smooth rolling wave that girls found very bewitching. He had a big and fleshy body, with heavy muscles, and was elegantly if somewhat flashily dressed. He smiled almost constantly, with a wide white grin under a thick and tilted nose, and it was this smile that antagonized Anthony, for he knew at once that Patrick Brogan was a rascal, a schemer and a budding reprobate even at his present age. Patrick was indeed a rogue, by natural inheritance, and ruthless, though he had no inherent cruelty or viciousness, but was rather possessed of cunning and monumental villainy. In short, a young reprobate, good-natured and colourful, brutal and humorous, with a loud and ingratiating voice full of meaningless affection.

But it was Rufus Hastings that Anthony instinctively detested. The son of an enormously wealthy gentleman associated with the Vanderbilts and their railroads, Rufus was constantly if silently impressing upon all who came in contact with him his vast superiority to others. He was about Patrick's own age, and slightly taller, very thin, almost lathelike, and dressed with exquisite taste. His face was neutral, long and thin and somewhat sallow, with a thin ridge of a long nose and close tight lips. Under sparse blond brows his eyes were a curious greenish yellow, intent and narrow. His hair was dun-coloured and thin, and he had large transparent ears. He moved slowly and impressively, and spoke in a low and almost inaudible voice, beautifully modulated and quiet. His manner was indifferent, supremely egotistic and regal, and he always gave the impression of pale ennui. In all physical attributes, he became dim in contrast to the more ebullient and flamboyant Patrick Brogan, but Anthony, young as he was, saw that here was pure wickedness, amoral and relentless, cold as death. He had seen this wickedness in his own father, and had recognized it at once, and the same subtlety. Here was a plotter, but not a schemer. What Rufus possessed was so superior to Patrick's jovial cunning as to make the latter appear lovable, in comparison. While Patrick was a good-natured bully, he might at times have generosity and warmth. But Rufus, though not a bully, was virulent.

His aloof glance quickened, after the first instant, upon Anthony. "I say," he murmured, "aren't you in the fourth form at Bullard's? I thought I'd seen you there. I am in the sixth form."

"Yes. That is right," replied Anthony. His gray eyes were piercing, but Rufus allowed no thought at all to touch his green eyes, and while he did not yawn, he gave that impression. "Beastly place, Bullard's," he murmured. "I'm to go to Exeter next September. One meets the most impossible people at Bullard's."

Anthony said nothing, but his nostrils widened for an instant.

Patrick laughed his rich and rollicking laugh. "I like Bullard's," he said. "I'm to go there myself, in September. Good playing fields, and boxing. I'm a good boxer," and he lifted his strong and meaty fists and gaily made a feinting motion at Rufus, who dropped his hooded eyelids and averted his head.

"Unless," added Patrick, heartily, "I decide to enlist."

"You!" cried Lavinia, hootingly. "You're too young! They aren't taking boys of sixteen."

"I look eighteen," said Patrick, with a complacent grin.

"Feel those muscles," and he flexed his arm and offered it to Lavinia. But she recoiled, very coyly. However, Louisa placed her little white fingers on the proffered member and looked properly impressed and admiring.

"Beastly thing, this war," said Rufus, with much ennui. "Very vulgar. Imagine white men fighting over blackamoors. Not to be thought of, really."

"Odious," said Anthony, mimicking the other's voice. "Really odious."

Rufus turned to him and stared at him with eyes suddenly deadly and quiet. The girls noticed nothing, but Patrick was not so obtuse. He laughed loudly. He took Anthony by the arm and shook him. "I like you!" he cried. "Damned if I don't!"

Louisa clapped her hands to her ears and looked horrified. "Patrick! What language! So unrefined, I do declare!"

Anthony shook off Patrick's friendly hand and said nothing. Lavinia's attention returned to him, and she gazed at him with frank admiration. "It's really entrancing, you know, to find you are our cousin. We didn't know at all."

"No, indeed," breathed Louisa, with a devastating smile in her blue eyes. "It's lovely, though."

Patrick, who was much smitten by Louisa, scowled suddenly at Anthony. These Protestants didn't mind marrying cousins, he reflected.

"What's your subjects at Bullard's?" he demanded, returning to his former sincere friendliness.

"The humanities," replied Anthony, coolly.

Patrick stared. "And what in hell are they, sir?"

Rufus smiled thinly. "You wouldn't know, Pat. Nebulous things. Brotherly love and such, history of human thought and religion. You wouldn't know."

"You wouldn't know," repeated Anthony, but he looked fixedly at Rufus.

"Sounds messy," said Patrick, frankly. But he looked from one to the other of the youths with his twinkling dark blue eyes.

A louder burst of music, accompanied by clapping, sounded from the parlours. It was a Virginia reel which had excited that applause. Patrick masterfully took Louisa's hand, and Rufus turned elegantly to Lavinia. With a last long look at their cousin, the girls drifted away with their cavaliers, Louisa pausing once at the door to flash Anthony a killing glance, provoking and inviting. But Anthony sat down again beside little Adelaide, whom every one had forgotten, as usual.

"So," he said, looking down at her and smiling quietly, "those are your sisters. They are very pretty."

"Yes," said Adelaide, dully.

"But not like you, my little love," said Anthony.

They paused and gazed at each other in a long and shining silence.

They began to talk, happily and contentedly. Adelaide shyly told Anthony of her music. He could play the violin, himself, he said, with enthusiasm. They must play a duet together. He was full of plans for the rest of the summer. And Adelaide, as she listened, saw heaven, glistening and rainbowed, opening before her.

But they did not see each other again for a very long time.

CHAPTER 32

MR. EVERETT LIVINGSTON was a very old man now, old and white and broken, his body bent and full of the slowness and heaviness of movement which is not entirely age, but also composed of a sickness of soul. Where he had once been erect, he was bowed. Where his face had once possessed a sunken and noble aristocracy, it was withered and shrunken now, small and ill under a white skull which had appeared to grow larger and more impressive as the countenance beneath it shrivelled.

He had called John Turnbull and Mr Wilkins in to see him. Behind him, on the bare wall, no longer hung the portrait of Queen Victoria, smugly and arrogantly staring before her. It had been replaced by a fine painting of President Lincoln, draped in the flag of the Union. He sat in his chair, huddled as if very cold, but his frosty blue eyes had taken on a living quality rare in these days. It was as if for the last time the hidden fires of him, so long banked under ashes, had leapt upwards in a final blaze. His hands, skeletal but distinguished old hands, clutched the arms of his chair convulsively, and he looked at John and Mr. Wilkins with bitter denunciation and wrath. His bluish lips shook.

"Mr. Turnbull, sir," he began, in a thin but burning tone, "I must ask you a most momentous question."

John inclined his head in respectful silence, and waited. Mr. Wilkins, however, leaned forward a little, with the most affable attention.

Mr. Livingston drew a deep breath, and put his hand to his forehead for a moment. Then he resumed in a stronger voice: "I must ask you how it is possible for you to secure cotton in these days of war, from the South."

John was silent for a little, then he said quietly and carefully: "We have much cotton stored in the warehouses, as you know, sir."

Mr. Livingston stared at him stonily, and then the blue fire flashed into his eyes again. He struck his desk with his trembling palm. "Do you dare to insult me, sir, with such a remark? We have been at war with the South for three years. How have you been able to store such vast amounts of cotton? I am well aware of the capacity of our warehouses, to the last cubic inch. You insult my intelligence, sir, you deride my common sense!"

John regarded the old man inscrutably, and still answered with neutral quietness: "I did not mean to do either, Mr. Livingston. However, I had hoped I might spare you some—unpleasantness. Too, I did not think the matter would disturb you." He paused. The blue fire quickened in Mr. Livingston's eyes, and he drew in his withered lips as if preparing to protect himself against a blow. John continued: "As you know, I have travelled extensively in the South, and have been entertained by wealthy cotton planters. I found my friends, and clients, very agreeable gentlemen. We had much in common. Their regard for England was very warm, for, after all, are not the best of the American people of English stock? In spite of the rabble which has poured into America, this country, thank God, is still controlled by the Anglo-Saxon, and will continue to be so controlled. I share that devout hope with you, sir.

"When war broke out between the States, my sympathies were with the South. They still are. I knew the underlying principle: the Northern industrialists wish to destroy slave-labour in the South, with which they cannot compete. Now, I was faced with a quandary. The South has always shipped vast quantities of cotton to the Lancastershire cotton mills, and I knew that after this war, if the South lost, her natural anger and vindictiveness would compel her to ship even larger quantities to England, and thus deprive our own mills of cotton. Again, we would run second to England in the manufacture of textiles. I did not want that. I am sure that you would not wish that, either."

He paused. Mr. Livingston listened with a frozen intensity which was almost agonized. But Mr. Wilkins, after his first apprehension, had begun to smile. John, however, was very grave, his voice candid with sincerity.

"What, then, was I to do? We faced ruin. The Livingston mills, after the war, would be deprived of everything except the minimum of raw cotton. As I said, I have always had the warmest relationships with the Southern planters. Knowing, then, that war was inevitable, I made my last tour among them, and bought up large quantities of cotton. Then," he hesitated, "I arranged with them for future deliveries, war or no war. Moreover, because of their personal regard for me, we are assured of deliveries after the war."

Mr. Livingston whispered painfully, putting his hand to his eyes for a moment: " 'War or no war.' "

John, his lips tightening, glanced impatiently at Mr. Wilkins, but he answered courteously enough: "Yes, Mr. Livingston."

The old man dropped his hand slowly, and there was a strange hard gleam in his eyes. "How do you contrive the deliveries, with the blockade interference?"

John was silent. Then he looked straightly at Mr. Livingston: "I cannot tell you that. It would mean ruin, probably imprisonment for me, and destitution for my friends, if not worse."

"And," said Mr. Livingston quietly, "you pay them with gold, of course?"

John inclined his head.

Mr. Livingston leaned back in his chair, and he looked fixedly at John. His eyes were like frozen lightning, bitter, and as sharp as swords.

"You are a traitor, sir!"

He stood up. His bent old back straightened. He towered over John, who remained seated for some moments, then rose also. The old man's face was bright and fierce with condemnation.

"You, sir, and other scoundrels like you, are guilty of murder! Each time that the blockade is run, and gold exchanged for contraband goods, you prolong this murder between brothers! For money, for expediency, you continue this war, this ghastly blood-letting of kinsmen! You are a murderer, sir, a conscienceless murderer, an assassin!"

He began to shake, and staggered. He caught at the edge of his desk, then fell again in his chair. He covered his eyes with his hands. John glanced at Mr. Wilkins, who was smiling malevolently. For one instant, John's fist clenched, and a black tide of hatred for the genial Lucifer rose up in him like a wash of poisonous gall. So often, he tasted this gall, felt the corrosive of hatred in his heart, so that the sensation was not new to him. But each time it left him more malignant, more corrupted, more eaten by corrosion. Then, he sat down and faced Mr. Livingston, a long and curious trembling running down every nerve in his body. A horrible sickness made him swallow convulsively.

He said, almost faintly: "I have saved the Livingston mills, sir."

He thought that the old man had not heard him. Then, very slowly, the veined and withered hands dropped, and the sunken face they revealed was petrified and appalling in its expression.

And out of those dry lips came a strangely quiet voice:

"It is not only this. I have heard so many things. Terrible, frightful things. About you, John Turnbull. They have filtered slowly to me."

He paused. He lifted one hand and pressed it heavily upon his chest. But there was no faltering in his voice, no fading of his appalling look:

"It is not only the Livingston mills. You have not stopped there, have you? I have heard about the ships in which you have an interest, which deal with the China Coast. I have heard of the Eastern Exporting and Importing Company."

John started.

"Opium," said Mr. Livingston, and his voice was a breath rather than a sound. Now his face had the aspect of a death's-head.

"From the first, I opposed the opening of Japan to trade. Why did we not leave Japan to her sleep of centuries? She did not want us. She hated and feared us, rightly. But the bankers, the industrialists, the usurers, the financiers, must have their way. Japan must be invaded by the giants of trade, for their advantage." He paused, drew a deep and shuddering breath: "Not expansion, not progress, was in the sails of Commodore Perry's invading ships. It was corruption that filled them, and cruelty, and murder, slavery and starvation, and exploitation. And death."

"Strange words for trade, and Occidental progress, sir," said John, with a peculiar smile.

"Progress!" cried Mr. Livingston, with fierce and shaking passion. "You call it 'progress,' this turning of contented and peaceful peasants into industrial slaves, this conniving with their powerful native enemies and rulers to enslave their people for the benefit and enrichment of American and English traders and merchants! You call it 'progress' to instil into the hearts of Japanese simple men military lust and the desire for conquest?" He rose again to his feet, and cried out in a loud and terrible voice: "For this, our children, and our children's children will pay! They will pay for the enslavement of Japan by our merchants and our industrialists! You have brought a virus to Japan, a profound and destroying pestilence! You have infected them with our own corruption and greed and lust! In your ships you carried the rats of destruction and death to a peaceful and slumbering people who wanted no part of you. Yes, for this our America will pay, with blood and nightmare, and it is only just!"

"This is extravagance," said John, coldly. He did not rise this time in respect to the old man. This was partly because of the trembling of his own legs, and the devouring sickness in him.

But Mr. Livingston did not hear him. His eyes were fixed in the distance, upon an affrighting vision.

"Why did you not leave them alone? Why did you not refrain from infecting them with dreams of conquest in their own right? Do you not know that it is because of these dreams that a peaceful island people have now set out to enslave and conquer their neighbours? That they now have nightmares of their own, bequeathed to them by our own murderers? In the wake of 'trade' and 'progress' come plagues of the spirit. You have brought them to Japan, you and others like you." He added, in a slow and terrible voice: "And they will return to you."

John had to swallow several times to moisten his dry throat. But he said steadily: "After the War between the States, we will have to find larger markets. We will have to find cheaper labour. We have them waiting for us in Japan. If we do not exploit them, England will. She has already taken advantage of this war. More and more of her fleet of ships sail for the China Coast, for Japan. We must do what we can, without nebulous idealism. Or, we shall go under."

But the old man did not appear to have heard him. He continued, his lips hardly moving: "Opium. The ships in which you have an interest carry opium to China. It was you merchants who suggested this to Japan, in order to enfeeble and destroy the Chinese, and thus lay them open to easier conquest. You have dealt in opium."

John was silent. He looked at his hands, first at the palms and then at the backs of them, as if they profoundly interested him.

"There is a disease in the West," said Mr. Livingston, in a whisper. "A disease of greed, pitiless and godless. You have taken it to the peaceful East. We will pay, in our death." Suddenly he cried out in an anguished voice: "Is there no end to the cruelty of men, to the virulence of men, to the horror of men?"

John muttered: "You are extravagant. You condemn America and England. Did you not know that Germany is competing with us, that if we had not opened Japan to trade, Germany would have done so? There was no stopping this. Had we, out of some silly squeamishness, not done it, Germany would not have been restrained by our own 'idealism.' Prussia has wicked dreams of her own. I know. I have heard. Do you want to see the world enslaved by Germans? I tell you, it would have happened."

He continued: "The Germans are ingenious. One of their more famous chemists has invented a way to make narcotic derivatives from opium, which take up less than one-fourth the bulk of opium, and are more deadly. This chemist has offered the formulae to Japan, and has suggested that they will be unbelievably valuable in the destruction of the morale of the Chinese. I tell you, nothing could have stopped the opening of Japan! We got there first, that is all. And it was necessary to our existence to get there first."

Mr. Livingston slowly turned the glacial fury of his horrified eyes upon John. He said: "We are not talking about the same things."

He sat down again, and stared emptily before him.

He said, in a deceptively quiet tone, full of despair: "I heard that your agents stole the formulae for the derivatives, that you are engaged in this now, yourself. You see, I know everything."

Now his voice mounted, and he cried out: "I know that the patents which you brought to me were stolen, also! I know that my company is part and parcel of this horrible conspiracy against mankind! My company, built by my fathers in honour and justice and decency!"

John glanced quickly at Mr. Wilkins, who was smiling gently as if engaged in contemplating the most innocent and rosy of dreams. Feeling John's glance at him, he lifted his head, and now the glassy hazel eyes pointed with glittering light. John drew a deep breath. His brow knotted as if in extreme pain, and blue lines sprang out about his mouth.

"Not your company any longer, sir," he said, softly.

The old man looked at him, and very slowly, he took on the sharper aspect of a death's-head. The fragile bones of his face seemed to pierce through the parchment skin; the bony forehead glistened as if flayed; the blue mouth sank in, and where the fiery blue eyes had been were only lightless holes. The silence in the room was full of dreadfulness.

John clenched his fists to control the rigours that raced over him. He could not look at the old man. He fixed his gaze on the desk.

"I did not want to tell you this, yet. I even thought you might never need to know. With the money I inherited from my father I bought up the mortgage bonds of Livingston from Mr. Jay Regan." He paused a moment, and the silence in the room became even more dreadful. "I am now Everett Livingston & Company."

Mr. Wilkins smiled sweetly, looking from John to Mr. Livingston as if the gentlest and most sentimental of words had been said, which touched him to his heart.

"In a way, sir," continued John in a stronger voice, though his brow gleamed, "this ought to be a relief for you. You are no longer connected with subsidiary activities which can only bring you pain."

A dry gape appeared in the death's-head, where a living mouth had been. There was a rustle of a whisper: "You—have stolen my company, my father's company."

John suddenly lifted his hand, and dropped his head on the back of it. His whole attitude strangely suggested deathly illness and weariness.

"I bought it," he said, dully. "This ought to bring you relief, and joy, under the circumstances."

Mr. Wilkins stared at him, and for a moment or two the most complete expression of contempt and disgust passed over his jovial countenance. This fool, this weak and shrinking fool, this craven and sentimental imbecile!

Mr. Livingston, too, stared at John. The young man seemed to have forgotten the others in the room. He was not aware of the silence, of the regard of the two men, one so old and broken, and the other so evil. And as Mr. Livingston stared, the strangest look came over his stricken and dying face, a look of compassion, of fright, of understanding, of ghastly and frantic despair. He half lifted his frail hands as if to touch John, to lift him from the abyss of mortal illness into which he was sinking.

"My God!" he whispered. "Why have you done all these things? John. John! Why have you done it? Did you want money so much? Did you want power? Did you want power more than anything else?"

John abruptly dropped his hand with a distraught gesture. He sprang to his feet. He began to pace up and down the room, as if in disordered flight.

And Mr. Wilkins watched him with a malignant smile. But Mr. Livingston watched him with mute pity and profound compassion.

"No," he said, gently, "it was none of these things. Was it? I know it was not."

Then his old face grew fixed with overwhelming terror. He grasped the edge of his desk and cried out sharply and loudly: "It was because you hated, John! You have become corrupted with hatred. You hate all men! That is so, isn't it, John?"

John did not answer. His hurried pace became more feverish, and his look more frightful.

"My God!" cried Mr. Livingston, with the omniscience of the old and the dying. "My God!" he repeated, and his voice sank into a deep whisper, as if he could no longer endure seeing what he had seen.

Mr. Wilkins stood up. He sighed, gently. He looked from John to Mr. Livingston with the sweetest and most benign of expressions.

"This is very painful to me, sir," he murmured. "Very painful. I gives you my word. I wouldn't 'ave 'ad it happen for the world. But now it's all been said. Wot's spoken can't be sucked back. Perhaps it's best, like."

At the sound of his voice, John halted abruptly in his tracks and turned to him. He looked steadily at Mr. Wilkins.

Mr. Wilkins, undisturbed, drew out his watch, visibly started, shook his head. "Time's passin'," he said, sadly. "We've concluded the business. I think me and my young friend had best go, with all regrets to you, Mr. Livingston," and he bowed humbly to the old man.

John picked up his hat, cane and gloves, and went with Mr. Wilkins to the door. He walked like a man in a trance. Mr. Wilkins opened the door. And then came Mr. Livingston's voice, strong and ringing and passionate: "John! John!"

The two men turned to him slowly, so impelling was his voice. The old man was standing up, leaning across his desk towards them. His face was living and flashing with light. He looked at John, but pointed an unshaking finger at Mr. Wilkins:

"John, leave this man at once! In the name of God, leave him!"

John did not answer. His dark face was closed and stony.

"For your own sake, leave him at once! Never see him again, before it is too late!" cried Mr. Livingston. "In the name of God!"

Mr. Wilkins chuckled gently. His eyes dwelt on Mr. Livingston with a fond and cunning expression.

"I allus gives 'em what they wants," he said. "You, too, sir, got wot you wanted, and no questions asked."

The door closed after him and John, and the old man was alone.

CHAPTER 33

MR. EVERETT LIVINGSTON sat for a long time, alone, in the office which he had visited so rarely during these past two years.

He did not move. He hardly seemed to breathe. His long patrician hands, veined and almost transparent now, clutched the arms of his chair rigidly. All of his elongated old body was transfixed in that rigour. He stared before him, and his eyes were as empty and glazed as the eyes of the dead, as they peered out under his white and frosty brows.

His thoughts were more like voices speaking to him than conscious activities in his own brain:

He said to me, that feller, that "I always give them what they want." It is true. All my life, I have been given what I wanted most. And in contemplating my friends, I know they have also been given what they wanted in their long and devious lives. No one can reach a great age without confessing to his inmost self that never has he been deprived of what he truly desired. That is our punishment. That is our tragedy. If there is a God, and if He cared for us, never, never would He give us our heart's desire. For in the fulfilment of our wish is our destruction, our endless agony, and our death.

Never have I believed in a Spirit of Evil. Now I know it exists. It is born in our hearts. It is invincible. What is its source? Does it come from the primordial depths from which we have emerged, from the dark jungles of unremembered antiquity, from our brute heritage which we share with other brutes? Is it part of our consciousness, and is that consciousness one with the nameless evil which permeates the sunken places of the world, the swamps of the world, the stony and bottomless abysses of the world? I do not know. But I know it floats in our minds and engulfs our hearts. We call upon it, we evoke it, when we desire one thing above all others. It is the cloudy genii of our souls.

When we desire passionately, we forget honour and goodness and virtue, we forget noble strength and abnegation. For these are the things of God, and are so feeble against our desires. Each man gets the thing he covets.

In all my life, I have desired one thing most: that never should I be humiliated and left to the laughter of my fellowmen. Why did I feel so? Because in common with all others, I hated my fellows. I dared not expose myself to them. One builds fortresses only against those he hates. We all build fortresses of one kind or another, but mine has been the most ignoble.

My life has been most frightfully lonely, cut off from living. Sometimes, I have pitied myself, commiserated with myself. I did not see, then, that that was the thing I desired above all others, which would protect me from other men.

Because of this desire, I plunged into dishonour. I used fine words and heroic gestures, but I knew in my heart that I had embraced that dishonour.

Now I am an old man, and I am dying. I am broken and left desolate. There is no hope in me. Because I got what I wanted.

He raised himself a little in his chair, and he cried out in a loud and terrible voice, which rang back from the walls of the room:

"My God, my God, have mercy upon me!"

Miss Hamlin had taken the girls to a picnic on this fine and golden September day. The sky had a dark blue brightness, the air was like warmed silk. Lilybelle leaned from her window to sniff the spicy air, and look at the trees, the tips of whose leaves were already rimmed with dry yellow. The pungent grass spread below her, rustling a little in a wind that whispered of far palms and glittering seas.

Lilybelle, though no one had ever thought to ask her opinion, loved New York. She loved America. The warmness, strength and generosity in her responded with passionate joy to these things in this new country. She did not analyse her sensations, for all Lilybelle's thoughts and reactions and emotions were sensations. She had never heard of "consciousness," for that is left to those who torture themselves with self-analysis. She only knew that she lived, that she loved and enjoyed. She had no more "consciousness" than a very young child. She was like the cup of a flower which is filled with the universal rain or sun. She accepted, not by will, but because that was part of her nature. She never questioned anything.

She was very happy that the girls were gone for a day. She did not reproach herself for this happiness, as would have a more sickly and sentimental woman. She was alone. She had the air and sun and house to herself, and that was cause for contentment. She did not consider the servants an intrusion, nor more of actual presences in the house than herself. In fact, she preferred their company much more than the company of the few people who visited her and her husband formally. She was uneasy in the presence of these "grand folks," and knew, without thinking about it, that John was also uneasy. Vaguely, she understood that his uneasiness sprang from another source than her own. She only knew that he was taut and sombre when the house was invaded by "friends," and that he had a dark and glowering look which he turned slowly from one to another. She was glad when they went, and experienced a mental sensation similar to the physical one when she removed her tight stays and rubbed her plump compressed flesh. Once, and only once, she said to herself, with simple and shrinking surprise: "Why, he hates 'em!" She went no further. John's hatred was an uncomplex fact, and she was incapable of questioning. The universe was full of iron-clad facts to Lilybelle, and there seemed no reason at all to her to ask the why and wherefore of them.

She never asked why John seemed to hate his youngest daughter. It was very sad to her, but not really bewildering. He hated. That was all. She would have been astounded if it had been suggested to her that she attempt to discover why.

But even this was forgotten today. She decided, guiltily, not to put on her stays. No one would come. Her home was never visited by gracious ladies during the day, "dropping" in during a leisurely ride in their carriages. She wrapped a blue dressing-gown about her, and humming hoarsely under her breath, picked up a mending-basket of the girls' long white stockings. She felt another guilt. Miss Hamlin had reproved her genteelly for this homely task. It was not "fitting." There were so many servants to do this. But when she sat like this by her sunny window Lilybelle was supremely content. The task gave her a sense of comfortable homeliness, of sturdy reality and affection. In truth, she would have preferred a much smaller house, where she would have had to do all the work herself. Sometimes the longing to feel hot bubbling soapsuds on her arms was as poignant and sad as another woman's longing for a lover. To serve her family with her two strong hands would have been the ultimate delight to Lilybelle, and so, when she could, she engaged in such work as this.

The girls sometimes distressed her, and bewildered her, for they were strange to her nature. But it would never have occurred to her to peer into their minds and their hearts. This did not spring from a delicate regard for their privacy. Privacy did not exist for Lilybelle. Her children's natures were facts, and she never questioned facts, though sometimes, but rarely, they worried her.

Humming as she rocked and darned, and tut-tutted under her breath at some new hole, she was entirely happy. The sun gilded the high masses of her bright hair, and lay on the warm and lustrous white flesh of her neck. Her humming rose to high singing, as artless as a child's melody.

She heard the grating of carriage wheels on the gravel driveway, and leaned forward to look through the window in surprise. Who could be calling at such an hour? She felt the old familiar shrinking. But, to her amazement, it was one of the carriages of the house, and John was descending near the door.

There were few times when Lilybelle's solid heart lunged with fear. But now it lunged. John never came home at noon, and rarely before five o'clock. She had only one thought: he was ill.

She dropped the heaped stockings from her lap. A ball of white thread rolled from the basket and galloped across the floor. Lilybelle, despite her bulk, was still young, and she rushed to the door, flung it open and hurtled down the stairs, her big plump face quite pale, her mouth open. John had hardly let himself into the cool dusky hall when he was confronted by his wife, leaping down the stairs, her tumbled masses of auburn hair uncoiling themselves from her head.

His first impulse upon ever seeing her was a frown, a turning away. But today, she saw in her tumult, he did not do this. He had closed the door behind him, and stood there, leaning against it, and staring blindly before him. He did not seem aware of her presence.

Lilybelle halted as if seized by inexorable hands. She stood on the last step and gazed at him. Then, catching her breath, and saying his name for the first time in all her married life, she whispered: "John! What is it? You are ill?"

He did not move. He continued to lean against the door and contemplate some point in space. Lilybelle crept down the stairs, approached him, then, greatly daring in her extremity of fear, she took him by the arm. That arm felt like rigid wood under her hand. She shook him, very gently.

He looked down at her, but hardly seemed to hear her. However, he said faintly: "I am not ill. Yes, I am ill. I will go upstairs."

He began to move towards the stairway. Her first thought was that he was drunk, as he so often was, for he wavered and stumbled as if his legs were giving way under him. She sniffed furtively. But there was no smell of whiskey about him. Her fear rose again on a great arch. He was ill. For a moment or two a wave of dizziness ran over her.

Without hesitating about it, she put her arm about him, and felt him give up his own strength to hers. This affrighted her. He leaned heavily against her as they slowly mounted step by step to the shining upper reaches of the hall. Lilybelle gasped a little, for all her strong young peasant strength. John appeared to grow weaker and weaker. Now he was leaning more heavily upon her. She could hardly support him. Halfway up he staggered, and she had to catch hold of the banister frantically to keep both of them from plunging downwards. When they finally reached the top, she was dripping with sweat, and tendrils of her hair clung wetly about her face.

Step by step, they reached John's room. Lilybelle guided him to the bed. He fell upon it as if struck weightily on the head. He lay, face down. Lilybelle raced to the window, closed the Venetian blinds. The blue gown clung stickily to her in the heat of her fear and the heat of the day. She tore it off, standing in her bodice, her white full shoulders and half her breasts revealed, her arms bare, her cambric petticoats standing out from her body, her hair tumbling about her. With swift strong hands she undressed her husband, moving and turning him as she would have done a child. He let her have her way with him, lying heavily with shut eyes, his breath loud and uneven. She brought him a fresh white nightshirt, pulled it deftly over his head and buttoned it. She tore away the lace bedspread, plumped up the pillows, half-lifted, half-dragged John under the cool white sheet. He lay there, and now his face was gray, deep clefts about his mouth, his nostrils pinched.

"I will send for the doctor," she said, panting from her exertions.

He did not stir or open his eyes, but he said weakly: "No. I don't want a doctor. I'm all right. Just leave me alone for awhile."

She stood and looked down upon him. She rarely had mystical intuitions, but now she thought to herself with dread: He's had a terrible shock.

Lilybelle was not acquainted, herself, with shocks to the spirit. But now in the presence of such a shock she felt a cold horror engulfing her, and a most dreadful impotence and desire to weep. She crept towards the door, soundlessly. Yet, he must have heard her, for he sluggishly opened his eyes and looked at her across the expanse of the dark red carpet. There was no expression on his face. But suddenly, as they regarded each other, a change came over his features. They became wild and distracted.

"Lilybelle!" he cried. "Don't leave me!"

Never had she heard such words from him before. Dazed, she moved back to him. She sat on the edge of the bed, and looked down at him. She saw that he was full of agony. He clutched her forearm with both his cold hands, and the fingers pressed almost to the bone. But she did not feel the pain.

"What is it? John, please tell me," she whispered. She could feel nothing but her fear, her aching compassion, her great and desperate love for him.

The wildness and anguish of his expression increased. Yet, when he spoke after a few moments' silence, he said quietly enough: "Old Livingston. I found him in the office a little while ago." He paused. "He was dead."

"Oh, what a pity!" cried Lilybelle, with new strength, her eyes filling with tears. She had only seen Mr. Livingston once, and thought him a cold and disagreeable old man. But John, apparently, had had some affection for him. She put her arms under his shoulders and raised him. His head fell slackly on her breast. She held him tightly and rocked back and forth, murmuring her pity incoherently. He felt as heavy as a dead man in her arms.

In her stress, as always, she relapsed into the vernacular of her childhood. "The poor old gentleman. Wot a pity, that it is. There, lovey, don't go on so. 'E was an old gentleman, that he was, and it was a shock to you. But 'e's got no woman, or lads or lasses to grieve over 'im, and he was alone, and it was best, like."

John did not answer. He leaned against her. His cheek was ice-cold against her warm moist breath. She hugged him closer, and her whole plump body thrilled with its contact with him. She felt almost happy that he could endure her like this. But there was a slackness and inertness about him which terrified her. Her strong arms pressed deeply about him.

Then he said, from her breast: "He didn't die naturally. He killed himself."

She stopped her rocking, rigid with shock. But her arms did not loosen. Then she breathed: "Now, that was terrible, wasn't it? Why? The poor old soul must've been ill, or barmy. No wonder it's upset you like this, lovey. But it's done, and there's no use bewailin' it."

He stirred in her arms, and moved away from her. He lay again on his pillows and stared at her. His mouth opened, as if he was about to speak, then closed again.

"It's best," she urged. "Who loved the old gentleman?

There wasn't no one, pet. When one's old, and there's no one, it's no use goin' on livin', like."

She went to his desk and lifted a decanter of whiskey from it. She filled a small glass half-full. Then remembering that John was, on occasion, a heavy drinker and a little swig would not do anything for him, she recklessly filled the glass to overflowing. She brought it back to him, and tenderly held it at his gray lips.

"Drink it, lovey," she said. "It'll do you good."

He drank obediently, thirstily. Lilybelle hesitated, then returned to the decanter and refilled the glass. John drank again. Lilybelle seated herself on the bed once more and earnestly and lovingly regarded her husband.

"It was a shock," she said, sorrowfully. "Finding him like that. It must have come all over you, like."

John said nothing. He just lay on his pillows and stared at her fixedly.

"No one knows why he did it?" she suggested. "There was no note? They allus leaves notes, they say."

With a visible physical effort, John replied quietly: "He left nothing. I saw him for the last time yesterday evening. We had a—talk. With Wilkins."

" 'E must've been barmy, poor old soul," said Lilybelle, with simple conviction. "And 'e bein' so old and all."

She was perplexed. It was terrible, of course. She could not understand John's prostration. She leaned over him, the warm sweetness of her flesh enfolding him. "There, lovey," she soothed him, "rest awhile. It does no good upsettin' yourself. Wot's done's done. I'll keep the 'ouse quiet for you. The lasses are away."

She smoothed the sheet coolly about him. She smiled down at him with deep love. He had come to her in his trouble; he had not turned away from her.

He said, speaking as if each word came from a throat transfixed with a knife: "You don't understand, Lily."

"I don't understand wot?" she murmured, as if he had been a feverish child.

But he was silent again. Only his burning eyes remained fixed on her face. Then he cried out as if in fresh agony: "Don't leave me, Lily!" and he half raised himself in the bed.

She took him in her arms again. She held him against her breast. She did not speak, only rocked him gently. Finally, when she looked down at him again after a long while, she saw that he slept. Inch by inch, she lowered him to his pillows. The grayness had begun to ebb from his face. It was relaxing. The misery remained, but a slow peace was washing over his mouth and closed eyes.

She slipped like a shadow from the room. As she closed the door, she heard the far pealing of the door-bell. Hastily running into her own room, she pulled on a muslin dress with swift and awkward hands. Then she descended the stairs again.

Mr. Wilkins stood in the hall, handing his cane and hat and gloves to a servant. Even in that duskiness she could see that he was perturbed and grim.

"Ah, Mrs. Turnbull, my dear," he said, upon seeing her.

Now a strange thing happened to Lilybelle. Her first impulse had been to go to him quickly, to tell this old friend of her husband's all about his trouble, to ask him his advice urgently and trustingly. But all at once, the strange thing happened, and she was on the last three steps and could not move. She stood there as if she was a fierce and relentless guardian of her husband, and could not speak.

He advanced towards her, and tried to smile with his old geniality.

"John, 'e's come home, eh?" he asked, cautiously.

Lilybelle moistened her full red lips, which were suddenly dry.

"Yes," she said, in a low voice. " 'E's 'ome. I've got him to sleep. He was upset."

Mr. Wilkins assumed a grave and lugubrious expression, and nodded. "It was sad. You know, ma'am?"

Lilybelle nodded her head slowly. In the duskiness her round and shallow blue eyes were very bright and intent.

Mr. Wilkins advanced another step. He looked up at her. "I'll see 'im, ma'am, and comfort him, like."

But Lilybelle did not move. She did not know why she stood there, so inexorably. Here was her old friend, her old protector, almost a father to her, and such a good friend to John, who had no other real companionship. Who but Mr. Wilkins could comfort him? But still, she could not move. Her heart felt chilled and enormous in her breast, and she was faint with her own perplexity.

" 'E's asleep," she said, firmly. One hand rested on the banister; she put the other hand on the wall, as if to bar passage. " 'E's got to rest, Mr. Wilkins."

Mr. Wilkins was silent. He looked up at her. His round pink face became closed and evil. How much did the wench know? What had that fool told her? That weak and craven fool who had not the fortitude to accept life and his own acts?

He coughed gently. "It was sad, wasn't it, ma'am? The old gentleman—shooting himself? Johnnie told you?"

"Aye," she answered. "'E' was proper upset. I gave him a swig or two. He fell asleep. 'E's not to be disturbed." She added: "I'm sorry, Mr. Wilkins."

He approached even closer, and spoke with cajoling firmness: "But I've got to talk to him, ma'am, asleep or no. There's plenty of time for that." He hesitated. "Johnnie didn't have no—idea—why the old gentleman did it, eh? He didn't tell you wot he thought, like?"

Lilybelle answered: " 'E didn't know." She frowned a little. "Leastways, 'e didn't say. Just that he killed himself." She repeated: " 'E's proper upset, sir. 'E's got to sleep." Then she exclaimed in bewilderment: "Was there a reason, as John didn't tell me? Does John know?"

Mr. Wilkins did not reply for a moment. Then he smiled with sad sweetness. "There warn't no reason, ma'am, that we know of. But you know Johnnie. Allus full of sensibility. It was a shock to 'im. So I thought I'd drop around and soothe 'im. Just as a friend."

Now his foot was on the first stair. Without any reason at all, Lilybelle began to tremble. She became very white. She sucked in her under lip like a child who is about to weep. But she did not stir from her position. She knew, with a strong and nameless knowledge, that John must not see his old "friend" now, that he was not to be allowed to enter that room, that something most frightful would happen to her husband if Mr. Wilkins came in upon him.

And then, with that knowledge, forceful and invincible, which comes only to the simple and pure of heart, she knew that Mr. Wilkins was evil. And she knew that that evil mortally threatened her husband.

The knowledge overwhelmed her with terrible fear. Her knees bent under her. And her eyes distended so that they seemed full of a glaring light. She stared at Mr. Wilkins with open and supreme terror.

"Go away!" she cried. "You must go away at once!"

A whole world of repudiation, of horror, was in her face. She confronted him, however, with white resolution, the resolution of good men confronted by a boundless evil, an evil which must not pass.

And Mr. Wilkins looked up at her, and a great silence fell between them.

Then, after a long time, Mr. Wilkins took up the hat and cane which the servant had left on a hall table. Looking at her steadily, and smiling just a little with a peculiar fondness, he pulled on his gloves. He bowed a little. He even seemed amused, in a genial fashion. But Lilybelle did not answer his smile. The white horror was a glare upon her face.

"You're right, ma'am," he said, humbly. "It's not the thing to disturb Johnnie just now. But you'll tell 'im I dropped in, and that he's not to upset 'imself? That I'll explain everything?"

Lilybelle did not speak. But she nodded dumbly.

Mr. Wilkins, after another bow, left the house.

Lilybelle could not move for a long time. Then, as if the strength had gone from her, she sank upon the stairs, huddling her folded arms upon her knees. After a few stark minutes, she bent her head on her arms and began to weep.

CHAPTER 34

THERE are some countenances that immediately inspire curiosity, and scandal, though in fact the possessors are usually persons of the utmost innocence and virtue. And there are other persons, who by some mysterious magic of demeanour, face or carriage inspire the belief that no calumny could touch them, that they could never be guilty of anything that in the slightest resembled infamy or dubiousness.

Such as the quiet slight lady, veiled and pale of manner and neutral of fashion, who came and went discreetly in the small blind white house with the green shutters on this street shadowed with trees. She was a lady of comfortable if small means, apparently, for she had no carriage, always arriving on foot at her low white gate, her head always bent as if in meditation or melancholy. She wore only gray or black garments, with a large bonnet and veil, and walked with aristocratic silence, attracting no attention by the slightest lift of a gloved hand, aware of no one. Her appearance was genteel, but not so excessively as to arouse comment. Behind that veil her face was nebulous, and only a few of her neighbours had caught even the faintest glimpse of a pair of brilliant gray eyes and straight pale mouth. No one could have said whether her hair was brown or gold or black, so carefully was it concealed under the bonnet, yet not so obviously concealed as to excite remark. Her long shawls and muffs blurred her figure. She might have been any age between

315

thirty or fifty. She fitted in perfectly with her background of "shabby genteel" neighbours.

Her landlord knew her as a Mrs. Johnson, but whether she was wife or widow even he did not know. Nor, hypnotized by that magic of manner, voice and quiet calm face, did he even dream of inquiring. By her very bearing she repudiated curiosity; the very suggestion that she might not be all that she seemed would have seemed blasphemous to a man even so cynical as a landlord. Her dignity and cold pride told him that here was a lady, who desired nothing more than seclusion and quietness. She implied that her health was not of the best, that she was a stranger, that she had no desire to know her neighbours, and all this without uttering a single word to this effect. Continuing the subtle, and indirect, implications, the landlord gathered that she had some small private means of her own, and that she might at times not be at home for days. "There were friends," she had murmured. Too, it might be expected that her brother would visit her occasionally, in order to cheer away the clouds of melancholy that perpetually floated about her. For references, she gave the landlord the name of a substantial city bank, and a note on perfumed stationery, crested and thick, from Mrs. Andrew Bollister, in which that lady firmly certified that "Mrs. Johnson" was a close friend who had suffered certain griefs and wished to retire to a quiet locality. The bank and the note quite overwhelmed the landlord, who was not inclined to be suspicious, anyway. He came to the sympathetic conclusion that here was a lady in sad and reduced circumstances, who wished to hide her sorrows and fallen fortunes in proud and silent seclusion.

A stout woman was hired by the day to keep the small house in neat order, and always left at six o'clock. The landlord, once calling to ascertain if the plumbing was in good order, had greatly admired the furnishings of the house. They were spare and elegant, the floors polished and bare, and while nothing was expensive or elaborate, the house had acquired a haughty and genteel atmosphere.

Nor were the neighbours curious. Even the fact that they rarely saw Mrs. Johnson did not excite them. When they did see her, she drifted so quietly in and out, and was so nebulous of appearance, that they came to the vague conclusion that when they did not see her for days she must, in reality, have been there all the time. They made no overtures to her. Her despondency and melancholy caused them to shrink from any contact with her, and so they "left her to her sorrows."

Once or twice they had seen a gentleman enter the house,

but they were so little interested in Mrs. Johnson that they paid him no heed. He was a "brother," they had gathered. Or perhaps a lawyer. Disinterested opinion was divided on the subject.

Mrs. Johnson had lived in the house for over fiften years now, and she might have been a ghost for all her neighbours. In the summer a small garden was tended by an old man, the father of the maid, but the garden was as neutral and orderly as Mrs. Johnson herself. Occasionally a tradesman came. No one had observed that the postman came only on rare occasions, and then with a single letter.

Had any one cared to notice, he would have discovered that he saw Mrs. Johnson only on those days when her "brother" or "lawyer" came later.

John frequently said to himself that in that discreet white house he found the only peace and contentment and rest he had ever known. Here he could talk with freedom, he told himself, confident of love and sympathy and subtle understanding. The quiet hand in his, the quiet eyes fixed on his own, the slow smile, were all means to escape, to recuperation and strength. He had told himself these things for over fifteen years.

It is strange, then, that his nameless anxiety, his ravaged emotions, his weariness and hidden despair, increased rather than decreased during the days following each visit to the lady of the secluded house. He thought all this the result of his discontent that he could not live with that lady entirely, and openly, without his furtive coming and going.

Sometimes he would sit with her in the loveseat before the fire, watching the long rosy flames licking the black bricks, and he would talk with her of their mutual childhood and memories in England. They would laugh a little, sigh a little, look at each other deeply. Sometimes they did not talk at all, only holding hands. Later they would go upstairs to the cool white bedroom above, and all lights would wink out silently and the house would be one with its dark neighbours.

He was never indiscreet. Cloaked in dark garments, his hat pulled well over his eyes, not carrying his cane, he would usually arrive at twilight. He had been nervous at first, not for his own sake, but for the lady's. However, he soon discovered that no one was interested. He too, arrived on foot, leaving his carriage some four streets away, and dismissing it.

So, he lived two lives: one of hot and aching misery and hatred, and the other, he believed, of peace and contentment and refreshment.

Sometimes he had dinner with the lady. She prepared

the finest delicacies with her own hands, and they would dine before the fire, quite alone in the house. She had excellent taste in wine and cordials, and for one who drank sparingly of these she was strangely lavish and insistent with them for her guest. There was an immediate large whiskey for him upon his arrival, to banish the dark tautness of his face and the taciturn restlessness in his eyes.

He would hurry eagerly to that house, leaving directly from the office. Sometimes she informed him that she could be with him only for an hour or two, and not long after his own departure she would steal away, unseen, to be gone for days. It was only once a month or so, that she remained overnight, and he with her.

It was spring again, now, and the sky was heliotrope over trees filled with pale green fog, and robins sang their silver threnodies in the wet branches. Spring always struck with unbearable poignancy on John's corroded heart. Then he could hardly control his restlessness and gloom, his urgent despair. The lady had an anxious time with him in the spring.

Sometimes she would muse that this explosive and bitterly violent man with the sombre eyes and gloomy mouth was not the hot and exigent young man she had known in England. Then he had been generous and warm, if violent, and all his faults were excessive but lovable. He had been ignorant and ingenuous, candid and open of heart, wishing only to be liked and included. A great bounding puppy of a youth, wistful for affection, and most frightfully lonely. His generosity and high humour had had a touching air about them. Hatred was a thing unknown to him. When he saw it in the faces of others for him, and their contempt, he was only angrily bewildered. He who hated no one could not understand why any one should hate him. Even his laughter at others had never been cruel or malicious, and was followed immediately by contrite compassion or lavish gifts.

The lady was not perplexed at this change in the man she loved. She only regretted that he had been so absurdly ingenuous, that upon contact with the realities of a world of men he had reacted with such bitterness, such hatred, such vengefulness and malignity. It was all so extravagant to her. She had known from earliest childhood the true character of the world, and it had not disconcerted or saddened her. But John was a full grown man before he had known, and his reaction had been both excessive and murderous, quite out of reason, importance or proportion.

She could not help but feel that he was weak. She had

always known he was weak, she told herself. Weakness was always violent in its reactions, never calm or considered.

The lady never considered that perhaps it is only the intrinsically pure of heart and simple of faith and truthful of soul who can become truly malignant and savage when confronted by a world composed mainly of men who are cruel, faithless, voracious and full of treachery. Those who are born disingenuous and cynical are never surprised. Neither have they known dreams and heroic passions.

Had any of this evenly faintly dawned upon her, she would have stated incisively that such men are weaklings, infuriated with reality when it is presented to them. Above all things, she detested weakness.

But she did not find John's "weakness" any deterrent to her love for him. In fact, she loved him the more for it. It was his "weakness" that put him so abjectly in her power, and there was in this lady a quite unfeminine passion for power. At all times, she must control any situation; others must be subjected to her, if only subjectively. If they would not be so subject, she ignored them, or detested them. She must be in authority at all costs. Anything else was a threat to her security.

Unlike John, her other life was not a confused and vicious and hateful dream to her. She operated in it quite competently, the cool and perfect wife and mother, the calm advisor and authority, the smiling and elegant hostess. She even enjoyed her other life. Too, this life with John was not an escape to peace and rest for her. It was a glorious diversion. It reaffirmed her egotism, her superiority, her control of all situations. Had she been deprived of it, she would have felt not only grief and desolation, but a destruction of her personality.

John, of course, guessed none of this. Like all who are intrinsically simple of heart, he believed that what he felt was shared by others. He believed that the lady found her other life as dreary and onerous and full of hatred as he found his own. She did not enlighten him. She was so much more subtle and intelligent than he. And, though she did not know it, she, Eugenia Bollister, was so much more base.

If John had changed, so had she. Or rather, in her case, her hidden and intrinsic qualities had been enhanced. Her pride and hauteur had increased enormously. Her coldness and selfishness had become monumental. Yet, (and this is not paradoxical) her integrity was more unshakable than ever. She had come to America to be with John, to regain him again. That was part of her integrity.

They rarely, if ever, mentioned their families to each

other. But sometimes John would fix a strange hard look upon her, scrutinizing and resentful, and she uneasily wondered of whom he was thinking, of whom he was reminded by her presence. Not that appalling coarse creature he had married, that servant, that abominable milkmaid! Was it his father? But he never spoke of his father without aching tenderness and sadness. However, she saw there was recognition in his look, and anger.

On this spring evening, so lovely and silent except for the robins, she had prepared a dainty and delicious meal. Tulips stood in a crystal vase on the table, whose stiff white damask held, in its folds, the rosy light of the fire. Her delicate china waited, gleaming as polished ivory. The heavy silver winked in the candlelight and firelight.

The key in the lock made her rise with that sudden blooming smile which made her pale calm face vivid with beauty. Once in the house, she always discarded her dun garments, and now she was arrayed in violet silk, pearls about her throat, her smooth brown hair shining with hidden bronze tints. Though she was past thirty now, she seemed a gracious lady in her early twenties. There was no line in the small quiet face with its round firm chin, and no weariness in those large and brilliant gray eyes. Her figure was still slight and perfect. She was all elegance, all hauteur, all composure.

John came in with his usual hasty and abrupt tread, throwing his coat and hat and gloves upon a chair, and advancing to her with outstretched hands. He smiled. Whenever he entered, she always gave a quick sharp glance, hidden under her dark lashes. How ravaged he was, how exhausted, yet how burning! He was hardly thirty-six, yet his temples were streaked with growing whiteness, and he was steadily growing thinner. This thinness was enhanced by his broad shoulders and his height. His black curls still grew thickly on his large round head, his manner was still hasty and exigent and seeking. But each time she saw him more tormented, more haggard, more consumed by the poison in himself. To all others he was pitiless and cruel and implacable. To her, he was the humble lover, the hesitant waiter upon her favours. She smiled contentedly, and with deep and sincere love.

He seized, rather than took her, in his arms. He bent his head and buried his face in her slim white neck. He was intoxicated by her rose scent, as delicate and fragile as herself. There was hunger in his grasping, and a frantic voracity. "Genie," he murmured, over and over.

Then he took her hands and held her off from him, delighted, as always, with her familiarity, her freshness and beauty. She smiled at him tenderly, but without his own passion.

She said: "I'm so sorry, love, but I can only stay three hours."

His face darkened, his hands tightened on hers. "But, it has been three weeks since I saw you. I thought tonight——"

Her expression became even more tender. "We have three hours," she reminded him with gentle serenity. "I could not help the three weeks."

There was a little silence. Then releasing her hands she moved to the table, gave it a last thoughtful glance, then left the room. John watched her go, his look darkening steadily. He sat down in the chair placed for him, then, as if stung by his chronic restlessness, he stood up, turned his back to the fire, and glowered before him. His preoccupied eye roved over the little room with its glimmering floors, its graceful chairs in the shadowy corners, its small but excellent Japanese prints on the white walls. Despite his anger, he began to relax. Three hours. Not much after a wretched three weeks. But it would have to do. When Eugenia returned with a covered silver dish in each hand, he was smiling.

They ate to the accompaniment of flickering candlelight and the dropping of bright coals. There was a lessening of the sick tension in John. He talked with amazing tranquillity, while Eugenia listened, intent and smiling. Everything she did was perfect and full of grace, whether it was the turning of her head, or the prosaic lifting of the cover of a dish to spoon out its steaming contents. John, as always, drank heavily. It seemed a necessity for him. Eugenia, understanding the cause, considered it weakness. Her dear John was so absurd. Her smile became even more soft.

They did not speak or think of their other lives. Nor was their conversation intellectual in the least. They said the smallest and silliest of things, and laughed, and covered the silences with long and passionate looks at each other. When they had finished the meal, they sat before the fire, hand in hand.

Then Eugenia said, gravely, and not looking at him: "I shall have to go to England in May, dear John. My son," and she hesitated briefly, "is finished with his school and I am to bring him home. He expects me to be there, to see him receive his honours."

John stiffened. He sat up and glared at her. "And how long?"

"Two months, at most," she said. She fixed her gray eyes upon him. That cool direct glance never failed to quell him before, make him submissive. But it failed now. His own dark eye sparkled with fury.

"You go alone?" he asked.

"No."

John clenched his teeth. He dropped her hand and stared at the fire.

"Two months is not too long," she said, as if he were a child. "I go by steamboat. I am so sorry. But I cannot refuse to go, you see. I am fond of my son."

John did not answer. His tight profile became more grim.

"I shall be so glad to see England again," continued Eugenia, and in spite of herself her voice became somewhat richer. "It is nearly seventeen years. A very long time to be away from home. I want to see my mother's grave, too."

She put her hand on his tense and unresponsive arm. "You have never been home, John. Don't you ever long for England? You have lived here so long, too."

Now he spoke through lips like iron: "I have never lived anywhere."

Suddenly she shivered. "I have never lived anywhere," he had said. She saw that it was true. All these years in America had meant nothing to him. How most horrible. She had many hours of enjoyment and pleasure in America, even away from him. She had become part of this country, and her longing for England only came to her occasionally. But John had not even been aware of America, except as a shifting background to his sick dream of hatred and vengefulness. He might have lived in China or Afghanistan for all this country had been to him. Nor did he suffer nostalgia for England, she knew. He lived suspended in space. The idea seemed gruesome and terrible to her. It was death in life. He had existed in a capsule.

She was overwhelmed with pity. And with impatience.

"But you have done so much here," she urged, her hand pressing his arm. "You are one of the richest men in New York."

"I have never lived anywhere," he repeated, as if to himself. And then he looked about the room. "Except here, for a few hours, perhaps."

But, to her mingled indignation and compassion, she saw that not even this was true. She, too, had been a dream to him.

"Oh, how could you ever endure it?" she cried, and there was an impatient anger in her voice. Then it seemed incredible to her. As usual, he was dramatizing himself. He could not have borne all these years, if he was telling the truth. He could not have gone on, doing the things he had done, if he had been engulfed in a perpetual nightmare. "Haven't you enjoyed anything, John? Your success? Your position? Your triumph over everything?"

He turned slowly and stared at her. Then all at once he began to laugh. It was a wild and dreary laugh. She moved a little away from him. He rubbed his eyes with the back of his hand.

"But that is so silly," she said, and became more firmly convinced that he was subconsciously acting. "You must have enjoyed something. Your new home on Fifth Avenue is considered priceless. You must have taken some interest in it, or you would not have cared whether you had it or not."

John seemed about to speak. Then he closed his livid lips. How could he put into words, how could he tell her, that even that fine new mansion was only an expression of his hatred, so universal, so all-embracing, and so mingled with revenge? He had no eloquent words. He could not tell her.

She said, almost repellently: "And you do have three lovely daughters."

He still did not answer. She looked away from him. "There is another difficulty, too. In the natural course of events, our children will meet. They met once. I sent Anthony to England for nearly four years after that. But there will be no more running away. He must eventually have to return home from college, even during the holidays. What then?"

He was still silent. He seemed suddenly broken and exhausted. He put his hands over his face, and she knew he neither cared about nor heard what she had said.

She was repulsed rather than touched by his foolishness. She said serenely, as if he had answered her question: "Perhaps you are right. If our children meet, it will do no harm, though it might cause a slight embarrassment under certain circumstances. However, it is not worth one's worry just yet."

She gazed at him expectantly. He had dropped his hands; they hung between his knees. He was staring emptily at the fire.

Now her impatience rose up so strong in her that her eyes flashed like steel. She pressed her lips together, and sitting stiffly beside him felt nothing now but scorn and icy contempt for his weakness, for his self-deliverance to emotion, frenzy and extravagance. She thought of her life apart from him. She had made many agreeable friends, had adjusted herself admirably. Her lonely girlhood was forgotten. She realized that loneliness had been abnormal, and had set out to change her life. She was the acknowledged leader among many friends and admirers, and enjoyed this position of social power. She dominated the household of Richard Gorth, who was now excessively fond of her. No one disputed her word, not even Andrew, though she realized she had her way with him because he was perpetually amused by her. But in this vigorous country she enjoyed her life greatly, mistress of a large fortune in her own name. Cool, sensible, astute and selfish, she was adored by scores, as is usually the case with people of her temperament. Never had pure emotion ridden over her calmer decisions.

The more she contemplated John, the more impatient and contemptuous and incredulous did she become. Finally her incredulity overcame everything else, and she was affronted that he dared so underestimate her intelligence as to pretend that nothing was of value to him, that he cared for nothing. He was an actor, and a very poor one at that, striking postures to engage her sympathy, weakly uttering heroics in order to melt her with pity for him. What weakness! What absurdity! How singularly unmanly! She glanced at his profile, dark and sombre, rigidly violent in the light of the fire, and was both embarrassed and irritated. But then, he had never been English. He had never realized the impropriety of dramatic pretense and cheap heroics.

Then she thought: Is it possible that in a smaller fashion he is telling the truth? She felt a moment's surge of gratified but appalled vanity. Her love for power made her feel quite heady for a few moments. And then, with a return of her affrontedness, she told herself that he had intended her to feel so, and was perhaps at times secretly amused that she so deceived herself. Her conceit was outraged.

She said sharply: "John, you aren't very sensible, you know."

He turned slowly and looked at her, and she knew he did not see her at all. His eyes were but empty if smoldering sockets. With a sudden chilling about her heart, she thought: I mean no more to him than anything else he has gained! But why did he wish to gain anything, if he felt this way, and is not only pretending?

She could not understand such madness. There was a disease in this man, a sick poison which had eroded him, leaving gaping holes behind. She was suddenly frightened, and now was not entirely sure that he was acting. Such a tormented expression could not possibly be assumed.

He stood up. He was more than a little drunk, and he swayed. Then he moved towards the door. She rose slowly, rustling in her violet silk. He went out into the hall. He was putting on his coat.

She could not believe it. He was leaving her! Why? Her face flushed scarlet.

"John," she said, in a peremptory voice.

But apparently he did not hear her. He picked up his hat and gloves, opened the door, stepped out, and closed the door behind him.

CHAPTER 35

LILYBELLE was very unhappy in the grand new mansion on Fifth Avenue, only half a mile from the home of Richard Gorth. Though she had lived here now for over six months, the great rooms and wide corridors were still strange and inimical to her. She hardly knew the army of servants. There was no more going down to the kitchen for an early and amiable conversation with the cook, sitting in the warmth of great iron ranges, gazing contentedly at red-tiled floors and walls. No more the delight of seeing bright reflections in the polished copper utensils hung all about; no more a last and lazy sipping of coffee in the morning sunshine while the cook grumbled, or joked or laughed or suggested new dishes. These new servants were cold and efficient automatons, and she feared and disliked them. She was afraid to speak to them, to give orders. She clung to Mrs. Bowden, who was not in the least intimidated by the servants. Miss Hamlin had gone. The two older girls had had their tutor, and Adelaide, Lilybelle's darling, had been sent away to school by her father's orders. That had broken Lilybelle's loving heart, but she had not presumed to interfere. The sadness had remained, however.

She had been so happy, despite John's indifference and contempt for her. She treasured the memories of the few occasions when he had called to her from the depths of his obscure but murderous despair. What did it matter if, remembering later, he was the more cruel, the more contemptuous, the more slighting? But, since that occasion, three years ago, when he had run to her in his mysterious and nameless agony, he had not approached her at all, had never even entered her rooms. Days passed without him speaking to her, or seeing her. Sometimes he entertained on so vast and lavish a scale that she was completely overcome, wandering among the grand guests as mute as a rosy and buxom ghost, her blue eyes shining with fear. Though the guests fawned upon John, even the best of them, they knew her for what she was, she would say humbly to herself. It was only right, then, that they should ignore her, or stare at her arrogantly.

She had no friends at all, except Mrs. Bowden and the aging Miss Beardsley. The latter came at least once a week, and then was full of cold and reproving remarks to Lilybelle. She was getting too fat. She must really control her appetite. The purple velvet made her look like a charwoman in borrowed finery. She did not insist upon proper respect from her children. She indulged Adelaide too much. She did not watch her speech constantly. All in all, Miss Beardsley forcibly impressed upon Lilybelle that her mentor was disappointed in her, that she was a poor stupid thing of low birth who had not profited by her magnificent opportunities. But she assured herself, when most depressed, that Miss Beardsley said all these things because of her fondness for her pupil, and that the fault lay entirely with herself.

When Mrs. Bowden came to her, however, Lilybelle had the most inexplicable urge to tears. Often, she indulged in them, with a tempestuous wildness which was quite hysterical. She often wept, these days, and would cling to Mrs. Bowden with aching arms. She was barely thirty-three now, but with her plumpness, now almost obesity, and her flamboyant garments, she appeared much older, even older than John. The brightness of her hair was fading, and she was becoming careless with its heavy masses.

In her fear of the servants, in her horror of the great and majestic mansion, she would retire immediately after dinner to her own rooms, lock the door against intrusion, and go to bed. There, upon her pillows, she would painfully pore over the newspapers, and try to read yellow-backed French novels of love and passion. Sometimes, she would surreptitiously bring to her rooms a box of bonbons or a rich cake or two, and in her fear and unhappiness and loneliness she would devour them avariciously. Tears would mingle with them, as her mouth opened and closed in its chewing. Crumbs would fill the bed, soil the satin pillows, much to the disgust of the immaculate chambermaid the next day.

Lilybelle had no control over the servants. They despised her.

The mansion was very quiet this pure spring night, blessedly so to Lilybelle. There was to be a huge dinner tomorrow, and she had gone to bed "so I'll have the strength for it." Lavinia and Louisa had departed for a party at the home of one of their legion of friends. Adelaide would not return from her school until June. Mrs. Bowden was not at home, having gone to visit some old friend of her own.

Lilybelle, on her pillows, began to cry. She had brought her hairbrush to bed with her, and was brushing her hair as she wept. Sometimes, with frank childishness she wiped her nose and wet cheeks and eyes on the backs of her large fat hands. She sniffled, looking about the large and handsome room as if it were a prison.

Though John had never entered here, he had furnished it, not even hearing Lilybelle's timid suggestions. There was a great white marble fireplace, over which hung an excellent landscape. The rug was of a thick yellow velvet, the walls ivory, the furniture of the heaviest mahogany, and draperies of a rich and lustrous green. Everything had been elegant and orderly, in the beginning. But Lilybelle, intimidated by the grandeur, had finally imposed her own personality upon it. The mantelpiece was cluttered with homely ornaments: a pottery cow all glazed brown and yellow, an excuse for a bed of earth in its back from which grew long streamers of ivy; several gay little figures of impudent gnomes, twinkling shepherdesses and dancing witches and little boys with striped trousers with cats in their arms. The dresser was strewn with the bright bottles which Lilybelle loved, dance programs which she had filched from the girls' rooms, little miniatures of her daughters, and brushes with mats of auburn hair clinging to them. She was not too orderly by nature, and the chairs, in spite of the chambermaid's strenuous efforts were always littered with undergarments, stays and stockings, and empty boxes of bonbons and fashion magazines. In a mood of exceptional daring, Lilybelle had smuggled a violent red hearthrug into the room, and this lay before the fire, fighting viciously with the yellow carpet. Because she was always so cold lately, a fire burned on the hearth almost into summer. It made the room very hot and stifling, especially as Lilybelle, in her nameless fear, kept the draperies drawn thickly across the windows. Now she feared dimness, and every candle-sconce burned brilliantly in the room, and her bedside lamp was lit.

But it was her own. No one came here, except Mrs. Bowden, when invited. When Adelaide was home, of course, she spent most of her time in her mother's room, and Lilybelle, in her loneliness, consoled herself with visions of that slight straight figure and gentle if stern pale face and light hanging hair. Sometimes she slept with Adelaide's miniature under her pillow.

Now, as she brushed her hair and sniffled, she felt despondent enough to die, she assured herself, with her old humble patience. She felt her friendlessness. Since that day, so long ago, when she had instinctively protected John from Mr. Wilkins, she had fled wildly from the latter whenever he came to this fine new mansion. For two months after that day, John had refused to see his old friend, and Lilybelle had rejoiced, without analysing her reasons for rejoicing. She had felt something sinister and ominous lifted from her heart, from John, from all she loved. Then, he had returned, and the old relationship had been resumed between the two men. But Lilybelle had never forgotten, had never been able to look upon Mr. Wilkins again with the old and childish affection. She had shrunk from him, growing pale and silent in his presence, however he tried too woo her. John had angrily reproved her for it, and she had looked at him mutely, despairingly, knowing herself for a stupid fool who had nothing but emotion to offer in place of a reasonable explanation. She only knew that when she saw Mr. Wilkins she experienced a sickening plunge of terror, and a kind of horror of him.

Lilybelle felt rather than thought. She began to sob, and her tears came faster.

Then, to her dismay, she heard a quick and urgent tapping at her door. Without thinking, she quavered: "Come in." The door opened, and John stood on the threshold, swaying, holding to the sides of the doorway with gripping hands. He was drunk, Lilybelle saw. But she did not care. Joy lifted her heart wildly. She smiled, and her big fat face was radiant, and she held out her arms instinctively.

He was looking at her emptily, his mouth sagging. She saw his torture. Slowly, half-stumbling, he came across the room to her. He sat heavily on the side of the bed. He looked at her. Then, very slowly, he looked about the room he had not entered for three years. His expression became wondering; he blinked a few times. He returned his eyes to Lilybelle, who was watching him in trembling and loving silence, hardly able to believe he had come to her.

Then he took her hand. He held it in both of his. Lilybelle caught her breath, and in her earthy wisdom, said nothing. He turned her hand about, examining it minutely, pressing its warmth and firmness, rubbing the skin between his thumbs. Then he smiled.

"It's real, isn't it?" he said, in a low voice.

Lilybelle did not speak, but she put her arms about him, and held him to her.

CHAPTER 36

"W HAT I can't understand," said Richard Gorth, pacing gloomily up and down the drawing-room of his home, and glancing savagely at his nephew, "is how he happened to let us exist. He could have destroyed us easily enough, if he had wanted to. We were tottering, three years ago. Why didn't he go on?"

Andrew answered indolently: "Auld Lang Syne, perhaps. Cousinly remembrance. Happy thoughts of his early association with you."

Richard Gorth uttered a foul word, then inclined his head apologetically at Eugenia, who sat serenely before the fire with her needlework. She acknowledged his apology with a faint amused jerking of her lips. Mrs. Gorth, however, tightened her yellowed face and jerked her dyed head.

"It puzzles me, curse it!" resumed Mr. Gorth, scowling. "During the war, he could have done us in. We had no cotton. He had. He's just the type of violent and turbulent devil that appealed to the Southerners. There's no doubt that he was smuggling the cotton in. But how? You reported your suspicions, Andy, but nothing was ever found out."

He paused to contemplate, with renewed savagery, the phenomenal progress of John Turnbull.

"Look what he's done in seventeen years! Built up Everett Livingston & Company to the largest cotton manufacturers in America. Cornered most of the trade. Look at his mills in New England. Almost impossible. But he wasn't satisfied with cotton and printing. He gets himself into the export and import trade. The China Coast. Japan, and building mills there for printing silk. The next thing will be cotton. We've begun to be flooded with cheap Japanese merchandise of all kinds. What's that going to do to our own economy? I hear he controls the Blue Crescent fleet of ships to the Orient. What's the devil after? Money? His father left him enough. He's got the Livingston mills, and their subsidiaries. Now, from what I hear, he's dealing in opium. He's using his ships for gun-running to Japan, too. A nefarious business, bound to do us enormous harm someday. How the hell does he keep his finger on so many enterprises? It's the devil's own work."

"Mr. Wilkins," suggested Andrew, languidly.

Mr. Gorth stared at him thoughtfully, and rubbed his chin.

"I've never known Wilkins to stick so long to any one man. Must have found him damned lucrative. And that's strange, too. I never thought him a particularly bright fellow; too emotional and unstable. Not the genius sort. Yet, I must have been mistaken. He must have had gifts I knew nothing about, I'm sorry to say."

"Mr. Wilkins," repeated Andrew, with an elegant yawn.

"Curse you and your Mr. Wilkins!" shouted Mr. Gorth. "Wilkins found something in him that was more valuable than he ever found in any one else! Surely you, you fine yawning gentleman, can see that for all your stupidity? What was it Wilkins found? That's what I'd like to know, I tell you."

"It wasn't wit. It wasn't an overpowering intellect. It wasn't inventiveness, nor great ambition, nor lust for power," said Andrew, smiling and unperturbed. "Yes, I agree with you. It was something else. He was not a chap that wanted money very much. He'd always had more than enough, thanks to his father. You intrigue me, Uncle Richard," and he sat up in his chair, and delicately dusted off his hands. "I've wondered, myself. I knew Johnnie very well in England. He wanted nothing but to be friendly with every one, and have a gay drinking companion. He liked people; he was a lonely devil. But he had no social graces, and most of us laughed at him. He was like a mongrel dog sniffing hopefully about. Once I asked him what he intended to do with his life, and the imbecile only blinked and gaped. The idea had never occurred to him. He was a hulking and handsome piece of flesh, wanting to be patted, and that was all." He turned to his wife gracefully. "I don't offend you by speaking so of your cousin, my dear?" His pale bright eyes were amused and affectionate.

Eugenia did not lift her head from her needlework. Her manner was very serene and gracious. She smiled. "Do go on, Andrew, you are always so clever in analysing others," she said, with gentle irony. But her heart was beating fast. Somewhere, in this conversation, lay the clue to the dark fastnesses of John Turnbull.

"It couldn't be only his unconscious marriage to that wench," said Richard Gorth, biting his lip. "Men aren't so damned wound up with women. There are always so many more of them, skitting about. It wasn't money; it wasn't power. Perhaps it was some instinct that Wilkins unearthed. Or he wouldn't have stuck. I hear Wilkins has made millions out of his association with Turnbull."

"Nothing to what Turnbull has made, then," commented Andrew nonchalantly.

Scowling, Richard Gorth resumed his pacing. "I still don't understand. Turnbull could have done us in many times, pulled the ground from under us. Why didn't he? Don't give me any more of your rot, Andy, about old remembrance. He hated me. Though, curse you, it was all your fault, and that wretch's, Wilkins. Nothing I could do or say could convince him that I knew nothing about it. Never will forget the look in the devil's eye. Murder. Yes, he hated me, hated all of us. And yet, he stepped aside each time he could have done us in. That isn't the way a man who hates normally acts. Why did he do it?"

"I've an idea," said Andrew, Suddenly he laughed, his low and toneless laugh that had something evil in it. "He thought, perhaps, that if you toppled I would go back to England. Then, I wouldn't be on hand to see his triumphs. I was convenient for him to flaunt everything he's done in my face. That's it! I knew I'd hit on it sooner or later."

Richard Gorth stared at him, his cold and colourless eyes narrowing.

"Perhaps you've hit it. And yet, he could have done better if he'd ruined us. That would be a greater satisfaction. Then you would have retreated back to England in complete confusion. That's the way a man's mind operates."

Andrew was silent. But his close and glittering smile grew even more amused. Out of the corner of his eye he saw his wife's profile, composed and aloof as always. Was it his imagination that she was slightly paler than usual? That the needle did not pursue its intricate work so quickly and deftly? He covered his smiling mouth with his hand. The little pet, the darling traitorous little creature and love!

Richard Gorth gave up in gloomy despair. "He knows I've got a million or two of my own, that the damned business means little to me now. He knows you've done well for yourself, too, Andy, in the business. Wiping out our firm wouldn't break our hearts. It's a rum affair."

He added sullenly: "I liked the devil. We'd have gone far together. Yet, from the start, I can see that Wilkins never intended that. He got him in to steal my patents, the ones he stole for me. That was the plot. I didn't think, when first I saw Turnbull, that he'd lend himself to such a nefarious business. It wasn't in his character, and I've never made a mistake in judging men. It's Wilkins, all over. But how did he get such power over Johnnie Turnbull? Blackmail? No, I don't think so. It is still something else."

He added: "I've seen him from a distance. He's changed

these years. He looks like a fiend. I've heard reports from all over. A savage and relentless brute. He's ruined dozens. Now he engages in businesses I wouldn't touch, not for a million pounds. I tell you, it wasn't in his character. Something changed him. Now, don't ascribe omnipotence to Wilkins, like an ass. He's no Mephisto."

"Johnnie looks as if he hates the whole damned world," commented Andrew, idly.

The needle stopped in Eugenia's suddenly cold fingers. Her pallor increased. Her eyes widened with a kind of still horror.

"I've no doubt of it," said Mr. Gorth, gloomily. He lit a cigar, and glared at it. "But why? I've no love for my dear fellow creatures. But I wouldn't drive myself mad hating 'em. The next thing you'll say is that Johnnie is daft."

"I'm sure of it," replied Andrew, smoothly.

He wasn't acting that night, thought Eugenia, the chill of her hands extending to her heart. He hated me, too. What extravagance. But extravagance or not, he hated me then, as he hated everybody else. He's come back to me. Everything is the same. Why can't he be sensible and adjust himself? Why does he hate so, and destroy himself in the hating?

Andrew was speaking to her with his usual quizzical fondness. She started, became aware that some time had passed, and John was no longer the object under discussion.

"I beg your pardon, Andrew, but I did not hear you," she said.

"I merely asked, where is our offspring?"

"He is out with some young friends, at a dance given by Mrs. William Chadwick," she answered. She glanced at the ormolu clock on the mantel. "Ten o'clock. He should be here shortly."

Mrs. Gorth was critically examining Eugenia's needlepoint. "You've taken some uneven stitches, Eugenia," she said, with a delight quite out of proportion to the matter.

"I did indeed," said Eugenia, tranquilly. "How very stupid of me." With steady fingers she daintily ripped out the work.

"One must keep one's mind on what one is doing," observed Andrew, lounging back easily in his chair, and studying his wife with his usual malicious affection.

"It is a very intricate pattern," said Eugenia, indifferently.

"Oh, not at all," exclaimed Mrs. Gorth, with her malevolent grin. "I've done much more difficult pieces. It is a matter of skill and concentration. You younger women don't have the patience, my dear. Everything is hasty, and done with. Have you examined the work on the chairs in my room? I've received many a compliment on them, from other ladies."

Eugenia smiled courteously, but did not reply. Andrew, through his narrow eyes, studied her. What poise, what calm, what control! The little serene devil! But how he loved her! How long must he wait for her to awake from her folly? He had waited seventeen years. He had long and deadly patience. There was only one sickly brother now between him and the peerage. That brother had married, but had produced only one child, a miserable ailing girl. It was time to go back to England. He, Andrew, wished it intensely. But he would not go and take his family with him until Eugenia awoke from her long and obstinate trance, her self-delusion. He loved her too much. There must be no looking back for her when she returned with him. He had his own knowledge of her true sentiments. She must have that knowledge, also, before he could take her away.

Anthony Bollister appeared in the archway of the room, a tall youth, as tall as his father, and with his father's graceful lean body and elegant manner, but with none of Andrew's smiling indolence and inertia. His reddish sandy hair lay thickly about his narrow head, and his slate-gray eyes, so dark and penetrating, saluted them gravely. Andrew never looked at his son without silent gratitude for his comeliness. How his lone brother must envy him this young man, he who could produce only a miserable whimpering girl! There was no fault in him from his alert and quietly intelligent expression, to his firm if somewhat too hard and keen mouth and cleanly cut nose. It pleased Andrew, perversely, that there was no craftiness in his son, no weakness, no explosive violence or deviousness. There was much of Eugenia in this young man, much of her hard integrity and reasonable composure and thoughtfulness. Andrew loved his son very much. Between them there was a deep understandering, in which there was no delusion about the character of the other. But, there'll come a day when we'll clash, thought Andrew, more pleased than anything else by this reflection.

He was also delighted by the excellent and patrician manner in which the young man's clothing draped about him. A good English tailor had made those fawn pantaloons, that long coat. His white shirt was exquisitely made, his full black cravat was tied expertly. Anthony was a gentleman, in the full meaning of the word, and again Andrew felt extreme gratitude. The young man had lived at the home of his uncle, Lord Brewster, during his years in England, and Andrew meditated with pleasure on his brother's envy, his clumsy letters to Andrew in which he more than hinted at a future marriage between Anthony and his daughter, Melissa. That was a most desirable arrangement, thought Andrew. If

Eric outlived him, Andrew, then the title would descend to Anthony's son as next in succession. Yes, it was very desirable.

With these thoughts in mind, Andrew greeted his son with amiable fondness. Anthony kissed his mother's cheek, bowed to Mrs. Gorth, greeted Mr. Gorth and then his father. His manners were perfection.

Eugenia asked him tranquilly how he had enjoyed the dance. Anthony replied politely. He seemed somewhat distrait, yet when his father spoke to him he turned courteously, and with attention.

"I have been discussing the matter with your mother, Tony," said Andrew. "We think Oxford will be best in September. That doesn't give you much time at home, does it? Unfortunately."

Anthony's wide thin mouth tightened. He replied with extreme quietness:

"I'd rather go to Harvard."

Andrew was jolted out of his indolence, and sat upright in his chair. He frowned, his pale brows drawing together. "Nonsense. A crude American university, not fit for an English gentleman, and especially no gentleman who will probably be Lord Brewster some day. Where in the name of God did you get that absurd idea?"

Eugenia looked from her husband to her son composedly. "Your father is quite right, Tony," she said. "Harvard! Ridiculous. It is not what we planned."

"Odious," remarked Mrs. Gorth.

But Richard Gorth, who had been gloomily staring at the night through the windows, turned abruptly and stared at Anthony as if seeing him for the first time.

"I'd rather go to Harvard," repeated Anthony, unmoved. But a sharp furrow appeared between his eyes. "I'm not interested in anything else. I shall stay here. I don't intend to go to England to study any longer." He looked at his father steadfastly. "You speak of me as an Englishman. You are mistaken, sir. I am an American."

Andrew stared with great amazement. Then he burst out laughing, his thin face becoming scarlet with his mirth. As for Eugenia, she appeared coldly shocked and affronted.

"Tony, don't be absurd," she said.

"You are a puppy, sir," said Andrew, wiping his forehead and nose delicately with his handkerchief. "What is this nonsense? I am sure you are quite aware that we intend to go to England, eventually, to live. That is our home. I never dreamed of becoming an American citizen. You know that. We have discussed it before."

"Nevertheless," said Anthony, in a clear hard voice, "I

334

was born here. This is my country. I am an American. I knew we would come to this discussion. I am sorry it had to come so soon, but it is best, probably. I am not interested in a moldy title, and a drafty old castle, or any part of that dead heritage. I shall stay in America, where I belong, and take my part in my own country."

His eyes remained on his father's, indomitable and relentless.

Eugenia, in her annoyance, was about to speak, when Andrew lifted his hand. "I don't know why I waste my time discussing this with you, Tony. How old are you? Not yet eighteen. You are still under my jurisdiction; the law recognizes your duty to obey. But, this is absurd! However, because I respect your dignity, and remember that you have always considered my own wishes first, I shall continue to discuss the matter with you.

"I am an Englishman, and will always be. Our home is in England, our roots, our duties, our privileges, our position. By accident, you were born in America. But you have had your higher education in England. You are the heir to an old and honourable title. It is my plan, or at least my hope, that some day you will marry your cousin, Melissa. You know her, and a moment's reflection will convince you of the desirability of this marriage. She is fifteen now. In two years, perhaps, the marriage can take place.

"There is nothing here for us. We do not belong here. Your Uncle Richard and I have concluded that the firm with which I am casually connected is no longer important."

At this, Mr. Gorth uttered an exclamation, but no one heard him. As for Anthony, his eyes became very narrow and intent. He had begun to smile faintly.

"I am sorry, father, but this doesn't interest me in the slightest. A year ago I knew that my place was in America, and here I intend to stay."

Andrew was seldom angry, but now he was enraged. He grasped the arms of his chair. "How dare you speak to me like this, you jackanapes! I was mistaken in your common sense. We shall discuss is no more. In September you go to Oxford. Before you have completed your studies, your mother and I will have joined you in England, and we will thereafter arrange your marriage to your cousin."

"This is 1869, father," said Anthony, calmly. "And, I am not a child. You can't force me to do anything I don't want to do. And I have no desire to comply with your wishes in this."

Mrs. Gorth, delighted at the sight of perturbation, anxiety, anger and discord among those about her, glanced from one to the other with gloating and happy eyes. She was never more at peace than when in the presence of hatred and apprehension.

Anthony turned courteously to Mr. Gorth. "This must be embarrassing to you, uncle, and I beg your pardon if I have precipitated a discussion here in your house that can only be annoying to you. So, if you will excuse me——"

But Mr. Gorth said slowly, and with a penetrating look at the young man: "No, not at all. I'm very interested. I'd like to hear everything you have to say, Tony."

Andrew said with venomous quiet: "You've forgotten one thing: I control everything until you are twenty-one. The money your grandmother left you will not come into your possession until then. You are entirely dependent on me, Tony. I'm not threatening you. I'm only pointing out things to you which you must be forced to consider."

Then Eugenia spoke in her neutral but compelling voice, fixing her eyes formidably upon her son:

"Tony, you are making a complete fool of yourself. Suppose we end this silliness here and now. We won't discuss it any longer. You may go to your room."

Eugenia always believed it was her strength of character, her indomitable will to authority, which always cowed others. It never occurred to her that others retreated before her, were silent before her, because they possessed greater sensibilities than hers, and did not, out of sheer courtesy of heart and civilization, wish to cause her the embarrassment a defiance would inflict upon her. When others gave way before her, she was convinced it was because they were either weaklings or were overpowered by her greater force of character, virtue or intelligence.

Therefore, she was astonished and angered by the amused smile with which Anthony turned to her. He had never opposed her before, but now his dark gray eyes held hers without flinching.

"Mother," he said, gently, "you've managed everything, and every one, before. In a delicate and ladylike fashion you've dominated every situation. With every success, you have become more and more insufferable. I've given way to you because I loved you, not because you cowed me. But I'm not a child now. I have my life to live, and I'm going to live it in accordance with my own convictions and desires."

Andrew stared at his son, his narrow and colourless face darkening. Then, suddenly, he bit his lip, and glanced at his wife, who was regarding her son with icy fury and complete embarrassment.

"You are a tyrant, Mama dear," continued Anthony, without malice. "And tyrants feed on the gentleness, submission and greater enlightenment of others. They become swollen, because they are uncivilized. I don't want to hurt you. But you are completely uncivilized. You aren't going to impose your barbarism any longer on me."

Andrew was incredulous. Under his fury at his son he stole a long and gleaming blade of malevolent amusement at the discomfiture of his wife. Eugenia's haughty face was a study. Her brilliant eyes flashed lightnings. But she was speechless. As for Mr. Gorth, he coughed once, violently, and studied the fire with deep intensity. Mrs. Gorth breathed loudly and deeply in her extreme joy. She stared, rapt, at Eugenia's face, in which the blood was rising like a tide.

"You are an impudent rascal," said Andrew, trying to keep the mirth out of his voice. "Later, you will apologize to your mother. But before you obey her, and go to your room, I want to ask you where you acquired your astounding and ridiculous chauvinism, this sudden devotion to America. Not in England, surely?"

"Yes," said Anthony, steadfastly. "In England. Not only in England, but in all of Europe. I've spent months, as you know, in France, Prussia, Italy and Spain. And what I saw there opened my eyes to America.

"I was born here, but I've lived in an English household. I never really knew America. You sent me to England four years ago. I've been hedged about with English customs and English taboos. I never knew I was smothering. I know now. When I was away from America, I could see her clearly for the first time. And what I saw convinced me that she was my country, and that here was my people."

He paused. His young face became grave and harder and full of resolution.

"I've heard the songs of every nation praising their land and their history and their people and kings. But who has sung the song of America? Who, eating her substance and enjoying her enlightenment, has paused long enough at his gorging and his grasping to know America, and say a prayer thanking God for her? Only a few, such a very few. But the others, gobbling and devouring, saw her only as a trough. The hundreds of thousands who are coming here now see her only a coffer to be emptied. Those who call themselves 'Americans' are no better. They only got here first, and have first place at the trough. And do you know what I've thought? I've thought that such ingratitude, such ugliness, such greed and stupidity ought to be punished!

"And then I knew that by punishment you can't make men

grateful or enlightened or good. You've got to educate them. You've got to pull them away from the trough and the gobbling long enough to shout in their ears that America means more than exploitation and gold. It means a chance at the real destiny of men. It means an opportunity to make the world into the kingdom of heaven. And I knew that this won't be accomplished by describing America as a land where the streets are paved with gold. It can only be done by making Americans love America, as Europeans love their starveling, filthy and oppressed countries.

"That's what I want to do in my country: teach Americans to know, understand and love America, as she deserves to be known, understood and loved. If this isn't done, then man's last hope for liberty, peace, happiness and justice will fall when America falls. And surely she will fall if the song of America remains the song of greed."

He paused. A profound silence filled the room. Andrew was smiling faintly, and examining his finger nails. Eugenia, haughty and affronted, looked at the floor, her lip curling. Mrs. Gorth, not understanding anything except that there was anger and discomfiture in this room, was still delighted. And Richard Gorth stared at Anthony with a fixed and inscrutable look.

Then Andrew said softly: "All this is very touching. Very. It quite moves me to the heart. You've got courage, Tony. But you're also a dreaming fool with shining eyes. I hate fools. I've always hated them. It is very humiliating to me to know that my son is a fool. I thought better of you. I knew you had intelligence and reason, and I was proud. But it is devastating to me to hear you sing like a nightingale and prance like a dervish. Yes, Tony, you are a fool."

He looked up now and regarded his son with that bland and evil look of his, derisive and mocking.

"Of course, you are young, Tony. You aren't a realist. Yet. But I still have hopes that you will eventually become a realist. At the present time, you are a feckless imbecile."

Then Gorth spoke, heavily: "You lie, Andrew. You know you lie. Tony isn't feckless. He's got courage. Courage. You know that. It takes courage to speak up to smooth liars like you, Andy. And smooth tyrants like you, ma'am," and he bowed deeply to Eugenia. "It always takes courage to look decadence in the face and tell it what it is."

Andrew slowly turned in his chair and gazed at his uncle. Eugenia, with a faint sound, rose and stood before Richard Gorth, trembling with outrage. But Mr. Gorth was not intimidated.

"Mind you," he continued, with a sour smile, "I don't

agree with this young buck. But he believes what he says. What does it matter if what he believes is foolish, and ridiculous? What does it matter if he calls me a rascal to my face? He's got courage. And I, for one, as an Englishman, like courage."

He turned to Anthony, who had been listening in grim silence, his eyes sparkling. "Young man," he said, "don't let your Papa's threats disturb you. If you want to stay here, stay. There's always room in my house for a chap with guts. There's always room at Richard Gorth for one who can look another man in the face and tell him he is a scamp or a liar. I've thought of shutting up shop and going back to England. But Richard Gorth is yours, if you want it. You can go into the firm tomorrow, if you wish. I'm with you."

Anthony looked down at the casklike short man standing before him on the hearth, at his pale and murderous eyes, at his square lined face and rough gray hair. Then he said: "Thank you, Uncle Richard."

"Oh!" cried Eugenia, "this is frightful!" She stared at her husband's uncle with cold but furious eyes. "Is this all the gratitude you have for Andrew, that you can encourage his son to rebellion and disobedience?"

"Gratitude, ma'am?" asked Gorth, pondering and knitting his shaggy brows at her. "You use the word foolishly, my dear. Don't flash those eyes at me; you don't frighten me in the least. If your husband had had any common sense, he would have beaten your folly out of you long ago. You start, ma'am. You wonder what I mean. Let your own conscience advise you. You've done with your petty tyranny in this house, ma'am. Hold your tongue in the future when men speak together."

Eugenia could not believe her ears. Then she burst into her rare and reluctant tears and turned to her husband. "Andrew," she faltered, reaching for him blindly. Andrew rose. He took her hand and drew her to him. He looked at his uncle over her head. His face was stern and hard, but his irrepressible mirth danced in his narrow slits of eyes.

"You know, of course, that we can't stay here any longer after this," he said.

Richard Gorth shrugged. "Please yourself, Andy. But don't be a damned fool. You've got money, but not enough for a blackguard like you. You've got control of your fine lady's fortune. But still that isn't enough for you. You've languished about here, and struck elegant attitudes, and professed to be amused at Turnbull's murdering successes. But, you haven't been amused. You've been damned mad. You've wanted to knife him. For a number of reasons. Leave this house, sever your connection with me, run back to England. But all the way you'll hear his loud and bellowing laughter at you. You know this.

"You've got a son who is a man. Thank whatever God you believe in for that. He'll help us. Help you. Someday," and he said this slowly, holding Andrew with his eyes and speaking with immense significance, "he'll help you do in Turnbull, for what he's done to you. I think you understand," he added.

Andrew's face turned livid. He drew in his mouth until it was a malignant slit. His eyes did not leave his uncle's.

Then Mr. Gorth turned heavily to Anthony, who had been listening with a dark and bewildered expression.

"Look here, you contentious brat. I've said Gorth is yours, in the future. I mean it. We've done rotten things in our day, I admit. I've made a fortune at it. I don't pretend I have any regrets. I haven't. But there are things we haven't done. You know that Turnbull is not only our competitor, but our enemy. He's built up Everett Livingston Company, so that it has outstripped us. But there are things about him you don't know. He's done things, for money, that sicken even me. Opium. Gun-running. And other things I won't mention for the sake of your gentle mother's sensibilities. He's the kind of man you spoke of: the kind that is ruining America. If you were sincere in what you said, you'll set out, when you are older, to expose such scoundrels.

"Well," he added, in the face of Anthony's fixed and steadfast silence, "what are you going to do now? Come in with us?"

Anthony drew a deep breath. "Yes," he said, very quietly. "After I have gone to Harvard. I'll come in with you, uncle."

Richard Gorth bowed gravely and profoundly to him, as if he had been an equal in age and experience and power. Then he looked at his nephew, and smiled grimly.

"Well, Andy?" he said, with a note of derision in his voice.

Andrew was holding Eugenia's hand. He looked down at her tear-stained and averted face. Then he said, still looking at her: "Yes, uncle. I'll stay. You know I couldn't go, under these circumstances."

CHAPTER 37

THERE was great excitement in the Turnbull household. On August 18th, Lavinia Amanda Turnbull was to marry Rufus Hastings, son of Robert Rufus Hastings, close associate of the Vanderbilts.

Rufus' parents had at first pretended horror and affront that their son had chosen this florid, red-cheeked, black-eyed daughter of John Turnbull as his future wife. They professed that John's repute was a stench in the nostrils of the more fastidious. Moreover, he was a sullen, surly devil with no social graces, no amiable presence, a man who stood aloof and made no attempt to ingratiate himself with any one. Though there was hypocrisy in their first pretenses, there was some sincerity too. John had ignored, openly flouted and treated with contempt those of New York society who had considered themselves the mighty. When he had bought and opened his great and impressive mansion on Fifth Avenue, they had waited eagerly and maliciously for invitations to dine there, intending to receive these invitations in insulting silence. But John had not given them this opportunity. He had continued to conduct himself as though unaware of their existence. They had called this "vulgar ignorance." John had failed to be impressed. Later, very much later, when he had finally condescended to issue a few indifferent invitations, all invited came in an angry rush. They had come to ridicule. But the magnificent and faultless grandeur of the mansion had silenced them. They sent the family invitations in return, but only the two older daughters accepted except for one or two scattered visits a year, when John and his wife arrived in dark silence, remained a little while, and then departed.

Finally, hostesses gloated when John could be induced to dine at their homes. It became quite a competition among the ladies to see who could secure this gloomy and irascible man and his wife as their guests. It also became an unwritten law that he was not to be invited when Andrew Bollister and his wife were given invitations. As a strange and ironical result, the Bollisters and Gorths discovered that their invitations decreased in quantity, and that they could not summon up sufficient distinguished personages at their own table when the Turnbulls entertained.

Lilybelle was no longer ridiculed in New York society. The ladies declared that she was a dear and unaffected "darling," so gracious and kind and attentive. Her simplicity, her eagerness to please and placate these formidable ladies, endeared her to them. It would have astonished her had she learned that a mysterious and distinguished ancestry had been invented for her by her new champions, that there was much significant nodding of heads and oblique hints that John had come to America because his wife, a lady of great consequence and ancient family, had been ostracized by her parents for marriage to a man much lower in station than herself.

So the parents of Rufus Hastings were only pretending that they objected to the marriage of their son to Lavinia Turnbull. In truth, they were delighted, and their demurrings were only uttered as a kind of boasting. When they so demurred, they listened with furtive pride to the protests of their friends. "Why, I have it on unimpeachable authority that Mrs. Turnbull is really the Honourable Lilybelle Brewster," they would say, firmly. "Of course, it is regrettable that Mr. Turnbull is of less distinguished ancestry, but one must remember that he is quite a power in America."

All in all, Lavinia's wedding promised to be the most brilliant event of the "season." Also, the most elaborate. In May, the bride and her sister, Louisa, went to Paris to purchase the nuptial wardrobe, accompanied by Miss Beardsley as duenna, at John's lavish expense. They returned with trunks and boxes filled to overflowing with gorgeous apparel, with hats, boots, gloves, furs and undergarments and perfumes beyond imagining. John's own gift to his favourite daughter (purchased at Cartiers in Paris by Lavinia, and chosen by herself) was a string of lustrous rosy pearls. Also, chosen by herself, was her mother's gift, a bracelet of glittering blue and white brilliants. The girls and their chaperone visited England briefly, there to pay their respects at the grave of their paternal grandfather and to visit Westminster Abbey and the Tower of London. They returned, chattering French volubly, and displaying elegant mannerisms acquired in London and Paris.

During the feverish tumult preceding the nuptials, (which were to be celebrated in the Turnbull mansion) Adelaide's pale and silent presence passed unnoticed by all save her mother. The only occasions when her sisters noticed her existence was when they commandeered her services, which was quite frequent. Adelaide must sew this, adjust this, carry this, bring that, go upon this errand, arrange matters and bear the brunt of tempers rapidly becoming more peremptory and hysterical. It was no wonder, therefore, that a new servant or two justifiably thought her a young lady's maid until they were belatedly and timidly disillusioned by Lilybelle. As for Adelaide, she would not have enlightened them, so detached and indifferent was her attitude to all that swirled, roared, screamed and shrieked about her. She was scarcely fourteen, but her composure and poise set her out in that household now rapidly becoming more chaotic as the days passed. She went about the house, slender, straight and silent, her light brown hair, (still straight and more shining than ever) streaming down her young back, her brown eyes liquid and still, her manners quiet and unhurried. There was a certain point beyond which even her distracted sisters dared not press her, and they had learned this point.

Had it not been for Adelaide's calmness and ability to keep order, Lilybelle would have gone quite mad.

John found it all amusing. He smiled more than usual. He would loiter in Lavinia's rooms, admiring her new wardrobe, looking upon his daughter with furtive affection and pride. Lavinia was very handsome, at eighteen, tall, with a splendid full figure, her black curling hair piled in masses on her head, her cheeks crimson, her manner spirited and impudent and excited, her eyes dancing with irascibility or anger or laughter, her pouting mouth very red and blooming. She would turn slowly before her father for his admiration, displaying one after another of her new gowns or frocks, demanding his opinion of the latest draped effect, the new bustle, the bodice, the lace or the glittering buttons. He must express his opinion about the plumed bonnets, the cloaks, the furs, gloves and boots. He must sniff every crystal bottle of scent. Once or twice, to Lilybelle's or Mrs. Bowden's horror, and to John's amusement, he was shown the heaps of lingerie, and even the lace-covered stays. Lavinia's loud delight in her purchases touched John's surly and restless heart. He looked at his vivid daughter, who was all life and vitality and exuberance, and he would feel a strong stirring of paternal pride and tender love. Who was there, among the dun daughters of his acquaintance, who could compare with this colourful girl, this handsome young creature who was his own? As a consequence, Lavinia's purse was always overflowing with gold and banknotes, and she constantly greeted her father with embraces and noisy emphatic kisses, and expressions of boisterous affection.

"Dearest Papa!" she would cry, "I cannot understand why

343

you are so deliciously good to me! I'm the naughtiest girl, really, and don't deserve you!"

For the first time, then, in many many years, John was reasonably happy in the happiness and excitement of his daughter. He took a deep interest in all her plans, gravely studied the guest-list, inspected minutely all the elaborate and expensive gifts that poured in every hour. Sometimes he would seize her and press his dark cheek against her own glowing cheek, in a kind of hunger which only young Adelaide found pathetic. He would say to her: "Are you happy, my darling?", and in return she would kiss him vigorously, exclaiming: "O dear Papa, so very happy!" As Lavinia was naturally of an ardent and lavish disposition, she did not find her father's affection tedious, and she was now in such high spirits as to be excessively amiable to every one, even to Adelaide.

As Louisa was to be her maid-of-honour, and Adelaide to be one of the six bridesmaids, Lavinia was very meticulous about their costumes. Louisa was to wear pale green silk, Adelaide, golden silk and lace. There were many violent quarrels between Lavinia and Louisa, for, with her yellow curls and large blue eyes, Louisia threatened to outshine even the flamboyant bride.

"Dearest, you are so unreasonable," Louisa would say gently, with her sweet smile and patient air. "You chose the green for me, yourself. However, if you don't like it, I could wear the blue again, though I'm really quite tired of it. Then Adelaide's yellow would be impossible."

Though Lavinia was his favourite daughter, John loved Louisa with a special tenderness. Lavinia's greatest fascination was her vitality; Louisa's, her femaleness. The soft blue light in her eyes, her daintiness and sweetness, her expression of patience, of sympathy, of deep interest in every one, of tolerance and gentleness, endeared her to her father. Her voice was always low and musical and beguiling, her touch tender and soothing. Whereas Lavinia was inclined to a certain robust untidiness on occasion, few ever saw Louisa ruffled or flustered; her clothing was always fresh and in order, her hair meticulously combed and brushed, her flesh delicately scented. "She never swears!" Lavinia would exclaim contemptuously, but with envy. All who knew Louisa loved her, except poor Lilybelle whose instincts, simple and unpolluted, recognized pure viciousness, cruelty and rapacity. Lilybelle fought against these instincts in horror. Surely none was so sweet, so good so reasonable and kind as Louisa, whose eye never flashed irately, whose voice never rose above a mellifluous murmur, whose touch was light and placating, whose smile was loving, gently amused or patient, and never malicious.

John considered his second daughter a superior angel, and could not understand the frequent savage attacks on her by Lavinia, who possessed considerable of her mother's instincts. When Lavinia cried, "hypocrite!" he was angered. Later, he would surreptitiously give Louisa a cheque or a sheaf of banknotes in order to soothe her female sensibilities. She would reward him for this with expressions of moved gratitude, or with scented embraces and the sweetest of kisses. He would hold her in his arms, and ask her the question he asked so often of Lavinia: "Do you love your old Papa, darling?"

But never did he ask this question of Adelaide, and never did he give her money or even a smile. That pale cold girl with the quiet and silent mouth, with the proud straight carriage and unobtrusive manners aroused only his obscure irritation and repulsion. He knew nothing about her, saw her only as a plain background for her beautiful sisters, and if he ever spoke to her it was with indifference, reproof or annoyance. Sometimes he would watch her furtively, feeling a hotness and rage in his heart for her resemblance to another and older woman. This resemblance appeared to him to be an outrage, an insult. He was convinced that Adelaide was all her sisters declared she was, a "sneak," a sly plotter, an ugly creature, a schemer and a fool.

And Lilybelle, always lurking in the shadow of his displeasure herself, had no words to tell him of Adelaide's honour and valour, of her courage and steadfastness, of her truth and pride and intelligence. He only knew, to his anger, that this miserable female creature was Lilybelle's love and joy.

"How you can endure the little wretch is beyond me!" he said once to his wife. "She goes sneaking and sliding about the house; her eyes are everywhere. It is evident that she envies and hates her sisters for their superior gifts. I tell you, she is poisonous! We ought to have sent her away long ago; it was foolish to keep her about the house until she was ten years old. She needs discipline and hard knocks to whip the insolence out of her. It is useless to hope she will ever get a decent husband. I suppose we'll be saddled with her for life, an ugly old maid slipping about and sneering at everything. A fine prospect!"

And once he quoted Lavinia: "There's no doubt the girl is a plotter and schemer, a sly piece. She has only to appear in her sisters' apartments to create discord between them."

He would grow nervous and almost hysterical in his denunciations of his younger daughter. As he operated only in his emotions, and rarely with his reason, he did not pause to analyse his reactions to Adelaide, to question whether his accusations were just or unjust. He only knew that when he discovered her brown eyes fixed unfathomably upon him there was a strange shaking in his nerves and about his heart, a depressing of his thoughts, a mysterious stirring in his instincts, at once savage and embarrassed. As she affected him so, he avoided her, refused to look at her. As he hated her so, he was convinced she hated him, and he felt the old uneasiness and tiredness in her presence which he felt among those by whom he was hated, and whom he hated in return.

"A stupid baggage," he would say, either to himself or his daughters, when Adelaide left the room when he entered it. "And hard-hearted, too, and too old for her years."

As he was convinced that the inferior are the natural servants of the superior, he approved when he discovered that Lavinia and Louisa regarded their sister as little better than one born to serve them. Even when the girl's young face was gray with weariness, he ordered her to accede to her sisters' constant demands for her services. "It is little enough for you to do," he would say to her brutally, when she hesitated. "You don't deserve such sweet sisters. I don't know how they can endure you."

In his will, he had left her only a small trust fund. It was quite enough for a drab and colourless little wretch who would never attract a husband.

In some mysterious way, he had detected that young Adelaide detested and feared Rufus Hastings, with his green eyes and sandy lifeless hair and grand manners. This infuriated him. He said to his daughter: "No wonder you look at him with such catlike aversion. You are envious. I don't blame you in a way. You'll never get a husband for yourself like young Hastings."

He was proud that Lavinia was to make such an excellent match, but it was no more than he expected of her. He unbent from his chronic suspicion with the young man, and was heavily paternal and affectionate with him. Though Rufus' father was immensely wealthy, as a result of his dealings with the railroad Vanderbilts, there was no nonsense about Rufus. He was to enter Everett Livingston & Company after his return from his honeymoon, as the first step in his initiation into the ramifications of John's enterprises. His manner towards his future father-in-law always pleased John immensely. He was courteous and polite, attentive and respectful, full of intelligent questions about the business, and given to low expressions of admiration.

All in all, John knew a measure of happiness these days.

It is true that Louisa was showing a deep interest in Patrick Brogan, "that Irishman!" But the Brogans were wealthy, and Patrick had a fond and ingratiating manner and a sly laughing twinkle in the depths of his intensely blue eyes, little and foxy though they were. He twitted John fearlessly; he had an affectionate way with him, and was given to linking his arm in John's and joking with him, quite openly and without timidity. John gave himself up to reconciling himself to accepting Patrick as a son-in-law, in spite of his natural aversion to the Irish. But he frequently hinted to Louisa that he would not countenance a marriage in the Catholic Church, and that if she was set on young Brogan she must induce him to marry her in the Protestant faith, with no future implications about children, and their religious allegiances. "In the end, perhaps, you may be able to wean him away from the priests," he would say. He invited Patrick's parents to his home and tried to overcome his deep dislike of their race and religion, for Louisa's sake. He treated them with benign superiority, and was pleased at their humility and eagerness to placate him. Moreover, in Timothy Brogan, he recognized an opportunist, a gay rascal, a man without a conscience, and a flexible and agreeable soul. He was able to suggest certain transactions in the Market which considerably augmented Brogan's fortune.

He took to returning home earlier during the last days before the marriage, for the pure delight of the flurry and noise all about the mansion. The hot and constant uneasiness of his spirit relaxed. There was a numbness in his mind, which he mistook for contentment. He became very amiable and easy, and was surprised that others responded to him in kind. It is true that his weariness increased, that the white rapidly spread in his hair, that there were dark hollows under his eyes, and that he frequently felt mortally ill.

But he was also convinced that he was very happy.

CHAPTER 38

Two days before the wedding, another crisis arose. Lavinia, with loud lamentations, discovered that the pale blue ribbons she had bought in Paris for her lingerie were not sufficient. Adelaide was immediately called, and intrusted with a slip of the ribbon and commanded to tour the shops in the burning August heat. She must match it exactly, Lavinia cried. And she must not dare return until she had found six yards more.

It was very hot this morning, the glittering air swirling with dust and chaff. Adelaide dressed herself in white muslin, tied a yellow Leghorn over her hair, and, pale with exhaustion, went out on foot to the shops on Fourteenth Street. Lilybelle urged a carriage upon her, and then it was discovered that Lavinia was to use one vehicle, Louisa another, and Lilybelle was to take lunch with Rufus' parents. John had taken the fourth carriage There was none for Adelaide.

The girl did not care. She walked through the hot closed streets, gasping a little in the heat. She took off her hat and let it hang by its ribbons over her arm. The flaying breeze lifted her long hair and blew it about her small pointed face. Flecks of black dust invaded her eyes and her nostrils, settled in the folds of the white muslin. But she hardly felt these discomforts. She was alone, away from the constant bickering of Lavinia, from Louisa's amused soft smile and gentle irony, from the uproar in the house. She might have been some quiet girl from the lower middle-class, out for a shopping stroll.

She looked at the blazing light sky, at the dusty trees, at the gritty hot streets, and felt some contentment. It was lovely to be alone, to think in peace. She even hummed a little under her breath, though her thoughts, as always, were vaguely sad. She could not recall a time in her life when she had not been sad and subdued in mind. No one ever knew what she thought, not even Lilybelle. But Adelaide's thoughts were very acute, subtle and mature. If she felt an emotion, she analysed it with irony, until it subsided, embarrassed. She had the wry inner mirth of the outcast, of the unloved. Later, she might grow bitter and inflexible, but she was still too young for these sorrows. She felt the sun on her face and her hands, the wind in her hair. If her heart was heavy, it was an old story, and she no longer questioned it. Today she was aware of her youth, the echo of her footsteps on the pavement, of the bright light falling all about her, of her rare freedom and happy solitary condition.

Next month, she would return to her boarding-school. A pang touched her heart, and she firmly quelled it. She disliked the school, the girls and the teachers, as much as they all disliked her. She thought her contemporaries stupid and vapid, the teachers steeped in gall. She would not think of it now, she told herself. There were six more weeks at home. In the previewing of misery was an augmentation of misery.

Lilybelle had furtively given her some money for herself

this morning, and she stopped at a curio shop to buy herself a little ivory box from China for her trinkets, a length of China silk for a frock, and two pairs of white silk stockings. In the meantime, she searched for the ribbon. It was a wearisome task. There was every shade of blue, but not the required one. Adelaide was not annoyed. A further search meant a longer absence from home. The shops were lively and gay, full of cool dusk, the smell of textiles and leathers, the brushing of women's garments, the voices of clerks, and a living busyness. Carriages rolled constantly on the cobbles of the streets, and the air outside was pungent with warm manure and acrid dust.

Adelaide bought her mother a beautiful ivory and lace fan to be used at the wedding. It was painted with tiny pink rosebuds. Adelaide privately thought it vulgar, but it would please Lilybelle inordinately. She was conscious of being hungry, now, but young ladies never entered restaurants alone, so Adelaide bought a bag of hot chestnuts to munch in doorways between shops. The chestnuts were delicious. She wiped her hand on her handkerchief, and was about to reenter the blazing light of the streets when she heard a masculine voice exclaiming at her elbow: "It's little Adelaide, isn't it? The little mouse?"

Flushing deeply, and hastily brushing away one or two hulls which remained on her bodice, she turned to her accoster. She saw a tall young man at her side, smiling down amusedly at her. She did not recognize him, and recovering herself, straightened haughtily, trying, with haste, to replace her hat.

"Don't you remember me?" he asked, touching her arm. "I'm your cousin, Anthony Bollister."

The ribbons were tangled. He helped her smooth them out. She was intensely mortified. Her heart began to beat with great rapidity.

"How pretty you've gotten," said Anthony, beaming at her affectionately. "And how glad I am to see you again."

The hat was in place now. Adelaide's trembling fingers fumbled with the bow, her cheeks bright with embarrassment. She looked up from under the brim of her hat, and her eyes gleamed like brown velvet. She tried to smile.

"How do you do?" she murmured, almost inaudibly.

"It's been six years," he said. "We're grown up now, aren't we? You are quite a young lady. How are your sisters? I've been away so long, over five years. I've often thought about you."

Adelaide was silent. The beating of her heart did not subside. The strangest tears were making a bright dazzle before her eyes. She heard Anthony's voice, and nothing else. It seemed to fill all the air about her, and little darting thrills ran over her legs and arms and young breasts. She had the oddest impulse to cry.

Then she stammered, her voice loud in her embarrassed ears: "I've often thought about you, too. And wondered where you were."

They looked at each other, as they stood in the doorway, apart from the hot and hurrying throngs in the street. They did not speak. Their eyes clung; Anthony was very close to the girl, and his sleeve brushed her bare forearm. Adelaide's mouth, now pink and moist, opened a little on a faint gasp.

After what appeared to be a long time, Anthony said gently, not taking his eyes from hers: "I've been in England. But now I'm home. I've been going to Harvard. We ought to see a lot of each other, Adelaide."

Adelaide had known such little joy in her life that she could not understand this pure and intoxicating ecstasy which flooded her, blinded her, and made her feel as if she had been lifted into radiant space. She began to laugh softly, quite without reason, and she felt her knees trembling. Her small and quiet face bloomed in tremulous beauty under the deep shadow of the Leghorn hat with its fluttering ribbons.

She had never forgotten her cousin. And how handsome he appeared to her now, tall and slender, almost as tall as her father. She had never forgotten those slate-gray eyes, intent and more than a little hard, that thick sandy-red hair under the round black hat, that slender sharp nose and quiet inflexible mouth. She felt his strength and purposefulness and strong assurance. She wanted, more than anything else, to touch his hand, to feel what she knew she would feel: warm familiarity and firmness, kindness and protection.

As if he knew what she thought, he extended his hand, and with a quick hunger, she laid her own in it. When his fingers pressed hers, her heart quaked with rapture, and the dazzle before her eyes splintered into rainbows.

"See here, this is no place to stand," she heard him say, from a long distance. "Let's go somewhere where we can sit down and have a cup of tea, or something."

She felt him take her arm. Obediently, her legs moved. She did not feel the ground under her feet. Her chin was at the level of his shoulder, and she brushed it strongly against the brown roughness of it, again and again, as a puppy would do. She clung to his side; people jostled her, and she was unaware. There was a sweet long singing in her ears. She was not alone now. She would never be alone again. Her desire to cry choked her, and she swallowed convulsively.

She found herself in a small restaurant with neat white tables, plated silver, dark panelled walls, crimson carpet underfoot, and very elderly waiters. The air was full of the smell of beef and onions, beer and coffee. But she hardly saw this background, discreet and dim and old. It was only the background of dreams wavering behind this glittering and ecstatic presence. She gazed about her, bemused, returning to Anthony to smile with shy radiance.

He leaned his elbows on the table and studied her with frank affection. What a strange pale little face it was, but so beautiful in its delicacy. And how like his mother's, too. But, there was a difference, he discerned. His mother's face might possess features like these, but this hauteur was timid rather than arrogant. His mother's eyes were cold; these brown soft eyes were quick, alive and warm. Pride might lie across that smooth clear forehead with its smooth wings of brows, but it was a simple and noble pride, rather than Eugenia's disdainful withdrawal. The mouth was very lovely in this girl's face, though its loveliness was in its expression and not in its colouring, which was pale, nor in its formation, which was somewhat wide and thin. He saw, however, that time and bitterness might change that expression, and leave the mouth exactly like Eugenia's: overbearing, full of hard authority, and disingenuousness. He hoped, with a sudden fierceness, that nothing would happen to Adelaide to change her into a replica of his mother. And he wondered, with sadness, if his mother might not once have been like this girl, naturally noble of temperament, sweetly intelligent and gently grave.

He felt a strong tenderness for Adelaide, a protectiveness and love. He reached across the table and took one of her little hands, so brown and thin and firm. She watched him with childish absorption, never looking away from his face. There were rare stains of colour on her cheek-bones.

Now she stammered, as she struggled to retain coherence over her wild emotions: "You remember Lavinia, Tony? She is to be married day after tomorrow."

He raised an eyebrow. "So I heard. I'm not invited, of course." And he smiled.

Adelaide's colour increased with sudden distress. But she said nothing.

"She is marrying Rufe Hastings, isn't she?" asked Anthony. "Well, it's a good match. What about Louisa? Is it true she is to marry Patrick Brogan?"

"I don't know," murmured Adelaide.

The waiter brought them a plate of cold beef, bread, a salad and some coffee. Adelaide was not aware of eating, though she watched Anthony intently as he filled her plate. All about her was a singing warmth and a passionate happiness.

"Now, tell me about yourself, my pet," said Anthony, leaning his elbows on the table and scrutinizing her fondly. "What have you been doing?"

Speech did not come readily to Adelaide, but soon she found herself talking, at first shyly, and then with quick eagerness. She told him of her years at school, barren and lonely years. She did not speak of this barrenness or loneliness, but he heard them in her words. And then all at once her expression became blank and sad. "There isn't really much to tell," she said. "Nothing happens to me."

"How old are you, Adelaide?"

"I will be fifteen next April."

Anthony was silent, still gazing at her. Then he began to tell her, in a light tone, of his experiences in England, of his school years there, of his uncle, Lord Brewster, and the simpering Melissa. Adelaide listened, enraptured. She hardly heard his words; she listened to his voice. Once or twice she closed her eyes as if her happiness was unendurable.

He was to go to Harvard for two more years, to complete his studies, he said. Then he was to go into Richard Gorth Company. "America is my home," he said. "I'm not going away again. So, we shall see each other often, Adelaide."

There was a sudden quenching of the light on her face. She began to murmur, and he leaned across the table the better to hear her. She had dropped her eyes, and was twisting her napkin in her hands.

"You know, Tony, that our parents don't like each other. I don't know why. It—it seems a little silly. I never understood. I questioned Mama, but she seemed so distressed that I changed the subject. You know they won't want us to meet —like this. Not ever."

She lifted her eyes now, and they were full of anguished tears. He took her hand again.

"Would you like us to meet, dear Adelaide?" he asked.

"Yes!" she cried, with quick despair.

He smiled. "Then we shall. I shall not ask you to disobey your parents. That would hurt you, you silly little creature. But I shall haunt you. I really shall. When we meet, it won't be your fault. I shall just come up behind you, and there we'll be! Just as simple as that. For instance, if every fourth Sunday you take a stroll down Fifth Avenue, I shall be strolling, too. If you should happen to wander past this restaurant on Friday afternoons, on the holidays, I shouldn't wonder if

I should be wandering along, also, remembering today. No one could blame you then if your cousin suddenly accosted you; no one would ask you to be so uncivil as to refuse to speak to me."

She returned his smile, but it was sad. "That would be sneaking," she said.

"What a conscientious little thing it is, to be sure! Well, I'll manage some way." Now he became very serious. "What is it to us if our parents are disagreeable to each other? Are we to build our lives on their prejudices?"

Adelaide said simply, looking him full in the eyes: "I love my Papa, Tony. I love him very much." And then her face became dark and sad, and she averted her eyes.

Though she had told him so little, he guessed with prescience, the circumstances and wretchedness of her life. He was filled with anger. So strange and quiet a little creature, with such flashing warm eyes and intelligent mouth and sweet dignified manners! Who could look at her and not love her?

And then he knew that such people as Adelaide are always hated, that the universality of the hatred that surrounded them was a terrible commentary on the nature of men. It is the liars, he reflected, that are loved, the hypocrites, the thieves, the false and the cruel, for they love only themselves. Those who are by temperament high and virtuous, just and gentle, good and honourable, inspire only detestation.

He walked with Adelaide down the street, insisted on helping her match the ribbon in the shops. He heard her slow and reluctant laughter. It delighted him to see how happiness and joy and amusement sparkled in her eyes. He became quite foolish and ridiculous, in order to see that light under her brown lashes. The shopgirls were entranced by him. Finally, the ribbon was matched, and they emerged in the long hot glow of the late afternoon.

He accompanied her almost to her home, and there he took her hand. They looked at each other with sudden gravity.

"We'll meet, my love," he said, gently but firmly. "I won't lose you. Remember that."

He hesitated. He glanced up and down the long quiet avenue with its frowning houses and clean swept steps. No one was about. Every window was shuttered against the heat. Before Adelaide could utter a sound, he drew her to him and kissed her shaking lips. She resisted a moment, then suddenly her hands seized his arms and clung to them, and her mouth pressed eagerly against his own.

CHAPTER 39

A DELAIDE found her mother with her sisters in Lavinia's sitting room when she entered the house.

Lavinia was in a great pet, flushed with heat and annoyance. Louisa sat calmly near the window, sorting out heaps of billowing petticoats and drawers and bodices. Lilybelle was in despair, a harried look on her big flushed face, which was pricked out with drops of sweat. She was sorting out Lavinia's French boots and placing them in proper bags. Two maids were there, also, packing enormous trunks with finery.

"Oh, there you are, you loitering little wretch!" cried Lavinia, advancing menacingly upon Adelaide. "Where have you been, for hours? Did you find the proper ribbon?"

She had discarded her outer clothing but her stays and stood in her great white drawers, dripping with wide bands of fine French lace. Her sturdy well-shaped legs were covered by thin black silk stockings. Her full bosom, splendid, and so like her mother's, appeared about to burst the confines of her lacy chemise. Her large white arms were damp and glistening, her black curls tied high on her head, her face crimson and her black eyes flashing ire and irritability.

She stretched out her hand impatiently for the little package Adelaide gave her. She tore the paper, and stared affrontedly at the coil of ribbon. "Why, this is outrageous! It doesn't match in the least!" She glared at Adelaide furiously, as if about to strike her. "Where on earth have you been, anyway? Wasting all that time! And then bringing me this abominable trash!"

Mrs. Bowden, who had been buried in a closet among dozens of stiff gowns, now emerged, several garments on her arms. She peered closely at the ribbon in Lavinia's hot wet hand. "It's a perfect match, Miss Lavinia," she said, firmly, adjusting the glasses on her nose. "Certainly it is. Let me show you."

She took the ribbon, and held it against the ribbon in the lingerie that lay heaped on the sofa. It was indeed a perfect match. Lavinia's fuming anger was only increased by this. "What do I care! But to waste hours, when we were waiting! Oh, it is intolerable!"

354

"Lovey, watch your nerves," urged Lilybelle, wiping her wet forehead with the back of her hand. "The little lass 'as done her best for you. It takes time to match ribbons."

"Oh—hell!" cried Lavinia, disgustedly, flinging the ribbon on the bed, from which it rolled to the floor. Louisa serenely picked it up, began to snip lengths for the petticoats and lace bodices. She glanced with tender humour at her older sister. "Such language. Not genteel at all. You will quite shock Mrs. Hastings. There, Linny, do sit down and stop breathing fire. I admit Adelaide's a trial with her laziness and indifference, but what is one to do? Adelaide, is it possible you can help me with the ribbons? Here is an extra bodkin."

Adelaide, her lips compressed and her eyes flashing, silently accepted the bodkin, sat on the edge of the bed and began to work. Lilybelle glanced at her with apologetic affection, and after a moment or two, Adelaide smiled at her mother.

Muttering fiercely, Lavinia began to fling the neat piles of frocks about, which the maids had just organized into some semblance of order. "That rag! It is contemptible! Mama, that is your doing. I told you the colour was abominable, but you would insist."

"It seemed prettier than the green you wanted," pleaded Lilybelle, exhausted. "Besides, you said it was, yourself, Linny. If you hadn't wanted it, you could've said so."

"You have no taste, Mama. You know you haven't. You always look like an overdressed washwoman. Why you insist so obstinately in choosing your own clothes, instead of allowing Aunt Amanda to do so—and she's offered often enough, God knows—is beyond me. Just consider the gown you've chosen for my wedding! It will be the laughter of New York. Violet and pale green! What an odious combination!"

"Miss Beardsley chose it," said Lilybelle, close to tears. "I didn't want it. There was such a pretty pink——"

"Pink!" screamed Lavinia, striking an attitude of exaggerated horror, and glaring at Louisa with a shocked expression. "Imagine pink! On Mama! With her hair and cheeks! Oh, how intolerable, how perfectly appalling! Did you ever!" And she burst into raucous and ribald laughter. "Mama, you are excruciating! Pink. You would look like a sunset, I declare you would. No wonder Papa is so humiliated by you, sometimes. You hurt his eyes with your horrible combinations. What a trial you must be to him!"

Adelaide looked up. Her face was white and quietly fierce. "Shut up," she said in a low and penetrating voice.

Lavinia swung on her, quite paling. "What did you say?" she asked, slowly, clenching her hands.

Adelaide flung aside the petticoat she was decorating with ribbon. She stared at her sister with an expression quite terrible in its intensity and anger.

"I said," she repeated clearly, "'shut up.'"

Lavinia gasped. Louisa lifted her head with an angelic smile of amusement. The two maids, repressing titters, stood in eager silence, looking from one girl to the other. Mrs. Bowden smiled to herself, continued about her business. As for Lilybelle, she was so frightened that she remained fixed in her attitude near the trunks, kneeling, her hands dropping to her sides.

Lavinia advanced with slow menace upon her younger sister, and Adelaide stood up to meet that advance. The two girls confronted each other in a sudden sharp silence. Lavinia was much taller than Adelaide, overpowering in her luscious figure, her black eyes on fire, her full ripe lips bared to display her glistening teeth.

"Why, you little wretch, you snivelling foul little creature!" she said, in a low voice of vicious wonder. "I should slap your face, pull your ugly hair!"

"Try it," said Adelaide quietly. Her own eyes were dilated, filled to the sockets with intense and dangerous light. "You're a coward and a beast, Lavinia. You attack Mama all the time. I'm tired of it. I said 'shut up.' I mean it. And, if you touch me, I tell you you'll regret it."

She suddenly reached down to the bed and picked up a long pair of pointed shears. It gleamed in her hand like a savage knife. Lilybelle screamed faintly, and put her fingers to her gaping mouth. Mrs. Bowden quickly and quietly reached Adelaide's side, but she made no attempt to take the scissors. The two maids, paralysed with terror and delight, stood with their arms full of garments, and stared joyously. As for Louisa, she laid her hands calmly on the underwear, and waited, with a sweet expression of evil.

Lavinia, enraged and beside herself, still could not move. She looked down at Adelaide, and was suddenly quite aghast at that small and appalling face, so white and fixed, with the eyes gleaming like steel. She saw murder in those eyes, wild and cold, and a thin icy tremor ran down her hot and sweating back.

Now Lavinia was no coward, no fool, nor was she truly vicious. She was not excessively frightened by this sudden glacial violence of her younger sister. Rather, Adelaide's look and attitude really gave her pause in the midst of her fury, and made her think. Very slowly, her cheeks resumed their florid tint, her eyes lost their fire, Her face began to manifest some shame, some sullen embarrassment.

She did not retreat. Her embarrassment increased. Then a dimple appeared near her pouting lips, and she regarded her little sister sheepishly.

"Oh, Addy, don't be a fool," she stammered awkwardly. "Do put down those shears. You might hurt yourself, or me, with them, when you don't intend any such thing." She paused. The dimple deepened, and her embarrassment made her eyes twinkle. "I'm sorry. I *am* a beast." She turned her head to her mother. "Mama, forgive me. I'm so damned hot, and things go wrong, and I say things I shouldn't."

Lilybelle burst into tears. She stumbled heavily to her feet, and came to her daughters. There was no diminution in Adelaide's wild and terrible look as she stared at her sister. Lilybelle put her burning wet hand on the girl's rigid arm.

"Lovey, it doesn't matter. It don't indeed, my pet. Your sister's tired. It's 'ard on females, getting married. Look, lovey, Linny's sorry." She gently laid her hand on the scissors, and tried to remove them. Adelaide's fingers were stiff and icy cold. One by one, Lilybelle lifted those fingers, and took away the scissors. Adelaide closed her eyes, but the stony whiteness of her face did not lessen. She felt the pressure of her mother's hand on her shoulders, and she sat down as if suddenly robbed of all strength.

Louisa laughed lightly and musically. "What bathos," she commented, in her sweet and trilling voice. "Do go on, Linny, with your work. What a vulgar display. Not that I blame you, Linny. The girl's exasperating. She deserved to be punished. And now, do try on this petticoat which I've finished."

Lavinia turned on her amiable sister with a gust of ferocity. "Shut up!" she shouted. "You and your honey! You're a pig, and I know all about you! Mind your own business, or I'll slap your teeth out!"

Louisa laughed with gentle restraint. She shook out the petticoat and extended it to her sister. "Now, don't be vulgar, there's a dear. Let me see if I've made the band narrow enough."

Muttering savagely, Lavinia snatched the garment, pulled it over her head, while Louisa regarded her with affectionate amusement. The maids resumed their work. Mrs. Bowden began to pack once again. But Lilybelle sat on the edge of the bed beside her youngest daughter, her big fat arm about those thin shoulders.

"Don't take on so, lovey," she murmured tearfully. "There

357

now, don't be so stiff. It's nothing, my pet. Nothing at all. Your Mama loves you."

But Adelaide, without a word or a look, rose and went from the room. Hardly seeing her way, she entered her own bedroom, and threw herself on the bed. Then, abruptly, she rose, and fled into the bathroom, where she was violently sick.

She returned to her bed and flung herself upon it, sinking her head deeply in the ruffled pillows. She felt deathly ill, prostrated. A still vast horror was in her heart, and a terrible sick anger. She lay there a long time.

She did not hear the door open, but at last she became aware that some one had rustled to the bed. She heard an embarrassed cough. Sluggishly, she lifted her head and looked dazedly at Lavinia, who was standing beside her.

"Look here," said Lavinia, sullenly. "I've said I was sorry. Now, why are you carrying on so, Addy?"

Adelaide pushed herself to a sitting posture with her thin and trembling arms. She gazed steadfastly at her sister. "I might have killed you," she said, quietly. "Yes, I'm sure I would have killed you if you had touched me. I wanted to kill you, Linny."

Lavinia stared down at her, incredulously. "Well, I'm damned," she said in a hushed voice. "I believe you. Why, Addy, you're a criminal at heart! Now, I've wanted to smack people, often, and black their eyes, but I never wanted to kill any one!"

She stammered with real horror: "Why, Addy, that isn't Christian!"

Adelaide said nothing. Then all at once she began to smile whitely. She passed her hand over her cold cheeks and ruffled hair.

Lavinia was truly horrified. Her violences were quick and hot, but never murderous. She moved a step away and regarded her sister with naively distended eyes.

"You're a murderess at heart, Addy," she said, in a subdued tone. Her face puckered as if she wanted to cry. "Oh, it's terrible. And I made you feel like that, Addy! I'm sorry, so very sorry. It was all my fault."

She suddenly thrust out her hand. In the palm lay one of her prized treasures, a beautiful cameo brooch surrounded by pearls and diamonds. Adelaide gazed at it, uncomprehending.

"I want you to have it, Addy. I brought it to you, because I was sorry," stammered Lavinia, flushing. "It will look so pretty with your yellow bridesmaid's gown. Right at the throat. Won't it?"

"I don't want your best brooch, Linny," said Adelaide. Her voice was faint and abstracted.

Lavinia laid it on the girl's lap. "Don't be an idiot. I want you to have it. I really do, Addy. I—I never liked it anyway. It's not my style. I knew it when Uncle Bob Wilkins gave it to me," she added, lying with generous hardihood.

Adelaide took the brooch in her hands. Then slow quiet tears stole down her cheeks. Lavinia, with rare timidity, approached her again, bent and awkwardly kissed her.

"We're beasts to you, Addy. Really we are. But, I do—like —you, Addy. I wouldn't let any one hurt you, even if I hurt myself."

Then she shouted angrily: "But you ought to be whipped! Wanting to kill your own sister! You ought to be whipped, you little wretch!"

Adelaide began to laugh. She could not stop. She fell back on the bed, in her extremity of unusual mirth. And Lavinia stared at her, affronted and outraged.

CHAPTER 40

THE WEDDING, held in the beautiful and formal gardens of the Turnbull mansion, was a magnificent affair. There were one hundred guests only. John spared nothing. For weeks, carpenters had been busy erecting flower-covered arbours in the gardens, stringing the trees with Chinese lanterns and transplanting rare shrubs and draining little ponds to be filled with fresh water and goldfish. The guests, who had fled to the seashore and other resorts to escape the heat, returned to the city for the ceremony.

The mansion was a bower of blooms, ferns and potted plants. In the vast dining-room a repast had been laid out that inspired wonder and envy. A river of champagne was damned up in its gilt bottles waiting for the moment of celebration. In another room, on a long white table, the gifts were laid out, gold and silver and laces like cobwebs, sedulously guarded by special constables. Every archway was festooned with flowers. Special red carpets were laid over the Oriental rugs.

A great hush descended on the fevered mansion on the day of the wedding. Lavinia slept till noon in her enormous white bedroom. The maids rustled about on tiptoe with dusters and mops, adding a last glitter to the rooms. Lilybelle was up at dawn, superintending the cooks in the kitchens, meticulously inspecting every corner of the house. Louisa, dreaming of Patrick Brogan, nestled in her silken sheets, her yellow hair a shaft of sunshine on her white pillows. Adelaide assisted her mother, her gray linen frock stained with wet flower-stems and dust, her light brown locks pinned high on her head. From the gardens came a last moment tapping of hammers, and the voices of workmen. It promised to be a fine hot day. The sky was already pale and glowing with morning heat. Delivery wagons rolled up the gravelled driveway, and men bustled out with baskets and delayed gifts. Confusion reigned in the kitchens, but the other great rooms of the mansion were hushed and dimmed and fragrant.

John wandered restlessly about the gardens, and inspected the white altar which was being covered with flowers for the ceremony. He sat for a few minutes at a time under the tall and bending trees, their green leaves already shimmering with a patina of golden dust. The grass breathed out its hot and poignant breath in the morning quiet. The silk-shrouded windows threw back rays of brilliant light.

John's dark and violent face was a little relaxed today. He seemed less feverish, less haunted and chronically wretched. He exchanged light words with the workmen, put his hand often in his pockets for extra tips. He gazed frequently at the rear of his great mansion with grim satisfaction. He tried not to think at all, to forget the constant nagging ache at the back of his head.

In the marriage of his daughter to Rufus Hastings there was a triumph. All his life had been a brutal flaunting in the face of his enemies. He had won against them. It was strange, therefore, that there was an unremitting sickness and ache in him, like a mortal disease. He saw the whitening of his hair, the furrows in his savage face, the tremor of his hands. His triumph was killing him, and he knew it, and hated the world more for it.

He would not think of Eugenia today, he had promised himself. For he knew when he thought of her the sickness increased in him. She was like a drug to him, which was destroying him, but which he could not resist, and which he had persuaded himself he would die without. But her face floated before him everywhere, and the old sick fever burned in his veins.

At noon, Lavinia was awakened, and the house seemed to stand on its feet in an uproar. Confusion rioted upstairs. Feet ran everywhere. There were shouts and wails, and much cursing from the bride. She cursed the heat, the fumbling of maids, her mother's stupidity, Adelaide's ineptness, Louisa's calm smiles, Mrs. Bowden's mild scolding. Miss Beardsley, in brown satin, arrived in the midst of the riot. She took charge, as always, and under her sternness and efficiency Lavinia regained some composure. Maids became more swift, Mrs. Bowden compressed her lips and ceased her scolding, Lilybelle miraculously became handier with needle and scissors, and Adelaide was packed off to dress. The musicians arrived, began to tune up in the gardens under the shade of the dusty trees.

After many repowderings, Lavinia managed to get into her bridal finery. The wedding-dress was a marvel of French lace and ivory silk, bustled and draped lavishly. Miss Beardsley had lent her mother's ancient lace veil for the occasion, and it billowed about Lavinia like a diaphanous cloud. Guests were arriving, filling the gardens with brightly coloured gowns, laughter, gleaming tall hats and canes. The tempo of the mansion increased deliriously. Louisa appeared in her soft green and lace, a tiny bonnet of forget-me-nots on her golden hair. Adelaide, harried and commandeered, wore a linen apron over her yellow silk. Lilybelle was florid and resplendent in her violet and green, her big red face stained with sentimental tears. She embraced the vexed Lavinia frequently, not intimidated by pettish cries and thrustings-off.

The girl was flamboyantly beautiful in her wedding dress and veil. She was obliged to coat her face with talc to subdue its brilliant colour. But she was pleased by her appearance, for she was tall and lavish of figure, and her black hair curled entrancingly.

Now the strains of the wedding march sounded from the garden. John knocked on the bedroom door for his daughter. The gardens bloomed hotly in the sun, crowded with guests. There was a last moment fluster, then Lavinia burst from the room, took her father's arm and descended the marble and gilt stairway. Her sisters followed her. They were joined by the other bridesmaids in the hall below.

Rufus was waiting for his bride at the altar, where the Episcopal bishop also waited in his black and white. The bridegroom, in black broadcloth, was a cool and elegant figure, his narrow green eyes smiling, his manner composed. The music swelled triumphantly.

John heard little of the solemn ceremony. He hardly glanced at his daughter and her distinguished bridegroom. He looked fixedly at his guests, and saw his own triumph in their polite and envious faces. It was strange then, that the old sickness assailed him in malignant intensity. And this happened whenever he caught the glassy and smiling eye of Mr. Bob Wilkins.

He saw the distinguished faces of Rufus' father and mother and relatives. He saw all that he had gained, not by ambition, not by a lust for power or money. But only by hatred. The pain in his head increased to frightful proportions. Mr. Wilkins, as if he knew everything, increased the wideness of his smile.

The rest of the day passed like an evil dream for John, too brilliant, too sickening, too noisy. By the time his daughter and her new husband had departed on their honeymoon, he was desperately ill, and went to his rooms.

It was there that Lilybelle found him, lying across his bed. She said nothing. But she slipped about the room softly, lowering blinds against the late afternoon sun. John seemed unaware of her presence.

She finally returned to him, and silently helped him undress. He submitted to her ministrations. She asked no questions. She brought him a glass of cold punch, plumped up his pillows, and assisted him under the cool sheets.

He reached up for her hand, smiled painfully, and as if ashamed. He put her rough kind palm under his cheek and closed his eyes. He slept. Lilybelle stood patiently beside him until she was certain that he was asleep. Then she bent over and kissed his cheek. There were tears on her face.

CHAPTER 41

IN THE cool green light of late April, Adelaide was recalled from her hated school to attend the wedding of her sister, Louisa, to Mr. Patrick Brogan.

It was also Louisa's seventeenth birthday, and so the occasion for a double celebration. There was less confusion about this wedding than there had been at Lavinia's, for Louisa was more calm, more authoritative, more assured. She had also decided on a less lavish affair, though with much more taste.

John's consent, for all his reluctant liking for young Brogan, was not easily obtained at the last. But after a long talk with Patrick, anent the religious matter, he consented. There were to be two brief ceremonies, first, by the Bishop, and then in the study of a Catholic priest. John permitted the latter, only after many tears on the part of Louisa, and pleadings by Lilybelle, and demands by Lavinia. He thought the second ceremony degrading and insulting, and was quite open in his opinions.

Patrick, who had no affection for the paving business of his father, and no particular aptitude for politics, that last and most effulent refuge of the Irish scoundrel, had shown considerable desire to enter the enterprises of his future father-in-law. This gave John secret satisfaction. He consulted long and earnestly with Mr. Wilkins, who assured him that the acquisition of another intelligent young man into the firm would "do it good."

"Now the Brogan lad," said Mr. Wilkins. "It'll give new life to the business. Mr. Hastings is clever, and all that, and does a good job. But we need imagination, Johnnie. And Brogan is one as 'as imagination. A lad after me own heart."

"He's a rascal," said John, surlily.

Mr. Wilkins beamed with his old sunniness. "That's it, Johnnie, that's it! You've got to 'ave rascals these days, or get your throat cut all proper."

After the ceremony, Lilybelle suddenly had a mysterious attack of hysterics and great grief, something which she had never betrayed before. Nothing would console her for the loss of her "lasses." Finally, after much impatient urging by John, she confessed that she would literally die if her last little lass were sent back to school. John was obdurate for a while, but he could not endure Lilybelle's loud wailings and sobbings. It was finally agreed that Adelaide was to remain at home, and have her education completed by a female tutor. Extensive search was made, and all applicants rejected. For Lilybelle, no doubt after subtle hints on the part of Miss Beardsley, finally suggested to her husband that that eminent and erudite lady would be "just the thing for little Addy."

So, Miss Beardsley, after she had sternly "resisted" all pleadings on the part of her old and beloved pupil, finally condescended to "consider" the matter. Then she came to Lilybelle and severely told her that it was only because she felt it was her duty that she would accept the position. "The girl is most gauche and awkward and immune to education," she said. "Besides, I am so fond of you, Lilybelle, and I cannot, I simply cannot, refuse to render you this service."

Adelaide, had she been consulted, would have passionately refused the favour of being educated by her ancient enemy. But she was not consulted. The onerousness of her new teacher's presence in her home was compensated for by her release from the detested school.

There was a coolness and narrowness in the girl which

precluded her from warm and wide friendships, and those easy relationships which make of existence a pleasant and sunny thing, if casual and meaningless. It was in her nature to love very few, but she loved them with an intensity and depth which were almost grim, and sombrely passionate. Life, indeed, for Adelaide, was a grave and momentous matter, not to be regarded with light smoothness and cheer. She had an immense feeling of responsibility, duty and honour, attributes of those of her temperament, and if she lacked robust humour, she possessed a wry subtlety and hidden wit.

She had never loved, or even liked her sisters, and this in part was the reason for their aversion to her. For it was impossible for any one to guess Adelaide's true depths of character unless she first loved them. Even then, it was not an easy thing.

When Adelaide had been but a baby, she had understood all about Lilybelle. It did not matter that her mother was stupid and illiterate, graceless and clumsy and vulgar. For, to Adelaide, everything could be forgiven if the other was kind, tender, sympathetic and honest. Lilybelle had true goodness, and for those who were good and pure of heart Adelaide had nothing but adoration and love.

While still very young, she had come to worship her father, for she, of all others except, strangely, Mr. Wilkins, knew that he had no slynesses, no real brutalities or cruelties, no hypocrisies or voracities, no reasonless savageries. She knew, too, that he had not been able to resist circumstance, which had wounded him beyond healing, and if, even as a child, she had thought this weak, she had also thought it tragic. Out of her early pity, she had come to love him passionately, with an incredible depth and devotion and protectiveness. She saw that no one really loved him except herself and her mother.

Now that Lavinia and Louisa were gone, Adelaide began to bloom, to expand. She exhibited a benign gentleness of disposition. She gained flesh, and colour. Her laughter was heard quite frequently about the great and echoing mansion. The thick lashes did not fall so heavily over her brown eyes; her manner was less restrained. Moreover, her silences were less evident, and sometimes she would chat quite readily and volubly to her mother and Mrs. Bowden. Only when she was in the schoolroom with Miss Beardsley did she become again that silent, grim and impassive girl which the noble lady found hateful and unendurable.

May came, sweet and warm and fragrant, and Adelaide felt an increasing peace in herself. It was when she was feeling happiest that the blow fell.

Since the departure of his daughters, (whom he believed loved him passionately) John had become increasingly restless and irascible and disconsolate. The mansion became hateful to him, and he stayed away more and more. He missed his daughters; he missed their laughter, their beauty, their excitement, the flutter of their pretty gowns, their jokes and freshness. He felt a deep resentment against the young men who had taken them away, and so displayed to them, in his offices, an irritability and unreasonableness which the astute Rufus Hastings was not long in analysing.

"The old man misses his daughters," he said, to Patrick Brogan. "He'll not have them away. There's something unhealthy in his feeling for them, and nothing complimentary to us. I'd say he resents us as rivals, who have won out against his superior attractions. If it goes on much longer, he'll be our enemy, and what will happen to us then? With the matters we have in mind," he added, with an expressionless wink at his brother-in-law.

Patrick Brogan, who was exuberant and heartily simple of temperament, for all his cunning and agreeable duplicity, was puzzled. He could not understand the implications behind Rufus' words. But he did know that John was daily becoming more sullen and resistive to suggestions, that he sometimes eyed his daughters' husbands with furtive hatred and resentment. Matters were not proceeding in the offices with that ease and delightful progress which Patrick had anticipated, and hence his perplexity. Being Irish, he might be a plotter or a schemer, but there was little dirtiness in his mind. So he said: "What would you suggest, Rufe?"

Rufus pretended to give the matter deep consideration and thoughtfulness. He pursed his thin and livid mouth, and narrowed his slits of green eyes. In the meantime, Patrick studied him cunningly, with a half smile. The young Irishman was not capable of virulent and unremitting hatreds; his temperament was too full of humour, and he had an innate laziness which precluded him from sustained enmities. Nevertheless, he was no fool, and was quite aware of the disguised implacability and rapacity of his brother-in-law. On the surface, they appeared great friends and confidants. Rufus had apparently overcome his aversion for the low birth and antecedents of Louisa's husband, and they worked together in charming amiability and efficiency, each recognizing the abilities of the other, and planning to use those abilities. No longer did Rufus condescend to Patrick. In the first place, that would have been impolitic under the circumstances, and in the second place, Patrick had a disconcerting habit of being loudly amused by such condescensions. Moreover, Patrick was of compelling handsomeness, and of commanding height and build, quite casting the dun and aristocratic Rufus Hastings into the shade.

Rufus, then, might cast his plotting nets with dexterity, but Patrick saw all the throws, and discerned, under the surface, the shadows of the fish which his astute brother-in-law had in mind to catch. He began to smile.

He waited while Rufus affected to give the matter close and serious thought. He was not surprised when Rufus sighed resignedly, and said, with a humorous shrug: "I presume the only thing I can do is to consent to return to that mausoleum on Fifth Avenue with Lavinia. At least, for a time. I haven't yet approached Lavinia with the idea, and I don't doubt I will have a struggle with her. She adores our new home, and has just finished furnishing it." He sighed again, and appealed with a wry smile to Patrick, for his sympathy.

Patrick was intensely titillated. He bit his lip to keep his smile from broadening. He even controlled himself enough so that he was able to nod sombrely, and then narrowed his little bright blue eyes and stared grimly into space.

"You're quite right, Rufe," he admitted, reluctantly. He pretended to hesitate. "Now that you mention it, I've got a thought of my own. Louisa, the little love, has been complaining of loneliness. She's often mentioned returning home. She misses her parents. Her Papa worshipped her, you know. So, I'll give it some thought, myself. It would be convenient for all of us, wouldn't it?"

You filthy Irishman, thought Rufus, fixing those wicked green eyes of his on Patrick, who returned the look with bland enthusiasm and great innocence.

You dirty little Machiavelli, thought Patrick, his expression becoming smoother and more boyish each instant.

"Splendid!" cried Rufus at last, with genteel pleasure, and striking his long bloodless hands together. He allowed his pleasure and enthusiasm to make his mask-life face quite mobile and brilliant for a moment. He thrust out his hand with an affectation of generous if restrained delight. Patrick took his hand, and shook it heartily. They beamed at each other with the most engaging affection, and understood each other completely. Rufus was enraged. Patrick was highly diverted.

They had their mutual schemes, their common villainy. They had hardly become relatives through their marriages before they had begun to plot. So far, the plots were still in a very nebulous state, but the outline of them was large on the horizon. Nevertheless, though they needed each other, and the harmony and consent of each other if each was to

366

succeed in his plots, they were mortal enemies, and each would have destroyed the other with immense satisfaction.

Rufus returned to the handsome if small house on East Ninth Street, and had a long consultation with his energetic and black-eyed wife. He told her everything, having a high opinion of her shrewdness, and her ability to visualize a situation.

"So you see, my dear," he ended in a tone of gloomy regret, "it will be necessary, for at least a time, to return to your old home. Your father will be delighted. If we do not—and God knows I don't wish it, myself—Pat will be there, with your sister. Now," he continued, closely watching the dark and enraged sparkle in Lavinia's eyes, "I have all brotherly regard for your dear sister, of course. But we must not blind ourselves to the dangers in the situation. Louisia is—er—a charming lady, who prefers herself first over any one else, even her devoted sister. She and Patrick will be in an excellent position to influence your father, to our later detriment. I would not adore you, my love, so much, if I did not have your just interests at heart, and a passionate desire to see to it that you are not forgotten, and pushed aside by the more immediate presence of your sister in your father's house. I am not implying that the thought originated with Louisa; I believe she is too gentle of temperament to plot and scheme to rob her beloved older sister. Females know nothing of business affairs, so how is it possible for her to originate these schemes? The fault lies with that cunning and conscienceless Irish scoundrel, Patrick Brogan. It is he who plans to do you in, and very completely, my love."

Lavinia was so choked with rage that she could not speak for a moment, and her round and handsome face turned crimson. Rufus smiled, and shrugged sadly.

"It is not that we'd be beggars, if your father forgot us completely, my dearest one. But there is the element of justice in this case. I cannot stand by and see your interests jeopardized. Nevertheless, if you do not desire to return to your father's house, I will accept your decision with, I confess, relief. I love our little home and our privacy too much, I am afraid."

Then Lavinia exploded with her violent rage. She shouted: "Make your excuses for Louisa, you fool! You, like all men, are taken in nicely by large blue eyes and yellow hair and hypocritical sweetness! But I tell you, it isn't Pat who plots all this. It is that smiling snake of a Louisa! Such a greedy baggage, you have no idea! Such a crafty scheming minx! I won't have it, I tell you." And she pounded her white fist on the arm of the chair. "We'll go back. And very soon, I can promise you that!"

Then she began to smile. "Besides, it is so tedious to manage a household and dilatory and impudent servants. It will be a relief to relegate all that to Mama again."

And Patrick said to his charming and gracious young wife: "So, my dear, you see how it is. He tried to pretend it was a disagreeable idea to him, to get on the ground floor of influence over your father. When I also suggested that we return, he could have murdered me. Indeed, if looks could have killed, you'd have been a widow by now. What do you say, then?"

Young Mrs. Brogan considered it all with the greatest care and thoroughness. She said at last, with meditative slowness: "It is not Lavinia, of course. Not that she is burdened by too many scruples, where her own advantage is concerned. But she has that loud and vulgar sort of temper which is neither clever nor malevolent. We have always been fond of each other, and she is really quite generous. I have no doubt that she would have repudiated, with much noise, any suggestion from Rufus that she enter into any conspiracy with him to rob me. In fact," Louisa added with an amused smile, "she would have doubtless rushed to me and told me all about it, with considerable anger. She never could keep her own counsel."

Ruus knew this also, so he took the precaution of warning Lavinia that she was not, by the slightest smile or word or flicker of eye, to allow her sister and Patrick to suspect that he, Rufus, had detected their "schemes." "Let them spin their rope until it is long enough to hang them," he advised.

So it was, then, that John was approached by the two young gentlemen, who assured him, in an effective chorus, that their wives were quite going into a decline over their grief at being separated from their beloved father.

"Louisa scarcely touches her plate," said Patrick, gravely.

"Lavinia is so irritable that I dare not invite guests," added Rufus.

To less wretched young rascals, John's sudden expression of joy and delight would have seemed pathetic. But these two merely exchanged glances of contemptuous amusement and congratulations. Neither of the two gentlemen was excessively happy in the situation. Rufus had intended that he and Lavinia, alone, return to John's house. When Patrick had also expressed his intentions to do likewise, Rufus had been infuriated, and had dared not retract his decision. Had he not been justly afraid of Patrick, he would have retreated, and remained in his own home. But he dared not do this. Patrick, too, was in the same position. So now they were caught in their own onerous plottings, and neither had the advantage. By nature, they preferred their own establishments. But their own scheming had forced them to abandon those establishments, without compensating advantages over each other.

Lilybelle, too, was overcome wth delight at the return of her "lasses." She gave up her own spacious and fine apartments to Lavinia and Rufus, and took much smaller and less convenient quarters on the third floor. John, in his generous pleasure, gave up his apartments to Louisa and Patrick, and contented himself with a single large room at the rear of the mansion. Lavinia expressed a desire for a sewing-room of her own, apart from the community sewing-room which she had shared with her sisters and mother. So Adelaide was compelled to surrender her pleasant bedroom to Lavinia. The two young matrons had become fond of their own personal maids, and so these dependents shared Adelaide's sitting-room. Adelaide was moved up to the fourth floor, where the servants, grumbling, were obliged to give up their sitting-room to be made into a bedroom for the girl. Lavinia, then, had four excellent rooms of her own, Louisa and Patrick three enormous rooms, not counting Adelaide's sitting-room which had been converted into a chamber for the new smart French maids.

Adelaide saw all these changes with a gray numbness of despair in her heart. She was hardly aware of her new quarters, which were drafty, inconvenient and dark. With acute prescience, she saw her new role in the life of this house. She would soon become a sort of upper servant, housekeeper and manager for her sisters. She had no court of appeal. Lilybelle would not have understood. John would not have listened.

Therefore, in her wretchedness, she appealed to her parents to send her away to school again. But poor Lilybelle was too engrossed in her delight at having her family with her again. And John, appealed to by his favourite daughters, refused to give his consent. Her sisters need her, he said, though heaven alone knew why they wanted such a silent and sullen young creature about them. Lavinia was pregnant, and she would need her sister's help in the months and years to come. It never occurred to John that Adelaide, herself, might marry. It was foreordained, he believed, that she would be the old maid of the family, and must make herself useful. She must pay for her ugliness and lack of personal attractions by services to her superior sisters. (John, himself, influenced by his daughters, was quite convinced that Adelaide was physically repellent. He never looked at her with awareness.)

Nor, said John, considering the future of service and selfless dedication in store for his youngest daughter, was it necessary to waste any further time on her education. She was nearly sixteen now, a great girl, and was none too good in her studies anyway. Miss Beardsley must be thanked, given a handsome gift, and alowed to return to her own home, (which she had advantageously rented out to a substantial family).

Miss Beardsley was aghast. She saw that she had "cut her own throat." She had constantly complained of Adelaide's stupidity to her parents, with the single desire of increasing John's displeasure with the girl. Adelaide might turn in a most excellent and complete paper, but Miss Beardsley would scrawl and slash at it viciously with a red pencil, and then take it grimly to John, watching, then, his scowl of disgust and irritation, with inner satisfaction. Now, he had taken Miss Beardsley seriously; had agreed with her that the girl was incapable of absorbing learning. So Miss Beardsley, then, was to be ousted from her excellent and comfortable quarters and the ministrations of fine servants, and deprived of a very substantial income. Her hatred for Adelaide increased. When she returned to her gaunt house with her baggage, she forgot the amazing cheque in her reticule, and concentrated all her malefic thoughts on Adelaide, who was responsible for her deprivations.

Adelaide was too engrossed in her despair to be happy over the dismissal of her old enemy. She went through the onerous days like one moving in a nightmare. At night, after the constant demands of her petulant sisters, she was too exhausted to sleep.

She could rarely escape. But one Sunday, on a clear sweet autumn day, she was able to elude her persecutors, and slip from the house. She moved swiftly down Fifth Avenue to Eighth Street, turned and approached Broadway. The little closed shops glittered in the sun. Clouds of sunlit chaff eddied about her feet, swirled in the bright air. Carriages rolled rapidly by, the ladies peering out haughtily from under their gay parasols. Gentlemen strolled, stood in knots on the wooden pavements to converse and smoke and exchange greetings. Adelaide, only, was alone. She quickened her pace steadily during the next hour, walking with her free and graceful step.

CHAPTER 42

Dｕｒｉｎｇ the months of emancipation from her sisters, Adelaide had indulged her true inclinations toward colour and fashion. She had dressed prettily and charmingly, had brushed her light brown hair into glimmers of chestnut light. Though no one had remarked on these changes, she had not been discouraged. She had a vague and diffused dream, shy and radiant, though apparently still without real hope.

Now, however, that her sisters had returned, they had taken on once more their old arrogance and dictatorial mannerisms towards Adelaide. Because she was so "colourless" and without "style," they said, she must dress in accordance with her natural characteristics. Too, they had in mind her new position as upper servant to them. In consequence, they selected dull grays, browns and blacks for her. They preferred black, for black added harmony to the shining black satins or bombazines of their French maids.

Louisa, who had a discerning eye, was not too satisfied about black. She saw that that sombre hue made Adelaide's complexion take on a luminous clarity, intensified the liquid brownness of her eyes, contrasted charmingly with her hair, which apeared to take on a shining vitality. Though the girl's lips had always appeared pale, black intensified their tint to a bright soft rose. One day, in fact, Louisa was annoyed to discover that Adelaide had a strange and vagrant beauty, as delicate as dawn, and completely rare and distinguished. But Louisa had always known that Adelaide was not ugly. She had insisted that Adelaide had no attractions because of her dislike for the girl. Lavinia, too emotional, always saw only what others desired her to see, especially if she had a desire to see in that fashion also. When Louisa suggested that black was "not the thing" for Adelaide, Lavinia disagreed vigorously. She was honestly convinced by Louisa that Adelaide was ugly, and black, in her estimation, was the fitting garb for ugliness.

Adelaide, therefore, this bright autumn day, was clad in black and severe silk, the bustle small, the skirt narrow and scarcely draped, the bodice tight over her breasts and fastened by a row of jet buttons. There was a frill of white about her throat. Her bonnet, too, was black, tied with

371

violet ribbons. Her appearance, unknown to herself, was distingiushed and elegant, for her slight figure was very fine and graceful, her walk dignified and slow, her manner composed and distant. Her hair took on a brightness in the pale autumn sun; her face looked transparently pearl-like under the black bonnet, and her mouth was warmly pink. The sun brought out amber flecks in her brown eyes which were so thoughtful and so sad and yet, so unresigned.

Her thoughts were not submissive. They were full of cold anger and hatred and despair. The lonely light under the trees that lined the pavement enhanced her sense of desolation and imprisonment. She had escaped for an hour, but she must return to that great mansion which had become a gaol to her. Strange ideas flashed into her mind. Thoughts of escape. But where? She received no allowance from her father; she had no money. She was less than a valued servant. Nor had she any jewels she might sell. Her trinkets were all composed of silver and semi-precious stones.

I am a servant, she thought, bitterly. Why, then, could she not sell her services? Surely there were many ladies in New York who would be only too willing to engage her. She had no references, it is true. But I am competent, God knows, she thought, wryly. Her family was reference enough. But who would engage the daughter of John Turnbull for menial tasks? And what a scandal there would be! Adelaide dismissed the real thought, on contemplating that scandal which would quite overwhelm her father. Daughters of rich and powerful men did not leave home to sell themselves as servants. At the last, prospective employers would be convinced that here was a wild and wayward girl, seeking to escape from parental discipline. A bad piece, they would call her.

She walked unseeingly, jostled by throngs that eyed her with speculative curiosity. Young ladies did not promenade unaccompanied through the streets of New York. Some young bucks thought, at first, that here was a female of the demimonde, but a glance at her quiet and abstracted face, so young and yet so embittered, dissuaded them from accosting her. Elderly ladies eyed her disapprovingly from their carriages, and then turned to discuss her with their daughters or sisters, remarking that they hardly knew what to think of young females these days, so bold and without modesty, and so entirely brazen.

"Is that not the Turnbulls' youngest daughter, Annie or something?" asked one old lady of her gay daughters, as they rolled by in their victoria. "The one who is so graceless and stupid and dull that they are not to bring her out?

The one who attends her sisters, those charming young matrons?"

But she did not believe this, herself. This lone and wandering young female could scarcely be the daughter of John Turnbull. He would not have allowed this shameless promenading.

Subconsciously aware, at last, of the stares and curiosity she excited, Adelaide drew her black veil over her face. Now the transparency of her face, and her delicate beauty, were greatly enhanced. She was not aware of this.

The fresh strong wind from the sea suddenly blew with accelerated boisterousness in her face. It carved her skirts about her, molded them to her thighs, to the great admiration of passing young gentlemen. Colour was stung into her cheeks. She held her bonnet with her hand, gloved in black kid. She moved steadily into the wind, with grace and sureness. Her heart began to beat with more calmness, and her depression lightened.

It was some moments before she became aware of an urgent voice calling her name. She turned about, confused. A young gentleman was leaning out towards her from the seat of his buggy, which was very bright and very new and stylish. His horse was black and shining also, and very spirited.

Adelaide started. Her face quickened into scarlet. She hesitated, then continued to walk, her heart beating furiously. The young gentleman followed, skillfully guiding his horse through the press of other carriages. He continued to call her. At last, he impatiently tossed aside his reins, leapt from the carirage, and raced after her, much to the amusement of other walkers.

He caught her arm. "Adelaide, you minx! Why are you running away?"

She tried to release her arm, then was suddenly quiet, and very pale. She looked up into the clean hard face of her cousin, Anthony Bollister. She tried to speak, and then fell into silence.

"What's the matter with you?" he demanded. He began to smile, but it was a shrewd and not too pleasant smile. "I haven't seen you for ages. Why didn't you meet me, as I suggested? All these months. Why, it's over a year!"

"I couldn't," she said, hoarsely. Her throat felt sick. Her pulses were beating with such rapidity that she was dazed. She felt the muddy pavement sway under her feet. There was a vivid dazzle before her eyes, and all at once they filled with tears.

"O, let me alone!" she cried, and to her horror, she sobbed drily. She tried to move on. She hurried, as if pursued. At last, panting, she was forced to pause. When she saw that Anthony had followed her, her heart rose in her breast and she heard its pounding in her ears.

She turned on him. "Please go away, Tony. This is impossible. I—I thought I'd forgotten you. It's no use, Tony. Look; you are making a spectacle on the street."

He looked down at her white face, her quivering lips, her brown eyes swimming with tears. He saw that she had unconsciously lifted her hands towards him. He took them and pressed them firmly.

"Dear little Adelaide," he said, with great gentleness. His hard mouth softened. His slate-gray eyes were strong and inflexible. "See here, let's get in my buggy. We'll go for a ride, and talk. You know, I just can't forget you, you little fool."

He took her arm in a resistless grip, and guided her back to his buggy. She found herself mounting the step, assisted by his hand. She sat down. There were tears on her cheeks, which she furtively wiped away with her handkerchief. He sprang up beside her, caught up the reins, and drove on towards the Battery. He did not speak. When she glanced furtively at his profile, she saw that it was stern and harder than ever, with deep lines about the mouth. He seemed much older that she remembered, surer and stronger, and she was frightened. This was not a kind face, or a tolerant one, nor even one with candour or honesty.

She looked away from him, and tried to fasten her attention on the streets and crowds they were passing. But all at once, she saw there was a glow and a vividness over the faces of the crowded buildings, a blinding glitter on their empty windows, a noise of confusion and joyousness all about her. She began to tremble, and clenched her hands together on her knees. She tried to control herself, but in spite of her efforts she was pervaded by an intoxicating ecstasy and fear. She shivered violently.

"Are you cold?" asked Anthony, in a curt but polite tone. He pulled a robe over her knees. She felt the touch of his hands, and a long and burning thrill ran over her body. She looked at him timidly, but still could not utter a word. He caught her look, tried to remain stern, and then could not help his smile.

"You little fool," he repeated, with more softness. He said nothing more for a long time, as they drove briskly through the streets for what seemed hours.

They reached the crowded Battery, surrounded by its ancient buildings and warehouses, its mud and piers. Beyond, the sea glittered and shimmered in its far immensity. The black outlines of Governors Island broke the line of the horizon. Gulls caught light on their white wings, circled and dived against the pale and brilliant sky. The wind was stronger here, and fresher, filled with salt and harshness. Far away were the sails of a great ship, then the low gray smoke of a liner moving out to sea. People stood on the piers, and shading their eyes, stared at the pale thread of the horizon and laughed to see the gulls dive for small fish in the turgid water. Vessels on the quays droned and whistled, while men hurried to fill them with cargo. The whole scene was filled with light, vivacity and vitality.

Anthony drew in his horse. There were many carriages about, guarded by grooms and coachmen, while their occupants strolled on the docks and held their bowlers and their bonnets. Only Adelaide and Anthony were silent. They gazed into the distance, avoiding looking at each other.

Then Anthony spoke in a neutral voice: "You know, Adelaide, you are medieval. You've avoided meeting me because of 'duty' to your worthy Papa, who, I've detected, seems totally unaware of your existence, or worse. You see, I've made some very pertinent inquiries about you. You are a young lady out of Jane Austen. A silly, foolish little baggage. I suppose it means nothing to you that I—like—you, and wanted to see you, and that you've liked me?"

Adelaide was at first angered and indignant at his words, and then she halted in the very midst of her emotions and stared at him incredulously. A soft rose flooded her face.

"You said, Tony, that you like me?" she whispered.

He tried to remain disgusted with her, but he could not. He reached for her hand under the robe and squeezed it warmly. He smiled. He loosened his grip, but she seized his hand and held it almost with despair, and pleaded with him with her eyes to repeat what he had said.

"My dear," he said, in a changed tone, "I more than like you. Don't you know that?"

"But, why?" she murmured, still disbelieving, still grasping his hand with feverish strength.

He shrugged. He moved closer to her, and their thighs touched. He felt her faint recoil.

"How should I know?" he asked, lightly, his eye travelling over her face and throat and breast. "I only know I do. From the first moment I saw you. What a mouse you were. I've only seen you three or four times in all my life, but it's been enough for me to know—" He paused.

"What?" she asked, with a curious thin intensity in her voice.

He was silent. What a strange innocent little creature this

375

was, and how infinitely pathetic. He leaned towards her, and then drew back.

"It's enough for me to know that I want to see you, very often," he replied at last.

She averted her face very slowly, and looked out at the sea, without truly seeing it. He saw her profile, delicate, clear and sad, and more than a trifle dark and embittered. And now he was filled with anger and violence against those who had so distorted her life and her youth. His expression darkened, became cruel and vindictive and full of relentlessness.

He felt her looking at him again, felt her start of apprehension at what she must have seen. He tried to smile reassuringly, but the congested look of violence about his eyes and mouth did not subside.

"I think it's about time that you and I had a little frank conversation, my pet," he said quietly, but with a note of implacability in his voice. "A very frank conversation indeed. Or, Adelaide, are you a coward and a liar?"

He was pleased at the indignant flash in her eyes. Then, the girl had spirit. She was not a feckless weakling as he had begun to suspect. In anger, truth will out, he remembered.

He held her eyes with his own strong and unrelenting eyes, and continued:

"You've avoided me, even though you wanted to see me. Out of duty to your father, or some other such foolishness. Not that your father would care, over much. I think he'd be glad if you got out of his house and out of his sight. Why? Because you resemble my mother, whom he once wanted to marry. Men like John Turnbull don't forget, you know. He hates my father. But he hates my mother worse."

He paused. He knew that he could not say what he wished to say, that he dared not say it. Not to this idiotic innocent little fool. He dared not say to her: "My mother is your accursed father's mistress. I've known that for two years. How, I shall not tell you. He keeps her as his mistress because he hates her. But he doesn't know it. There are many things about your blessed father which I know, and he doesn't. He couldn't stand up to life. Now, he keeps my mother because she represents to him a wicked black triumph. He doesn't love her, and neither does she love him. Those two fools live in some fine and imbecile delusion of their own. And to this man, who persecutes and hates you because you remind him of someone whom he knows deep in his twisted soul that he hates, you give your loyalty and your idiot's devotion. This man who has ruined and destroyed many men far better than he, who has spread misery to the ends of the world, and who has started a train of events that future generations will have to bear in increased enormity. This man who destroys and creates havoc because he hates."

"How can you say my father hates your mother?" cried Adelaide, with anger. "She's his cousin, but he never sees her at all!"

"You must take my word for it," he insisted, inflexibly. "I know. Well, are you going to cater to his insanity, or are you going to live for yourself?"

She stared at him with cold and fulminating fury, and he was delighted at the blaze of her eye, the stiff whiteness of her face, the arch of her pale lips. Then, even as she gathered words to devastate him, a dark shadow ran over her features, and they became pinched and wizened. She looked away.

" 'Live for myself!' " she repeated, with intense bitterness and scorn. "Such nice easy words. How can I? Don't you know that I've thought about it, until my head spun around, and I was sick to death? I have no money; I never had any. Who would give me money to go away? You say my father wants me out of his sight. I was to much of a coward to admit it before—I couldn't bear to admit it though it was there to see—but now I know it. I think I always knew it. Go away? Where? With what? If I asked my father to give me money so I could remove myself, he would know I couldn't bear things any longer. I—I think that would please him," and now her voice faltered, broke, and when she resumed, it was quite hoarse: "He would watch to see that I couldn't get away. Besides," she added, with such fierceness and hatred that Anthony frowned, "my dear sisters need me. I am their servant. They'd see to it that I'd never get away."

He took her hand quickly. It was ice cold and rigid as steel. He felt the clenched curve of her fingers. He pressed firmly upon her hand until it relaxed out of sheer pain. He looked into her eyes penetratingly, and said with slow cold intensity:

"Stop that, Adelaide. You've had reason for hatred, I admit. But, for your sake, in the name of God, don't hate. Or, don't acquire the kind of hatred which will destroy you. There's a healthy hatred that sets about reasonably to right things, a righteous hatred. But, that isn't the kind that's in you. You just hate, wildly and murderously. I suppose, perhaps, it is because you feel trapped. Adelaide, do you know what that kind of hatred will do to you? Look at your father."

She stared at him, her face tragic and convulsed, and overcome with horror. He took her other hand, held them both as if he were trying to prevent her from doing some mad and terrible thing.

377

He made his voice very quiet and steadfast: "I hate many things, too, Adelaide. I've seen so much. I've studied the men all about me. Robbers, thieves, murderers and exploiters. America is rotten with them. I know what they are doing, and I know what will happen to my country if they are not stopped. I know that the very principles upon which this nation was founded are endangered, that liberty and freedom and the dignity of man are being menaced. It is an international plotting, and American malefactors are beginning to lead all the world, to enmesh it in such a web of plotting, lies, crimes and intrigue that it will take a hundred generations before men can extricate themselves from their slavery. I've talked to politicians, to Senators and Governors, in my father's house, and they all have one thing in common: a hatred for all other men. America, based on freedom and the principle that man is a creature of dignity and soul, is being destroyed by rapacity."

He paused. His hold on her hands tightened. He looked away from her at the sea, and his face was black with violence and anger.

"Yes, I hated them. I still hate them. But I didn't stay locked in my room chewing my nails and concentrating on my hatred. As you do. I didn't let the poison destroy me, and fill me with eroded cavities brimming with vitriol. I looked about me to see what I could do.

"My beginning will be small. There's Richard Gorth & Company. I'm in it now, with my uncle. He likes me. He's intimated he'll leave the business to me. My father is against it. We scarcely speak now. He had other plans. But his plans are not my plans."

He was silent a moment. Then he continued: "My uncle's company is not so bad as others. Not as bad as it might have been. And now I've planned to make it a fair and decent company, in competition with the thieves and the exploiters in other businesses. I'll make Richard Gorth & Company a sample of what American business might and can be. Honest, fair and honourable. Perhaps I won't make much money. It is hard, competing with robber barons, as they call themselves grandiloquently. But I have faith in the American people. It will take time, but eventually they will come to have faith in us. That is a good beginning."

He turned to the girl and smiled at her. "You see, Adelaide? There is destructive hatred, which solves nothing but only murders the harbourer, and there is the kind of pure and constructive hatred which sets out to right wrongs, to undo justices, to liberate and to cleanse. I think the good men of all the ages had that hatred, from Jesus to Lincoln, from Luther to Washington."

She had listened, hardly breathing, absorbing his words like messages of peace and cleanness and sanity. Her fierce young face softened; her eyes were dim. Her throat worked, and finally she dropped her chin on her breast.

But her voice was low and despairing when she spoke: "You're a man, Tony. You can do so many things. But, I'm a female. What can I do?"

He drew nearer to her. He put his arm about her. "You can marry me, you little idiot," he said.

Her shoulders became rigid with shock against his arm. She flung up her head and stared at him incredulously. But a great light broke out in her eyes.

"Marry you!" she cried.

He nodded, pressing her shoulders with his arm to calm the hysteria he felt mounting in her.

"Why not? You know I've always loved you, my little love."

She looked at him in a tremendous shining silence, disbelieving, searching his face for mockery, for lightness. But he looked back at her with passion and tenderness, and touched her cheek gently with his finger.

Then, without warning, she burst into tears. She turned and pushed her face against the broadcloth of his chest. She clutched him with shaking hands.

"O, take me away, Tony," she cried. "Take me away."

CHAPTER 43

FOR A long time they were conscious of nothing but themselves. They leaned back in the shadow cast by the hood of the buggy, and held each other in strong and passionate silence. Adelaide had laid her head on Anthony's shoulder. Her eyes were closed. She felt his gentle hand on her cheek and throat and hair, and a smile, rare in its sweetness, curved her lips.

What an innocent little darling it is, thought the young man. And how peaceful she is now, and free from her misery and hatred. Please God, I'll protect her from them from now on. Nothing will touch her again.

The evening was falling swiftly. The crowds were thinning. Now, few remained on the piers. The evening sky was paling, and the gulls fluttered lower to the water. The sea turned

379

gray and shadowy. Carriage wheels rolled away with a hollow sound on the wooden pavement. The wind had the chill of coming winter in it, rank and salt and bitter.

In their absorption in each other, and what they had said in this last hour, they had not been aware that one man, at least, had been greatly interested in them, had drawn close enough to them, from the rear, to hear much of what had passed between them. And this man was Mr. Wilkins.

He had seen them almost from the moment when they had rolled up near the water, and then, circling with apparent aimlessness, had approached the rear of the buggy, then, reaching the back wheels, had stood there, listening with profound interest and intensity.

He had recognized young Bollister, and had been surprised at the sight of Adelaide. No mere curious desire to eavesdrop had brought him to this carriage. But he was very fond of Adelaide, and indeed his fondness had increased to a real love. He had spent many hours plotting how to extricate her from her misery, and visit vengeance on her oppressors. When he discovered her in the company of young Bollister he was apprehensive. It was a real desire to protect her that had brought him to this vantage point.

Mr. Wilkins was very gay and gallant today in his handsome brown wardrobe. He never aged. He was more rotund and rubicund than ever. Now, as he listened, the most cherubic and peaceful smile came over his rosy round face. He nodded, pursed his lips, lifted his eyebrows, as if he was carrying on with himself a most delightful and satisfactory conversation. There was a gloating gleam in his glassy hazel eyes. When Adelaide had collapsed in Anthony's arms, Mr. Wilkins had discreetly lifted apart a flap of the leather hood, and had feasted on the sight. He winked once or twice, quite violently, and had an inordinate desire to clear his throat.

He heard Adelaide speak in a faint shaken voice: "But, Tony. I do love my father, you know. What shall I do? He'll never consent."

"What do we care for that?" asked Anthony lightly. "Look here, you aren't a coward, are you? We can go away quietly, tomorrow, for a few hours, and be married. What do you say?"

The girl was silent. Mr. Wilkins could hear her quiet sobbing. Then she said: "O, Tony. I don't know what to do. I've had the strangest feeling. I've felt that something quite terrible is threatening Papa. It is foolish, I know. But, I've felt it. How can I leave him?"

Mr. Wilkins heard Anthony utter a vulgar word of disgust. He cleared his throat loudly, stamped vigorously on the wooden planks as if he was approaching the carriage, hummed a little, and circled round to the front. He glanced with the utmost casualness into the carriage, tipped his hat, murmured a word of apology. Then he allowed a pleased expression of amazement to come over his glowing countenance.

"Well, now, if it isn't Miss Adelaide!" he exclaimed, with a look of supreme sunniness. Then he pretended to start, to become nonplussed, upon meeting Anthony's cold gray eyes and forbidding look of impatience. Anthony had seen the amiable Mr. Wilkins at a distance, but had never met him. His look was not amiable upon his recognition.

Adelaide blushed deeply. She sat up, touched her disordered hair. Her eyes were both embarrassed and frightened. She drew away from Anthony.

"Uncle Bob," she murmured, distractedly, smoothing her rumpled clothing. The tears had left wet streaks on her face.

Mr. Wilkins appeared ineffably unaware of the hiatus that his appearance had caused. He regarded Adelaide with affection.

"I was 'opin' I'd meet some one on such a fine day," he said, with a beaming smile. "And I'm proper glad to see you out, Miss Adelaide, taking the air." He spoke more slowly and clearly: "You were lookin' quite pale lately, what with the work and all, and the responsibilities. 'Not right, Bob,' I says to myself, many's the time. 'Not right for the little lass to stay shut up like a blasted prisoner in a gaol. She should be out, gettin' roses in her cheeks, she being so young.' I've thought to speak to your Papa about it."

He turned to Anthony, whose eyes had narrowed. He spoke with great and blushing frankness: "The little lass needs a firm 'and to take her out of herself, that she does. Too much work, too conscientious like. You agree with me, sir?"

Adelaide, more confused than ever, could still remember the amenities of society. "Oh, Uncle Bob," she stammered, her colour mounting, "this is my cousin, Mr. Bollister. Anthony, you've heard me speak of Uncle Bob?"

Mr. Wilkins pretended immense surprise and pleasure. He swept his round brown hat with a flourish to his breast, and bowed. Anthony, smiling secretly, returned the bow from his seat, with fitting ceremony.

"Well, Mr. Bollister!" exclaimed the rosy Lucifer, with visible delight. "It's a pleasure, I'm sure! Not that I haven't heard about you, with many compliments."

"That's very kind of you," returned Anthony, with some irony. "I've heard of you, too, Mr. Wilkins."

His gray eyes were sharp and quizzical, glinting with a hidden smile. Mr. Wilkins lowered his own eyes modestly for a moment, then said: "Good things, I 'opes, Mr. Bollister? Not that one can expect good words from a world like this."

"Oh, I assure you the comments were quite strong," said Anthony.

Mr. Wilkins chuckled gently. "I'll wager they were," he responded, with humour. He eyed Anthony keenly, taking complete inventory of every feature. What he saw pleased him. A hard young devil, he thought, and one for Wilkins' money.

In the meantime, Adelaide had recovered her composure. She had smoothed her hair, adjusted her bonnet, straightened her skirts, put on her gloves, all with surreptitious speed.

"Now that we've met, as I've always wished it, sir, I 'opes we improves the acquaintance?" said Mr. Wilkins, with the sweetest of looks.

"Very agreeable of you, I'm sure," said Anthony. He put his hat on his thick sandy-red hair, and picked up the reins. But Mr. Wilkins, suddenly earnest, laid his hand restrainingly on the buggy. Anthony looked down at him with darkening impatience. He knew all about Mr. Wilkins. He felt that there was a bad odour swirling about the carriage.

But, as he looked down at the fat and evil cherub of a man, his attention was arrested by a strange and penetrating gleam in the glassy eyes, full of meaning and significance.

"I want you to remember this, sir," said Mr. Wilkins, in an odd and very slow and purposeful voice, full of import, "that if you needs Bob Wilkins, I'm at your service. There's few as I've said that to, and I never says it lightly. I'm not one as talks idly, but there's many a man I've made and broken."

"I've no doubt of that," said Anthony, coldly. But he was both puzzled and interested at the contemptible rascal's manner.

"I don't go abaht offerin'," continued Mr. Wilkins, in that same peculiar tone. "But, there's things I can do."

"Yes, I've heard of them," returned Anthony, with some grimness. But Mr. Wilkins' hand tightened more strenuously on the buggy, which had begun to move. He walked along with it. He peered up at Anthony, and his eyes seemed phosphorescent in the gathering twilight. Because of the dimness, those eyes appeared disembodied, malevolent and full of power.

"I just arsks you to remember, Mr. Bollister," said Mr. Wilkins, and his voice had some fatefulness in it.

"I won't forget," said Anthony, with grim contempt. He

slapped the reins sharply on the horse's back, and the animal broke into a sudden trot.

"Good arfternoon, Miss Adelaide!" shouted Mr. Wilkins, waving his hat.

"Good afternoon, Uncle Bob," she called faintly, leaning out of the buggy to look back at Mr. Wilkins. The Battery was completely deserted now. Against the background of darkening sky and dark gray sea Mr. Wilkins was a rigid and lonely fat figure, his hat held high in his hand. He was, even to Adelaide's confused senses, a strange and sinister figure, and the loneliness and desolation all about him increased that strange and sinister quality, as if he were part of them. She had the most unfathomable and nightmarish thought that he would remain there eternally, one with the eternal sea and sky, that his emergence into the world of men was only for brief intervals.

They were clattering through the quiet evening streets before Anthony spoke again, and then with quiet determination:

"Well, Adelaide, what have you decided? Remember, you can't play with me. It's yes or no, now. If it is no, I assure you we won't meet again. I won't see you again, ever. Well, what is it?"

Adelaide was silent for a long moment, then in a trembling voice, she murmured: "It's 'yes,' Tony. Whenever you say. Tomorrow, if you wish. But I must ask you this: let me stay in my home until I am sure that all is well, there."

Mr. Wilkins never wrote anything on paper. He knew the dangers too well. But he sent a discreet and anonymous messenger to Messieurs Hastings and Brogan to call upon him at his home on Monday evening, on a matter of grave importance. They would understand, said the messenger, that no one was to be taken into confidence about the matter.

CHAPTER 44

AFTER the messenger had gone, Rufus Hastings and Patrick Brogan looked at each other in a long and peculiar silence. The dun and haughty Rufus' eyes were glinting green slits, and there were streaks of scarlet on his sharp and sallow cheek-bones. But Patrick faintly smiled, and smoked one of his strong cheroots. He knew that Rufus expected him to make a voluble comment, while he kept his own thoughts to himself.

Rufus opened his cruel slash of a mouth, and a nerve in his cheek twitched.

"Well?" he was goaded to say, with impatience.

Patrick laughed gently. His little eyes, so cunning and bright vivid blue, sparkled mirthfully. "Well?" he repeated. "You, of course, expected something like this would happen, eventually?"

But Rufus refused to answer this. He frowned, tapped his lean fingers on his desk, and pretended to give the matter great thought. "What the hell can he want?" he muttered.

Patrick, however, was not deceived. Rufus was a fox. Indeed, there was a foxlike look about him, from his thin straight hair with the tawny streaks in it, to his long sharp nose and sinuous length of body. Patrick understood all about foxes. They doubled on their tracks. They feinted and twisted.

Rufus sat up at length with an air of reluctant decision. "It can't be important. I don't think it necessary for both of us to go, do you? After all, the old codger is getting ancient. He's probably worried about his investments, now that our dear Papa-in-law comes less and less to the offices, and looks more like complete disintegration every day. One of us is sufficient to reassure him, I think." He picked up a sheaf of papers and frowned at it. "The Blue Crescent Line is doing very well," he continued, with interest.

"It ought to do," said Patrick, with his easy Irish affability. "It's now the sole line engaged in gun-running to Japan. One of these days all that ammunition is going to explode in the face of Europe."

His smile became broader. He arose with his lazy grace, which was pronounced despite the bulk of his handsome body. "Well, apparently you're right. No use both of us going. I'll run over to his house this evening, and see what the old devil wants."

Rufus still studied the papers in his hand. He frowned in concentration. He spoke in an abstracted tone: "Yes. You go, Pat." Then he dropped the papers, and sighed. "But he asked both of us, didn't he? So, I presume I ought to go, too."

Patrick smiled so broadly that his big white teeth glittered in the autumn sunshine that streamed through the windows.

"As if you'd let me go alone," he said, in his rich and affectionate voice. He touched his forehead in a mocking salute, and strolled gracefully out of the office, returning to his own. Rufus looked after him with a deadly expression in his eyes. His fingers resumed their devil's tattoo on the desk, and now that he was alone he made no further pretense of being absorbed in the reports of the Blue Crescent Line. The air about him seemed to congeal, to become static with its own intensity, as he stared fixedly at the door through which Patrick had disappeared.

That night the two worthy young men strolled amiably together to Mr. Bob Wilkins' pleasant little house. They did not mention that sunny gentleman, nor his probable conversation with them. They commented, rather, on the condition of John Turnbull.

"There's no doubt he's desperately ill," said Patrick. "It's my opinion he's going mad. Have you noticed his eyes lately? Like balls of fire, sunk deep in his skull. He scarcely touches his plate at dinner. But how he can drink! I'm an Irishman, but he could put me under the table any night. And what a confounded temper he's developing. He runs from maudlin to furious, to wild accusations of everybody, to threats, then to cajolings. Dr. Conway is seriously disturbed, Lavinia says."

"He's neglecting the business, too," replied Rufus. "It's practically all in our hands now."

"Not that we object," commented Patrick, lightly.

Rufus shook his head. "I'm not so sure of that, Pat. It's too much responsibility. We're hamstrung when it comes to decisions. But he'll give us no authority. There's a cunning streak in the Old Man. You'd think he'd have more trust in us."

"Wouldn't you, though?" replied Patrick, with a grin.

"I object to your tone," said Rufus, with injured severity. "It's true that I am first vice-president, and you are secretary and treasurer. But they're empty titles, at the best. Look at what the enterprises have lost this past year. It's appalling, really it is. Now, had we the proper authority, instead of resounding titles, that could have been prevented. It's infuriating for us to have to stand by and watch the decay of the enterprises solely because the Old Man keeps the final decisions in his own hands. Have you seen the pile of papers on his desk? Vital decisions, needing his signatures. The dust gathers thicker on them every day."

He continued, with a note of thin irony: "It's an impossible situation! I've long thought of resigning and going in with my father. I'm not a child. If Turnbull continues to distrust me, I shall throw up everything."

Like hell you will, thought Patrick, mirthfully. But he matched Rufus' tone with a serious one of his own: "You are quite right, of course. After all, the enterprises will eventually fall into our hands, when he dies. It is only his cursed egotism and suspicion of everybody and his desire to keep everything under his own thumb which prevent him from letting us take the whole load of responsibility. Now, I've got some mighty fine ideas of my own, but I won't advance them unless there is something in it for me."

"Have you indeed?" said Rufus, with friendly interest. "We're in this together, Pat. Let's have a little talk to-morrow."

Patrick could hardly restrain his laughter. But he replied in an ingenuous voice: "I may tell you, at that. I'm sure you will consider them remarkable."

Rufus was not in the least demonstrative, but now he linked his arm in Patrick's in the most confidential manner imaginable. Patrick felt a faint thrill of disgust, for all his amusement. This sly sinewy fox, this dexterous doubler, this poisonous twisting bastard! Now, he, Patrick, had no objection to opportunism, to exigency, to exploitation. These were all necessary to business. A man had to compete with a world of wolves, and Patrick Brogan was quite a hardy wolf himself. But he liked to meet fellow wolves on an open battlefield, to tear and rend in equal and exhilarating combat, with loud howls of exultation and joy. But Rufus, he reflected, was not like this. He preferred the stealthy and lethal approach, the fawning and grinning, the soft touch, the gentle treacherous word A foul yellow hypocrite. It was loathsome to Patrick Brogan to pretend sweet friendship the while the knife was inserted.

It enraged him that Rufus was John's favourite, and for no other reason than that Rufus deferred to the sick man, treated him with exquisite respect, listened to him with rapt and serious attention, gave way before him courteously. But Patrick's harsh sense of humour, ribald smiles, combative temperament, sudden furies and quick rages, and, moreover, his race and religion, did not endear him to John. Patrick's only advantage over Rufus was his ability to make John laugh. In truth, the only time John laughed these strange and darkly confused days of his, was when Patrick induced him to do so. Even that was rare. John's silences were becoming blacker and more dangerous as the months passed, and sometimes he appeared quite beside himself. Patrick's gay blandishments were met with increasing resistance and with red and sombre looks. But Rufus soothed him, placated and eased him.

The man's a fool, thought Patrick, with hot disgust and rage. If he had the wit of an imbecile he'd know what Rufe is up to, and how the fox hates him. Now, I don't hate him. I pity him. He's been a fine figure of a man but he's full of holes and fissures now. I could be his friend. But I'm prevented from that by the plottings of this suave and yellow thief, this gentlemanly bastard.

He shrugged in the darkness, as he walked beside his brother-in-law, and his handsome merry face, so coarse and thick, blackened with disgust.

I've got to keep my end up, he thought, much as it makes me want to puke. I've got to be ruthless, and ruthlessness sits badly on an Irishman. We prefer a bout with the shilallah, and then shake hands all around and have a drink. He knew he had the full and robust capacity for wickedness and plotting. But he knew, simply, that he was not evil.

They came to Mr. Wilkins' house, the windows streaming with yellow light, the white door gleaming in the light of the street-lamps, the brass knocker shining like gold. They were admitted by the ancient crone of a housekeeper, and conducted into the pleasant living room where Mr. Wilkins awaited them near the fire. Everything was in simple and beguiling chintzes, and all exposed wood was polished to extreme brightness. On a table near Mr. Wilkins reposed decanters of whiskey and bottles of soda. He rose when his young guests entered, beaming upon them with delighted affability, and extending both his fat rosy hands to them.

"Excellent! Excellent!" he exclaimed. "It does me old heart good to see young faces abaht! That it does. It was kind of you young chaps to visit an old codger like me."

He implied, in every tone and gesture and radiant expression, that the gentlemen had paid an unexpected call upon him, for which he was artlessly grateful. He flurried about them, drawing comfortable chairs to the fire, adjusting lamps for better light, dashing whiskey and soda into glittering crystal glasses. The bright gay curtains were now drawn over the windows. Mr. Wilkins bustled with exclamations of delight and pleasure and hospitality. The fire danced in its grate. Everything was excessively cosy.

Mr. Wilkins seated himself on the edge of a blue wing-chair and rested his hands on his fat knees. His large bald head, so pink and still so unwrinkled, shone in the lamplight with moisture. His face was crimson with his recent exertions. There was scarcely a line on its genial and cherubic expanse. He regarded his guests with fond excitement and paternal affection. Patrick momentarily expected him to clap his hands together in an excess of childish ecstasy at this call upon him by his dear young friends. The hazel eyes, so glassy, so protuberant, and so opaque, were luminous with the sweetest and brightest of expressions. His plump thighs strained against the sleekness of his brown broadcloth pantaloons;

across his round belly the thick links of his gold watch-chain were quite agitated. Over the stiff linen of his high collar three rosy moist chins spilled, the first deeply dimpled. He was in his middle sixties now, yet he appeared ageless.

He refilled his guests' glasses, and talked happily of inconsequential things. With deep interest, he inquired as to the health of the gentlemen's ladies, and listened to their replies as if they were of momentous importance. He expressed his artless delight that Rufus was soon to become a father, and winked at that young man archly, wagging one index finger as if Rufus had accomplished something unusual and delicious, but just slightly naughty. When Patrick expressed his own hopes, Mr. Wilkins could hardly contain himself for rapture. He clapped his hands over and over, rolling his eyes, and then slapping his hands vigorously on his knees, rocking himself back and forth on the edge of his chair, to the imminent danger of finding himself on the floor.

Then his face sobered dramatically, and with a kind of tragedy. He brought out a large white kerchief, and mopped his brow and eyes. From behind the thick folds his voice came, deep and sombre:

"Ah, I shouldn't be envious, that I shouldn't. It's not in me to complain against the decrees of Providence. Wot's to be will be, 'as always been my motto. Not that it don't pain this old heart of mine, and set me to wonderin' just what Providence 'ad in mind for me to do, to replace wife and little ones in me arms."

Patrick turned a ribald grimace upon Rufus, who replied with one of his sedate and expressionless winks.

Mr. Wilkins removed the handkerchief, replaced it, with heavy sighs, in his pocket, then assumed a brave and shining expression of renunciation and resigned sweetness. He straightened himself in his chair, like a gallant old soldier who has told himself that he must not bewail his fate, and then turns his face nobly and with fortitude to the arid future. It was extremely touching.

Then, he allowed his expression to become sad and thoughtful again. He passed his hand over his eyes, then left it there, shading those orbs as if what he was about to say pained him beyond endurance.

"Gentlemen, you must wonder why I've sent for you, and wot I've got to say. You must understand that it's a painful task, just. Not wot I'd 'oped would 'ave to happen. But one must face one's duty, is my motto. Allus face duty, brave like and unflinchin'."

Patrick again exchanged a quick look with Rufus, who idly turned his glass in hs prehensile fingers.

"Gentlemen," resumed Mr. Wilkins, in a louder voice with

a note of desperation, "I'm not one to shirk. Not Bob Wilkins. But I'm an old man now. Tired and worn like. Weary in the shafts. I've done me work, and all I wants now is peace and contentment. It's little enough for a life of struggle, you'll agree with me. But it seems like it's not to be."

The young men eyed him with alert respect and commendable attention. But Mr. Wilkins kept his eyes dolorously hidden. His fat rotund body slumped in the chair. He seemed overcome with exhaustion and sorrow.

"It's 'ard," sighed Mr. Wilkins, " 'ard to see the efforts of a lifetime come to nothing. Labourin' in the vineyard in the hot sun, and then seeing the wine poured out just when a chap's old lips reaches for it. That's Bob Wilkins, today."

"Surely not, sir," said Patrick, in a tone of rich and concerned sympathy. "It's not as bad as that."

Mr. Wilkins looked at him with simple and dignified despair. "It is, indeed, Mr. Brogan. I'm not one as complains unjustly. You'll grant me, gentlemen, that I've been Mr. Turnbull's benefactor, his friend, his power behind the throne, if I may be allowed to say it."

His Nemesis more likely, thought Patrick, with some grimness.

But he nodded gravely, as did Rufus.

"Wot I've done for that gentleman!" exclaimed Mr. Wilkins, rolling his eyes and throwing up his hands in eloquent despair. "No word can tell. I lifted him from nothing. I put him in the way of making his fortun. Now, it's not that he's ungrateful. Don't misquote me or misunderstand me. That would be unfair like. But, I've got a proper pride, gentlemen. I'm one as likes to see the edifice he's built stand up against all the storms of fate and bad fortun. Too, bein' human, I like the satisfaction of just deserts. No one can deny that I've got just deserts comin' to me.

"And then, just as I thinks me weary old bones can rest, wot happens? Mr. Turnbull goes into a decline. He becomes ill. Not just ill in body, you see. But ill in his mind. Things begin to go to pot. I 'ad an income from his firm and his subsidiaries that brought me in a tidy fifty thousand a year, clear. But wot've I got last year? A bare ten thousand. And things goin' steadily from bad to worse. This year, I don't expect five thousand. Gentlemen, I ask you, is that fair after a lifetime of devotion and service to Mr. Turnbull?"

The young men were silent. But they fixed their eyes sharply upon Mr. Wilkins.

"You don't condemn me, gentlemen?" pleaded Mr. Wilkins, with great pathos, and extending his hands to them. "There may be old panic in me. But I was never one as shut his eyes to facts. I know my business affairs. I've talked to

Mr. Jay Regan. He tells me things are very serious indeed."

"We know that only too well," said Rufus, quietly. "In fact, Patrick and I have discussed the matter thoroughly. But, what can we do? Mr. Turnbull keeps all power and authority in his own hands. We have titles, but they are empty ones. He reserves all decisions to himself, signs all matters of importance. Perhaps, Mr. Wilkins, you have something to suggest? If fame speaks rightly, you aren't the kind to sit back and watch ruin overcome you. You aren't without resources." And he smiled intimately at Mr. Wilkins.

Patrick satup slowly but alertly. He looked from Rufus to Mr. Wilkins. There was a sharp blue light in his small and cunning eyes.

And now Mr. Wilkins was silent. He smiled sweetly and sadly. But in his own eyes there was a brilliant point deep within their hazel recesses. The air grew tense. The young men expected some observation from Mr. Wilkins that would immeasurably excite them.

But Mr. Wilkins slowly allowed his expression to become heavy with sympathy and indignation as he regarded them. "I've talked to Johnnie, serious like, as an old friend. 'Johnnie,' I've said, 'those lads of yours are fine young chaps. Trust 'em. Let 'em take over. Relieve you of burdens. After all, they are your nateral heirs. You can't deny that. You've worked 'ard. You're in your forties. Men as works as 'ard as you've done deserves rest. Retire. Before things go to ruin. Trust the lads.' And wot do you think he answered, roaring like, a lion: "I'll 'ave no part in their foolishness! The business's mine. I'll keep me 'and on the rudder until I drop. That's my final word.' " He paused, and gazed at Patrick and Rufus in final despair.

Now neither Patrick nor Rufus believed a single word of this. But they pretended that they did, and shook their heads sombrely. They felt a thrill of excitement rush over them.

He knows we know he's lying, thought Patrick. Damn it, why all this play-acting, this skirmishing? Let him come to the damn point.

"So," ended Mr. Wilkins, "wot was I to do? I've racked my brains. Finally, it come to me. It's the only thing I can do. I've got to take you lads into my confidence, and suggest things. Or, we're all done in."

What the hell is he up to? thought Patrick, knitting his thick black brows. He's got millions tucked away. He can't really be upset about his picayune fifty thousand a year. He's got something else up his sleeve. I think I see part of it. He wants to ruin the Old Man. Why?

Rufus was speaking. "Mr. Wilkins, talk to us freely. We're

with you." And he glanced at Patrick soberly. But the eye turned nearest to Patrick winked again.

Mr. Wilkins looked down. He slowly pressed the palms of his hands together. He spoke in a low voice:

"This is breakin' me 'art, gentlemen. But it's no time for personal feelin's. You'll grant me that."

He drew a deep breath, and looked at the young men with stern resolution.

"First of all, Johnnie's very close to our 'arts. His welfare touches us. We can't look at him, the way he is these days, without pangs. Can we? He's got to get away. He's got to take a journey. Out of New York. To quiet spots, on ships. For a long time. Your ladies, gentlemen, as is lovin' daughters to Johnnie, can persuade him. He is breakin' their 'arts. They can't sleep of nights, worryin' about him. Wot'll they do without their dear Papa, if he dies off and leaves 'em alone in the world? 'Aven't they always adored him like? He's got to go away for a time, for their sakes. They demands it."

"Lavinia," said Rufus, in a deep and worried tone, "has spoken of this often, to me. She is very grieved. It isn't the best thing in the world for a lady in her condition to worry so excessively about any one. I shall surely speak to Lavinia."

"And I," said Patrick, "shall speak to Louisa. She, too, is very concerned." He could not look at Rufus, or he would have burst out into ribald laughter.

Mr. Wilkins was beaming again, his eyes suffused tenderly. "Ah, I can see what good 'arts and understandin' you gentlemen have! You'll do this for Johnnie. He'll come back, right as rain. He won't get ill again. You'll have taken on all the responsibility."

Again, there was a sudden pregnant silence in the warm and pleasant room. Rufus and Patrick sat as still as statues. But there were streaks of rough red on Rufus' sallow cheekbones. Patrick's eyes were so narrowed that they could not be seen.

"But how?" asked Rufus, very softly, at last. His lean veined hands clenched on the arms of his chair.

Mr. Wilkins regarded him fixedly. "Easy enough," he said. He was smiling now. And now he was a fat and rotund and very evil Buddha, smiling out from the recesses of his dark and devious mind.

He spoke in a thin and shrilling whisper, leaning towards the young men:

"I've kept up with matters. You two have large blocks of stock in Johnnie's firm and subsidiares. Very large. Your ladies have received them from their Papa, for birthday and

Christmas and other presents. Very large blocks. Makin' up to thirty percent of the stock. That is correct, ain't it?"

Patrick did not move. But Rufus nodded carefully.

"And I," continued Mr. Wilkins, "have another thirty percent."

He paused. Rufus and Patrick sat immobile. The veins sprang out more sharply on Rufus' gripping hands. Patrick's face was tense and white.

"Sixty percent all together," said Mr. Wilkins, in a soft and loving voice. "And Jay Regan has another ten. Seventy percent. Think wot that means, gentlemen."

But the young men did not speak.

"You'll get Johnnie away," said Mr. Wilkins, so softly, so balefully. "But before he goes, you'll get 'im to give you, Mr. Rufus, power of attorney, with all actions to be approved by Mr. Patrick. You'll negotiate, then, in your own names. Wilkins is behind you. Regan is behind you. You'll begin to buy in the open market, too." He looked from one to the other, and laughed gently. His tongue thrust itself out and lapped his fat under lip, and his eyes were swimming with evil laughter.

"You two gentlemen will enter into a secret partnership agreement. Then, you've got things by the tail, and swingin' them."

"You mean," said Rufus, almost inaudibly, "that you'll throw your shares in with us?"

"Exactly," beamed Mr. Wilkins, with an artless look.

Rufus and Patrick looked at each for a long time, while Mr. Wilkins watched them with ecstatic cunning. He had not underestimated them.

Patrick had to clear his throat several times before he could speak, and then his voice was thick and hoarse. "You know what that means, Mr. Wilkins? Mr. Turnbull will be out. For all time. Completely done in. Everything he possesses is in his companies. He'll have nothing left. Is that what you want?"

Mr. Wilkins leaned back in his chair, and folded his hands placidly on his round belly. He looked from Rufus to Patrick very slowly, and his eyes were shining with malefic radiance.

"That's wot you gentlemen want, ain't it?" he asked, tenderly.

Rufus smiled slightly. His malignant expression was equal to Mr. Wilkins'. "I wouldn't mind," he said, easily. "I've always hated him. He's a fool. Without you, sir, he'd have gotten nothing. He's had a handsome life, with your help. It's enough for a man."

But Patrick's face turned black and heavy, the ruddy folds thickening and swelling. His big meaty fists clenched.

"Wait a moment," he said, with ominous quiet. "I've got a word to say. It's not going to be that bad, for the Old Man. I'm not a complete snake. I want to do this with you, Rufus, and with you, Mr. Wilkins. I'll do it. But the Old Man is going to have a nominal income. I'll insist on that."

Mr. Wilkins exchanged a subtle wink with Rufus. He turned to Patrick. He shook his head slowly and ponderously. Now his look was lethal, and Patrick saw all his Satanic wickedness, open and unembarrassed.

"Mr. Patrick, I commends your sentiments. But I've got a word to say abaht this. You'll go all the way with me, or none of the way. That's my final word." He shrugged. "Of course, I'm not one to interfere with private arrangements, Mr. Patrick. You can spare Johnnie somethin' from your own pocket. I won't interfere."

Patrick sank back into black silence, gnawing his under lip savagely. Rufus gave him a bland and amused look, then said to Mr. Wilkins:

"Of course, you have something in mind for yourself? You aren't going to be so magnificently generous without some personal gain?"

"Certainly not," said Mr. Wilkins, simply. " 'Aven't I told you that I've got to protect myself? I'm an old man, now." He paused, then continued: "This is my first and final suggestion. Take it or leave it, gentlemen. I demands sixty thousand a year clear for meself, and thirty-five thousand a year for Miss Adelaide Turnbull. For Miss Adelaide, as is my goddaughter."

Had the room suddenly dissolved into fire and smoke, and had Mr. Wilkins suddenly emerged, dancing in flames in accordance with his true character, the two young men could not have been more astounded, more taken aback, more shaken and confused. They gazed at him with distended eyes and gaping mouths. There was a long and ringing silence in the room, in which the dropping of the coals in the grate could be heard distinctly, and the whisper of autumn leaves drily rustling on the window sills.

Then all at once Patrick burst into a shout of wild laughter. He bent almost double, shaking his black head until his thick dark waves of hair were greatly agitated. But Rufus sat, pale and frozen, in his chair, and tried to stare Mr. Wilkins down.

"Little Addy!" shouted Patrick. "Holy Mother! So, that's it!"

Rufus was white with rage and hatred. But Patrick was

393

convulsed with his obscene delight. He threw himself back in his chair, stretched out his legs and literally screamed with rapture.

"That's impossible, of course," said Rufus, ignoring his obstreperous brother-in-law's immense laughter. He spoke with a slight dry gasp. "Sixty thousand a year clear for you, Mr. Wilkins. That is reasonable. But not thirty-five thousand for that—that livid little monster. We'll go further with you. Make it seventy-five thousand for you. You can't refuse that."

Mr. Wilkins slowly clasped his hands again. His expression was grave and thoughtful. "Miss Adelaide is my goddaughter," he repeated, in a sorrowful tone. "It's thirty-five thousand for her, me lads. Or nothing for either of you. You can't do nothin' without me. I've got the upper hand. It's time to be frank. You'll do as I say, or go about your business."

Now he smiled sweetly. "And don't think you'll act on my suggestions and get power of authority from Johnnie on your own. I'll spike that. I'll go to Johnnie tomorrow and tell 'im the whole plot. Where'll you be, then?" He shook his head gently. He continued in the most benign tone, as if the two young men were beloved sons. "Don't think I won't do it. I will. You'll never get the upper hand of Johnnie, then."

Patrick was choking and coughing violently, as he tried to control himself. He attempted to speak, but his voice was a dwindled squeal. He finally gave up, and gave himself up to raucous peals of mirth, throwing himself about in his chair. But Rufus still looked at Mr. Wilkins with helpless malignance.

Mr. Wilkins rose, and went to a chest of drawers near by, and withdrew from it a long page of foolscap. He returned to his chair, and eyed the printed characters on it with great love.

"It's all here," he said. "The whole agreement between you gentlemen and meself. Written out clear like. To the last item. You'll sign it tonight. Then I'll tuck it away where it'll be all cosy and safe. Not to be used unless necessary." He looked at Rufus with sweet meaning. "And you'll not go back on your agreement. Not one inch. Or Johnnie sees the paper."

Patrick found his voice. He cried out with a squeaking sound: "Mr. Wilkins, don't tell me that you don't trust us! You're breaking our damned hearts!"

Mr. Wilkins regarded him thoughtfully. "Mr. Patrick," he said, in a meaning voice, "I've operated on one principle in me life: 'Trust no one. Signed and sealed, only.' And I've never found reason to doubt my judgment."

Rufus compressed his white lips. His eyes were a bitter green gleam. He held out a steady hand. "We'll sign it," he said.

"That's the ticket, lads!" cried Mr. Wilkins, jovially, rising with great alertness to get pen and ink. "I'm one as likes to do business with sensible men."

He dipped the pen in the ink. Rufus took it. With steady fingers he signed the agreement, after glancing briefly at the contents of the paper. Patrick watched him, silent now, but with open grinning mouth.

Then Rufus extended the pen to Patrick. Patrick stared at it, then at his brother-in-law's haggard and malevolent face, so fixed and deadly. He seemed about to burst into laughter again, but controlled himself. Shaking his head from side to side, he signed the paper.

The business done, Mr. Wilkins suggested, with fine and exuberant ardour, that they all " 'ave a drink on it!"

Rufus accepted, but drank steadily in sullen and brooding silence. But Patrick drank wildly, laughing with great violence quite frequently. As for Mr. Wilkins, he sipped at his glass, beaming on each of them impartially.

It was almost midnight before they left him. He closed the door softly after them. Then he slipped silently to a window, and looked after them until the darkness of the night obliterated their figures.

Then he shook with lewd and silent laughter, his tongue lapping his lips. He performed a brief hornpipe with an agility remarkable for his age. Once or twice he paused to shake his fist exultantly at the ceiling. And in those moments his large pink face was quite frightful to see.

CHAPTER 45

ON THE morning of this, her wedding day, Adelaide awoke with a strange disoriented sensation, confused and aching. There was a beating pain in her head, which her throbbing heart choroused, and a nameless malaise in her body impelling listlessness and yet, a feverish excitement. The excitement mounted as she came to full consciousness in her bed, so that all her flesh seemed incandescent with heat; her head swam alarmingly. When she looked in her mirror, she was vaguely alarmed to see the dull scarlet in her cheeks.

Her eyes were sunken and heavy, with dark and graven lines under them. She put icy hands to hot forehead, and then had to press those hands quickly on the back of her chair to keep herself from falling in a wave of giddiness. Now the malaise was stronger. She alternately shivered with paralyzing cold and burned with fever. Did all these symptoms assail every bride? she wondered.

She was sick with fear and dread, also, and these almost overcame the brief and vivid ecstasy that occasionally flooded her. She determined not to think, only to act. Later, there was enough time for thought and plan.

She could eat nothing of her breakfast but some hot tea. Her body was one long tremor in the quite brown broadcloth frock and jacket in which she had dressed herself. A dreamlike thought floated through her mind: later, she would slip out to the greenhouse and clip enough blossoms for a nosegay for her jacket. The still dining-room floated in vague shadow. Outside, torrents of spring rain dashed themselves like cataracts against the windows. Adelaide ate alone. Her parents had not yet come down to breakfast. Her sisters would have trays later in their own apartments. It was Adelaide's duty to carry the tray to Lavinia and Louisa, for neither would presume to ask their French maids to do this homely duty, and there was a household feud below stairs between the house servants and those elegant young ladies who served the Mesdames Hastings and Brogan.

The cook, herself, stout, short and florid, brought in Lavinia's tray to the dining-room and plumped it down irately near Adelaide, who was holding her tea cup in a trembling hand. Adelaide was a great favourite with Mrs. Courtney, who declared, in the kitchen, that it was a "sickening sin and shame" that the girl had to wait upon her sisters like a common servant.

Adelaide looked at the tray of hearty breakfast, and had to grip the edge of the table to hold back a plunge of nausea that seized her stomach. The odours of hot fresh rolls, strips of bacon, two eggs, oatmeal and coffee made her violently ill. She closed her eyes.

"Miss Lavinia's," said Mrs. Courtney, regarding the breakfast with a grim eye, as if she would have liked to have included ground glass among the viands. "And how a lady that's soon to have a baby can eat all those victuals's beyond me."

Adelaide compressed her lips as she endeavoured to control her physical sensations. Then she rose and took up the heavy clanking tray and climbed the stairs to Lavinia's apartments. She found Lavinia lolling luxuriously in bed, yawning over a yellow-backed French novel, while her maid lovingly brushed and combed the thick black curls. Lavinia, dressed in a beribboned and belaced cambric gown, was a handsome sight on her ruffled pillows. A fire had been lit against the chill of the wet spring morning. The curtains were looped back to show the wide quiet stretch of the drenched avenue.

Lavinia smiled with eager pleasure as the fragrance of her breakfast was wafted to her. She stared at it avidly the while Adelaide disposed it on her knees. The maid deftly straightened silken sheet, plumped up the pillows. Then Lavinia became aware that there was something strange about her sister. She buttered a roll thickly and stuffed part of it in her mouth. Then she widened her large black eyes at Adelaide.

"What!" she exclaimed, her articulation somewhat impeded by the buttered roll. "You're dressed up. You don't intend to go out this morning, do you?"

"Yes," said Adelaide, briefly, turning away.

"But you can't," remarked Lavinia, crossly. "You promised to finish putting the lace on the christening dress. Besides, there is so much mending to do. You really can't go, Addy, so you might as well take off those clothes."

Adelaide had turned back a moment, near the door. Now Lavinia saw her feverish face and dull sunken eyes. She sat up, the better to scrutinize her sister.

"What's the matter with you?" she demanded. "You look ill."

Adelaide pressed the back of her cold hand against her burning cheek. "I'm not too well this morning," she admitted.

Lavinia scowled. "Good God. I hope you aren't sickening for something, Addy. With the baby soon coming, and everything. Dr. Burney will be here presently. He'd better see you, so he can reassure me."

"I'm not sickening," answered Adelaide, curtly. She drew a deep breath. Her heart was a fixed knife in her chest.

She closed the door after her, went downstairs again for Louisa's tray, a more dainty affair, and less heavy. Nevertheless, by the time Adelaide had reached Louisa's apartments, she was drenched in cold sweat, and the smooth roll of her hair was wet near her neck.

Louisa's apartments were less flamboyant than Lavinia's, and in much better and more discreet taste. She sat on a chaise longue near the window, a vision in floating white lace and yellow flowing hair. A small fire burned on the marble hearth. The maid puttered about, rearranging flowers in jade green bowls, and smoothing the white, lace-hung poster bed.

Louisa smiled with languid sweetness at her sister, and thanked her graciously for the tray. She inspected the coffee, rolls and marmalade which composed her breakfast, poured cream and sugar into the cup. Then she, too, noticed Adelaide's strangeness.

"An errand?" she murmured. "On such a morning? What a shame. I suppose Linny's forgotten something as usual. Will you be long? I wanted to use Mama's victoria. Are you using it?"

"No," said Adelaide, moving towards the door.

"Do wait, darling," said Louisa. "While you are out, will you stop at Britton's and get me a box of those candied fruits? I simply crave them all the time."

"Yes," answered Adelaide.

"Are you ill?" asked Louisa, with sudden sharpness, like an acid under the honey of her voice. "You look very peculiar, Adelaide. And there's so much typhoid about. You have quite a fever, it appears."

"I'm not ill," said Adelaide, with bitterness. She turned at the door and looked at her sister with wide dark eyes full of contempt and pain. For a long moment the two young women regarded each other across the dainty expanse of the room. Louisa's blue eyes narrowed with cunning acuteness. She tapped her lips with a white finger.

"Well, you are certainly not yourself, Adelaide," she said. She paused. "On second thought, please don't go out. There is my nightgown to finish, and I do wish the baby's blankets to be completed with that satin ribbon. No, you really must not go out."

The bitterness and hatred swelled in Adelaide's heart. She came closer to her sister, and her eyes were no longer dull, but were flashing with fire.

"I suppose it never occurs to either of you that I might have errands of my own to do," she said, in a quick and breathless voice. "It never occurs to you that I'm not your slave, not your hired servant. I am going out. What I have to do is no concern of yours."

Again, there was silence in the room. Then Louisa smiled gently.

"Do forgive me, dearest," she said, in her sweet and contrite tone which she could use so effectively on occasion. "I am so thoughtless. You are quite right. I was only just a little worried because you appeared slightly ill, and it is no morning for one to be out who might be coming down with a cold or chill. Won't you wear my furs over your jacket? Please?"

But Adelaide did not reply. She swung about and left the room.

By the time she had reached the lower hall she was swaying, and there were dark floating clouds of mist before her eyes. She put on her bonnet and gloves, which she had left on a chair in readiness. She heard her father's step on the upper reaches of the stairs, and she turned and fled through a passageway to the kitchen. There was no time now to requisition a carriage. She snatched up Mrs. Courtney's umbrella in the kitchen closet, and stepped out into the areaway. The rain had now increased in violence. Adelaide hurried to the street, holding up her heavy brown skirts. Near the corner she found a hansom, and stepped into it. She sank back on the seat, trying to control the laboured pain of her breathing. Once or twice she coughed tightly, and at each cough she winced and shivered with cold. The drone of the rain on the roof and windows took on a nightmare quality. Long brown rivers of water washed down the avenue. There was hardly a soul about at this time, which was ten o'clock.

She reached a little gray church on Broadway, standing lonely and streaming in the rain. The door was open. And in the doorway stood Anthony, waiting and smiling. Despite the rain, he ran down the steps to meet her, and when he clasped her hands and looked down into her eyes, she forgot everything in the sudden brilliant rapture and joy which assailed her.

He led her into the church. As he did so, the lone organist struck up the wedding march. The long dolorous notes echoed against the simple groined roof, rolled back to meet the bride. The clergyman waited at the altar, stifling a yawn. There were two young men present, Anthony's friends.

Adelaide walked up to the altar with her groom, who was certainly committing a faux pas in not waiting for his bride decorously. But the girl did not mind. She saw nothing, felt nothing, but the pressure and strength of Anthony's hand and the slate-gray eyes fixed so comfortingly and tenderly upon her.

Then it was over. Adelaide faintly remembered words and questions, to which she answered. Then Anthony's lips were upon hers, and his arms were about her. She burst into inexplicable weeping, and clung to him. The new gold ring upon her finger was a circlet of fire.

In the meantime, two interesting conversations had taken place in the apartments of Louisa and Lavinia.

Rufus Hastings knew that with Lavinia he had to use the utmost tact and guile. She was not naturally suspicious of the motives of others. But he understood well enough that a straightforward suggestion to her of guile and treachery would infuriate her, would elicit nothing but her angry and tumultuous refusal. Now, he reflected, as he sat beside her bed and kissed her warm hand, if she only had the sense of Louisa, who understood everything, and had the subtlety to read the lift of an eyebrow and the lift of a shoulder. Too, there was a conscience hidden under all the noisy violence of Lavinia, and Rufus knew he dared not arouse it. He did not respect his young wife for this conscience, for the inconvenient scruples which she possessed. They only made him impatient, and contemptuous.

So, he began by sighing. Lavinia, none too subtle at the best, never saw what was to be seen until it was thrust directly before her eyes. So she finished up the last of her breakfast with hearty enjoyment, while Rufus increased the tempo of his sighing. Lavinia was feeling exceptionally well this morning, and when she finally discerned that Rufus was in a very low state of mind, her first emotion was impatient annoyance. It was just like Rufus to come in with a long face and spoil her pleasant morning.

"Do stop heaving like a winded horse, Rufe," she said, wiping her hands vigorously on her napkin. "What's the matter? Tell me. I don't like fatal looks, you know that."

Rufus took her hand again, and smoothed it tenderly, each finger separately. Then he looked up and fixed his green eyes upon her, and shook his head. But all this did not alarm Lavinia. She made a mouth of resigned irritation, and waited.

"Have you noticed how ill your dear Papa is these days?" he asked at last, just when she had reached the explosive point.

She gaped at him, scowling. Now she looked excessively like John, and, in spite of her anger, there was his own vulnerable appearance about her.

"Well, he certainly doesn't appear to be enjoying bounding health," she said, with ill-nature. "But one can't expect it. After all, he is in his forties, and that is quite elderly."

"It is more than that," said Rufus, with deep gravity. "I believe he suffers from some affection of the heart. There was my grandfather, you know. He had a similar appearance before his last illness. I might as well confess to you, my dear, that I am seriously concerned about your father. I have had a consultation with Burney. He agrees with me that your Papa needs a long rest, and that the most dangerous consequences might take place if that rest is too long delayed."

Lavinia knitted her thick black brows together and stared at her husband with gloomy anxiety. She started to say something, then bit her lip.

"Patrick and I have talked with your Papa, but he is adamant. He will not go away. He is suspicious, it seems, of us." He allowed himself a reflective and melancholy smile. "He thinks we plot, or something. He cannot conceive that we have only the deepest regard for him, and that our protestations that he must rest are genuine."

"Are they?" asked Lavinia, with that disconcerting bluntness of hers. "Rufe, I know you. You never really felt concern for anybody but yourself. I want the truth." She snatched her hand away from her husband, and threw herself back against her pillows. Her black eyes were sharp and narrowed points.

Rufus smiled boyishly. He rose. He walked to the window, then returned to the bed. He sat down again. "I will be frank with you, my love," he said.

"Impossible," murmured Lavinia, satirically.

Rufus ignored this. "As you know, we have access to all your Papa's affairs. We have discovered that he has not made the slightest outline of a will. We have suggested that he do this. He was quite violent when he advised us to mind our own business. This becomes serious when one remembers that your grandpapa's will specifically requires that in the event of your Papa's death the entire estate left to your Papa is to be divided equally among all his children.

"The money left to your Papa is now completely invested in your Papa's affairs. Now, suppose for a moment that your Papa does not take his necessary rest, and dies suddenly, and very soon. What then? Adelaide, whom we all know is a sly baggage and has nothing but hatred for all of us, can really ruin us if she decides—and well she might—to liquidate that part of her share of the estate invested in your Papa's enterprises and businesses. And I might as well tell you now, my pet, that such a demand on us by Adelaide would ruin us.

"Moreover, your dear Mama would have her share, her widow's dower. One-third of the estate. We all know that she is much under Adelaide's influence. Think, then, what it will mean if not only Adelaide demands liquidation of her share, but influences your Mama to do likewise. I can tell you frankly, that everything would collapse. You and Louisa would not inherit enough from the estate to save the businesses."

He straightened, and drew a deep breath. "Our only hope

is to prolong your Papa's life, and restore him to a state of mental and physical health in which he can reasonably be approached and his duty laid before him. At the present time it is hopeless to approach him with this thought. Therefore, I am asking you now, as his favourite daughter, to induce him to recuperate his health. You have two reasons: your natural affection for your father, and the danger in which we all stand."

Lavinia, though shrewdly doubting that her husband had told her the complete truth, nevertheless recognized the validity of his arguments. She was consumed by the deepest and most enraged anxiety. She muttered savagely under her breath, and Rufus heard the vicious mention of Adelaide's name.

Then she said aloud, in her noisy and hectoring voice: "It is a stinking mess. No wonder you are upset, Rufe. But what if he won't go? You know how obstinate Papa is at times."

Rufus, delighted at his success, stroked his wife's dark and vivid cheek.

"He can't resist you, my love. You have only to weep on his neck, and kiss him hysterically, and beg him to listen to reason. You know how he adores you. When he sees that his obstinacy is causing you such great distress, he will soften. For your sake, he will do as you ask. He can't help but be touched."

Lavinia regarded him in brooding and violent silence. Her face had flushed. Then she averted her eyes.

"I do love Papa," she muttered. "Even without the other— Oh, it is intolerable of Papa! It is odious! He must realize in what jeopardy he has placed us. Still, if it were only that I wouldn't bother." She dropped her eyelids. Her husband did not see the thick hot tears that threatened to run over her cheeks.

Rufus smiled secretly.

Now Patrick needed no such subtlety in his approach towards Louisa. (Rufus often wondered into what chaos the business would be plunged had fate been evil enough to have given Lavinia to Patrick as a wife. Their mutual dislike of the ultimate ruthlessness would have betrayed all of them into ruin. People who possessed a furtive generosity and humour could never deal the final murderous blow.)

Patrick came to his pretty and dainty wife, and kissed her with enthusiasm. He adored her immaculate fastidiousness, her graciousness, her apparent pliancy and exquisite manners. Nevertheless, as he looked at her this morning he felt a faint thrill of repellent dislike for her. He would not need, he reflected, to play on her affections for her father, for she had none. He need only talk to her bluntly and cynically, and she would laugh mellifluously and nod her golden head. For this, then, he felt a quite hot and inexplicable dislike.

He did not waste time, therefore, in Rufus' dramatics. He said, bluntly:

"Look here, my golden bird, I've got to talk to you. Straight. No beatings about the bush."

Louisa smiled at him sweetly, lifted his hand and placed it against her cool fresh cheek. As she did so, the lace dropped back from her arm, and showed it in all its dainty whiteness and smoothness. She was not unaware of the effect. Nor was she unaware, from Patrick's sudden frown, the sudden heaviness and surliness about his mouth, that he had come on serious business. She detected the uneasiness in him, the angry impatience against himself. Her smile was now hidden. She despised Patrick a little, for she knew there was a rotten spot of weakness in him, a soft spot of conscience. Her astuteness was so keen that she half guessed at what he was about to say.

"What gravity," she murmured. She leaned back against her cushions and regarded him with the blue luminosity of her eyes. Her golden hair framed her lovely face. It was an angel's face, rapt and innocent.

"It is grave," he said, and his dislike for her increased, for he knew that however brutal he might be, however despicable, she would not really care.

He said: "I want you to get your father away from the city for a long time. Frankly, he is ill. Burney has already told me that he needs a prolonged rest. If he doesn't the consequences can be quite terrible. Fatal."

The angel's face became meditative, with a curious sharpness about the faultless features, a curiously wizened tightness around the soft rosy mouth.

"And," she said, musically, "if he does die, that will leave us all in a very precarious state, won't it? With no will at all? I know all that. I know the conditions of grandpapa's will. I know Adelaide's influence on Mama. A quite dangerous influence. Yes, I see."

Patrick rose abruptly, with a really unreasonable gesture of disgust, considering that he ought to have been relieved by Louisa's acumen, which had spared him much uneasy maneuvering. He actually glared down at his pretty wife.

"Yes," he said, shortly. "That's it."

Louisa dropped the too revealing light of her blue eyes. She played with a ruffle of lace on her peignoir. Patrick was absurd, she reflected, with contemptuous amusement. He did not appreciate a clever wife. He really meant all sorts of skullduggery, cruelty and malignancy, and yet, because she did not fall into what he conceived was her proper attitude, because she would not pretend to female alarm over her father and perhaps swoon a little, daintily, he disliked her and resented her. What weak hypocrites gentlemen were, to be sure. They had their preconceived notions of feminine reactions, and if women were too clever, too honest, to carry out those notions, the gentlemen were quite annoyed. They seemed to think a female was hard if she were astute.

It was very tedious, but there was nothing to do but pretend, she reflected. So she lifted her lace handkerchief and put it to her eyes. She allowed her soft breast to become momentarily agitated. Seeing all this, a vast relief flooded Patrick. He sank down again on the edge of the chaise longue and put his arm about his wife.

"I'm sure that your Papa will recover his health completely, if he takes the recommended rest," he urged, elaborately consoling her. What a dear little thing it was, to be sure. How he had misjudged her. She was so delicate, so defenseless. He loved her passionately again.

She dropped her kerchief and looked at him radiantly through a freshet of adorable tears. She put her head on his shoulder.

"Dear Papa," she sighed, the music in her voice breaking effectively. "I really must persuade him to go away for a while. What should I do without him?"

Patrick pressed her to him with an ardour in which there was as much gratitude as love. And against the breadth of his handsome shoulder Louisa smiled. Had Patrick seen that smile he would surely have hated her.

CHAPTER 46

WHEN Adelaide returned, she climbed up the great stairway to her cramped and uncomfortable quarters where the servants lived. She had lost all ability to feel now, at least emotionally. She could experience only those sensations appertaining to her body, and these were all strangely and frighteningly painful and confused. The stairway stretched far before her, winding and curving like a stairway of mist and smoke, without end or beginning, and without substance. She could feel its tenuous webs of fog swaying under her feet. Her head roared, seemed to expand enormously, to contract to a pinpoint, all in a horrible rhythm. Moreover, a trembling weakness had laid hold of her legs, and a spinning emptiness whirled within her.

She had reached halfway to the top, when she halted, clutching the balustrade, and for the first time she said to herself, in fear: I am not just excited. I am ill.

She was quite overwhelmingly frightened, for she had never been truly ill before, and she had no memory of fortitude. Nor was she able to gauge how severe was her illness. She found herself sitting on the stairs with her head in her hands. She had removed her bonnet, and it lay on the step beside her. Because of the complete misery that was in and about her, she forgot everything, forgot the circlet on her finger and the withering nosegay on her bodice, and the fact that she had married Andrew Bollister only an hour ago.

Vaguely, as she sat there, she had a faint memory of his last words: "Only a little while, and then you come to me. Only a little while."

Now her head hummed and screamed the refrain, until it lost all meaning.

She did not know how much time had passed, but she came to herself with a shivering start. The day was dark; the wind and the rain had increased. She forced herself to her feet, her one desire to reach her bedroom and collapse upon the bed. She could see it before her, white and cool and quiet. Her flesh burned like fire. She heard herself sobbing heavily. She hungered for her bed with an almost savage desire.

She had reached the second floor when a door opened, and Lavinia's French maid, Eloise, accosted her with a superior expression. "Ah, there you are, Mamselle. Madame Hastings wishes you at once, in her sitting-room."

Then Adelaide, to her intense astonishment, said: "Please give Madame my compliments, and tell her to go to hell."

The girl's expression became so ludicrously blank and shocked at this remark that Adelaide began to laugh wildly. The girl stared at her, retreated a step. Adelaide's face, so white and so strange, with the spots of bright red colour on the cheek-bones, her eyes blazing with fever, was a most peculiar sight to Eloise, and a terrifying one. Her hair was damp and rumpled; the soft brown roll sprawled on her shoulders.

This is absurd, thought Adelaide. I must be mad. She controlled herself, and said in a hoarse weak voice: "Don't mind, Eloise. I'll be down directly."

Still controlling herself, gritting her teeth against the waves of faintness and giddiness that attacked her, she reached her own room. She looked at her face in the mirror. The room was dim, and the image cast back at her seemed entirely normal. But bubbles of laughter kept rising to her parched lips, so that she giggled senselessly. She changed her clothing to a frock of black silk, fastened the lace collar, and combed her hair. Then, glancing at her trembling hands, she saw the golden ring.

Her heart seemed to pause in its beating. Tears dazzled her eyes. She kissed the ring frantically, and something painful and yearning opened in her like a wound. "O Tony," she murmured, catching her breath. "O Tony, Tony," and now the tears were hot and scalding. There was such a sorrow and a pang in her breast, such a bitterness of longing and desire.

She removed the ring, placed it under a pile of her underclothing in the great chest between the windows. Then, drawing her courage and fortitude together with a truly physical effort, she went downstairs to her sister's sitting-room.

By the time she had reached the door, the shivering had subsided, the trembling had gone. Now her body was incandescent with heat, her mind preternaturally sharp and clear, so that the door, the door handle, the very carpet under her feet, the figures on the wallpaper, were so vivid, so imminent, that new fright took hold upon her. She seemed to float as she walked. She touched the molding of the door, and its substance seemed too solid, immovable to her. She wondered if she would have the strength to open the door.

When she entered Lavinia's sitting-room, she found her sisters and mother in what had apparently been a heated and tempestuous conversation. At least, Lavinia's bold beautiful face was black and violent, Lilybelle was in weak and copious tears, and Louisa's usually sweet calm expression betrayed impatient annoyance.

"Oh, there you are," said Lavinia, angrily. "What a sneak you are, Addy. Slipping off like an eel just when I need you most. Miss Gurtz could not come this morning, and the sewing is simply miles high. One can't rely upon any one these days. Do sit down and sort over those petticoats and chemises."

Lilybelle, upon seeing her dearest daughter, wept again, rocking back and forth on her ample haunches, and rubbing her eyes frenziedly with a ball of a handkerchief. She was never any match for her daughters, who cowed her ruthlessly. Her bright masses of hair were in disorder, and showed faded streaks and threads of gray, and she revealed a blotched and piteous face to Adelaide, who went to her instinctively.

Lilybelle clutched her with her big fat hands, and her large ripe mouth shook.

"Really, Adelaide, you are so inconsiderate," murmured Louisa, crossly, lifting her lovely blue eyes to her sister. "And we've so needed you, with Mama. Mama is being very difficult."

"You aren't surely asking Addy's opinion?" cried Lavinia, flinging herself back in her chair. "As if that counted, with Papa."

"Nevertheless," said Louisa, coolly, "she has some sort of underhanded influence with Mama."

The two young women regarded their sister without amiability. Louisa's regard became more intent. "I believe you are ill," she said, slowly, as if Adelaide had been guilty of some enormity. "How strange you look, Adelaide. Wild and feverish. Are you certain you are not sickening? I've thought you appeared to be going into a decline for some time." She shrank back from the girl to escape any infection.

"I am not ill," said Adelaide, hoarsely. She paused. "I've seen the doctor. He assures me I am perfectly well, though somewhat tired."

"Tired!" shrilled Lavinia, with a snorting laugh. "Why should you be tired? You are such a lazy minx, really you are. You do nothing at all. Now, if you were a married woman, in a certain condition, one would not wonder."

Lilybelle was weeping in Adelaide's arms. The girl forced herself to concentrate upon her mother, for the strangest things were happening to her. Voices, scenes, faces, all had a most disconcerting habit of retreating and advancing, of blurring and sharpening. She suppressed a cough.

"What have you been doing to Mama?" she asked, and now her burning eyes gleamed with anger. "Hush, Mama, dear, for just a minute." She stared at her sisters with a hard look.

When she wore such an aspect, even the bold Lavinia was quelled momentarily. She shrugged. "I suppose it is foolish to speak to you of it, Addy, but I can see no other way of bringing Mama to her senses. Papa is ill. Surely even you can see that? He needs a rest. His health is very bad. We've seen it for sometime. Now we've decided he and Mama must go away for awhile, at once. He must forget everything. Otherwise, there is no telling what will happen."

"I don't want to go away!" wailed Lilybelle. Her two elder daughters exchanged pent looks. "Mr. T. will refuse, I know he will. There's no use. He won't listen to me, even if I ask him."

"I've told you, we'll ask him, in fact, urge him, make demands," said Lavinia. "You have only to say nothing, Mama.

Do be reasonable. You make things so very hard."

Lilybelle struck her big heaving breast dramatically. "I have my feelin's, Linny. I've told you: I'm afraid to ask your Papa to go away. Something'll happen, mark my words."

"What nonsense," sighed Louisa. Her blue eyes sparkled with a narrow light. "You'll have to stand with us, Mama. Otherwise, there is no doubt you'll be a widow before long."

Adelaide listened to all this, looking intently from one face to another. Again, everything was preternaturally sharp and clear, as if magnified. Of course, it is my illness, she thought. But, she, too, had the strangest and darkest foreboding. Her heart had begun to beat heavily, like an ominous drum. Her ears were filled with its mounting and menacing sound. She caught a look passing between Lavinia and Louisa, a secret and cunning look, and in her condition it had something malefic about it.

A sick terror seized her. She saw her father as clearly as if he had stood before her, and it seemed to her that some terrible danger, some ruin and catastrophe, had thrown a black aura about him. Her fever rose to extreme heights, and, in its intoxication she appeared endowed with a second sight, lucid and frightful.

"You say Papa is ill," she said, and her voice seemed to echo throughout all the aching bones of her skull. "Who will take his place? Who will manage things for him? That must be considered, of course."

Lavinia started to speak, then, colouring heavily, was silent. But Louisa, the imperturbable and logical, looked steadily at her sister and said in a calm tone: "That can surely be arranged. Rufus and Patrick are quite competent to manage, I assure you."

Louisa had great control, but she could not prevent her blue eyes from glinting with amused evil as she regarded Adelaide, nor could she restrain the secret tightening of her pretty features.

Ah, thought Adelaide. The drum was pounding all about her. She saw in more than the three dimensions. Everything appeared to her sharpened as under lighted water.

"Have they said they could?" she asked, very quietly.

Louisa's delicate nostrils dilated, but it was Lavinia who answered with loud and hasty impatience. "Certainly, they've said they could! They understand everything. It was their idea, in the very beginning."

Louisa bestowed a look of real hatred and contempt upon Lavinia for this indiscretion, for, unlike Lavinia, she did not consider Adelaide a fool. That odious Lavinia, with her loose and dangerous tongue, her frank stupidity! She, herself, would have said hesitatingly: "Now, that is something we don't know. But it is our intention to urge them to consider the possibilities, when we assure them that Papa is ill." But that idiot of a Lavinia usually ruined everything.

In an effort to retrieve the situation, she said coldly: "Does it matter, really? What if things are not run so expertly while Papa is away? It is his health we must consider, Adelaide. You would realize that if you weren't so selfish, and so completely wrapped up in yourself. As a matter of fact, Rufus and Patrick are very doubtful, for Papa usually keeps things in his own hands. But we intend to persuade them to undertake the responsibilities in order to help Papa regain his health."

But the mischief had been done. Adelaide's face had become as still and pale as granite. Fever was running in fiery liquid through her veins. She spoke, and her voice was hard and clear.

"Since when have you and Linny ever considered Papa, except as a source of revenue? Since when have you cared what became of him? If he died, you and your husbands would be in an excellent situation. You must have considered that fully. You would, with the minds you possess. Why, then, all this solicitude, this eagerness to protect and preserve Papa?"

The young women exchanged swift looks. Lavinia was momentarily embarrassed, and, in consequence, was infuriated. She even appeared slightly ashamed. But Louisa, poised and restrained as always, mistress of herself as always, was not too disconcerted. The eyes she fixed on Adelaide were wicked and smooth and blue as stone.

"I may ask that of you, Adelaide: 'Why all this passionate running to Papa's defense?' You've never been—congenial, to speak as charitably as possible. You've never endeared yourself to Papa. Nor has Papa shown you any overpowering affection. We must look at things as honestly as possible. Our own feelings for Papa are surely more tender than yours, all things considered. As for your crude denunciations, I pass over them in silence. I do not care to discuss anything so absurd with you.

"You speak of our minds. I assure you they are cleaner than yours, and kinder. All your life, you have displayed an obstinacy and selfishness that are truly contemptible. You've never tried to ingratiate yourself with Papa, or to please him. You have done nothing but antagonize him with your stupid silences and your determination to have your own way. You have no graces whatsoever, either of person or of character. You are secretive and sly, and one never knows where he is with you. You annoy Papa at every turn, until he can't endure the sight of you." She paused. "We were foolish to discuss this matter with you in the first place."

Never before, in all her cool, sweet and gracious life had she used such calm and deadly words to any one. Lavinia, hearing them, cringed internally, then, very slowly, she felt a heat in her cheeks, a sick rage in her heart against her lovely sister. Lilybelle listened, and her vital organs felt squeezed to the suffocation point. But Louisa gazed tranquilly at Adelaide after these words, with such a bland and indifferent expression that it only enhanced the lethal quality of what she had said.

But Adelaide had always known. Her eyes did not drop away from Louisa's steadfast regard. Their brownness took on a molten golden quality, as if incandescent. The words had struck her like repeated dagger blows, and she felt a great aching anguish in her heart. But she did not look away from her sister.

"Now," she said, "we are out in the open, aren't we, Louisa? I've always known what you were. I've always known you were malevolent and without heart or goodness or charity. I've known you for a monster. You've smiled and simpered your way through life, deceiving honest people; but you've never deceived me. I've known all about you."

She drew a deep breath into lungs that felt aflame. Her voice grew stronger, even ringing.

"You've got to reckon with me, Louisa. I don't know all the plot, but I've guessed enough to realize it is a little terrible. Perhaps I can't do much. But I'll do what I can. Papa shall not go away and leave everything in your husbands' hands. Not if I can help it!"

"What plot!" cried Lavinia, pulling herself upright.

But neither Louisa nor Adelaide heard or noticed her. Their eyes were locked together in a hideous fixity. Then, very slowly, Louisa smiled. She lay back in her chair. Her lips curved in lovely meditation, without looking away from Adelaide.

"What can you do?" she asked, with honey sweetness, even tenderness. "Papa hates you, deservedly. What can you do, my darling sister? You are a liar, a sneak, a secretive and ugly thing. Do you think he would believe your ravings?

"Yes, I've suspected you weren't a fool. I think that is why I've hated you, my dear pet. But, I've the upper hand over you. You'll stand by. You can do nothing else."

Lilybelle, ashen with terror, gaped from one girl to the other. She blinked her eyes. She saw Adelaide beside her, straight and slight, with such a white fixed face and glowing eyes; she saw Louisa, serene and smiling, as lovely and tender as an angel. She began to whimper, deep in her fat throat.

But Lavinia also looked from one to the other. The heavy flush was darker than ever on her cheeks. Her thoughts were clamouring. She was sick with their import. She turned to Louisa.

"You are a filthy beast, Louisa," she said. "A foul and filthy wretch. I hate you."

Her voice was muffled, thick and confused. She struck her clenched fists repeatedly on the arms of her chair. Louisa turned to her, her pink and white face alight with malicious mirth.

"Dear Lavinia, are you championing Adelaide? How very surprising. Please don't be so absurd. You know how things are without any elaborating on my part. Do control yourself. I've told the truth to Adelaide for the first time in her life. I assure you it will do her good. She was becoming entirely too arrogant, and it is about time that she realized her position in this house."

"Her position is the same as ours!" bellowed Lavinia.

Louisa reached over and indulgently patted her sister's hands, with the most luminous affection. "My dear dear," she murmured. "Haven't we discussed all this? I really can't understand you, Linny. Only an hour ago you agreed with me. And here you are, all confused and dangerously excited, championing Adelaide against me, for something I can't understand. What have I done, except protect ourselves? You know very well how things would be, under certain other circumstances——"

Lavinia, swollen and scarlet, was silent. But her glittering black eyes were held by Louisa's in a kind of horrid and frightened hypnotism. Louisa smiled internally. How weak every one was, except herself! How stupid, confused, vacillating and contemptible! Only Rufus was equal to her. But Rufus, the fool, had preferred this imbecile of a Lavinia to herself, despite her efforts. What she and Rufus might not have accomplished together! She resolved to have a quiet talk with him that evening. They understood each other perfectly.

She saw the world as a herd of fat sheep, needing only a shepherd and a slaughterer. So few there were who were wise, clear-sighted and detached. These were the natural leaders, the natural manipulators, the inheritors of the earth. She saw herself as one of these supreme ones. She looked fleetly from her mother to Lavinia, and from Lavinia to Adelaide, so fragile, so straight, so silent, and with such burning eyes. All stupid, all idiots. The internal smile widened to

411

deep laughter.

If she were clever enough, in the future, she would have everything, and these fools would have nothing. To the wise belonged the spoils. Where money was concerned, no quarter should be granted.

She disliked the necessity for open combat, for vulgar struggle. She had long anticipated that some day she must face Adelaide, whom she hated with malignance, but without violence. Her only fear had been that perhaps some day John might recognize his youngest daughter for what she was. Now that fear had vanished.

Now Adelaide was speaking again, and her voice hardly moved her parched lips. "Yes, we are out in the open now. I'm not done. You've not finished with me. You intend to ruin Papa. After all the love he's given you, and the things he's heaped upon you. But I'm standing between him and you. You won't get past me, Louisa."

Louisa laughed, merrily, with a sound of ringing crystal. "Such dramatics. We have been discussing Papa's health, and here you are, my sweet Adelaide, tilting ferociously at windmills, until you've forced me to defend myself and show you up for what you really are. Do go along, my darling, or I'll expire of laughter, and I'm in no condition."

She waved her white and dainty fingers at Adelaide with graceful and pretty dismissal, as one might wave at an annoying dog. She picked up her needlework, and shook her head to herself, smiling brightly.

But Lavinia looked at her with sick and heavy suspicion, her heart labouring. She had always evaded questions of conscience, of self-examination, as her father had done before her. Now she knew that she was soft, a weakling. She had no steel. Only violence. She wished, vehemently, that this scene had never taken place. It had compelled her to think. She was suddenly exhausted, in spite of her great vitality.

Adelaide's words, her own uneasy thoughts and conjectures, filled her with panic. She saw the shapes of things she had denied. She felt a poisoned wound in her breast, and shame, and fear. Now she knew that despite all her lifetime of fury and noise and tempestuousness she had always evaded issues, had refused to think of them. She had seen injustice and cruelty done, and dirtiness, and malice, and had reacted to them only with boisterous noise and belligerence, because she dared not face and fight them. She dared not do this now. She had no real strength.

She thought: I have only to say to Louisa: I'll have no part in this. I am looking at things squarely. I am nauseated; I am sick of myself, and of you, and of every one. I'll not evade;

I'll examine. And then, you'll have me as well as Addy to reckon with.

But even as she thought these things she knew she dared not say them. Why? She did not know. Confusion came over her again.

She turned to Adelaide, and said in a changed voice: "Addy, you do look ill. Don't mind Louisa, who has the nastiest tongue. Go and lie down. Never mind the sewing. We'll discuss all this later."

Adelaide looked at her long and intently, and now there was scorn in her blazing eyes, and pity and understanding. Before that look, Lavinia averted her head.

Adelaide bent over her mother, and kissed her cheek.

"Don't worry, Mama. We'll have the doctor look at Papa, and if he must rest, he can do so at home. With you to care for him, dearest, he will soon be well."

She straightened and gazed steadfastly at the smiling and sedate Louisa.

"But, he shall not go away!"

CHAPTER 47

ADELAIDE walked up and down her dark and narrow room in a frenzy and confusion.

She had always had a logical and analytical mind, but now she saw that in the dark forest of human machinations, human passions, logic was useless, a feeble little candle that the smallest black wind could extinguish in one gust.

Where was there reason for the frantic terror that engulfed her, for the fear and suspicion that roared in her feverish mind? Her sisters had said her father was ill; she knew this. Why, then, did wild repudiation choke her throat, torment her, make her wish to cry out meaningless and incoherent warnings? She only knew that she was afraid; that her fear was a fire in her spirit. She wondered, confusedly, if there were not warnings delivered to the soul that could not be diagrammed or explained in cool and reasonable words. Were there forces that could not be phrased, passions and ominously felt threats that overwhelmed analysis?

She felt there were. Like all reasonable people, she foundered when confronted by the inexplicable, which, despite its inexplicability, was stronger than rationality. The neat borders of philosophy were destroyed in the upheaval of instinct. A well-defined syllogism became the veriest insanity when an

413

unfathomable truth confronted it. One started with a clear premise, controlled and orderly, but the argument ended in madness, even if that madness was valid.

She saw at last that instinct and passion were the basic premises upon which all students of humanity must construct their syllogisms, if the conclusion were to be true as well as valid. There was no neatness in the human soul.

She put her ice cold hands against her burning forehead. If I could only think clearly, she thought, in despair, conscious, meanwhile, of the intangible mists that floated about her. Then, she gave herself up to instinct, to feeling, to sensation, and the disorder became order, even if a terrible one. Her father was mortally threatened. She must protect him. But out of the chaos she must find intelligible words with which to warn him.

To warn him! How could she force him to listen to her, he who hardly spoke to her except to reprimand or sneer? He had ignored her for nearly seventeen years. Why had he hated her? His dislike, it is true, had set up a counter defense against him in her, of silence, of apparent sulkiness and obdurateness and injured vanity. And of assaulted love. But she had always loved him.

Mama and I are the only ones who have ever loved him, she thought, pain and compassion tearing at her heart. And Mama has loved him as a dog loves, without understanding.

She had wanted to protect him, to soothe him, to defend him. But, from what? Even that was hidden from her. However, it only enhanced the yearning and compassionate love she had for him.

He had seen her searching and penetrating eyes upon him, and he had reacted to them as all turbulent and emotional people reacted: with anger and uneasiness.

Now, as she thought of all these things, her agony was intense and desperate. John was threatened, this time dangerously, mortally. He would go down, unless she helped him. But who threatened him so terribly? Who wished to destroy him? His daughters? Their husbands? It was absurd, when looked at reasonably. But she had surmounted reason in this hour.

She thought of Rufus, whom she instinctively hated, as she hated all slyness and evil and calculation. She thought of Patrick, whom she vaguely liked. Patrick had always treated her with cavalier affection and amusement. She had found no pure evil in him, even if there was malice, and expediency and plotting. Once, in her hearing, he had said: "Now, there is a clever baggage," and he had said this without animosity, and even with an amused admiration.

But even as she thought of him and Rufus, doubting the screaming affirmation that clamoured in her, she knew that her instinct was to be trusted. These two would destroy her father.

Her compassion, her love, her anguish, made her burst into wild and uncontrolled weeping. Her father, in spite of what he had accomplished, in spite of his imposing presence and his strength, was vulnerable, helpless, a child in the midst of malignant adults. He could never understand them. There was no virulence in him to recognize the virulence of others. He hated. And that hatred, to Adelaide, seemed the most piteous of all. The hater was the most helpless of men, the most injured, the most tormented. Those who had made him hate were the wicked ones.

Hatred seemed to her the most pathetic of the vices. It was a scar over wounds inflicted by the cruel and the merciless.

She experienced no resentment, no anger, against John for all the years of indifference and dislike he had heaped upon her. If he could only know that she loved him, understood him, he must love her in return. But she had no words to tell him. She saw, clearly, that when Lavinia and Louisa had mauled him, embraced and kissed him, protesting their affection for him (and he was so hungry for reassurance of human love, and the security it gave) she had stood apart, apparently willful and scornful, and always silent. What if she had run to him then, flung her arms about him, cried out her real love, begged for his love in return? Might he not then have responded, in grateful amazement? She could not know. But she had had her awkward pride, her miserable reticence, her fear. She saw now that when he had looked at her over the warm young arms of Lavinia and Louisa, he had seen nothing but a stubborn pale little face, and an arching lip. He had believed she disliked him. He believed her to be a stranger.

Her confusion grew. The heat and pain in her head was a swirling delirium. She threw herself across her bed, and in a moment or two she was in a stupor, ridden by meaningless nightmares. She heard fury and clamour all about her, and was conscious of some fateful sickness in herself. But all else was confusion.

And then, in the chaos, she dreamt of Anthony, or thought of him. A sweet and powerful yearning opened in her breast. She must go to Anthony, whom she had married that morning, and whom she had forgotten she had married. Anthony would help her. He would understand the full import of only a few faltering words and aimless gestures. Now a warm sense of protection enveloped her. No one could hurt her now. She had only to dress, to go to him, and he would take her in his arms, and she would rest. Then he would listen to her, and everything would become clear again, and reasonable.

She pressed the finger that had worn his ring against her lips. She smiled in her fever and sickness. Now she slept, though it was a hot and uneasy sleep. She was faintly conscious of fear, but the thought of Anthony exorcised it, like the touch of a father's hand.

When she awoke, the room was in complete twilight, and she was shivering violently. Her head felt weighted with hot lead. The soreness in her chest was so severe that every breath was painful. There was no sound of servants about her, and so she knew they had gone downstairs to prepare dinner. She rose, staggering a little, and looked at the small clock on her dresser. It was nearly six. Her father must be home. Within an hour the dinner bell would ring.

Now faintness and weakness so appalling took hold upon her that she fell against the dresser. Swimming points of light floated before her eyes. But she controlled herself. She knew she was ill. But before succumbing, she had work to do.

She bathed, changed her frock, combed her hair. The comb felt heavy and thick in her trembling hand. Her hair was a weight of iron. Her face, in the lighted mirror, had a sunken look, livid and wizened.

Suddenly a spasm of coughing wracked her. She put her handkerchief to her lips, and stared affrightedly at the stain of blood upon it. Perhaps she had lung fever. A convulsion of shivering shook her from head to foot. She forced herself to drink a glass of water, and the resulting nausea was so intense that she had to lie down for a few moments.

She heard the dinner bell, pealing softly and musically through the house. Forcing herself to rise, clenching her teeth on her lip to control the waves of weakness that flowed over her, she left the room and descended the stairway. Now all her efforts were concentrated on retaining her footing.

The family was already at the table when she entered the room. Lavinia, in cerise velvet, Louisa in angelic blue silk, Lilybelle in a muddy brown, sat waiting. John was at the head of the table, his daughters' husbands on each side of him. Patrick must have said one of his usual light jests, for all were laughing agreeably. Even John was smiling.

It was at her father that Adelaide's burning eye directed itself. Yes, he was truly ill. Haggard, livid, furrowed and sunken of look, there was no doubt that he was a sick man. His hands fumbled as they carved the roast. Candlelight flickered over the great room with its beamed ceiling, its massive oaken furniture, its heavy silver on the sideboard. The butler and the maids stood at his elbow.

He did not glance at Adelaide when she entered. Lavinia saw her out of the corner of her eye, and averted her head with a sullen expression. Louisa smiled and dimpled like a cherub. Patrick rose gallantly and drew out the girl's chair. Lilybelle eyed her timidly.

Adelaide seated herself. She gripped her hands together in her lap. The smell and sight of food made her violently ill. She closed her eyes. She heard the placing of her plate before her, the apologetic and humble touch of her mother's hand. A swimming and heady unreality assaulted her, and she felt herself being softly wafted about in space.

Moments passed in complete unconsciousness for the girl. Darkness closed about her. She heard and felt movements, as one under drugs feels them. But they had no connection with her.

Then, clear and sharp, she heard Rufus' voice:

"So, father, you really must consider it. We've talked it over with Lavinia and Louisa, and they agree with us. However, you must make the final decision. We've given you our opinion, out of our concern for you, our anxiety."

CHAPTER 48

As she awakened to full consciousness, lightning seemed to break before Adelaide's eyes. Again, everything became abnormally brilliant and clear, so that the edges of the silverware, the contours of dish and bowl, the shimmer of the white damask cloth, the light-shadows on wall and ceiling, took on a blinding luminousness and dazzling intensity. She saw every face ringed in sharp brightness, full of significant meaning not otherwise apparent. Rufus' veined buff hand, lying elegantly by his plate, Patrick's vivid little blue eyes and half smile, Lavinia's sullen and averted face, Louisa's dimpled celestial smile, Lilybelle's puffy florid face, and John's febrile and sultry eyes, impinged so closely upon her senses that she felt that she could not endure their closeness, that she must scream and force them to retreat.

Then she realized what had awakened her. She heard the echo of Rufus' words as if they had been repeated over and over in her ears. She turned her aching eyes from one face to another, and tried to speak. But Louisa was talking eagerly to her father, leaning across the table to him, her blue eyes shining with passionate affection:

"Dear Papa, won't you listen to me a moment, and to Lavinia? You know how we love you, and how frightened we are about your apparent illness."

"I'm not ill!" shouted John, thrusting back his chair from the table. Nevertheless, when he looked at his tender and dainty daughter, his look softened in spite of himself, and he passed his worn hand over his face.

"Papa dear, you are," insisted Louisa, and now she allowed tears to suffuse her eyes. "You know you are. You are breaking our hearts. What should we do without you? I can't bear it, really I can't," and she touched her lashes with her handkerchief, and sobbed delicately.

And then Adelaide, to her inner rage and despair, realized that a conversation had long been in progress of which she, in her illness, had been unaware and unconscious. All her inner resources came painfully to her aid now. She concentrated on the swimming brilliance of the table and faces before her. Her head felt enormous and swollen. It was a truly physical agony to listen, to try to comprehend. And it was so horribly necessary to listen, to comprehend.

"My love, don't cry," mumbled John pleadingly. Adelaide saw how his brown hands were shaking on the cloth.

"O Papa, you are breaking our hearts," sobbed Louisa. She turned blindly to Patrick, who took her hand and held it tightly. His face was quite red and peculiar. Rufus listened calmly, with a faint half-smile, and shrugged.

Louisa appealed to Lavinia, whose face was sullen and obstinate. That young woman played with her silver, as if distressed and uneasy. "Linny, darling, do say something." There was steel under the honey of Louisa's voice.

Lavinia looked at her father, and said surlily: "Yes, Papa. You know you are ill. We've consulted Dr. Burney." She paused, then added in a rush of loud words: "It—it doesn't matter about anything else. But you are ill. We've got to realize that. You ought to have a rest. We don't know what will happen if you don't——"

Lilybelle spoke then, timidly and hoarsely: "Mr. T. The lasses are right. I know you won't listen to me. But I've seen. We could go away to the mountains for a little, or the seashore."

John said nothing. He looked at his beloved daughters, and his mouth jerked. He was profoundly touched at their solicitude, and he admitted to himself that life had at least temporarily become too much for him. He had thought he was alone, that no one realized his condition, the constant malaise and sick horror that had him without surcease. And all at once the idea of a brief escape was like a sudden easing of pain. He closed his eyes as the full deliciousness of the thought came to him. But what of his business, and the fear and suspicion he had of any one else conducting it for him? He looked at Patrick and Rufus, and his heart was squeezed with foreboding. Nevertheless, the delight he experienced at his daughters' love and solicitude was a warm fire in his spirit.

He looked slowly about the table, met Louisa's sweet and melting gaze, Rufus' stern and anxious eye, Patrick's affected concern, Lavinia's brooding look, Lilybelle's tears. And then he saw Adelaide's face, blazing white and strange. He was struck by that face. He had so rarely seen his youngest daughter clearly. There was anger in her eyes, denial, challenge, and a breathless eagerness. He turned away from her, his old dislike twisting in him.

Now he felt truly ill, truly prostrated. Darkness passed in streaks before him, a sensation of surrender, of a giving up and turning aside. Before he was aware of it, Louisa and Lavinia were beside him, embracing him, wetting his face with their tears. Louisa had seated herself on his knee, and had laid her head on his breast. His hand rose and pressed itself on her golden curls. The delight came to him again, a shaking and wondering delight, that these children of his loved him so intensely.

"Now, now," he said, striving for lightness. "It isn't as bad as that, my pets. I'm tired, I admit. But I'm an old horse in harness. No one can undertake my responsibilities."

He paused. He thought of his decaying affairs, and was terrified. Perhaps he was, in truth, much more ill than he realized. He thought of the passed dividends, the restlessness of his stockholders, the severe alarm of Jay Regan. He had pushed these matters aside, thinking that tomorrow, or tomorrow, he would face them, take them in hand again, subdue and control them. But the tomorrows had passed, helpless and fruitless, and nothing had been accomplished. He recalled his indifference, his falling into bed into a deep stupor, in order to escape them. Now, his terror rose, and he saw the imminent ruin completely. How had he been so blind, so obtuse?

As clearly as if they were before him, he saw the heaps of dusty papers on his desk, and recalled that for weeks now he had sat before them dully every day, without the will or the desire to touch them. He knew that he must turn his efforts to them, but his will had been flaccid. His hands had shook so violently when reaching for the papers that he had been obliged to halt them in mid passage. His legs had turned to water. He had arisen a dozen times, making for the windows as if choking, and had fallen against chairs, tables and desks on his way. How had he forgotten all these things? How had he continued to hope?

Now, if he should leave, if only for a little while, the confusion and nightmare might be overcome. The stupefaction might be blown away.

But even as he thought these things, a dark swirling fog entered his mind, and unconscious of those who watched, two with love, four with cunning calculation, he pressed his hands over his forehead in a gesture of distraction. Everything fell away before him. Through the fog he saw Mr. Wilkins' moist rosy face and round grave eyes:

"Well, now, Johnnie, things is comin' to a pretty pass. You 'aven't looked at Regan's letters. You 'aven't noticed how things is gettin' along. And they're bad, very bad. Not like they should be, I don't think. You've got to get things in 'and, I warns you, as a friend. Rest. That's wot you need. Rest."

That had been only this afternoon. Nothing was clear to him but Mr. Wilkins. He remembered how he had shouted and cursed at the fat little man with the ageless affable face. How he had struck the desk until the dusty papers flew. Mr. Wilkins had left, shaking his head dolorously.

Rest. He had never rested in twenty-five years. He had not dared to rest. For, with rest, he would think. He was in terror of the thoughts that would assault him in idleness. So, he had driven himself. He could not remember why, or what the threatening thoughts might be. He felt the ache and burning of his body, the knifing pain in his head, his passionate eagerness for sleep, for forgetfulness.

Now, in his panic, he was most enormously frightened. What had Regan said in his ignored letters? What of the directors' meetings he had avoided? What had been decided there? He remembered that he had refused to attend, that all that day he had sat before his desk, numb, blind, unfeeling. He saw the procession of the sightless futile days, when nothing had been done. Was he really only tired? What had come over him, to make him a lump of flesh without sensation, decision or thought?

It must be that he was tired. That was all—tired. He must go away.

He dropped his hands. His face had a livid moistness over it. But he smiled. He pressed his daughters convulsively to him. "Come with me, my darlings," he said.

Lavinia and Louisa exchanged a swift look. Then Louisa said gently: "Yes, Papa, dear. Anywhere. We have thought only of ourselves for a long time. We'll go away with you. We've been such selfish beasts, and it is time to think of you, now." She hesitated, then continued joyously: "You needn't worry about your affairs, dearest Papa. What does anything matter, but you?"

But John was frightened again. It is true that Rufus and Patrick could conduct his affairs adequately enough. But he had made all the decisions so long that he feared to relegate them to young and inexperienced hands. He looked at the two young men doubtfully. And the old sensation of disintegration, impotence, despair and weariness swept over him. The old suspicion of every one, the distrust of every voice and every face, the old wary hatred. He thrust his daughters away roughly, but it was the roughness of despair.

"How can I?" he cried. "Who will manage things for me? You talk like a fool, Louisa!"

Rufus leaned forward, spoke softly and soothingly: "A few weeks away won't matter. We can manage things. Of course," he added, with a slight cough, "we have no real authority to make decisions. We must just mark time."

Patrick looked at him, and his mouth tightened. His was a more forthright nature, but he saw that subtlety must be used in dealing with this frightened sick man who suspected every shadow and shied at every slight gesture.

Rufus sighed. John was regarding him with dilated and shining eyes, full of fear and anger and indecision.

"You know enough," he said, brutally. "You've hung around enough. Why can't you manage? Not that I've fully decided, but it seems to me that you've faddle-daddled long enough to know an invoice from an order, Rufus."

Rufus spread out his hands resignedly. "That's true. But, I repeat: we have no authority. What if a matter of importance comes up, father? We'd be helpless." He lifted his sharp fox-like chin resolutely. "And I can assure you that we won't annoy you with the details. We'll let it go, until you return. That is all we can do."

John was silent. He gnawed his lip. A lifetime of doubt and caution, of suspicion and fear, could not be overcome in a moment. In the meanwhile, his feeling of disintegration, stupor and forgetfulness increased. What the hell did it all matter, anyway? He studied the faces of the two young men with feverish concentration. They returned his look with resolute artlessness and concern.

Then he flung out his hand. He said dully: "I can't leave things with you, as they are. What can you do?"

The look that passed between Rufus and Patrick was a thin rapier of darting triumph. But Rufus remained sober, and very serious.

"What do you then suggest, sir?" asked Rufus, with grave

421

courtesy. "We are only anxious to help you. Would it be best to curtail all activities until your recovery?"

John did not speak. His look was more black and lowering each moment, as the sharp pin-pricks of his eyes pressed in upon each face.

Then he said explosively: "Nonsense! You talk like fools. Why do you hide and skulk, when you know exactly what you want? You want me to put authority in your hands, don't you? You want authority instead of a gilt pen which duplicates what I first write? Well, why can't you speak up like men?"

It was Patrick who spoke now, with a lumbering heaviness which duplicated honesty very adequately: "Well, then, it's out. You need to rest, sir. We've agreed on that. We know what we can do, if you will allow us to do it. Rufe is Vice-President; I am Treasurer. You wouldn't have given us these positions if you doubted our native wit. Or, at least, I flatter myself that you wouldn't. Now, we must go further than that. We can't act as your office boys while you are away." He flung aside his napkin and pushed back his chair, as if angrily impatient and disgusted. He turned his handsome flushed face, which in its thick lines and sullenness resembled John's quite remarkably, slowly from one face to another. Rufus, watching intently, was faintly annoyed. He admitted to himself that there was much more to acting than the deft touch, the subtle gesture.

"No," continued Patrick, "I'll be an errand boy no longer. The position is onerous. It wasn't so bad when you were there, sir. We had you to look to. But, if you go away, I want some manly authority, if I'm to do my best and keep things in hand. If I have no authority, I'll not have the ridicule that I'll have if I am given no freedom of my own. What is the matter? Do you distrust us? And, if so, why? That seems the first thing to be settled before we go any further. If you distrust me, I'm done. I've wanted to be done for a long while."

"Oh!" mourned Louisa, bursting into tears, "how can you talk to Papa like that, Patrick? How can you say such cruel things to him when he is so ill?"

But John had listened with profound attention to Patrick's rough and angry words, which had mounted in a stentorious volume towards the last. He held his lower lip with his teeth, with that vulnerable and savage look he had when confused and disconcerted.

Patrick pressed his wife's hand strongly and fondly, but looked at John.

"Let's be frank," he said. "Do you distrust us? We've got

to settle that now."

John's eyes met Patrick's, and he saw the fiery blue in the young man's eyes, the boldness of his look, the resolute irritation. His brows drew together.

"Have I said I distrust you?" he asked. "If I distrusted you, you'd never have gotten in, you jackanapes."

Patrick's expression spoke of robust impatience hardly restrained. He gave the table a sharp blow with his clenched fist.

"This is as good a time as ever to weigh anchor. I've wanted to, for a long time. You'll give us authority, sir, to act in your absence, or I'm getting out. Tonight."

Rufus turned his narrow green eye upon Lavinia. But she would not look at him. She was twisting her handkerchief over her fingers with John's own savagery. Her full and beautiful face was dark crimson, with a curiously swollen look. For a sickening instant, her husband felt for her a blasting hatred. What was wrong with the wench? Why did she not add her lamentations and pleas to Louisa's?

None, of course, heeded Adelaide in the least. She sat in her chair, her white face ablaze, her glittering eyes fixed on her father. Once or twice her parched lips moved, as if she was about to speak, to cry out.

Patrick had neatly infused a loud and discordant atmosphere into the discussion, an anger and fury which must needs impress the naïve John with their honesty. He felt acute embarrassment. His confusion was growing. He could not even question anything in his own mind. He only felt the necessity of placating his daughters' husbands for the insult he had implied.

He tried to bluster, sheepishly. "Come now, what's all the row about? I've not said I would go. On second thought, I probably won't."

"Well, then," said Patrick, heavily. He slapped down his hand with a sound of finality. "That's settled. Forget we spoke, sir. We'll do the best we can under the circumstances. You can't go away and leave things as they are. And, we aren't equipped to take on the burden, with our hands tied behind us. We hope you'll recover your health without a rest. That's all we can hope."

The damned Irish gambler! thought Rufus, with evil fury. He's ruined everything. He cast, and he lost. I could have managed this.

Patrick rose, and held out his hand to his wife. Her wet blue eyes were sharp and shining, full of malignance. But an instant later, as she studied his face, the malignance died, and her eyes were like hyacinths again, sweet and moist.

She accepted his hand, and rose meekly. Patrick's air was all grave and affronted finality, aloof and unconcerned. He gave John to understand that it would be a long time before he would be appeased.

"Wait," said John. Patrick, standing near him, took on a look of suspicious surprise.

John cleared his throat. He moved his head as if choking, and a livid tint replaced the last of his congested colour. He spoke with difficulty. "I haven't said it was over—this discussion. You're right, I suppose. Have I distrusted you? It is just that I've never acquired the habit of trusting any one. I can see I've got to do that. Trust. It's hard for me. You've to give me a little time."

Patrick shook his head slowly and sombrely. "No. Don't. I've changed my mind. I can't go on. You have my resignation, sir, in the event you go away and give us no authority. I may even tender my resignation without any more discussion. That's what I've got to think about, tonight."

Rufus listened with penetrating and sudden attention. He ran the tip of his tongue over his lips, and his narrow face narrowed still more.

John began to shout, all at once, as if his last control was gone. His face was contorted. He struggled to his feet. "Damn you! I'll give you what you want! I'm sick of it all. And of all of you! D'ye know that? I'll go away. You'll get what you want, curse you! Tonight!"

He flung back his chair so violently that it crashed behind him. But Patrick was not intimidated. The servants, however, who had been listening avidly, retreated to the doorway. Patrick stood before the sick man and shouted back as furiously: "I don't want it! I'm through! You can do as you wish for all of me! After this, I wouldn't touch any damn part of it!"

They shouted at each other incoherently, while the women, frightened now, whimpered in their throats. The two men stood almost chest to chest, bellowing at each other with threatening gestures, so that the sound of their voices mingled together thunderously. But Rufus smiled faintly, covered his lips with his thin buff fingers.

Then, very suddenly, John paused, then laughed boisterously. His mood changed. He put his hand on Patrick's shoulder, and the young man restrained a movement as if to throw off that hand. John's grip tightened. He regarded Patrick with surprised affection, and his sheepish look increased.

"Come upstairs with me, both of you, and I'll talk it over," he said. "I'll send for that skulking sheep of a lawyer of mine.

Tonight. We'll do it all, within the hour. Is that enough for you, you fool, you Irish navvy?"

There was a sharp silence in the room. Patrick's face was still congested, and his eye flashed fire. His mouth settled into sullen and resistive lines. Then he shrugged, turned away. Rufus rose swiftly, and stood at John's side.

But before he could speak, there was a loud cry shattering the sinking violence of the air. Adelaide was on her feet. She leaned towards her father, and her white face was terrible and wild.

"No!" she cried. "No! You mustn't do that, Papa! Not now; not ever. Don't you see?" And she made a desperate motion with her hands. "Don't you see it all? They want to ruin you, to take everything away from you. They've been plotting it all the time!"

CHAPTER 49

ADELAIDE's light voice, with its lack of resonance and depth, was very seldom heard loquaciously in family conferences or gatherings. Even when she did speak, and that was rare, the absence of strength and power in her tones made what she said inconsequential in a household where determined and loud enunciation was conspicuous. Therefore, her silences had become longer through the years, and her family was apt to be unconscious of her presence.

Now her voice, as she cried out, was so strong, so passionate, so ringing and wild in its intensity that all, including her father, stared at her in motionless stupefaction. Too, her blazing white face and glittering eyes were so extraordinary that these alone, if she had not spoken, would have grasped their amazed attention. She was transfigured. Her orderly brown hair was suddenly dishevelled, as if unfelt winds were blowing it violently.

They looked at her, and none could move. Lilybelle's fat and florid face became the shade and contour of wet putty. Louisa had paled excessively, but her blue eyes shone with that stonelike and malefic radiance that very few ever saw. Lavinia's face changed strangely, her black eyes dilated, her nostrils widening. Quickly, she moistened her slack lips, and they composed themselves in a peculiar pent expression of intense concentration. Patrick had been frozen in the very midst of a movement, and stood there, rigid and astounded, his hand half lifted, his head turned over his shoulder as he stared at the girl. But Rufus seemed to tighten down the whole length of his fox-like body, and his supple back bent forward a little, in the curve of a spring. His lean and pointed face narrowed to a wedge, and his green eyes sparkled with malignance and cold fury.

John looked at his daughter as if she was some appalling and hateful thing suddenly sprung up in his path, some monster, some creature of whose existence he had never been aware.

He shook off the entrancement that had seized him at Adelaide's look and words, and his hands doubled murderously into fists. Now his big body leaned forward, and it was implicit with mad hatred and fulminating rage. He took a single step towards his daughter, and they faced each other across a small space that seemed to crackle with monstrous passion. Somewhere in the background there was a gasp and whimper from Lilybelle, who had covered her open lips with her hand, and who was staring at her husband and child with terror and agony.

Adelaide was not intimidated at her father's look and gesture, however frightful they were. Her slight body appeared to expand with the vehemence of her thoughts and her despair. She flung out her hands towards him.

"Papa! Think. Think for just a moment, in the name of God! Think what they want to do to you! I've talked with her," and she turned her hand in Louisa's direction without looking at her sister. "She was shameless. She as much as admitted it all. That was only this morning. Papa, they will ruin you, take everything from you! I know it. I know all about it!"

The tragic and disordered appeal in her voice, her face and her eyes, would have moved a less violent and more reasonable man. But John was both violent and without reason. Moreover, in these moments, Adelaide expressed so much that was familiar to him in another, in her every look, tone and gesture, that he was suddenly beside himself, suddenly seized with frenzy and disorder.

Yet, he spoke very quietly, and with appalling slow virulence:

"You baggage. You—dirty thing. You liar. How dare you open your mouth? Get out of my sight, you hussy!"

All through him he felt the pounding of giant pulses, gathering, rushing to an unbearable and excruciating crescendo of thunder and insanity. And now all this seemed not only in himself, but all about him, a universe of agonized pain. Everything darkened before his eyes, and he saw nothing but the swimming and spectral whiteness of Adelaide's face, disembodied, imploring, and soundless.

Having been the victim all his life of sensation and emotion, and rarely of reason, he did not understand what he was experiencing, nor the cause of the fixed pang which stood in his chest like a sword. He felt only madness and rage and frenzy.

His words had brought a profound silence into the room. Adelaide gazed at him, starkly. Her lips moved, but she could not speak. Then she put her hands over her face and broke into desperate weeping.

Lilybelle then was stirred into action. She lumbered to her daughter's side, and put her great fat arm about the girl's trembling shoulders. Tears ran over her shaking cheeks, rolled into the corners of her twisted mouth.

"You sha'n't talk to my lassie like that, Mr. T.," she said, hoarsely. "My lassie. My little love. It's best you hear her out——"

Louisa smiled, relaxed. The blue glow of her eyes softened; she glanced at Rufus, who returned her look with a faint and evil smile. But Patrick's face had thickened, become congested and furtive. He dropped his eyes. As for Lavinia, the strangeness of her expression increased. She took one step towards Adelaide, then paused. She began to tremble with the oddest of emotions.

But John's eyes were fixed upon Adelaide, and he saw no one else. He did not hear what Lilybelle had said. His concentration had something inhuman and ghastly in it.

Then Adelaide dropped her hands. She looked at her father again. The wildness had disappeared from her sick face, and it was full of stern resolution. And so, for a long moment she gazed at him.

"I've loved you so, all my life," she said, in a low voice. "I've been the only one who's loved you. I've always hoped you'd know, and understand. But it's useless. You can't help yourself. You won't let me help you."

Now she turned swiftly to Louisa, who smiled at her gently and maliciously, and with triumph. Adelaide's expression quickened with a kind of noble hatred and fortitude.

"You haven't got what you want. Not yet. You won't have it. I'm still here to see you don't."

The blazing scorn in her face, its strength in her voice, made the smile disappear from Louisa's lips. Now it was replaced by a wary and calculating look, watchful and conjecturing.

Very gently, then, Adelaide disengaged herself from her mother's arm and walked swiftly from the room. And John looked after her as if she were drawing his eyes with her.

The others, too, looked after the girl, with fascination, and so they did not see John's expression, how blank and changed it had become, how confused and still, how his fists slackened, and his hands dropped helplessly to his sides.

It was a long moment before any one moved, and then there was an audible intake of breath. Louisa began to laugh lightly and sweetly.

"Whatever has gotten into Adelaide?" she asked. "Did you ever hear anything like it? I know she's always hated us, and been jealous of us, but I thought she had more sense than this."

John came to himself. All colour had gone from his face. He turned to Rufus and Patrick.

"Come with me," he said, and turned and walked away with a step that had a slight stagger in it.

The young men followed him quickly, after a brief flashing glance at each other. The women were left alone. Louisa was laughing again, idly. Lavinia did not speak, but she bent the most fixed and furious eyes upon her sister. Her hands were clenched against her breast.

Lilybelle broke into hoarse sobbing. "My lassie!" she said. "I must go to my lassie."

With a step remarkably swift and agile for one of her ponderous weight, she hurried from the room and followed her daughter.

CHAPTER 50

A COLD resolution and intense clarity had come to Adelaide. They were so profound that she completely overcame her increasing illness, and forgot it. She rushed up the stairs to her room, seized a bonnet and tied it under her chin with hands as icy as death, but firm and untrembling. She caught up a thick dark shawl and flung it over her shoulders.

She must go for help. She must go to Anthony, now, before this terrible thing was irretrievably done to her father. Anthony would know what to do. He would return with her. A curious light elation rushed over her at the very thought. Her step was without weakness as she turned towards the door.

Then the door opened, and Lilybelle, sobbing, disordered and dishevelled, appeared on the threshold, her arms outspread. Incoherent words gushed to her lips, then halted at the sight of her daughter, prepared to go out into the cool windiness of the night. Her round blue eyes, so faded and tear-filled, widened blankly. She had lifted her hands, and they remained in the air, stupefied.

Adelaide came to her mother, and said clearly: "Mama, I must go out for a little. Just an hour. I've got to get help for Papa, you see."

Lilybelle stared at her in terrified and uncomprehending silence. Now her maternal instinct rushed warningly all through her senses. She had not perceived it before, but now she saw everything. She saw that the girl was frightfully ill, and she forgot everything else. She saw the sunken and stricken face under the brown bonnet, the feverish eyes, the parched lips, and she knew it was no emotion that had caused these, but some ominous sickness.

The poor foolish woman had never been very courageous in all her life. Others had always done what they would with her. She had experienced very little emotion throughout her years but love and sorrow. But these had always been powerful and invincible. Through them, she had interpreted all things.

She stood, massive and unmoving, on the threshold, like a mountain of love and courage.

"No, my pet, my little love," she said, in a breaking voice. "You're not to go out. It's some sickness, that's wot it is. I can see it with my own eyes."

Adelaide regarded her mother intently in a momentary silence. Then, all at once, she was shaken with a sense of desperate and terrible hurry, such as one feels below a breaking dam. Something was looming behind her, gigantic and awful, something which would overwhelm her. She had not a minute to lose. She felt the crumbling of the dam of her resistance, the surging and arching flood of death behind it. Hurry! Hurry! warned her body, her senses, her stern and iron mind. She had the sensation of looking behind her, and up, at a tilting and enormous wall.

"Mama," she said, "I must go. Only for a few minutes. I'll come back directly. Please step aside." Her hands reached out as if to seize her mother and thrust her away by sheer strength of will. She cried out: "Can't you see I can't wait any longer? Can't you see what I've got to do?"

Then she took her mother by the arms and shook her furiously. "Mama, I'll bring help. Go to Papa. Now. Tell him to wait. Just an hour. Just half an hour. I'll bring some one here who will convince him, help him!"

Lilybelle stared at her, overcome with terror. But she did not move. Her loving instinct screamed aloud in her heart. Her great round eyes glittered affrightedly in the feeble light of the single lamp on a distant table. She caught Adelaide's hands.

"Lovey, you can't go out of this house. Not tonight. You must go to bed, and your Mama will undress you and send for the doctor." Her voice was broken, wheedling, as she attempted to push the girl back into the room. "Come to your Mama, my little lamb. Mama will take care of you. Tomorrow, when you're better, we'll both talk to your Papa."

But Adelaide had become a thin shaft of steel in her hands. The girl spoke softly and inflexibly: "Mama, you don't understand. Tomorrow will be too late. I've got to go now." The light from the corridor shone on her face, and fresh terror overwhelmed Lilybelle, fresh and paralysing alarm.

Adelaide's eyes darted beyond Lilybelle. They were away from the threshold now. With a swift and sinuous movement, Adelaide twisted under her mother's arm, and then bounded from the room. Lilybelle, after one despairing cry, listened to the girl's light and racing footsteps retreating down the stairway.

She tried to follow, shouting aloud. But she had hardly reached the second landing with her lumbering and trembling tread, than she heard the great heavy street door open and shut with a loud crash.

Now all her strength left her. She was compelled to lower her massive body on the stairs. She shivered over and over. She wrapped her arms about her knees, and a vast sickness flowed over her. She saw below her the wide hall, brightly lighted, the oak and crimson chairs lined against the walls, the paintings in their gilt frames, the lighter crimson of the carpet. There was no sound. Now the immense and lighted emptiness took on a strange and awful quality to her, static and breathless. Every object, every chair, every edge of gilt on the paintings, every lamp on long oaken tables between the chairs, every downward sweep of the stairway below her, acquired a dreadful and waiting life of its own.

Now she heard the poignant ticking of the great grandfather's clock under the angle of the stairway below her. It was a mechanical and gloating voice, indifferent, merciless and savage. She heard it as the bereaved hear it, and each tick struck upon her heart like a lash. She put her hands to her ears and moaned. She rolled her head from side to side. Her enormous body was a million porous openings from which suffering and anguish poured forth, and voiceless grief.

She saw the carved molding of the door through which Adelaide had fled, and it was like the door through which a beloved corpse had been carried, never to be seen again. She had all the sensatory powers of those to whom thought is a stranger, and the door, as she gazed at it, took on the aspect of finality, the aspect of a stone covering the opening of a sepulcher. Her heart seemed to stream from a thousand wounds, draining the life from her.

She did not know she was weeping. But the bodice of her brown dress was dark with a slowly spreading moisture. She wept as the bereaved weep, hopelessly, unknowingly, the salt of her tears carrying with it the final resignation of those who can endure no more.

She thought only in symbols, in impressions and emotions. Now it appeared to her that all her life had been focussed towards this moment of loss and desolation, of agony and giving-up. It had been turned to this moment when the dear thing she had loved was gone through an impassable door into darkness, and beyond recall. There had been no meaning to her life but sorrow. That one fact was like a shining sword held before her in complete emptiness. All the years had gone into the formation of this sword which had finally entered into her heart and had transfixed it forever.

She did not know how long she sat there, enduring and motionless. But all at once she heard the distant pealing of a bell, and then the soft quick tread of a servant approaching the street door below. She saw it open. A little wizened man briskly entered, carrying a dispatch case. She watched, with distended eyes, as the servant took cane, coat and hat, heard, as one hears an echo, the quick exchange of greetings and directions.

The servant disappeared. The little man, with the weasel face of the astute and the slyly ruthless, began to ascend the stairway. He did not see Lilybelle until he was actually upon her. Then he started quite violently.

For she was a very strange sight indeed, this big fat woman with the bodice of her gown wet as if soaked in water, her faded mass of auburn hair dishevelled about her great livid face, her eyes streaming. Cold and withered though he was, he saw and felt the tragedy in her posture, her aspect. He saw strange bright eyes fixed upon him, flaccid lips, crouching attitude.

He fell back a step. "Mrs. Turnbull!" he exclaimed, and he glanced behind him with a curious alarm.

She moved then, and all her movements were implicit with a mortal weariness. Her voice came to him, without resonance, dull and heavy. "Mr. Blakely."

He stood and stared at her, overcome with the oddness of all this. He had seen her but seldom, and had taken little heed of her. To him, she was a dull and stupid woman, aging and useless, not quite the wife for Mr. John Turnbull. His brows knitted. What was he to do? She blocked his way with her solid sprawling limbs and body. It was absurd. Then he had a thought. Was Turnbull ill, dying, that he had been sent for with such urgency? Some changes in the will, perhaps? No doubt this was correct. This enormous bloated woman, this figure of stupid and shapeless tragedy, was a creature about to be widowed. But why was there no one about to guide him, no sound, nothing but this woman staring at him out of some blackness of her own?

He composed his features, cleared his throat. "Mr. Turnbull?" he said, delicately, in a thin sad tone. "It is not so very bad, is it?"

She did not answer. She only looked at him. And then it appeared to him that within those swollen and streaming eyes a bright spark of light began to glitter. She stretched up her large arm to him and caught his wrist. He felt her sudden and frantic strength. She glanced up and behind her, with a hunted expression, which, as it returned to him, had a slyness and secrecy about it.

She began to whisper, and he had to bend his head to hear the fumbling and hissing words that came through her shaking lips.

"Go away, Mr. Blakely. Mr. T. doesn't want you. He wants you to go away. I—I've waited for you. It's all done, Mr. Blakely."

She heaved herself to her feet, and swayed. He had an instant's fright that that immense bulk would fall upon him and he tried to step aside. But she retained her grip on his bony wrist, and looked down upon him. Now she was urgent, frenzied, hurried.

"Good night, Mr. Blakely," she said, and she pushed downwards upon him, so that he fell back, and had to grip the balustrade to keep from falling. He looked up at her, and she appeared even larger to him than she was, menacing, frightful, and even her fatness had in it a sinister meaning and mountainous power.

But he had a courage of his own. He stood his ground. "Mrs. Turnbull, ma'am, Mr. Turnbull sent for me less than an hour ago. It was very urgent. I must come at once. I will see him for just a moment——"

"Good night, Mr. Blakely," she repeated, as if she had not heard. She smiled. There was something terrible to him in that smile. Something more than a little mad, and frenetic. Confusedly he wondered if he should shout, bring help. He was being pushed downwards on the steps, and she was following him, holding his wrist so firmly that he heard the bones creaking in her hand. In a moment he would be on the last step. He felt there was something nightmarish, inexplicable, in all this.

The whole damned house was so silent, so still. He heard the ticking of the clock. He saw the lighted hall just below him. He saw the shadows of the light on the towering wall to his left, the shimmering gilt of the balustrade which he was gripping with his free hand. And above him, this horrible, this swelling and gigantic woman, pushing him down.

Then, blessedly, he heard a door open on the upper hall, saw a gush of light, heard an impatient masculine voice. John's voice. Mr. Blakely was so relieved that he burst into hot sweat.

"Mr. Turnbull!" he shouted. "It's me, Blakely! I'll be up directly!"

He felt the grip on his wrist slackening. He looked up at Lilybelle. She appeared to be dissolving. She shrank back, as if lashed. She thrust her body against the wall. Mr. Blakely, with one bound, was past her. He rushed up the stairs as if all hell was at his heels. Only at the top did he pause.

Lilybelle's body was in shadow. Her face was only a large shapeless form. But her eyes glowed, incandescent, as if lighted with a fire of their own, as they stared up after him. And even he saw their terror, their despair, their hopelessness.

Shrugging, shivering a little, he raced down the hallway to John's room.

CHAPTER 51

Mr. Hiram Blakely was convinced that there was something extremely peculiar in the whole situation. However, his advice was not requested. It seemed to him somewhat indiscreet that John Turnbull should so lavishly grant power of attorney to his daughters' husbands, and with such haste and lack of careful thought. Had he been able to attain John's ear, he would have murmured a suggestion that these new powers be bestowed only until such time as he returned to his business, and that they were to terminate on that very instant. But there was an air of disorder and chaos in John's apartments tonight, of noise and confusion. Mr Blakely shook his head slowly, and pursed his lips. He did not like the crackling atmosphere about the two young gentlemen. No doubt they were estimable and trust-worthy—certainly. Otherwise, John Turnbull would never have allowed himself to sign such a paper without glancing at the contents. But it was unheard of that a man should be so hasty, so noisy, so boisterous, and blind to the possibility of quite a number of contingencies. Recklessness, to Mr. Blakely, was the supreme vice in business. Now, if he could have had John's ear, he would have suggested a sober meeting in his law offices, among his associates, and a long discussion, hedged about by wherefores and whereases, all iron-clad, all safe and orderly. There was no common sense in putting all that power into another man's hands, no matter how closely attached to one. Witnesses, foolscap paper, long documents, files and leather-bound briefs might all be tedious, but they had saved many a man from folly and ruin.

But, within a very few moments the clever Mr. Blakely clearly saw that the young gentlemen had no intention of allowing him to gain John's private ear. He felt conspiracy in the room. Each time that he lifted the ominous paper, cleared his throat, and with a gnarled finger was about to point out to the loud and riotous John some sinister implication in a phrase, the young gentlemen would "surge" about the little lawyer, and talk very rapidly and confusingly, appealing to John about the most irrelevant things, laughing, filling his glass (which had been filled too often and too significantly in Mr. Blakely's opinion), and slapping his back with the utmost affection. They did not trust Mr. Blakely, it was very evident.

This was all very improper, even alarming. He recalled Lilybelle waiting on the stairs, and frowned. He cleared his throat again, then met Rufus' slit of a green eye. There was some warning, there, but fellowship and promise, also. Mr. Blakely tapped on the shining table before him, frowned again.

He had thought he had come to make some changes in the will of a sick or dying man. Well, it was very evident that Mr. Turnbull was ill, perhaps mortally so. Mr. Blakely had never cared for Mr. Turnbull, personally. A reckless, heedless, violent chap, with business genius, perhaps, but no business head. The kind of feller that was dangerous. Business, like the mills of the gods, should grind slowly and ponderously, but grind exceeding small. John never ground. He exploded in the mills, set all the wheels to whirling rapidly and with tremendous row, his vitality infusing a kind of delirium into all proceedings. Not proper in the least. It showed a serious lack of respect for the machinery of business. Mr. Blakely did not like buccaneers. They generally resembled

Roman rockets, spraying the air all about them with sparks, fire and detonations. Then they fizzled out into blackness, or worse, ignited more sober structures and blew them up in the general ruin.

Well, Mr. Blakely had heard whispers, of course. Winds of rumour and conjecture blew all up and down Wall Street. He had heard that Jay Regan (whom Mr. Blakely revered as he had never revered God) was seriously concerned with Mr. Turnbull's wildness, lack of forethought, and the probable collapse of his enterprises. Rumour said that Mr. Turnbull was very ill, that he was mad, that he no longer appeared to know what he was doing, that he had become excessively violent and explosive, and then had habits of sinking into black despondencies and silences during which he seemed drugged or stupefied. Mr. Blakely had a theory that Mr. Turnbull drank too much. Men who drank should not be allowed to build the business structure of a nation. Pioneering, buccaneering, vividness and recklessness were no longer necessary in America. The dynamite had blown out the holes for the foundations, but now sober bricklayers and carpenters were needed to erect the solid buildings where commerce and trade and finance could be carried on reasonably and with respectability, and by men in quiet garments and watch-chains, with beards and noble paunches.

He studied John, who was signing the papers with a hand visibly trembling. A sick man; a terribly sick man. A mad man. Yes, there was no doubt he had become mad, in a riotous, noisy, incoherent kind of way. Those sunken delirious eyes, that congested colour, that twitching mouth, the eyelids jerking, veins beating in the dark forehead under the streaked black curls: all these were the signs of a man on the edge of collapse, of raving, of delirium.

Mr. Blakely, who was a stern teetotaler, was convinced that John owed all this to his excessive drinking. Who ever heard of a drunkard in business! The very idea was obscene to Mr. Blakely. John's bouts of constant drinking were no news on Wall Street. He had become so quarrelsome, so unreasonable, so violent, that all avoided him who could.

Well, then, reflected Mr. Blakely, perhaps all this was for the best. He regarded Rufus acutely. Yes, this one would become the proper business man. Perhaps a trifle too elegant, too refined. But there was steel there, too, yes, indeed. A schemer and a liar, it was said, a vicious feller. But no fool. And, in Mr. Blakely's opinion, a man who was not a fool was halfway to heaven. As for Mr. Brogan there, grinning, sipping at his glass, his little bright blue eyes darting everywhere restlessly as if something prevented them from

435

focussing, Mr. Blakely did not trust him at all. But this distrust had nothing to do with personality. It was just that here was another man similar to Mr. Turnbull. Mr. Brogan was an Irishman, and every one knew that Irishmen could not be relied upon, that they were wild and unpredictable, untrustworthy and rascals, vivid and expedient. Mr. Blakely had nothing against expediency, but he preferred the colder and more thoughtful expediency of Mr. Hastings. The Irish expediency was delirious, also, and explosive. It was said that Mr. Turnbull was an Englishman by birth. But there was nothing English in that dark and mercurial face, those turbulent eyes, that air of haste and violence. Mr. Blakely darkly suspected that Mr. Turnbull was really Irish. Yes, that explained a great deal.

And Mr. Blakely cleverly reflected that the coming race of giants were to be men of iron and ice, not such as Turnbull and Brogan. They would make a predictable world, these giants. The Turnbulls and the Brogans were finished. They were anachronisms. They were passing, as the dinosaurs had passed, because the climate was now one in which they would perish. They could not adapt themselves.

Mr. Blakely, then, breathed a sigh of relief. He no longer desired to warn John. He glanced at Rufus, sitting near his father-in-law, languidly, elegantly, quietly at ease, and again he saw that amiable flash, that promise, in those green eyes. Mr. Blakely was suddenly quite abnormally excited.

He looked again at Patrick, who was moving restlessly up and down the long and handsome room, pausing to stare absently at some ornament, some lamp, in which he could not possibly be interested. Sometimes his eyebrows jerked, as if his thoughts were tempestuous and uneasy. A handsome big devil, like John Turnbull. Mr. Blakely did not like handsome big devils. They were not really gentlemen. They were actors. Actors in business! Mr. Blakely shook his head sombrely.

He became aware that Rufus was studying him intently. He turned slowly and met the young man's eyes again. In his mind he said to him: You know, of course, that I could have stopped all this? Rufus nodded almost imperceptibly, and smiled his thin spasmodic smile, very amiably. Yes, he replied to that silent question, I know you could have stopped it. I shall not forget it; I will talk with you soon. We are clever men, together.

And then, as if struck, Mr. Blakely turned quickly and met Patrick's eyes. They were pinpoints of blue fire, and his expression was sour and lowering, full of contempt and knowledge. Mr. Blakely was startled. He had not thought this big and flamboyant young Irishman possessed any subtlely at all. A pirate, but unsubtle. Now Mr. Blakely was not so sure. What was the matter with the feller? He had wanted this, had he not? He had conspired all this, most certainly, with Mr. Hastings? Why, then, this dangerous look, this twisted mouth, this nasty expression in the eyes? Mr. Blakely had never encountered a man with any conscience before. Surely this feller had no conscience, or he would not have begun this! Mr. Blakely was full of cool disdain. He despised men who began things and then halted irresolutely in the very midst of events to hate themselves and hate others. Weaklings. Feckless fools. Mr. Blakely smiled thinly. No doubt Mr. Hastings understood all this, however. No doubt he had his own plans.

Mr. Blakely was suddenly alarmed and tense. Brogan had moved quickly behind John, was staring over his shoulder as the final sheet was being signed. His hand lifted. His expression was something quite ominous and hideous to see. All this happened in an instant, but it seemed hours to Mr. Blakely. He did not observe that Rufus had sprung silently to his feet, had dexterously swept up the papers, and was now extending them to Mr. Blakely. Mr. Blakely was very adequate. He literally snatched the papers, slid them swiftly into his dispatch case. Patrick stood there, blinking, his face crimson, his eyes flickering.

John began to laugh, loudly, raucously. He flung himself back into his chair. Rufus politely filled his glass again. John drank. Patrick stood in the middle of the floor, cleverly shut out from everything, fuming, scowling, biting his lip. But slowly, a look of relief, of indifferent resignation, came over his face, and he smiled darkly. Yes, indeed, a weakling, a wastrel, a fool.

It was more than two hours later that John, staggering quite heavily, was escorted by two affectionate young gentlemen to the door of his apartments. They wished to go in with him, and assist him into bed. But he shook his head, grinning at them. They went away, but as they retreated down the corridor, they turned and saw him still watching them, and his grin was like a flash of light on his dark face.

He opened the door and stumbled into the warm, lamplighted dusk of his sitting-room. At first his confused and reeling senses did not warn him that he had a visitor. He felt his way to the bed, and sat down upon it, and rubbed his damp hands over his forehead, blinking, trying to catch his thoughts in the whirling confusion of his drunken mind. He heard a little sound, a little movement. He lifted his head and could hardly believe what he saw. Lilybelle was standing in the center of the room, a wet shawl about her shoulders, her bonnet awry on her head, her tumbled hair streaming about her ghastly face. Drunk though he was, he had an instant of terror, of fear, for never had Lilybelle looked like this, so distraught, so unafraid, and with such an affrighting expression.

She stood before him, mountainous, looming, and silent. Again, he could hardly believe it. She had never dared enter here before, and now here she was, and she looked at him as if he was a hated stranger. There was stark denunciation in her face and eyes, tragedy, and awfulness.

Now he heard her voice. "John," she said, and she spoke very quietly, but with an echoing immensity of tone, "where is my lassie? You have driven away my lass. My little one. I've searched through the streets for her. You've driven away my child, your child, John Turnbull. What have you done with her?"

It was a dream, thought John, confusedly. He had never seen Lilybelle like this before. She advanced a step towards him, and there was distracted grief and agony in her voice as she repeated:

"Where is my lass?"

She clasped her big hands convulsively before her, and wrung them. He heard her breath, anguished, torn. Her eyes glowed upon him. She regarded him with awful hatred.

She loomed over him, gigantic, crushing, expanding until all the room seemed filled with her presence. There was turbulence about her, and menace, and huge passion.

John shook his head to clear away the fumes that darkened his vision. Then, suddenly, he was quite sober. He saw everything with clarity, sharp and outlined with light.

"What are you talking about, Lily?" he asked, dully. "You mean Adelaide has gone? Where? That's impossible."

He heard the rushing of her breath. "She's gone. She said she was to go for help, for you. Only for you. Into the wind and the rain she went. I saw it in her face. Her sickness. I tried to hold her back. But she would go. There was no holding her. It was for you."

Suddenly she cried out in a loud broken voice, and wrung her hands again: "My God! God! Where is my lass? What has become of her?"

Her face was flooded with tears, contorted. She shook violently.

"My baby, my poor little one. It was for you, John Turnbull. You who drove her away. As you allus drove her away. Year after year, since she was born, you drove her away!

Do you remember how you did it? You bad, you wicked bad man!"

She was only a step from him now. He saw that she was near collapse, near insanity from grief and fear. And now he saw as she looked at him that she hated him, loathed him.

He gaped at her incredulously. He forced himself to his feet and grasped a post of the bed to hold himself up. So many things there were to see now in this poor enormous creature, this terrified and agonized mother, this repudiating woman who hated him at last and saw him clearly.

"Lily," he said. His throat was dry and thick as he swallowed. "She can't have gone far, the little fool. Where could she go? To whom? To help me? Who does she know?" He paused, swallowed again. His heart was beating with a fateful foreboding, close to terror. "Have you—have you seen the police?"

But she was staring at him as if she had never seen him before. Words poured like a solemn and deathly cataract from her lips.

"All her life, you drove her away. As you drove me away. You never wanted us. That was because we loved you. You never wanted a body to love you, did you, John Turnbull? You searched out those that hated you, because you hated, too. You had your fancy woman, as was a poison in your heart, and she a wife and mother. You had your Mr. Wilkins, as is a wicked man. Allus, you surrounded yourself with bad men and women, because there was badness in you, and hate, and all sorts of hellish things."

She paused. A wave of purple rolled over her features. She gasped and pressed her hand to her enormous breast. All the careful enunciation, all the proper false grammar which Miss Beardsley had taught her, was washed away in the flood of her passion and anguish, and it was the Lilybelle Botts of over a quarter of a century ago that stood before John now.

Her voice, raucous, tearing, crude, assaulted him like fists. "Why'd'ye hate us, John? Only because we loved you? You couldn't abide that, could you? You was afraid we'd heal you. You didn't want to be healed. You was allus a coward. Only cowards hate. Wot did they take from you? A woman as never cared for you, a bad woman in her heart. I've known it all for over ten years.

"You've 'ad your Mr. Wilkins, as killed your spirit. Because you wanted it to be killed. You wanted to hug your hate, like a serpint. Not to hate would have been too much for you. Every man must've a reason to live. You thought your reason to live was to hate. And for such a little thing! For such a silly bloody thing! Somethin' you never even

439

wanted!"

She seemed inspired with the wildest passion, hatred and loathing. She was so close to him now that he could smell the wet woolen scent of her drenched shawl, her sweat, the damp silk of her gown, her very flesh.

"Wot've you done to yourself, John? And to me, whose only fault was lovin' you? And to my little lass, as loved you, too? You've killed us, John Turnbull, and you'll answer to God for it!"

The carpeted floor seemed to move under John's feet. He clutched the post with a slipping hand. He heard the ominous rolling of his heart, and there was a fierce sickness somewhere in the center of it. He stretched out his free hand to his wife.

"Lily. Don't talk like that. I—I haven't hated you, my dear." A strange and startled look flashed into his eyes, and he stared at her, moistening his lips. "Why, damn you, I've loved you! I love you! I never knew it before."

She looked at his hand, at his face, and shuddered. She retreated from him. But he stared at her in amazed wonder, as at a revelation. Something like a fiery wound opened in his chest, and he felt its heat run all along his nerves.

Her voice bore in upon his disordered senses like a crash of thunder:

"D'ye think the others—the other lassies—ever loved you, John? They hated you! Wot do you think of that? They hated you. They and their men. They plotted against you. That's wot they've done to you, tonight, and me and my little lass tried to save you! We couldn't. Because there's a judgment on you, for your badness. God wouldn't let us help you. There's a hard and terrible way for you to walk, my man! A hard and terrible way. And you'll go it alone. Me and my little lass won't walk it with you."

Again, grief and agony overwhelmed her, and she gasped for breath. "Where is my little lass? Give me back my little lass!"

Everything darkened, wavered, expanded, blazed with light before John. He pressed his hands to his throat.

He tried to speak calmly:

"Lily, my dear, my love, try to control yourself. The child can't have gone far in two or three hours. Lily, try to listen to me. We'll call the police. We'll find her. We'll bring her home."

He paused. He saw Adelaide before him, as she had faced him that night. And again the wound opened in his heart, like a flame. Terror seized on him. He could not bear the immensity of his new revelations.

440

He caught up one of Lilybelle's hands. She did not struggle with him. She was spent, broken. Her hand was very cold and leaden, and full of tremor. He looked at it, then carried it to his lips. But it did not warm, nor move.

"My lass," she repeated, looking at him. "My little lass."

"I'll bring her home, my love," he said, rubbing her hand in his palms. "Sit down, Lily. Let me call some one. Rest. I'll go for her, myself. We'll find her."

She was silent. She did not stir. She was a great figure of stone.

CHAPTER 52

ONCE out in the dark windy street, Adelaide was again impressed with the sense of desperate hurry which had assaulted her a few moments ago. The cold damp gale struck at her hot and feverish body, and she shivered automatically. She hardly felt the discomfort, however, and her thoughts were so urgent that the pounding pain in her head, and the knife in her breast were only vaguely apparent to her.

There were few about, and she raced swiftly down the street in the direction of Anthony Bollister's home. The wind caught at her shawl, almost tore it from her shoulders. Her bonnet wrenched at her head, loosened her hair. Mud and water splashed over her boots and skirt, and once she tripped, falling on her knees in an icy puddle. She sprang to her feet again, the dirty water saturating her skirt. Faster, faster, until it seemed to her that she was soaring, and her urgency was a hot blaze in her mind.

Within the hour, Mr. Blakely would be at her father's house, and the damage and ruin would be hopelessly accomplished. It was a race between her and the lawyer. How Anthony was to work a miracle she did not yet know, but the thought of his face, keen, sharp, coldly watchful and hard, filled her with hope and resolution. Someway, when she appealed to him, he would know. He would not fail. Of this she was certain.

She gave no thought to the vision of herself bursting in upon Anthony and his astounded family, crying out to him for help, seizing his hand, and racing back with him to her father's house. She only knew that he would come, must come.

She reached the broad white steps of the Gorth home. The

flickering light of the street-lamp shone on their dripping wetness. Gaunt bare trees, only just beyond the bud, cast heaving and dancing spectral shapes on the pavement. She flew up the stairs and pulled the bell with almost delirious vigour, and then grasped the iron grilling in avid hands, and shook it. Beyond the glass she could see the long white hall, the lamps, the curving staircase.

A shadow intervened between her and the light. The door opened. Adelaide sprang at the door, pushed it open, and catapulted herself into the hall.

She was a strange and astonishing and alarming sight to the old butler. He saw before him a panting young woman dressed in quiet sober garments of an upper servant, or, at the best, a governess. Her wet shawl slipped off one shoulder; her bonnet was askew on her falling roll of light brown hair; her skirt was drenched with mud and water to the knees. She was gloveless, disheveled, wild. It was her face, however, which alarmed the old man the most, so blazing white was it, the eyes distended and glittering, her whole aspect febrile and urgent and disordered.

She was hurling incoherent words at him: "Mr. Anthony! I must see Mr. Anthony at once! Tell him to come to me directly!"

The old man stepped back a pace or two. The young female's garments were dripping, saturated. She had left dreadful footsteps of mud and water on the pale carpet. She was quite insane, he thought, this young person in her plain garments, and with her stormy gestures and fierce agitation, and terrible leaping eyes.

He stammered, trying to recover his composure: "That is impossible, ma'am. Mr. Anthony is not at home. He has gone with Mr. and Mrs. Bollister and Mr. and Mrs. Gorth to the Academy of Music. From there, I understand, they are to visit some friends——"

She was still now, and speechless. But she vibrated with her hurry and passion. He took this opportunity to approach her again and seize her arm. He must eject this impossible young female immediately. What could such as she have to do with Mr. Anthony? A most odious young creature, and obviously drunk. Young men would insist upon associating with dreadful female persons, and then wondered afterwards why they were embarrassed and discommoded.

She wrung her gloveless hands.

"You've got to find him! Immediately!" she cried, trying to wrench her arm free. She felt herself being remorselessly backed towards the door, and cast about her a glance of the most tragic frenzy. "You must find him, tell him that Adelaide needs him——!"

"Yes, yes," said the butler, soothingly, deftly opening the door behind her. "I'll tell him, ma'am, as soon as he comes home. No doubt he'll go to Miss—Adelaide——"

She struggled with him, tearing at his firm hand on her arm with frantic fingers. Her knees shook under her.

"I must stay! I'll wait, while you send for him." She cried this wailingly into his face, and her look frightened him.

"No, no, ma'am," he replied. They were on the threshold now, and Adelaide stumbled. He tried to release her, but it was she now who gripped his arm with drowning hands, to regain her step, to keep herself inside the house. "You go home, there's a good girl, and when Mr. Anthony returns, I'll tell him all about it."

Fearing, for a moment, that he was being injudicious, he glanced down behind her at the street to see if it was possible that she had come in a private carriage. But the street was empty except for the wind and the rain and the twisting shadows of the trees. Now his efforts to free himself were more brutal, and he shouted: "There now, be off with you, or I'll call the police, that I will. No nonsense, now. Let go of my arm, or I warn you it will be the worse for you, my fine girl."

He twisted his arm, wrenching it from her grasp. She tottered on the step, fell backward, flailing the air outside with her arms. He shut the door in her face. She lost her balance, fell on her knees and hands, her head striking the grill-work. She was stunned. The sharp edge had cut her forehead, and while she knelt there, shaking her head from side to side to recover herself, a thin trickle of blood spurted through the skin and flesh and began to drip down her cheek. She gasped aloud. The light rain had increased in fury, and fell over her in an icy stream.

But the water revived her. She caught hold of the grill and pulled herself to her feet, one heel tearing a long slit in her skirt. Then she screamed. She shook the grill madly. She tore at the bell, and heard its long pealing inside the house. She saw the empty white hall. It remained empty. She screamed over and over, until her throat closed, and her breath stopped.

Somewhere near by a window opened and she heard a shout of "Police!" She put her hand to her mouth. She was trembling so strongly that she staggered. Then she turned and rushed down the steps, and raced down the street again, her shawl and bonnet strings streaming behind her. She thought she heard pursuing footfalls, and fled like the very wind itself.

She could go no further. Shafts of light and darkness stabbed her eyes. She leaned against the wet trunk of a tree and tried to fumble with her shawl. Rain and tears ran down her cheeks. She looked about her with distended eyes, sobbing aloud in hoarse gasps. A lonely carriage came on echoing wheels down the street, and she shrank back into the shadows.

She heard a hollow groaning near her. "O Papa. O Tony. O God." She did not know it was herself.

Now the urgency was closer upon her, like a visible and awful presence. She began to run again, weaving from side to side on the running pavement. Then she stopped so suddenly she almost fell.

Uncle Bob Wilkins! Why had she not thought of him before, her father's friend, her own dear friend? She cried aloud, with joy, sobbing with relief and new hope.

It hardly seemed possible that one in her condition of mind and body could find her way safely through the streets. She never remembered that journey; she only remembered the darkness, floating mists of white clouds colliding with what must have been lamp-posts and trees and iron fences. It was a journey through an eternity of agony and haste, led by instinct and the singleness of her desperate purpose. As she hurried, her eyes staring blindly ahead, her cold wet hand impatiently wiping away the blood that ran down her cheek, her breath a wrenched hoarse clamour in her throat, she thought of nothing, saw nothing, but what she must do.

Then she saw bright lights, the bulk of Mr. Wilkins' pleasant small house. The curtains had not been drawn. She hurried up the flagged walk, and was faintly aware of mingled firelight and lamplight on the glistening windows. She did not wait to ring the bell or lift the knocker. She turned the handle of the door and it opened, and she burst into the small warm parlour and the cold wet wind in with her.

Mr. Wilkins, who liked happy quiet evenings alone occasionally, was sitting nodding and yawning over his newspapers before the fire. He heard the door open, felt the draft, and, startled, rose to his feet, the papers spilling, crackling, upon the hearth. There were several dogs dozing on the hearthrug, and they leapt up, snarling, and rushed towards the girl.

It was a moment or two before Mr. Wilkins could believe that this disordered and streaming young woman with the bloody cheek and brow, the fallen hair, the torn skirt and muddy boots, was his pet, his little lass, his Adelaide. When he did so, he cried out, incredulously, and with horror, and ran towards her with his little fat hands outstretched.

"Adelaide!" he exclaimed. "My God! Wot the bloody hell, my child! Wot is it?"

She stood before him, speechless, panting, swaying. He put out his arms and caught her before she fell. Half-carrying her, half-dragging her, he got her to a chair near the fire, dropped her into it. She was barely conscious now. She lay back in the chair, her nostrils dilating and closing with her efforts to breathe. The blood dripped unheeded by her over her cheek and chin, and then her throat. Kneeling beside her, cursing, terrified, Mr. Wilkins removed her shawl, wiped away the blood, rubbed her hands and cheeks. The dogs, alarmed and uneasy, sniffed about her, looked at her and then their master. There were deep growls in their throats, as they tried to understand this extraordinary thing.

Her clothing was drenched to the flesh. There was a terrible rough sound in her breathing. She lay back, her eyes closed and bruised, her body slack. Mr. Wilkins heard the frightened beating of his heart, and increased the vigour of his rubbing of her hands. Over his shoulder he shouted for his old housekeeper, and when she came, hastily fastening a dressing-gown over her nightgown, he ordered her to bring wine, a dry shawl, some water.

But before the old woman could return, Adelaide had recovered her consciousness. She sat upright in her chair. She grasped Mr. Wilkins by his wide fat shoulders, and bent her face, so wild, so distraught, so fierce, towards him.

"Papa!" she cried. "It's Papa, Uncle Bob."

He sat back on his heels and regarded her with open horror and amazement. He looked at the blood which continued to drip down her cheek. Then his face wrinkled, ape-like, drew together, and his eyes narrowed to slits with inhuman savagery and hatred.

"He did this to you, Adelaide, my little lass? He struck you? He drove you out?"

Black murder rose in him. He caught her hands away from his shoulders and held them tightly.

But she was shaking her head wildly. "No, no! It's Rufus, it's Patrick! They're getting him to sign papers, tonight, right now, to ruin him. Uncle Bob, you've got to help him, you've got to stop them!"

He knelt before her, speechless. The wrinkles smoothed themselves away from his large round face, in which the ruddiness slowly began to return. She had seized his hands, twisting her own away from him in order to grasp them in a grip of cold iron.

"Uncle Bob, I've been to Tony. But he's not there. They

—threw me out. They wouldn't send for him, or let me wait for him." Her voice had dwindled, had become a thin husky whine. "Tony would help me. I'm his wife, Uncle Bob. But he wasn't there. They threw me out. You've got to go, Uncle Bob, and help Papa. Now. You mustn't wait."

Mr. Wilkins was astounded. He blinked and gaped. He shook his head as if to clear it. Then he drew the girl to him and held her tightly. "You're married, Addy? To Mr. Bollister? Gad, this is unbelievable." She struggled to release herself, but his grasp strengthened. He kissed her poor white cheek, smoothed her hair with one hand. "There, there, my little lovey. Don't upset yourself. They threw you out, eh? Tell your Uncle Bob all about it. There now, quiet yourself, my pet. Uncle Bob's 'ere, ain't he? Did Uncle Bob ever refuse his lass anything?"

She was weeping uncontrollably. She clung to him. Her speech was incoherent, but Mr. Wilkins soon grasped it all.

"Uncle Bob," she groaned, "you mustn't wait another minute. You must go at once. Before they ruin Papa——"

Damn your bloody Papa, thought Mr. Wilkins. Damn him all to hell, the black-faced bastard. Help him? I'll push him deeper into perdition, that I will. So, the lads lost no time, did they?

"Yes, yes, lovey," he said. "I'll go immejate. Your uncle Bob won't fail his lass. There, there now, it's a bad cut you've got on your sweet little head. Uncle Bob loves his little pet. There, now, up we go, and rest awhile, and then Uncle Bob goes."

The old housekeeper had returned with bowls and cloths and bottles, accompanied by her husband. But Mr. Wilkins winked at them, shook his head. He lifted Adelaide to her feet, motioned to the old people.

"You'll take Miss Adelaide upstairs and put her to bed. I've got work to do."

He gently turned Adelaide over to his servants. But she struggled to leave them, straining in their arms towards him.

"Uncle Bob! You'll go? Now?"

"Yes, lovey, I said immejate, didn't I? You'll go with Mrs. Downey, and rest, and I'll come back after I've done me work."

But the girl no longer heard him. She had collapsed. The two old people carried her between them up the narrow polished stairs. Mr. Wilkins watched them go. To the last, he saw Adelaide's white trailing hand over the old man's shoulder, the fallen mass of her light shining hair. Again his face darkened, wrinkled, became monstrous.

He found his hat and coat, his umbrella and gloves. He let himself out of the house and went at once to his near neighbour, Dr. Walker.

CHAPTER 53

A NTHONY BOLLISTER was dressing for dinner in the gloomiest of moods, wrathful and full of resentment. This was his wedding day, but he had no bride. He had nothing at all but the memory of a pale and feverish little creature who had stood beside him briefly, murmuring a few incoherent words, a hasty kiss, shy and strangely burning, and then a plea, uttered in a breathless voice about her damned Papa, and the necessity of her "saving" him from some nebulous and ridiculous trouble.

He despised himself for his weakness. He ought to have refused to listen to her, to have forced her into his carriage, to have driven away with her, anywhere. Yet, when she had spoken so to him, fixing her large brown eyes pleadingly upon his, he had said nothing, had only taken on a harsh and formidable look. Perhaps it was because of something in her eyes, too bright, too glowing, too restless. He had felt a curious apprehension when he had looked into them. And this apprehension had stilled him as a warning might have done. He had finally said: "Only a day or two, then, my sweet. And then, if you don't come to me, I shall go for you. I mean this."

She had smiled quite convulsively, he remembered, his hands pausing as they folded his cravat. He looked intently in the mirror, trying to recall other things about Adelaide that morning. She had been very white, not in the least the "blushing bride." He remembered the touch of her hand, hot and tremulous, and her breath, a little too loud and quick. His hands dropped to his sides, as he frowned with concentration. He had been so absorbed in his anger and resentment against her, against his weakness in allowing her to leave him, that he had forgotten things that ought to have had some significance for him.

"She was ill," he said aloud, incredulously, his heart beating faster. That was it! It was a stricken girl who had stood beside him that morning, and he had not known in his selfish folly and excitement. But, why had she not told him? Such a foolish little creature, so steely, so soft, so quiet, but with such passion when she was aroused. It was such a nature

447

that concealed danger to itself from others.

He stared unseeingly at the mirror. This damned nonsense! He had never been frightened before in his life, but now a coldness of fear possessed him. Tomorrow, he would go to her, go to the house of her blessed damnable Papa, and look the scoundrel in the eye and say to him: "I have come for my wife. I want my wife."

The sharp, somewhat hard and inflexible face in the mirror tightened, and his slate-gray eyes sparkled. He brushed his thick sandy hair. The line of his chin had turned bony white and glistened in the light of the lamp. It was not a good face that glimmered back at him, not even a kind one. It had a cold ruthlessness about it, an intellectual implacability. He put on his coat and fastened it, and he was frowning again, his thin cheeks drawn in sombrely.

Tomorrow morning he and Adelaide would be together. Nothing would stop him now. He had never feared the opinion or the anger of others, had never allowed them to halt or restrain him.

He heard a soft tapping at the door, and turned. His mother was entering, in her favourite dove-gray, her white shoulders and neck and chest gleaming like polished marble. Her gown, draped and bustled, was distinguished and elegant. She was always so elegant, he thought, regarding her in silence and detachment, and without love. She moved perfectly; all her slight and beautiful figure was perfect. There was no error, no blurring, in the cool shape of her small pointed face, the resolute shining of her gray and brilliant eyes. Nor was there the slightest fading in the smooth high sweep of her brown hair, in the pale tint of her haughty thin mouth. He could not recall that she had grown the least older since his boyhood. Ageless, aristocratic, cold and indomitable, she was always the same. He had rarely seen her disturbed or agitated, and even then there had been something intimidating about her, as though the cause of her disturbance or agitation had been the sheerest impertinence, the worse *lèse majesté* committed against her person.

Yet, though he looked at her in silence, without emotion, he saw Adelaide's resemblance to her. Adelaide could become such another delicate ruthlessness, such another fragile tyranny, such another steely egotist. It was a matter of exquisite balance of circumstances. She, Eugenia, had been a woman deprived of what she thought she had wanted, and she had become a frozen fury in consequence. What egotism! What absurdity! Was it possible that such creatures could exist, who, thwarted, could become such fools out of their impossible vanity? As if the world was not full of frustrations, of lost dreams, of defeats and retreats. He saw that he must become ever watchful of Adelaide, lest circumstances, lest conceit, lest egotism, turn the goodness he knew was in her to such patrician decay and hateful selfishness.

He was so absorbed in his thoughts that he started when Eugenia repeated impatiently: "Tony, I have been talking to you, and you have been staring at me as if I am an image. Surely you owe your mother the courtesy of listening to her."

"I'm sorry, mother," he said, coldly.

She stood near him, rigid and straight, her face turned to him with glacial calm.

"This is my last appeal to you, Tony. We, your father and I, have not mentioned the matter for a long time, hoping you would come to your senses. We are going back to England, perhaps very soon. We wish you to come with us."

He was surprised, and incredulous. Had she tired of her stupid and violent lover, then? He regarded her intently, but saw nothing changed in her look, in the steadfast brilliance of her eyes. He felt a new contempt for her.

He shrugged. "Mother, I also thought you would come to your senses, and at least respect my dignity and my own decisions. I hope you will be happy in England. You never really lived in America, did you? I shall miss you, of course. But I stay here. This is my country, as England is yours. I have work to do here." He paused. "However, I hope you will invite me to visit you."

She gazed at him in her inflexible silence that so often intimidated weaker characters. Her mouth lost even its pale tint. It became hard and fixed as stone, and the gray shining of her eyes was like twilight on ice.

"Cannot we discuss this like intelligent beings, and not fools?" she asked, and her voice was low and brittle.

Anthony smiled. He saw all through all her tricks. He knew that so many became excited and incoherent, and lost, when his mother said this to them, in such a tone, which implied that her antagonist was a weak and tremulous fool, all heedless excitement, all childishness and vulnerability. The antagonist, the opposer, might be, in the beginning, as calm and self-possessed as herself, and just as inflexible, but her imputation that he was wallowing in emotion and extravagance was invariably his undoing. Then, she was triumphant, carrying the spoils off the field, leaving the other bewildered and fuming, hating her, hating himself, confusedly wondering what had happened.

Yes, it was a clever trick. She was really the fool. She

would never learn that he, perhaps one of only a few, could not be deluded into believing that he was emotional and excited, and that she alone, because of her coolness and restraint, had right and justice on her side.

His smile was very unpleasant, its amusement malicious.

"No one ever disputed my intelligence," he said, deliberately lowering his voice to a murmur so that it was almost inaudible, and very infuriating to her. "Nor am I aware that I am a fool. Do sit down, mother, and we'll go all over this again." He looked at his watch with elaborate concentration. "We have exactly fourteen minutes before the final dinner bell, and I am willing to give them to you and your really tedious arguments."

Eugenia flushed. It was not a warming flush. It darkened her cheeks so that they appeared sunken, and her years became evident. However, she forced herself to sit down. Enthroned like this, like a queen, she felt her power, and her silly son was a suppliant before her. Her gray gown rustled richly as she sat; the pearls about her throat glistened. She was very angry, and infuriated against Anthony for having deftly turned her trick aside, and smiling that hateful smile.

"You are impertinent, Tony. Impertinent and brash, like a child. Will you ever become fully adult? I doubt it. I really doubt it. I have hoped that you would eventually reach a man's stature. It is very humiliating to me to believe that you will remain in a perpetual childhood."

"Give me time, dear mother," he urged, nastily. He would not deny anything. She had a habit of saying such outrageous and well-bred things, which confounded others, set them excitedly to denying them, thus giving her the advantage.

Eugenia paused. Their eyes clashed. Anthony retained his smile, a little disdainful, and very removed and untouched.

"You have had time, years of time," she pointed out, in a thin hard voice. "Your juvenility has not decreased in the slightest. Nevertheless, I want to point out to you some facts which even your childishness must take heed of. When we go to England, you will have only a small income of your own."

"I'll have my work, with Uncle Richard," said Anthony. He had laid his watch on the commode near him. "Ten minutes now, mother. No, eleven, I beg your pardon."

Eugenia's small and delicate hands clenched briefly on her knees.

"What he can give you, even if he gives you all, is not what you will have in England. Are you an idealist, Tony?" and she smiled disagreeably. "Do you think that 'money is nothing'"?

"Oh, I'm all the rosy idealist," answered Anthony airily. "A crust of bread in peace and quiet and contentment, and all that——"

Eugenia's nostrils dilated dangerously. She regarded her son with open dislike and contempt.

"I ignore your impertinence, your stupidity. I wish to recall to your attention that you have an aunt, your father's aunt, Arabella. She has a claim on a great part of Uncle Richard's fortune. It is she who produced the money which he invested, which, I admit, he has increased. But law, and decency on his own part, makes it imperative that she be his chief heir, if she survives him."

"Which I devoutly hope will not happen," said Anthony. "I can conceive nothing worse than being Aunt Arabella's henchman, as I would be, in that event. Nevertheless, it is a chance I must take. Besides, has she not some chronic 'inward' trouble, as she calls it, which she darkly threatens will end her life any day—please God?"

For an instant a dark and involuntary smile twitched at Eugenia's lips, but it was gone in an instant. "Need I tell you that you are excessively vulgar, Tony? You are not clever. You are only disgusting. Your Aunt Arabella has been kind to you." She made a slight gesture with her little graceful hand, on which the diamonds flashed. "No matter. If you are ungrateful, that is your loss. Too, it has been my experience that invalids have a certain toughness of fibre, of vitality, which insures them a long if onerous life. It would surprise me very much if she did not survive Uncle Gorth for many years."

"It would annoy me very much if she did," said Anthony, with good temper.

"It is a contingency you cannot ignore," continued Eugenia, overlooking this remark, which, however, caused another dark twitching of her lips. "Now, your aunt has been kind. But that is out of her nature, and not out of an impulse of real affection towards you. Moreover, she has lineal descendants of her own, and it will be only natural if she prefers them to you. Where will you be then, Tony? I assure you the cold street is a very unpleasant place on which to find one's self."

"But an intriguing one," said Anthony, assuming an extravagant posture of head that gazed shiningly into the future. He struck an attitude. "Can you not see me going forward into the years, mother, resolute, uncowed, brave of soul, a Galahad or something, 'whose strength is as the strength of ten, because his heart is pure'?" He turned to Eugenia, and smiled with wide ingenuousness. "Isn't that an attractive, a noble, picture? Doesn't it stir your emotions?"

Eugenia's only stirring of emotion at all this folly was anger and active dislike.

"If you are going to play the buffoon, Tony," she said. "You are very naive. I assume, of course, that you are only acting? Or, is it possible you are serious?"

"I was never more serious in my life," he said, with a sudden black change of attitude towards her, which startled her into quick alertness. "Look here, mother, it is you who is being the obdurate fool. You've known what I've wanted for a long time. You've known my decision. To hell with the Gorth money, if I can't get it. I want it, damn bad. I'll let nothing be left undone to get it, Aunt Arabella or no Aunt Arabella. Outside of actual embezzlement or theft, I mean. But, if I don't get it, I simply don't get it. I've got a small income of my own, as you know. It isn't enough for me. I want money; I'll get it some way. A life of simplicity is not in the least to my taste. And a man who wants money above anything else invariably gets it. That's one lesson my father, and others, have taught me. I am grateful for the lesson."

He paused, fixed his sparkling harsh eyes upon her, and continued: "I still have my hope that Uncle Richard will survive his wife. I'm going to concentrate all my will upon it. Short of giving her poison, myself, I'll continue to bank on her early demise. Have you noticed her colour, lately? Like a piece of spoiled liver."

Eugenia shuddered, averted her face.

"And," concluded the young man, mercilessly, "I have my hopes. I'll stay with Uncle Gorth. I've had many conversations with him. I've seen his will, in the event he survives his wife. Everything goes to me. He is very certain that my father will not remain in America."

He hesitated, then smiled disagreeably. "Besides, am I not personable? I may marry a rich young lady, and make my fortune that way."

Eugenia rose. She moved across the floor to the doorway. There, she paused, looked back at her son with haughty withdrawal and contempt.

"I have said all I can ever say," she said. "I'll not bring it up again, I assure you."

"I hope that is a promise," returned Anthony. "It is one you haven't kept before."

Eugenia closed the door firmly behind her. As she did so, the last dinner bell rang. Anthony laughed softly to himself, gave himself a brief inspection in the mirror, and, humming under his breath, ran quickly down the stairs.

CHAPTER 54

A FTER dinner, Anthony accompanied his parents and his aunt and uncle to the Academy of Music. It was a gracious gesture on his part, for he did not particularly admire music, especially some of the more sentimental passages. But he was feeling in high good temper now, excitedly remembering Adelaide, for whom he would go tomorrow. He laughed a little to himself, when he thought of presenting her to his parents, and of then hearing Richard Gorth's loud outburst of lewd and enjoying laughter.

He wondered a little about his mother's hints of returning soon to England. Was she really fed up, then, with John Turnbull, whose black decay and disintegration were now notorious knowledge in the business world? He was a weakling. She must have discerned that long ago. She had always hated weakness. Now, Andrew, his father, was not weak. He saw things with sudden clarity. There had been open soft affection, sincere and gentle, in her manner lately, towards her husband.

Well, that was proper. But if he, Anthony, had had such a wife he would never have endured her for so long, nor would never, in the final triumph, have taken her back. But Andrew was something quite different, enigmatic. Anthony had not particularly cared for his father, but lately he had acquired a fondness for him, a deep understanding, silent and mirthful, and Andrew had shown signs of comprehension towards his son. Andrew was an impersonally evil and amused man, as suave, elegant, languid and distinguished as ever. It had been only recently that Anthony had possessed a sudden sharp appreciation of his intellect, breeding and extreme poise. How he must love his wife, then, for all her folly, and the underlying stupidity beneath her keenness and subtlety! But he, Anthony, would have been bored by her very shortly. Her tricks annoyed him. They did not annoy Andrew, who found in them a constant diversion, and variety. They both saw through Eugenia's tricks. The only difference was that Andrew was tenderly amused by them. Was it possible, if one loved a woman, to accept her tricks and sillinesses as part and parcel of her charm?

Andrew no longer annoyed his son with imperative suggestions that they all return to England together. He granted him that dignity. Whatever he thought, he kept to himself.

He would accept Adelaide as Anthony's wife, perhaps with enjoyment. But Eugenia would never forgive him. Perhaps the very fact that she had been Adelaide's father's mistress would be the impassable barrier to her acceptance. The whole affair to her would seem excessively degrading, untenable.

Eugenia was surprised at Anthony's decision to accompany them. And very pleased. She began to hope that he had given her remarks consideration, that this was the first step towards her triumph. Anthony did not disillusion her. He had begun to feel some compassion for his mother, who was so absurd.

He sat beside her in the carriage, solicitously covering her silken knees with the robe. As he did so, she caught his hand and delicately pressed it, and, by the light of a street-lamp he saw the gray bright flash of her subtle eyes. He felt again a quickening of his pity. He was her only child, her only son, and in her way she loved him with the cool hard possessiveness of her nature. But he would not be possessed by her, and so was sorry for her, knowing how frightened, embarrassed and enraged she could be when frustrated and denied. There was some urge in her nature which could not endure resistance. Perhaps it was because of hidden fear of defeat. Defeat, in some natures, he reflected, might be a veritable threat to the integration of the personality. How like his father, then, she was! He had never thought of that before.

He looked at his father, long and thin and so always polished and contained. He was a little taken aback by Andrew's expression, thoughtful, conjecturing, and amused. To his further embarrassment, Andrew winked at him, without changing his expression in the least. What had happened to Andrew in these years, he who, like Eugenia, could not endure defeat? Was it that he felt a greater victory at hand, beyond which all others meant nothing? Did a man, as he grew older, decide that one could not have a multiplicity of desires and attain a single one of them?

The music, as Anthony had feared, bored him, made him restless. He preferred German music, passion and fury and uproar. The massive tread of gods that shook the pillars of the earth. The sounding of terrible trumpets against boiling heavens. The rumbling of earthquakes which originated in some profound cosmic space and convulsed all the universe in tormented travail. The cries of demi-gods against the stupidity of man and the inexorability of cause and effect. But there was none of this tonight. The light sweet suavity of French music only irritated Anthony. There was the perfumed and fetid taint of decadence in it, he thought. There was nothing here to transfix or strike the soul. The French masters, especially, seemed to have reduced all fundamental passion to civilized gestures and epigrams of graceful sound. The Germans were more elemental. They scorned, or were unaware of, epigrams. They dealt with emotion, the savage heart, the strange and terrible exaltation of the spirit which accompanied savagery. Flesh and soul in gigantic combat, Jacob and the Angel.

Anthony amused himself with his thoughts until he could endure the sweetness and graciousness of the music no longer. At the second intermission, he whispered to his mother that he had a headache, and wished to go home. Before she could protest, he slipped away, reached the cool dark windiness of the street. A light rain was falling. He turned up the velvet collar of his coat, pressed his tall black hat more firmly on his head, and turned homeward. He had missed a tedious party also, he congratulated himself. He wanted to prepare for tomorrow, when he would go and demand Adelaide.

The rain was heavy and determined by the time he reached his uncle's house. He ran up the steps, saw the white glimmer of a handkerchief near the door. His mother's, doubtless. He rang the bell, holding the silken square of linen, and as he waited, he saw the neat white A embroidered at the edge. He eyed it with distaste. Aunt Arabella. But no whiff of musky perfume rose from it. He remembered that she drowned all her belongings with this sickening scent, as if to hide the smell of decay that pervaded her diseased body.

Still wondering vaguely, he entered the hall, and let the butler assist him in removing his wet garments. "Any calls, William?" he asked, without interest, but from habit.

The old man stood near him, the coat and hat in his hands. He hesitated, fixed a stern if respectful eye on the young gentleman. He had not thought this of Mr. Anthony. Always so correct and refined, so proper and unmuddied.

He spoke reluctantly: "Nothing important, Mr. Anthony. Except that a young—person, a really objectionable young person, came here in the wildest state and demanded to see you about two hours ago. A female person. I suspect she was a little—intoxicated sir, if I may be permitted to say so."

"Eh?" said Anthony, absently, examining the handkerchief again. Then he started. He turned abruptly upon William. "What did you say? A young lady? Did she leave a message for me? Where is she?"

The old man was alarmed. His wrinkled face paled. Anthony was eying him with an excited sparkle in his eyes, a flushing of the face.

He stammered: "Why, sir, I had to put her out. She was in a state. No carriage. Muddy and wet. A servant, I judged, from her garments. Not quite herself. Rushed in, screaming." He was terribly frightened. "I—I had to persuade her to leave. She was violent. When she was outside the door again, she began to scream like a witch. It was very unnerving. No carriage, sir," he repeated, in extenuation.

Anthony's face was darkly flushed now. He caught the old man by the arm.

"Her name? She left her name?"

The old man's fright was so great that he trembled, tried to withdraw from Anthony's grip. "She said to tell you it was Adelaide," he whimpered.

There was a sudden silence, while Anthony regarded him with mounting ferocity. His eyes had paled to the glint and colour of light stone. His hands had clenched. But he spoke with pent calm:

"I want to know about this, William. Everything. You say you threw her out?"

The old man was reduced to shaking terror. Incoherently he exclaimed: "Mr. Anthony, what shall I do? It—it was a very disorderly young person. Not a lady at all. One could see that. Dirty, wild, quite, quite excited. No carriage, sir. Not a sign of one. Wet shawl and bonnet, hair all of a tumble. Quite frightening. And screaming, outside the door when I persuaded her to leave. What a state, sir. She quite aroused the street, and some one called the police. She stopped screaming then, then ran away—" He could not go on. His whimpering stopped his words.

"Why, you damnable old fool," said Anthony, with vicious calm. "You filthy old wretch. That was my wife. Miss Adelaide Turnbull."

The old man was overwhelmed. He staggered back against the wall. He regarded Anthony with abject horror. "I didn't know, sir, before God, I didn't know," he mumbled.

"And you threw her out," repeated Anthony, advancing upon him. "My wife."

"There was no carriage," pleaded William, moaning, throwing up his arm as if to defend himself.

Anthony caught that withered old arm and pressed his fingers almost to the bone. His face was very ugly. "Be quiet. Did she say where she was going? Try to think."

William swallowed convulsively, his eyes fixed with affright on the young man.

"No. I tell you, sir, it was quite awful. Screaming, and all that. Wet and muddy. You can see the footprints yourself. Quite beside herself." He swallowed. "Did you say your wife, sir?" he asked, in incredulous terror.

"My God," said Anthony, dropping the arm he held. So Adelaide had come for him in that condition, "beside herself," distracted and lost. What had happened? Had she told her father? Had he driven her out, in true melodramatic fashion? What had forced her to a confession? Had they been seen? And where was she now?

The ugly expression of his face increased, and the glitter of his eye was murderous. He snatched up his hat and coat from the old man's paralysed grasp, opened the door, and ran out into the streaming darkness.

He felt naked with fear under the rain. What had happened to that poor distracted child? What had they done to her? His throat suddenly choked with his rage and hatred. The few streets he ran seemed endless to him. He saw red dots whirling before him. He would kill Turnbull. He would kill any one who had injured her, who had driven her to such a condition.

When he reached the Turnbull mansion, he saw that the whole house was blazing with lights. Despite its outward quietness, it had a sinister look to the young man's excited eyes. He tore at the bell, then shook the grill of the door, and shouted. He saw the forms of three men in the hallway, with its crimson carpet, its oaken furniture, its portraits and white marble busts on pedestals. He saw that they were dressed for the street.

One of them loomed up against the door, and opened it. He did not move fast enough for Anthony, who pushed the door open and precipitated himself into the hallway, panting with his haste and fury.

The lights dazzled him. He saw that the men were Turnbull, himself, ghastly and gray, Patrick Brogan and Rufus Hastings. They stared at him, astounded.

It was Patrick who spoke first. "Tony. Tony Bollister. What the hell—" The big Irishman was very pale, and had a sullen and violent look. Even Rufus seemed disturbed.

John stared at Anthony, and his face seemed to wither, to take on a wrinkled and wizened look. Eugenia's son, whom he had seen once or twice, and then only at a distance. Andrew Bollister's son. The thought brought no surge of emotion to him now. He felt nothing but emptiness, after the first shock.

Anthony looked at them all with bottomless hatred and rage.

"Where is Adelaide?" he demanded, advancing upon them. His appearance, so disordered, so furious, took them aback. Only John did not retreat. He only stared at the young man, and did not move.

Now Anthony had always considered that what his mother had done with years of her life was a matter between herself and her own peculiar God. He did not share the fallacy that women were fragile and innocent creatures, seduced against their will by villains stalking in darkened doorways or in perfumed drawing-rooms. He believed that vice and treachery were mutual, that rarely was one a victim and the other a destroyer. Especially not in the case of his mother, he had reflected wryly, except that perhaps there was little doubt that she was certainly never a victim. There had even been times when he had felt some contemptuous pity for John Turnbull, so obviously and abjectly at the mercy of this small but terrible luster for power with the illumined gray eyes.

And yet now, as he looked at John Turnbull staring at him so motionlessly, with no expression at all upon his face, Anthony felt the sudden surging of an atavistic gorge and loathing, a primordial fury, the murderous outrage of a man who sees another male creature who has violated his own personal pride, sanctity and integrity. All his cool reason and indifferent tolerance were lost in the whirlpool welter of his chaotic emotions like helpless straws. Much of what he was enduring (and in fact he was enduring rather than thinking) must have been starkly evident, for John, though he still did not move, appeared to wince, and his eyes retreated far back in their sockets as at the sight of an upspringing and relentless enemy, full of contempt and balefulness.

All the passions of his flesh, and his flesh alone, assailed Anthony. This was the contemptible and fulminating creature who had lain with his mother, and so assaulted the decency and dignity of her son and her husband, and in so doing had destroyed their self-respect. Anthony's maleness rose up in towering repudiation and gorge against the destructive maleness of John Turnbull. His face became darkly congested, his eyes glittered. He was filled with lust, with the crushing desire to batter his fists against the flesh of this man, to kick him and tear him.

Patrick and Rufus, regarding them in silence, were struck into a kind of waiting breathlessness. But it was Patrick who struck into a kind of waiting breathlessness. But it was Patrick who smiled first, with malicious satisfaction, and a glance at his father-in-law.

John broke a silence which was fast approaching the explosive point, and he spoke in a dull voice without resonance, and even with listlessness.

"Adelaide? What do you know about my daughter, Adelaide? What have you got to do with Adelaide?"

It was the tone of his voice, his weariness, his dreary denial of the young man's passions, that quieted Anthony, rather than his words. He replied as quietly, feeling the glowing heat leave him, with no residue left behind except a hard beating in his temples.

"Adelaide is my wife. We were married this morning."

"Married?" cried John, with a blank and idiotic look. "You? My daughter?"

"Married!" exclaimed Rufus and Patrick, in unison. The two young men turned quickly and faced each other. Then Patrick burst out in his sudden boisterous laugh, and threw back his head in his convulsions of mirth. But Rufus became deadly pale.

"Married?" repeated John. He had quickened. He approached Anthony, and looked at him with hard steadfastness. Then all at once, he flushed, and his mouth fell open as if he was stifling, and must struggle for breath.

"My God!" shouted Patrick, slapping the shining broadcloth of his large and shapely thighs. "It can't be! It's impossible! It's delicious!"

But neither Anthony or John heard him. They were saying unfathomable things to each other in silence. It was John, not Anthony, who had forgotten Eugenia, and to whom she no longer existed. It was Anthony who remembered. And he saw no remembrance in this man's look. He was only trying to understand, to orient himself. This baffled and disconcerted the young man. He knew that John was seeing him as his daughter's husband, and not as the son of Andrew and Eugenia Bollister.

John's hand reached out, and he gripped Anthony's shoulder, and shook him roughly. "I don't believe it. She would have told her mother." Now his features were suffused and thick again, and full of incredulous agitation.

"Take your hand off me," said Anthony, in a low and contemptuous tone. He did not try to shake off John's grip, but he turned on that hand a look ineffable scorn and distaste.

John's hand fell away. It dropped to his side. He did not remove his black and jerking eyes from Anthony's face.

"I don't believe it," he mumbled. He pressed his fingers suddenly to his wrinkling forehead. "Why should she do that? She would have told her mother. Her mother said nothing—"

Then he had a thought. He dropped his hand and regarded Anthony with vivid and rising excitement.

"If this is true, you can perhaps tell us where she is? She disappeared some hours ago. We are going out to look for her. She had only a few friends!" His voice rose to a hurried cry, and hope. "You can tell us where she can be found? Her mother is in a state of collapse——"

"What did you do to her?" asked Anthony, ruthlessly. "You've always hated her. You must have done something. And if you have, I'll make you pay for it, someway."

"Where is she?" cried John. "You must know? She must have gone to you, in the beginning." It was apparent that he had heard nothing of what Anthony had said.

"I don't know. She did come to me. But—I was not there, and she went away again." Now his first fear, and the first terror he had ever known, rushed back into him like the plunge of steel.

"We're trying to find her," said Patrick, advancing and standing near the young man. He regarded Anthony with sparkling curiosity and some hidden amusement. He coughed, and touched his hand to his mouth and bent his head a little. "This is all somewhat disorderly, and very melodramatic. The little baggage, the clever little baggage! Well, I always liked her, anyway. I suppose this is not just the time and place to offer you my congratulations?"

Anthony was silent. He glanced at Rufus Hastings, who had apparently fallen into some vicious and hating reverie.

"Let's be sensible," resumed Patrick, taking command of the whole situation, which had elements of absurdity in it to him. "She can't have gone far. Her mother is convinced she is ill. Perhaps she is; I thought so myself, tonight. Look here, we haven't done anything to Adelaide. She was feverish. She imagined things. She took exception to a certain—business procedure between her father and us. What does a little baggage like that know of men's affairs? She presumed that she did. It annoyed her. I never thought her very violent, and it could only be that she was sickening with something that made her burst out of the house without any one seeing her or attempting to restrain her." He shrugged, spread out his hands in an eloquent and humorous gesture, as if inviting Anthony to join him in a tender smile at Adelaide's expense.

But Anthony was staring at him fixedly. So, he thought, the poor child was quite right, in spite of everything. They've done this to him, and she suspected they would try it. And she came to me for help, in her terror and illness.

He forced himself to be calm. He looked only at Patrick, whom he knew as a rascal, but as a good-tempered and generous devil besides. One could not trust him on an impersonal basis, of course, especially where money was involved. But on the basis of human and personal equations, he could be all that was helpful and sympathetic.

"You have the names of her friends? No doubt she has gone to one of them. As you say, she can't have gone far."

But even as he said this, he felt a cold lump in his chest. Adelaide, alone, sick, in the rain and the windy night. She might have collapsed in some side street, some alley, and might remain there until morning before she was discovered.

John had forgotten them. He was staring emptily at the floor. If he was thinking anything at all, it was not evident. He started when Patrick gently touched his arm.

"Look here, father, we'd better begin to search at once. It's a nasty night. And, if Addy's ill, we'd best get her home as soon as possible."

He paused. He glanced at Rufus, and then at Anthony.

"I suggest we divide into pairs. You, father, go with Rufe. I'll go with Tony." He grinned, and slapped Anthony lightly on the chest with the back of his hand. "Well, 'brother'?" he added.

John came slowly back to life with a sickened look. He stared at Anthony.

"I've got to talk to you," he mumbled, with a vague gesture.

"Not now," said Patrick, briskly, wrapping his muffler about his neck. "Later. When we bring Addy home."

CHAPTER 55

Mr. WILKINS found Miss Beardsley's house shut and dark and retired for the night. But in her upper chamber he saw a last light burning. Without the slightest qualm he set the knocker to thundering, awakening echoes in the dark street with its wet pavements and flickering lamps.

Miss Beardsley, who had been in the midst of her censorious and rigorous prayers, came downstairs to him in the cold bleak parlour. She had taken the time, as was proper, to comb and brush her hair, which she had removed from their thin gray plaits, and to knot it as usual on the back of her head. She had dressed, also. She entered, august, stately, withered and inflexible as ever, old now, but as ageless in her way as Mr. Wilkins. He might have been calling upon her in broad daylight, so composed was her manner, so unsurprised. She held out her hand to him.

"Well, Mr. Wilkins," she said, in her harsh and brittle voice. "A very bad evening, it seems."

He took her hand, gravely. "Indeed it is, ma'am," he answered, with significance. Miss Beardsley felt a prickling all

461

over her dried parchment skin. Nevertheless, with dignity and majesty, she motioned him to a seat, and sat down near him.

"Most unseasonable weather for this time of the year," she said, in her best drawing-room manner. She observed that he had come hastily, not waiting for a carriage. His light brown greatcoat was streaked with black moisture. His polished boots were dulled with mud and water.

The room was as cold as a mausoleum. No fire had burned that day, or for days previous. Miss Beardsley observed the seasons by calendar rather than by temperature. There was a dankness, a chill and closeness in the air that struck at Mr. Wilkins' bones. The cold had penetrated the very furniture, the sombre draperies, the rugs, the bric-a-brac, so that they exhaled a deathliness of their own. It was hard to imagine that this room was ever warm. The awakened servant had lit a single lamp in a distant shadowy corner, and it only enhanced the gloom and chill with a wan white glare.

Mr. Wilkins laid his hands on his umbrella, and leaned towards Miss Beardsley, who waited with a sense of arid excitement.

"It's a long and nasty story that I've got to tell you, ma'am, about a certain young person."

Miss Beardsley became straighter and more rigid than ever. She had folded her gaunt veined hands on her lap. Now, under her gray brows her eyes quickened, took on their old hard and virulent expression.

"Yes, Mr. Wilkins?" she murmured.

But Mr. Wilkins was silent for a moment. His big rosy face became excessively grave and still. His glassy hazel eyes shone like agates in the light of the distant lamps.

"It is Miss Adelaide Turnbull of whom I speak, ma'am," he said at last.

Miss Beardsley made a slight movement. The malefic look about her mouth and sunken cheeks took on new life.

"Ah," she breathed. "Something quite bad, I presume? I've always feared it, suspected it, warned her foolish mother against it. But what was one to do? It was useless, all the warnings and abjurations. No one would listen, least of all Lilybelle, who is an excessive fool. Now, at last it seems, I am justified." All her hatred for Adelaide was like a phosphorescent glow on her face, and she smiled malevolently. "What is it, Mr. Wilkins? You are keeping me in such suspense. You are asking me to go to Lilybelle, and attempt to comfort her? What has Adelaide done? It must be very terrible indeed," she added, with eager hope.

Mr. Wilkins stared at her massively. Then he said: "There's

462

a story I've got to tell you, ma'am, as will stir your heart, one I knows as is a good and virtuous heart." He coughed gently. "There are those as believes, wrongly, that yours is a cold and indifferent heart." He tapped himself softly on the breast, shook his head. "But those are them as 'ave never taken the time to consider you, or observe close like. But you never deceived me, ma'am, in spite of you being the perfect leddy. I've allus known that under it all there was virtue and sensibility and the tenderest feelin's."

Miss Beardsley bridled. A faint and unaccustomed blush passed over her cheeks. She simpered, inclined her head. "That is because you have understanding, Mr. Wilkins. That is because you are a true friend. Understanding comes only with intelligent friendship." She made a motion as if to rise, and the motion was quick and lively. "If you'll excuse me a moment, Mr. Wilkins, I'll get my shawl and bonnet, and I'll go with you to my poor dear Lilybelle. What a trial! What a tragedy! And it could all have been avoided, if my advice had been taken."

Mr. Wilkins ignored all this. He was speaking as if thinking aloud: "When the trouble came to me tonight, ma'am, I was bewildered. I confess it: Bob Wilkins was bewildered. Didn't know where to turn. A funny thing for Bob Wilkins! Then I says to meself: 'Who is the one that one'd naterally turn to in a crisis? Who is the one as 'as a heart of gold and goodness? Who is the friend?' And then it came to me. 'Bob Wilkins!' I cried to meself, 'it's Miss Beardsley!' And here I am."

So sad, so sorrowful, so agitated and pleading was his manner, that Miss Beardsley was caught in the very act of rising. She subsided upon her chair with some impatience. But she said quietly: "Yes, Mr. Wilkins? Do tell me, please. You are quite overwhelming me." She put her hand to her withered breast and drew a deep breath as if she was about to swoon with fear and concern.

"It's a long story, ma'am. I'll try to make it short. It seems, tonight, that Johnnie Turnbull decided as he was ill, and must go away for a rest. I suggested it; his doctor suggested it; his friends and loved ones suggested it. He was persuaded. All but the little lass, Adelaide. She suspected something very nasty, indeed. That her lovely sisters as were plottin' with their 'usbands to take advantage of Johnnie, and do him in, while he rested comfortable somewheres."

"Oh!" cried Miss Beardsley, in a tone of horror and anger and disgust. "That is just like Adelaide! I warned them! I warned them! What did the little hussy do? Please tell me, Mr. Wilkins!"

Mr. Wilkins shook his head. "Miss Beardsley," he said in a hollow voice. "It is nateral that one as 'as your heart would not suspect evil of any one. But," he added, sombrely and slowly, "you are wrong. Wot Miss Adelaide suspected is true. I've my ways of finding out. It's quite true, ma'am. The little lass knew it."

"Impossible!" exclaimed Miss Beardsley, looking very old and shocked. "I don't believe it! It is one of Adelaide's lies. She was always a liar. Mr. Wilkins, you don't actually put credence in the words of a little nasty creature like that?"

Mr. Wilkins rose and stood before her, bending down upon her a shining and sorrowful look. "Miss Beardsley, I knowed as you would say that. Not from conviction, but from the evil works and lies to you of others, as I won't name just now. You 'aven't had much fondness for the little lass? Why? Not because it was your heart that turned against her, but because others tried to turn away that golden heart from one as 'as allus needed a friend, and understanding. Ma'am," he continued, solemnly raising a finger and shaking it at her, "you've been deceived. You've been had. You've been lied to, and turned aside, and had your kindest feelin's violated. There's no punishment great enough for that, ma'am, the deceivin' of a good kind heart and aturnin' of its nateral milk of human kindness into gall."

Now Miss Beardsley was a very shrewd lady indeed, and it took her only an instant to be advised by her own intelligence to go exceedingly slow here, and watch her every step. After a moment or two, she tossed her head primly.

"You are implying that I am a fool, Mr. Wilkins. Pardon me, allow me to finish, if you please. You are implying that others deceived me as to the true character of Adelaide Turnbull. I am not prepared to admit that. It hurts me, Mr. Wilkins, it hurts me excessively." And again she pressed her hand to her breast, and let her shoulders sag under her black shawl. Her eyes implored him to enlighten her, to reassure her.

Mr. Wilkins shook his head dolorously, as he stood before her. He regarded her with compassion. In an indignant voice he resumed: "'Ow like you it is, ma'am, to say that, to repudiate the falseness of evil people! 'Ow easy it is for the good and the kind to be deceived, and given wrong impressions. Ma'am, I can forgive many things, but there is one as I can't forgive: the deception practiced on generosity and goodness. Ma'am, it is you as 'as been the victim of bad people, you and Adelaide Turnbull."

He struck his umbrella resoundingly on the bare polished floor. He seemed to expand with his righteous anger. He lifted one hand as if to invoke a malediction against all the evil in the world. He was inspired.

"But, ma'am, they'll 'ave to reckon with Bob Wilkins! I warns you of that! They'll 'ave to reckon with him, they as 'ave injured my little lass, and my best friend, Miss Amanda Beardsley! Bob Wilkins will avenge them!" And he shook his head at the ceiling in an ecstasy of passionate promise.

Miss Beardsley felt quite tremulous, quite maidenly, quite fragile and deliciously helpless, in the presence of her avenger. She clasped her hands to her breast. She closed her eyes. She rocked slightly on her chair, and moaned softly in her throat.

Mr. Wilkins had seated himself again, had dragged his chair close to hers. He leaned towards her, and she saw the glittering of his eyes, his wide and gloating smile. He began to whisper.

"Ma'am, I'll tell you a secret as is known to only me and my lawyers. Little Addy is my heir. My heir to all I possess, and, ma'am, that's not inconsiderable!" He nodded his head delightedly. "You'd be surprised, ma'am! And it's all for the little lass, when Bob Wilkins is safely laid away, and at rest. All I possess. Ma'am, I can trust your discretion?"

Miss Beardsley was petrified. She stared at Mr. Wilkins, astounded, her bleak mouth fallen open in an imbecile expression. She was an image of shattered astonishment.

Mr. Wilkins appeared not to see this. He was grinning widely. "They'll not go far this time, with Mr. Wilkins! Not after wot they've done. It's justice Bob Wilkins is after. And I need you, ma'am, to help me."

"I'm sure," murmured Miss Beardsley, faintly, really shaken this time, "that you can depend upon me." She sucked in her lips, let her eyelids tremble. "Poor little Adelaide. To think that I have been so deceived! She needs me, Mr. Wilkins, I who have been her teacher, her guide, her philosopher——?"

He nodded grimly. "Yes, ma'am, she needs you.

"Tonight, knowing wot it was all abaht, the poor little creature runs from her home for help, for her Papa as is a fool, and is abaht to be ruined. Now where would she run to, ma'am? To her friend, her lovin' Uncle Bob, one as loves her like a father. She comes to me, all agitated like, wet and shivering and cold, bruised and not in her right mind. I sees it all at once. I see a lot more. I sees that the little lass is ill, besides her mind bein' agitated. I 'as my old housekeeper put her to bed. I calls my good friend, Dr. Walker." He paused, then resumed in a choked and trembling voice, in which there was now nothing but sincerity, and rage. "Ma'am, Dr. Walker informs me that the little lass is at death's door.

465

Lung fever. She must've 'ad it for a day or two, not knowin', and the rain tonight, and the wind, and her state, 'ave brought her to a low pass. Only the lovin' ministrations of her friends, their prayers, and the help of the Almighty, can save her now."

"Gracious heavens!" cried Miss Beardsley, weakly. She clasped her hands in great agitation before her. "The poor child! The poor helpless little creature! Where are her parents, Mr. Wilkins, her unfeeling father, her foolish mother?"

He became very grim. "They've not been informed, ma'am. Not yet. Let them suffer a bit. They deserves it. They'll not know till tomorrow, and perhaps not then. They don't know where she is. You see 'ow I trust you, ma'am? 'As she friends in her father's 'ouse? I ask you, in all honesty, ma'am. And I knows your answer: 'No.'"

"Oh, oh," moaned Miss Beardsley. "Let us go to her at once, Mr. Wilkins! She needs us."

Mr. Wilkins was silent for a short space. Then he leaned even closer to Miss Beardsley, and whispered: "There's another piece of news I've got for you, ma'am. The little lass married Mr. Anthony Bollister this morning. Not a soul knows but you and me. Mr. Anthony Bollister, as is 'is Uncle Gorth's heir, one of the richest men in Ameriky."

Miss Beardsley thought she had passed the boundaries of astonishment, but now she was completely paralysed. She gaped blankly at Mr. Wilkins, who nodded gloatingly.

"Now then, ma'am, ain't that a fine bright piece of news where we thought all was darkness? Ma'am, with my money, and her 'usband's position, little Adelaide will be the greatest leddy in New York! 'Old that to your kind heart, ma'am! And I promises you you'll never be forgotten by Bob Wilkins."

CHAPTER 56

MR. WILKINS had sat there a long time in his carriage, near the Gorth mansion. But he had a long and deadly patience.

He listened to the sound of the dripping water splashing on the roof of his carriage from the glistening trees. He heard an occasional distant hollow footstep on the pavement. He watched the shadows of the lamps. He lay back on the seat of his carriage and stared fixedly at the street, waiting.

He had been there over an hour. Before that, he had been informed by the stricken William that Mr. Bollister had left home hastily over two hours ago, and had not yet returned.

Somewhere there was a dolorous clanging of a church-bell. One o'clock. Mr. Wilkins moved on the plush seat. He heard the weary lifting and dropping of his horse's hoofs. Above him, the coachman coughed, muttered, slapped the reins, scuffled his feet.

No doubt the young devil had heard that Adelaide had called to see him, thought Mr. Wilkins. And then he had rushed off to find her. Well, he would look long and far, without the help of Mr. Wilkins.

Mr. Wilkins had other thoughts, also, and he chuckled over them evilly in the dark recesses of the carriage. His mind had never been so clear, so sharp, so swift. Ah, he had them all now! And what he would not do to them!

Then, he was silent. He pressed the head of his cane against his lips, and peered out into the darkness. His little lass! She dared not die, must not die, now. She was all he had. The little good creature, the little helpless thing, the foolish, heedless little baggage, whom he loved with such a strange and obscure passion!

He heard quick and disordered footsteps, running towards the house. Again, he peered out. Ah, yes, there was young Bollister, rushing homewards, perhaps to see if Adelaide had returned there for him. Mr. Wilkins saw his face in the struggling lamplight: white, drawn, distracted with fear, intent and thrust ahead of his racing body. He was alone.

Mr. Wilkins lowered the window of his carriage. Anthony had just reached the steps of the house, when he heard a soft and urgent voice: "Mr. Bollister!"

He wheeled swiftly. He had not seen the carriage before. But at the sight of its dark bulk in the shadow, his heart sprang up in his throat. He rushed towards it, grasped the sill of the window, peered within, swaying with exhaustion.

"Adelaide?" he cried. "Are you there, Adelaide?"

He was streaming with water. Somewhere, he had lost his hat. His thick sandy hair was wet and drenched, and stood up on his head like a crest.

Mr. Wilkins pressed his fingers firmly on the clutching hands on the window-sill.

"No, Mr. Bollister, it ain't Addy. It's Mr. Wilkins."

Anthony started. He tried to tear away his hand. His face involuntarily took on a look of disgust, profound disappointment and despair.

"What do you want here, Wilkins?" he exclaimed.

"Hush," said Mr. Wilkins, softly. "I've got news of Addy. There, now, calm yourself. The little lass is safe. But none's to know. Look ye, go into the house and change your clothing. I'll wait. But hurry. And when you come out, I'll take you to Addy."

"You've got Adelaide? You know where she is?" The joy and the agony of relief on the young man's face was quite piteous to see. "Take me to her at once!"

"No, sir, you'll get your death. One invalid's enough on Bob Wilkins' hands. I'll wait. Just you change."

Without another word, Anthony swung about, raced up the stairs, fumbled for his keys, and rushed into the house. Mr. Wilkins leaned back and smiled to himself.

Within an incredibly short space of time Anthony reappeared, dragging on a dry coat over his fresh clothing. He plunged into the carriage, hurtling over Mr. Wilkins. He fell on the seat. Mr. Wilkins could feel his trembling, his pent emotions.

The carriage rolled away, and there was a silence. Then, gently, slowly, Mr. Wilkins began to speak. Before they had arrived at his own home, Anthony was very white and still.

"And so," concluded Mr. Wilkins, pressing his hand on Anthony's knee, "that's 'ow it all is. You can see, Mr. Bollister, sir, that you and I 'ave got work to do, together."

During this last half hour, Anthony experienced most of the rage and hatred and fury and vengefulness he was ever to feel in his whole life. He was exalted with his passions. "My God, my God!" he said, over and over, aloud.

They entered the warm brightness of Mr. Wilkins' pleasant house, and mounted up the polished stairs to a narrow white bedroom on the second floor. There, in the gay little room, all firelight and soft lamplight, in a ruffled white bed with a canopy, lay Adelaide. As Mr. Wilkins and Anthony entered, there was a harsh rustle near the fireplace, and a tall harridan of an elderly lady rose primly, and advanced towards them.

"She is resting quite comfortably, Mr. Wilkins," she said. She turned regally, to be introduced formally to Anthony Bollister, but he had darted away to the bedside, and was now kneeling beside it.

Adelaide was half sleeping, half delirious. She moaned softly in her throat, struggling feebly for breath. Her long shining brown hair was lying in braids over the gay quilts and the white sheets. She had been propped up on ruffled pillows, in order to ease her breathing. Her face was very dwindled and small, child-like in its simplicity of pain and hovering death. When Anthony took her hand, its tremulous heat startled and horrified him. He bent over her, whispering her name.

"I wouldn't advise that, sir," said Miss Beardsley, severely.

"She has only just fallen asleep. She needs much rest to gather strength for the crisis, which we expect in a few days."

But a quickened look of listening alertness had come to Adelaide's pinched and pallid cheeks. Her eyelids fluttered. She drew in a breath, and held it. Her lips parted. Slowly, the lashes lifted and her eyes, feverish and glazed, peered out helplessly seeking from between them.

Anthony bent closely over her. "Adelaide, my dear, my dearest," he whispered. "It's I. Tony. Do you hear me, darling?"

His heart was swelling. His eyes were dazzled with the first tears he had shed since his boyhood. He pressed his lips against her hot cheek as if to infuse into them his own life and strength. Miss Beardsley was much affected. She put her handkerchief to her eyes, and swayed so alarmingly that Mr. Wilkins was compelled, with generous gallantry, to put his arm about her waist. She leaned against him.

Adelaide slowly turned her head to her young husband. The glazed look in her eyes remained for some moments. Then it was suddenly dissipated in the clear shining of her consciousness and awareness. She moved a little towards him.

"Tony," she whispered, hoarsely. Her other hand lifted. He caught it up and pressed it warmly in his palms, with the first one.

"Yes, dear, yes, my sweet," he said. There was a thickness in his throat. "Everything is well, my love. Just sleep. Just rest. I won't leave you."

But now wild anxiety darkened the light of her eyes.

"Papa?" she groaned. "Papa?"

Mr. Wilkins advanced to the bed, and beamed down upon her. He wagged a loving finger at her.

"There, now, my little lass, we've not to be agitated. We've to sleep. We've to get well. We mustn't worry about our Papa. Everything is in good order. We've to trust our Uncle Bob."

She smiled again, closed her eyes. Still holding to Anthony's hands, she fell asleep.

CHAPTER 57

LAVINIA and Louisa sat near their mother as she lay silently, in a stuporous half-sleep, on their father's bed. It was there that John had laid his wife when she had suddenly collapsed, and it was he, now, who undressed her, comforted her, drew the sheets and silken quilts over her, with a tenderness that had been given him in such full measure. She had allowed him to do all this; but she had not been really aware, obeying, not resisting, in a kind of heavy and languid stupor. She had listened to his voice as he soothed her and promised her, her eyes fixed upon his face, their blueness filmed over and glazed, her mouth sagging. When finally, before leaving on the search for Adelaide, he had bent over and kissed her cold dry lips, she had not stirred, but had continued to gaze at him emptily.

He had looked down at her for a moment, and had cried out to her from the deepest wretchedness of his heart.

"Lily, my dear! It's not too late, Lily? We'll find Adelaide. But for us, Lily—tell me it isn't too late?"

But she had looked at him speechlessly, in her unmoving misery, as if she had died, or become dumb. It was as if the outpourings of her vehement denunciations of him had entered her own consciousness, and she could not speak for its stupefied horror. She had finally closed her eyes wearily, sighing deeply, and had turned away her head. Her rumpled but still gleaming masses of auburn hair lay spread over pillows where they had never lain before, and her big tired hands curled upwards on the satin quilt. He saw her profile, fat, large and fallen, and her expression, full of dreary resignation, pain and hopelessness. With a shaking hand he smoothed her hair; one curl of it lifted a little and wound itself over his fingers. He bent and kissed it.

He sent for his daughters, and told them to watch their mother until he and their husbands returned after their search for Adelaide.

"How tiresome, how dramatic, of Adelaide," said Louisa, pettishly, then immediately resumed her automatic sweet smile. "And on such a night, too. Really, it is a silly play. No doubt she has told everybody that you drove her out, Papa, into the night."

"I did," said John, quietly.

Louisa laughed gently. "Now, Papa, you know you did not. You merely told the chit to get out of your sight. It is just a play of words, and means nothing."

But Lavinia looked steadily at her father and was silent. Her florid colouring had paled. Her mouth was tight and bluish, and there was an uncontrollable twitching about her black eyes as if tears urged to be released.

"And how thoughtless and selfish of her to create a scandal," resumed Louisa. "She has so few friends, thank heavens. But friends gossip and exaggerate. Whatever can she have told people? I always knew that Adelaide was vengeful; she will take advantage of this little situation to make a frightful hullabaloo."

"You are a liar, Louisa," said Lavinia, softly. Now she looked sick and stricken. But her eyes were ablaze. She turned to John. "We'll stay with Mama." She hesitated, then clasped her hands impulsively over her father's arm, and gazed up at him. "Papa, bring Adelaide home. We've a lot to do to reconcile her to us. We all know it. We needed this to happen to us. Bring her home to Mama. For her sake. For our sake, too."

"How absurd," murmured Louisa. But she eyed her sister reflectively. Was Lavinia going to be ridiculous, obstructive, now that matters were shaping themselves so satisfactorily? It was a mercy that she was married to Rufus, rather than to her own unpredictable Patrick. What weaklings those two were! Weaklings, for all their bluster and noise and expressions of violence. Louisa had long ago discerned that the relentless plotter, the truly intellectual schemer and manipulator, was never noisy, but moved on velvet feet and struck in silence. She thought suddenly of Rufus, and her blue eyes shone like hard sapphires under her golden lashes. She could trust Rufus; they understood each other. But one could never trust the stormy of temperament, the clamorous. There was a weak and rotten spot in them.

She was much annoyed at the vigil at her mother's bed in her father's rooms. She had already retired for the night. One must guard herself when in a delicate condition. Tomorrow, she would have quite a headache, and be indisposed all day, and her colour would be dull. It was perfectly all right for Lavinia, the robust and vulgar. Nothing ever impaired the brilliance of her vitality.

Too, she, Louisa, rather dreaded that vigil with her sister. Lavinia had a cruel and wounding tongue. No doubt she would be full of rumbling and incoherent reproaches when alone with Louisa. Louisa sighed petulantly. She was in no mood to combat disordered words and vehement gestures.

She sat down near her mother, and yawned delicately, touching her lips with her fingers. Her yellow hair lay richly on the shoulders of her blue peignoir. She leaned back in the chair, and indicated, by her closed eyes, that she was very weary, and she would thank Lavinia not to disturb her.

But, to her surprise, Lavinia did not speak at all. She sat near her sister and fixed her eyes on her mother's vast and empty face. She appeared to have forgotten Louisa entirely; she was alone with Lilybelle.

The fire was burning briskly on the hearth, throwing up shafts of orange light, to touch, with restless spear-heads,

471

the ceiling, the walls, the polished wood of the furniture. A lamp was burning dimly near the great ponderous bed. The heavy folds of the curtains were drawn over the windows. Lilybelle lay as the dead lie, not moving, the sound of her breathing not to be heard even in the deep silence. She had withdrawn into some sick far vortex of her own, no longer caring for those she loved, occupied with an agony that was crushing and numbing. Lavinia saw the bulging curve of the cheek on the pillow, the bronze lashes catching little gleams of light from the fire, the sturdy large hands quiet now with a dreadful and resigned quietness. Lavinia pressed her eyelids closely together, and shook her head slightly.

Then Lilybelle sighed. The bulk of her body trembled on the bed; her mountainous breasts heaved piteously. Lavinia rose and bent over her. But Lilybelle, after that one convulsion of suffering, was still again, unconscious of her daughter. Louisa watched all this from under her lashes. She pretended to sleep.

Why did not Lavinia speak? There was something ominous in her silence. She sat in her chair again, tall, plump, already giving evidence of becoming like her mother in figure. Her crimson velvet peignoir stretched over her body, eloquent of the new life beneath it. Louisa peered at her sister. How sombre and grim and changed was her face! Its expression was heavy and meditative. She stared before her with the strangest look. I really must speak to Rufus, thought Louisa. Lavinia is becoming too dangerous.

An hour went by, slowly, weighted with silence. And still Lavinia sat there, sometimes glancing at her mother, sometimes leaning back wearily in her chair. Louisa's uneasiness increased. How unlike Lavinia, this motionless grim woman! What were her thoughts? The thoughts of the violent, when they are speechless, are quite terrible, reflected Louisa. She felt the impact of Lavinia's thoughts like blows upon her keen sensibilities. She darted a furtive glance at her sister. Lavinia's profile had assumed an iron and rigid quality, full of threat. Her colour had not returned. Her thick black curls were disordered about her neck and shoulders.

Then Louisa dozed. She awoke with a start. The ormolu clock on the mantelpiece chimed a delicate one. The room had cooled. Sighing, Louisa rose and poked at the dying embers on the hearth. Lavinia had not moved. She appeared as unconscious of her mother. Louisa would have thought she slept, except that her black eyes were still open, staring unblinkingly at the bed. Why had she not stirred the fire, the fool?

472

The thoughts she had thought were like scattered and broken stones all through the large and silent room. Louisa had an impression that something had changed, had been broken down, and that there were jagged and shattered fragments thrown everywhere. How like Lavinia to make the very air disorderly and untidy! To strew the psychic atmosphere with the evidence of her hasty sorting and throwing-over. And now the smell of danger was everywhere, like a gas.

Louisa heard the opening and shutting of the door downstairs, and the distant rumble of men's voices. They had returned, and had, no doubt, brought that wicked nasty little creature with them. How very tedious, indeed, all this was. Lavinia rose quickly; her pale face deeply lined and hard. The two young women glanced at each other, then softly left the room, together. They had reached the landing, when they saw their father and their husbands ascending. One glance at their faces assured Louisa that they had not found Adelaide. John was climbing the stairway, slowly, like an old man, holding to the balustrade. Rufus wore a tight and impatient look. But Patrick's face resembled Lavinia's in its close grimness.

John looked up and saw his waiting daughters. His expression changed, dissolved, and then his features took on an aspect of deathly despair and exhaustion. He shook his head.

"Now, ladies, no hysterics, please," said Rufus in a low and peremptory tone. His green eyes glittered up at the young women, and his foxlike countenance narrowed warningly. "We'll find the girl in the morning. We've been to the police. We've talked to the Chief of Police, himself, and he has his men searching every corner of the city."

The men reached the landing. John turned to Lavinia. "Your mother?" he muttered.

Lavinia put her hand on his arm. Now her sombre mouth shook. "She is still asleep. You aren't going to wake her and tell her, Papa?"

"No, my dear." He seemed to see her for the first time, and now she saw a desperate appeal in his eyes, and a dark anguish. He patted the hand on his arm. "Go to bed now, my darlings. We can do nothing more until morning."

Patrick did not speak. He walked away to his own bed-chamber and closed the door firmly. John entered his room, and went directly to his bed to see Lilybelle, and to sit near the window where he could watch her.

Rufus and the two young women were alone together in the dim hall.

He spoke softly, glancing swiftly at the closed doors all

about them.

"Look here, there has been a remarkable development. Your gay little sister married Anthony Bollister yesterday morning." His face was suffused with malevolent mirth. "What do you think about that?"

"No!" exclaimed Louisa, in her hushed sweet voice. Her eyes became alive and unpleasant. "That's incredible! I can't believe it!" She indicated, by the look of her mouth and dilated nostrils, that this was most disagreeable and disconcerting news. "What a little sneak! And Tony Bollister! Every girl in town has been after him. How could she have inveigled him into marriage? And without telling us, too." She paused, then added delicately: "I hope there was no scandal——?"

"On the contrary. It seems rather sudden, and suddenness is always suspect, isn't it? They've met less than half a dozen times, Bollister told me tonight. He said," and Rufus coughed thinly, as if to suppress a vicious laugh, "that he had decided to marry her when she was eight years old!"

Lavinia seized his arm urgently. "Rufe! Could it be Adelaide is with him?"

"No," he answered, impatiently, trying to withdraw from her vulgar and robust grasp. "He came here, looking for her. It seems that she first went to him, after her melodramatic flight, but he was not at home. After that, she simply vanished into thin air. We've been all over. I assure you," he added with nasty significance, "that her dear friends will talk. The town will have a delicious morsel to eat with its breakfast. A very nice situation for all of us."

"Tony Bollister!" repeated Louisa, with incredulous amazement, and outrage. "What possessed him? Really! I thought he had wit and discrimination."

"He did," said Lavinia, with great quietness. Then tears filled her large dry eyes, and she turned and walked to her own apartments, leaving Rufus and Louisa alone together.

Louisa was silent. Her face, caught off guard by her astonishment and annoyance, was not a nice thing to see. Rufus watched her, as her thoughts whirled. He smiled tightly, the corners of his thin mouth sinking inwards, his nose sharpening.

"So, we've got the enemy of the family for a brother, now," he said, in a light, hushed tone. "What a contretemps! What an anti-climax! You should have seen your dear Papa's face when Bollister burst in upon us, shouting for his little child-wife. And what a confusion all this is going to make! I'd like to see what Tony's elegant Papa is going to say this morning, when the glad tidings are made manifest to him."

He coughed delicately. "And Tony's most distinguished and aloof Mama."

Louisa suddenly coloured violently, and stared at her brother-in-law. But she said nothing.

"You were quite right, Louisa," continued Rufus, with tact, and inner amusement. "It is an artful little baggage. Carrying on clandestinely with Bollister. We ought to be thankful that the scandal didn't break over our heads—without benefit of clergy. Though we must admit that she has made a brilliant marriage. New York forgives anything if the marriage is spectacular enough."

Louisa was close to acid tears. Her mouth clenched in envy and hatred. She had wanted Anthony Bollister very urgently, herself, and there had been once or twice when she believed that she had entranced him. And now it was that hideous little baggage that had captured him, that pale shrivelled little snail, that odious and contemptible little creature, who was without style, without the slightest beauty, without the smallest wit! It was not to be borne.

"How like Adelaide!" she whispered, in a virulent tone. "She never had any consideration at all for us. She could not have made a more awkward marriage. If she had thought for one moment, how Papa detests the whole family," she faltered a moment, and glanced downwards, "she could not have done this to us. It is the richest tale in New York, the family feud."

"But New York will love this," urged Rufus, delightedly. "Quite like Romeo and Juliet. All that is needed is the balcony."

Louisa glanced at him swiftly, with such a flash of blue malignance that he, who knew her very well, was startled.

"It pleases you to make fun of the Turnbulls, Rufus," she said, bitterly. "I don't find it in the least amusing. But we might have known that Adelaide would disgrace us one day."

"I don't call it 'disgrace,' my dear," he said, delighted more than ever. "After all, Tony Bollister isn't exactly a pauper, or a chimney-sweep. I, for one, am excessively pleased."

Louisa drew a deep breath, and her features became momentarily wizened. "I'm sure you won't be overly pleased to know that your wife is plotting something quite violent. I saw it in her face. You'd best have a little talk with her."

She turned and walked towards her own rooms, her golden head shining in the dim lamplight. Rufus watched her go, and drew in his lips against his teeth. He had married Lavinia because she was the eldest daughter of John Turnbull, and his obvious favourite. Now, he was not certain that he had not made a mistake. Louisa was much more to his taste. As

475

things had now developed, her situation was quite as favourable as her sister's.

He remembered what she had said about Lavinia, and was disquieted. There was Patrick, who was of a similar and equally dangerous temperament. He paused and listened at Patrick's door. Louisa, then, had not entered her husband's apartments, but had quickly retired. He knocked softly, then entered.

Patrick had not yet made the slightest gesture towards undressing. He had lit one lamp. He was standing near a window with undrawn curtains, and staring gloomily out into the darkness. He turned when he saw Rufus, and glowered at him intimidatingly. But he said nothing. His dark face was drawn and strangely ferocious.

Rufus shut the door after him. "A pretty kettle of fish," he remarked, in a low light tone. "The running away. The marriage to Bollister. The ladies aren't taking it in the most graceful manner."

Patrick did not answer. He went to a table, opened a silver box, and withdrew a cheroot. He put a taper into the fire, lit it, then applied it to the cheroot, and drew upon it vigorously.

Rufus watched him closely.

"A clever little baggage," he mused. "What gave her the idea in the first place—about us?"

Patrick shrugged his big shoulders. He leaned his arm on the mantel, and stared at the fire. His features, rough but handsome, were crudely revealed in the glow of red and black. Rufus did not like his expression.

"It was fortunate that Blakely came—before we heard the bad news," continued Rufus, tentatively.

Patrick lifted his head and turned it in Rufus' direction. Now his face was in darkness, and dangerously inscrutable.

"I've just been thinking," pursued Rufus, very delicately, and he laughted a little. "Of course, the baggage will be found. But, if it is not—" and he coughed, "remembering our small agreement with Wilkins about her income, it will be rather awkward——."

Patrick moved so fast that his arm was only a blur. Rufus felt the impact of his fist against his chin. Scarlet stars exploded before his eyes, and he had an impression that he was flying through space. A moment later, he found himself on the floor, on his back.

"Get out!" said Patrick, in a soft and savage tone. His foot lifted, drew back on the arch of a kick. Then he halted it. He smiled viciously. "No, Pat," he admonished himself, gently. "Don't kick a pig when it's on the ground. That isn't

Queensbury rules, you know. Or, is it? You're an Irishman, Pat Brogan. You aren't an English gentleman. So, Pat, you must remember never to kick a fallen swine, no matter how badly it smells."

CHAPTER 58

J OHN sat near his wife, and watched her as she slept. He lay in his chair in a supine attitude which told more than any words or gestures might do. When she sighed in her sleep, his heart rose on a crest of pain and yearning. He watched her profile, the occasional slight lifting of her helpless and muted hands.

He no longer worried about Adelaide. Some mysterious reassurance had come to him in this room that she would be found, and all would be well. He did not think of her now. He thought of himself, and Lilybelle. He thought of so many things. It seemed to him that a most solemn hour had arrived, when he must understand.

He went back over the last years of his life. He thought of the slow and lethal illness of mind, rather than body, which had come over him. And, with a stern panic, he knew that he was mortally ill, or at least, dangerously ill.

He had known, all his life, that he had a strong and pre-possessing body, but as his nature was not naturally introspective, he had not mused upon the fact, nor congratulated himself smugly. He was aware of his body as an animal is aware, with naturalness and indifferent acceptance. Though he had known headaches and the mysterious achings and malaise of a strong body sometimes, and briefly, not in full working order, true and devastating illness of the flesh had never touched him. He had heard, with contemptuous lack of comprehension, of the diseases of others, of sudden deaths and failures, of long and chronic collapses. Vaguely, he had believed that in these sufferers there was some weakness, some flaccidity of will, some lack of determined resistance, some ignominious surrender. He had known collapse, himself, but not that fatal disintegration of the flesh which afflicted others. He always rose from these collapses with recovering strength, and then forgot them.

Now, as he sat near Lilybelle tonight, waiting for the morning, it came to him with sudden and frightful knowledge that some vital virtue in him, some profound strength and resistance, had drained out of him like blood, and that the draining was no new thing but had persisted over a long and unconscious period. He was like a man who had been slowly bleeding to death for years, without much discomfort, or knowledge, and then reaches the time where it is borne in upon him that the limit of life and endurance has come, and he is abandoned in extremis.

Faintly, he remembered that he had felt increasing exhaustion over the past few years. But he had ignored the deep and silent warnings in himself. He had believed that by ignoring them they would cease to exist. He sat near his wife, and thought: What has brought this about? He did not deny any longer. He did not make the frenzied excuses other men might make. Without question, without denial, he accepted the verdict that he was close to death. And that before he died, before he finally gave up, he must understand everything, his life, himself, Lilybelle, his family, his relation to all the world. Otherwise he would die in the confusion in which he had lived.

The great and magnificent room about him was in semi-darkness. He saw the looming of the pier mirror, a glimmering ghost in the dimness. He saw the outline of his wardrobe, the edge of his chairs, the spectral glimmer of his fireplace, and the three or four crimson and expiring coals on the hearth. The windows were rectangles of empty gloom, framed in their draperies. And as he looked at them all, slowly, they seemed to be imbued with his own deathliness, to be the shapes of his own disintegration and fatal decay. They stood about him in silence, as if listening.

He felt no despair, only a kind of heavy sickness and abandonment.

Though he had experienced rages, hatreds and violences, confusions and furies, he had never delved in himself to explain these things to an indifferent mind that cared for nothing but emotion. The calm self-analysis of a less virile man was not his. Emotions and passions rose out of him like spiralling storms, and it had been enough for him that they were, and not why they were. He had been blasted and torn by them, involved only in sensation.

But now, in this grave hour, he asked himself why he was dying, he who was only in his middle forties. He rose heavily, went to a table near his mirror. He felt his lethargy, his iron weariness, the slowness of his step. He peered in the mirror, and saw his ravaged face, his feverish sunken eyes, so fierce and so restless, his mouth bitter and heavy, locked in deep lines. He saw the wide streaks of whiteness in his hair. He leaned forward, the better to confront himself, and then he saw that never before had he looked at his own image so intently. And he thought: Why, I've never looked at myself before!

The visual image blurred before him, yet he seemed to see what was real so much more clearly. It was almost as if a brilliant light had been turned on. He saw John Turnbull for the first time in all his life.

And he was profoundly astonished, and saddened.

The moments passed, and in his eyes there appeared a steadfast and burning light. He did not move. He saw himself through all the years, bewildered, infuriated, fulminating, wretched and rootless. He was like one who has died, and who is now standing apart, watching his life depicted before him like a living and blurred frieze of meaningless pictures.

Many a man has asked himself: What has motivated me through these feverish eons of my life? And John asked himself this question now, as he had never before asked himself. His question seemed asked of him by another, and he waited a little, wondering, confused, trying to remember, childishly urgent and simply perplexed, feeling a faint embarrassment as if the questioner were actually at hand, full of stern demand and inexorable waiting.

Then he said aloud, in a dull and marvelling voice: "It was hatred."

Silence engulfed the room again. John looked into his mirror, and it seemed to him that the vague image in its fading depths was a small and uncertain shadow, utterly without substance or significance.

He said aloud, again: "And it is hatred that has killed me."

He was overcome with amazement, as if some one else had uttered this sorrowful condemnation, this incredible thing. He wanted to cry out, half in laughter, and half in rage, repudiating this foolishness, this colossal stupidity imputed to him. And then, he was still as stone, still gazing at himself, not believing it was himself that stood there so impotent, so lonely, so wretched and contemptible before him.

What had he hated? He had been wronged. But so many millions had been wronged before him and would be wronged again. Had he been so egotistic, so imbecile, that he had let a wrong distort and cripple, and finally destroy him? The wrong had been done in laughter and youth and contempt, by an insignificant man of no consequence. Had the wrong been so very terrible, so very devastating and overwhelming?

John leaned his hands on the table heavily, but still stared at the mirror to the left of him. He asked himself this question again, and the room appeared to ring with its implacable sound. And now beside that image in the mirror crept

Eugenia's image, and it was the form of a stranger, its face only slightly familiar, its dumb gestures arousing in him only weariness and indifference.

He said aloud: "I never loved you. I do not love you now. I have killed myself because of you, because of what you never were. I never knew you. You are nothing to me."

The dim face seemed to change, to dissolve, and then it was gone.

Then, all at once, John was overcome with rage against himself, and fury. He felt a hoarse wild laughter in every organ, every cell, of his body. For a dream, a lie, for a creature that never existed, he had destroyed his life, had made of it a barren and sterile wilderness, a hopeless dull horror, filled with enemies. He had hurt and injured those who had loved him, had driven them away. Now he was all alone in the wilderness, and not even the lying image was there with its empty words and imagined comfort.

Then, strangely, he knew that his father was standing beside him, living and vital. He could not hear his words, but the sound of his faint and echoing voice was sad and urgent and very tender. Standing there, hardly breathing, not moving, John listened.

Then he said, simply: "But, I am dying. I am done. I've killed myself. My God, I have wasted all my life. I have gotten things I never wanted; I have struck away those who loved me; I have abandoned everything that had in it the least joy and hope. I have done things that sickened me, that were never a part of me. For what? For hatred."

He turned away, filled with the acrid poison of despair. He sat upon his chair again. Lilybelle stirred on the bed, moaned feebly. He went to her for a moment, looked down upon her, and his heart heaved. And now he knew what hatred could do for a man, or a world.

It seemed to him that it was hatred, not love, not compassion, not peace or justice or understanding, that lived among men, and in himself. He saw how it was deadlier than the most appalling virus that ever came from the mouths of the plague-stricken, a more lethal poison than any brewed by a chemist. It was an actual thing, an actual venom, an actual malignance. It literally corroded the cells of the brain, convulsed the vital organs, thickened blood, diseased the very breath. It made a man a pestilence, deadly to all other men, a danger and a madness that should be regarded with horror, and quickly destroyed. A man who walked abroad with hatred in his flesh was a leper. Corruption, decay, degeneration and death walked with him. If it debased and twisted the soul, it did not less with the body. The man of hatred had a fire in his eye, murder in his hand. He infected the innocent as well as the guilty. He was all sin.

Moreover, he was the first victim of his own pestilence.

He saw now how all his life had been made a hideous thing by his hatred. (He thought to himself: How terribly I have hated for so little!) And then he comprehended that it need not matter if the thing be small or great that made a man hate others. The focus of infection must have lived with him from the beginning, born of his own egotism, his own ignorance, his own stupidity. Then came the first lesion, and the poison spewed out into it, making the man a festering mass of corruption.

The first victim of a man's hatred was always himself—yes. John saw himself as a putrid and pestilential creature, streaming with his own festerings. He saw the faces of those he had injured over all these years. He saw old Everett Livingston. What had he had against all these wretches? Nothing. He had struck out at them in his madness, and they had fallen away before him, confused, bewildered, mortally hurt. He had watched their suffering. Had it given him pleasure? No. Only for a moment had he felt some alleviation, some numbness. When he remembered later, he was filled with agony.

He had hated poor Lilybelle, not for what she was, but because of what he was. Now he knew that she had been the only reality in his life, the only love and purity. She alone of any had loved him.

But no, there had been another. He had always known it. His daughter, Adelaide, had loved him. And he had hated her. Why? Because she reminded him of some one whom he knew in his heart did not really love him. She reminded him of a lie, was a testament to his own degradation. What he had seen in her eyes had been love, and because, in his condition, he could not bear to be loved, he had hated.

And then he was stupefied with horror.

He could find nothing to pity in himself. The wild turbulence of his nature rushed out to engulf all those he had hated in a writhing torrent of pity and remorse. He bent his head and grasped his hair fiercely in his hands, and rolled his head from side to side.

There is no hope for me anywhere, he thought. What I have done is too much for a single man to stop.

He thought of Mr. Wilkins, and in his feverish eyes the vision of that affable gentleman was a vision ringed in fire. This was his Lucifer, his destroyer.

And then, because he was now, in spite of his despair, so near to sanity, he burst into dreary laughter. "I allus gives 'em wot they wants." It was not Mr. Wilkins who had done these things, but himself. Satan is powerless before a man who does not hate. Mr. Wilkins had known from the start that he was a man of hatred. He had given him what he wanted.

I can't stop things now, thought John.

He seemed to see his own corrupted wounds. But, as he looked at them, they no longer drained. They were healthy. They were healing.

There was a sudden strange beating near his heart now. It grew stronger. He lifted his head, as if listening. His heart no longer moved with the old and familiar sluggishness, as if reluctant of every drop of blood entering or leaving it. Now it pulsed with aching strength, and a lightness flooded him.

He could not believe it. He felt his eyes fill with terrible moisture.

"God," he said, simply, in a voice as low as prayer, "help me."

He sat for a long time, while the windows became faintly gray, and the stillness seemed as intense as the stillness at the bottom of the ocean. He looked about him. The forms and shapes, so hardly discerned, were not emanations of sickness and death, as they had been before. They were warm and close and friendly, and full of compassion.

His body was tired, but no longer heavy. It felt very porous and light. He heard the soft dropping of the last embers on the hearth. A wind murmured beyond the windows. Lilybelle stirred on the bed, and muttered something. John rose and went to her, leaning over her, smoothing her cold damp forehead.

She opened her dull eyes, so hopeless and so drained, and looked at him.

"Adelaide will be here, in the morning," he whispered. He kissed her chilled cheek, and then her poor dry lips. She watched him, emptily. He knelt beside her, and spoke in the softest of voices, holding her eyes urgently with his own.

"Lily, my darling, do you hate me so much? Isn't there any hope for me, with you? I haven't been much to you. I've despised you, cursed you, driven you away. That was my blindness and cruelty. But I suffered, too, for a lie. Can't you pity and understand a little, Lily?"

She still stared at him, as if he were a stranger, and he had not spoken. But was it his imagination that a faint sparkle of blue light had appeared in the shallow depths of her round and stricken eyes?

He continued: "You've loved me, my dearest. I've always known it. Is it too much to ask you to believe that I've loved you, too, all these years? For it is true. It was only my folly that prevented me from knowing. I've wronged you, Lily. But I've wronged myself, too. I've been worse than a wicked man: I've been a fool." His voice became thick and strangulated. "Lily, do you hear me? I love you. I need you. I want you."

Her hand stirred. He felt its aimless weak fluttering. He caught it strongly, and held it, then put it to his lips. Something seemed breaking in him, with an unbearable pain.

Her eyes were bright and clear now, and very shining. She was smiling, trying to speak. He bent his head near her mouth, to hear the fumbling words. But all she said was "Johnnie."

But that was all he needed. He laid his head on the pillow beside hers, and pressed his lips into the soft masses of her hair. Her hand lifted, laid itself on his neck, warmly, protectingly. He heard her sigh, over and over.

Then she tucked his hand under her cheek, and slept again, as simply as a child.

CHAPTER 59

A NTHONY let himself into his Uncle's home just when the gray dawn was brightening into pink and hyacinth radiance. The cool and pristine freshness of the morning blew in his weary face as he mounted the steps. There was a silver mist in the bare branches of the trees; the pavements steamed in the first light. He heard the poignant voice of robins on the little plot of grass before the houses, and the thin ecstasy of the sound seemed to pierce his consciousness with unbearable and exquisite pain. Far up the quiet street he heard the rumbling of milk wagons on the cobbles, and the clank of tin vessels echoed up and down. He looked at the silk shrouding of the windows of the mansion; the first rays of light gleamed on the brass door handles and step behind the grillwork. The soft and sleeping silence, cool and pure, permeated everything.

He was suddenly conscious of exhaustion, and his hands fumbled with the keys. But he was no longer afraid. The vigil at Adelaide's bed had been long, but two hours ago her breathing had become easier, and she had slept with more naturalness. He could put his fear for her aside, for he had very unpleasant work to do in the next few hours.

He crept upstairs to his bedroom, undressed, and lay on his bed. He would not be able to sleep, he thought. But the next thing of which he was conscious was the discreet opening of the door, and the appearance of a maid with his breakfast on a tray. The bright sunlight of midmorning was streaming through the curtains. Anthony sat up abruptly, glanced at the clock on the mantel, and saw that it was just after eleven.

When he saw the tray and the demure chambermaid, his brows drew together quickly. He had never missed breakfasting with his father and Richard Gorth unless he was ill. This tray was evidence that the whole house knew that he had been absent the entire night. Now, this was not exactly an unheard-of thing. He had been absent all night during the past year for at least once a month, and when he had appeared at breakfast, no comment had been made, no tray had been brought to his room. Nor had Richard Gorth nor Andrew ever, by so much as a glance, betrayed their knowledge of his discreet disappearances. They accorded him the dignity of being another man.

But now the tray, as it was laid on his knees without comment, had a sharp significance. Some one had directed that he was not to be awakened before the usual breakfast hour. The only conclusion at which he could arrive was that his company was not desired at the usual time, that no one wished to assume, tactfully, that he had been home all night. He found something ominous in the whole situation.

He had a thought. Just as the maid was retreating, he said: "Alice, have Mr. Gorth and Mr. Bollister left for the offices?"

By the girl's expression, puzzled and mutely excited, he knew the worst, and was not surprised when she answered quickly: "No, Mr. Anthony. They are downstairs in the library, with Mrs. Gorth and Mrs. Bollister."

Ah, thought Andrew, the judges are in session.

He sent for William, who came in furtive and cringing. It was evident that the old man had had a bad night. He shrank at the sight of Anthony frowning on his pillows. But the young man said equally enough: "Come in, William. Look here, I'm not annoyed with you. How were you to know, anyway, that the young lady was my wife? Under the circumstances," and he coughed shortly, "you did only what was your duty to do. Stop shaking. Sit down there near me. I want to ask you a few questions."

William sat down on a chair near by, and pressed his hands on his ancient knees, and gazed at Anthony piteously, and with fear.

"Mr. Anthony, if the young lady had just spoken—I beg your pardon, sir, but the young lady was so—distraught. If she had said: 'I am Mrs. Anthony Bollister,' why then, sir, the matter would have been very different——"

"Doubtless, doubtless," replied Anthony, impatiently. "Now, to the questions: When the ladies and Mr. Gorth and Mr. Bollister arrived home last night, what did you say to them?"

The old man's face became gray and pinched, and he averted his eyes. "I was that excited, sir. I—I thought it was a matter of private knowledge with them—I told them that your lady wife, the former Miss Adelaide Turnbull, had come here for you, had gone away, and that you had left to go to her. Sir," he added pleadingly, "I had no thought but what they knew, knowing you to be a young gentleman not given to—to——"

"To strange and impulsive things," finished Anthony, for him. "Yes, I see. For God's sake, stop looking as if you were about to be hung, William. You know, I ought to thank you. You've saved me some awkward preliminary moments and explanations."

"I thought," continued William, with more confidence, "that the marriage was being kept quiet, sir, for personal family reasons." He flushed, and stammered: "I mean——"

So the family feud is common knowledge, thought Anthony. "It was," he said, frankly. "It was being kept quiet between Miss Turnbull and myself. No one else knew. Never mind, William. As I said, you've saved me some unpleasantness. The family has gotten over the shock by now, without the necessity of me watching the painful process. I don't like painful situations, William. I'm really a coward, when it comes to them. Love an agreeable atmosphere at all time; saves wear and tear."

He paused, and smiled. The terror and anxiety of the night had aged him, had made haggard his face, had turned his eyes to steadfast grimness. He reached over to where his damp coat had been thrown over a chair near the bed. He drew out his purse, sought through it for an appropriate bill, and tossed it to William, who gaped at it with incredulous delight.

"You couldn't," pursued Anthony, with delicacy, "inform me what the weather is downstairs?"

The old man was beaming with joy. Then he assumed a sober look, and shook his head. "I would say, on the ladies' part, that it is slightly ominous, sir. The gentlemen, as usual, are more composed." He continued, tactfully: "I would suggest, Mr. Anthony, that the sooner the situation is confronted, the less—unpleasantness. Ladies gather irritation as time goes on."

"They certainly do," assented Anthony. He drank his coffee, then threw back the bed clothing. "I'll go down at once."

He bathed and dressed, then went downstairs, to the library. He suppressed an impulse to whistle softly to himself. "Graveyard courage," he thought.

The library had been appropriately darkened by Mrs. Gorth's orders, and lamps were lit, though outside the sun was brilliant with spring.

Anthony thrust his pale smiling face into the room, and whispered:

"Is the body properly laid out and ready to be seen?"

The sombre room, vast and beamed of ceiling, lined with dark books, filled with heavy oaken furniture and thick Oriental carpets, was filled with gloomy shadows and denseness. Apart from the ladies waited Mr. Gorth and Andrew. Richard Gorth's expression was closed and sour, the jowls tight and knotty in the wan lamp light, his fingers tapping the arm of his chair. Andrew sat near him, as languid and graceful as ever, and seemingly bored. But when he saw Anthony in the archway of the room, his narrow eyes glinted with a pale cold light. As for Mrs. Gorth, she alone displayed any violent emotion, and was sobbing rapturously in her handkerchief, and when she discerned Anthony, the look she turned upon him was positively baleful in its loathsome malice. Eugenia, sitting near her husband's aunt, was pallid, her face very haggard and quiet. She was perfect, as always, reflected Andrew, with a swift look at her. Gowned in severe black, with a fragile white collar at her throat, her hair drawn austerely behind her ears, she was the most formidable personage in the room despite her slightness and quiet straight attitude.

"Let us have some light in the damned room," said Andrew, quietly, and rose with swift grace to draw back the curtains. The sunlight assaulted the duskiness of the library like noisy shouts, and the lamps flickered, turned yellow. The sun streamed over the carpets, picking out vivid jade green and crimson tints, brightening bowls of flowers on the tables, glancing back from the scrolled gold edges of the portraits on the walls, turning the backs of hundreds of books to rich and ruddy colours. All these things impinged sharply on Anthony's awareness. He walked into the room, chose a chair not too close to any one. He looked from one formidable face to the other, and waited.

No one spoke for a long time. Every eye was fixed on

him. And then, all at once, Richard Gorth's harsh pale lips twitched; he coughed; stared down at his feet. Andrew regarded his son in icy immobility, without expression. He wore a most dangerous aspect, without violence. Mrs. Gorth sobbed aloud.

"Oh, the disgrace!" she moaned.

But Eugenia did not move. Her face became paler than ever, and quite old.

"This isn't a Star Chamber, nor the Inquisition," said Andrew at last, with a light gesture of his bloodless hand. "Suppose, Tony, that you give us the whole story."

His manner was cool and reasonable, but the pale glint in his eyes did not abate.

"Shut up," said Richard Gorth to his wife, as her moans gained in intensity. His voice was savage, full of murderous contempt. Eugenia moved slightly on her chair, moistened lips that were as smooth and cold as stone.

"There isn't much to say," Anthony said, very composedly. There was no bravado in his words, no defiance. He looked steadily at his father. "I met Adelaide when she was a child. I didn't see her for years. Then I met her again on the street, when she was about fourteen. That was before her sister Lavinia's marriage to Rufus Hastings."

"And thereafter, you met her clandestinely?" said Andrew. "In a disgraceful and furtive manner? That is in accord with the general Turnbull character."

Anthony flushed. A vein beat in his forehead, but he retained his composed tone. "You are quite wrong. I've seen Adelaide less than half a dozen times since I first met her. But from the beginning, I've wanted her. There was nothing sly or secretive about the whole thing. We met accidentally. I asked her to meet me casually, but she did not. It was I who looked for her, walked past her home many times on the chance that she would appear. Sometimes I even thought she had seen me, and so would come out into the street. She had a strange loyalty to her dear Papa." He paused. His face darkened, tightened. Andrew observed this with a curious relief and secret satisfaction, and these mounted when Anthony continued:

"I discovered, not from what the poor little creature said, but from others, and my own infrequent observations, that the child was persecuted, and hated by her father, that he treated her abominably." He paused, then added in a low but penetrating voice, and each word came from him with bitter significance, though he did not look at his mother: "I think I know the reason, though apparently the drunken fool did not. I think that Adelaide reminds him of some one

—a woman. She is slight and small; I doubt if you have seen her. She is very fragile, but full of steel. She is a pale girl, very quiet and composed, with character and dignity. I know only one thing for certain: she resembles, remarkably, some one whom I know also, and know very well."

Eugenia uttered no sound, but the air about her appeared to take on disorder and confusion, and appalled awareness. As for Andrew, his thin hand clenched on the arm of his chair; he did not look at his wife. He regarded his son with intense fixity, and an unfathomable look caused his eyes to draw closer together.

"I think," pursued Anthony, "that this woman—perhaps—was one Turnbull hated. I think he inflicted on Adelaide the cruelties he'd like to inflict on this—person. Whether she—or, perhaps, he—had ever really wronged him or not, I don't know. That is unimportant. But the cruelty was there, the sadism, the irresponsible violence of the whole man. Her life was a curse to the poor child. Instinctively, she understood him. She knows him to be vulnerable and impotent, for all his wild bluster, and the things he thinks he has accomplished. I think she is the only one who ever really cared for him.

"And so, knowing of the—lack of compatibility between her family and ours, she avoided me. Only last Sunday I saw her, after a long interval. I think it must be almost two years since last I saw her. I then persuaded her to marry me. And so, we were married yesterday morning. She would not go with me. She must return to her darling Papa, she said. There was some trouble, some ruin, perhaps, hanging over his damned head."

At this, Andrew and Richard Gorth appeared to turn to him quickly, though, in fact, they hardly moved. Anthony watched them closely a moment, then continued:

"And I have strong reason, perhaps strong surety, that she is right, though I laughed at her in the beginning. Something was told me last night which made me believe that there is a real plot against him, that he is now completely ruined. By his daughters' husbands."

"Impossible," said Richard Gorth, hoarsely. He coughed heavily. He rubbed his hand over his mouth, glanced at Andrew.

Anthony's eyes narrowed subtly; he tried not to smile. He shrugged. "Nevertheless, it is true.

"Last night, it seems, the whole plot was exposed, without the apparent understanding of that stupid fool, Turnbull. But Adelaide saw it. She came to me for help. What wild scheme she had in mind, how she could possibly conceive I could save her darling Papa, I don't know. She came here;

I wasn't at home, as you know. The worst part of the whole thing was that she was sickening with lung fever. After she left this inhospitable house, she ran to another friend. There she collapsed. I went looking for her. First of all—I went to Turnbull."

He paused. Now electricity crackled in the room. Even Mrs. Gorth halted her mechanical and continued moaning. Anthony, out of his compassion, did not look at his mother. He fixed his attention upon his father and Gorth. The two men were sitting up in their chairs now, bent stiffly towards him, their faces illumined by the sunlight. Then, very slowly, very cruelly, Andrew began to smile. The smile was evil and incandescent in his pale eyes.

"Yes?" he said, softly. "You saw Turnbull? He knew you?" He did not glance at Eugenia, but he saw her rigidly lifted hands, risen just an inch or two above her knees, as if they had frozen in the midst of a distracted gesture.

"Yes," said Anthony, shortly, now disgusted at the trick he had employed to distract his parents' attention from his marriage. "At least, he stared at me like a petrified bull. I didn't leave him in doubt. I told him. I demanded my wife."

"And," said Andrew, with even more softness, "what did he say then?"

Anthony hesitated. He was infuriated against himself. He could not stomach the evil in his father's eyes, the sudden dark wide smile of Richard Gorth, the sudden gloating malignance of Mrs. Gorth, the sudden awful frozenness of his mother.

"Well, I'll give the devil his due. My identity, my revelation of my marriage to his daughter, didn't seem to impress him very much. I gathered that he was in a state about her disappearance. This confused me a little. I'd have thought him just angrily indifferent. Then I remembered that Adelaide had told me that she and her mother were quite devoted to each other, that her mother had been victimized by Turnbull almost as much as she had been victimized. It must have been something else which had awakened him. Or, perhaps, he was afraid that Adelaide would run about the city, crying out that her sister's husbands had robbed him, or ruined him. He couldn't stand that, you know. At any rate, he looked at me in a confused and broken state, tried to speak to me, and then went away with Hastings to look for Adelaide. I went with Pat Brogan."

"My God," whispered Andrew. Now the evil was sharp, vivid, on his features. It was a very ugly expression, with something of exultation and huge mirth in it.

No one looked, with a strange mercy, at Eugenia, except

489

Mrs. Gorth. She had the aspect of death itself. Her full white lids half dropped over her eyes. Her mouth had fallen open a little as if she was unconscious. But she sat as straight and still as before, and her hands now lay on her black silk knees, palm up, in an attitude of prostration.

"I found Adelaide," concluded Anthony, hurriedly, "at the home of that slimy scoundrel, Wilkins, whom she calls 'Uncle Bob.' Wilkins is in a murderous state, I assure you. I shouldn't wonder if he had something to do with the whole thing about Turnbull, in the beginning. And I shouldn't wonder if his attention isn't now set on Hastings and Brogan —" He halted, alarmed and enraged at his indiscretion. He had been lavishly throwing sops to his father and Gorth, with a craven desire to placate them, perhaps to draw them with him into some inner satisfaction and amusement. He hated himself. Then he shrugged, sullenly, without an abatement, however, of his inner digust and aversion for himself.

"Well," he concluded, shortly, "Adelaide is with Wilkins, with an elderly female friend, who is nursing her. She is very ill. I stayed with her all through the night, until she seemed easier. In a few minutes, I will go back to her."

Again, there was a great silence in the room. Andrew, still staring at his son, appeared to be thinking rapidly. Then he cleared his throat, gently.

"And, if I may inquire, what is the attitude of Wilkins towards your—towards Miss Turnbull?"

Anthony knew the trend of his father's thoughts, and said in a loud hard voice: "I am given to understand that she is his god-daughter, his pet, that he would do practically anything for her. He was much aroused at the whole thing. He—he told me last night: 'We've a lot of work to do together.'" He stopped, abruptly, turning a bright scarlet with his anger against himself for these revelations. It infuriated him that he was so weak, so soft, that he wished to appease his father and his uncle, that he wished them to look upon Adelaide with approval and pleasure, even for a nefarious and exigent reason.

Andrew turned in his chair towards Mr. Gorth, and Mr. Gorth turned in his, to meet his nephew's look. They regarded each other in a long silence, faintly smiling, and secret.

"'We've a lot of work to do together,'" repeated Andrew, in a rich tone.

"Mr. Wilkins," replied Mr. Gorth, to Andrew, "is a very remarkable man, indeed. Very remarkable."

It was hard for Anthony to restrain an impulse to shout out in fury: "Damn it, I'll have nothing to do with Wilkins!"

But he halted himself. He knew this was not true. He would have a lot to do with Wilkins. There was no tolerance in him for cruelty, for ugly deceit, for the wickedness of men like Hastings and Brogan. Besides, there was Adelaide to avenge, and Anthony was hungry for limitless revenge. In the hour before he had left Mr. Wilkins, there had been a long talk between the two men, in which Mr. Wilkins had outlined a very subtle and merciless plot.

"Let 'em enjoy their gains for a bit, me lad," he had said. "They've got it coming to 'em, they have. Then, we'll move in. It's all clear in me mind. But wait a bit. A month, two months, three, and then we'll 'ave 'em in the palms of our hands." And he had made a vicious squeezing gesture with his fat rosy fingers, infinitely slow and terrible. Perhaps Anthony was the first man to discern that Mr. Wilkins had a strangler's hands.

He was still fuming, still red, when Andrew turned to him. His father's manner was singularly friendly, amused and tolerant.

"Mr. Wilkins isn't a man to speak idly, or on impulse," he observed, watching his son, closely. He was silent a moment. "What he sets out to do, he does, as you have perhaps discerned before, in our own affairs. But he's a lethal devil. I'd advise you to watch him like the thief he is. Could you tell me," he added, "whether this affection he has for your wife is something new, born of his endless schemes, or something on which the young lady can rely?"

Anthony was silent. He would have liked to answer that Mr. Wilkins' affection was tepid, or only a by-product of the Wilkins' scheming. Then, with a last disgusted surrender he said: "I've told you she is his god-daughter. He told me frankly that he loves her 'like a father.' That he's intended all his life to avenge her on her father, some day. That she is his sole heir."

Andrew glanced again, swiftly, at his uncle. Gorth was chuckling hoarsely, deep in his throat. He was rubbing his rough harsh palms together.

"The mills of the gods," he observed.

Eugenia, as if smothering, placed her trembling hand to her throat. Mrs. Gorth was studying her with avid viciousness and delight. The poor woman would not have spoken if she could. There was about her a complete collapse and sinking.

Then Andrew spoke to his son, with an air of tolerance, amusement and resignation: "Well, Tony, it seems that you've gotten yourself into quite a situation. Not one I'd have chosen for you. For a young man whom I've always thought clear-headed, cool and expedient, and hard as iron, you've involved yourself in circumstances that are turbulent, to say the least. And very exciting. Perhaps even interesting."

He continued after a moment's silence: "You know what I'd planned for you. No matter. This is your own life, to do with as you please. I've always granted you that. My own wishes have been disappointed. Nothing can undo this indiscreet marriage. Now, I wish to say that I have no doubt that Miss Turnbull is a very estimable young lady. I hope— I know—that you'd have married no other sort of young female. I ask you, now, not to consider too much my own feelings in the matter, my own disappointments. I ask you to believe that I wish you happiness."

With a look of supreme forgiveness, of repressed mirth, of evil satisfaction, he extended his bloodless hand to his son, who stared at him grimly for a few moments before taking it. He was surprised at the warm grip of his father's hand. He tried not to see the pale sparkling of Andrew's eye.

Mr. Gorth rose ponderously, and approached Anthony, who stood up courteously. Mr. Gorth held out his hand, and Anthony took it. Mr. Gorth was smiling widely.

"A fine kettle of fish! But, congratulations, young man. Wilkins, and the young lady, didn't exaggerate about her condition in her father's house. It was fairly well known. I understand, too, that she is a female of discretion and intelligence, and quite comely. You have my permission to bring her home to us."

He pressed Anthony's hand with significance. He regarded the young man with real affection.

"Could you tell me one thing? What is Wilkins' attitude towards you? You know, he's not been exactly a friend to us. Did he appear—ah—to resent Miss Turnbull's entanglement with you?"

Anthony clenched his teeth a moment before replying, then he said sullenly: "No. Last Sunday he saw us together. He asked me, in very ambiguous language, to call upon him at any time, that he would be happy to serve me. He seemed to be pleased to see us, Adelaide and me, in close conversation. However, I'm sure whoever she had chosen would have been equally acceptable to him. His first consideration, he assured me, is her happiness." He hesitated. "It's no choice of mine to be stirred up in the same pot with him. He is loathsome. But I've Adelaide to consider; I've to remember what has been done to her." He added, roughly: "I'll not engage in any dirtiness, except perhaps in this one instance. Anything else I do, in conjunction with our Mr. Wilkins, isn't going to have a smell about it. And I have an idea that whatever I want, the scoundrel will work to give me. I assured him, very bluntly, that beyond this one occasion, I'll not engage in filth with him. And he said: 'That's right, me lad. I allus give 'em wot they wants. If you want all fair and aboveboard, we'll do it together. It'll be a relief for a change, somethink different, and interestin'.'"

Anthony imitated Mr. Wilkins to perfection, in his furious annoyance. Andrew and Mr. Gorth burst out laughing.

"'I allus give 'em wot they wants,'" repeated Mr. Gorth, quite purple in the face with his uncontrollable mirth.

Anthony discerned that he could ignore his poor mother no longer. He turned to her, flushing.

"Mama," he said in a changed voice, "I hope this hasn't been too terrible for you? I hope——"

Eugenia looked at him with strange fixed eyes, in which the brilliance was too intense. A long tremor ran over her. Then, without a word, and with infinite dignity and pride, she rose, turned away from Anthony, and left the room, walking as composedly and regally as ever, her head held high.

Anthony watched her go.

His attention was caught by Mrs. Gorth plucking at his sleeve, and simpering up at him, her liver-coloured face alight with malice and satisfaction.

"What a young man it is, to be sure!" she exclaimed. "It seems, then, that you've done excellently for yourself, Tony. Do let me give you a kiss and my best wishes."

CHAPTER 60

Even if Andrew had felt an impulse to go at once to his wife, an impulse he did not feel in the least, he would have been delayed by Richard Gorth's insistence that he, his nephew and his nephew's son, join him for a glass of wine "for the health and happiness of the young couple, and especially the bride."

Anthony, fuming with his haste to be out of this house, where all now seemed chuckling contentment, secret and malevolent delight, and great good fellowship, and to return to Adelaide, was forced to smile, to listen to the toasts, and to express his thanks. His disgust at the whole past hour rose in strength. He saw himself the prisoner of forces which he could not oppose, even if he had wished. And he was not certain that he wanted to oppose them.

He was finally allowed to go, after a knowing remark from Mr. Gorth that "of course, one should not keep a bridegroom from his bride, and give her our love, my dear lad, our best wishes for her recovered health, and extend to her the hospitality of our home."

Thereafter, Mr. Gorth and his nephew had a long and edifying conversation, during which they laughed much together, and congratulated each other. Anthony would certainly not have enjoyed the discussion.

It was much later, more than two hours, before Andrew lightly ascended the staircase to the apartments he shared with his wife. Another man would have shrunk from confronting the poor woman in her agony, her humiliation and shame and ruin. But Andrew did not shrink. This was the last, the final punishment, he would inflict upon her: these hours alone with her thoughts. Thereafter, matters would be quite different between them. He smiled a little, as he opened the door.

Eugenia was sitting near the window, in the shadow. In that large plush chair her figure was very small, but straight and rigid and calm. She turned her pale and haughty face to Andrew when he entered, but did not move or speak.

He drew a chair near her and studied her silently. He saw the gray shining of her eyes, her firm pointed chin, the smooth white brow, the quiet hands on her dove-gray silk lap. She appeared the same to him, as always. Yet his acuteness, the subtlety of his perceptions, assured him that some catastrophic change had overtaken her. Her eyes met his; he saw their abysmal shame. Her head was erect; he saw her broken pride and misery. All about her were broken pillars and fallen walls, the ruin of her life.

He must be careful, he warned himself. He must not let her say the things her anguish and despair might force her to say, and her shame and humiliation. He must not let her say the things that would rush to her lips, things of terrible confession that would make it impossible to take her hand thereafter and lead her away. The impossibility would be in herself, not in him. The spoken word was sometimes a sword that forever barred the way to peace and reconstruction. That word must not be said.

He began to speak very softly and gently: "My dear, it is not so awful. Of course, I understand. The girl cannot come here. Our welcome was only allegorical. Moreover, I believe that the impasse will never occur. Eugenia, will you go back to England with me?"

Her white lips parted; her eyes flashed. He saw them suddenly filled with proud tears.

"Andrew, there is much I must tell you. It is my duty to

494

tell it to you." Her voice was low and neutral, but it shook uncontrollably.

He lifted his hand. "Let me speak first, my dear. I'm not a man of great volubility. You will grant me that? Then, let me speak."

Her mouth moved, but she was silent. However, the eyes so steadfastly fixed on his were filled with humble grief, with a prayer for forgiveness, with the hopelessness that such forgiveness would be granted.

"Tony has disappointed us," Andrew resumed. "However, that is his own life. The young cannot carry on the quarrels of the old. For that, I must confess, I am thankful. Think of us going on into old age, keeping alive our dislikes and our feuds and our resentments! How very tedious! How boring! Can you imagine anything less exciting than rereading old books until one's yawns lift the top of one's head?"

He continued, without giving her a chance to speak, though she lifted her hand in a slight and helpless gesture.

"I, for one, confess that John Turnbull no longer interests me. He did, at one time. A natural phenomenon. Now I find him tiresome. Let Tony contend with him. But I have the thought that Tony will find John as tedious as I now find him, and that John is as weary as I am.

"It all happened a long time ago, did it not? A very long time ago." He paused, then said musingly: "It is strange that the huge immensity and tragedy of life pass, and others say indifferently: 'It happened a long time ago. It is no longer of significance, and certainly of no significance to us.'"

Eugenia clasped her hands tightly together.

"One makes errors; one is engulfed in pain and anguish; one does evil things. And one believes that in these moments he is the center of the universe. Instead, he shares the common impulses of all men, and perhaps of all animals, and even insects. However, he cannot believe it. Such was never endured before; such will never be endured again. But years later, others say: 'It was so long ago.' They say that, if there was any memory left at all of the one who suffered or erred or endured spectacular death. For the majority of us: well, we are forgotten, along with our passions and our mistakes and our pain. There is nothing left. We should remember that, and not take ourselves too seriously. At the very least, we should be silent."

Eugenia could not control herself any longer, and cried out in a thin wild tone: "I can't keep silent! I must tell you!"

He reached out and took her hand and held it strongly. Her face was alive with a moving hysteria, a desperate bleakness. He controlled her by his own will. She subsided. Now her expression was all desolation, all pleading. And, he saw, all humble love.

He continued as if she had not spoken: "Therefore, we must not take this matter of Tony and the girl very seriously. We have approached the richest part of our lives, when we may have peace and contentment. Tony is in the midst of the riot and the confusion. Do you wish to share it with him? Do you wish to engage in it again? As for myself, never!" His voice rose with amused emphasis.

He said: "We have had our disappointment in our son. But, he is a full human being, and his life is his own. Let him live it in whatever peace he can. He did not disturb our lives. Let us refrain from disturbing his. We must respect his dignity.

"Of course, I know it is humiliating for you to accept as a daughter the child of a drunken fool and a barmaid. However, this is America. Such things are not of importance here, fortunately. It will not affect us. We shall return to England. Very shortly, I shall inherit my uncle's title. We shall have a life there of richness and fullness. America was never for us. We both realize that. It was not because we were old when we came. We were, in fact, very young. Yet, in our minds, we were old and fixed and grooved to fit one pattern. We never fitted here. We must return to the only place where we can be happy."

She was weeping now, her head bent and averted. His strongest impulse was to take her in his arms and comfort her. He restrained himself, but held her hand tightly.

"It is not an eternal separation, Eugenia, my dear. Ships go constantly to and fro across the ocean. Later, Tony will visit us, with his wife. In another setting, she may not appear so impossible. Too, she is a young lady of fortune, and that is very pleasant. From Tony's description, she cannot be hideous. I grant him some taste. Her manners are probably very agreeable."

"Andrew, I must tell you something," she whispered, not looking at him.

He pretended not to have heard her. "Eugenia, there is a new life for us. You have not been happy. I have thought, perhaps, that you knew, that you suspected——" He paused, as if in the greatest embarrassment.

She heard the change in his voice, and turned to him quickly. He dropped her hand and stood up. He stood near the window, half turned from her.

"I have given this matter much thought. I have thought that things are best left unspoken. I am still wondering if this is not true."

He spoke in a low and reluctant voice, very convincing if its intonations were only assumed.

"Eugenia, as I have said, there is a new life for us. Now, assume for a moment, that I say to you: 'I am sorry. I am devastated. But some devil in me urges me to confess that I have often betrayed you in the past. These infidelities came from my ignorance, my errors, my foolishnesses. Nevertheless, they exist. Let me pour them all out to you, even if they forever destroy our future life together, our peace, and make it impossible for us to continue together.' What would you say to that, my dear?"

She was silent for a long time. For so long indeed, that he thought that she had fainted, or had risen and left him. And then he heard a soft movement at his side, a light touch on his arm. He turned to her slowly. She was looking up, and her gray eyes were wet and radiant, her mouth shaking and smiling.

"I would say, Andrew," she whispered, "that you must not tell me of those things. I would ask you not to burden me with them. I would ask you to save our lives for us, and not cloud them all over with confessions that cannot be taken back, with things that can only corrode and ruin."

He took her hands quickly, and held them with hard strength. He looked down into her face. She returned his look with high head, with courage, with sadness. And with supreme love.

"I will not say them, then," he said, with a catch in his voice. "They are dead. They never happened. The—man who did them does not exist any longer. There is just you, now, my dearest, and I. We were born today."

He took her in his arms now, and kissed her lips with passion. She clung to him, weeping again, nestling her head on his shoulder.

CHAPTER 61

ANTHONY was part way to the home of Mr. Wilkins, when he had a thought which caused him to hesitate, and frown to himself. His thought appeared weak to him, and then he smiled. He remembered that it is the weak man who fears a demonstration of weakness; the courageous are cautious about nothing.

Therefore, he turned abruptly, and hurried through the

streaming mid-day streets to the Turnbull mansion. Arriving there, he was halted at the grill-work by a servant who protested that Mr. and Mrs. Turnbull were ill, and resting, and that the Madams Hastings and Brogan could see no one.

Impatiently, Anthony cried: "Nonsense. Tell Mr. Turnbull immediately that I have news of Miss Adelaide. I am Mr. Bollister."

At once, the grill sprang open, and Anthony entered the house. The servant rushed off with an eager look. Anthony stood alone in the massive hall, then sat down on one of the tall oaken chairs. He heard a quick soft footstep, and saw a lady approaching him from the rear hall. She was an old woman, sedate yet dignified, small and neat, with brown eyes and gray hair under a white cap. She wore a black apron over her brown cloth dress, and a large bunch of keys jingled at her belt. Anthony rose. Was this royal old lady Adelaide's mother? It was very evident that she was a lady, so calm was her manner, so composed her withered features in spite of the agitation so evident in the eyes behind the steel-rimmed spectacles.

She came up to him with remarkable swiftness, and said in a low voice: "Did I hear: Mr. Bollister?"

"Yes, ma'am," he answered. She studied him with acute gravity and intentness, sorrowful yet keen. Then she said: "I am Mrs. Bowden, the housekeeper."

He could not resist extending his hand to her, and she took it with dignity. Now her lip trembled, and her eyes filled with tears.

"I have heard that you are Miss Adelaide's husband. I am correct?"

"Yes. We were married yesterday," he answered, simply.

She clasped her hands tightly together, and wrung them. Her scrutinizing eyes did not leave his face. Whatever she saw must have satisfied her, for eventually she smiled faintly, and with sadness.

"I am very happy," she said, softly. This hard-faced young man with the gray eyes, the harsh and bony line of chin, the inflexible yet not obstinate mouth, was exactly the sort of husband she, Mrs. Bowden, would have chosen for Adelaide. No one would hurt her now, except, perhaps, himself, and it would not be a hurt given in cruelty. To Mrs. Bowden the supreme and deadly sin, the unpardonable crime, was cruelty. From its noxious root all other crimes and vices rose, like twisted and blasted trees. She might have liked more gentleness about the lips and eyes, more tolerance in the glance, more softness in the smile. But one could not have everything. It was enough for her that this man was not cruel by nature, even if he was not kind. He would be good to Adelaide. He would protect and guard and cherish her.

Tears moistened her eyelids, as she smiled at him.

"Miss Adelaide is very dear to me," she said. "We are very fond of each other. And now, I also hear that you have news of her." She paused, then said with quick and pleading urgency: "Tell me: is she well? You have found her?"

"Yes, I have found her, Mrs. Bowden. She is not exactly well. Exposure to last night's weather increased a fever she must have had for a day or two before. However, her doctor believes that the crisis will come within a short time, and that we must hope."

Mrs. Bowden turned very white. "Lung fever? She—isn't dying, Mr. Bollister?"

He tapped her shoulder reassuringly, grateful to her for her look of anguish and grief. "No, not at all. But these things need careful nursing. There is no reason to doubt that she will recover."

"Such a tragedy," said Mrs. Bowden, in a whisper and through shaking lips. "One cannot tell— Be good to her, my dear Mr. Bollister. Love her. The poor child——"

She stopped abruptly. Footsteps, slow, halting, were coming down the stairway. She turned swiftly and went to the rear of the hall where she opened a door and disappeared.

Anthony watched the bottom of the curving stairway. He felt some awkwardness, and some discomfort, and was, in consequence, inclined to be angry and annoyed. Now two figures appeared around the sweeping bend of the stairway. They were John Turnbull, and a massive great woman, clinging to the balustrade as the man supported her on the other side. She moved on shaking limbs, staring blindly and wildly ahead, seeking with her round shallow blue eyes, which darted on every side. Anthony knew that this was Adelaide's mother, this tall and immense woman with her untidy masses of auburn hair, her bulging white face, her open panting lips, her mountainous figure which once must have been luscious. Her clothing had been donned hastily; her black gown was fastened awry at the great swelling breasts, the collar pinned in a crooked fashion, the edge of a white lace petticoat peeping down over the insteps of her boots.

Her husband helped her down each step, for she was tottering. "Now, Lily dear, be careful. Be slow. Here is another step. You must not tremble so. All is well. Another step, my darling."

Nothing could have exceeded the infinite tenderness and comfort of his voice. Anthony listened in amazement. This was not the voice of cruel hatred he had expected. He saw John's haggard face, so seamed and sunken, and it was filled with love and yearning and absorption in this large tragic woman, moving with such blind and desperate eyes. Anthony involuntarily moved forward to the base of the stairway, to assist John with his wife, for it was evident that it was taking all his exhausted strength to hold her, so passionately was she surging forward.

She saw him now, a step or two below her, with lifted arms to help her. She halted abruptly, swayed perilously, then caught at the balustrade. Tears rushed to her swollen eyes; they spilled over her cheeks. She smiled at him with such a face. Then she extended her hands to him, and came down the last two steps with a rush. He caught her hands. She was almost as tall as he. He was embarrassed before the passion of her look, her strange gleaming smile, her imploring eyes and quivering lips.

"Addy? My little lass?" she asked, brokenly, now clutching his arms.

Her voice was hoarse and common. But Anthony did not hear its intonations. He saw only the tragic mother, driven by terror, given a promise of relief and comfort. He could not endure the searching eagerness of her eyes.

Now Anthony had only intended to inform the parents of Adelaide that he "believed" she had been found, that he would bring them any later news, that they were not to be overly anxious. He owed Adelaide's parents that, he had thought. She would wish it, herself. Later on, he would consult with Mr. Wilkins and decide at a time when they were to be given the entire story. Perhaps not for days. Mr. Wilkins had spoken with virulence of them, and had been very eloquent upon the subject of Adelaide's sufferings, the stupidity of her mother who had not protected her or given her much comfort. It had been decency which had brought Anthony here, not compassion.

But now, as he looked at Lilybelle, with such unendurable joy and anguish and hope on her ruined face, and at John, who was looking at him with indescribably imploring and humble eyes, all his stern resolution was destroyed.

"Adelaide has been found," he said, with unusual gentleness. "She—she is a little ill. She must be quiet."

John said quickly, putting his arm about his wife: "We will go to her at once. Lilybelle," he said, urgently, trying to attract her attention for she was gazing as if fascinated at Anthony, "if you will get your bonnet and your shawl, Mr. Bollister will take us to Adelaide." He turned to Anthony again. "She—she is with you, at your home?" His mouth contracted painfully.

"No, with Mr. Wilkins. She went there last night." Anthony's voice hardened in spite of himself. "He came and told me."

A wave of dark colour ran over John's face. His eyes gleamed with sudden savagery. His arm dropped from his wife's shoulders. "Wilkins! And the scoundrel, the swine, never came to me and told me!"

"You forget," said Anthony, looking at him coldly and fixedly, "or do not know." Lilybelle was clinging to him; the pressure of her hands, feverish and drowning, hurt his arms, but he did not remove them. "Adelaide was ill. She went to Wilkins to—to get help for you." He smiled contemptuously, and with a meaning glance at John, who stood in sudden and rigid silence. "Her own needs were more immediate than yours, Mr. Wiklins and I decided. Whatever those needs were. She was desperately ill. She is still very ill. We have only hope to sustain us now."

He flung these words brutally into John's congested face, like stones, for he knew that Lilybelle was too dazed to understand much of them. She was still gazing at him like a devoted dog, who hears and sees nothing but its master. Her hands were pressing his arms convulsively, opening and shutting. Her eyes were filled with adoring light.

"He—he told me. My little lass's husband! She didn't tell me. No matter," she whispered. "No matter. You love my lass, Mr. Bollister? You will take care of my lass? Such a pretty little thing, such a little creature! So gentle and good! You've no idea, Mr. Bollister."

He turned his attention to her. After a moment, he bent his head and kissed her streaming cheek. She flung her arms about his neck and clung to him, sobbing, her hands moving over his neck, his shoulders, his back, in passionate motherhood and love and joy. He held her to him, a mysterious sorrow in his heart, and his arms were gentle.

"God bless you, my dear, my dear!" she sobbed, pressing her lips against his cheek, his chin. Then she drew away a little, took one of his hands and kissed it, and wet it with her tears. Her humility, her ecstasy, her simplicity, were so touching and so pathetic, that John looked away, and Anthony could feel nothing but pain and tenderness.

Then John said at last, putting his hand on her shoulder: "Compose yourself, my darling. Go to your room and bathe your eyes. Then dress for the street, and I will have the carriage brought. We'll go at once to Adelaide."

"Yes, yes!" she cried, transported, looking at them with her wet and radiant face. "At once!"

She sprang away from them, and like a girl she ran up the stairs and disappeared.

Anthony and John were alone in an embarrassed and speechless silence. They could not look at each other. John bit his lips and clenched and unclenched his hands. He had aged years in one night. The marks of violence were imprinted betrayingly on his forehead, about his mouth, so heavy and sullen, in the flaring of his nostrils and the modelling of his chin. But Anthony saw how vulnerable was that face, how stricken, and how, now that immediate anxiety was relieved, how ashamed and confused.

Then John cleared his throat, and asked hoarsely: "You say Adelaide is very ill? She has a good physician? I prefer to bring our family physician. I shall send for him at once."

"She is in good hands," answered Anthony, more and more embarrassed. "I sent for our own physician, before I returned home early this morning. There is also a doctor called by Wilkins."

At the sound of that name, John turned abruptly to Anthony, and the violence came out again on his features, and his mouth was brutal.

"I'll never forgive him for this," he muttered, almost inaudibly.

"You owe Adelaide's life to him," Anthony reminded John, with a satirical contempt. "He is very fond of her. She had no other friend."

"Friend!" cried John, with sudden savagery. "He was no one's friend! He was my worst enemy. I'll twist the rascal's neck!"

"What damned nonsense," said Anthony, with disgust, and a shrug. "I'm not concerned with your feelings for the estimable Mr. Wilkins. But I do know that Adelaide is not to be disturbed. If any shouting it going to go on, or any nasty remarks at that house, I shall refuse to allow you to see my wife."

John halted abruptly. He stared at Anthony incredulously, and with fury. His clenched fist lifted. Anthony did not move. He looked into John's eyes with disdain and indifference. The dangerous moment passed impotently.

Then John's livid mouth slowly smiled. He stared searchingly at the young man, but not intimidatingly. A slow quiet sparkle appeared in his exhausted eyes. He studied Anthony intently.

"A jackanapes," he said, and his voice was amused and affectionate. "By God, it's a whippersnapper!" Some thought made him colour with renewed embarrassment, and he raised the hand that had been a fist and rubbed his chin. "You are impudent, young man," he added, but it was in an absent tone.

He averted his eyes and fixed them on a point behind Anthony. "I suppose you know that we are relatives? We are second cousins?"

I should feel renewed hatred, and disgust and rage, thought Anthony, with surprise that he felt none of these. He was conscious of a faint liking and understanding for this broken and weary man who had so ruined his own life and the lives of others, not with vicious intent, but because he was like an impersonal storm twisting in his own agony.

He said, calmly: "Yes, I know." Then with wryness he added: "Shall I call you father, or Cousin John?"

John, still not looking at him, smiled sheepishly. Now he scratched his cheek. Then he stared at the young man.

"You know, I ought to horsewhip you for running off with my daughter, without my permission. I could have the law on you. I could make it very unpleasant. I could bring my daughter home, and lock her up away from you."

"But you won't," said Anthony. He smiled broadly.

John thrust out his hand. "Call me whatever you damned please, you young bounder!" he said, and he suddenly laughed, loudly and recklessly. "But mind your tongue, and use the names to yourself!"

Anthony laughed also. He took John's hand. He felt a sudden pang of pity for this man. He was childish, he was violent, he was unpredictable and savage. But he was no scoundrel, even if he was a fool.

They shook hands warmly, with no embarrassment now. Is it possible he remembers nothing of my mother? thought Anthony. There was no sign of memory on John's grinning face, in which the lines of wildness and suffering and tempest were so deeply graven.

Then John, with one of the sudden and stormy changes of mood characteristic of him, said in a hard and sombre voice:

"Look here, you'll be good to Adelaide? You'll make—things—up to her?"

"Certainly. Why do you suppose I married her?" asked Anthony, bluntly. "Do you think I've been blind? Well, no matter. I suppose you wonder how this all came about? I've seen Adelaide not more than half a dozen times in my life. But I've always wanted her. I assure you, she'll not want for anything."

"She might have told her mother, at least," said John, after a moment, with childish resentment and relentlessness. "It was a cruel thing to do to Mrs. Turnbull."

"We were married only yesterday," replied Anthony, impatiently. "Last Sunday I saw her again, after perhaps a year or two of complete silence from her. I practically forced her to marry me. She wanted it kept secret for a few days—while she did something or other to prevent ruin from coming down on you. Then, she was to tell her mother, and you."

John's eyes narrowed to glittering pinpoints. "Ruin? What do you mean?"

Then he visibly started. He stared at Anthony, but did not see him.

"It was the girl's imagination," he said at last, in a difficult voice.

"You are wrong," said Anthony, with blunt decision. "She suspected the truth. Now Wilkins informs me that she was quite right. Your precious sons-in-law——"

He stopped, abruptly. Lilybelle had reappeared, dressed for the street, her eyes pools of round blue radiance. Her hands were ungloved; her shawl was bunched on her shoulders.

But John did not look at her. He was staring at Anthony, and his features were pinched and wizened, and a great revelation was darkening on his face. It was aghast, full of complete knowledge.

CHAPTER 62

THE WINDOWS of Adelaide's room faced the street. The two physicians were in consultation over the girl, testing her, listening to her breathing, counting her pulse. Miss Beardsley had returned to her home for a rest; she would come back in the evening. In the meanwhile the old housekeeper, assisted by a strong middle-aged woman, was in attendance over the sick girl. The room smelled of cool fresh air and chemicals.

Mr. Wilkins was at the window, watching for young Anthony, who would be here shortly. A carriage drove up to the house, and at the sight of it, recognizing it, Mr. Wilkins started. His suspicions were justified when Anthony opened the carriage door and stepped out into the April sunshine, followed by John, and then by Lilybelle. Both men assisted her to alight, handling her gently and firmly. The sunlight struck the auburn masses of her hair, untidily piled under the tipsy bonnet. Mr. Wilkins saw her shapeless white face, huge and shining.

"Why," he said aloud, slowly and heavily, "the bloody

young beggar. The blasted young bastard."

So, Anthony Bollister had told them, had brought them here. It had been Mr. Wilkins' intention to keep Adelaide's whereabouts a secret for several days, until the Turnbulls had turned New York upside down looking for her. One could trust no one, it seemed. That young Bollister chap had seemed a hard 'un; yet, he had gone soft. Why? He surely had no love for John Turnbull. Was it possible he didn't know about his mother? But there had been a sudden harsh flushing of his cheek when John's name had been mentioned, which had shrewdly led Mr. Wilkins to believe that he knew. Was it possible that they had sought him out, had threatened him, had followed him? Mr. Wilkins shook his head and scowled. He knew men. No one could threaten Anthony into compliance. He had done this all by himself.

Well, he, Mr. Wilkins, had no desire to see Johnnie Turnbull just at this time, though certainly Johnnie ought to be grateful. But there was omniscience in Mr. Wilkins; he had had it at birth; he had cultivated it, thereafter. There was a look on the devil's dark face as he glanced at the house before starting up the flagged walk. A very nasty look indeed. Mr. Wilkins suddenly suspected that this look had more to do than just with little Addy.

He turned abruptly and beckoned to his housekeeper, who came, her hands in her apron. He pointed silently outside; she glanced, and nodded. He whispered: "Look ye, I'm not to 'ome. I've gone out for a bit of fresh air."

She nodded again, curiously. Mr. Wilkins whisked himself out of the room just as the knocker resounded furiously on the door. He entered his own room, closed the door, then, as an afterthought, he locked it. He sat down on the bed.

Well, it was all over. He had done with Johnnie. He had given Johnnie what he wanted. Johnnie had not been the man to keep it. Johnnie had always been the fool. Now, Johnnie, no doubt, had lost his hatred. He was not the chap for Mr. Wilkins any longer, even if what had happened last night had not occurred. He had washed his hands of Johnnie. A stupid violent devil. The future would go on without Johnnie. It would go on with the little lass, with Tony Bollister. Mr. Wilkins frowned reflectively. A hard 'un, yes. Not one to be led easily. Liked money like the rest of 'em; but there would be things he wouldn't do. No chap for Mr. Wilkins' money. Nevertheless, there was the little lass to protect. Mr. Wilkins began to smile. A tender look overspread his rosy face, suffusing it with a brighter colour. It might be interesting to be an honest man for a change, to satisfy a curiosity he had always had: whether an honest man could succeed in the world.

Mr. Wilkins doubted it very much. An honest man in a den of thieves was invariably stripped to the eyebrows, and a good thing. An honest man was a fool. He deserved the last crust of charity thrown to him. The wages of sin was a rich old age. The wages of honesty was the workhouse. Still, the experiment might be exciting. He, Mr. Wilkins, would try it. He would be Anthony's right hand man. Later, the young ass would be convinced by experience that honesty was a virtue no one but the dying and the dead could afford, but in the meantime it would have its elements of novelty, and the ageless Mr. Wilkins loved novelty.

"Mr. Wilkins," he said aloud, slapping himself on his cask-like chest, "from this day henceforth, you're an honest man. Honest Bob: that's wot they'll call you."

He heard a confusion of footsteps on the polished stairs, but no voices. He rose and pressed his ear against the wall, and listened.

The physicians, recognizing the formidable Mr. Turnbull, hastened forward to greet him with important and solemn faces. If they were highly astonished and diverted at the mysterious presence of Miss Turnbull in this house, and in a dangerous condition of illness, they tactfully refrained from referring to it. They bowed to him and his lady with great ceremony, and immediately launched into a learned discussion of the young lady's disease, symptoms and condition, interrupting each other impatiently as they did so.

"In cases of lung fever, sir," said Dr. Walker, portentously.

"Pneumonia, my dear doctor," urged Dr. Gorman, with a bow to his colleague, and a faintly smug smile.

Dr. Walker drew himself up with hauteur, and fingered his pince-nez. "I hold no brief for modern and pretentious terminology in medicine," he replied, scathingly, but still with the utmost politeness. "I have never considered it necessary to confuse, with the idea of impressing, the layman, employing Greek and Roman obscurities. It is rather a cheap attempt to subdue the layman, force him to accord the medical profession a kind of spurious respect in lieu of real respect for our knowledge. Lung fever, my dear colleague," he added, with a wintry smile, "is as bad under any other name, and the layman, upon hearing it, has a definite picture of the syndrome, its symptoms, its probable mortalities, its chances for recovery. What does he see when he hears the affected word: 'Pneumonia?' A mysterious malady, with which he is not familiar, and which terrifies him as though it were some strange and unfamiliar disease which will certainly terminate the life of his loved one with dispatch."

"Lung fever is ambiguous," contradicted Dr. Gorman. "Lung. Fever. A hundred diseases might come into that category. In every such disease there is inflammation of the lung; there is fever. The layman should have a clear picture: yes. But he also should know the true character of the disease from which he or his loved ones suffer."

John interrupted impatiently, trying to see Adelaide over their shoulders: "Gentlemen, call the disease what you will, for all of me. I am interested only in knowing the full extent of my daughter's illness, and the chances for her recovery."

With more abruptness than politeness, he pushed the doctors aside, supported the trembling and pallid Lilybelle on one side as Anthony supported her on the other, and approached the bed.

Adelaide was either in a deep sleep or a stupor. John could not tell. Her face was very small and pinched, the skin bluish where it was not streaked with scarlet on the sharp cheekbones. Her hoarse breathing filled the room. She was lifted high on pillows. A kettle, filled with some sort of medicinal ingredient, permeated the room with a strong odour. Its steam was directed, by means of a sheet, to the girl. There was a strange and removed dignity in her expression; her eyelids were bruised in appearance, and twitched, as if she was absorbed in some gigantic struggle deep within herself. Her neatly plaited hair coiled on the pillows; they saw the red dried cut on her forehead. There was about her an arching tenseness; her hands on the quilt were clenched so that the knuckles sprang out under the skin.

Lilybelle began to whimper. She sagged in John's and Anthony's arms, and fell on her knees beside the bed. She said nothing. But she lifted Adelaide's cold blue hands and pressed them deep within her bosom, to warm them. She fixed her eyes upon the girl's face. Now her whimpering was still. Long convulsions ran over her mountainous flesh in visible ripples. But she did not move, nor speak. All the power of her love, grim, indomitable, passionate, was focussed upon Adelaide, denying her death and peace, urging her, in some mysterious and desperate and silent communication, to return, to come back, to see and hear again.

John stood beside the bed, holding to a bed-post. He, too, was completely silent. He looked down upon his child. The hand tightened on the bed-post. His closed dark face had become almost emaciated in appearance. Like Lilybelle, he fixed his eyes upon Adelaide, and did not remove them. Under them, there were purple pockets, swollen and heavy.

He saw Adelaide as he had never seen her before. He

watched her struggle for life, a struggle implicit with gravity and soundless courage. The hand on the bed-post tightened. His eyes closed, and there was a sunken appearance about his mouth that gave him the look of an old and exhausted man, full of despair, knowledge, self-hatred and over-powering sorrow.

Anthony, too, bent over Adelaide, touching her forehead and her cheek. But he found Lilybelle's expression, her iron passion and misery, far more pathetic than his young wife's heroic battle for her life. Slow tears, each one rounded and unhurried, ran down from Lilybelle's eyes, but there was no contortion or squeezing of her eyelids, no distortion of her mouth such as appear in facile emotion. There was a great dignity, and immeasurable anguish, in those tears, but also, very strangely, an immense fortitude and resolution. She would not let Adelaide die. She would fight every inch of the perilous way with the frightful enemy; she would not go down. Her spiritual arms clutched her child, and she lifted her face in steadfast denial to the enemy that would snatch away that child.

John had turned away. He approached the doctors, and said in a hoarse swift voice: "I want the truth. Will she live?"

The doctors exchanged with each other a look of superior resignation at the stupidity of the layman. They rose to their full heights, and regarded John gravely.

"There are a number of possibilities, my dear sir," said the unctuous Dr. Walker. "She may—expire—of exhaustion, of suffocation, at any moment. You have asked for a frank and manly opinion; we are giving you that. Then, again, she may survive to the crisis, which may occur in five, in seven, or even in nine days, if exhaustion does not terminate her sufferings before that. At the crisis, there may occur, if conditions are favourable, the strength maintained, a rapid fall in temperature and a profuse perspiration. Thereafter, in these favourable cases, convalescence slowly begins. However, should the crisis not be favourable, there is increasing brief fever, then a falilng of the temperature, a heightening of the exhaustion, an increase in the cough, more difficult breathing, coma, suffocation—collapse."

John seized the doctor's arm and shook him roughly. His livil lips parted and showed the savage glisten of his teeth. "I did not ask you for a list of symptoms. You see my daughter. What chance has she for—living——?"

Dr. Walker looked at the hand that gripped him with severe affront, but did not try to free himself. "My dear sir, we are only physicians. We are not God. I understand that

508

she suffered prolonged exposure last night, when already in the throes of the disease. That has not increased the possibilities of her recovery. We can only wait and see; we can only pray. She is young, we must remember."

John released the doctor's arm. His hand fell heavily to his side. He stared at the man with eyes suddenly fiery.

He began to speak in a low pent voice: "There are hundreds of thousands of people in this city—millions. There are dogs and rats, too. All kinds of superfluous and ugly life. There are thousands of worthless creatures here who walk the street in health and safety. Yet, my daughter, my daughter, lies here, and may die. From your faces, I understand that she will not live!"

He paused, as if smothering. He drew a loud and grating breath. "Life all around us, hateful and vicious and useless life, but my daughter will not live! A city full of physicians, and you cannot save her!"

His hands clenched into fists. The fire in his eyes was wild and infuriated.

"A little life—you can't save it. A poor little life, that never harmed a soul, that was never guilty of a crime, and you are impotent! Look you, there is no end to money, if you save her. Ask what you wish; you will get it. But you cannot let her die! Before God, you can't let her die!"

He is mad, thought the physicians, glancing at each other again. Dr. Walker tried to speak soothingly: "My dear sir, we are doing all we can. Nothing more can be done. If it will help your natural sensibilities, the sensibilities of a stricken father, I will remain with her constantly, until Dr. Gorman can take up the vigil in turn. We shall leave nothing undone——"

"The foulest life," muttered John. "That is safe. But my daughter——"

"There is no bargaining with God," said Dr. Gorman, with some pity. "We cannot say to Him: 'Here is a rat, that has life, or a criminal, or a drab. Take such a life and leave that which is precious.' We can only pray to him that this beloved life be spared."

John was silent. His head dropped on his breast. He felt some one take his arm. He heard Anthony say: "Please. This is no use. They are doing what they can. Sit down, I beg of you."

He felt himself in a chair. Some one was beside him; an arm lay on his shoulders, pressing it. He covered his face with his hands, and broke out into the most terrible sobbing, dry and tearless. Anthony glanced at the doctors, who shook their heads gravely. They were startled into pity for this desperate and broken man, who, in the supreme moment, had nothing to offer but his agony, and no courage but impotent rage and torment, and desolation.

His hands dropped from his face. It was ravaged, distorted. He clenched his hands and beat them on his knees, soundlessly now, but with slow heavy blows. He was conscious of nothing but his anguish, his helplessness, and his remorse which burned and blasted his heart.

The doctors, much touched, thought that here was a father whose pet, whose darling, lay just within the gray grasp of death, that nothing could reconcile him in his vehement and almost insane sorrow. But Anthony knew it was more than this. He knew it was a crushing and frantic remorse. If Adelaide died, then John would die, expiring of his unbearable agony. The young man forgot his own torture in his attempts to calm the man who really deserved his utmost hatred.

The housekeeper and the nurse, who had been watching this scene avidly, were extremely affected, and wept, in the manner of their kind. Only Lilybelle was removed and quiet, as if no one was in this room but herself and her child, as if nothing else existed but her supreme stern struggle with the enemy that was dragging at one hand as she held the other. In her dedication, in her stern and heroic concentration, was the nobility and the grandeur and the inflexible strength of a prayer.

She, alone, heard Adelaide sigh and stir on her pillows. She alone saw the fluttering of the tired eyelids, the indrawing of breath that dilated the transparent nostrils. She saw the weary eyes open and look at her with slow recognition.

"Yes, my little love, my little lass," whispered Lilybelle, and she lifted the girl in her arms and held her against her breast. Adelaide's head lay on her mother's shoulder; the warmth and strength of her mother's arms were about her.

"Mama," whispered the girl, in her great exhaustion.

"Yes, yes, little lovey. We must rest now," said Lilybelle with infinite tenderness. She gently laid the girl back on her pillows. She took the small hands and pressed and rubbed them. There was a faint warmth in them now. Adelaide was smiling.

The doctors became aware of movement near the bed. They came at once, bent over the girl, holding her pulse, listening intently to her breathing. John and Anthony were alone.

Anthony was speaking to John in a low voice. "Don't give up. She is fighting, still. She won't die. I know it. Can you hear me? She won't die. Not now."

John did not appear to hear at first. Then, as Anthony's

repeated words slowly entered his consciousness, he lifted his head and looked at the young man. There was hopeless pleading on his face, simple and moved. Anthony nodded, pressed his arm strongly about John's shoulders.

Dr. Walker was at his side now, his face quite excited for all its dignity. "The girl is conscious," he whispered. "It is too early to say. But there has been a marked improvement— a very small, but marked improvement. You might speak to her. But only for a moment, I beg of you."

Anthony helped John to his feet. The older man swayed and staggered. The doctor and Anthony guided him as one might guide a half conscious man. They reached the bed. Adelaide opened her eyes again and saw them together. A smile, surprised, delighted and very soft, parted her pale and swollen lips.

John knelt beside her, opposite Lilybelle. He looked long into his daughter's eyes. His hand was against her cheek, smoothing it. He tried to smile, and his look was unbearably poignant even to the doctors.

"Yes, my dear, it's Papa. Papa understands everything. You must rest. And then, you must come home."

His voice, low and hoarse, came falteringly, feebly. Adelaide listened, her eyes fixed on his face. Then, she weakly turned her head and kissed the hand that lay along her cheek. She tried to speak.

"Nothing matters," said John. "Nothing matters but my darling."

She had never heard such a tone from him, nor such words. Wonder and delight shone in her poor eyes, and brightened her colour. She could not look away from him.

"Forgive me, my love," said John, brokenly.

Lilybelle, kneeling opposite him, timidly extended her hand across the white bed, and he felt the movement rather than saw it. He grasped her hand, held it convulsively. His fingers were chill and stiff as ice, hers warm and strong. He clung to her hand, almost crushing it.

Adelaide hardly moved, but she seemed to curve towards her father, to lay in the circle of his arm. Anthony stood near John, and smiled down at her. She returned his smile. She tried to speak, and then, in the midst of her whispering words, she fell asleep.

"I think she will do now," said Dr. Walker, rubbing his glasses vigorously. "Yes, I think she will do now. With care, with rest, with devotion."

Mr. Wilkins had listened to everything, with much interest and satisfaction. After a long time, he heard a door open, and Anthony and Dr. Walker came out into the hall. They talked together long and earnestly. Mr. Wilkins listened frankly at the key-hole. Dr. Walker went down the polished stairs with a firm and distinguished tread. Mr. Wilkins opened the door, and saw Anthony alone, musing thoughtfully. The young man frowned when he saw the affable old gentleman.

"Ah," whispered Mr. Wilkins. "The little lass will do, eh? Very good, very good. Like a 'appy endin' to a fairy tale. Reconciliations, and such. Very affectin'. I'm a kind man, Mr. Bollister. I 'ave a heart. This does me good."

Anthony could not help smiling a little. His hand was on the door handle of Adelaide's room. Mr. Wilkins plucked his sleeve. He winked amiably. He tapped the young man on the chest.

"And you and me, eh? We've got a lot of blasted work to do? Eh?"

Anthony was silent a moment. Then his smile broadened. He nodded slowly. His gray eyes were hard as new steel. He extended his hand to Mr. Wilkins who took it and shook it warmly.

Mr. Wilkins stood alone for a long moment or two staring at the white door closed in his face. He nodded over and over, played with his watch-chain, smiled.

The blasted young beggar would not fail him. There was iron there, and stone. If there was also a curious honesty and integrity, this would not prevent vengeance. No softness. It would be very interesting, indeed. Mr. Wilkins chuckled richly.

"I allus give 'em wot they wants," he whispered to himself.

He rubbed his hands together with slow delight. He felt new life in him, new excitement. Life had taken on its old richness once again.

A shaft of sunlight struck from the high skylight upon his face. It was evil and rosy, and full of chuckling mirth. And very terrible.